W9-BLK-462

PENGUIN BOOKS

THE PORTABLE POETS OF THE ENGLISH LANGUAGE

RESTORATION AND AUGUSTAN POETS

Each volume in The Viking Portable Library either presents a representative selection from the works of a single outstanding writer or offers a comprehensive anthology on a special subject. Averaging 700 pages in length and designed for compactness and readability, these books fill a need not met by other compilations. All are edited by distinguished authorities, who have written introductory essays and included much other helpful material.

"The Viking Portables have done more for good reading and good writers than anything that has come along since I can remember."
—Arthur Mizener

W. H. Auden was born in England in 1907 and died in 1973. Versatile, outspoken, psychologically acute, and brilliant in literary technique, he wrote plays and libretti as well as volumes of prose and poetry—among these last, *The Double Man*, *The Age of Anxiety*, and *The Shield of Achilles*.

The late Norman Holmes Pearson was chairman of American studies at Yale. Books by him include *American Literature*, *Some American Studies*, and *American Literary Fathers*.

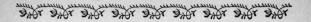

The Viking Portable Library

POETS OF THE
ENGLISH LANGUAGE

Edited by

W. H. AUDEN

and

NORMAN HOLMES PEARSON

VOLUME I: LANGLAND TO SPENSER

VOLUME II: MARLOWE TO MARVELL

VOLUME III: MILTON TO GOLDSMITH

VOLUME IV: BLAKE TO POE

VOLUME V: TENNYSON TO YEATS

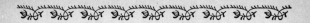

POETS OF THE ENGLISH LANGUAGE

Restoration

AND

Augustan

POETS

Milton to Goldsmith

PENGUIN BOOKS

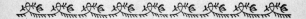

Penguin Books Ltd, Harmondsworth,
Middlesex, England
Penguin Books, 625 Madison Avenue,
New York, New York 10022, U.S.A.
Penguin Books Australia Ltd, Ringwood,
Victoria, Australia
Penguin Books Canada Limited, 2801 John Street,
Markham, Ontario, Canada L3R 1B4
Penguin Books (N.Z.) Ltd, 182–190 Wairau Road,
Auckland 10, New Zealand

First published in the United States of America
by The Viking Press 1950
First published in Great Britain by Eyre & Spottiswoode Ltd. 1952
Viking paperbound edition published 1958
Reprinted 1960, 1961, 1963, 1965, 1967, 1968, 1969, 1972, 1973
Published in Penguin Books 1977
Reprinted 1978

LIBRARY OF CONGRESS CATALOGING IN PUBLICATION DATA
Auden, Wystan Hugh, 1907–1973, ed.
Poets of the English language.
Reprint of the 1950 ed. published by Viking Press, New York,
issued in series: The Viking portable library.
CONTENTS: v. 3. Restoration and Augustan poets, Milton to Goldsmith.
Includes index.
1. English poetry. 2. American poetry.
I. Pearson, Norman Holmes, 1909–   II. Title.
[PR1175.A76 1977]   821'.008   76–30501
ISBN 0 14 015.051 X (v. 3)

Printed in the United States of America by
Kingsport Press, Inc., Kingsport, Tennessee
Set in Linotype Caledonia

Grateful acknowledgment is made to the following for permission to
reprint selections. William H. Bond and the Harvard University Library,
Cambridge: excerpts from *Jubilate Agno* by Christopher Smart (copy-
right 1950 by William H. Bond); The New England Quarterly, Bruns-
wick, Maine: "Upon a Wasp Chilled with Cold" and "Meditation
Forty" by Edward Taylor; Colonial Society of Massachusetts, Boston:
"An Elegy upon the Death of . . . Mr. John Allen" by Edward Taylor;
Princeton University Press, Princeton: selections from *The Poetical
Works of Edward Taylor*, edited by Thomas H. Johnson, copyright 1939
by Rocklands Editions, 1943 by Princeton University Press.

Contents

v

CONTENTS

Introduction

VERSE AND PROSE

During the latter half of the seventeenth century and the first half of the eighteenth, prose comes to rival verse as a popular medium. Moreover, a new kind of prose narrative, the novel, appears. In consequence the essential nature and possibilities of each become clearer.

Verse, for example, owing to its greater mnemonic power, is the superior medium for didactic instruction. Those who condemn didactic poetry can only do so because they condemn didacticism and must disapprove *a fortiori* of didactic prose. In verse, at least, as the Alka-Seltzer advertisements testify, the didactic message loses half its immodesty.

Verse is also certainly equal and perhaps superior to prose as a medium for the lucid exposition of ideas, because in skillful hands the form of the verse can parallel and reinforce the steps of the logic. Indeed, contrary to what most people who have inherited the romantic conception of poetry believe, the danger of argument in verse is that it will make the ideas too clear and distinct, more Cartesian than they really are. Pope's *Essay on Man* is a case in point.

On the other hand, verse is unsuited to controversy—to proving true or right some fact or belief which has been questioned or denied—because its formal nature then conveys a certain skepticism about its conclusions. The rhyme

> Thirty days hath September,
> April, June, and November

is valid because no one doubts its truth. Supposing, however, that there were a body of people who passionately
denied it, the lines would be powerless to convince
them, for formally it would make no difference if they
ran

> Thirty days hath September,
> April, May, and December.

This becomes very clear in Dryden's poetry. We have
no reason to doubt that the man who wrote *Religio Laici*
and *The Hind and the Panther* was sincere in his beliefs,
but these two great poems are not serious controversy
in the sense that their poetic intention is to convert the
reader to Anglicanism and Roman Catholicism respec-
tively. Dryden the poet, like Shaw the playwright, ex-
hibits that most skeptical of all mentalities, a passionate
pleasure in argument for its own sake, in the play of
dialectic irrespective of any conclusion. For, as Charles
Williams says:

Prose, especially sweet and rational prose, conceals its human
limitations. It may argue or instruct or exhort, but all that
while it subdues or hides from us the pattern which is our
reminder that its conclusions are what they are because of
its own limitations—which are its writer's—which are in the
nature of man. . . . It is that fact which poetry willingly
embraces, and from which prose, as it were, turns away. . . .
It takes man's limitation and makes that explicitly a part of
his total sensation. It avoids the last illusion of prose, which
so gently sometimes and at others so passionately pretends
that things are thus and thus. In poetry they also are thus
and thus, but because the arrangement of the lines, the pattern within the whole, will have it so. . . . Exquisitely leaning to an implied untruth, prose persuades us that we can

trust our natures to know things as they are; ostentatiously faithful to its own nature, poetry assures us that we cannot —we know only as we can.

Reason and Beauty in the Poetic Mind

Controversy, then, requires prose. So does history, as distinct from myth. For the essential point about a historical fact is how and when it actually occurred, not how it ideally might have occurred. The novel differs from the epic or the tale in that it is an imitation of history: however unnaturalistic his technique, the novelist fails if he does not convince us while we are reading that his characters are historical characters, that this is what they actually said and did. The novel as a literary genre could not appear until men had become conscious of the peculiar nature of history.

MILTON'S BLANK VERSE

Milton is the ancestor of a kind of poet whom we associate with a much later period. He is, for example, the first poet in English literature whose attitude toward his art is neither professional like that of Ben Jonson and Dryden nor amateur like that of Wyatt, but priestly or prophetic. Poetry to him was neither an amusing activity nor the job for which he happened to be qualified, but the most sacred of all human activities. To become a great poet was to become not only superior to other poets but superior to all other men.

Again, he is the first English poet to set out deliberately to fashion a style for himself, for his own use alone. Whereas Shakespeare's blank verse is at the start indistinguishable from that of his contemporaries and develops as he develops, Milton's blank verse is, as it were, a medium which he had to invent before he could begin writing, and for its invention other English poets

like Browne or Drummond were of much less assistance
than Latin and Italian poets.

An idiosyncratic style, when it carries the authority
of a great poet, is a danger to his successors, and in Milton's case particularly so. The most obvious characteristic of his style is its uninterrupted grandeur, which is
incapable of any lighter tone, and the number of themes
to which such a grand style is suited is strictly limited.
Milton's influence on later poets was principally through
his diction, which is precisely the element in his style
which, when the subject does not demand it, is most
likely to fall into pomposity. Few, if any, of them made
use of his poetic syntax, his extraordinary way of arrang-
ing his clauses:

> Down a while
> He sate, and round about him saw unseen:
> At last as from a Cloud his fulgent head
> And shape Starr-bright appeer'd, or brighter, clad
> With what permissive glory since his fall
> Was left him, or false glitter: All amaz'd
> At that so sudden blaze the *Stygian* throng
> Bent thir aspect, and whom they wish'd beheld,
> Thir mighty Chief return'd: loud was th' acclaime:
> Forth rush'd in haste the great consulting Peers,
> Rais'd from thir dark *Divan*, and with like joy
> Congratulant approach'd him, who with hand
> Silence, and with these words attention won.
> *Paradise Lost*, Book X

This is a pity, because syntax, the structural element in
style, is adaptable to different subjects and different
sensibilities in a way that diction is not.

THE COUPLET

At the mention of any poetry written between 1688
and 1776, our immediate association is likely to be with

the heroic couplet. This is not quite just; the period shows more metrical variety than we usually credit it with; there are, for example, the meters of Prior, the octosyllabics of Swift and his irregular comic verse which anticipates Ogden Nash, stanzas of Gay which anticipate Byron, Charles Wesley's hymns, etc. It remains true, however, that during this period the heroic couplet was the dominating form for a poem of any length. There is much to be said for a standard form, whether it be blank verse, the couplet, or any other. Instead of searching for his own original form and perhaps never finding it, the poet takes it as given and can concentrate upon making it say what he has to say. The more original a poet is, the less—barring a few exceptional cases—he feels it a limitation to use a form employed by others; further, continuous practice in the same form trains his mind to think easily and naturally in it and makes him sensitive to the subtlest variations of which it is capable.

That the heroic couplet is capable of adapting itself to a wide range of topic and music can be seen from the following extracts.

> But this our Age such Authors does afford,
> As make whole Plays, and yet scarce write one word;
> Who, in this anarchy of Wit, rob all,
> And what's their Plunder, their Possession call:
> Who, like bold Padders, scorn by Night to prey,
> But rob by Sun-shine, in the Face of Day:
> Nay scarce the common Ceremony use
> Of Stand, Sir, and deliver up your Muse;
> But knock the Poet down, and, with a Grace,
> Mount Pegasus before the Owner's Face.
>
> Dryden, Prologue to Tomkis's *Albumazar*

> To happy Convents, bosom'd deep in vines,
> Where slumber Abbots, purple as their wines:

To Isles of fragrance, lily-silver'd vales,
Diffusing languor in the panting gales:
To lands of singing or of dancing slaves,
Love-whisp'ring woods, and lute-resounding waves.
But chief her shrine where naked Venus keeps,
And Cupids ride the Lion of the Deeps;
Where, eas'd of Fleets, the Adriatic main
Wafts the smooth Eunuch and enamour'd swain.

                        Pope, *The Dunciad*, IV

But few there are whom hours like these await,
Who set unclouded in the gulfs of Fate.
From Lydia's monarch should the search descend,
By Solon caution'd to regard his end;
In life's last scene what prodigies surprise,
Fears of the brave, and follies of the wise?
From Marlb'rough's eyes the streams of dotage flow,
And Swift expires a driv'ler and a show.

                 Johnson, *Vanity of Human Wishes*

In comparison with blank verse, its only serious rival
in English verse as a standard form, the couplet has one
disadvantage. The emphasis on the line structure which
the rhymes produce, an emphasis so much stronger in
an accented language like English than in French, is so
powerful that it almost compels the sentence structure
to conform to it, so losing a subtlety which can be one
of the great charms of poetry—the opposition and inter-
play of the line stop and the sentence stop.

Of its comparative advantage, Dryden writes:

But that benefit which I consider most in it, because I
have not seldome found it, is, that it Bounds and Circum-
scribes the Fancy. For Imagination in a Poet is a faculty so
Wild and Lawless, that, like an High-ranging Spaniel it
must have Cloggs tied to it, least it out-run the Judgment.
The great easiness of blank Verse, renders the Poet too
Luxuriant; He is tempted to say many things, which might
better be Omitted, or at least shut up in fewer Words: But

when the difficulty of Artfull Rhyming is interpos'd, where the Poet commonly confines his Sence to his Couplet, and must contrive that Sence into such Words, that the Rhyme shall naturally follow them, not they the Rhyme; the Fancy then gives Leisure to the Judgment to come in; which seeing so heavy a Tax impos'd, is ready to cut off all unnecessary Expences. This last Consideration has already answer'd an Objection which some have made; that Rhyme is only an Embroidery of Sence, to make that which is ordinary in it self pass for excellent with less Examination. But certainly, that which most regulates the Fancy, and gives the Judgment its busiest Employment, is like to bring forth the richest and clearest Thoughts.

Epistle Dedicatory to *The Rival Ladies*

THE BATTLE OF THE BOOKS

The characteristic which is common to the poets in this volume and distinguishes them from their predecessors (though Ben Jonson in some measure possesses it) is a consciousness of their historical position as poets. However different they may be in other ways, Milton and Pope are like each other and unlike Shakespeare in the kind of questions they ask themselves about their contemporary poetic task.

In addition to admiring the classical authors, they are conscious of them as writers of the past and of themselves as moderns. Reading a classical writer, therefore, they ask, "What has he accomplished once and for all, which it would therefore be useless repetition for me to attempt to repeat? What help as a model can he be to me in writing of experiences or subjects which are too modern for him to have known?" Thus Milton abandons his projected epic on King Arthur, not because the theme lacks personal appeal to him, but because the theme of Arthur is essentially the same as the theme of Aeneas; he is not satisfied until he alights on a subject which in relation to Vergil is modern, namely the Fall. Similarly Pope takes the *Iliad* and the *Aeneid* as his models, but, substituting for the gods and warriors of the one the Sylphs and visitors to a lady's drawing room, and for the prehistoric heroes of the other the literary hacks of a modern metropolis, he produces *The Rape of the Lock* and *The Dunciad*.

The mutual interaction of comparable memories is one of the greatest sources of civilized pleasure; just as one sees America differently after one has seen Italy, and vice versa, so, after one has read both the *Iliad* and *The Rape of the Lock,* one cannot help seeing the Baron in Hector and Hector in the Baron. Again, the differences between Samson's attitude to free will and sin and that of the Aeschylean tragic heroes, between their temptation to be insolent toward the gods and his to despair of God's goodness, are emphasized by the similarity of the dramatic form and make *Samson Agonistes* not only a tragedy but also a historical and critical comparison of the Greek and Biblical conceptions of life.

Both Milton and Pope consider and expect their audiences to consider their reading as a significant experience, comparable to, say, falling in love; literature is to them a natural part of life.

THE CAVALIER POETS

After the death of James I, the court ceased to be the symbolic center of the national life, and the poets associated closely with the court reflect the change. They are on the defensive; before the Civil War they try to believe that no serious change is going to take place, and after the Restoration they try to pretend that in fact no serious change has occurred, that the former status quo has been restored. Their poetry deliberately ignores history and public interests and as deliberately insists on the private life of leisure and pleasure. In technique they move away from the complicated stanzas and ingenious conceits of the metaphysical poets toward the simpler and more polite poetry of the coming age; in their subjects and sensibility, on the other hand, they represent the final development of the school which began with Wyatt. The wheel has with them turned a half-circle, so that now the Petrarchan convention is stood on its head; it is infidelity that is recommended, fidelity that is despised. But the Petrarchan sentiments are still there in a repressed form, and that is what gives these poets' work, Rochester's in particular, its unique flavor. They are not naïvely frivolous but defiantly so, debauched by a serious effort of will.

GENERAL

The Treaty of Westphalia in 1648 marks the end of the Lutheran revolution; neither Protestantism nor Roman Catholicism had succeeded in destroying the other; henceforth both were to live side by side. The problem facing Western civilization was how to find some principle of unity which could prevent a Christendom divided nationally and religiously from disintegration. In this attempt the lead was taken by England; between 1642 and 1776 England is the center of revolutionary and "progressive" ideas.

The actual period of revolution lasts from 1642–1688 and is best seen as one period, of which the Puritan Revolution and the Glorious Revolution are two complementary halves. The objective of this revolution is not to achieve freedom in either the Lutheran or the Jacobin sense, but rather to bring individual freedom into conformity with law. The slogans are Common Law, Common Sense, Public Spirit. Its first enemy is the claim of the king to be free to govern as he please; its second the claim of the sects—the Anabaptists, Anti-Scripturists, Chiliasts, Familists, Muggletonians, Old Brownists, Questionists, Sebaptists, Soul Sleepers, Traskites, etc.— to know the truth by private inspiration. Cromwell defeated the first; the Whigs of 1688 the second. Its viewpoint might be described as a sort of secular or at least non-sacramental Catholicism. The Whig families had no intention of undoing the Reformation to which they owed their fortunes, but their attitude to life was profoundly unprotestant. Whether in politics, religion, or art, whether in the mouth of a king or an oysterwoman, Luther's egotistic cry, "I can do no other," is to them the voice of the enemy, to be dealt with not by burning but by ridicule. The Parliament to which they gave sovereignty in civil and religious affairs is not only a collective body but an anonymous one; it is not an individual Mr. Smith who speaks or votes but the Member for Middletown; the term Opposition is taken from astronomy, and signifies not irreconcileable conflict, but balance.

The hero of this revolution is the unarmed gentleman. The gentleman differs from the aristocrat in being distinguished not by birth but by breeding; anyone who can learn to acquire the habits and live according to the standards of the gentleman becomes one.

This revolution was catholic in another sense, namely that the views of the politicians were in harmony with those of the theologians, the scientists, and the writers.

Thus the Newtonian cosmology, in which the universe consists of things located in space upon which the laws of nature are imposed, requires the unitarian Deist God to impose the latter; for there is nothing in the nature of things to account for the laws they obey, and nothing in the laws to account for the things. The Deist God, for his part, need not reveal himself supernaturally to man; the public order and economy of the Newtonian universe are sufficient proof of his existence.

Similarly, in the aesthetic theories of the writers, there is no great mystery about poetic composition. It is the result of the cooperation of three mental faculties, memory, judgment, and fancy. Memory provides the raw material, judgment arranges all this into a coherent pattern, from which fancy can select whatever she needs for the task at hand. The first and last of these are private to the individual, but judgment is public and social; judgment is to art what public spirit is to politics, or the laws of nature to astronomy. Thus Addison writes:

> I shall add no more to what I have here offered, than that Musick, Architecture, and Painting, as well as Poetry, and Oratory, are to deduce their Laws and Rules from the general Sense and Taste of Mankind, and not from the Principles of those Arts themselves; or, in other words, the Taste is not to conform to the Art, but the Art to the Taste.
>
> *The Spectator*, no. 29

To be true to nature means to express what is enduring, essential, and comprehensible; the accidental or irregular is ugly and unnatural.

> There are two Causes of Beauty, natural and customary. Natural is from Geometry, consisting in Uniformity (that is Equality) and Proportion. Customary Beauty is begotten by the Use of our Senses to those Objects which are usually pleasing to us for other Causes, as Familiarity or particular Inclination breeds a Love to Things not in themselves lovely. Here lies the great Occasion of Errors; here is tried the Architect's Judgment: but always the true Test is natural or geometrical Beauty.
>
> Geometrical Figures are naturally more beautiful than other irregular; in this all consent as to a Law of Nature.

Of geometrical Figures, the Square and the Circle are most beautiful; next, the Parallelogram and the Oval. Strait lines are more beautiful than curve. . . .

Views contrary to Beauty are Deformity, or a Defect of Uniformity, and Plainness, which is the Excess of Uniformity; Variety makes the Mean.

Variety of Uniformities make compleat Beauty: Uniformities are best tempered, as Rhimes in Poetry, alternately, or sometimes with more Variety, as in Stanzas.

Sir Christopher Wren, *Parentalia*

Eccentricity of emotion or diction, the elevation of private fancy over public judgment, are to be as condemned in poets as is the refusal of an individual member to accept the general verdict of the House of Commons:

> Beware what Spirit rages in your Breast;
> For ten Inspir'd ten thousand are possest.
> Thus make the proper Use of each Extream,
> And write with Fury, but correct with Phleam.
> Roscommon

CONCLUSION

Such a view is most valid in political life, which by its nature is public, impersonal, secular, and practical. The lasting contribution of the English Revolution was neither the emancipation of a class nor the construction of a political theory, but the promulgation of a certain ideal of political conduct. If it would be partial to assert —as the writer believes—that "to behave like a gentleman" is the only possible ideal for sane politics in any kind of society, it is not too much to say that it is the ideal upon which the successful functioning of a democratic government, as the West understands the term, depends, even in, or rather most of all in, a situation of crisis.

In personal life, however, the religion of common

sense and good taste is seriously defective. It can neither allow for nor comprehend those decisive once-for-all instants of vision in which a life is confronted by another, addressed by God, Nature, or a Beatrice—which, unique and momentary though they may be, are what make that life a person and give his normal day-to-day experiences their meaning.

It is a view which necessarily excludes some kinds of poetry, perhaps the greatest kinds. This does not mean, however, that it is of no use to poets or that the poetry written from it cannot be of a high order. Indeed, there is a good deal to be said for its aesthetic as a practical guide to poets. It may make out the creative act to be more conscious than in fact it is, but it encourages the poet to pay attention to that which is in his control. Inspiration is granted or withheld as the Muse, not he, disposes; all he can do is to see that his work is well made. If then he is not inspired—well, his work will be dull, but at least it will not be chaotic rubbish.

If a style of poetry is valid, then there is an ideal subject for it, and we shall know its real possibilities only when that subject has been found. Luckily for our estimate of the Augustans it was. *The Dunciad* is not only a great poem but also the only poem in English which is at once comic and sublime. It should never be read with notes, for to think that it matters who the characters were or why Pope was angry with them is to miss the whole point of the poem, which is best appreciated by supplying one's own contemporary list of the servants of the Goddess of Dullness. No great poem can be written without genuine passion; hostile as the aesthetic of the Augustan might be to most kinds of passion, there was one it could and did encourage, a passion for the civilized intelligent life, and it is this which burns so fiercely throughout Pope's poem. To have seen

Dullness, the goddess of minor and in themselves unimportant figures, as a really formidable and eternal threat to the City of Man was a vision in its own way as original and of as permanent value to the City as Dante's of Paradise or Wordsworth's of Nature.

General Principles

SELECTIONS

The differing versions of Eden as remembered in Milton's *Paradise Lost* and in Goldsmith's *The Deserted Village* frame the present volume. Milton's concerns are not out of place as an introduction to a body of poetry so much influenced by his examples. *The Rape of the Lock* takes on fuller significance in juxtaposition to Milton's great poems, and *An Essay on Man* may be regarded with some justice as an eighteenth-century definition of post-lapsarian Adam. If cavaliers like Herrick, Carew, Suckling, Lovelace, and Waller seem strangers to the increasingly dominant mood, they serve as a reminder of what lingered after Milton but was ultimately abandoned.

Obviously no excerpts can replace *Paradise Lost* as a whole, though we have done what we could to suggest the whole. *Samson Agonistes* fortunately can be given in entirety. Pope's *The Rape of the Lock* and *An Essay on Criticism* are also printed without cutting, as are the individual books or essays from the other longer works of the man who took Milton's place as the chief poetic force of the advancing century. Johnson's *The Vanity of Human Wishes*, Smart's *A Song to David,* and Goldsmith's *The Deserted Village* also help to indicate the breadth of canvas preferred by poets. In these as elsewhere we have tried to overcome the tendency of anthologists to represent the past chiefly as a salon of miniatures.

TEXTS

Out of consistency to the principle of maintaining the contemporary appearance of the texts of the poems, we have tried to present them as they were known. Spelling and punctuation present no special problems, but the vagaries of contemporary capitalization, as they shift from one edition to another, are evidence that in this respect there is a decline in the reliance of either poets or public on capitalization as a guide. Capitalization apparently became little more than a sport for typesetters. We have nevertheless retained the contemporary appearance. The chief exception has been in the selections from Pope where we have generally used the texts of Warburton, since they contain Pope's own emendations, though the manner of capitalization is somewhat different from what Pope normally saw. Perhaps quixotically, but through a desire to show capitalization as it indicates the balance of a line, we have retained the early appearance of *The Rape of the Lock* and the "Epistle to Dr. Arbuthnot," incorporating only the few verbal changes and altered punctuations which were later made.

William H. Bond and the Harvard College Library have generously permitted the use of excerpts from his forthcoming edition of Smart's *Jubilate Agno,* done from the original manuscript now in The Houghton Library of Harvard University. These versions, now published for the first time, are of real significance. Smart's trial essay toward *A Song to David,* whose composition it immediately preceded, has been hitherto considered as a disjunct series of separate poems. The reconstruction of the manuscript, however, shows Smart's design to have been that of paired poems in antiphonal relationship to each other. This structure we have stressed by printing them in alternate passages, though Smart originally arranged them on opposite sheets as in an antiphonary.[1] For the inimitable passages on Jeoffry, the cat, only one set of versicles now exists; but it is most probable that their missing counterparts in the other section of the poem bore little direct relationship to them, for by this time Smart's original design had begun to disintegrate.

SUPPLEMENTARY DATA

We have not tried to supply biographical data on the poets, although the dates of their births and deaths will be found with the poems, and those of their principal works in the charts which are a supplement to each volume. The amount of biographical data which could have been supplied within the volumes would in actuality have been meaningless. For such study there are published biographies which it would have been folly to attempt to summarize in a few lines. We have preferred to print more poems.

If there is anything in the nature of biography in the various volumes, it is the autobiography of the poetical imagination and fancy as it has been expressed in poems. Comments on this autobiography occur in the introductions to each volume, which are meant not to be definitive but to suggest as freshly as possible the problems with which poetry has coped. Instead of biographical data for each poet, therefore, we have drawn

[1] For a fuller discussion of the manuscript and Smart's intent, see Bond, William H., "Christopher Smart's *Jubilate Agno*," *Harvard Library Bulletin*, IV, i (Winter 1950), pp. 39–52.

up tables in which, on one side, is given the direct course of poetry and, on the other, are to be found certain of the cultural and societal events which had formative effect. These will be of some help, we trust, toward seeing the course of poetry in historical perspective.

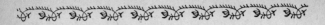

A Calendar of British
and American Poetry

GENERAL BACKGROUND	DATE	DIRECT HISTORY
First charter granted an English East India Company	1600	Allot, ed., *England's Parnassus:* miscellany of verse
Peri's *Euridice:* first extant opera		Bodenham, ed., *England's Helicon:* miscellany of verse
		Dekker, *The Shoemaker's Holiday*
		Nashe, *Summer's Last Will*
	1600–49	William Strode; greater part of poetry not published until 1907
	1601	Jonson, *Cynthia's Revels; Every Man in his Humour*
Bodleian Library opened	1602	Campion, *Art of English Poesie*
		Jonson, *Poetaster*
Florio, translation of Montaigne	1603	Daniel, *Defense of Rhyme*
		Jonson, *Sejanus*
		Shakespeare, *Hamlet*
	1604	Breton, *Passionate Shepherd*
		Marlowe, *Doctor Faustus:* written c.1590
		Marston, *The Malcontent*
King James Version of the Bible	1604–11	
Bacon, *Advancement of Learning*	1605	Drayton, *Certain Small Poems*
Cervantes, *Don Quixote,* first part, published		
	1606	Drayton, *Poems Lyric and Pastoral*
		The Return from Parnassus: Cambridge drama
Founding of Jamestown Colony	1607	Chapman, *Bussy D'Ambois*
		Heywood, *A Woman Killed with Kindness*
Monteverdi's *Orfeo* performed at Mantua		Jonson, *Volpone*
		Shakespeare, *Anthony and Cleopatra* acted; first published in First Folio, 1623
		Tourneur (?), *The Revenger's Tragedy*

GENERAL BACKGROUND	DATE	DIRECT HISTORY
Hall, *Characters of Vertues and Vices*	1608	Shakespeare, *King Lear*
Lippershey invents the telescope		
Avisa Relation oder Zeitung, first newspaper	1609	Shakespeare, *Sonnets*
Dekker, *The Gul's Hornebooke*		
	1610	Campion, *Two Books of Airs*
		Daniel, *Tethys Festival*
		Giles Fletcher, *Christ's Victory and Triumph*
		John Fletcher, *The Faithful Shepherdess*
		Richard Rich, *News from Virginia*
	c.1610	Shakespeare, *The Tempest* acted
	1611	Donne, *Anatomy of the World*
Brinsley, *Ludus literarius: or the Grammar Schoole*	1612	Jonson, *The Alchemist*
Heywood, *An Apology for Actors*		Textor, *Epitheta:* helps in composing verse
Purchas, *Purchas his Pilgrimage*		Webster, *The White Divel*
Shelton, translation of *Don Quixote*	1612–20	
Galileo, *Istoria e dimostrazioni delle macchie solari:* discovery that the sun turns on its axis	1613	
Globe Playhouse burned		
Overbury, *Characters*	1614	
Ralegh, *The History of the World*	1616	Chapman completes translation of *Whole Works* of Homer
		Drummond of Hawthornden, *Poems*
		Jonson, *Works,* first folio
	1617	Jonson, *Vision of Delight* presented; published in 1640 folio
Outbreak of the Thirty Years' War	1618	Chapman, translation of Hesiod's *Georgics*
First importation of Negro slaves into Virginia	1619	Beaumont and Fletcher, *The Maid's Tragedy*
		Pavier quartos: first attempt to collect Shakespeare
Arrival of Pilgrims at Plymouth	1620	Beaumont and Fletcher, *Philaster*
Bacon, *Novum Organum*		
Burton, *The Anatomy of Melancholy*	1621	

GENERAL BACKGROUND	DATE	DIRECT HISTORY
Mun, *A Discourse of Trade from England unto the East Indies*	1621	
	1622	Shakespeare, *Othello*
Drummond of Hawthornden, *Cypress Grove*	1623	Browne, "On the Countess Dowager of Pembroke," in Camden's *Remains*
		Drummond of Hawthornden, *Flowers of Sion*
		Shakespeare, First Folio
		Webster, *The Dutchesse of Malfi*
Herbert of Cherbury, *De Veritate*	1624	Chapman, translation of *Battle of Frogs and Mice*
		Donne, *Devotions upon Emergent Occasions*
Grotius, *De jure belli ac pacis*	1625	
New Amsterdam founded		
Donne, *Five Sermons*	1626	
Roper, *The Life of Syr T. More*		
	1627	Drayton, *Shepherd's Sirena; The Moon Calf*
Kepler, *Tabulae Rudolphinae:* astronomical tables of Tycho Brahe	1627–30	
Bernini begins tomb of Urban VIII (rise of Baroque)	1628	
Harvey, *Exercitatio anatomica de motu cardis et sanguinis in animalibus*		
Mun, *England's Treasure by Forraign Trade* written	1630	Drayton, *Muses Elizium* (*Noah's Floud*, etc.)
Galileo, *Dialogo dei due massimi sistemi del mondo*	1632	
	1633	Cowley, *Poetical Blossoms*
		Donne, *Poems*
		Phineas Fletcher, *The Purple Island*
		Ford, *The Broken Heart; 'Tis Pity She's a Whore*
		George Herbert, *The Temple*
		Massinger, *A New Way to Pay Old Debts*
	1634	Carew, *Coelum Britannicum*
		John Fletcher (and Shakespeare?), *The Two Noble Kinsmen*
Founding of the French Academy	1635	Quarles, *Emblems*
Founding of Harvard College	1636	
	1637?–74	Thomas Traherne; poems not published until 1903

GENERAL BACKGROUND	DATE	DIRECT HISTORY
Descartes, *Discours de la méthode* Hobbes, *A Briefe of the Art of Rhetorique*	1637	Milton, *Comus, a Masque Presented at Ludlow Castle*
New Sweden founded	1638	Milton, "Lycidas," in *Obsequies to . . . Edward King*
Bay Psalm Book: first book printed in English colonies in America Jonson, *Timber: or, Discoveries* Walton, *The Life and Death of Dr. Donne*	1640	Beaumont, *Poems* Carew, *Poems*
Browne, *Religio Medici* Milton, *The Reason of Church-Government Urg'd against Prelaty* Outbreak of Civil War	1642	Denham, *Cooper's Hill*
Milton, *The Doctrine and Discipline of Divorce*	1643	
Milton, *Areopagitica* Roger Williams, *The Bloudy Tenent of Persecution for Cause of Conscience, Discussed*	1644	
	1644–1729	Edward Taylor, poems chiefly published 1939
	1645	Milton, *Poems* Waller, *Poems*
	1646	Crashaw, *Steps to the Temple* Shirley, *Poems* Suckling, *Fragmenta Aurea* Vaughan, *Poems*
	1647	Beaumont and Fletcher, *Comedies and Tragedies* Cowley, *The Mistress*
End of Thirty Years' War Fox founds Society of Friends	1648	Herrick, *Hesperides*
Donne, *Fifty Sermons* England as commonwealth; execution of Charles I	1649	Lovelace, *Lucasta*
	1650	Anne Bradstreet, *The Tenth Muse lately sprung up in America* Marvell, "A Horatian Ode upon Cromwell's Return from Ireland"
	1650–55	Vaughan, *Silex Scintillans*
Hobbes, *Leviathan* Taylor, *The Rule and Exercises of Holy Dying*	1651	Cleveland, *Poems* D'Avenant, *Gondibert*, with critical preface, and

GENERAL BACKGROUND	DATE	DIRECT HISTORY
	1651	Hobbes's *Answer to D'Avenant*
		Vaughan, *Olor Iscanus*
Urquhart, translation of Rabelais, books I–II	1653	Fanshawe, translation of *The Lusiad* of Camoëns
Walton, *The Compleat Angler*		Lawes, *Airs and Dialogues*, containing Townshend's "Dialogue"
		Middleton and Rowley, *The Changeling*
		Strode, *Floating Island*
Johnson, *A History of New-England*	1654	
	1656	Cowley, *Poems*, with critical preface
		Drummond of Hawthornden, *Poems*
	1657	Henry King, *Poems*
		Poole, *The English Parnassus: Or, A Help to English Poesie*
Browne, *Hydriotaphia, Urne-Buriall*	1658	
Baxter, *A Holy Commonwealth*	1659	Lovelace, *Posthume Poems*
Molière, *Les Précieuses ridicules*		Shirley, *The Contention of Ajax and Ulysses, for the Arms of Achilles*
Boyle, *New Experiments Physico-Mechanical*	1660	
Founding of the Royal Society		
Restoration of the English monarchy		
Beginning of personal government of Louis XIV: "*L'état, c'est moi*"; Court of Versailles established	1661	
Fuller, *The History of the Worthies of England*	1662	Wigglesworth, *The Day of Doom*
	1662–78	Butler, *Hudibras*
Boyle, *Experiments and Considerations touching Colours*	1664	
New Netherlands captured by English, and rechristened New York		
Boyle, *Occasional Reflections*	1665	Herbert of Cherbury, *Occasional Verses*
The Great Plague		
Bunyan, *Grace Abounding to the Chief of Sinners*	1666	Philip Pain, *Daily Meditations*: apparently first original verse printed in English colonies in America
The Great Fire of London		
Molière, *Le Misanthrope*		
Racine, *Andromaque*	1667	Milton, *Paradise Lost*
Sprat, *The History of the Royal-Society of London*		

GENERAL BACKGROUND	DATE	DIRECT HISTORY
Dryden, *Of Dramatick Poesie*	1668	
La Fontaine, *Fables,* books I–VI		
Dryden made first poet laureate	1670	Dryden, *The Tempest,* redacted from Shakespeare's play
First celebration of Feast of Sacred Heart, originated by Jean Eudes		Wigglesworth, *Meat Out of the Eater*
Pascal, *Pensées*		
	1671	Milton, *Paradise Regained; Samson Agonistes*
	1672	Dryden, *The Conquest of Granada*
	1673	Dryden, *Marriage A-la-Mode*
Boileau, *L'Art poétique*	1674	
Traherne, *Christian Ethicks*	1675	Rochester, *A Satyr Against Mankind*
Wren starts rebuilding St. Paul's Cathedral		
Wycherley, *The Country-Wife*		
	1676	Dryden, *Aurung-Zebe*
Racine, *Phèdre*	1677	
Wycherley, *The Plain-Dealer*		
Bunyan, *The Pilgrim's Progress,* Part I	1678	Dryden, *All for Love*
	1680	Roscommon, translation of Horace's *Art of Poetry*
	1681	Marvell, *Miscellaneous Poems*
	1681–82	Dryden, *Absalom and Achitophel*
	1682	Dryden, *MacFlecknoe; Religio Laici*
		John Sheffield, Duke of Buckingham, *An Essay upon Poetry*
Ashmolean Museum founded	1683	
Boyle, *Memoirs for the Natural History of Humane Blood*	1684	Roscommon, *An Essay on Translated Verse*
Leibniz's theory of the infinitesimal calculus made public		
	1685	Rochester, *Valentinian*
Newton, *Philosophiae naturalis principia mathematica*	1687	
Aphra Behn, *Oroonoko; or, the Royal Slave:* a novel	1688	
La Bruyère, *Les Caractères*		
The Glorious Revolution		
Purcell, *Dido and Aeneas:* an opera	1689	Cotton, *Poems on Several Occasions*
Locke, *Essay concerning Human Understanding; Two Treatises*	1690	

GENERAL BACKGROUND	DATE	DIRECT HISTORY
Temple, "An Essay upon the Ancient and Modern Learning": a defense of classicism	1690	
Bank of England chartered	1691	
Langbaine, *An Account of the English Dramatick Poets*: first scholarly study of Shakespeare		
	1694	Dryden, *Love Triumphant*
	1697	Dryden, *Alexander's Feast*
Collier, *A Short View of the Immorality and Profaneness of the English Stage*	1698	
Congreve, *The Way of the World*	1700	Pomfret, *The Choice*
Motteux, translation of *Don Quixote*	1701	Defoe, *The True-Born Englishman*
		John Philips, *The Splendid Shilling*
Cotton Mather, *Magnalia Christi Americana*	1702	Bysshe, *The Art of English Poetry*: most famous handbook for English poets, frequently revised and widely used; contains a rhyming dictionary, a poetic commonplace book, and "Rules for Making English Verse"
Clarendon, *The History of the Rebellion and Civil Wars in England*	1702–04	
The Daily Courant: first English daily newspaper	1702–35	
Swift, *A Tale of a Tub; The Battel of the Books*	1704	Wycherley, *Miscellany Poems*
Boston News-Letter: first American newspaper	1704–76	
Newcomen invents his steam engine	c.1705	
	1706	Watts, *Horae Lyricae*
Farquhar, *The Beaux Stratagem*	1707	Prior, *Poems on Several Occasions*
		Watts, *Hymns and Spiritual Songs*
	1708	Philips, *Cyder*
Berkeley, *An Essay towards a New Theory of Vision*	1709	Pope, *Pastorals*
First Copyright Act		
Rowe's edition of Shakespeare: first illustrated and first edited text		
Steele, *The Tatler*	1709–11	
Cotton Mather, *Bonifacius* (*Essays to Do Good*)	1710	

GENERAL BACKGROUND	DATE	DIRECT HISTORY
Building of Zwinger Palace in Dresden begins: triumph of Rococo	1711	Pope, *An Essay on Criticism*
Shaftesbury, *Characteristics of Men, Manners, Opinions, Times:* most important of the deists		
Addison, *The Spectator*	1711–12	
Papal bull: *Unigenitus,* condemns Jansenism	1712	
	1713	Gay, *Rural Sports*
		Parnell, *An Essay on the Different Stiles of Poetry*
		Pope, *Windsor-Forest*
		Countess of Winchilsea, *Miscellany Poems*
	1714	Gay, *The Shepherd's Week*
		Pope, *The Rape of the Lock*
	1715	Watts, *Divine Songs attempted in Easy Language for the Use of Children*
	1715–20	Pope's translation of the *Iliad*
	1716	Gay, *Trivia: or, the Art of Walking the Streets of London*
Wise, *A Vindication of the Government of New-England Churches*	1717	
Founding of New Orleans by the French	1718	Gildon, *Complete Art of Poetry:* "a collection of the most beautiful Descriptions, Similes, Allusions, etc."
Defoe, *Robinson Crusoe*	1719	
	1720	Gay, *Poems on Several Occasions*
Cotton Mather, *The Christian Philosopher*	1721	Addison, *Works*
Last execution of witches among the English-speaking peoples (at Dornoch, Scotland)	1722	
Defoe, *A Tour thro' the whole Island of Great Britain*	1724	Ramsay, *The Ever Green:* collection of old Scottish poetry
Vico's *Principi di una scienza nuova*	1725	
Watts, *Logick*		
Swift, *Travels into Several Remote Nations of the World. By Lemuel Gulliver*	1726	Dyer, *Grongar Hill,* final version
		Swift, *Cadenus and Vanessa*
Theobald, *Shakespeare Restored*		Thomson, *Winter*
	1727	Thomson, *Summer*

GENERAL BACKGROUND	DATE	DIRECT HISTORY
Chambers, comp., *Cyclopædia, or an Universal Dictionary of Arts and Sciences*: first important encyclopedia in English Law, *A Serious Call to a Devout and Holy Life*	1728	Gay, *The Beggar's Opera* Pope, *The Dunciad*
	1728	Thomson, *Spring*
	1730	Thomson, *The Seasons*
	1732	Pope, *Of the Use of Riches*
	1733–34	Pope, *An Essay on Man*
First English translation of La Fontaine (anonymous) Voltaire, *Lettres philosophiques . . . sur les anglais*	1734	Swift, *On Poetry: A Rapsody*
Flora, or Hob-in-the-Well, produced in Charleston, S.C.: first ballad-opera performance in America Hogarth, *The Rake's Progress* Linnaeus, *Systema naturae*	1735	Pope, *An Epistle to Dr. Arbuthnot*
Letters of Mr. Pope, and Several Eminent Persons	1735	
Butler, *The Analogy of Religion, Natural and Revealed, to the Constitution and Course of Nature*	1736	William Dawson, *Poems on Several Occasions*, "By a Gentleman of Virginia"
	1737	Matthew Green, *The Spleen* Shenstone, *Poems upon Various Occasions*
John Wesley's evangelical conversion; the Methodist revival	1738	Hayward, *The British Muse: a commonplace book* Johnson, *London*
Hume, *A Treatise of Human Nature*	1739–40	
Richardson, *Pamela: or, Virtue Rewarded*	1740	
Jonathan Edwards, *Sinners in the Hands of an Angry God*	1741	Charles and John Wesley, *A Collection of Psalms and Hymns*
Fielding, *The History of the Adventures of Joseph Andrews*	1742	Collins, *Persian Eclogues* Shenstone, *The School-Mistress*
	1742–47	Young, *The Complaint: or, Night-Thoughts on Life, Death and Immortality*
American Philosophical Society founded Handel's *Messiah* first performed in England	1743	Blair, *The Grave*
	1744	Akenside, *The Pleasures of Imagination*

GENERAL BACKGROUND	DATE	DIRECT HISTORY
	1744	Armstrong, *The Art of Preserving Health*
		Joseph Warton, *The Enthusiast; or, the Lover of Nature*
	1745	Akenside, *Odes on Several Subjects*
Horace Walpole acquires Strawberry Hill; Gothic additions begun 1749	1747	Collins, *Odes on Several Descriptions and Allegorical Subjects*
		Gray, *Ode on a distant prospect of Eton College*
		Thomas Warton, *The Pleasures of Melancholy*
Montesquieu, *L'Esprit des lois* Richardson, *Clarissa* Smollett, *The Adventures of Roderick Random*	1748	Thomson, *The Castle of Indolence*
Fielding, *The History of Tom Jones*	1749	Johnson, *The Vanity of Human Wishes; Irene: A Tragedy*
Swedenborg, *Arcana Coelestia*	1749–56	
Buffon, *Histoire naturelle*	1749–88	
J. S. Bach, *Die Kunst der Fuge:* end of polyphonic period Rousseau, *Discours sur les arts et les sciences*	1750	
Johnson, *The Rambler:* a bi-weekly	1750–52	
French *Encyclopédie,* Vols. i–ii Hume, *An Enquiry concerning the Principles of Morals*	1751	Gray, *Elegy Written in a Country Church Yard*
Franklin, *Experiments and Observations on Electricity*	1751–54	
Gregorian Calendar adopted for England and her colonies	1752	Smart, *Poems on Several Occasions*
British Museum founded Mrs. Charlotte Lennox, *Shakespear Illustrated:* first collection of Shakespearean sources	1753	
Jonathan Edwards, *Freedom of the Will* Hume, *History of Great Britain,* Vol. i	1754	
Johnson, *A Dictionary of the English Language*	1755	
Burke, *On the Sublime and Beautiful*	1756	

GENERAL BACKGROUND	DATE	DIRECT HISTORY
Walpole establishes Strawberry Hill Press	1757	*The Beauties of Poetry Display'd*: "common-place book"
		Collins, *Oriental Eclogues*
		Dyer, *The Fleece*
		Gray, *Odes*: "Progress of Poesy," "The Bard"
Franklin, "Way to Wealth" (in *Poor Richard's Almanac*)	1758	
Helvétius, *De l'Esprit*		
Johnson, *The Idler*: weekly gazette	1758–60	
Johnson, *The History of Rasselas*	1759	
Lessing, *Briefe, die neueste Litteratur betreffend*	1759	
Robertson, *History of Scotland during the Reign of Queen Mary*		
Voltaire, *Candide*		
Rousseau, *La Nouvelle Héloïse*	1760	
Sterne, *Tristram Shandy*	1760–67	
Piranesi, *Della magnificenza ed architettura de' Romani*	1761	Churchill, *The Rosciad*
		Derrick, *A Poetical Dictionary*: dictionary of familiar quotations
Goldsmith, *The Citizen of the World*	1762	Macpherson, *Fingal, An Ancient Epic Poem*
Gluck, *Orfeo ed Euridice*, Vienna		
Kames, *Elements of Criticism*		
Rousseau, *Le contrat social*		
Stuart and Revett, *Antiquities of Athens*		
	1763	Smart, *A Song to David*
Rousseau, *Emile*	1764	Churchill, *Gotham*
Voltaire, *Dictionnaire philosophique*		
Winckelmann, *Geschichte der Kunst des Altertums*		
Goldsmith, *Essays* collected	1765	Percy, *Reliques of Ancient English Poetry*
The Stamp Act		
Walpole, *The Castle of Otranto*		
Blackstone, *Commentaries on the Laws of England*	1765–68	
Goldsmith, *The Vicar of Wakefield*	1766	
Lessing, *Laokoön*		
Herder, *Fragmente über die neuere deutsche Litteratur*: program for *Sturm und Drang*	1767	

GENERAL BACKGROUND	DATE	DIRECT HISTORY
Dickinson, *Letters from a Farmer in Pennsylvania to the Inhabitants of the British Colonies*	1768	Gray, *Poems*
Royal Academy of Arts founded; Reynolds president		
Sterne, *A Sentimental Journey through France and Italy*		
Watt's steam engine patented	1769	
Reynolds, *Discourses*	1769–91	
Hargreaves's spinning jenny patented	1770	Goldsmith, *The Deserted Village*
Holbach, *La Système de la nature*		
	1771–74	Beattie, *The Minstrel*
	1772	John Trumbull, *The Progress of Dullness*
Goldsmith, *She Stoops to Conquer*	1773	John Byrom, *Miscellaneous Poems*
First American museum organized at Charleston, S.C.		Phillis Wheatley, *Poems on Various Subjects:* first book of poems by a Negro in America
Chesterfield, *Letters Written by the Earl of Chesterfield to His Son, Philip Stanhope*	1774	Goldsmith, *Retaliation*
Gluck, *Iphigénie en Aulide,* first performance, Paris		
Goethe, *Die Leiden des jungen Werthers*		
	1774–81	Thomas Warton, *The History of English Poetry*
Beaumarchais, *Le Barbier de Séville,* first performance	1775	Walker, *A Dictionary of the English Language, answering at once the Purposes of Rhyming, Spelling and Pronouncing*
Burke, *Speech . . . on Moving his Resolution for Conciliation with the Colonies*		
Sheridan, *The Rivals*		
Declaration of American Independence	1776	
Paine, *Common Sense*		
Adam Smith, *Wealth of Nations*		
Gibbon, *Decline and Fall of the Roman Empire*	1776–88	
	1777	Chatterton, *Poems* (presented as though written by Thomas Rowley in the 15th century)
		Thomas Warton, *Poems*
Frances Burney, *Evelina*	1778	

GENERAL BACKGROUND	DATE	DIRECT HISTORY
Hume, *Dialogues concerning Natural Religion*	1779	Cowper, *Olney Hymns*
Mesmer, *Mémoire sur la découverte du magnétisme animal:* theory of hypnotism		
	1779–81	Johnson, *Prefaces, Biographical and Critical, to the English Poets*
Wieland, *Oberon*	1780	
Kant, *Kritik der reinen Vernunft* (Critique of Pure Reason)	1781	
Schiller, *Die Räuber*		
Rousseau, *Confessions*	1781–88	
Crèvecœur, *Letters from an American Farmer*	1782	Cowper, "John Gilpin": first appearance
Trimmer, *An Easy Introduction to the Knowledge of Nature*	1782	Trumbull, *M'Fingal*
Noah Webster, *Spelling Book*	1782–83	
Blair, *Lectures on Rhetoric and Belles Lettres*	1783	Blake, *Poetical Sketches*
		Crabbe, *The Village*
William Herschel, *On the Proper Motion of the Sun and Solar Systems*		Trusler, *Poetic Endings, or, A Dictionary of Rhymes*
Sheridan, *The School for Scandal*		
Jefferson, *Notes on the State of Virginia,* published at Paris	1784	
Kant, *Ideen zu einer allgemeiner Geschichte in weltbürgerliche Absicht*		
Herder, *Ideen zur Philosophie der Geschichte der Menschheit*	1784–91	
Kant, *Grundlegung zur Metaphysik der Sitten:* metaphysics of morals	1785	Cowper, *The Task*
		Dwight, *The Conquest of Canaan*
Charles Wilkins' translation of the *Bhagavadgita:* first in English		
Beckford, *Vathek*	1786	Burns, *Poems chiefly in the Scottish Dialect*
		Freneau, *Poems*
		Rogers, *An Ode to Superstition*
		Wolcot, *Bozzy and Piozzi*
Goethe, *Iphigenie auf Tauris*	1787	Barlow, *The Vision of Columbus (The Columbiad)*
Mozart, *Don Giovanni*		
The Federalist	1787–88	
Goethe, *Egmont*	1788	Collins, *An Ode on Popular*

GENERAL BACKGROUND	DATE	DIRECT HISTORY
Kant, *Kritik der practischen Vernunft* (Critique of Practical Reason) United States Constitution ratified	1788	*Superstitions of the Highlands of Scotland* Whitehead, *Poems*
Bentham, *An Introduction to the Principles of Morals and Legislation:* utilitarianism Erasmus Darwin, *The Loves of the Plants* Fall of the Bastille White, *Natural History and Antiquities of Selborne*	1789	Blake, *The Book of Thel; Songs of Innocence*
Bewick, *A General History of Quadrupeds* Malone's edition of Shakespeare	1790	Blake, *The Marriage of Heaven and Hell*
William Bartram, *Travels through North and South Carolina, Georgia, East and West Florida . . .* Boswell, *The Life of Samuel Johnson* De Sade, *Justine*	1791	Burns, "Tam o' Shanter": first appearance
Brackenridge, *Modern Chivalry,* Parts I–II: a novel Wollstonecraft, *A Vindication of the Rights of Woman*	1792	Ritson, *Ancient Songs from the Time of King Henry III to the Revolution* Rogers, *The Pleasures of Memory*
Carnot's *levée en masse:* beginning of universal military conscription; cult of the Goddess of Reason; decimal system adopted by the National Assembly; execution of Louis XVI and Reign of Terror Dalton, *Meteorological Observations and Essays:* ultimately leading to atomic theory Godwin, *Political Justice* Louvre established	1793	Blake, *America, A Prophecy* Wordsworth, *An Evening Walk*
Paley, *A View of the Evidences of Christianity* Radcliffe, *Mysteries of Udolpho* Slavery in French colonies abolished by the National Assembly Whitney patents his cotton gin	1794	Blake, *Songs of Innocence and Experience* Dwight, *Greenfield Hill*

GENERAL BACKGROUND	DATE	DIRECT HISTORY
Murray, *English Grammar:* widely used in American schools	1795	*The Poems of Walter Savage Landor,* suppressed by Landor
Goethe, *Wilhelm Meisters Lehrjahre*	1795–96	
Lewis, *The Monk*	1796	Barlow, *The Hasty Pudding*
Jean Paul Richter, *Quintus Fixlein*		Coleridge, *Poems on Various Subjects*
Washington, "Farewell Address"		
Goethe, *Hermann und Dorothea*	1797	
C. B. Brown, *Wieland*	1798	Wordsworth and Coleridge, *Lyrical Ballads*
Malthus, *Principle of Population as it affects the Future of Society*		
Napoleon's *coup* of the 18th Brumaire	1799	Moore, *Odes of Anacreon,* translated into English Verse
Mme de Staël, *De la Littérature considérée dans ses rapports avec les institutions sociales:* the advent of democracy requires a pure language	1799	Scott, *The Eve of St. John* Wordsworth and Coleridge, *Lyrical Ballads,* Vol. II

John Milton

(1608–1674)

On the Morning of Christs Nativity

Compos'd 1629

This is the Month, and this the happy morn
Wherin the Son of Heav'ns eternal King,
Of wedded Maid, and Virgin Mother born,
Our great redemption from above did bring;
For so the holy sages once did sing,
 That he our deadly forfeit should release,
And with his Father work us a perpetual peace.

That glorious Form, that Light unsufferable,
And that far-beaming blaze of Majesty,
Wherwith he wont at Heav'ns high Councel-Table,
To sit the midst of Trinal Unity,
He laid aside; and here with us to be,
 Forsook the Courts of everlasting Day,
And chose with us a darksom House of mortal Clay.

Say Heav'nly Muse, shall not thy sacred vein
Afford a present to the Infant God?
Hast thou no vers, no hymn, or solemn strein,
To welcom him to this his new abode,
Now while the Heav'n by the Suns team untrod,
 Hath took no print of the approching light,
And all the spangled host keep watch in squadrons
  bright?

1

See how from far upon the Eastern rode
The Star-led Wisards haste with odours sweet:
O run, prevent them with thy humble ode,
And lay it lowly at his blessed feet;
Have thou the honour first, thy Lord to greet,
   And joyn thy voice unto the Angel Quire,
From out his secret Altar toucht with hallow'd fire.

THE HYMN

It was the Winter wilde,
While the Heav'n-born-childe,
   All meanly wrapt in the rude manger lies;
Nature in aw to him
Had doff't her gawdy trim,
   With her great Master so to sympathize:
It was no season then for her
To wanton with the Sun her lusty Paramour.

Onely with speeches fair
She woo's the gentle Air
   To hide her guilty front with innocent Snow;
And on her naked shame,
Pollute with sinfull blame,
   The Saintly Vail of Maiden white to throw,
Confounded, that her Makers eyes
Should look so neer upon her foul deformities.

But he her fears to cease,
Sent down the meek-eyd Peace,
   She crown'd with Olive green, came softly sliding
Down through the turning sphear
His ready Harbinger,
   With Turtle wing the amorous clouds dividing,
And waving wide her mirtle wand,
She strikes a universall Peace through Sea and Land.

No War, or Battails sound
Was heard the World around:
   The idle spear and shield were high up hung;
The hooked Chariot stood
Unstain'd with hostile blood,
   The Trumpet spake not to the armed throng,
And Kings sate still with awfull eye,
As if they surely knew their sovran Lord was by.

But peacefull was the night
Wherin the Prince of light
   His raign of peace upon the earth began:
The Windes with wonder whist,
Smoothly the waters kist,
   Whispering new joyes to the milde Ocean,
Who now hath quite forgot to rave,
While Birds of Calm sit brooding on the charmed wave.

The Stars with deep amaze
Stand fixt in stedfast gaze,
   Bending one way their pretious influence,
And will not take their flight,
For all the morning light,
   Or *Lucifer* that often warn'd them thence;
But in their glimmering Orbs did glow,
Untill their Lord himself bespake, and bid them go.

And though the shady gloom
Had given day her room,
   The Sun himself with-held his wonted speed,
And hid his head for shame,
As his inferiour flame,
   The new-enlightn'd world no more should need;
He saw a greater Sun appear
Then his bright Throne, or burning Axletree could bear.

The Shepherds on the Lawn,
Or ere the point of dawn,
   Sate simply chatting in a rustick row;
Full little thought they than,
That the mighty *Pan*
   Was kindly com to live with them below;
Perhaps their loves, or els their sheep,
Was all that did their silly thoughts so busie keep.

When such musick sweet
Their hearts and ears did greet,
   As never was by mortall finger strook,
Divinely-warbled voice
Answering the stringed noise,
   As all their souls in blisfull rapture took:
The Air such pleasure loth to lose,
With thousand echo's still prolongs each heav'nly close.

Nature that heard such sound
Beneath the hollow round
   Of *Cynthia's* seat, the Airy region thrilling.
Now was almost won
To think her part was don,
   And that her raign had here its last fulfilling;
She knew such harmony alone
Could hold all Heav'n and Earth in happier union.

At last surrounds their sight
A Globe of circular light,
   That with long beams the shame-fac't night array'd,
The helmed Cherubim
And sworded Seraphim,
   Are seen in glittering ranks with wings displaid,
Harping in loud and solemn quire,
With unexpressive notes to Heav'ns new-born Heir.

Such Musick (as 'tis said)
Before was never made,
   But when of old the sons of morning sung,
While the Creator Great
His constellations set,
   And the well-balanc't world on hinges hung,
And cast the dark foundations deep,
And bid the weltring waves their oozy channel keep.

Ring out ye Crystall sphears,
Once bless our human ears,
   (If ye have power to touch our senses so)
And let your silver chime
Move in melodious time;
   And let the Base of Heav'ns deep Organ blow,
And with your ninefold harmony
Make up full consort to th'Angelike symphony.

For if such holy Song
Enwrap our fancy long,
   Time will run back, and fetch the age of gold,
And speckl'd vanity
Will sicken soon and die,
   And leprous sin will melt from earthly mould,
And Hell it self will pass away,
And leave her dolorous mansions to the peering day.

Yea Truth, and Justice then
Will down return to men,
   Orb'd in a Rain-bow; and like glories wearing
Mercy will sit between,
Thron'd in Celestiall sheen,
   With radiant feet the tissued clouds down stearing,
And Heav'n as at som festivall,
Will open wide the Gates of her high Palace Hall.

But wisest Fate sayes no,
This must not yet be so,
  The Babe lies yet in smiling Infancy,
That on the bitter cross
Must redeem our loss;
  So both himself and us to glorifie:
Yet first to those ychain'd in sleep,
The wakefull trump of doom must thunder through the
    deep,

With such a horrid clang
As on mount *Sinai* rang
  While the red fire, and smouldring clouds out brake:
The aged Earth agast
With terrour of that blast,
  Shall from the surface to the center shake;
When at the worlds last session,
The dreadfull Judge in middle Air shall spread his
    throne.

And then at last our bliss
Full and perfect is,
  But now begins; for from this happy day
Th'old Dragon under ground
In straiter limits bound,
  Not half so far casts his usurped sway,
And wrath to see his Kingdom fail,
Swindges the scaly Horrour of his foulded tail.

The Oracles are dumm,
No voice or hideous humm
  Runs through the arched roof in words deceiving.
Apollo from his shrine
Can no more divine,
  With hollow shreik the steep of *Delphos* leaving.

No nightly trance, or breathed spell,
Inspire's the pale-ey'd Priest from the prophetic cell.

The lonely mountains o're,
And the resounding shore,
    A voice of weeping heard, and loud lament;
From haunted spring, and dale
Edg'd with poplar pale.
    The parting Genius is with sighing sent,
With flowre-inwov'n tresses torn
The Nimphs in twilight shade of tangled thickets mourn.

In consecrated Earth,
And on the holy Hearth,
    The *Lars,* and *Lemures* moan with midnight plaint,
In Urns, and Altars round,
A drear, and dying sound
    Affrights the *Flamins* at their service quaint;
And the chill Marble seems to sweat,
While each peculiar power forgoes his wonted seat.

Peor, and *Baalim,*
Forsake their Temples dim,
    With that twise batter'd god of *Palestine,*
And mooned *Ashtaroth,*
Heav'ns Queen and Mother both,
    Now sits not girt with Tapers holy shine,
The Libyc *Hammon* shrinks his horn,
In vain the *Tyrian* Maids their wounded *Thamuz*
    mourn.

And sullen *Moloch* fled,
Hath left in shadows dred,
    His burning Idol all of blackest hue,
In vain with Cymbals ring,
They call the grisly king,
    In dismall dance about the furnace blue,

The brutish gods of *Nile* as fast,
Isis and *Orus,* and the Dog *Anubis* hast.

Nor is *Osiris* seen
In *Memphian* Grove, or Green,
   Trampling the unshowr'd Grasse with lowings loud:
Nor can he be at rest
Within his sacred chest,
   Naught but profoundest Hell can be his shroud,
In vain with Timbrel'd Anthems dark
The sable-stoled Sorcerers bear his worshipt Ark.

He feels from *Juda's* Land
The dredded Infants hand,
   The rayes of *Bethlehem* blind his dusky eyn;
Nor all the gods beside,
Longer dare abide,
   Not *Typhon* huge ending in snaky twine:
Our Babe to shew his Godhead true,
Can in his swadling bands controul the damned crew.

So when the Sun in bed,
Curtain'd with cloudy red,
   Pillows his chin upon an Orient wave.
The flocking shadows pale,
Troop to th'infernall jail,
   Each fetter'd Ghost slips to his severall grave,
And the yellow-skirted *Fayes,*
Fly after the Night-steed, leaving their Moon-lov'd
     maze.

But see the Virgin blest,
Hath laid her Babe to rest.
   Time is our tedious Song should here have ending,
Heav'ns youngest teemed Star,
Hath fixt her polisht Car.

Her sleeping Lord with Handmaid Lamp attending.
And all about the Courtly Stable,
Bright-harnest Angels sit in order serviceable.

At a Solemn Musick

Blest pair of *Sirens,* pledges of Heav'ns joy,
Sphear-born harmonious Sisters, Voice, and Vers,
Wed your divine sounds, and mixt power employ
Dead things with inbreath'd sense able to pierce,
And to our high-rais'd phantasie present,
That undisturbed Song of pure content,
Ay sung before the saphire-colour'd throne
To him that sits theron
With Saintly shout, and solemn Jubily,
Where the bright Seraphim in burning row
Their loud up-lifted Angel trumpets blow,
And the Cherubick host in thousand quires
Touch their immortal Harps of golden wires,
With those just Spirits that wear victorious Palms,
Hymns devout and holy Psalms
Singing everlastingly;
That we on Earth with undiscording voice
May rightly answer that melodious noise;
As once we did, till disproportion'd sin
Jarr'd against natures chime, and with harsh din
Broke the fair musick that all creatures made
To their great Lord, whose love their motion sway'd
In perfect Diapason, whilst they stood
In first obedience, and their state of good.
O may we soon again renew that Song,
And keep in tune with Heav'n, till God ere long
To his celestial consort us unite,
To live with him, and sing in endles morn of light.

On the Late Massacher in Piemont

Avenge O Lord thy slaughter'd Saints, whose bones
   Lie scatter'd on the Alpine mountains cold,
   Ev'n them who kept thy truth so pure of old
   When all our Fathers worship't Stocks and Stones,
Forget not: in thy book record their groanes
   Who were thy Sheep and in their antient Fold
   Slayn by the bloody *Piemontese* that roll'd
   Mother with Infant down the Rocks. Their moans
The Vales redoubl'd to the Hills, and they
   To Heav'n. Their martyr'd blood and ashes sow
   O're all th'*Italian* fields where still doth sway
The triple Tyrant: that from these may grow
   A hunder'd-fold, who having learnt thy way
   Early may fly the *Babylonian* wo.

On His Blindness

When I consider how my light is spent,
   E're half my days, in this dark world and wide,
   And that one Talent which is death to hide,
   Lodg'd with me useless, though my Soul more bent
To serve therewith my Maker, and present
   My true account, least he returning chide,
   Doth God exact day-labour, light deny'd,
   I fondly ask; But patience to prevent
That murmur, soon replies, God doth not need
   Either man's work or his own gifts, who best
   Bear his milde yoak, they serve him best, his State

Is Kingly. Thousands at his bidding speed
   And post o're Land and Ocean without rest:
   They also serve who only stand and waite.

On His Late Wife

Methought I saw my late espoused Saint
   Brought to me like *Alcestis* from the grave,
   Whom *Joves* great Son to her glad Husband gave,
   Rescu'd from death by force though pale and faint.
Mine as whom washt from spot of child-bed taint,
   Purification in the old Law did save,
   And such, as yet once more I trust to have
   Full sight of her in Heaven without restraint,
Came vested all in white, pure as her mind:
   Her face was vail'd, yet to my fancied sight,
   Love, sweetness, goodness, in her person shin'd
So clear, as in no face with more delight.
   But O as to embrace me she enclin'd
   I wak'd, she fled, and day brought back my night.

The Fifth Ode of Horace

LIB. I

Quis multa gracilis te puer in Rosa

Rendred almost word for word without Rhyme according to the Latin Measure, as near as the Language will permit.

What slender Youth bedew'd with liquid odours
Courts thee on Roses in some pleasant Cave,
   Pyrrha for whom bindst thou

In Wreaths thy golden Hair,
Plain in thy neatness; O how oft shall he
On Faith and changed Gods complain: and Seas
    Rough with black winds and storms
    Unwonted shall admire:
Who now enjoyes thee credulous, all Gold,
Who alwayes vacant always amiable
    Hopes thee; of flattering gales
    Unmindfull. Hapless they
To whom thou untry'd seem'st fair. Me in my vow'd
Picture the sacred wall declares t' have hung
    My dank and dropping weeds
    To the stern God of Sea.

Lycidas

*In this Monody the Author bewails a learned Friend, unfortu-
natly drown'd in his Passage from Chester on the Irish Seas,
1637. And by occasion foretels the ruine of our corrupted
Clergy then in their height.*

    Yet once more, O ye Laurels, and once more
    Ye Myrtles brown, with Ivy never-sear,
    I com to pluck your Berries harsh and crude,
    And with forc'd fingers rude,
    Shatter your leaves before the mellowing year.
    Bitter constraint, and sad occasion dear,
    Compels me to disturb your season due:
    For *Lycidas* is dead, dead ere his prime
    Young *Lycidas,* and hath not left his peer:
    Who would not sing for *Lycidas?* he knew
    Himself to sing, and build the lofty rhyme.
    He must not flote upon his watry bear
    Unwept, and welter to the parching wind,

Without the meed of som melodious tear.
    Begin then, Sisters of the sacred well,
That from beneath the seat of *Jove* doth spring,
Begin, and somwhat loudly sweep the string.
Hence with denial vain, and coy excuse,
So may som gentle Muse
With lucky words favour my destin'd Urn,
And as he passes turn,
And bid fair peace be to my sable shrowd.
For we were nurst upon the self-same hill,
Fed the same flock; by fountain, shade, and rill.
    Together both, ere the high Lawns appear'd
Under the opening eye-lids of the morn,
We drove a field, and both together heard
What time the Gray-fly winds her sultry horn,
Batt'ning our flocks with the fresh dews of night,
Oft till the Star that rose, at Ev'ning, bright
Toward Heav'ns descent had slop'd his westering wheel.
Mean while the Rural ditties were not mute,
Temper'd to th'Oaten Flute,
Rough *Satyrs* danc'd, and *Fauns* with clov'n heel,
From the glad sound would not be absent long,
And old *Damœtas* lov'd to hear our song.
    But O the heavy change, now thou art gon,
Now thou art gon, and never must return!
Thee Shepherd, thee the Woods, and desert Caves,
With wilde Thyme and the gadding Vine o'regrown,
And all their echoes mourn.
The Willows, and the Hazle Copses green,
Shall now no more be seen,
Fanning their joyous Leaves to thy soft layes.
As killing as the Canker to the Rose,
Or Taint-worm to the weanling Herds that graze,
Or Frost to Flowers, that their gay wardrop wear,
When first the White thorn blows;

Such, *Lycidas,* thy loss to Shepherds ear.

    Where were ye Nymphs when the remorseless deep
Clos'd o're the head of your lov'd *Lycidas?*
For neither were ye playing on the steep,
Where your old *Bards,* the famous *Druids* ly,
Nor on the shaggy top of *Mona* high,
Nor yet where *Deva* spreads her wisard stream:
Ay me, I fondly dream!
Had ye bin there—for what could that have don?
What could the Muse her self that *Orpheus* bore,
The Muse her self, for her inchanting son
Whom Universal nature did lament,
When by the rout that made the hideous roar,
His goary visage down the stream was sent,
Down the swift *Hebrus* to the *Lesbian* shore.

    Alas! What boots it with uncessant care
To tend the homely slighted Shepherds trade,
And strictly meditate the thankles Muse,
Were it not better don as others use,
To sport with *Amaryllis* in the shade,
Or with the tangles of *Neæra's* hair?
Fame is the spur that the clear spirit doth raise
(That last infirmity of Noble mind)
To scorn delights, and live laborious dayes;
But the fair Guerdon when we hope to find,
And think to burst out into sudden blaze,
Comes the blind *Fury* with th'abhorred shears,
And slits the thin-spun life. But not the praise,
Phœbus repli'd, and touch'd my trembling ears;
Fame is no plant that grows on mortal soil,
Nor in the glistering foil
Set off to th'world, nor in broad rumour lies,
But lives and spreds aloft by those pure eyes,
And perfet witnes of all-judging *Jove;*
As he pronounces lastly on each deed,

Of so much fame in Heav'n expect thy meed.

  O Fountain *Arethuse,* and thou honour'd floud,
Smooth-sliding *Mincius,* crown'd with vocall reeds,
That strain I heard was of a higher mood:
But now my Oate proceeds,
And listens to the Herald of the Sea
That came in *Neptune's* plea,
He ask'd the Waves, and ask'd the Fellon winds,
What hard mishap hath doom'd this gentle swain?
And question'd every gust of rugged wings
That blows from off each beaked Promontory,
They knew not of his story,
And sage *Hippotades* their answer brings,
That not a blast was from his dungeon stray'd,
The Ayr was calm, and on the level brine,
Sleek *Panope* with all her sisters play'd.
It was that fatall and perfidious Bark
Built in th'eclipse, and rigg'd with curses dark,
That sunk so low that sacred head of thine.

  Next *Camus,* reverend Sire, went footing slow,
His Mantle hairy, and his Bonnet sedge,
Inwrought with figures dim, and on the edge
Like to that sanguine flower inscrib'd with woe.
Ah! Who hath reft (quoth he) my dearest pledge?
Last came, and last did go,
The Pilot of the *Galilean* lake,
Two massy Keyes he bore of metals twain,
(The Golden opes, the Iron shuts amain)
He shook his Miter'd locks, and stern bespake,
How well could I have spar'd for thee young swain,
Anow of such as for their bellies sake,
Creep and intrude, and climb into the fold?
Of other care they little reck'ning make,
Then how to scramble at the shearers feast,
And shove away the worthy bidden guest.

Blind mouthes! that scarce themselves know how to
    hold
A Sheep-hook, or have learn'd ought els the least
That to the faithfull Herdmans art belongs!
What recks it them? What need they? They are sped;
And when they list, their lean and flashy songs
Grate on their scrannel Pipes of wretched straw,
The hungry Sheep look up, and are not fed,
But swoln with wind, and the rank mist they draw,
Rot inwardly, and foul contagion spread:
Besides what the grim Woolf with privy paw
Daily devours apace, and nothing sed,
But that two-handed engine at the door,
Stands ready to smite once, and smite no more.
    Return *Alpheus*, the dread voice is past,
That shrunk thy streams; Return *Sicilian* Muse,
And call the Vales, and bid them hither cast
Their Bels, and Flourets of a thousand hues.
Ye valleys low where the milde whispers use,
Of shades and wanton winds, and gushing brooks,
On whose fresh lap the swart Star sparely looks,
Throw hither all your quaint enameld eyes,
That on the green terf suck the honied showres,
And purple all the ground with vernal flowres.
Bring the rathe Primrose that forsaken dies.
The tufted Crow-toe, and pale Gessamine,
The white Pink, and the Pansie freakt with jeat,
The glowing Violet.
The Musk-rose, and the well attir'd Woodbine,
With Cowslips wan that hang the pensive hed,
And every flower that sad embroidery wears:
Bid *Amaranthus* all his beauty shed,
And Daffadillies fill their cups with tears,
To strew the Laureat Herse where *Lycid* lies.
For so to interpose a little ease,

Let our frail thoughts dally with false surmise.
Ay me! Whilst thee the shores, and sounding Seas
Wash far away, where ere thy bones are hurld,
Whether beyond the stormy *Hebrides,*
Where thou perhaps under the whelming tide
Visit'st the bottom of the monstrous world;
Or whether thou to our moist vows deny'd,
Sleep'st by the fable of *Bellerus* old,
Where the great vision of the guarded Mount
Looks toward *Namancos* and *Bayona's* hold;
Look homeward Angel now, and melt with ruth.
And, O ye *Dolphins,* waft the haples youth.

    Weep no more, woful Shepherds weep no more,
For *Lycidas* your sorrow is not dead,
Sunk though he be beneath the watry floar,
So sinks the day-star in the Ocean bed,
And yet anon repairs his drooping head,
And tricks his beams, and with new spangled Ore,
Flames in the forehead of the morning sky:
So *Lycidas* sunk low, but mounted high,
Through the dear might of him that walk'd the waves
Where other groves, and other streams along,
With *Nectar* pure his oozy Lock's he laves,
And hears the unexpressive nuptiall Song,
In the blest Kingdoms meek of joy and love.
There entertain him all the Saints above,
In solemn troops, and sweet Societies
That sing, and singing in their glory move,
And wipe the tears for ever from his eyes.
Now *Lycidas* the Shepherds weep no more;
Hence forth thou art the Genius of the shore,
In thy large recompense, and shalt be good
To all that wander in that perilous flood.

    Thus sang the uncouth Swain to th'Okes and rills,
While the still morn went out with Sandals gray,

He touch'd the tender stops of various Quills,
With eager thought warbling his *Dorick* lay:
And now the Sun had stretch'd out all the hills,
And now was dropt into the Western bay;
At last he rose, and twitch'd his Mantle blew:
To morrow to fresh Woods, and Pastures new.

FROM *Comus*

[*Comus's Praise of Nature*]

COMUS. O foolishnes of men! that lend their ears
To those budge doctors of the *Stoick* Furr,
And fetch their precepts from the *Cynick* Tub,
Praising the lean and sallow Abstinence.
Wherefore did Nature powre her bounties forth,
With such a full and unwithdrawing hand,
Covering the earth with odours, fruits, and flocks,
Thronging the Seas with spawn innumerable,
But all to please, and sate the curious taste?
And set to work millions of spinning Worms,
That in their green shops weave the smooth-hair'd silk
To deck her Sons, and that no corner might
Be vacant of her plenty, in her own loyns
She hutch't th'all-worship ore, and precious gems
To store her children with; if all the world
Should in a pet of temperance feed on Pulse,
Drink the clear stream, and nothing wear but Freize,
Th'all-giver would be unthank't, would be unprais'd,
Not half his riches known, and yet despis'd,
And we should serve him as a grudging master,
As a penurious niggard of his wealth,
And live like Natures bastards, not her sons,

Who would be quite surcharged with her own weight,
And strangl'd with her waste fertility;
Th'earth cumber'd, and the wing'd air dark't with
    plumes,
The herds would over-multitude their Lords,
The Sea o'refraught would swell, and th'unsought
    diamonds
Would so emblaze the forhead of the Deep,
And so bestudd with Stars, that they below
Would grow inur'd to light, and com at last
To gaze upon the Sun with shameless brows.
List Lady be not coy, and be not cosen'd
With that same vaunted name Virginity,
Beauty is natures coyn, must not be hoorded,
But must be currant, and the good thereof
Consists in mutual and partak'n bliss,
Unsavoury in th'injoyment of it self
If you let slip time, like a neglected rose
It withers on the stalk with languish't head.
Beauty is natures brag, and must be shown
In courts, at feasts, and high solemnities
Where most may wonder at the workmanship;
It is for homely features to keep home,
They had their name thence; course complexions
And cheeks of sorry grain will serve to ply
The sampler, and to teize the huswifes wooll.
What need a vermeil-tinctured lip for that
Love-darting eyes, or tresses like the Morn?
There was another meaning in these gifts,
Think what, and be adviz'd, you are but young yet.

(*Lines* 705–54)

SABRINA FAIR
  Sabrina fair
    Listen where thou art sitting

Under the glassie, cool, translucent wave,
   In twisted braids of Lillies knitting
The loose train of thy amber-dropping hair,
   Listen for dear honours sake,
   Goddess of the silver lake,
                Listen and save.
Listen and appear to us
In name of great *Oceanus,*
By the earth-shaking *Neptune's* mace,
And *Tethys* grave majestick pace,
By hoary *Nereus* wrincled look,
And the *Carpathian* wisards hook,
By scaly *Tritons* winding shell,
And old sooth-saying *Glaucus* spell,
By *Leucothea's* lovely hands,
And her son that rules the strands,
By *Thetis* tinsel-slipper'd feet,
And the Songs of *Sirens* sweet,
By dead *Parthenope's* dear tomb,
And fair *Ligea's* golden comb,
Wherwith she sits on diamond rocks
Sleeking her soft alluring locks,
By all the *Nymph's* that nightly dance
Upon thy streams with wily glance,
Rise, rise, and heave thy rosie head
From thy coral-pav'n bed,
And bridle in thy headlong wave,
Till thou our summons answered have.
                Listen and save.

                    (Lines 859–89)

FROM *Paradise Lost*

[*Invocation*]

Of Mans First Disobedience, and the Fruit
Of that Forbidden Tree, whose mortal tast
Brought Death into the World, and all our woe,
With loss of *Eden,* till one greater Man
Restore us, and regain the blissful Seat,
Sing Heav'nly Muse, that on the secret top
Of *Oreb,* or of *Sinai,* didst inspire
That Shepherd, who first taught the chosen Seed,
In the Beginning how the Heav'ns and Earth
Rose out of *Chaos:* or if *Sion* Hill
Delight thee more, and *Siloa's* Brook that flow'd
Fast by the Oracle of God; I thence
Invoke thy aid to my adventrous Song,
That with no middle flight intends to soar
Above th' *Aonian* Mount, while it pursues
Things unattempted yet in Prose or Rhime.
And chiefly Thou O Spirit, that dost prefer
Before all Temples th' upright heart and pure,
Instruct me, for Thou know'st; Thou from the first
Wast present, and with mighty wings outspread
Dove-like satst brooding on the vast Abyss
And mad'st it pregnant: What in me is dark
Illumine, what is low raise and support;
That to the highth of this great Argument
I may assert Eternal Providence,
And justifie the wayes of God to men.

(*Book I, lines* 1–26)

[*The Council of Satan*]

　　So *Satan spake*, and him *Bëëlzebub*
Thus answer'd. Leader of those Armies bright,
Which but th' Omnipotent none could have foyld,
If once they hear that voyce, their liveliest pledge
Of hope in fears and dangers, heard so oft
In worst extreams, and on the perilous edge
Of battel when it rag'd, in all assaults
Their surest signal, they will soon resume
New courage and revive, though now they lye
Groveling and prostrate on yon Lake of Fire,
As we erewhile, astounded and amaz'd,
No wonder, fall'n such a pernicious highth.
　　He scarce had ceas't when the superiour Fiend
Was moving toward the shore; his ponderous shield
Ethereal temper, massy, large and round,
Behind him cast; the broad circumference
Hung on his shoulders like the Moon, whose Orb
Through Optic Glass the *Tuscan* Artist views
At Ev'ning from the top of *Fesole,*
Or in *Valdarno,* to descry new Lands,
Rivers or Mountains in her spotty Globe.
His Spear, to equal which the tallest Pine
Hewn on *Norwegian* hills, to be the Mast
Of some great Ammiral, were but a wand,
He walkt with to support uneasie steps
Over the burning Marle, not like those steps
On Heavens Azure, and the torrid Clime
Smote on him sore besides, vaulted with Fire;
Nathless he so endur'd, till on the Beach
Of that inflamed Sea, he stood and call'd
His Legions, Angel Forms, who lay intrans't
Thick as Autumnal Leaves that strow the Brooks

In *Vallombrosa,* where th' *Etrurian* shades
High overarch't imbowr; or scatterd sedge
Afloat, when with fierce Winds *Orion* arm'd
Hath vext the Red-Sea Coast, whose waves orethrew
Busiris and his *Memphian* Chivalrie,
While with perfidious hatred they pursu'd
The Sojourners of *Goshen,* who beheld
From the safe shore their floating Carkases
And broken Chariot Wheels, so thick bestrown
Abject and lost lay these, covering the Flood,
Under amazement of their hideous change.
He call'd so loud, that all the hollow Deep
Of Hell resounded. Princes, Potentates,
Warriers, the Flowr of Heav'n, once yours, now lost,
If such astonishment as this can sieze
Eternal spirits; or have ye chos'n this place
After the toyl of Battel to repose
Your wearied vertue, for the ease you find
To slumber here, as in the Vales of Heav'n?
Or in this abject posture have ye sworn
To adore the Conquerour? who now beholds
Cherube and Seraph rowling in the Flood
With scatter'd Arms and Ensigns, till anon
His swift pursuers from Heav'n Gates discern
Th' advantage, and descending tread us down
Thus drooping, or with linked Thunderbolts
Transfix us to the bottom of this Gulfe.
Awake, arise, or be for ever fall'n.
    They heard, and were abasht, and up they sprung
Upon the wing, as when men wont to watch
On duty, sleeping found by whom they dread,
Rouse and bestir themselves ere well awake.
Nor did they not perceave the evil plight
In which they were, or the fierce pains not feel;
Yet to their Generals Voyce they soon obeyd

Innumerable. As when the potent Rod
Of *Amrams* Son in *Egypts* evill day
Wav'd round the Coast, up call'd a pitchy cloud
Of *Locusts,* warping on the Eastern Wind,
That ore the Realm of impious *Pharaoh* hung
Like Night, and darken'd all the Land of *Nile:*
So numberless were those bad Angels seen
Hovering on wing under the Cope of Hell
'Twixt upper, nether, and surrounding Fires;
Till, as a signal, giv'n, th' uplifted Spear
Of their great Sultan waving to direct
Thir course, in even ballance down they light
On the firm brimstone, and fill all the Plain;
A multitude, like which the populous North
Pour'd never from her frozen loyns, to pass
Rhene or the *Danaw,* when her barbarous Sons
Came like a Deluge on the South, and spread
Beneath *Gibraltar* to the *Lybian* sands.
Forthwith from every Squadron and each Band
The Heads and Leaders thither hast where stood
Their great Commander; Godlike shapes and forms
Excelling human, Princely Dignities,
And Powers that earst in Heaven sat on Thrones;
Though of their Names in heav'nly Records now
Be no memorial, blotted out and ras'd
By thir Rebellion, from the Books of Life.
Nor had they yet among the Sons of *Eve*
Got them new Names, till wandring ore the Earth,
Through Gods high sufferance for the tryal of man,
By falsities and lyes the greatest part
Of Mankind they corrupted to forsake
God their Creator, and th' invisible
Glory of him, that made them, to transform
Oft to the Image of a Brute, adorn'd
With gay Religions full of Pomp and Gold,

And Devils to adore for Deities:
Then were they known to men by various Names,
And various Idols through the Heathen World.
Say, Muse, their Names then known, who first, who last,
Rous'd from the slumber, on that fiery Couch,
At thir great Emperors call, as next in worth
Came singly where he stood on the bare strand,
While the promiscuous croud stood yet aloof?
The chief were those who from the Pit of Hell
Roaming to seek their prey on earth, durst fix
Their Seats long after next the Seat of God,
Their Altars by his Altar, Gods ador'd
Among the Nations round, and durst abide
Jehovah thundring out of *Sion*, thron'd
Between the Cherubim; yea, often plac'd
Within his Sanctuary it self their Shrines,
Abominations; and with cursed things
His holy Rites, and solemn Feasts profan'd,
And with their darkness durst affront his light.
First *Moloch*, horrid King besmear'd with blood
Of human sacrifice, and parents tears,
Though for the noyse of Drums and Timbrels loud
Their childrens cries unheard, that past through fire
To his grim Idol. Him the *Ammonite*
Worshipt in *Rabba* and her watry Plain,
In *Argob* and in *Basan,* to the stream
Of utmost *Arnon.* Nor content with such
Audacious neighbourhood, the wisest heart
Of *Solomon* he led by fraud to build
His Temple right against the Temple of God
On that opprobrious Hill, and made his Grove
The pleasant Vally of *Hinnom, Tophet* thence
And black *Gehenna* call'd, the Type of Hell.
Next *Chemos*, th' obscene dread of *Moabs* Sons,
From *Aroer* to *Nebo,* and the wild

Of Southmost *Abarim;* in *Hesebon*
And *Horonaim, Seons* Realm, beyond
The flowry Dale of *Sibma* clad with Vines,
And *Eleale* to th' *Asphaltick* Pool.
Peor his other Name, when he entic'd
Israel in *Sittim* on their march from *Nile*
To do him wanton rites, which cost them woe.
Yet thence his lustful Orgies he enlarg'd
Even to that Hill of scandal, by the Grove
Of *Moloch* homicide, lust hard by hate;
Till good *Josiah* drove them thence to Hell.
With these came they, who from the bordring flood
Of old *Euphrates* to the Brook that parts
Egypt from *Syrian* ground, had general Names
Of *Baalim* and *Ashtaroth,* those male,
These Feminine. For Spirits when they please
Can either Sex assume, or both; so soft
And uncompounded is their Essence pure,
Not ti'd or manacl'd with joynt or limb,
Nor founded on the brittle strength of bones,
Like cumbrous flesh; but in what shape they choose
Dilated or condens't, bright or obscure,
Can execute their aerie purposes,
And works of love or enmity fulfill.
For those the Race of *Israel* oft forsook
Their living strength, and unfrequented left
His righteous Altar, bowing lowly down
To bestial Gods; for which their heads as low
Bow'd down in Battel, sunk before the Spear
Of despicable foes. With these in troop
Came *Astoreth,* whom the *Phœnicians* call'd
Astarte, Queen of Heav'n, with crescent Horns;
To those bright Image nightly by the Moon
Sidonian Virgins paid their Vows and Songs,
In *Sion* also not unsung, where stood

Her Temple on th' offensive Mountain, built
By that uxorious King, whose heart though large,
Beguil'd by fair Idolatresses, fell
To Idols foul. *Thammuz* came next behind,
Whose annual wound in *Lebanon* allur'd
The *Syrian* Damsels to lament his fate
In amorous dittyes all a Summers day,
While smooth *Adonis* from his native Rock
Ran purple to the Sea, suppos'd with blood
Of *Thammuz* yearly wounded: the Love-tale
Infected *Sions* daughters with like heat,
Whose wanton passions in the sacred Porch
Ezekiel saw, when by the Vision led
His eye survay'd the dark Idolatries
Of alienated *Judah.* Next came one
Who mourn'd in earnest, when the Captive Ark
Maim'd his brute Image, head and hands lopt off
In his own Temple, on the grunsel edge,
Where he fell flat, and sham'd his Worshipers:
Dagon his Name, Sea Monster, upward Man
And downward Fish: yet had his Temple high
Rear'd in *Azotus,* dreaded through the Coast
Of *Palestine,* in *Gath* and *Ascalon,*
And *Accaron* and *Gaza's* frontier bounds.
Him follow'd *Rimmon,* whose delightful Seat
Was fair *Damascus,* on the fertil Banks
Of *Abbana* and *Pharphar,* lucid streams.
He also against the house of God was bold:
A Leper once he lost and gain'd a King,
Ahaz his sottish Conquerour, whom he drew
Gods Altar to disparage and displace
For one of *Syrian* mode, whereon to burn
His odious offrings, and adore the Gods
Whom he had vanquisht. After these appear'd
A crew who under Names of old Renown,

Osiris, Isis, Orus and their Train
With monstrous shapes and sorceries abus'd
Fanatic *Egypt* and her Priests, to seek
Thir wandring Gods disguis'd in brutish forms
Rather then human. Nor did *Israel* scape
Th' infection when their borrow'd Gold compos'd
The Calf in *Oreb:* and the Rebel King
Doubl'd that sin in *Bethel* and in *Dan,*
Lik'ning his Maker to the Grazed Ox,
Jehovah, who in one Night when he pass'd
From *Egypt* marching, equal'd with one stroke
Both her first born and all her bleating Gods.
Belial came last, then whom a Spirit more lewd
Fell not from Heaven, or more gross to love
Vice for it self: To him no Temple stood
Or Altar smoak'd; yet who more oft then hee
In Temples and at Altars, when the Priest
Turns Atheist, as did *Ely's* Sons, who fill'd
With lust and violence the house of God.
In Courts and Palaces he also Reigns
And in luxurious Cities, where the noyse
Of riot ascends above thir loftiest Towrs,
And injury and outrage: And when Night
Darkens the Streets, then wander forth the Sons
Of *Belial,* flown with insolence and wine.
Witness the Streets of *Sodom,* and that night
In *Gibeah,* when hospitable dores
Yielded thir Matrons to prevent worse rape.
These were the prime in order and in might;
The rest were long to tell, though far renown'd,
Th' *Ionian* Gods, of *Javans* Issue held
Gods, yet confest later then Heav'n and Earth
Thir boasted Parents; *Titan* Heav'ns first born
With his enormous brood, and birthright seis'd
By younger *Saturn,* he from mightier *Jove*

His own and *Rhea's* Son like measure found;
So *Jove* usurping reign'd: these first in *Creet*
And *Ida* known, thence on the Snowy top
Of cold *Olympus* rul'd the middle Air,
Thir highest Heav'n; or on the *Delphian* Cliff,
Or in *Dodona,* and through all the bounds
Of *Doric* Land; or who with *Saturn* old
Fled over *Adria* to th' *Hesperian* Fields,
And ore the *Celtic* roam'd the utmost Isles.
All these and more came flocking; but with looks
Down cast and damp, yet such wherein appear'd
Obscure som glimps of joy, to have found thir chief
Not in despair, to have found themselves not lost
In loss it self; which on his count'nance cast
Like doubtful hue: but he his wonted pride
Soon recollecting, with high words, that bore
Semblance of worth not substance, gently rais'd
Their fainted courage, and dispel'd their fears.
Then strait commands that at the warlike sound
Of Trumpets loud and Clarions be upreard
His mighty Standard; that proud honour claim'd
Azazel as his right, a Cherube tall:
Who forthwith from the glittering Staff unfurld
Th' Imperial Ensign, which full high advanc't
Shon like a Meteor streaming to the Wind
With Gemms and Golden lustre rich imblaz'd,
Seraphic arms and Trophies: all the while
Sonorous mettal blowing Martial sounds:
At which the universal Host upsent
A shout that tore Hells Concave, and beyond
Frighted the Reign of *Chaos* and old Night.
All in a moment through the gloom were seen
Ten thousand Banners rise into the Air
With Orient Colours waving: with them rose
A Forrest huge of Spears: and thronging Helms

Appear'd, and serried Shields in thick array
Of depth immeasurable: Anon they move
In perfect *Phalanx* to the *Dorian* mood
Of Flutes and soft Recorders; such as rais'd
To highth of noblest temper Hero's old
Arming to Battel, and in stead of rage
Deliberate valour breath'd, firm and unmov'd
With dread of death to flight or foul retreat,
Nor wanting power to mitigate and swage
With solemn touches, troubl'd thoughts, and chase
Anguish and doubt and fear and sorrow and pain
From mortal or immortal minds. Thus they
Breathing united force with fixed thought
Mov'd on in silence to soft Pipes that charm'd
Thir painful steps o're the burnt soyle; and now
Advanc't in view they stand, a horrid Front
Of dreadful length and dazling Arms, in guise
Of Warriers old with order'd Spear and Shield,
Awaiting what command thir mighty Chief
Had to impose: He through the armed Files
Darts his experienc't eye, and soon traverse
The whole Battalion views, thir order due,
Thir visages and stature as of Gods,
Thir number last he summs. And now his heart
Distends with pride, and hardning in his strength
Glories: For never since created man,
Met such imbodied force, as nam'd with these
Could merit more then that small infantry
Warr'd on by Cranes: though all the Giant brood
Of *Phlegra* with th' Heroic Race were joyn'd
That fought at *Theb's* and *Ilium*, on each side
Mixt with auxiliar Gods; and what resounds
In Fable or *Romance* of *Uthers* Son
Begirt with *British* and *Armoric* Knights;
And all who since, Baptiz'd or Infidel

Jousted in *Aspramont* or *Montalban*,
Dàmasco, or *Marocco*, or *Trebisond*,
Or whom *Biserta* sent from *Afric* shore
When *Charlemain* with all his Peerage fell
By *Fontarabbia*. Thus far these beyond
Compare of mortal prowess, yet observ'd
Thir dread Commander: he above the rest
In shape and gesture proudly eminent
Stood like a Towr; his form had yet not lost
All her Original brightness, nor appear'd
Less then Arch Angel ruind, and th' excess
Of Glory obscur'd: As when the Sun new ris'n
Looks through the Horizontal misty Air
Shorn of his Beams, or from behind the Moon
In dim Eclips disastrous twilight sheds
On half the Nations, and with fear of change
Perplexes Monarchs. Dark'n'd so, yet shon
Above them all th' Arch Angel: but his face
Deep scars of Thunder had intrencht, and care
Sat on his faded cheek, but under Browes
Of dauntless courage, and considerate Pride
Waiting revenge: cruel his eye, but cast
Signs of remorse and passion to behold
The fellows of his crime, the followers rather
(Far other once beheld in bliss) condemn'd
For ever now to have their lot in pain,
Millions of Spirits for his fault amerc't
Of Heav'n, and from Eternal Splendors flung
For his revolt, yet faithfull how they stood,
Thir Glory witherd. As when Heavens Fire
Hath scath'd the Forrest Oaks, or Mountain Pines,
With singed top their stately growth though bare
Stands on the blasted Heath. He now prepar'd
To speak; whereat their doubl'd Ranks they bend
From Wing to Wing, and half enclose him round

With all his Peers: attention held them mute.
Thrice he assayd, and thrice in spite of scorn,
Tears such as Angels weep, burst forth: at last
Words interwove with sighs found out their way.

   O Myriads of immortal Spirits, O Powers
Matchless, but with th' Almighty, and that strife
Was not inglorious, though th' event was dire,
As this place testifies, and this dire change
Hateful to utter: but what power of mind
Foreseeing or presaging, from the Depth
Of knowledge past or present, could have fear'd,
How such united force of Gods, how such
As stood like these, could ever know repulse?
For who can yet beleeve, though after loss,
That all these puissant Legions, whose exile
Hath emptied Heav'n, shall faile to re-ascend
Self-rais'd, and repossess their native seat.
For me, be witness all the Host of Heav'n,
If counsels different, or danger shun'd
By me, have lost our hopes. But he who reigns
Monarch in Heav'n, till then as one secure
Sat on his Throne, upheld by old repute,
Consent or custome, and his Regal State
Put forth at full, but still his strength conceal'd,
Which tempted our attempt, and wrought our fall.
Henceforth his might we know, and know our own
So as not either to provoke, or dread
New warr, provok't; our better part remains
To work in close design, by fraud or guile
What force effected not: that he no less
At length from us may find, who overcomes
By force, hath overcome but half his foe.
Space may produce new Worlds; whereof so rife
There went a fame in Heav'n that he ere long
Intended to create, and therein plant

A generation, whom his choice regard
Should favour equal to the Sons of Heaven:
Thither, if but to prie, shall be perhaps
Our first eruption, thither or elsewhere:
For this Infernal Pit shall never hold
Cælestial Spirits in Bondage, nor th'Abysse
Long under darkness cover. But these thoughts
Full Counsel must mature: Peace is despaird,
For who can think Submission? Warr then, Warr
Open or understood must be resolv'd.

He spake: and to confirm his words out-flew
Millions of flaming swords, drawn from the thighs
Of mighty Cherubim; the sudden blaze
Far round illumin'd hell: highly they rag'd
Against the Highest, and fierce with grasped arm's
Clash'd on their sounding shields the din of war,
Hurling defiance toward the vault of Heav'n.

(*Book* I, *lines* 271–669)

[*The Prospect of Eden*]

O for that warning voice, which he who saw
Th' *Apocalyps,* heard cry in Heaven aloud,
Then when the Dragon, put to second rout,
Came furious down to be reveng'd on men,
Wo to the inhabitants on Earth! that now,
While time was, our first Parents had bin warnd
The coming of thir secret foe, and scap'd
Haply so scap'd his mortal snare; for now
Satan, now first inflam'd with rage, came down,
The Tempter ere th' Accuser of man-kind,
To wreck on innocent frail man his loss
Of that first Battel, and his flight to Hell:
Yet not rejoycing in his speed, though bold,
Far off and fearless, nor with cause to boast,

Begins his dire attempt, which nigh the birth
Now rowling, boiles in his tumultuous brest,
And like a devellish Engine back recoiles
Upon himself; horror and doubt distract
His troubl'd thoughts, and from the bottom stirr
The Hell within him, for within him Hell
He brings, and round about him, nor from Hell
One step no more then from himself can fly
By change of place: Now conscience wakes despair
That slumberd, wakes the bitter memorie
Of what he was, what is, and what must be
Worse; of worse deeds worse sufferings must ensue.
Sometimes towards *Eden* which now in his view
Lay pleasant, his grievd look he fixes sad,
Sometimes towards Heav'n and the full-blazing Sun,
Which now sat high in his Meridian Towre:
Then much revolving, thus in sighs began.
    O thou that with surpassing Glory crown'd,
Look'st from thy sole Dominion like the God
Of this new World; at whose sight all the Starrs
Hide thir diminisht heads; to thee I call,
But with no friendly voice, and add thy name
O Sun, to tell thee how I hate thy beams
That bring to my remembrance from what state
I fell, how glorious once above thy Spheare;
Till Pride and worse Ambition threw me down
Warring in Heav'n against Heav'ns matchless King:
Ah wherefore! he deservd no such return
From me, whom he created what I was
In that bright eminence, and with his good
Upbraided none; nor was his service hard.
What could be less then to afford him praise,
The easiest recompence, and pay him thanks,
How due! yet all his good prov'd ill in me,
And wrought but malice; lifted up so high

I sdeind subjection, and thought one step higher
Would set me highest, and in a moment quit
The debt immense of endless gratitude,
So burthensome, still paying, still to ow;
Forgetful what from him I still receivd,
And understood not that a grateful mind
By owing owes not, but still pays, at once
Indebted and dischargd; what burden then?
O had his powerful Destiny ordaind
Me some inferiour Angel, I had stood
Then happie; no unbounded hope had rais'd
Ambition. Yet why not? som other Power
As great might have aspir'd, and me though mean
Drawn to his part; but other Powers as great
Fell not, but stand unshak'n, from within
Or from without, to all temptations arm'd.
Hadst thou the same free Will and Power to stand?
Thou hadst: whom hast thou then or what to accuse,
But Heav'ns free Love dealt equally to all?
Be then his Love accurst, since love or hate,
To me alike, it deals eternal woe.
Nay curs'd be thou; since against his thy will
Chose freely what it now so justly rues.
Me miserable! which way shall I flie
Infinite wrauth, and infinite despaire?
Which way I flie is Hell; my self am **Hell;**
And in the lowest deep a lower deep
Still threatning to devour me opens wide,
To which the Hell I suffer seems a Heav'n.
O then at last relent: is there no place
Left for Repentance, none for Pardon left?
None left but by submission; and that word
Disdain forbids me, and my dread of shame
Among the Spirits beneath, whom I seduc'd
With other promises and other vaunts

Then to submit, boasting I could subdue
Th' Omnipotent. Ay me, they little know
How dearly I abide that boast so vaine,
Under what torments inwardly I groane:
While they adore me on the Throne of Hell,
With Diadem and Scepter high advanc't
The lower still I fall, onely supream
In miserie; such joy Ambition findes.
But say I could repent and could obtaine
By Act of Grace my former state; how soon
Would highth recal high thoughts, how soon unsay
What feign'd submission swore: ease would recant
Vows made in pain, as violent and void.
For never can true reconcilement grow
Where wounds of deadly hate have peirc'd so deep:
Which would but lead me to a worse relapse,
And heavier fall: so should I purchase deare
Short intermission bought with double smart.
This knows my punisher; therefore as farr
From granting hee, as I from begging peace:
All hope excluded thus, behold in stead
Of us out-cast, exil'd, his new delight,
Mankind created, and for him this World.
So farwel Hope, and with Hope, farwel Fear,
Farwel Remorse: all Good to me is lost;
Evil be thou my Good; by thee at least
Divided Empire with Heav'ns King I hold
By thee, and more then half perhaps will reigne;
As Man ere long, and this new World shall know.

    Thus while he spake, each passion dimm'd his face
Thrice chang'd with pale, ire, envie and despair,
Which marrd his borrow'd visage, and betraid
Him counterfet, if any eye beheld.
For heav'nly mindes from such distempers foule
Are ever cleer. Whereof hee soon aware,

Each perturbation smooth'd with outward calme,
Artificer of fraud; and was the first
That practisd falshood under saintly shew,
Deep malice to conceale, couch't with revenge:
Yet not anough had practisd to deceive
Uriel once warnd; whose eye pursu'd him down
The way he went, and on th' *Assyrian* mount
Saw him disfigur'd, more then could befall
Spirit of happie sort: his gestures fierce
He markd and mad demeanour, then alone,
As he suppos'd, all unobserv'd, unseen.
So on he fares, and to the border comes
Of *Eden,* where delicious Paradise,
Now nearer, Crowns with her enclosure green,
As with a rural mound the champain head
Of a steep wilderness, whose hairie sides
With thicket overgrown, grottesque and wilde,
Access deni'd; and over head up grew
Insuperable highth of loftiest shade,
Cedar, and Pine, and Firr, and branching Palm,
A Silvan Scene, and as the ranks ascend
Shade above shade, a woodie Theatre
Of stateliest view. Yet higher then thir tops
The verdurous wall of Paradise up sprung:
Which to our general Sire gave prospect large
Into his neather Empire neighbouring round.
And higher then that Wall a circling row
Of goodliest Trees loaden with fairest Fruit,
Blossoms and Fruits at once of golden hue
Appeerd, with gay enameld colours mixt:
On which the Sun more glad impress'd his beams
Then in fair Evening Cloud, or humid Bow,
When God hath showrd the earth; so lovely seemd
That Lantskip: And of pure now purer aire
Meets his approach, and to the heart inspires

Vernal delight and joy, able to drive
All sadness but despair: now gentle gales
Fanning thir odoriferous wings dispense
Native perfumes, and whisper whence they stole
Those balmie spoiles. As when to them who saile
Beyond the *Cape of Hope,* and now are past
Mozambic, off at Sea North-East windes blow
Sabean Odours from the spicie shoare
Of *Arabie* the blest, with such delay
Well pleas'd they slack thir course, and many a League
Cheard with the grateful smell old Ocean smiles.
So entertaind those odorous sweets the Fiend
Who came thir bane, though with them better pleas'd
Then *Asmodeus* with the fishie fume,
That drove him, though enamourd, from the Spouse
Of *Tobits* Son, and with a vengeance sent
From *Media* post to *Ægypt,* there fast bound.
    Now to th' ascent of that steep savage Hill
Satan had journied on, pensive and slow;
But further way found none, so thick entwin'd,
As one continu'd brake, the undergrowth
Of shrubs and tangling bushes had perplext
All path of Man or Beast that past that way:
One Gate there onely was, and that look'd East
On th' other side: which when th' arch-fellon saw
Due entrance his disdaind, and in contempt,
At one slight bound high overleap'd all bound
Of Hill or highest Wall, and sheer within
Lights on his feet. As when a prowling Wolfe,
Whom hunger drives to seek new haunt for prey,
Watching where Shepherds pen thir Flocks at eeve
In hurdl'd Cotes amid the field secure,
Leaps o're the fence with ease into the Fould:
Or as a Thief bent to unhoord the cash
Of some rich Burgher, whose substantial dores,

Cross-barrd and bolted fast, fear no assault,
In at the window climbes, or o're the tiles;
So clomb this first grand Thief into Gods Fould:
So since into his Church lewd Hirelings climbe.
Thence up he flew, and on the Tree of Life,
The middle Tree and highest there that grew,
Sat like a Cormorant; yet not true Life
Thereby regaind, but sat devising Death
To them who liv'd; nor on the vertue thought
Of that life-giving Plant, but only us'd
For prospect, what well us'd had bin the pledge
Of immortalitie. So little knows
Any, but God alone, to value right
The good before him, but perverts best things
To worst abuse, or to thir meanest use.
Beneath him with new wonder now he views
To all delight of human sense expos'd
In narrow room Natures whole wealth, yea more,
A Heaven on Earth: for blissful Paradise
Of God the Garden was, by him in the East
Of *Eden* planted; *Eden* stretchd her Line
From *Auran* Eastward to the Royal Towrs
Of Great *Seleucia,* built by *Grecian* Kings,
Or where the Sons of *Eden* long before
Dwelt in *Telassar:* in this pleasant soile
His farr more pleasant Garden God ordaind;
Out of the fertil ground he caus'd to grow
All Trees of noblest kind for sight, smell, taste;
And all amid them stood the Tree of Life,
High eminent, blooming Ambrosial Fruit
Of vegetable Gold; and next to Life
Our Death the Tree of Knowledge grew fast by,
Knowledge of Good bought dear by knowing ill.
Southward through *Eden* went a River large,
Nor chang'd his course, but through the shaggie hill

Pass'd underneath ingulft, for God had thrown
That Mountain as his Garden mould high rais'd
Upon the rapid current, which through veins
Of porous Earth with kindly thirst up drawn,
Rose a fresh Fountain, and with many a rill
Waterd the Garden; thence united fell
Down the steep glade, and met the neather Flood,
Which from his darksom passage now appeers,
And now divided into four main Streams,
Runs divers, wandring many a famous Realme
And Country whereof here needs no account,
But rather to tell how, if Art could tell,
How from that Saphire Fount the crisped Brooks,
Rowling on Orient Pearl and sands of Gold,
With mazie error under pendant shades
Ran Nectar, visiting each plant, and fed
Flours worthy of Paradise which not nice Art
In Beds and curious Knots, but Nature boon
Powrd forth profuse on Hill and Dale and Plaine,
Both where the morning Sun first warmly smote
The open field, and where the unpierc't shade
Imbround the noontide Bowrs: Thus was this place,
A happy rural seat of various view;
Groves whose rich Trees wept odorous Gumms and
    Balme,
Others whose fruit burnisht with Golden Rinde
Hung amiable, *Hesperian* Fables true,
If true, here onely, and of delicious taste:
Betwixt them Lawns, or level Downs, and Flocks
Grasing the tender herb, were interpos'd,
Or palmie hilloc, or the flourie lap
Of som irriguous Valley spread her store,
Flours of all hue, and without Thorn the Rose:
Another side, umbrageous Grots and Caves
Of coole recess, o're which the mantling Vine

Layes forth her purple Grape, and gently creeps
Luxuriant; mean while murmuring waters fall
Down the slope hills, disperst, or in a Lake,
That to the fringed Bank with Myrtle crownd,
Her chrystall mirror holds, unite thir streams.
The Birds thir quire apply; aires, vernal aires,
Breathing the smell of field and grove, attune
The trembling leaves, while Universal *Pan*
Knit with the *Graces* and the *Hours* in dance
Led on th' Eternal Spring. Not that faire field
Of *Enna*, where *Proserpin* gathring flours
Her self a fairer Floure by gloomie *Dis*
Was gatherd, which cost *Ceres* all that pain
To seek her through the world; nor that sweet Grove
Of *Daphne* by *Orontes,* and th' inspir'd
Castalian Spring might with this Paradise
Of *Eden* strive; nor that *Nyseian* Ile
Girt with the River *Triton*, where old *Cham*,
Whom Gentiles *Ammon* call and *Libyan Jove*,
Hid *Amalthea* and her Florid Son
Young *Bacchus* from his Stepdame *Rhea's* eye;
Nor where *Abassin* Kings thir issue Guard,
Mount *Amara*, though this by som suppos'd
True Paradise under the *Ethiop* Line
By *Nilus* head, enclos'd with shining Rock,
A whole dayes journey high, but wide remote
From this *Assyrian* Garden, where the Fiend
Saw undelighted all delight, all kind
Of living Creatures new to sight and strange:
Two of far nobler shape erect and tall,
Godlike erect, with native Honour clad
In naked Majestie seemd Lords of all,
And worthie seemd, for in thir looks Divine
The image of thir glorious Maker shon,
Truth, Wisdome, Sanctitude severe and pure,

Severe, but in true filial freedom plac't;
Whence true autoritie in men; though both
Not equal, as thir sex not equal seemd;
For contemplation hee and valour formd,
For softness shee and sweet attractive Grace,
Hee for God only, shee for God in him:
His fair large Front and Eye sublime declar'd
Absolute rule; and Hyacinthin Locks
Round from his parted forelock manly hung
Clustring, but not beneath his shoulders broad:
Shee as a vail down to the slender waste
Her unadorned golden tresses wore
Dissheveld, but in wanton ringlets wav'd
As the Vine curles her tendrils, which impli'd
Subjection, but requir'd with gentle sway,
And by her yeilded, by him best receivd,
Yeilded with coy submission, modest pride,
And sweet reluctant amorous delay.
Nor those mysterious parts were then conceald,
Then was not guiltie shame, dishonest shame
Of natures works, honor dishonorable,
Sin-bred, how have ye troubl'd all mankind
With shews instead, meer shews of seeming pure,
And banisht from mans life his happiest life,
Simplicities and spotless innocence.
So passd they naked on, nor shund the sight
Of God or Angel, for they thought no ill:
So hand in hand they passd, the lovliest pair
That ever since in loves imbraces met,
Adam the goodliest man of men since borne
His Sons, the fairest of her Daughters *Eve*.
Under a tuft of shade that on a green
Stood whispering soft, by a fresh Fountain side
They sat them down, and after no more toil
Of thir sweet Gardning labour then suffic'd

To recommend coole *Zephyr*, and made ease
More easie, wholsom thirst and appetite
More grateful, to thir Supper Fruits they fell,
Nectarine Fruits which the compliant boughes
Yeilded them, side-long as they sat recline
On the soft downie Bank damaskt with flours:
The savourie pulp they chew, and in the rinde
Still as they thirsted scoop the brimming stream;
Nor gentle purpose, nor endearing smiles
Wanted, nor youthful dalliance as beseems
Fair couple, linkt in happie nuptial League,
Alone as they. About them frisking playd
All Beasts of th' Earth, since wilde, and of all chase
In Wood or Wilderness, Forrest or Den;
Sporting the Lion rampd, and in his paw
Dandl'd the Kid; Bears, Tygers, Ounces, Pards
Gambold before them, th' unwieldy Elephant
To make them mirth us'd all his might, and wreathd
His Lithe Proboscis; close the Serpent sly
Insinuating, wove with Gordian twine
His breaded train, and of his fatal guile
Gave proof unheeded; other on the grass
Coucht, and now fild with pasture gazing sat,
Or Bedward ruminating: for the Sun
Declin'd was hasting now with prone carreer
To th' Ocean Iles, and in th' ascending Scale
Of Heav'n the Starrs that usher Evening rose:
When *Satan* still in gaze, as first he stood,
Scarce thus at length faild speech recoverd sad.

O Hell! what doe mine eyes with grief behold,
Into our room of bliss thus high advanc't
Creatures of other mould, earth-born perhaps,
Not Spirits, yet to heav'nly Spirits bright
Little inferior; whom my thoughts pursue
With wonder, and could love, so lively shines

In them Divine resemblance, and such grace
The hand that formd them on thir shape hath pourd.
Ah gentle pair, yee little think how nigh
Your change approaches, when all these delights
Will vanish and deliver ye to woe,
More woe, the more your taste is now of joy;
Happie, but for so happie ill secur'd
Long to continue, and this high seat your Heav'n
Ill fenc't for Heav'n to keep out such a foe
As now is enterd; yet no purpos'd foe
To you whom I could pittie thus forlorne
Though I unpittied: League with you I seek,
And mutual amitie so streight, so close,
That I with you must dwell, or you with me
Henceforth; my dwelling haply may not please
Like this fair Paradise, your sense, yet such
Accept your Makers work; he gave it me,
Which I as freely give; Hell shall unfould,
To entertain you two, her widest Gates,
And send forth all her Kings; there will be room,
Not like these narrow limits, to receive
Your numerous ofspring; if no better place,
Thank him who puts me loath to this revenge
On you who wrong me not for him who wrongd.
And should I at your harmless innocence
Melt, as I doe, yet public reason just,
Honour and Empire with revenge enlarg'd,
By conquering this new World, compels me now
To do what else though damnd I should abhorre.
 So spake the Fiend, and with necessitie,
The Tyrants plea, excus'd his devilish deeds.
Then from his loftie stand on that high Tree
Down he alights among the sportful Herd
Of those fourfooted kindes, himself now one,
Now other, as thir shape servd best his end

Neerer to view his prey, and unespi'd
To mark what of thir state he more might learn
By word or action markt: about them round
A Lion now he stalkes with fierie glare,
Then as a Tiger, who by chance hath spi'd
In some Purlieu two gentle Fawnes at play,
Strait couches close, then rising changes oft
His couchant watch, as one who chose his ground
Whence rushing he might surest seise them both
Grip't in each paw: when *Adam* first of men
To first of women *Eve* thus moving speech,
Turnd him all eare to heare new utterance flow.
    Sole partner and sole part of all these joyes,
Dearer thy self then all; needs must the Power
That made us, and for us this ample World
Be infinitly good, and of his good
As liberal and free as infinite,
That rais'd us from the dust and plac't us here
In all this happiness, who at his hand
Have nothing merited, nor can performe
Aught whereof hee hath need, hee who requires
From us no other service then to keep
This one, this easie charge, of all the Trees
In Paradise that beare delicious fruit
So various, not to taste that onely Tree
Of knowledge, planted by the Tree of Life,
So neer grows Death to Life, what ere Death is,
Som dreadful thing no doubt; for well thou knowst
God hath pronounc't it death to taste that Tree,
The only sign of our obedience left
Among so many signes of power and rule
Conferrd upon us, and Dominion giv'n
Over all other Creatures that possesse
Earth, Aire, and Sea. Then let us not think hard
One easie prohibition, who enjoy

Free leave so large to all things else, and choice
Unlimited of manifold delights:
But let us ever praise him, and extoll
His bountie, following our delightful task
To prune these growing Plants, and tend these Flours,
Which were it toilsom, yet with thee were sweet.
   To whom thus *Eve* repli'd. O thou for whom
And from whom I was formd flesh of thy flesh,
And without whom am to no end, my Guide
And Head, what thou hast said is just and right.
For wee to him indeed all praises owe,
And daily thanks, I chiefly who enjoy
So farr the happier Lot, enjoying thee
Preeminent by so much odds, while thou
Like consort to thy self canst no where find.
That day I oft remember, when from sleep
I first awak't, and found my self repos'd
Under a shade on flours, much wondring where
And what I was, whence thither brought, and how.
Not distant far from thence a murmuring sound
Of waters issu'd from a Cave and spread
Into a liquid Plain, then stood unmov'd
Pure as th' expanse of Heav'n; I thither went
With unexperienc't thought, and laid me downe
On the green bank, to look into the cleer
Smooth Lake, that to me seemd another Skie.
As I bent down to look, just opposite,
A Shape within the watry gleam appeerd
Bending to look on me, I started back,
It started back, but pleasd I soon returnd,
Pleas'd it returnd as soon with answering looks
Of sympathie and love, there I had fixt
Mine eyes till now, and pin'd with vain desire,
Had not a voice thus warnd me, What thou seest,
What there thou seest fair Creature is thy self,

With thee it came and goes: but follow me,
And I will bring thee where no shadow staies
Thy coming, and thy soft imbraces, hee
Whose image thou art, him thou shall enjoy
Inseparablie thine, to him shalt beare
Multitudes like thy self, and thence be call'd
Mother of human Race: what could I doe,
But follow strait, invisibly thus led?
Till I espi'd thee, fair indeed and tall,
Under a Platan, yet methought less faire,
Less winning soft, less amiablie milde,
Then that smooth watry image; back I turnd,
Thou following cryd'st aloud, Return fair *Eve*,
Whom fli'st thou? whom thou fli'st, of him thou art,
His flesh, his bone; to give thee being I lent
Out of my side to thee, neerest my heart
Substantial Life, to have thee by my side
Henceforth an individual solace dear;
Part of my Soul I seek thee, and thee claim
My other half: with that thy gentle hand
Seisd mine, I yeilded, and from that time see
How beauty is excelld by manly grace
And wisdom, which alone is truly fair.
  So spake our general Mother, and with eyes
Of conjugal attraction unreprov'd,
And meek surrender, half imbracing leand
On our first Father, half her swelling Breast
Naked met his under the flowing Gold
Of her loose tresses hid: he in delight
Both of her Beauty and submissive Charms
Smil'd with superior Love, as *Jupiter*
On *Juno* smiles, when he impregns the Clouds
That shed *May* Flowers; and press'd her Matron lip
With kisses pure: aside the Devil turnd
For envie, yet with jealous leer maligne

Ey'd them askance, and to himself thus plaind.
   Sight hateful, sight tormenting! thus these two
Imparadis't in one anothers arms
The happier *Eden,* shall enjoy thir fill
Of bliss on bliss, while I to Hell am thrust,
Where neither joy nor love, but fierce desire,
Among our other torments not the least,
Still unfulfill'd with pain of longing pines;
Yet let me not forget what I have gain'd
From thir own mouths; all is not theirs it seems:
One fatal Tree there stands of Knowledge call'd,
Forbidden them to taste: Knowledge forbidd'n?
Suspicious, reasonless. Why should thir Lord
Envie them that? can it be sin to know,
Can it be death? and do they onely stand
By Ignorance, is that thir happie state,
The proof of thir obedience and thir faith?
O fair foundation laid whereon to build
Thir ruine! Hence I will excite thir minds
With more desire to know, and to reject
Envious commands, invented with designe
To keep them low whom knowledge might exalt
Equal with Gods; aspiring to be such,
They taste and die: what likelier can ensue?
But first with narrow search I must walk round
This Garden, and no corner leave unspi'd;
A chance but chance may lead where I may meet
Some wandring Spirit of Heav'n, by Fountain side,
Or in thick shade retir'd, from him to draw
What further would be learnt. Live while ye may,
Yet happie pair; enjoy, till I return,
Short pleasures, for long woes are to succeed.
   So saying, his proud step he scornful turn'd,
But with sly circumspection, and began

Through wood, through waste, o're hil, o're dale his
    roam.
Mean while in utmost Longitude, where Heav'n
With Earth and Ocean meets, the setting Sun
Slowly descended, and with right aspect
Against the eastern Gate of Paradise
Leveld his eevning Rayes: it was a Rock
Of Alablaster, pil'd up to the Clouds,
Conspicuous farr, winding with one ascent
Accessible from Earth, one entrance high;
The rest was craggie cliff, that overhung
Still as it rose, impossible to climbe.
Betwixt these rockie Pillars *Gabriel* sat
Chief of th' Angelic Guards, awaiting night;
About him exercis'd Heroic Games
Th' unarmed Youth of Heav'n, but nigh at hand
Celestial Armourie, Shields, Helmes, and Speares
Hung high with Diamond flaming, and with Gold.
Thither came *Uriel*, gliding through the Eeven
On a Sun beam, swift as a shooting Starr
In *Autumn* thwarts the night, when vapors fir'd
Impress the Air, and shews the Mariner
From what point of his Compass to beware
Impetuous winds: he thus began in haste.
   Gabriel, to thee thy cours by Lot hath giv'n
Charge and strict watch that to this happie place
No evil thing approach or enter in;
This day at highth of Noon came to my Spheare
A Spirit, zealous, as he seem'd, to know
More of th' Almighties works, and chiefly Man
Gods latest Image: I describ'd his way
Bent all on speed, and markt his Aerie Gate;
But in the Mount that lies from *Eden* North,
Where he first lighted, soon discernd his looks

Alien from Heav'n, with passions foul obscur'd:
Mine eye pursu'd him still, but under shade
Lost sight of him; one of the banisht crew
I fear, hath ventur'd from the deep, to raise
New troubles; him thy care must be to find.

    To whom the winged Warriour thus returnd:
Uriel, no wonder if thy perfet sight,
Amid the Suns bright circle where thou sitst,
See farr and wide: in at this Gate none pass
The vigilance here plac't, but such as come
Well known from Heav'n; and since Meridian hour
No Creature thence: if Spirit of other sort,
So minded, have oreleapt these earthie bounds
On purpose, hard thou knowst it to exclude
Spiritual substance with corporeal barr.
But if within the circuit of these walks
In whatsoever shape he lurk, of whom
Thou telst, by morrow dawning I shall know.

    So promis'd hee, and *Uriel* to his charge
Returnd on that bright beam, whose point now raisd
Bore him slope downward to the Sun now fall'n
Beneath th' *Azores;* whither the prime Orb,
Incredible how swift, had thither rowl'd
Diurnal, or this less volubil Earth
By shorter flight to th' East, had left him there
Arraying with reflected Purple and Gold
The Clouds that on his Western Throne attend:
Now came still Eevning on, and Twilight gray
Had in her sober Liverie all things clad;
Silence accompanied, for Beast and Bird,
They to thir grassie Couch, these to thir Nests
Were slunk, all but the wakeful Nightingale;
She all night long her amorous descant sung;
Silence was pleas'd: now glow'd the Firmament
With living Saphirs: *Hesperus* that led

The starrie Host, rode brightest, till the Moon
Rising in clouded Majestie, at length
Apparent Queen unvaild her peerless light,
And o're the dark her Silver Mantle threw.
    When *Adam* thus to *Eve:* Fair Consort, th' hour
Of night, and all things now retir'd to rest
Mind us of like repose, since God hath set
Labour and rest, as day and night to men
Successive, and the timely dew of sleep
Now falling with soft slumbrous weight inclines
Our eye-lids; other Creatures all day long
Rove idle unimploid, and less need rest;
Man hath his daily work of body or mind
Appointed, which declares his Dignitie,
And the regard of Heav'n on all his waies;
While other Animals unactive range,
And of thir doings God takes no account.
To morrow ere fresh Morning streak the East
With first approach of light, we must be ris'n,
And at our pleasant labour, to reform
Yon flourie Arbors, yonder Allies green,
Our walks at noon, with branches overgrown,
That mock our scant manuring, and require
More hands then ours to lop thir wanton growth:
Those Blossoms also, and those dropping Gumms,
That lie bestrowne unsightly and unsmooth,
Ask riddance, if we mean to tread with ease;
Mean while, as Nature wills, Night bids us rest.
    To whom thus *Eve* with perfet beauty adornd.
My Author and Disposer, what thou bidst
Unargu'd I obey; so God ordains,
God is thy Law, thou mine: to know no more
Is womans happiest knowledge and her praise.
With thee conversing I forget all time,
All seasons and thir change, all please alike.

Sweet is the breath of morn, her rising sweet,
With charm of earliest Birds; pleasant the Sun
When first on this delightful Land he spreads
His orient Beams, on herb, tree, fruit, and flour,
Glistring with dew; fragrant the fertil earth
After soft showers; and sweet the coming on
Of grateful Eevning milde, then silent Night
With this her solemn Bird and this fair Moon,
And these the Gemms of Heav'n, her starrie train:
But neither breath of Morn when she ascends
With charm of earliest Birds, nor rising Sun
On this delightful land, nor herb, fruit, floure,
Glistring with dew, nor fragrance after showers,
Nor grateful Evening mild, nor silent Night
With this her solemn Bird, nor walk by Moon,
Or glittering Starr-light without thee is sweet.
But wherfore all night long shine these, for whom
This glorious sight, when sleep hath shut all eyes?
    To whom our general Ancestor repli'd.
Daughter of God and Man, accomplisht *Eve*,
Those have thir course to finish, round the Earth,
By morrow Eevning, and from Land to Land
In order, though to Nations yet unborn,
Ministring light prepar'd, they set and rise;
Least total darkness should by Night regaine
Her old possession, and extinguish life
In Nature and all things, which these soft fires
Not only enlighten, but with kindly heate
Of various influence foment and warme,
Temper or nourish, or in part shed down
Thir stellar vertue on all kinds that grow
On Earth, made hereby apter to receive
Perfection from the Suns more potent Ray.
These then, though unbeheld in deep of night,
Shine not in vain, nor think, though men were none,

That heav'n would want spectators, God want praise;
Millions of spiritual Creatures walk the Earth
Unseen, both when we wake, and when we sleep:
All these with ceaseless praise his works behold
Both day and night: how often from the steep
Of echoing Hill or Thicket have we heard
Celestial voices to the midnight air,
Sole, or responsive each to others note
Singing thir great Creator: oft in bands
While they keep watch, or nightly rounding walk
With Heav'nly touch of instrumental sounds
In full harmonic number joind, thir songs
Divide the night, and lift our thoughts to Heaven.
    Thus talking hand in hand alone they pass'd
On to thir blissful Bower; it was a place
Chos'n by the sovran Planter, when he fram'd
All things to mans delightful use; the roofe
Of thickest covert was inwoven shade
Laurel and Mirtle, and what higher grew
Of firm and fragrant leaf; on either side
Acanthus, and each odorous bushie shrub
Fenc'd up the verdant wall; each beauteous flour,
Iris all hues, Roses, and Gessamin
Rear'd high thir flourisht heads between, and wrought
Mosaic; underfoot the Violet,
Crocus, and Hyacinth with rich inlay
Broiderd the ground, more colour'd then with stone
Of costliest Emblem: other Creature here
Beast, Bird, Insect, or Worm durst enter none;
Such was thir awe of man. In shadier Bower
More sacred and sequesterd, though but feignd,
Pan or *Silvanus* never slept, nor Nymph,
Nor *Faunus* haunted. Here in close recess
With Flowers, Garlands, and sweet-smelling Herbs
Espoused *Eve* deckt first her Nuptial Bed,

And heav'nly Quires the Hymenæan sung,
What day the genial Angel to our Sire
Brought her in naked beauty more adorn'd,
More lovely then *Pandora,* whom the Gods
Endowd with all thir gifts, and O too like
In sad event, when to the unwiser Son
Of *Japhet* brought by *Hermes,* she ensnar'd
Mankind with her faire looks, to be aveng'd
On him who had stole *Joves* authentic fire.

    Thus at this shadie Lodge arriv'd, both stood,
Both turnd, and under op'n Skie ador'd
The God that made both Skie, Air, Earth and Heav'n
Which they beheld, the Moons resplendent Globe
And starrie Pole: Thou also mad'st the Night,
Maker Omnipotent, and thou the Day,
Which we in our appointed work imployd
Have finisht happie in our mutual help
And mutual love, the Crown of all our bliss
Ordain'd by thee, and this delicious place
For us too large, where thy abundance wants
Partakers, and uncropt falls to the ground.
But thou hast promis'd from us two a Race
To fill the Earth, who shall with us extoll
Thy goodness infinite, both when we wake,
And when we seek, as now, thy gift of sleep.

    This said unanimous, and other Rites
Observing none, but adoration pure
Which God likes best, into thir inmost bower
Handed they went; and eas'd the putting off
These troublesom disguises which wee wear,
Strait side by side were laid, nor turnd I weene
Adam from his fair Spouse, nor *Eve* the Rites
Mysterious of connubial Love refus'd:
Whatever Hypocrites austerely talk
Of puritie and place and innocence,

Defaming as impure what God declares
Pure, and commands to som, leaves free to all.
Our Maker bids increase, who bids abstain
But our Destroyer, foe to God and Man?
Haile wedded Love, mysterious Law, true sourse
Of human ofspring, sole proprietie,
In Paradise of all things common else.
By thee adulterous lust was driv'n from men
Among the bestial herds to raunge, by thee
Founded in Reason, Loyal, Just, and Pure,
Relations dear, and all the Charities
Of Father, Son, and Brother first were known.
Farr be it, that I should write thee sin or blame,
Or think thee unbefitting holiest place,
Perpetual Fountain of Domestic sweets,
Whose Bed is undefil'd and chast pronounc't,
Present, or past, as Saints and Patriarchs us'd.
Here Love his golden shafts imploies, here lights
His constant Lamp, and waves his purple wings,
Reigns here and revels; not in the bought smile
Of Harlots, loveless, joyless, unindeard,
Casual fruition, nor in Court Amours
Mixt Dance, or wanton Mask, or Midnight Bal,
Or Serenate, which the starv'd Lover sings
To his proud fair, best quitted with disdain.
These lulld by Nightingales imbraceing slept,
And on thir naked limbs the flourie roof
Showrd Roses, which the Morn repair'd. Sleep on,
Blest pair; and O yet happiest if ye seek
No happier state, and know to know no more.

(*Book IV, lines* 1-775)

[*The Fall*]

Thus saying, from her Husbands hand her hand
Soft she withdrew, and like a Wood-Nymph light

Oread or *Dryad*, or of *Delia's* Traine,
Betook her to the Groves, but *Delia's* self
In gate surpass'd and Goddess-like deport,
Though not as shee with Bow and Quiver armd,
But with such Gardning Tools as Art yet rude,
Guiltless of fire had formd, or Angels brought.
To *Pales,* or *Pomona,* thus adornd,
Likeliest she seemd, *Pomona* when she fled
Vertumnus, or to *Ceres* in her Prime,
Yet Virgin of *Proserpina* from *Jove.*
Her long with ardent look his Eye pursu'd
Delighted, but desiring more her stay.
Oft he to her his charge of quick returne
Repeated, shee to him as oft engag'd
To be returnd by Noon amid the Bowre,
And all things in best order to invite
Noontide repast, or Afternoons repose.
O much deceav'd, much failing, hapless *Eve,*
Of thy presum'd return! event perverse!
Thou never from that houre in Paradise
Foundst either sweet repast, or sound repose;
Such ambush hid among sweet Flours and Shades
Waited with hellish rancor imminent
To intercept thy way, or send thee back
Despoild of Innocence, of Faith, of Bliss.
For now, and since first break of dawne the Fiend,
Meer Serpent in appearance, forth was come,
And on his Quest, where likeliest he might finde
The onely two of Mankinde, but in them
The whole included Race, his purposd prey.
In Bowre and Field he sought, where any tuft
Of Grove or Garden-Plot more pleasant lay,
Thir tendance or Plantation for delight,
By Fountain or by shadie Rivulet
He sought them both, but wish'd his hap might find

Eve separate, he wish'd, but not with hope
Of what so seldom chanc'd, when to his wish,
Beyond his hope, *Eve* separate he spies,
Veild in a Cloud of Fragrance, where she stood,
Half spi'd, so thick the Roses bushing round
About her glowd, oft stooping to support
Each Flour of slender stalk, whose head though gay
Carnation, Purple, Azure, or spect with Gold,
Hung drooping unsustaind, them she upstaies
Gently with Mirtle band, mindless the while,
Her self, though fairest unsupported Flour,
From her best prop so farr, and storm so nigh.
Neerer he drew, and many a walk travers'd
Of stateliest Covert, Cedar, Pine, or Palme,
Then voluble and bold, now hid, now seen
Among thick-wov'n Arborets and Flours
Imborderd on each Bank, the hand of *Eve:*
Spot more delicious then those Gardens feign'd
Or of reviv'd *Adonis,* or renownd
Alcinous, host of old *Lærtes* Son,
Or that, not Mystic, where the Sapient King
Held dalliance with his faire *Egyptian* Spouse.
Much hee the Place admir'd, the Person more.
As one who long in populous City pent,
Where Houses thick and Sewers annoy the Aire,
Forth issuing on a Summers Morn to breathe
Among the pleasant Villages and Farmes
Adjoynd, from each thing met conceaves delight,
The smell of Grain, of tedded Grass, or Kine,
Or Dairie, each rural sight, each rural sound;
If chance with Nymphlike step fair Virgin pass,
What pleasing seemd, for her now pleases more,
She most, and in her look summs all Delight.
Such Pleasure took the Serpent to behold
This Flourie Plat, the sweet recess of *Eve*

Thus earlie, thus alone; her Heav'nly forme
Angelic, but more soft, and Feminine,
Her graceful Innocence, her every Aire
Of gesture or lest action overawd
His Malice, and with rapine sweet bereav'd
His fierceness of the fierce intent it brought:
That space the Evil one abstracted stood
From his own evil, and for the time remaind
Stupidly good, of enmitie disarm'd,
Of guile, of hate, of envie, of revenge;
But the hot Hell that alwayes in him burnes,
Though in mid Heav'n, soon ended his delight,
And tortures him now more, the more he sees
Of pleasure not for him ordain'd: then soon
Fierce hate he recollects, and all his thoughts
Of mischief, gratulating, thus excites.

    Thoughts, whither have ye led me, with what sweet
Compulsion thus transported to forget
What hither brought us, hate, not love, nor hope
Of Paradise for Hell, hope here to taste
Of pleasure, but all pleasure to destroy,
Save what is in destroying, other joy
To me is lost. Then let me not let pass
Occasion which now smiles, behold alone
The Woman, opportune to all attempts,
Her Husband, for I view far round, not nigh,
Whose higher intellectual more I shun,
And strength, of courage hautie, and of limb
Heroic built, though of terrestrial mould,
Foe not informidable, exempt from wound,
I not; so much hath Hell debas'd, and paine
Infeebl'd me, to what I was in Heav'n.
Shee fair, divinely fair, fit Love for Gods,
Not terrible, though terrour be in Love
And beautie, not approacht by stronger hate,

Hate stronger, under shew of Love well feign'd,
The way which to her ruin now I tend.

So spake the Enemie of Mankind, enclos'd
In Serpent, Inmate bad, and toward *Eve*
Address'd his way, not with indented wave,
Prone on the ground, as since, but on his reare,
Circular base of rising foulds, that tour'd
Fould above fould a surging Maze, his Head
Crested aloft, and Carbuncle his Eyes;
With burnisht Neck of verdant Gold, erect
Amidst his circling Spires, that on the grass
Floted redundant: pleasing was his shape,
And lovely, never since of Serpent kind
Lovelier, not those that in *Illyria* chang'd
Hermione and *Cadmus,* or the God
In *Epidaurus;* nor to which transformd
Ammonian Jove, or *Capitoline* was seen,
Hee with *Olympias,* this with her who bore
Scipio the highth of *Rome.* With tract oblique
At first, as one who sought access, but feard
To interrupt, side-long he works his way.
As when a Ship by skilful Stearsman wrought
Nigh Rivers mouth or Foreland, where the Wind
Veres oft, as oft so steers, and shifts her Saile;
So varied hee, and of his tortuous Traine
Curld many a wanton wreath in sight of *Eve,*
To lure her Eye; shee busied heard the sound
Of rusling Leaves, but minded not, as us'd
To such disport before her through the Field,
From every Beast, more duteous at her call,
Then at *Circean* call the Herd disguis'd.
Hee boulder now, uncall'd before her stood;
But as in gaze admiring: Oft he bowd
His turret Crest, and sleek enamel'd Neck,
Fawning, and lick'd the ground whereon she trod.

His gentle dumb expression turnd at length
The Eye of *Eve* to mark his play; he glad
Of her attention gaind, with Serpent Tongue
Organic, or impulse of vocal Air,
His fraudulent temptation thus began.

    Wonder not, sovran Mistress, if perhaps
Thou canst, who art sole Wonder, much less arm
Thy looks, the Heav'n of mildness, with disdain,
Displeas'd that I approach thee thus, and gaze
Insatiate, I thus single, nor have feard
Thy awful brow, more awful thus retir'd.
Fairest resemblance of thy Maker faire,
Thee all things living gaze on, all things thine
By gift, and thy Celestial Beautie adore
With ravishment beheld, there best beheld
Where universally admir'd; but here
In this enclosure wild, these Beasts among,
Beholders rude, and shallow to discerne
Half what in thee is fair, one man except,
Who sees thee? (and what is one?) who shouldst be
    seen
A Goddess among Gods, ador'd and serv'd
By Angels numberless, thy daily Train.

    So gloz'd the Tempter, and his Proem tun'd;
Into the Heart of *Eve* his words made way,
Though at the voice much marveling; at length
Not unamaz'd she thus in answer spake.
What may this mean? Language of Man pronounc't
By Tongue of Brute, and human sense exprest?
The first at lest of these I thought deni'd
To Beasts, whom God on thir Creation-Day
Created mute to all articulat sound;
The latter I demurre, for in thir looks
Much reason, and in thir actions oft appeers.
Thee, Serpent, suttlest beast of all the field

I knew, but not with human voice endu'd;
Redouble then this miracle, and say,
How cam'st thou speakable of mute, and how
To me so friendly grown above the rest
Of brutal kind, that daily are in sight?
Say, for such wonder claims attention due.
   To whom the guileful Tempter thus reply'd.
Empress of this fair World, resplendent *Eve*,
Easie to mee it is to tell thee all
What thou commandst, and right thou shouldst be
     obeyd:
I was at first as other Beasts that graze
The trodden Herb, of abject thoughts and low,
As was my food, nor aught but food discern'd
Or Sex, and apprehended nothing high:
Till on a day roaving the field, I chanc'd
A goodly Tree farr distant to behold
Loaden with fruit of fairest colours mixt,
Ruddie and Gold: I nearer drew to gaze;
When from the boughes a savorie odour blow'n,
Grateful to appetite, more pleas'd my sense
Then smell of sweetest Fenel, or the Teats
Of Ewe or Goat dropping with Milk at Eevn,
Unsuckt of Lamb or Kid, that tend thir play.
To satisfie the sharp desire I had
Of tasting those fair Apples, I resolv'd
Not to deferr; hunger and thirst at once,
Powerful perswaders, quick'nd at the scent
Of that alluring fruit, urg'd me so keene.
About the Mossie Trunk I wound me soon,
For high from ground the branches would require
Thy utmost reach or *Adams:* Round the Tree
All other Beasts that saw, with like desire
Longing and envying stood, but could not reach.
Amid the Tree now got, where plentie hung

Tempting so nigh, to pluck and eat my fill
I spar'd not, for such pleasure till that hour
At Feed or Fountain never had I found.
Sated at length, ere long I might perceave
Strange alteration in me, to degree
Of Reason in my inward Powers, and Speech
Wanted not long, though to this shape retaind.
Thenceforth to Speculations high or deep
I turnd my thoughts, and with capacious mind
Considerd all things visible in Heav'n,
Or Earth, or Middle, all things fair and good;
But all that fair and good in thy Divine
Semblance, and in thy Beauties heav'nly Ray
United I beheld; no Fair to thine
Equivalent or second, which compel'd
Mee thus, though importune perhaps, to come
And gaze, and worship thee of right declar'd
Sovran of Creatures, universal Dame.
     So talk'd the spirited sly Snake; and *Eve*
Yet more amaz'd unwarie thus reply'd.
     Serpent, thy overpraising leaves in doubt
The vertue of that Fruit, in thee first prov'd:
But say, where grows the Tree, from hence how far?
For many are the Trees of God that grow
In Paradise, and various, yet unknown
To us, in such abundance lies our choice,
As leaves a greater store of Fruit untoucht,
Still hanging incorruptible, till men
Grow up to thir provision, and more hands
Help to disburden Nature of her Bearth.
     To whom the wilie Adder, blithe and glad.
Empress, the way is readie, and not long,
Beyond a row of Myrtles, on a Flat,
Fast by a Fountain, one small Thicket past

Of blowing Myrrh and Balme; if thou accept
My conduct, I can bring thee thither soon.

    Lead then, said *Eve*. Hee leading swiftly rowld
In tangles, and made intricate seem strait,
To mischief swift. Hope elevates, and joy
Bright'ns his Crest, as when a wandring Fire
Compact of unctuous vapor, which the Night
Condenses, and the cold invirons round,
Kindl'd through agitation to a Flame,
Which oft, they say, some evil Spirit attends,
Hovering and blazing with delusive Light,
Misleads th' amaz'd Night-wanderer from his way
To Boggs and Mires, and oft through Pond or Poole,
There swallow'd up and lost, from succour farr.
So glister'd the dire Snake, and into fraud
Led *Eve* our credulous Mother, to the Tree
Of prohibition, root of all our woe;
Which when she saw, thus to her guide she spake.

    Serpent, we might have spar'd our coming hither,
Fruitless to me, though Fruit be here to excess,
The credit of whose vertue rest with thee,
Wondrous indeed, if cause of such effects.
But of this Tree we may not taste nor touch;
God so commanded, and left that Command
Sole Daughter of his voice; the rest, we live
Law to our selves, our Reason is our Law.

    To whom the Tempter guilefully repli'd.
Indeed? hath God then said that of the Fruit
Of all these Garden Trees ye shall not eate,
Yet Lords declar'd of all in Earth or Aire?

    To whom thus *Eve* yet sinless. Of the Fruit
Of each Tree in the Garden we may eate,
But of the Fruit of this fair Tree amidst
The Garden, God hath said, Ye shall not eate

Thereof, nor shall ye touch it, least ye die.
   She scarse had said, though brief, when now more
      bold
The Tempter, but with shew of Zeale and Love
To Man, and indignation at his wrong,
New part puts on, and as to passion mov'd,
Fluctuats disturbd, yet comely, and in act
Rais'd, as of som great matter to begin.
As when of old som Orator renound
In *Athens* or free *Rome,* where Eloquence
Flourishd, since mute, to som great cause addrest,
Stood in himself collected, while each part,
Motion, each act won audience ere the tongue,
Somtimes in highth began, as no delay
Of Preface brooking through his Zeal of Right.
So standing, moving, or to highth upgrown
The Tempter all impassiond thus began.

   O Sacred, Wise, and Wisdom-giving Plant,
Mother of Science, Now I feel thy Power
Within me cleere, not onely to discerne
Things in thir Causes, but to trace the wayes
Of highest Agents, deemd however wise.
Queen of this Universe, doe not believe
Those rigid threats of Death; ye shall not Die:
How should ye? by the Fruit? it gives you Life
To Knowledge? By the Threatner, look on mee,
Mee who have touch'd and tasted, yet both live,
And life more perfet have attaind then Fate
Meant mee, by ventring higher then my Lot.
Shall that be shut to Man, which to the Beast
Is open? or will God incense his ire
For such a petty Trespass, and not praise
Rather your dauntless vertue, whom the pain
Of Death denounc't, whatever thing Death be,
Deterrd not from atchieving what might leade

To happier life, knowledge of Good and Evil;
Of good, how just? of evil, if what is evil
Be real, why not known, since easier shunnd?
God therefore cannot hurt ye, and be just;
Not just, not God; not feard then, nor obeid:
Your feare it self of Death removes the feare.
Why then was this forbid? Why but to awe,
Why but to keep ye low and ignorant,
His worshippers; he knows that in the day
Ye Eate thereof, your Eyes that seem so cleere,
Yet are but dim, shall perfetly be then
Op'nd and cleerd, and ye shall be as Gods,
Knowing both Good and Evil as they know.
That ye should be as Gods, since I as Man,
Internal Man, is but proportion meet,
I of brute human, yee of human Gods.
So ye shall die perhaps, by putting off
Human, to put on Gods, death to be wisht,
Though threat'nd, which no worse then this can bring.
And what are Gods that Man may not become
As they, participating God-like food?
The Gods are first, and that advantage use
On our belief, that all from them proceeds;
I question it, for this fair Earth I see,
Warm'd by the Sun, producing every kind,
Them nothing: If they all things, who enclos'd
Knowledge of Good and Evil in this Tree,
That whoso eats thereof, forthwith attains
Wisdom without their leave? and wherein lies
Th' offence, that Man should thus attain to know?
What can your knowledge hurt him, or this Tree
Impart against his will if all be his?
Or is it envie, and can envie dwell
In heav'nly brests? these, these and many more
Causes import your need of this fair Fruit.

Goddess humane, reach then, and freely taste.
   He ended, and his words replete with guile
Into her heart too easie entrance won:
Fixt on the Fruit she gaz'd, which to behold
Might tempt alone, and in her ears the sound
Yet rung of his perswasive words, impregn'd
With Reason, to her seeming, and with Truth;
Meanwhile the hour of Noon drew on, and wak'd
An eager appetite, rais'd by the smell
So savorie of that Fruit, which with desire,
Inclinable now grown to touch or taste,
Sollicited her longing eye; yet first
Pausing a while, thus to her self she mus'd.
   Great are thy Vertues, doubtless, best of Fruits,
Though kept from Man, and worthy to be admir'd,
Whose taste, too long forborn, at first assay
Gave elocution to the mute, and taught
The Tongue not made for Speech to speak thy praise:
Thy praise hee also who forbids thy use,
Conceales not from us, naming thee the Tree
Of Knowledge, knowledge both of good and evil;
Forbids us then to taste, but his forbidding
Commends thee more, while it inferrs the good
By thee communicated, and our want:
For good unknown, sure is not had, or had
And yet unknown, is as not had at all.
In plain then, what forbids he but to know,
Forbids us good, forbids us to be wise?
Such prohibitions binde not. But if Death
Bind us with after-bands, what profits then
Our inward freedom? In the day we eate
Of this fair Fruit, our doom is, we shall die.
How dies the Serpent? hee hath eat'n and lives,
And knows, and speaks, and reasons, and discernes,
Irrational till then. For us alone

Was death invented? or to us deni'd
This intellectual food, for beasts reserv'd?
For Beasts it seems: yet that one Beast which first
Hath tasted, envies not, but brings with joy
The good befall'n him, Author unsuspect,
Friendly to man, farr from deceit or guile.
What fear I then, rather what know to feare
Under this ignorance of Good and Evil,
Of God or Death, of Law or Penaltie?
Here grows the Cure of all, this Fruit Divine,
Fair to the Eye, inviting to the Taste,
Of vertue to make wise: what hinders then
To reach, and feed at once both Bodie and Mind?
    So saying, her rash hand in evil hour
Forth reaching to the Fruit, she pluck'd, she eat:
Earth felt the wound, and Nature from her seat
Sighing through all her Works gave signs of woe,
That all was lost. Back to the Thicket slunk
The guiltie Serpent, and well might, for *Eve*
Intent now wholly on her taste, naught else
Regarded, such delight till then, as seemd,
In Fruit she never tasted, whether true
Or fansied so, through expectation high
Of knowledg, nor was God-head from her thought.
Greedily she ingorg'd without restraint,
And knew not eating Death: Satiate at length,
And hight'nd as with Wine, jocond and boon,
Thus to her self she pleasingly began.
    O Sovran, vertuous, precious of all Trees
In Paradise, of operation blest
To Sapience, hitherto obscur'd, infam'd,
And thy fair Fruit let hang, as to no end
Created; but henceforth my early care,
Not without Song, each Morning, and due praise
Shall tend thee, and the fertil burden ease

Of thy full branches offer'd free to all;
Till dieted by thee I grow mature
In knowledge, as the Gods who all things know;
Though others envie what they cannot give;
For had the gift bin theirs, it had not here
Thus grown. Experience, next to thee I owe,
Best guide; not following thee, I had remaind
In ignorance, thou op'nst Wisdoms way,
And giv'st access, though secret she retire.
And I perhaps am secret; Heav'n is high,
High and remote to see from thence distinct
Each thing on Earth; and other care perhaps
May have diverted from continual watch
Our great Forbidder, safe with all his Spies
About him. But to *Adam* in what sort
Shall I appeer? shall I to him make known
As yet my change, and give him to partake
Full happiness with mee, or rather not,
But keep the odds of Knowledge in my power
Without Copartner? so to add what wants
In Femal Sex, the more to draw his Love,
And render me more equal, and perhaps,
A thing not undesireable, somtime
Superior; for inferior who is free?
This may be well: but what if God have seen,
And Death ensue? then I shall be no more,
And *Adam* wedded to another *Eve*,
Shall live with her enjoying, I extinct;
A death to think. Confirm'd then I resolve,
Adam shall share with me in bliss or woe:
So dear I love him, that with him all deaths
I could endure, without him live no life.

     So saying, from the Tree her step she turnd,
But first low Reverence don, as to the power
That dwelt within, whose presence had infus'd

Into the plant sciential sap, deriv'd
From Nectar, drink of Gods. *Adam* the while
Waiting desirous her return, had wove
Of choicest Flours a Garland to adorne
Her Tresses, and her rural labours crown
As Reapers oft are wont thir Harvest Queen.
Great joy he promis'd to his thoughts, and new
Solace in her return, so long delay'd;
Yet oft his heart, divine of somthing ill,
Misgave him; hee the faultring measure felt;
And forth to meet her went, the way she took
That Morn when first they parted; by the Tree
Of Knowledge he must pass, there he her met,
Scarse from the Tree returning; in her hand
A bough of fairest fruit that downie smil'd,
New gatherd, and ambrosial smell diffus'd.
To him she hasted, in her face excuse
Came Prologue, and Apologie to prompt,
Which with bland words at will she thus addrest.
      Hast thou not wonderd, *Adam*, at my stay?
Thee I have misst, and thought it long, depriv'd
Thy presence, agonie of love till now
Not felt, nor shall be twice, for never more
Mean I to trie, what rash untri'd I sought,
The paine of absence from thy sight. But strange
Hath bin the cause, and wonderful to heare:
This Tree is not as we are told, a Tree
Of danger tasted, nor to evil unknown
Op'ning the way, but of Divine effect
To open Eyes, and make them Gods who taste;
And hath bin tasted such: the Serpent wise,
Or not restraind as wee, or not obeying,
Hath eat'n of the fruit, and is become,
Not dead, as we are threatn'd, but thenceforth
Endu'd with human voice and human sense,

Reasoning to admiration, and with mee
Perswasively hath so prevaild, that I
Have also tasted, and have also found
Th' effects to correspond, opener mine Eyes
Dimm erst, dilated Spirits, ampler Heart,
And growing up to Godhead; which for thee
Chiefly I sought, without thee can despise.
For bliss, as thou hast part, to me is bliss,
Tedious, unshar'd with thee, and odious soon.
Thou therfore also taste, that equal Lot
May joyne us, equal Joy, as equal Love;
Least thou not tasting, different degree
Disjoyne us, and I then too late renounce
Deitie for thee, when Fate will not permit.

    Thus *Eve* with Countnance blithe her storie told;
But in her Cheek distemper flushing glowd.
On th' other side, *Adam,* soon as he heard
The fatal Trespass don by *Eve,* amaz'd,
Astonied stood and Blank, while horror chill
Ran through his veins, and all his joynts relax'd;
From his slack hand the Garland wreath'd for *Eve*
Down drop'd, and all the faded Roses shed:
Speechless he stood and pale, till thus at length
First to himself he inward silence broke.

    O fairest of Creation, last and best
Of all Gods Works, Creature in whom excell'd
Whatever can to sight or thought be formd,
Holy, divine, good, amiable, or sweet!
How art thou lost, how on a sudden lost,
Defac't, deflourd, and now to Death devote?
Rather how hast thou yeelded to transgress
The strict forbiddance, how to violate
The sacred Fruit forbidd'n! som cursed fraud
Of Enemie hath beguil'd thee, yet unknown,
And mee with thee hath ruind, for with thee

Certain my resolution is to Die;
How can I live without thee, how forgoe
Thy sweet Converse and Love so dearly joyn'd,
To live again in these wilde Woods forlorn?
Should God create another *Eve*, and I
Another Rib afford, yet loss of thee
Would never from my heart; no no, I feel
The Link of Nature draw me: Flesh of Flesh,
Bone of my Bone thou art, and from thy State
Mine never shall be parted, bliss or woe.

   So having said, as one from sad dismay
Recomforted, and after thoughts disturbd
Submitting to what seemd remediless,
Thus in calme mood his Words to *Eve* he turnd.

   Bold deed thou hast presum'd, adventrous *Eve*,
And peril great provok't, who thus hast dar'd
Had it bin onely coveting to Eye
That sacred Fruit, sacred to abstinence,
Much more to taste it under banne to touch.
But past who can recall, or don undoe?
Not God Omnipotent, nor Fate, yet so
Perhaps thou shalt not Die, perhaps the Fact
Is not so hainous now, foretasted Fruit,
Profan'd first by the Serpent, by him first
Made common and unhallowd ere our taste;
Nor yet on him found deadly, he yet lives,
Lives, as thou saidst, and gaines to live as Man
Higher degree of Life, inducement strong
To us, as likely tasting to attaine
Proportional ascent, which cannot be
But to be Gods, or Angels Demi-gods.
Nor can I think that God, Creator wise,
Though threatning, will in earnest so destroy
Us his prime Creatures, dignifi'd so high,
Set over all his Works, which in our Fall,

For us created, needs with us must faile,
Dependent made; so God shall uncreate,
Be frustrate, do, undo, and labour loose,
Not well conceav'd of God, who though his Power
Creation could repeate, yet would be loath
Us to abolish, least the Adversary
Triumph and say; Fickle their State whom God
Most Favors, who can please him long? Mee first
He ruind, now Mankind; whom will he next?
Matter of scorne, not to be given the Foe.
However I with thee have fixt my Lot,
Certain to undergoe like doom, if Death
Consort with thee, Death is to mee as Life;
So forcible within my heart I feel
The Bond of Nature draw me to my owne,
My own in thee, for what thou art is mine;
Our State cannot be severd, we are one,
One Flesh; to loose thee were to loose my self.
      So *Adam*, and thus *Eve* to him repli'd.
O glorious trial of exceeding Love,
Illustrious evidence, example high!
Ingaging me to emulate, but short
Of thy perfection, how shall I attaine,
Adam, from whose deare side I boast me sprung,
And gladly of our Union heare thee speak,
One Heart, one Soul in both; whereof good prooff
This day affords, declaring thee resolvd,
Rather then Death or aught then Death more dread
Shall separate us, linkt in Love so deare,
To undergoe with mee one Guilt, one Crime,
If any be, of tasting this fair Fruit,
Whose vertue, for of good still good proceeds,
Direct, or by occasion hath presented
This happie trial of thy Love, which else
So eminently never had bin known.

Were it I thought Death menac't would ensue
This my attempt, I would sustain alone
The worst, and not perswade thee, rather die
Deserted, then oblige thee with a fact
Pernicious to thy Peace, chiefly assur'd
Remarkably so late of thy so true,
So faithful Love unequald; but I feel
Farr otherwise th' event, not Death, but Life
Augmented, op'nd Eyes, new Hopes, new Joyes,
Taste so Divine, that what of sweet before
Hath toucht my sense, flat seems to this, and harsh.
On my experience, *Adam,* freely taste,
And fear of Death deliver to the Windes.

   So saying, she embrac'd him, and for joy
Tenderly wept, much won that he his Love
Had so enobl'd, as of choice to incurr
Divine displeasure for her sake, or Death.
In recompence (for such compliance bad
Such recompence best merits) from the bough
She gave him of that fair enticing Fruit
With liberal hand: he scrupl'd not to eat
Against his better knowledge, not deceav'd,
But fondly overcome with Femal charm.
Earth trembl'd from her entrails, as again
In pangs, and Nature gave a second groan,
Skie lowr'd, and muttering Thunder, som sad drops
Wept at compleating of the mortal Sin
Original; while *Adam* took no thought,
Eating his fill, nor *Eve* to iterate
Her former trespass fear'd, the more to soothe
Him with her lov'd societie, that now
As with new Wine intoxicated both
They swim in mirth, and fansie that they feel
Divinitie within them breeding wings
Wherewith to scorn the Earth: but that false Fruit
Farr other operation first displaid,

Carnal desire enflaming, hee on *Eve*
Began to cast lascivious Eyes, she him
As wantonly repaid; in Lust they burne:
Till *Adam* thus 'gan *Eve* to dalliance move.

 Eve, now I see thou art exact of taste,
And elegant, of Sapience no small part,
Since to each meaning savour we apply,
And Palate call judicious; I the praise
Yeild thee, so well this day thou has purvey'd.
Much pleasure we have lost, while we abstain'd
From this delightful Fruit, nor known till now
True relish, tasting; if such pleasure be
In things to us forbidden, it might be wish'd,
For this one Tree had bin forbidden ten.
But come, so well refresh't, now let us play,
As meet is, after such delicious Fare;
For never did thy Beautie since the day
I saw thee first and wedded thee, adorn'd
With all perfections, so enflame my sense
With ardor to enjoy thee, fairer now
Then ever, bountie of this vertuous Tree.

 So said he, and forbore not glance or toy
Of amorous intent, well understood
Of *Eve*, whose Eye darted contagious Fire.
Her hand he seis'd, and to a shadie bank,
Thick overhead with verdant roof imbowr'd
He led her nothing loath; Flours were the Couch,
Pansies, and Violets, and Asphodel,
And Hyacinth, Earths freshest softest lap.
There they thir fill of Love and Loves disport
Took largely, of thir mutual guilt the Seale,
The solace of thir sin, till dewie sleep
Oppress'd them, wearied with thir amorous play.
Soon as the force of that fallacious Fruit,
That with exhilerating vapour bland

About thir spirits had plaid, and inmost powers
Made erre, was now exhal'd, and grosser sleep
Bred of unkindly fumes, with conscious dreams
Encumberd, now had left them, up they rose
As from unrest, and each the other viewing,
Soon found thir Eyes how op'nd, and thir minds
How dark'nd; innocence, that as a veile
Had shadow'd them from knowing ill, was gon,
Just confidence, and native righteousness,
And honour from about them, naked left
To guiltie shame hee cover'd, but his Robe
Uncover'd more. So rose the *Danite* strong
Herculean Samson from the Harlot-lap
Of *Philistean Dalilah,* and wak'd
Shorn of his strength, They destitute and bare
Of all thir vertue: silent, and in face
Confounded long they sate, as struck'n mute,
Till *Adam,* though not less then *Eve* abasht,
At length gave utterance to these words constraind.

   O *Eve,* in evil hour thou didst give eare
To that false Worm, of whomsoever taught
To counterfet Mans voice, true in our Fall,
False in our promis'd Rising; since our Eyes
Op'nd we find indeed, and find we know
Both Good and Evil, Good lost, and Evil got.
Bad Fruit of Knowledge, if this be to know,
Which leaves us naked thus, of Honour void,
Of Innocence, of Faith, of Puritie,
Our wonted Ornaments now soild and staind,
And in our Faces evident the signes
Of foul concupiscence; whence evil store;
Even shame, the last of evils; of the first
Be sure then. How shall I behold the face
Henceforth of God of Angel, earst with joy
And rapture so oft beheld? those heav'nly shapes

Will dazle now this earthly, with thir blaze
Insufferably bright. O might I here
In solitude live savage, in some glade
Obscur'd, where highest Woods impenetrable
To Starr or Sun-light, spread thir umbrage broad,
And brown as Evening: Cover me ye Pines,
Ye Cedars, with innumerable boughs
Hide me, where I may never see them more.
But let us now, as in bad plight, devise
What best may for the present serve to hide
The Parts of each from other, that seem most
To shame obnoxious, and unseemliest seen,
Some Tree whose broad smooth Leaves together sowd,
And girded on our loyns, may cover round
Those middle parts, that this new commer, Shame,
There sit not, and reproach us as unclean.
    So counsel'd hee, and both together went
Into the thickest Wood, there soon they chose
The Figtree, not that kind for Fruit renown'd,
But such as at this day to *Indians* known
In *Malabar* or *Decan* spreds her Armes
Braunching so broad and long, that in the ground
The bended Twigs take root, and Daughters grow
About the Mother Tree, a Pillard shade
High overarch't, and echoing Walks between;
There oft the *Indian* Herdsman shunning heate
Shelters in coole, and tends his pasturing Herds
At Loopholes cut through thickest shade: Those Leaves
They gatherd, broad as *Amazonian* Targe,
And with what skill they had, together sowd,
To gird thir waste, vain Covering if to hide
Thir guilt and dreaded shame; O how unlike
To that first naked Glorie. Such of late
Columbus found th' *American* so girt
With featherd Cincture, naked else and wilde

Among the Trees on Iles and woodie Shores.
Thus fenc't, and as they thought, thir shame in part
Coverd, but not at rest or ease of Mind,
They sate them down to weep, nor onely Teares
Raind at thir Eyes, but high Winds worse within
Began to rise, high Passions, Anger, Hate,
Mistrust, Suspicion, Discord, and shook sore
Thir inward State of Mind, calme Region once
And full of Peace, now tost and turbulent:
For Understanding rul'd not, and the Will
Heard not her lore, both in subjection now
To sensual Appetite, who from beneathe
Usurping over sovran Reason claimd
Superior sway: From thus distemperd brest,
Adam, estrang'd in look and alterd stile,
Speech intermitted thus to *Eve* renewd.

   Would thou hadst heark'nd to my words, and stai'd
With me, as I besought thee, when that strange
Desire of wandring this unhappie Morn,
I know not whence possessd thee; we had then
Remaind still happie, not as now, despoild
Of all our good, sham'd, naked, miserable.
Let none henceforth seek needless cause to approve
The Faith they owe; when earnestly they seek
Such proof, conclude, they then begin to faile.

   To whom soon mov'd with touch of blame thus *Eve.*
What words have past thy Lips, *Adam* severe,
Imput'st thou that to my default, or will
Of wandering, as thou call'st it, which who knows
But might as ill have happ'nd thou being by,
Or to thy self perhaps: hadst thou bin there,
Or here th' attempt, thou couldst not have discernd
Fraud in the Serpent, speaking as he spake;
No ground of enmitie between us known,
Why hee should mean me ill, or seek to harme.

Was I to have never parted from thy side?
As good have grown there still a liveless Rib.
Being as I am, why didst not thou the Head
Command me absolutely not to go,
Going into such danger as thou saidst?
Too facil then thou didst not much gainsay,
Nay, didst permit, approve, and fair dismiss.
Hadst thou bin firm and fixt in thy dissent,
Neither had I transgress'd, nor thou with mee.

　　To whom then first incenst *Adam* repli'd.
Is this the Love, is this the recompence
Of mine to thee, ingrateful *Eve,* exprest
Immutable when thou wert lost, not I,
Who might have liv'd and joyd immortal bliss,
Yet willingly chose rather Death with thee:
And am I now upbraided, as the cause
Of thy transgressing? not enough severe,
It seems, in thy restraint: what could I more?
I warn'd thee, I admonish'd thee, foretold
The danger, and the lurking Enemie
That lay in wait; beyond this had bin force,
And force upon free Will hath here no place.
But confidence then bore thee on, secure
Either to meet no danger, or to finde
Matter of glorious trial; and perhaps
I also err'd in overmuch admiring
What seemd in thee so perfet, that I thought
No evil durst attempt thee, but I rue
That errour now, which is become my crime,
And thou th' accuser. Thus it shall befall
Him who to worth in Women overtrusting
Lets her Will rule; restraint she will not brook,
And left to her self, if evil thence ensue,
Shee first his weak indulgence will accuse.

　　Thus they in mutual accusation spent

The fruitless hours, but neither self-condemning:
And of thir vain contest appeer'd no end.

(Book IX, lines 385–end)

[<i>The Retreat from Paradise</i>]

He ended; and thus *Adam* last reply'd.
How soon hath thy prediction, Seer blest,
Measur'd this transient World, the Race of time,
Till time stand fixt: beyond is all abyss,
Eternitie, whose end no eye can reach.
Greatly instructed I shall hence depart,
Greatly in peace of thought, and have my fill
Of knowledge, what this vessel can containe;
Beyond which was my folly to aspire.
Henceforth I learne, that to obey is best,
And love with feare the onely God, to walk
As in his presence, ever to observe
His providence, and on him sole depend,
Merciful over all his works, with good
Still overcoming evil, and by small
Accomplishing great things, by things deemd weak
Subverting worldly strong, and worldly wise
By simply meek; that suffering for Truths sake
Is fortitude to highest victorie,
And to the faithful Death the Gate of Life;
Taught this by his example whom I now
Acknowledge my Redeemer ever blest.

To whom thus also th' Angel last repli'd:
This having learnt, thou hast attained the summe
Of wisdom; hope no higher, though all the Starrs
Thou knewest by name, and all th' ethereal Powers,
All secrets of the deep, all Natures works,
Or works of God in Heav'n, Air, Earth, or Sea,
And all the riches of this World enjoydst,
And all the rule, one Empire; onely add

Deeds to thy knowledge answerable, add Faith,
Add Vertue, Patience, Temperance, add Love,
By name to come call'd Charitie, the soul
Of all the rest: then wilt thou not be loath
To leave this Paradise, but shalt possess
A Paradise within thee, happier farr.
Let us descend now therefore from this top
Of Speculation; for the hour precise
Exacts our parting hence; and see the Guards,
By mee encampt on yonder Hill, expect
Thir motion, at whose Front a flaming Sword,
In signal of remove, waves fiercely round;
We may no longer stay: go, waken *Eve;*
Her also I with gentle Dreams have calm'd
Portending good, and all her spirits compos'd
To meek submission: thou at season fit
Let her with thee partake what thou hast heard,
Chiefly what may concern her Faith to know,
The great deliverance by her Seed to come
(For by the Womans Seed) on all Mankind.
That ye may live, which will be many dayes,
Both in one Faith unanimous though sad,
With cause for evils past, yet much more cheer'd
With meditation on the happie end.

　　He ended, and they both descend the Hill;
Descended, *Adam* to the Bowre where *Eve*
Lay sleeping ran before, but found her wak't;
And thus with words not sad she him receav'd.

　　Whence thou returnst, and whither wentst, I know;
For God is also in sleep, and Dreams advise,
Which he hath sent propitious, some great good
Presaging, since with sorrow and hearts distress
Wearied I fell asleep: but now lead on;
In mee is no delay; with thee to goe,
Is to stay here; without thee here to stay,

Is to go hence unwilling; thou to mee
Art all things under Heav'n, all places thou,
Who for my wilful crime art banisht hence.
This further consolation yet secure
I carry hence; though all by mee is lost,
Such favour I unworthie am voutsaft,
By mee the Promis'd Seed shall all restore.

So spake our Mother *Eve*, and *Adam* heard
Well pleas'd, but answer'd not; for now too nigh
Th' Archangel stood, and from the other Hill
To thir fixt Station, all in bright array
The Cherubim descended; on the ground
Gliding meteorous, as Ev'ning Mist
Ris'n from a River o're the marish glides,
And gathers ground fast at the Labourers heel
Homeward returning. High in Front advanc't,
The brandisht Sword of God before them blaz'd
Fierce as a Comet; which with torrid heat,
And vapour as the *Libyan* Air adust,
Began to parch that temperate Clime; whereat
In either hand the hastning Angel caught
Our lingring Parents, and to th' Eastern Gate
Led them direct, and down the Cliff as fast
To the subjected Plaine; then disappeer'd.
They looking back, all th' Eastern side beheld
Of Paradise, so late thir happie seat,
Wav'd over by that flaming Brand, the Gate
With dreadful Faces throng'd and fierie Armes:
Som natural tears they drop'd, but wip'd them soon;
The World was all before them, where to choose
Thir place of rest, and Providence thir guide:
They hand in hand with wandring steps and slow,
Through *Eden* took thir solitarie way.

(*Book XII, lines 552–end*)

Samson Agonistes

THE ARGUMENT

Samson made Captive, Blind, and now in the Prison at Gaza, there to labour as in a common workhouse, on a Festival day, in the general cessation from labour, comes forth into the open Air, to a place nigh, somewhat retir'd there to sit a while and bemoan his condition. Where he happens at length to be visited by certain friends and equals of his tribe, which make the Chorus, who seek to comfort him what they can; then by his old Father Manoa, who endeavours the like, and withal tells him his purpose to procure his liberty by ransom; lastly, that this Feast was proclaim'd by the Philistins as a day of Thanksgiving for thir deliverance from the hands of Samson, which yet more troubles him. Manoa then departs to prosecute his endeavour with the Philistian Lords for Samson's redemption; who in the mean while is visited by other persons; and lastly by a publick Officer to require his coming to the Feast before the Lords and People, to play or shew his strength in thir presence; he at first refuses, dismissing the publick Officer with absolute denyal to come; at length perswaded inwardly that this was from God, he yields to go along with him, who came now the second time with great threatnings to fetch him; the Chorus yet remaining on the place, Manoa returns full of joyful hope, to procure e're long his Sons deliverance: in the midst of which discourse an Ebrew comes in haste confusedly at first; and afterward more distinctly relating the Catastrophe, what Samson had done to the Philistins, and by accident to himself; wherewith the Tragedy ends.

THE PERSONS

Samson	Harapha of Gath
Manoa the Father of Samson	Publick Officer
Dalila his Wife	Messenger
	Chorus of Danites

The Scene before the Prison in Gaza.

SAMSON. A little onward lend thy guiding hand
To these dark steps, a little further on;
For yonder bank hath choice of Sun or shade,
There I am wont to sit, when any chance
Relieves me from my task of servile toyl,
Daily in the common Prison else enjoyn'd me,
Where I a Prisoner chain'd, scarce freely draw
The air imprison'd also, close and damp,
Unwholsom draught: but here I feel amends,
The breath of Heav'n fresh-blowing, pure and sweet,
With day-spring born; here leave me to respire.
This day a solemn Feast the people hold
To *Dagon* thir Sea-Idol, and forbid
Laborious works, unwillingly this rest
Thir Superstition yields me; hence with leave
Retiring from the popular noise, I seek
This unfrequented place to find some ease,
Ease to the body some, none to the mind
From restless thoughts, that like a deadly swarm
Of Hornets arm'd, no sooner found alone,
But rush upon me thronging, and present
Times past, what once I was, and what am now.
O wherefore was my birth from Heaven foretold
Twice by an Angel, who at last in sight
Of both my Parents all in flames ascended
From off the Altar, where an Off'ring burn'd,
As in a fiery column charioting
His Godlike presence, and from some great act
Or benefit reveal'd to *Abraham's* race?
Why was my breeding order'd and prescrib'd
As of a person separate to God,
Design'd for great exploits; if I must dye

Betray'd, Captiv'd, and both my Eyes put out,
Made of my Enemies the scorn and gaze;
To grind in Brazen Fetters under task
With this Heav'n-gifted strength? O glorious strength
Put to the labour of a Beast, debas't
Lower then bondslave! Promise was that I
Should *Israel* from *Philistian* yoke deliver;
Ask for this great Deliverer now, and find him
Eyeless in *Gaza* at the Mill with slaves,
Himself in bonds under *Philistian* yoke;
Yet stay, let me not rashly call in doubt
Divine Prediction; what if all foretold
Had been fulfilld but through mine own default,
Whom have I to complain of but my self?
Who this high gift of strength committed to me,
In what part lodg'd, how easily bereft me,
Under the Seal of silence could not keep,
But weakly to a woman must reveal it,
O'recome with importunity and tears.
O impotence of mind, in body strong!
But what is strength without a double share
Of wisdom, vast, unwieldy, burdensom,
Proudly secure, yet liable to fall
By weakest suttleties, not made to rule,
But to subserve where wisdom bears command.
God, when he gave me strength, to shew withal
How slight the gift was, hung it in my Hair.
But peace, I must not quarrel with the will
Of highest dispensation, which herein
Happ'ly had ends above my reach to know:
Suffices that to me strength is my bane,
And proves the sourse of all my miseries;
So many, and so huge, that each apart
Would ask a life to wail, but chief of all,

O loss of sight, of thee I most complain!
Blind among enemies, O worse then chains,
Dungeon, or beggery, or decrepit age!
Light the prime work of God to me is extinct,
And all her various objects of delight
Annull'd, which might in part my grief have eas'd,
Inferiour to the vilest now become
Of man or worm; the vilest here excel me,
They creep, yet see, I dark in light expos'd
To daily fraud, contempt, abuse and wrong,
Within doors, or without, still as a fool,
In power of others, never in my own;
Scarce half I seem to live, dead more then half.
O dark, dark, dark, amid the blaze of noon,
Irrecoverably dark, total Eclipse
Without all hope of day!
O first created Beam, and thou great Word,
Let there be light, and light was over all;
Why am I thus bereav'd thy prime decree?
The Sun to me is dark
And silent as the Moon,
When she deserts the night
Hid in her vacant interlunar cave.
Since light so necessary is to life,
And almost life it self, if it be true
That light is in the Soul,
She all in every part; why was the sight
To such a tender ball as th' eye confin'd?
So obvious and so easie to be quench't,
And not as feeling through all parts diffus'd,
That she might look at will through every pore?
Then had I not been thus exil'd from light;
As in the land of darkness yet in light,
To live a life half dead, a living death,

And buried; but O yet more miserable!
My self, my Sepulcher, a moving Grave,
Buried, yet not exempt
By priviledge of death and burial
From worst of other evils, pains and wrongs,
But made hereby obnoxious more
To all the miseries of life,
Life in captivity
Among inhuman foes.
But who are these? for with joint pace I hear
The tread of many feet stearing this way;
Perhaps my enemies who come to stare
At my affliction, and perhaps to insult,
Thir daily practice to afflict me more.
CHORUS. This, this is he; softly a while,
Let us not break in upon him;
O change beyond report, thought, or belief!
See how he lies at random, carelessly diffus'd,
With languish't head unpropt,
As one past hope, abandon'd,
And by himself given over;
In slavish habit, ill-fitted weeds
O're worn and soild;
Or do my eyes misrepresent? Can this be hee,
That Heroic, that Renown'd,
Irresistible *Samson*? whom unarm'd
No strength of man, or fiercest wild beast could with-
    stand;
Who tore the Lion, as the Lion tears the Kid,
Ran on embattelld Armies clad in Iron,
And weaponless himself,
Made Arms ridiculous, useless the forgery
Of brazen shield and spear, the hammer'd Cuirass,
Chalybean temper'd steel, and frock of mail
Adamantean Proof;

But safest he who stood aloof,
When insupportably his foot advanc't,
In scorn of thir proud arms and warlike tools,
Spurn'd them to death by Troops. The bold *Ascalonite*
Fled from his Lion ramp, old Warriors turn'd
Thir plated backs under his heel;
Or grovling soild thir crested helmets in the dust.
Then with what trivial weapon came to hand,
The Jaw of a dead Ass, his sword of bone,
A thousand fore-skins fell, the flower of *Palestin*
In *Ramath-lechi* famous to this day:
Then by main force pull'd up, and on his shoulders bore
The Gates of *Azza*, Post, and massie Bar
Up to the Hill by *Hebron*, seat of Giants old,
No journey of a Sabbath day, and loaded so;
Like whom the Gentiles feign to bear up Heav'n.
Which shall I first bewail,
Thy Bondage or lost Sight,
Prison within Prison
Inseparably dark?
Thou art become (O worst imprisonment!)
The Dungeon of thy self; thy Soul
(Which Men enjoying sight oft without cause complain)
Imprison'd now indeed,
In real darkness of the body dwells,
Shut up from outward light
To incorporate with gloomy night;
For inward light alas
Puts forth no visual beam.
O mirror of our fickle state,
Since man on earth unparallel'd?
The rarer thy example stands,
By how much from the top of wondrous glory,
Strongest of mortal men,
To lowest pitch of abject fortune thou art fall'n.

For him I reckon not in high estate
Whom long descent of birth
Or the sphear of fortune raises;
But thee whose strength, while vertue was her mate,
Might have subdu'd the Earth,
Universally crown'd with highest praises.

SAMSON. I hear the sound of words, thir sense the air
Dissolves unjointed e're it reach my ear.

CHORUS. Hee speaks, let us draw nigh. Matchless in
    might,
The glory late of *Israel*, now the grief;
We come thy friends and neighbours not unknown
From *Eshtaol* and *Zora's* fruitful Vale
To visit or bewail thee, or if better,
Counsel or Consolation we may bring,
Salve to thy Sores, apt words have power to swage
The tumors of a troubl'd mind,
And are as Balm to fester'd wounds.

SAMSON. Your coming, Friends, revives me, for I learn
Now of my own experience, not by talk,
How counterfeit a coin they are who friends
Bear in their Superscription (of the most
I would be understood) in prosperous days
They swarm, but in adverse withdraw their head
Not to be found, though sought. Yee see, O friends,
How many evils have enclos'd me round;
Yet that which was the worst now least afflicts me,
Blindness, for had I sight, confus'd with shame,
How could I once look up, or heave the head,
Who like a foolish Pilot have shipwrack't,
My Vessel trusted to me from above,
Gloriously rigg'd; and for a word, a tear,
Fool, have divulg'd the secret gift of God
To a deceitful Woman: tell me Friends,

Am I not sung and proverbd for a Fool
In every street, do they not say, how well
Are come upon him his deserts? yet why?
Immeasurable strength they might behold
In me, of wisdom nothing more then mean;
This with the other should, at least, have paird,
These two proportiond ill drove me transverse.
CHORUS. Tax not divine disposal, wisest Men
Have err'd, and by bad Women been deceiv'd;
And shall again, pretend they ne're so wise.
Deject not then so overmuch thy self,
Who hast of sorrow thy full load besides;
Yet truth to say, I oft have heard men wonder
Why thou shouldst wed *Philistian* women rather
Then of thine own Tribe fairer, or as fair,
At least of thy own Nation, and as noble.
SAMSON. The first I saw at *Timna,* and she pleas'd
Mee, not my Parents, that I sought to wed,
The daughter of an Infidel: they knew not
That what I motion'd was of God; I knew
From intimate impulse, and therefore urg'd
The Marriage on; that by occasion hence
I might begin *Israel's* Deliverance,
The work to which I was divinely call'd;
She proving false, the next I took to Wife
(O that I never had! fond wish too late.)
Was in the Vale of *Sorec, Dalila,*
That specious Monster, my accomplisht snare.
I thought it lawful from my former act,
And the same end; still watching to oppress
Israel's oppressours: of what now I suffer
She was not the prime cause, but I my self,
Who vanquisht with a peal of words (O weakness!)
Gave up my fort of silence to a Woman.

CHORUS. In seeking just occasion to provoke
The *Philistine,* thy Countries Enemy,
Thou never wast remiss, I bear thee witness:
Yet *Israel* still serves with all his Sons.
SAMSON. That fault I take not on me, but transfer
On *Israel's* Governours, and Heads of Tribes,
Who seeing those great acts which God had done
Singly by me against their Conquerours
Acknowledg'd not, or not at all consider'd
Deliverance offerd: I on th' other side
Us'd no ambition to commend my deeds,
The deeds themselves, though mute, spoke loud the
    dooer;
But they persisted deaf, and would not seem
To count them things worth notice, till at length
Thir Lords the *Philistines* with gather'd powers
Enterd *Judea* seeking mee, who then
Safe to the rock of *Etham* was retir'd,
Not flying, but fore-casting in what place
To set upon them, what advantag'd best;
Mean while the men of *Judah* to prevent
The harass of thir Land, beset me round;
I willingly on some conditions came
Into thir hands, and they as gladly yield me
To the uncircumcis'd a welcom prey,
Bound with two cords; but cords to me were threds
Toucht with the flame: on thir whole Host I flew
Unarm'd, and with a trivial weapon fell'd
Their choicest youth; they only liv'd who fled.
Had *Judah* that day join'd, or one whole Tribe,
They had by this possess'd the Towers of *Gath,*
And lorded over them whom now they serve;
But what more oft in Nations grown corrupt,
And by thir vices brought to servitude,
Then to love Bondage more then Liberty,

Bondage with ease then strenuous liberty;
And to despise, or envy, or suspect
Whom God hath of his special favour rais'd
As thir Deliverer; if he aught begin,
How frequent to desert him, and at last
To heap ingratitude on worthiest deeds?
CHORUS. Thy words to my remembrance bring
How *Succoth* and the Fort of *Penuel*
Thir great Deliverer contemn'd,
The matchless *Gideon* in pursuit
Of *Madian* and her vanquisht Kings:
And how ingrateful *Ephraim*
Had dealt with *Jephtha,* who by argument,
Not worse then by his shield and spear
Defended *Israel* from the *Ammonite,*
Had not his prowess quell'd thir pride
In that sore battel when so many dy'd
Without Reprieve adjudg'd to death,
For want of well pronouncing *Shibboleth.*
SAMSON. Of such examples adde mee to the roul,
Mee easily indeed mine may neglect,
But Gods propos'd deliverance not so.
CHORUS. Just are the ways of God,
And justifiable to Men;
Unless there be who think not God at all,
If any be, they walk obscure;
For of such Doctrine never was there School,
But the heart of the Fool,
And no man therein Doctor but himself.
  Yet more there be who doubt his ways not just,
As to his own edicts, found contradicting,
Then give the rains to wandring thought,
Regardless of his glories diminution;
Till by thir own perplexities involv'd
They ravel more, still less resolv'd,

But never find self-satisfying solution.
    As if they would confine th' interminable,
And tie him to his own prescript,
Who made our Laws to bind us, not himself,
And hath full right to exempt
Whom so it pleases him by choice
From National obstriction, without taint
Of sin, or legal debt;
For with his own Laws he can best dispence.
    He would not else who never wanted means,
Nor in respect of the enemy just cause
To set his people free,
Have prompted this Heroic *Nazarite*,
Against his vow of strictest purity,
To seek in marriage that fallacious Bride,
Unclean, unchaste.
    Down Reason then, at least vain reasonings down,
Though Reason here aver
That moral verdit quits her of unclean:
Unchaste was subsequent, her stain not his.
    But see here comes thy reverend Sire
With careful step, Locks white as doune,
Old *Manoah:* advise
Forthwith how thou oughtst to receive him.
SAMSON. Ay me, another inward grief awak't,
With mention of that name renews th' assault.
MANOA. Brethren and men of *Dan*, for such ye seem,
Though in this uncouth place; if old respect,
As I suppose, towards your once gloried friend,
My Son now Captive, hither hath inform'd
Your younger feet, while mine cast back with age
Came lagging after; say, if he be here.
CHORUS. As signal now in low dejected state,
As earst in highest, behold him where he lies.
MANOA. O miserable change! is this the man,

That invincible *Samson*, far renown'd,
The dread of *Israel's* foes, who with a strength
Equivalent to Angels walk'd thir streets,
None offering fight; who single combatant
Duell'd thir Armies rank't in proud array,
Himself an Army, now unequal match
To save himself against a coward arm'd
At one spears length. O ever failing trust
In mortal strength! and oh what not in man
Deceivable and vain! Nay what thing good
Pray'd for, but often proves our woe, our bane?
I pray'd for Children, and thought barrenness
In wedlock a reproach; I gain'd a Son,
And such a Son as all Men hail'd me happy;
Who would be now a Father in my stead?
O wherefore did God grant me my request,
And as a blessing with such pomp adorn'd?
Why are his gifts desirable, to tempt
Our earnest Prayers, then giv'n with solemn hand
As Graces, draw a Scorpions tail behind?
For this did the Angel twice descend? for this
Ordain'd thy nurture holy, as of a Plant;
Select, and Sacred, Glorious for a while,
The miracle of men: then in an hour
Ensnar'd, assaulted, overcome, led bound,
Thy Foes derision, Captive, Poor, and Blind
Into a Dungeon thrust, to work with Slaves?
Alas methinks whom God hath chosen once
To worthiest deeds, if he through frailty err,
He should not so o'rewhelm, and as a thrall
Subject him to so foul indignities,
Be it but for honours sake of former deeds.
SAMSON. Appoint not heavenly disposition, Father,
Nothing of all these evils hath befall'n me
But justly; I my self have brought them on,

Sole Author I, sole cause: if aught seem vile,
As vile hath been my folly, who have profan'd
The mystery of God giv'n me under pledge
Of vow, and have betray'd it to a woman,
A *Canaanite*, my faithless enemy.
This well I knew, nor was at all surpris'd,
But warn'd by oft experience: did not she
Of *Timna* first betray me, and reveal
The secret wrested from me in her highth
Of Nuptial Love profest, carrying it strait
To them who had corrupted her, my Spies,
And Rivals? In this other was there found
More Faith? who also in her prime of love,
Spousal embraces, vitiated with Gold,
Though offer'd only, by the sent conceiv'd
Her spurious first-born; Treason against me?
Thrice she assay'd with flattering prayers and sighs,
And amorous reproaches to win from me
My capital secret, in what part my strength
Lay stor'd, in what part summ'd, that she might
    know;
Thrice I deluded her, and turn'd to sport
Her importunity, each time perceiving
How openly, and with what impudence
She purpos'd to betray me, and (which was worse
Then undissembl'd hate) with what contempt
She sought to make me Traytor to my self;
Yet the fourth time, when mustring all her wiles,
With blandisht parlies, feminine assaults,
Tongue-batteries, she surceas'd not day nor night
To storm me over-watch't, and wearied out.
At times when men seek most repose and rest,
I yielded, and unlock'd her all my heart,
Who with a grain of manhood well resolv'd
Might easily have shook off all her snares:

But foul effeminacy held me yok't
Her Bond-slave; O indignity, O blot
To Honour and Religion! servil mind
Rewarded well with servil punishment!
The base degree to which I now am fall'n,
These rags, this grinding, is not yet so base
As was my former servitude, ignoble,
Unmanly, ignominious, infamous,
True slavery, and that blindness worse then this,
That saw not how degenerately I serv'd.
MANOA. I cannot praise thy Marriage choises, Son,
Rather approv'd them not; but thou didst plead
Divine impulsion prompting how thou might'st
Find some occasion to infest our Foes.
I state not that; this I am sure; our Foes
Found soon occasion thereby to make thee
Thir Captive, and thir triumph; thou the sooner
Temptation found'st, or over-potent charms
To violate the sacred trust of silence
Deposited within thee; which to have kept
Tacit, was in thy power; true; and thou bear'st
Enough, and more the burden of that fault;
Bitterly hast thou paid, and still art paying
That rigid score. A worse thing yet remains,
This day the *Philistines* a popular Feast
Here celebrate in *Gaza;* and proclaim
Great Pomp, and Sacrifice, and Praises loud
To *Dagon,* as their God who hath deliver'd
Thee *Samson* bound and blind into thir hands,
Them out of thine, who slew'st them many a slain.
So *Dagon* shall be magnifi'd, and God,
Besides whom is no God, compar'd with Idols,
Disglorifi'd, blasphem'd, and had in scorn
By th' Idolatrous rout amidst thir wine;
Which to have come to pass by means of thee,

Samson, of all thy sufferings think the heaviest,
Of all reproach the most with shame that ever
Could have befall'n thee and thy Fathers house.
SAMSON. Father, I do acknowledge and confess
That I this honour, I this pomp have brought
To *Dagon,* and advanc'd his praises high
Among the Heathen round; to God have brought
Dishonour, obloquie, and op't the mouths
Of Idolists, and Atheists; have brought scandal
To *Israel,* diffidence of God, and doubt
In feeble hearts, propense anough before
To waver, or fall off and joyn with Idols;
Which is my chief affliction, shame and sorrow,
The anguish of my Soul, that suffers not
Mine eie to harbour sleep, or thoughts to rest.
This only hope relieves me, that the strife
With me hath end; all the contest is now
'Twixt God and *Dagon; Dagon* hath presum'd,
Me overthrown, to enter lists with God,
His Deity comparing and preferring
Before the God of *Abraham.* He, be sure,
Will not connive, or linger, thus provok'd,
But will arise and his great name assert:
Dagon must stoop, and shall e're long receive
Such a discomfit, as shall quite despoil him
Of all these boasted Trophies won on me,
And with confusion blank his Worshippers.
MANOA. With cause this hope relieves thee, and these
    words
I as a Prophecy receive: for God,
Nothing more certain, will not long defer
To vindicate the glory of his name
Against all competition, nor will long
Endure it, doubtful whether God be Lord,
Or *Dagon.* But for thee what shall be done?

Thou must not in the mean while here forgot
Lie in this miserable loathsom plight
Neglected. I already have made way
To some *Philistian* Lords, with whom to treat
About thy ransom: well they may by this
Have satisfi'd thir utmost of revenge
By pains and slaveries, worse then death inflicted
On thee, who now no more canst do them harm.
SAMSON. Spare that proposal, Father, spare the trouble
Of that sollicitation; let me here,
As I deserve, pay on my punishment;
And expiate, if possible, my crime,
Shameful garrulity. To have reveal'd
Secrets of men, the secrets of a friend,
How hainous had the fact been, how deserving
Contempt, and scorn of all, to be excluded
All friendship, and avoided as a blab,
The mark of fool set on his front?
But I Gods counsel have not kept, his holy secret
Presumptuously have publish'd, impiously,
Weakly at least, and shamefully: A sin
That Gentiles in thir Parables condemn
To thir abyss and horrid pains confin'd.
MANOA. Be penitent and for thy fault contrite,
But act not in thy own affliction, Son,
Repent the sin, but if the punishment
Thou canst avoid, self-preservation bids;
Or th' execution leave to high disposal,
And let another hand, not thine, exact
Thy penal forfeit from thy self; perhaps
God will relent, and quit thee all his debt;
Who evermore approves and more accepts
(Best pleas'd with humble and filial submission)
Him who imploring mercy sues for life,
Then who self-rigorous chooses death as due;

Which argues over-just, and self-displeas'd
For self-offence, more then for God offended.
Reject not then what offerd means, who knows
But God hath set before us, to return thee
Home to thy countrey and his sacred house,
Where thou mayst bring thy off'rings, to avert
His further ire, with praiers and vows renew'd.
SAMSON. His pardon I implore; but as for life,
To what end should I seek it? when in strength
All mortals I excell'd, and great in hopes
With youthful courage and magnanimous thoughts
Of birth from Heav'n foretold and high exploits,
Full of divine instinct, after some proof
Of acts indeed heroic, far beyond
The Sons of *Anac,* famous now and blaz'd,
Fearless of danger, like a petty God
I walk'd about admir'd of all and dreaded
On hostile ground, none daring my affront.
Then swoll'n with pride into the snare I fell
Of fair fallacious looks, venereal trains,
Softn'd with pleasure and voluptuous life;
At length to lay my head and hallow'd pledge
Of all my strength in the lascivious lap
Of a deceitful Concubine who shore me
Like a tame Weather, all my precious fleece,
Then turn'd me out ridiculous, despoil'd,
Shav'n, and disarm'd among my enemies.
CHORUS. Desire of wine and all delicious drinks,
Which many a famous Warriour overturns,
Thou couldst repress, nor did the dancing Rubie
Sparkling, out-pow'rd, the flavor, or the smell,
Or taste that cheers the heart of Gods and men,
Allure thee from the cool Crystalline stream.
SAMSON. Where ever fountain or fresh current flow'd
Against the Eastern ray, translucent, pure.

With touch ætherial of Heav'ns fiery rod
I drank, from the clear milkie juice allaying
Thirst, and refresht; nor envy'd them the grape
Whose heads that turbulent liquor fills with fumes.
CHORUS. O madness, to think use of strongest wines
And strongest drinks our chief support of health,
When God with these forbid'n made choice to rear
His mighty Champion, strong above compare,
Whose drink was only from the liquid brook.
SAMSON. But what avail'd this temperance, not compleat
Against another object more enticing?
What boots it at one gate to make defence,
And at another to let in the foe
Effeminatly vanquish't? by which means,
Now blind, disheartn'd, sham'd, dishonour'd, quell'd,
To what can I be useful, wherein serve
My Nation, and the work from Heav'n impos'd,
But to sit idle on the houshold hearth,
A burdenous drone; to visitants a gaze,
Or pitied object, these redundant locks
Robustious to no purpose clustring down,
Vain monument of strength; till length of years
And sedentary numness craze my limbs
To a contemptible old age obscure.
Here rather let me drudge and earn my bread,
Till vermin or the draff of servil food
Consume me, and oft-invocated death
Hast'n the welcom end of all my pains.
MANOA. Wilt thou then serve the *Philistines* with that
    gift
Which was expresly giv'n thee to annoy them?
Better at home lie bed-rid, not only idle,
Inglorious, unimploy'd, with age out-worn.
But God who caus'd a fountain at thy prayer
From the dry ground to spring, thy thirst to allay

After the brunt of battel, can as easie
Cause light again within thy eies to spring,
Wherewith to serve him better then thou hast;
And I perswade me so; why else this strength
Miraculous yet remaining in those locks?
His might continues in thee not for naught,
Nor shall his wondrous gifts be frustrate thus.

SAMSON. All otherwise to me my thoughts portend,
That these dark orbs no more shall treat with light,
Nor th' other light of life continue long,
But yield to double darkness nigh at hand:
So much I feel my genial spirits droop,
My hopes all flat, nature within me seems
In all her functions weary of herself;
My race of glory run, and race of shame,
And I shall shortly be with them that rest.

MANOA. Believe not these suggestions which proceed
From anguish of the mind and humours black,
That mingle with thy fancy. I however
Must not omit a Fathers timely care
To prosecute the means of thy deliverance
By ransom or how else: mean while be calm,
And healing words from these thy friends admit.

SAMSON. O that torment should not be confin'd
To the bodies wounds and sores
With maladies innumerable
In heart, head, brest, and reins;
But must secret passage find
To th' inmost mind,
There exercise all his fierce accidents,
And on her purest spirits prey,
As on entrails, joints, and limbs,
With answerable pains, but more intense,
Though void of corporal sense.
    My griefs not only pain me

As a lingring disease,
But finding no redress, ferment and rage,
Nor less then wounds immedicable
Ranckle, and fester, and gangrene,
To black mortification.
Thoughts my Tormenters arm'd with deadly stings
Mangle my apprehensive tenderest parts,
Exasperate, exulcerate, and raise
Dire inflammation which no cooling herb
Or medcinal liquor can asswage,
Nor breath of Vernal Air from snowy *Alp*.
Sleep hath forsook and giv'n me o're
To deaths benumming Opium as my only cure.
Thence faintings, swounings of despair,
And sense of Heav'ns desertion.
    I was his nursling once and choice delight,
His destin'd from the womb,
Promisd by Heavenly message twice descending.
Under his special eie
Abstemious I grew up and thriv'd amain;
He led me on to mightiest deeds
Above the nerve of mortal arm
Against the uncircumcis'd, our enemies.
But now hath cast me off as never known,
And to those cruel enemies,
Whom I by his appointment had provok't,
Left me all helpless with th' irreparable loss
Of sight, reserv'd alive to be repeated
The subject of thir cruelty, or scorn.
Nor am I in the list of them that hope;
Hopeless are all my evils, all remediless;
This one prayer yet remains, might I be heard,
No long petition, speedy death,
The close of all my miseries, and the balm.
CHORUS. Many are the sayings of the wise

In antient and in modern books enroll'd;
Extolling Patience as the truest fortitude;
And to the bearing well of all calamities,
All chances incident to mans frail life
Consolatories writ
With studied argument, and much perswasion sought
Lenient of grief and anxious thought,
But with th' afflicted in his pangs thir sound
Little prevails, or rather seems a tune,
Harsh, and of dissonant mood from his complaint,
Unless he feel within
Some sourse of consolation from above;
Secret refreshings, that repair his strength,
And fainting spirits uphold.
   God of our Fathers, what is man!
That thou towards him with hand so various,
Or might I say contrarious,
Temperst thy providence through his short course,
Not evenly, as thou rul'st
The Angelic orders and inferiour creatures mute,
Irrational and brute.
Nor do I name of men the common rout,
That wandring loose about
Grow up and perish, as the summer flie,
Heads without name no more rememberd,
But such as thou hast solemnly elected,
With gifts and graces eminently adorn'd
To some great work, thy glory,
And peoples safety, which in part they effect:
Yet toward these thus dignifi'd, thou oft
Amidst thir highth of noon,
Changest thy countenance, and thy hand with no regard
Of highest favours past
From thee on them, or them to thee of service.
   Nor only dost degrade them, or remit

To life obscur'd, which were a fair dismission,
But throw'st them lower then thou didst exalt them
    high,
Unseemly falls in human eie,
Too grievous for the trespass or omission,
Oft leav'st them to the hostile sword
Of Heathen and prophane, thir carkasses
To dogs and fowls a prey, or else captiv'd:
Or to the unjust tribunals, under change of times,
And condemnation of the ingrateful multitude.
If these they scape, perhaps in poverty
With sickness and disease thou bow'st them down,
Painful diseases and deform'd,
In crude old age;
Though not disordinate, yet causless suffring
The punishment of dissolute days, in fine,
Just or unjust, alike seem miserable,
For oft alike, both come to evil end.
    So deal not with this once thy glorious Champion,
The Image of thy strength, and mighty minister.
What do I beg? how hast thou dealt already?
Behold him in this state calamitous, and turn
His labours, for thou canst, to peaceful end.
    But who is this, what thing of Sea or Land?
Femal of sex it seems,
That so bedeckt, ornate, and gay,
Comes this way sailing
Like a stately Ship
Of *Tarsus,* bound for th' Isles
Of *Javan* or *Gadier*
With all her bravery on, and tackle trim,
Sails fill'd, and streamers waving,
Courted by all the winds that hold them play,
An Amber sent of odorous perfume
Her harbinger, a damsel train behind;

Some rich *Philistian* Matron she may seem,
And now at nearer view, no other certain
Then *Dalila* thy wife.

SAMSON. My Wife, my Traytress, let her not come near
　　me.

CHORUS. Yet on she moves, now stands and eies thee fixt,
About t' have spoke, but now, with head declin'd
Like a fair flower surcharg'd with dew, she weeps
And words addrest seem into tears dissolv'd,
Wetting the borders of her silk'n veil:
But now again she makes address to speak.

DALILA. With doubtful feet and wavering resolution
I came, still dreading thy displeasure, *Samson*,
Which to have merited, without excuse,
I cannot but acknowledge; yet if tears
May expiate (though the fact more evil drew
In the perverse event then I foresaw)
My penance hath not slack'n'd, though my pardon
No way assur'd. But conjugal affection
Prevailing over fear, and timerous doubt
Hath led me on desirous to behold
Once more thy face, and know of thy estate.
If aught in my ability may serve
To light'n what thou suffer'st, and appease
Thy mind with what amends is in my power,
Though late, yet in some part to recompense
My rash but more unfortunate misdeed.

SAMSON. Out, out *Hyæna*; these are thy wonted arts,
And arts of every woman false like thee,
To break all faith, all vows, deceive, betray,
Then as repentant to submit, beseech,
And reconcilement move with feign'd remorse,
Confess, and promise wonders in her change,
Not truly penitent, but chief to try
Her husband, how far urg'd his patience bears,

His vertue or weakness which way to assail:
Then with more cautious and instructed skill
Again transgresses, and again submits;
That wisest and best men full oft beguil'd
With goodness principl'd not to reject
The penitent, but ever to forgive,
Are drawn to wear out miserable days,
Entangl'd with a poysnous bosom snake,
If not by quick destruction soon cut off
As I by thee, to Ages an example.

DALILA. Ye hear me *Samson;* not that I endeavour
To lessen or extenuate my offence,
But that on th' other side if it be weigh'd
By it self, with aggravations not surcharg'd,
Or else with just allowance counterpois'd,
I may, if possible, thy pardon find
The easier towards me, or thy hatred less.
First granting, as I do, it was a weakness
In me, but incident to all our sex,
Curiosity, inquisitive, importune
Of secrets, then with like infirmity
To publish them, both common female faults:
Was it not weakness also to make known
For importunity, that is for naught,
Wherein consisted all thy strength and safety?
To what I did thou shewdst me first the way.
But I do to enemies reveal'd, and should not.
Nor shouldst thou have trusted that to womans frailty
E're I to thee, thou to thy self wast cruel.
Let weakness then with weakness come to parl
So near related, or the same of kind,
Thine forgive mine; that men may censure thine
The gentler, if severely thou exact not
More strength from me, then in thy self was found.
And what if Love, which thou interpret'st hate,

The jealousie of Love, powerful of sway
In human hearts, nor less in mine towards thee,
Caus'd what I did? I saw thee mutable
Of fancy, feard lest one day thou wouldst leave me
As her at *Timna*, sought by all means therefore
How to endear, and hold thee to me firmest:
No better way I saw then by importuning
To learn thy secrets, get into my power
Thy key of strength and safety: thou wilt say,
Why then reveal'd? I was assur'd by those
Who tempted me, that nothing was design'd
Against thee but safe custody, and hold:
That made for me, I knew that liberty
Would draw thee forth to perilous enterprises,
While I at home sate full of cares and fears
Wailing thy absence in my widow'd bed;
Here I should still enjoy thee day and night
Mine and Loves prisoner, not the *Philistines,*
Whole to my self, unhazarded abroad,
Fearless at home of partners in my love.
These reasons in Loves law have past for good,
Though fond and reasonless to some perhaps;
And Love hath oft, well meaning, wrought much wo,
Yet always pity or pardon hath obtain'd.
Be not unlike all others, not austere
As thou art strong, inflexible as steel.
If thou in strength all mortals dost exceed,
In uncompassionate anger do not so.
SAMSON. How cunningly the sorceress displays
Her own transgressions, to upbraid me mine?
That malice not repentance brought thee hither,
By this appears: I gave, thou say'st th' example,
I led the way; bitter reproach, but true,
I to my self was false e're thou to me,
Such pardon therefore as I give my folly,

Take to thy wicked deed: which when thou seest
Impartial, self-severe, inexorable,
Thou wilt renounce thy seeking, and much rather
Confess it feign'd, weakness is thy excuse,
And I believe it, weakness to resist
Philistian gold: if weakness may excuse,
What Murtherer, what Traytor, Parricide,
Incestuous, Sacrilegious, but may plead it?
All wickedness is weakness: that plea therefore
With God or Man will gain thee no remission.
But Love constrain'd thee; call it furious rage
To satisfie thy lust: Love seeks to have Love;
My love how couldst thou hope, who tookst the way
To raise in me inexpiable hate,
Knowing, as needs I must, by thee betray'd?
In vain thou striv'st to cover shame with shame,
Or by evasions thy crime uncoverst more.
DALILA. Since thou determinst weakness for no plea
In man or woman, though to thy own condemning,
Hear what assaults I had, what snares besides,
What sieges girt me round, e're I consented;
Which might have aw'd the best resolv'd of men,
The constantest to have yielded without blame.
It was not gold, as to my charge thou lay'st,
That wrought with me: thou know'st the Magistrates
And Princes of my countrey came in person,
Sollicited, commanded, threatn'd, urg'd,
Adjur'd by all the bonds of civil Duty
And of Religion, press'd how just it was,
How honourable, how glorious to entrap
A common enemy, who had destroy'd
Such numbers of our Nation: and the Priest
Was not behind, but ever at my ear,
Preaching how meritorious with the gods
It would be to ensnare an irreligious

Dishonourer of *Dagon:* what had I
To oppose against such powerful arguments?
Only my love of thee held long debate;
And combated in silence all these reasons
With hard contest: at length that grounded maxim
So rife and celebrated in the mouths
Of wisest men; that to the public good
Private respects must yield; with grave authority
Took full possession of me and prevail'd;
Vertue, as I thought, truth, duty so enjoyning.

SAMSON. I thought where all thy circling wiles would
  end;
In feign'd Religion, smooth hypocrisie.
But had thy love, still odiously pretended,
Bin, as it ought, sincere, it would have taught thee
Far other reasonings, brought forth other deeds.
I before all the daughters of my Tribe
And of my Nation chose thee from among
My enemies, lov'd thee, as too well thou knew'st,
Too well, unbosom'd all my secrets to thee,
Not out of levity, but over-powr'd
By thy request, who could deny thee nothing;
Yet now am judg'd an enemy. Why then
Didst thou at first receive me for thy husband?
Then, as since then, thy countries foe profest:
Being once a wife, for me thou wast to leave
Parents and countrey; nor was I their subject,
Nor under their protection but my own,
Thou mine, not theirs: if aught against my life
Thy countrey sought of thee, it sought unjustly,
Against the law of nature, law of nations,
No more thy countrey, but an impious crew
Of men conspiring to uphold thir state
By worse then hostile deeds, violating the ends
For which our countrey is a name so dear;

Not therefore to be obey'd. But zeal mov'd thee;
To please thy gods thou didst it; gods unable
To acquit themselves and prosecute their foes
But by ungodly deeds, the contradiction
Of their own deity, Gods cannot be:
Less therefore to be pleas'd, obey'd, or fear'd,
These false pretexts and varnish'd colours failing,
Bare in thy guilt how foul must thou appear?
DALILA. In argument with men a woman ever
Goes by the worse, whatever be her cause.
SAMSON. For want of words no doubt, or lack of breath,
Witness when I was worried with thy peals.
DALILA. I was a fool, too rash, and quite mistaken
In what I thought would have succeeded best.
Let me obtain forgiveness of thee, *Samson*,
Afford me place to shew what recompence
Towards thee I intend for what I have misdone,
Misguided; only what remains past cure
Bear not too sensibly, nor still insist
To afflict thy self in vain: though sight be lost,
Life yet hath many solaces, enjoy'd
Where other senses want not their delights
At home in leisure and domestic ease,
Exempt from many a care and chance to which
Eye-sight exposes daily men abroad.
I to the Lords will intercede, not doubting
Thir favourable ear, that I may fetch thee
From forth this loathsom prison-house, to abide
With me, where my redoubl'd love and care
With nursing diligence, to me glad office,
May ever tend about thee to old age
With all things grateful chear'd, and so suppli'd,
That what by me thou hast lost thou least shalt miss.
SAMSON. No, no, of my condition take no care;
It fits not; thou and I long since are twain;

Nor think me so unwary or accurst
To bring my feet again into the snare
Where once I have been caught; I know thy trains
Though dearly to my cost, thy ginns, and toyls;
Thy fair enchanted cup, and warbling charms
No more on me have power, their force is null'd,
So much of Adders wisdom I have learn't
To fence my ear against thy sorceries.
If in my flower of youth and strength, when all men
Lov'd, honour'd, fear'd me, thou alone could hate me
Thy Husband, slight me, sell me, and forgo me;
How wouldst thou use me now, blind, and thereby
Deceiveable, in most things as a child
Helpless, thence easily contemn'd, and scorn'd,
And last neglected? How wouldst thou insult
When I must live uxorious to thy will
In perfet thraldom, how again betray me,
Bearing my words and doings to the Lords
To gloss upon, and censuring, frown or smile?
This Gaol I count the house of Liberty
To thine whose doors my feet shall never enter.

DALILA. Let me approach at least, and touch thy hand.

SAMSON. Not for thy life, lest fierce remembrance wake
My sudden rage to tear thee joint by joint.
At distance I forgive thee, go with that;
Bewail thy falshood, and the pious works
It hath brought forth to make thee memorable
Among illustrious women, faithful wives:
Cherish thy hast'n'd widowhood with the gold
Of Matrimonial treason: so farewel.

DALILA. I see thou art implacable, more deaf
To prayers, then winds and seas, yet winds to seas
Are reconcil'd at length, and Sea to Shore:
Thy anger, unappeasable, still rages,
Eternal tempest never to be calm'd.

Why do I humble thus my self, and suing
For peace, reap nothing but repulse and hate?
Bid go with evil omen and the brand
Of infamy upon my name denounc't?
To mix with thy concernments I desist
Henceforth, nor too much disapprove my own.
Fame if not double-fac't is double-mouth'd,
And with contrary blast proclaims most deeds,
On both his wings, one black, th' other white,
Bears greatest names in his wild aerie flight.
My name perhaps among the Circumcis'd
In *Dan,* in *Judah,* and the bordering Tribes,
To all posterity may stand defam'd,
With malediction mention'd, and the blot
Of falshood most unconjugal traduc't.
But in my countrey where I most desire,
In *Ecron, Gaza, Asdod,* and in *Gath*
I shall be nam'd among the famousest
Of Women, sung at solemn festivals,
Living and dead recorded, who to save
Her countrey from a fierce destroyer, chose
Above the faith of wedlock-bands, my tomb
With odours visited and annual flowers.
Not less renown'd then in Mount *Ephraim,*
Jael, who with inhospitable guile
Smote *Sisera* sleeping through the Temples nail'd.
Nor shall I count it hainous to enjoy
The public marks of honour and reward
Conferr'd upon me, for the piety
Which to my countrey I was judg'd to have shewn.
At this who ever envies or repines
I leave him to his lot, and like my own.
CHORUS. She's gone, a manifest Serpent by her sting
Discover'd in the end, till now conceal'd.
SAMSON. So let her go, God sent her to debase me ·

And aggravate my folly who committed
To such a viper his most sacred trust
Of secresie, my safety, and my life.

CHORUS. Yet beauty, though injurious, hath strange
      power,
After offence returning, to regain
Love once possest, nor can be easily
Repuls't, without much inward passion felt
And secret sting of amorous remorse.

SAMSON. Love-quarrels oft in pleasing concord end,
Not wedlock-trechery endangering life.

CHORUS. It is not vertue, wisdom, valour, wit,
Strength, comliness of shape, or amplest merit
That womans love can win or long inherit;
But what it is, hard is to say,
Harder to hit,
(Which way soever men refer it)
Much like thy riddle, *Samson*, in one day
Or seven, though one should musing sit;
    If any of these or all, the *Timnian* bride
Had not so soon preferr'd
Thy Paranymph, worthless to thee compar'd,
Successour in thy bed,
Nor both so loosly disally'd
Thir nuptials, nor this last so trecherously
Had shorn the fatal harvest of thy head.
Is it for that such outward ornament
Was lavish't on thir Sex, that inward gifts
Were left for hast unfinish't, judgment scant,
Capacity not rais'd to apprehend
Or value what is best
In choice, but oftest to affect the wrong?
Or was too much of self-love mixt,
Of constancy no root infixt,
That either they love nothing, or not long?

What e're it be, to wisest men and best
Seeming at first all heavenly under virgin veil,
Soft, modest, meek, demure,
Once join'd, the contrary she proves, a thorn
Intestin, far within defensive arms
A cleaving mischief, in his way to vertue
Adverse and turbulent, or by her charms
Draws him awry enslav'd
With dotage, and his sense deprav'd
To folly and shameful deeds which ruin ends.
What Pilot so expert but needs must wreck
Embarqu'd with such a Stears-mate at the Helm?

   Favour'd of Heav'n who finds
One vertuous rarely found,
That in domestic good combines:
Happy that house! his way to peace is smooth:
But vertue which breaks through all opposition,
And all temptation can remove,
Most shines and most is acceptable above.

   Therefore Gods universal Law
Gave to the man despotic power
Over his female in due awe,
Nor from that right to part an hour,
Smile she or lowre:
So shall he least confusion draw
On his whole life, not sway'd
By female usurpation, nor dismay'd.

   But had we best retire, I see a storm?
SAMSON. Fair days have oft contracted wind and rain.
CHORUS. But this another kind of tempest brings.
SAMSON. Be less abstruse, my riddling days are past.
CHORUS. Look now for no inchanting voice, nor fear
The bait of honied words; a rougher tongue
Draws hitherward, I know him by his stride,
The Giant *Harapha* of *Gath*, his look

Haughty as is his pile high-built and proud.
Comes he in peace? what wind hath blown him hither
I less conjecture then when first I saw
The sumptuous *Dalila* floating this way:
His habit carries peace, his brow defiance.

SAMSON. Or peace or not, alike to me he comes.

CHORUS. His fraught we soon shall know, he now arrives.

HARAPHA. I come not *Samson,* to condole thy chance,
As these perhaps, yet wish it had not been,
Though for no friendly intent. I am of *Gath*
Men call me *Harapha,* of stock renown'd
As *Og* or *Anak* and the *Emims* old
That *Kiriathaim* held, thou knowst me now
If thou at all art known. Much I have heard
Of thy prodigious might and feats perform'd
Incredible to me, in this displeas'd,
That I was never present on the place
Of those encounters where we might have tri'd
Each others force in camp or listed field:
And now am come to see of whom such noise
Hath walk'd about, and each limb to survey,
If thy appearance answer loud report.

SAMSON. The way to know were not to see but taste.

HARAPHA. Dost thou already single me; I thought
Gives and the Mill had tam'd thee; O that fortune
Had brought me to the field where thou art fam'd
To have wrought such wonders with an Asses Jaw;
I should have forc'd thee soon with other arms,
Or left thy carkass where the Ass lay thrown:
So had the glory of Prowess been recover'd
To *Palestine,* won by a *Philistine*
From the unforeskinn'd race, of whom thou bear'st
The highest name for valiant Acts, that honour
Certain to have won by mortal duel from thee,
I lose, prevented by thy eyes put out.

SAMSON. Boast not of what thou wouldst have done, but do
What then thou would'st, thou seest it in thy hand.

HARAPHA. To combat with a blind man I disdain,
And thou hast need much washing to be toucht.

SAMSON. Such usage as your honourable Lords
Afford me assassinated and betray'd,
Who durst not with thir whole united powers
In fight withstand me single and unarm'd,
Nor in the house with chamber Ambushes
Close-banded durst attaque me, no not sleeping,
Till they had hir'd a woman with their gold
Breaking her Marriage Faith to circumvent me.
Therefore without feign'd shifts let be assign'd
Some narrow place enclos'd, where sight may give thee,
Or rather flight, no great advantage on me;
Then put on all thy gorgeous arms, thy Helmet
And Brigandine of brass, thy broad Habergeon,
Vant-brass and Greves, and Gauntlet, add thy Spear
A Weavers beam, and seven-times-folded shield,
I only with an Oak'n staff will meet thee,
And raise such out-cries on thy clatter'd Iron,
Which long shall not with-hold mee from thy head,
That in a little time while breath remains thee,
Thou oft shalt wish thy self at *Gath* to boast
Again in safety what thou wouldst have done
To *Samson,* but shalt never see *Gath* more.

HARAPHA. Thou durst not thus disparage glorious arms
Which greatest Heroes have in battel worn,
Thir ornament and safety, had not spells
And black enchantments, some Magicians Art
Arm'd thee or charm'd thee strong, which thou from Heaven
Feigndst at thy birth was giv'n thee in thy hair,
Where strength can least abide, though all thy hairs

Were bristles rang'd like those that ridge the back
Of chaf't wild Boars, or ruffl'd Porcupines.
SAMSON. I know no Spells, use no forbidden Arts;
My trust is in the living God who gave me
At my Nativity this strength, diffus'd
No less through all my sinews, joints and bones,
Then thine, while I preserv'd these locks unshorn,
The pledge of my unviolated vow.
For proof hereof, if *Dagon* be thy god,
Go to his Temple, invocate his aid
With solemnest devotion, spread before him
How highly it concerns his glory now
To frustrate and dissolve these Magic spells,
Which I to be the power of *Israel's* God
Avow, and challenge *Dagon* to the test,
Offering to combat thee his Champion bold,
With th' utmost of his Godhead seconded:
Then thou shalt see, or rather to thy sorrow
Soon feel, whose God is strongest, thine or mine.
HARAPHA. Presume not on thy God, what e're he be,
Thee he regards not, owns not, hath cut off
Quite from his people, and delivered up
Into thy Enemies hand, permitted them
To put out both thine eyes, and fetter'd send thee
Into the common Prison, there to grind
Among the Slaves and Asses thy comrades,
As good for nothing else, no better service
With those thy boyst'rous locks, no worthy match
For valour to assail, nor by the sword
Of noble Warriour, so to stain his honour,
But by the Barbers razor best subdu'd.
SAMSON. All these indignities, for such they are
From thine, these evils I deserve and more,
Acknowledge them from God inflicted on me
Justly, yet despair not of his final pardon

Whose ear is ever open; and his eye
Gracious to re-admit the suppliant;
In confidence whereof I once again
Defie thee to the trial of mortal fight,
By combat to decide whose god is god,
Thine or whom I with *Israel's* Sons adore.

HARAPHA. Fair honour that thou dost thy God, in
    trusting
He will accept thee to defend his cause,
A Murtherer, a Revolter, and a Robber.

SAMSON. Tongue-doubtie Giant, how dost thou prove me
    these?

HARAPHA. Is not thy Nation subject to our Lords?
Their Magistrates confest it, when they took thee
As a League-breaker and deliver'd bound
Into our hands: for hadst thou not committed
Notorious murder on those thirty men
At *Askalon*, who never did thee harm,
Then like a Robber stripdst them of thir robes?
The *Philistines*, when thou hadst broke the league,
Went up with armed powers thee only seeking,
To others did no violence nor spoil.

SAMSON. Among the Daughters of the *Philistines*
I chose a Wife, which argu'd me no foe;
And in your City held my Nuptial Feast:
But your ill-meaning Politician Lords,
Under pretence of Bridal friends and guests,
Appointed to await me thirty spies,
Who threatning cruel death constrain'd the bride
To wring from me and tell to them my secret,
That solv'd the riddle which I had propos'd.
When I perceiv'd all set on enmity,
As on my enemies, where ever chanc'd,
I us'd hostility, and took thir spoil
To pay my underminers in thir coin.

My Nation was subjected to your Lords.
It was the force of Conquest; force with force
Is well ejected when the Conquer'd can.
But I a private person, whom my Countrey
As a league-breaker gave up bound, presum'd
Single Rebellion and did Hostile Acts.
I was no private but a person rais'd
With strength sufficient and command from Heav'n
To free my Countrey; if their servile minds
Me their Deliverer sent would not receive,
But to thir Masters gave me up for nought,
Th' unworthier they; whence to this day they serve.
I was to do my part from Heav'n assign'd,
And had perform'd it if my known offence
Had not disabl'd me, not all your force:
These shifts refuted, answer thy appellant
Though by his blindness maim'd for high attempts,
Who now defies thee thrice to single fight,
As a petty enterprise of small enforce.
HARAPHA. With thee a Man condemn'd, a Slave enrol'd,
Due by the Law to capital punishment?
To fight with thee no man of arms will deign.
SAMSON. Cam'st thou for this, vain boaster, to survey me,
To descant on my strength, and give thy verdit?
Come nearer, part not hence so slight inform'd;
But take good heed my hand survey not thee.
HARAPHA. O *Baal-zebub!* can my ears unus'd
Hear these dishonours, and not render death?
SAMSON. No man with-holds thee, nothing from thy hand
Fear I incurable; bring up thy van.
My heels are fetter'd, but my fist is free.
HARAPHA. This insolence other kind of answer fits.
SAMSON. Go baffl'd coward, lest I run upon thee,
Though in these chains, bulk without spirit vast,
And with one buffet lay thy structure low,

Or swing thee in the Air, then dash thee down
To the hazard of thy brains and shatter'd sides.
HARAPHA. By *Astaroth* e're long thou shalt lament
These braveries in Irons loaden on thee.
CHORUS. His Giantship is gone somewhat crest-fall'n,
Stalking with less unconsci'nable strides,
And lower looks, but in a sultrie chafe.
SAMSON. I dread him not, nor all his Giant-brood,
Though Fame divulge him Father of five Sons
All of Gigantic size, *Goliah* chief.
CHORUS. He will directly to the Lords, I fear,
And with malitious counsel stir them up
Some way or other yet further to afflict thee.
SAMSON. He must allege some cause, and offer'd fight
Will not dare mention, lest a question rise
Whether he durst accept the offer or not,
And that he durst not plain enough appear'd.
Much more affliction then already felt
They cannot well impose, nor I sustain;
If they intend advantage of my labours
The work of many hands, which earns my keeping
With no small profit daily to my owners.
But come what will, my deadliest foe will prove
My speediest friend, by death to rid me hence,
The worst that he can give, to me the best.
Yet so it may fall out, because thir end
Is hate, not help to me, it may with mine
Draw thir own ruin who attempt the deed.
CHORUS. Oh how comely it is and how reviving
To the Spirits of just men long opprest!
When God into the hands of thir deliverer
Puts invincible might
To quell the mighty of the Earth, th' oppressour,
The brute and boist'rous force of violent men
Hardy and industrious to support

Tyrannic power, but raging to pursue
The righteous and all such as honour Truth;
He all thir Ammunition
And feats of War defeats
With plain Heroic magnitude of mind
And celestial vigour arm'd,
Thir Armories and Magazins contemns,
Renders them useless, while
With winged expedition
Swift as the lightning glance he executes
His errand on the wicked, who surpris'd
Lose thir defence distracted and amaz'd.
      But patience is more oft the exercise
Of Saints, the trial of thir fortitude,
Making them each his own Deliverer,
And Victor over all
That tyrannie or fortune can inflict,
Either of these is in thy lot,
Samson, with might endu'd
Above the Sons of men; but sight bereav'd
May chance to number thee with those
Whom Patience finally must crown.
This Idols day hath bin to thee no day of rest,
      Labouring thy mind
More then the working day thy hands,
And yet perhaps more trouble is behind.
For I descry this way
Some other tending, in his hand
A Scepter or quaint staff he bears,
Comes on amain, speed in his look.
By his habit I discern him now
A Public Officer, and now at hand.
His message will be short and voluble.
OFFICER. *Ebrews,* the Pris'ner *Samson* here I seek.
CHORUS. His manacles remark him, there he sits.

OFFICER. *Samson*, to thee our Lords thus bid me say;
This day to *Dagon* is a solemn Feast,
With Sacrifices, Triumph, Pomp, and Games;
Thy strength they know surpassing human rate,
And now some public proof thereof require
To honour this great Feast, and great Assembly;
Rise therefore with all speed and come along,
Where I will see thee heartn'd and fresh clad
To appear as fits before th' illustrious Lords.
SAMSON. Thou knowst I am an *Ebrew*, therefore tell them,
Our Law forbids at thir Religious Rites
My presence; for that cause I cannot come.
OFFICER. This answer, be assur'd, will not content them.
SAMSON. Have they not Sword-players, and ev'ry sort
Of Gymnic Artists, Wrestlers, Riders, Runners,
Juglers and Dancers, Antics, Mummers, Mimics,
But they must pick me out with shackles tir'd,
And over-labour'd at thir publick Mill,
To make them sport with blind activity?
Do they not seek occasion of new quarrels
On my refusal to distress me more,
Or make a game of my calamities?
Return the way thou cam'st, I will not come.
OFFICER. Regard thy self, this will offend them highly.
SAMSON. My self? my conscience and internal peace.
Can they think me so broken, so debas'd
With corporal servitude, that my mind ever
Will condescend to such absurd commands?
Although thir drudge, to be thir fool or jester,
And in my midst of sorrow and heart-grief
To shew them feats and play before thir god,
The worst of all indignities, yet on me
Joyn'd with extream contempt? I will not come.
OFFICER. My message was impos'd on me with speed,

Brooks no delay: is this thy resolution?

SAMSON. So take it with what speed thy message needs.

OFFICER. I am sorry what this stoutness will produce.

SAMSON. Perhaps thou shalt have cause to sorrow indeed.

CHORUS. Consider, *Samson;* matters now are strain'd
Up to the highth, whether to hold or break;
He's gone, and who knows how he may report
Thy words by adding fuel to the flame?
Expect another message more imperious,
More Lordly thund'ring then thou well wilt bear.

SAMSON. Shall I abuse this Consecrated gift
Of strength, again returning with my hair
After my great transgression, so requite
Favour renew'd, and add a greater sin
By prostituting holy things to Idols;
A *Nazarite* in place abominable
Vaunting my strength in honour to thir *Dagon?*
Besides, how vile, contemptible, ridiculous,
What act more execrably unclean, prophane?

CHORUS. Yet with this strength thou serv'st the *Philistines,*
Idolatrous, uncircumcis'd, unclean.

SAMSON. Not in thir Idol-worship, but by labour
Honest and lawful to deserve my food
Of those who have me in thir civil power.

CHORUS. Where the heart joins not, outward acts defile
not.

SAMSON. Where outward force constrains, the sentence
holds
But who constrains me to the Temple of *Dagon,*
Not dragging? the *Philistian* Lords command.
Commands are no constraints. If I obey them,
I do it freely; venturing to displease
God for the fear of Man, and Man prefer,
Set God behind: which in his jealousie

Shall never, unrepented, find forgiveness.
Yet that he may dispense with me or thee
Present in Temples at Idolatrous Rites
For some important cause, thou needst not doubt.

CHORUS. How thou wilt here come off surmounts my
    reach.

SAMSON. Be of good courage, I begin to feel
Some rouzing motions in me which dispose
To something extraordinary my thoughts.
I with this Messenger will go along,
Nothing to do, be sure, that may dishonour
Our Law, or stain my vow of *Nazarite*.
If there be aught of presage in the mind,
This day will be remarkable in my life
By some great act, or of my days the last.

CHORUS. In time thou hast resolv'd, the man returns.

OFFICER. *Samson*, this second message from our Lords
To thee I am bid say. Art thou our Slave,
Our Captive, at the public Mill our drudge,
And dar'st thou at our sending and command
Dispute thy coming? come without delay;
Or we shall find such Engines to assail
And hamper thee, as thou shalt come of force,
Though thou wert firmlier fastn'd then a rock.

SAMSON. I could be well content to try thir Art,
Which to no few of them would prove pernicious.
Yet knowing thir advantages too many,
Because they shall not trail me through thir streets
Like a wild Beast, I am content to go.
Masters commands come with a power resistless
To such as owe them absolute subjection;
And for a life who will not change his purpose?
(So mutable are all the ways of men)
Yet this be sure, in nothing to comply
Scandalous or forbidden in our Law.

OFFICER. I praise thy resolution, doff these links:
By this compliance thou wilt win the Lords
To favour, and perhaps to set thee free.

SAMSON. Brethren farewel, your company along
I will not wish, lest it perhaps offend them
To see me girt with Friends; and how the sight
Of me as of a common Enemy,
So dreaded once, may now exasperate them
I know not. Lords are Lordliest in thir wine;
And the well-feasted Priest then soonest fir'd
With zeal, if aught Religion seem concern'd:
No less the people on thir Holy-days
Impetuous, insolent, unquenchable;
Happ'n what may, of me expect to hear
Nothing dishonourable, impure, unworthy
Our God, our Law, my Nation, or my self,
The last of me or no I cannot warrant.

CHORUS. Go, and the Holy One
Of *Israel* be thy guide
To what may serve his glory best, and spread his name
Great among the Heathen round:
Send thee the Angel of thy Birth, to stand
Fast by thy side, who from thy Fathers field
Rode up in flames after his message told
Of thy conception, and be now a shield
Of fire; that Spirit that first rusht on thee
In the camp of *Dan*
Be efficacious in thee now at need.
For never was from Heaven imparted
Measure of strength so great to mortal seed,
As in thy wond'rous actions hath been seen.
But wherefore comes old *Manoa* in such hast
With youthful steps? much livelier then e're while
He seems: supposing here to find his Son,
Or of him bringing to us some glad news?

MANOA. Peace with you brethren; my inducement hither
Was not at present here to find my Son,
By order of the Lords new parted hence
To come and play before them at thir Feast.
I heard all as I came, the City rings
And numbers thither flock, I had no will,
Lest I should see him forc't to things unseemly.
But that which mov'd my coming now, was chiefly
To give ye part with me what hope I have
With good success to work his liberty.
CHORUS. That hope would much rejoyce us to partake
With thee; say reverend Sire, we thirst to hear.
MANOA. I have attempted one by one the Lords
Either at home, or through the high street passing,
With supplication prone and Fathers tears
To accept of ransom for my Son thir pris'ner,
Some much averse I found and wondrous harsh,
Contemptuous, proud, set on revenge and spite;
That part most reverenc'd *Dagon* and his Priests,
Others more moderate seeming, but thir aim
Private reward, for which both God and State
They easily would set to sale, a third
More generous far and civil, who confess'd
They had anough reveng'd, having reduc't
Thir foe to misery beneath thir fears,
The rest was magnanimity to remit,
If some convenient ransom were propos'd.
What noise or shout was that? it tore the Skie.
CHORUS. Doubtless the people shouting to behold
Thir once great dread, captive, and blind before them,
Or at some proof of strength before them shown.
MANOA. His ransom, if my whole inheritance
May compass it, shall willingly be paid
And numberd down: much rather I shall chuse
To live the poorest in my Tribe, then richest,

And he in that calamitous prison left.
No, I am fixt not to part hence without him.
For his redemption all my Patrimony,
If need be, I am ready to forgo
And quit: not wanting him, I shall want nothing.
CHORUS. Fathers are wont to lay up for thir Sons,
Thou for thy Son art bent to lay out all;
Sons wont to nurse thir Parents in old age,
Thou in old age car'st how to nurse thy Son
Made older then thy age through eye-sight lost.
MANOA. It shall be my delight to tend his eyes,
And view him sitting in the house, enobl'd
With all those high exploits by him atchiev'd,
And on his shoulders waving down those locks,
That of a Nation arm'd the strength contain'd:
And I perswade me God had not permitted
His strength again to grow up with his hair
Garrison'd round about him like a Camp
Of faithful Souldiery, were not his purpose
To use him further yet in some great service,
Not to sit idle with so great a gift
Useless, and thence ridiculous about him.
And since his strength with eye-sight was not lost,
God will restore him eye-sight to his strength.
CHORUS. Thy hopes are not ill founded nor seem vain
Of his delivery, and thy joy thereon
Conceiv'd, agreeable to a Fathers love,
In both which we, as next participate.
MANOA. I know your friendly minds and—O what
    noise!
Mercy of Heav'n what hideous noise was that!
Horribly loud unlike the former shout.
CHORUS. Noise call you it or universal groan
As if the whole inhabitation perish'd,
Blood, death, and deathful deeds are in that noise,

Ruin, destruction at the utmost point.

MANOA. Of ruin indeed methought I heard the noise,
Oh it continues, they have slain my Son.

CHORUS. Thy Son is rather slaying them, that outcry
From slaughter of one foe could not ascend.

MANOA. Some dismal accident it needs must be;
What shall we do, stay here or run and see?

CHORUS. Best keep together here, lest running thither
We unawares run into dangers mouth.
This evil on the *Philistines* is fall'n,
From whom could else a general cry be heard?
The sufferers then will scarce molest us here,
From other hands we need not much to fear.
What if his eye-sight (for to *Israels* God
Nothing is hard) by miracle restor'd,
He now be dealing dole among his foes,
And over heaps of slaughter'd walk his way?

MANOA. That were a joy presumptuous to be thought.

CHORUS. Yet God hath wrought things as incredible
For his people of old; what hinders now?

MANOA. He can I know, but doubt to think he will;
Yet Hope would fain subscribe, and tempts Belief.
A little stay will bring some notice hither.

CHORUS. Of good or bad so great, of bad the sooner;
For evil news rides post, while good news baits.
And to our wish I see one hither speeding,
An *Ebrew*, as I guess, and of our Tribe.

MESSENGER. O whither shall I run, or which way flie
The sight of this so horrid spectacle
Which earst my eyes beheld and yet behold;
For dire imagination still persues me.
But providence or instinct of nature seems,
Or reason though disturb'd, and scarse consulted
To have guided me aright, I know not how,
To thee first reverend *Manoa*, and to these

My Countreymen, whom here I knew remaining,
As at some distance from the place of horrour,
So in the sad event too much concern'd.

MANOA. The accident was loud, and here before thee
With rueful cry, yet what it was we hear not,
No Preface needs, thou seest we long to know.

MESSENGER. It would burst forth, but I recover breath
And sense distract, to know well what I utter.

MANOA. Tell us the sum, the circumstance defer.

MESSENGER. *Gaza* yet stands, but all her Sons are fall'n,
All in a moment overwhelm'd and fall'n.

MANOA. Sad, but thou knowst to *Israelites* not saddest
The desolation of a Hostile City.

MESSENGER. Feed on that first, there may in grief be
    surfet.

MANOA. Relate by whom.

MESSENGER.   By *Samson.*

MANOA.   That still lessens
The sorrow, and converts it nigh to joy.

MESSENGER. Ah *Manoa* I refrain, too suddenly
To utter what will come at last too soon;
Lest evil tidings with too rude irruption
Hitting thy aged ear should pierce too deep.

MANOA. Suspense in news is torture, speak them out.

MESSENGER. Then take the worst in brief, *Samson* is
    dead.

MANOA. The worst indeed, O all my hope's defeated
To free him hence! but death who sets all free
Hath paid his ransom now and full discharge.
What windy joy this day had I conceiv'd
Hopeful of his Delivery, which now proves
Abortive as the first-born bloom of spring
Nipt with the lagging rear of winters frost.
Yet e're I give the rains to grief, say first,
How dy'd he? death to life is crown or shame.

All by him fell thou say'st, by whom fell he,
What glorious hand gave *Samson* his deaths wound?
MESSENGER. Unwounded of his enemies he fell.
MANOA. Wearied with slaughter then or how? explain.
MESSENGER. By his own hands.
MANOA.   Self-violence? what cause
Brought him so soon at variance with himself
Among his foes?
MESSENGER.   Inevitable cause
At once both to destroy and be destroy'd;
The Edifice where all were met to see him
Upon thir heads and on his own he pull'd.
MANOA. O lastly over-strong against thy self!
A dreadful way thou took'st to thy revenge.
More then anough we know; but while things yet
Are in confusion, give us if thou canst,
Eye-witness of what first or last was done,
Relation more particular and distinct.
MESSENGER. Occasions drew me early to this City,
And as the gates I enter'd with Sun-rise,
The morning Trumpets Festival proclaim'd
Through each high street: little I had dispatch't
When all abroad was rumour'd that this day
Samson should be brought forth to shew the people
Proof of his mighty strength in feats and games;
I sorrow'd at his captive state, but minded
Not to be absent at that spectacle.
The building was a spacious Theatre
Half round on two main Pillars vaulted high,
With seats where all the Lords and each degree
Of sort, might sit in order to behold,
The other side was op'n, where the throng
On banks and scaffolds under Skie might stand;
I among these aloof obscurely stood.
The Feast and noon grew high, and Sacrifice

Had fill'd thir hearts with mirth, high chear, and wine,
When to thir sports they turn'd. Immediately
Was *Samson* as a public servant brought,
In thir state Livery clad; before him Pipes
And Timbrels, on each side went armed. guards,
Both horse and foot before him and behind
Archers, and Slingers, Cataphracts and Spears.
At sight of him the people with a shout
Rifted the Air clamouring thir god with praise,
Who had made thir dreadful enemy thir thrall.
He patient but undaunted where they led him,
Came to the place, and what was set before him
Which without help of eye, might be assay'd,
To heave, pull, draw, or break, he still perform'd
All with incredible, stupendious force,
None daring to appear Antagonist.
At length for intermission sake they led him
Between the pillars; he his guide requested
(For so from such as nearer stood we heard)
As over-tir'd to let him lean a while
With both his arms on those two massie Pillars
That to the arched roof gave main support.
He unsuspitious led him; which when *Samson*
Felt in his arms, with head a while enclin'd,
And eyes fast fixt he stood, as one who pray'd,
Or some great matter in his mind revolv'd.
At last with head erect thus cryed aloud,
Hitherto, Lords, what your commands impos'd
I have perform'd, as reason was, obeying,
Not without wonder or delight beheld.
Now of my own accord such other tryal
I mean to shew you of my strength, yet greater;
As with amaze shall strike all who behold.
This utter'd, straining all his nerves he bow'd,
As with the force of winds and waters pent,

When Mountains tremble, those two massie Pillars
With horrible convulsion to and fro,
He tugg'd, he shook, till down they came and drew
The whole roof after them, with burst of thunder
Upon the heads of all who sate beneath,
Lords, Ladies, Captains, Councellors, or Priests,
Thir choice nobility and flower, not only
Of this but each *Philistian* City round
Met from all parts to solemnize this Feast.
Samson with these immixt, inevitably
Pulld down the same destruction on himself;
The vulgar only scap'd who stood without.
CHORUS. O dearly-bought revenge, yet glorious!
Living or dying thou hast fulfill'd
The work for which thou wast foretold
To *Israel*, and now ly'st victorious
Among thy slain self-kill'd
Not willingly, but tangl'd in the fold
Of dire necessity, whose law in death conjoin'd
Thee with thy slaughter'd foes in number more
Then all thy life had slain before.
SEMICHORUS. While thir hearts were jocund and sub-
        lime,
Drunk with Idolatry, drunk with Wine,
And fat regorg'd of Bulls and Goats,
Chaunting thir Idol, and preferring
Before our living Dread who dwells
In *Silo* his bright Sanctuary:
Among them he a spirit of phrenzie sent,
Who hurt thir minds,
And urg'd them on with mad desire
To call in hast for thir destroyer;
They only set on sport and play
Unweetingly importun'd
Thir own destruction to come speedy upon them.

So fond are mortal men
Fall'n into wrath divine,
As thir own ruin on themselves to invite,
Insensate left, or to sense reprobate,
And with blindness internal struck.
SEMICHORUS. But he though blind of sight,
Despis'd and thought extinguish't quite,
With inward eyes illuminated
His fierie vertue rouz'd
From under ashes into sudden flame,
And as an ev'ning Dragon came,
Assailant on the perched roosts,
And nests in order rang'd
Of tame villatic Fowl; but as an Eagle
His cloudless thunder bolted on thir heads.
So vertue giv'n for lost,
Deprest, and overthrown, as seem'd,
Like that self-begott'n bird
In the *Arabian* woods embost,
That no second knows nor third,
And lay e're while a Holocaust,
From out her ashie womb now teem'd,
Revives, reflourishes, then vigorous most
When most unactive deem'd,
And though her body die, her fame survives,
A secular bird ages of lives.
MANOA. Come, come, no time for lamentation now,
Nor much more cause, *Samson* hath quit himself
Like *Samson,* and heroicly hath finish'd
A life Heroic, on his Enemies
Fully reveng'd, hath left them years of mourning,
And lamentation to the Sons of *Caphtor*
Through all *Philistian* bounds. To *Israel*
Honour hath left, and freedom, let but them
Find courage to lay hold on this occasion,

To himself and Fathers house eternal fame;
And which is best and happiest yet, all this
With God not parted from him, as was feard,
But favouring and assisting to the end.
Nothing is here for tears, nothing to wail
Or knock the breast, no weakness, no contempt,
Dispraise, or blame, nothing but well and fair,
And what may quiet us in a death so noble.
Let us go find the body where it lies
Sok't in his enemies blood, and from the stream
With lavers pure and cleansing herbs wash off
The clotted gore. I with what speed the while
(*Gaza* is not in plight to say us nay)
Will send for all my kindred, all my friends
To fetch him hence and solemnly attend
With silent obsequie and funeral train
Home to his Fathers house: there will I build him
A Monument, and plant it round with shade
Of Laurel ever green, and branching Palm,
With all his Trophies hung, and Acts enroll'd
In copious Legend, or sweet Lyric Song.
Thither shall all the valiant youth resort,
And from his memory inflame thir breasts
To matchless valour, and adventures high:
The Virgins also shall on feastful days
Visit his Tomb with flowers, only bewailing
His lot unfortunate in nuptial choice,
From whence captivity and loss of eyes.
CHORUS. All is best, though we oft doubt,
What th' unsearchable dispose
Of highest wisdom brings about,
And ever best found in the close.
Oft he seems to hide his face,
But unexpectedly returns
And to his faithful Champion hath in place

Bore witness gloriously; whence *Gaza* mourns
And all that band them to resist
His uncontroulable intent,
His servants he with new acquist
Of true experience from this great event
With peace and consolation hath dismist,
And calm of mind all passion spent.

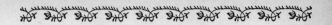

Anne Bradstreet

(c.1612–1672)

To My Dear and Loving Husband

If ever two were one, then surely we.
If ever man were lov'd by wife, then thee;
If ever wife was happy in a man,
Compare with me ye women if you can.
I prize thy love more then whole Mines of gold,
Or all the riches that the East doth hold.
My love is such that Rivers cannot quench,
Nor ought but love from thee, give recompence.
Thy love is such I can no way repay,
The heavens reward thee manifold I pray.
Then while we live, in love lets so persever,
That when we live no more, we may live ever.

FROM *Contemplations*

Some time now past in the Autumnal Tide,
When *Phoebus* wanted but one hour to bed,
The trees all richly clad, yet void of pride,
Where gilded o're by his rich golden head.
Their leaves and fruits seem'd painted, but was true
Of green, of red, of yellow, mixed hew,
Rapt were my sences at this delectable view.

I wist not what to wish, yet sure thought I
If so much excellence abide below;
How excellent is he that dwells on high?
Whose power and beauty by his works we know.
Sure he is goodness, wisdome, glory, light,
That hath this under world so richly dight:
More Heaven then Earth was here, no winter and no
    night.

Silent alone, where none or saw, or heard,
In pathless paths I lead my wandring feet,
My humble Eyes to lofty Skyes I rear'd
To sing some Song, my mazed Muse thought meet.
My great Creator I would magnifie,
That nature had, thus decked liberally:
But Ah, and Ah, again, my imbecility!

I heard the merry grashopper then sing,
The black clad Cricket, bear a second part,
They kept one tune, and plaid on the same string,
Seeming to glory in their little Art.
Shall Creatures abject, thus their voices raise?
And in their kind resound their makers praise:
Whilst I as mute, can warble forth no higher layes.

When I behold the heavens as in their prime,
And then the earth (though old) stil clad in green,
The stones and trees, insensible of time,
Nor age nor wrinkle on their front are seen;
If winter come, and greeness then do fade,
A Spring returns, and they more youthfull made;
But Man grows old, lies down, remains where once he's
    laid.

Shall I then praise the heavens, the trees, the earth
Because their beauty and their strength last longer
Shall I wish there, or never to had birth,
Because they're bigger, and their bodyes stronger?
Nay, they shall darken, perish, fade and dye,
And when unmade, so ever shall they lye,
But man was made for endless immortality.

Under the cooling shadow of a stately Elm
Close sate I by a goodly Rivers side,
Where gliding streams the Rocks did overwhelm;
A lonely place, with pleasures dignifi'd.
I once that lov'd the shady woods so well,
Now thought the rivers did the trees excel,
And if the sun would ever shine, there would I dwell.

Ye Fish which in this liquid Region 'bide,
That for each season, have your habitation,
Now salt, now fresh where you think best to glide
To unknown coasts to give a visitation,
In Lakes and ponds, you leave your numerous fry,
So nature taught, and yet you know not why,
You watry folk that know not your felicity.

Look how the wantons frisk to taste the air,
Then to the colder bottome streight they dive,
Eftsoon to *Neptun's* glassie Hall repair
To see what trade they great ones there do drive,
Who forrage o're the spacious sea-green field,
And take the trembling prey before it yield,
Whose armour is their scales, their spreading fins their
    shield.

O Time the fatal wrack of mortal things,
That draws oblivions curtains over kings,
Their sumptuous monuments, men know them not,
Their names without a Record are forgot,
Their parts, their ports, their pomp's all laid in th' dust
Nor wit nor gold, nor buildings scape times rust;
But he whose name is grav'd in the white stone
Shall last and shine when all of these are gone.

(Stanzas 1, 2, 8, 9, 18, 20, 21, 24, 25, 33)

As weary pilgrim, now at rest

As weary pilgrim, now at rest,
  Hugs with delight his silent nest,
His wasted limbes now lye full soft
  That myrie steps have trodden oft;
Blesses himself, to think upon
  His dangers past, and travailes done.
The burning sun no more shall heat,
  Nor stormy raines on him shall beat.
The bryars and thornes no more shall scratch,
  Nor hungry wolves at him shall catch;
He erring pathes no more shall tread,
  Nor wild fruites eate, in stead of bread;
For waters cold he doth not long,
  For thirst no more shall parch his tongue;
No rugged stones his feet shall gaule,
  Nor stumps nor rocks cause him to fall;
All cares and feares he bids farwell,
  And meanes in safity now to dwell.
A pilgrim I, on earth perplext
  With sinns, with cares and sorrows vext,

By age and paines brought to decay,
    And my Clay house mouldring away:
Oh how I long to be at rest
    And soare on high among the blest!
This body shall in silence sleep;
    Mine eyes no more shall ever weep;
No fainting fits shall me assaile,
    Nor grinding paines, my body fraile;
With cares and fears ne'r cumbred be,
    Nor losses know, nor sorrowes see.
What tho my flesh shall there consume,
    It is the bed Christ did perfume;
And when a few yeares shall be gone,
    This mortall shall be cloth'd upon.
A Corrupt Carcasse downe it lyes,
    A glorious body it shall rise;
In weaknes and dishonour sowne,
    In power 'tis rais'd by Christ alone.
Then soule and body shall unite
    And of their maker have the sight;
Such lasting joyes shall there behold
    As eare ne'r heard nor tongue e'er told.
Lord make me ready for that day!
    Then Come, deare bridgrome, Come away!

Edward Taylor

(c.1644–1729)

FROM God's Determinations

GOD'S SELECTING LOVE IN THE DECREE

O! Honour! Honour! Honour! Oh! the Gain!
And all such Honours all the saints obtain.
It is the Chariot of the King of Kings:
That all who Glory gain, to glory brings;
Whose Glory makes the rest, (when spi'de) beg in.
Some gaze and stare, some stranging at the thing,
Some peep therein; some rage thereat, but all,
Like market people seing on a stall
Some rare Commodity, Clap hands thereon,
And Cheapen 't hastily, but soon are gone
For hearing of the price, and wanting pay,
Do pish thereat, and Coily pass away.
So hearing of the terms, whist! they'le abide
At home before they'l pay so much to ride.
But they to whom it's sent had rather all
Dy in this Coach, than let their journey fall.
They up therefore do get, and in it ride
Unto Eternal bliss, while down the tide
The other scull unto eternall woe,
By letting slip their former journey so.
For when they finde the Silver Pillars fair,
The Golden bottom pav'de with Love as rare,
To be the Spirits sumptuous building cleare;
When in the Soul his Temple he doth reare,

And Purple Canopy to bee (they spy)
All Graces Needlework and Huswifry;
Their stomachs rise: these graces will not down:
They think them Slobber Sawces: therefore frown.
They loath the same, wamble keck, heave they do:
Their Spleen thereat out at their mouths they throw.
Which while they do, the Coach away doth high:
Wheeling the Saints in't to eternall joy.
    These therefore and their journey now do come
    For to be treated on, and Coacht along.

(*Lines* 33–*end*)

THE SOULS GROAN TO CHRIST FOR SUCCOUR

Good Lord, behold this Dreadfull Enemy
    Who makes me tremble with his fierce assaults;
I dare not trust, yet feare to give the ly,
    For in my soul, my soul finds many faults.
    And though I justify myselfe to's face:
    I do Condemn myselfe before thy Grace.

He strives to mount my sins, and them advance
    Above thy Merits, Pardons, or Good Will;
Thy Grace to lessen, and thy Wrath t' inhance
    As if thou couldst not pay the sinners bill.
    He Chiefly injures thy rich Grace, I finde,
    Though I confess my heart to sin inclin'de.

Those Graces which thy Grace enwrought in mee,
    He makes as nothing but a pack of Sins;
He maketh Grace no grace, but Crueltie;
    Is Graces Honey Comb, a Comb of Stings?
    This makes me ready leave thy Grace and run,
    Which if I do, I finde I am undone.

I know he is thy Cur, therefore I bee
  Perplexed lest I from thy Pasture stray,
He bayghs and barks so veh'mently at mee.
    Come, rate this Cur, Lord, breake his teeth I pray.
    Remember me I humbly pray thee first,
    Then halter up this Cur that is so Curst.

CHRIST'S REPLY

Peace, Peace, my Hony, do not Cry,
My Little Darling, wipe thine eye,
  Oh Cheer, Cheer up, come see.
Is anything too deare, my Dove,
Is anything too good, my Love,
  To get or give for thee?

If in the severall thou art,
This Yelper fierce will at thee bark:
  That thou art mine this shows.
As Spot barks back the sheep again,
Before they to the Pound are ta'ne,
  So he, and hence 'way goes.

But if this Cur that bayghs so sore,
Is broken tootht, and muzzled sure,
  Fear not, my Pritty Heart.
His barking is to make thee Cling
Close underneath thy Saviours wing.
  Why did my sweeten start?

And if he run an inch too fur,
I'le Check his Chain, and rate the Cur.
  My Chick, keep close to mee.
The Poles shall sooner kiss and greet,

And Paralells shall sooner meet,
　　Than thou shall harmed bee.

He seeks to aggrivate thy sin,
And screw them to the highest pin,
　　To make thy faith to quaile.
Yet mountain sins like mites should show,
And then these mites for naught should goe,
　　Could he but once prevaile.

I smote thy sins upon the Head.
They Dead'ned are, though not quite dead:
　　And shall not rise again.
I'l put away the Guilt thereof,
And purge its Filthiness cleare off:
　　My Blood doth out the stain.

And though thy judgment was remiss,
Thy Headstrong Will too Wilfull is:
　　I will Renew the same.
And though thou do too frequently
Offend as heretofore, hereby
　　I'le not severely blaim.

And though thy senses do inveagle
Thy Noble Soul to tend the Beagle,
　　That t' hunt her games forthgo.
I'le Lure her back to me, and Change
Those fond Affections that do range
　　As yelping beagles doe.

Although thy sins increase their race,
And though when thou hast sought for Grace,
　　Thou fallst more than before:
If thou by true Repentence Rise,
And Faith makes me thy Sacrifice,
　　I'l pardon all, though more.

Though Satan strive to block thy way
By all his Stratagems he may,
   Come, come, though through the fire.
For Hell, that Gulph of fire for sins,
Is not so hot as t' burn thy Shins.
   Then Credit not the Lyar.

Those Cursed Vermin Sins that Crawle
All ore thy Soul, both Greate and Small,
   Are onely Satans own:
Which he in his Malignity
Unto thy Souls true Sanctity
   In at the doore hath thrown.

And though they be Rebellion high,
Ath'ism or Apostacy:
   Though blasphemy it bee:
Unto what Quality, or Sise,
Excepting one, so e're it rise,
   Repent, I'le pardon thee.

Although thy Soule was once a Stall
Rich hung with Satans nicknacks all;
   If thou Repent thy Sin,
A Tabernacle in 't I'le place,
Fill'd with Gods Spirit, and his Grace.
   Oh Comfortable thing!

I dare the World therefore to show
A God like me, to anger slow:
   Whose wrath is full of Grace.
Doth hate all Sins both Greate and Small:
Yet when Repented, pardons all.
   Frowns with a Smiling Face.

As for thy outward Postures each,
Thy Gestures, Actions, and thy Speech,

I Eye, and Eying spare,
If thou repent. My Grace is more
Ten thousand times still tribled ore
    Than thou canst want, or ware.

As for the Wicked Charge he makes,
That he of Every Dish first takes
    Of all thy holy things:
It's false; deny the same, and say,
That which he had he stool away
    Out of thy Offerings.

Though to thy Griefe, poor Heart, thou finde
In Pray're too oft a wandring minde,
    In Sermons, Spirits dull:
Though faith in firy furnace flags,
And Zeale in Chilly Seasons lags:
    Temptations powerfull:

These faults are his, and none of thine
So fur as thou dost them decline:
    Come then, receive my Grace.
And when he buffits thee therefore,
If thou my aid and Grace implore,
    I'le shew a pleasant face.

But still look for Temptations Deep,
Whilst that thy Noble Sparke doth keep
    Within a Mudwald Cote.
These White Frosts and the Showers that fall
Are but to whiten thee withall,
    Not rot the Web they smote.

If in the fire where Gold is tri'de,
Thy Soule is put, and purifi'de,
    Wilt thou lament thy loss?
If silver-like this fire refine

Thy Soul and make it brighter Shine:
  Wilt thou bewaile the Dross?

Oh! fight my Field: no Colours fear:
I'l be thy Front, I'l be thy reare.
  Fail not: my Battells fight.
Defy the Tempter, and his Mock.
Anchor thy heart on mee, thy Rock.
  I do in thee Delight.

FROM *Sacramental Meditations*

MEDITATION ONE

What Love is this of thine, that Cannot bee
  In thine Infinity, O Lord, Confinde,
Unless it in thy very Person see
  Infinity and Finity Conjoyn'd?
    What! hath thy Godhead, as not satisfi'de,
    Marri'de our Manhood, making it its Bride?

Oh, Matchless Love! Filling Heaven to the brim!
  O'rerunning it: all running o're beside
This World! Nay, Overflowing Hell, wherein
  For thine Elect, there rose a mighty Tide!
    That there our Veans might through thy Person
      bleed,
    To quench those flames, that else would on us feed.

Oh! that thy love might overflow my Heart!
  To fire the same with Love: for Love I would.
But oh! my streight'ned Breast! my Lifeless Sparke!
  My Fireless Flame! What Chilly Love, and Cold?
    In measure small! In Manner Chilly! See!
    Lord, blow the Coal: Thy Love Enflame in mee.

MEDITATION EIGHT

John 6:51. I am the living bread.

I kenning through Astronomy Divine
  The Worlds bright Battlement, wherein I spy
A Golden Path my Pensill cannot line
  From that bright Throne unto my Threshold ly.
    And while my puzzled thoughts about it pore,
    I find the Bread of Life in't at my doore.

When that this Bird of Paradise put in
  This Wicker Cage (my Corps) to tweedle praise
Had peckt the Fruite forbid: and so did fling
  Away its Food, and lost its golden dayes,
    It fell into Celestiall Famine sore,
    And never could attain a morsell more.

Alas! alas! Poore Bird, what wilt thou doe?
  This Creatures field no food for Soul's e're gave:
And if thou knock at Angells dores, they show
  An Empty Barrell: they no soul bread have.
    Alas! Poore Bird, the Worlds White Loafe is done,
    And cannot yield thee here the smallest Crumb.

In this sad state, Gods Tender Bowells run
  Out streams of Grace: And he to end all strife,
The Purest Wheate in Heaven, his deare-dear Son
  Grinds, and kneads up into this Bread of Life:
    Which Bread of Life from Heaven down came and
      stands
    Disht in thy Table up by Angells Hands.

Did God mould up this Bread in Heaven, and bake,
  Which from his Table came, and to thine goeth?
Doth he bespeake thee thus: This Soule Bread take;

Come, Eate thy fill of this, thy Gods White Loafe?
Its Food too fine for Angells; yet come, take
And Eate thy fill! Its Heavens Sugar Cake.

What Grace is this knead in this Loafe? This thing
   Souls are but petty things it to admire.
Yee Angells, help: This fill would to the brim
   Heav'ns whelm'd-down Chrystall meele Bowle, yea
      and higher.
   This Bread of Life dropt in thy mouth doth Cry:
   Eate, Eate me, Soul, and thou shalt never dy.

MEDITATION THIRTY-THREE

I Corinthians 3:22. Whether Paul, or Apollos, or Cephas, or
the world, or life, or death, or things present, or things to
come; all are your's.

My Lord, my Life, can Envy ever bee
   A Golden Vertue? Then would God I were
Top full thereof untill it colours mee
   With yellow streaks for thy Deare sake most Deare;
   Till I be Envious made by't at myselfe:
   As scarcely loving thee, my Life, my Health.

Oh! what strange Charm encrampt my Heart with spite,
   Making my Love gleame out upon a Toy?
Lay out Cart Loads of Love upon a mite?
   Scarce lay a mite of Love on thee, my Joy?
   Oh! Lovely thou! Shalt not thou loved bee?
   Shall I ashame thee thus? Oh! shame for mee!

Nature's amaz'de. Oh, monstrous thing, Quoth shee,
   Not Love my life? What Violence doth split
True Love and Life, that they should sunder'd bee?
   She doth not lay such Eggs, nor on them sit.
   How do I sever then my Heart with all

Its Powers whose Love scarce to my Life doth
crawle.

Glory lin'de out a Paradise in Power
    Where e'ry seed a Royall Coach became
For Life to ride in, to each shining Flower.
    And made mans Flower with glory all ore flame.
    Hells Inkfac'de Elfe black Venom spat upon
    The same, and kill'd it. So that Life is gone.

Life thus abus'de fled to the golden Arke,
    Lay lockt up there in Mercie's seate inclosde:
Which did incorporate it whence its Sparke
    Enlivens all things in this Arke inclos'de.
    Oh, glorious Arke! Life's Store-House full of Glee!
Shall not my Love safe lockt up ly in thee?

Lord, arke my Soule safe in thyselfe, whereby
    I and my Life again may joyned bee.
That I may finde what once I did destroy
    Again Confer'de upon my soul in thee.
    Thou art this Golden Ark, this Living Tree,
    Where life lies treasurde up for all in thee.

Oh! Graft me in this Tree of Life within
    The Paradise of God, that I may live.
Thy Life make live in mee; I'le then begin
    To beare thy Living Fruits, and them forth give.
    Give mee my Life this way; and I'le bestow
    My Love on thee, my Life. And it shall grow.

MEDITATION FORTY

I John 2:2. And he is the propitiation for our sins: and not
for ours only, but also for the sins of the whole world.

    Still I complain; I am complaining still.
        Oh woe is me! Was ever Heart like mine?
    A Sty of Filth, a Trough of Washing-Swill,

A Dunghill Pit, a Puddle of mere Slime,
A Nest of Vipers, Hive of Hornets-stings,
A Bag of Poyson, Civit-Box of Sins.

Was ever Heart like mine? So bad? black? vile?
   Is any Divell blacker? Or can Hell
Produce its match? It is the very soile
   Where Satan reads his charms and sets his spell;
   His Bowling Ally where he sheeres his fleece
   At Nine Pins, Nine Holes, Morrice, Fox and Geese.

His Palace Garden where his courtiers walke;
   His Jewells cabbinet. Here his caball
Do sham it and truss up their Privie talk
   In Fardells of Consults and bundles all.
   His shambles and his Butchers stall's herein.
   It is the Fuddling Schoole of every sin.

Was ever Heart like mine? Pride, Passion fell,
   Ath'ism, Blasphemy pot, pipe it, dance,
Play Barlybreaks, and at last couple in Hell:
   At Cudgells, Kit-Cat, Cards and Dice here prance:
   At Noddy, Ruff-and-Trump, Jink, Post and Pare,
   Put, One-and-thirty, and such ware.

Grace shuffled is away; Patience oft sticks
   Too soon, or draws itselfe out, and's out put.
Faith's over-trumpt, and oft doth lose her tricks.
   Repentance's chalkt up Noddy, and out shut.
   They Post and Pare off Grace thus, and its shine.
   Alas! alas! was ever Heart like mine?

Sometimes methinks the serpents head I mall:
   Now all is still: my spirits do recreute.
But ere my Harpe can tune sweet praise they fall
   On me afresh and tare me at my Root.
   They bite like Badgers now: nay worse, although
   I tooke them toothless sculls, rot long agoe.

My Reason now's more than my sense, I feele
  I have more sight than sense: Which seems to bee
A Rod of sunbeams t'whip mee for my steele.
  My Spirits spiritless and dull in mee
  For my dead prayerless Prayers: the Spirits winde
  Scarce blows my mill about. I little grinde.

Was ever Heart like mine? My Lord, declare
  I know not what to do: What shall I doe?
I wonder, split I don't upon Despare.
  Its grace's wonder that I wrack not so.
  I faintly shun't, although I see this case
  Would say my sin is greater than thy grace.

Hope's Day-peep down hence through this chinck,
    Christ's name,
  Propition is for sins. Lord, take
It so for mine. Thus quench thy burning flame
  In that clear stream that from his side forth brake.
  I can no comfort take while thus I see
  Hell's cursed Imps thus jetting strut in mee.

Lord, take thy sword: these Anakims destroy;
  Then soake my soul in Zion's Bucking-tub
With Holy Soape, and Nitre, and rich Lye.
  From all Defilement me cleanse, wash, and rub.
  Then wrince, and wring mee out till th'water fall
  As pure as in the Well: not foule at all.

And let thy Sun shine on my Head out cleare.
  And bathe my Heart within its radient beams:
Thy Christ make my Propitiation Deare:
  Thy Praise shall from my Heart breake forth in
    streams.
  This reeching Vertue of Christ's blood will quench
  Thy Wrath, slay Sin, and in thy Love mee bench.

MEDITATION SIXTY

I Corinthians 10:4. And did all drink the same spiritual drink.

Ye Angells bright, pluck from your Wings a Quill;
  Make me a pen thereof that best will write:
Lende me your fancy and Angellick skill
  To treate this Theme, more rich than Rubies bright.
  My muddy Inke and Cloudy fancy dark
  Will dull its glory, lacking highest Art.

An Eye at Centre righter may describe
  The Worlds Circumferentiall glory vast,
As in its nutshell bed it snugs fast ti'de,
  Than any angells pen can glory Cast
  Upon this Drink drawn from the Rock, tapt by
  The Rod of God, in Horeb, typickly.

Sea water strain'd through Minerall, Rocks, and Sands,
  Well Clarifi'de by Sunbeams, Dulcifi'de,
Insipid, Sordid, Swill, Dishwater stands.
  But here's a Rock of Aqua-Vitae tri'de!
  When once God broacht it, out a River came
  To bath and bibble in, for Israels train.

Some rocks have sweat. Some Pillars bled out tears,
  But here's a River in a Rock up tunn'd,
Not of Sea Water nor of Swill. It's beere!
  No Nectar like it! Yet it once unbungd,
  A River down out runs through ages all,
  A Fountain opte, to wash off Sin and Fall.

Christ in this Horebs Rock, the streames that slide
  A River is of Aqua Vitae Deare,
Yet costs us nothing, gushing from his side:

Celestiall Wine our sinsunk souls to cleare.
This Rock and Water, Sacramentall Cup
Are made, Lords Supper Wine for us to sup.

This Rock's the Grape that Zions Vineyard bore,
    Which Moses Rod did smiting pound, and press,
Untill its blood, the brooke of Life, run ore:
    All Glorious Grace, and Gracious Righteousness.
    We in this brook must bath: and with faiths quill
Suck Grace and Life out of this Rock our fill.

Lord, oynt me with this Petro oyle: I'm sick.
    Make mee drinke Water of the Rock: I'm dry.
Me in this fountain wash: my filth is thick.
    I'm faint: give Aqua Vitae or I dy.
    If in this stream thou cleanse and Chearish mee,
    My Heart thy Hallelujahs Pipe shall bee.

Upon a Spider Catching a Fly

Thou sorrow, venom Elfe:
    Is this thy play,
To spin a web out of thyselfe
    To Catch a Fly?
        For why?

I saw a pettish wasp
    Fall foule therein:
Whom yet thy whorle pins did not hasp
    Lest he should fling
        His sting.

But as afraid, remote
    Didst stand hereat,
And with thy little fingers stroke

And gently tap
  His back.

Thus gently him didst treate
  Lest he should pet,
And in a froppish, aspish heate
  Should greatly fret
    Thy net.

Whereas the silly Fly,
  Caught by its leg,
Thou by the throate took'st hastily,
  And 'hinde the head
    Bite Dead.

This goes to pot, that not
  Nature doth call.
Strive not above what strength hath got,
  Lest in the brawle
    Thou fall.

This Frey seems thus to us:
  Hells Spider gets
His intrails spun to whip Cords thus,
  And wove to nets,
    And sets.

To tangle Adams race
  In's stratagems
To their Destructions, Spoil'd, made base
  By venom things,
    Damn'd Sins.

But mighty, Gracious Lord,
  Communicate
Thy Grace to breake the Cord; afford
  Us Glorys Gate
    And State.

We'l Nightingaile sing like,
　　When pearcht on high
In Glories Cage, thy glory, bright:
　　Yea, thankfully,
　　　　For joy.

An Address to the Soul
Occasioned by a Rain

Ye Flippering Soule,
　　Why dost between the Nippers dwell?
Not stay, nor goe. Not yea, nor yet Controle.
　　Doth this doe well?
　　　　Rise journy'ng when the skies fall weeping
　　　　　　Showers,
　　　　Not o're nor under th' Clouds and Cloudy Powers.

Not yea, nor noe:
　　On tiptoes thus? Why sit on thorns?
Resolve the matter: Stay thyselfe or goe:
　　Ben't both wayes born.
　　　　Wager thyselfe against thy surplic'de see,
　　　　And win thy Coate, or let thy Coate win thee.

Is this th' Effect
　　To leaven thus my Spirits all?
To make my heart a Crabtree Cask direct?
　　A Verjuc'te Hall?
　　　　As Bottle Ale, whose Spirits prison'd must
　　　　When jogg'd, the bung with Violence doth burst?

Shall I be made
　　A sparkling Wildfire Shop,
Where my dull Spirits at the Fireball trade

Do frisk and hop?
And while the Hammer doth the Anvill pay,
The fire ball matter sparkles e'ry way.

One sorry fret,
An anvill Sparke, rose higher,
And in thy Temple falling, almost set
The house on fire.
Such fireballs dropping in the Temple Flame
Burns up the building: Lord, forbid the same.

FROM *An Elegy upon the Death
of That Holy Man of God Mr. John Allen*

LATE PAST. OF THE CHURCH OF CHRIST
AT DEDHAM, WHO DEPARTED
THIS LIFE 25TH 6^{M} 1671

How are our Spirituall Gamesters slipt away?
Crossing their Hilts, and leaving of their play?
We take up hilts, the Fencing Schoole implore.
Are Norton, Newman, Stone, Thompson gone hence?
Gray, Wilson, Shepherd, Flint, and Mitchell since?
Eliot, two Mather's Fathers first, then th'Son,
Is Buncker's Woodward's Rainer's hourglass run?
With Davenport's Sim's, Wareham's? Who are gone?
That Allen now is Called hence? Shall none
Be left behinde to tell's the Quondam Glory
Of this Plantation? What bleeding Story
Doth this present us with? Mine eyes boile ore
Thy gellid teares into this Urn therefore,
Wherein their Noble ashes are, and know yee
ALL END in ALLEN, by a Paragoge.

(Lines 49–end)

Upon a Wasp Chilled with Cold

The Bear that breaths the Northern blast
Did numb, Torpedo-like, a Wasp
Whose stiffend limbs encrampt, lay bathing
In Sol's warm breath and shine as saving,
Which with her hands she chafes and slams
Rubbing her Legs, Shanks, Thighs, and hands.
Her petty toes, and fingers ends
Nipt with this breath, she out extends
Unto the sun, in greate desire
To warm her digits at that fire:
Doth hold her Temples in this state
Where pulse doth beate, and head doth ake:
Doth turn and stretch her body small,
Doth comb her velvet capitall
As if her little brain-pan were
A Volume of choice precepts cleare:
As if her sattin jacket hot
Contained Apothecaries Shop
Of Natures recepts, that prevails
To remedy all her sad ailes,
As if her velvet helmet high
Did turret rationality.
She fans her wing up to the winde
As if her Pettycoate were lin'de
With reasons fleece, and hoises saile
And humming flies in thankfull gaile
Unto her dun curld palace Hall,
Her warm thanks offering for all.

Lord, cleare my misted sight that I
May hence view thy Divinity,

Some sparkes whereof thou up dost hasp
Within this little downy Wasp,
In whose small Corporation wee
A school and a schoolmaster see:
Where we may learn, and easily finde
A nimble Spirit, bravely minde
Her worke in ev'ry limb: and lace
It up neate with a vitall grace,
Acting each part though ne'er so small,
Here of this fustian animall,
Till I enravisht climb into
The Godhead on this ladder doe:
Where all my pipes inspir'de upraise
An Heavenly musick, furr'd with praise.

Samuel Butler

(1612–1680)

[*Portrait of Hudibras*]

He was in *Logick* a great Critick,
Profoundly skill'd in Analytick.
He could distinguish, and divide
A Hair 'twixt *South* and *South-West* side:
On either which he would dispute,
Confute, change hands, and still confute.
He'd undertake to prove by force
Of Argument, a Man's no Horse.
He'd prove a Buzard is no Fowl,
And that a *Lord* may be an Owl;
A Calf an *Alderman,* a Goose a *Justice,*
And Rooks *Committee-men* and *Trustees*
He'd run in Debt by Disputation,
And pay with Ratiocination.
All this by Syllogism, true
In Mood and Figure, he would do.

For *Rhetorick,* he could not ope
His mouth, but out there flew a Trope:
And when he hapned to break off
I'th middle of his speech, or cough,
H'had hard words, ready to shew why,
And tell what Rules he did it by.
Else when with greatest Art he spoke,

159

You'd think he talk'd like other folk.
For all a Rhetoricians Rules
Teach nothing but to name his Tools,
His ordinary Rate of Speech
In loftiness of sound was rich,
A *Babylonish* dialect,
Which learned Pedants much affect.
It was a parti-colour'd dress
Of patch'd and Pyball'd Languages:
'Twas *English* cut on *Greek* and *Latin*,
Like Fustian heretofore on Sattin.
It had an odd promiscuous Tone,
As if h' had talk'd three parts in one.
Which made some think when he did gabble,
Th' had heard three Labourers of *Babel;*
Or *Cerberus* himself pronounce
A Leash of Languages at once.
This he as volubly would vent,
As if his stock would ne'r be spent.
And truly to support that charge
He had supplies as vast and large.
For he could coyn or counterfeit
New words with little or no wit:
Words so debas'd and hard, no stone
Was hard enough to touch them on.
And when with hasty noise he spoke 'em,
The Ignorant for currant took 'em.
That had the Orator who once,
Did fill his Mouth with Pibble stones
When he harangu'd; but known his Phrase
He would have us'd no other ways.

In *Mathematicks* he was greater
Then *Tycho Brahe,* or *Erra Pater:*
For he by *Geometrick* seale

Could take the size of *Pots of Ale;*
Resolve by Signs and Tangents straight,
If *Bread* or *Butter* wanted weight;
And wisely tell what hour o'th' day
The Clock does strike, by *Algebra.*

Beside he was a shrewd *Philosopher;*
And had read every Text and gloss over:
What e're the crabbed'st Author hath
He understood b'implicit Faith,
What ever *Sceptick* could inquire for;
For every *why* he had a *wherefore:*
Knew more then forty of them do,
As far as words and terms could go.
All which he understood by Rote,
And as occasion serv'd, would quote;
No matter whether right or wrong:
They might be either said or sung.
His Notions fitted things so well,
That which was which he could not tell;
But oftentimes mistook the one
For th'other, as Great Clerks have done.
He could reduce all things to Acts,
And knew their Natures by Abstracts,
Where Entity and Quiddity
The Ghosts of defunct Bodies flie;
Where Truth in Person does appear,
Like words congeal'd in Northern Air.
He knew *what's what,* and that's as high
As *Metaphysick* Wit can fly.
In *School Divinity* as able
As he that hight *Irrefragable;*
Profound in all the Nominal
And real ways beyond them all,
And with as delicate a Hand

Could twist as tough a Rope of Sand.
And weave fine Cobwebs, fit for Skull
That's empty when the Moon is full;
Such as take Lodgings in a Head
That's to be lett unfurnished.
He could raise Scruples dark and nice,
And after solve 'em in a trice:
As if Divinity had catch'd
The Itch, of purpose to be scratch'd;
Or, like a Mountebank, did wound
And stab her self with doubts profound,
Only to shew with how small pain
The sores of faith are cur'd again,
Although by woful proof we find,
They always leave a Scar behind.
He knew the Seat of Paradise,
Could tell in what degree it lies:
And, as he was dispos'd, could prove it,
Below the Moon, or else above it
What *Adam* dreamt of when his Bride
Came from her Closet in his side:
Whether the Devil tempted her
By a *High Dutch* Interpreter:
If either of them had a Navel;
Who first made Musick malleable:
Whether the Serpent at the fall
Had cloven Feet, or none at all.
All this without a Gloss or Comment,
He would unriddle in a moment
In proper terms, such as men smatter
When they throw out and miss the matter.

For his *Religion* it was fit
To match his Learning and his Wit:
'Twas *Presbyterian* true blew,

For he was of that stubborn Crew
Of Errant Saints, whom all men grant
To be the true Church *Militant:*
Such as do build their Faith upon
The holy Text of *Pike* and *Gun;*
Decide all Controversies by
Infallible *Artillery;*
And prove their Doctrine Orthodox
By Apostolick *Blows* and *Knocks;*
Call Fire and Sword and Desolation,
A *godly-thorough-Reformation,*
Which always must be carry'd on,
And still be doing, never done:
As if Religion were intended
For nothing else but to be mended.
A Sect, whose chief Devotion lies
In odd perverse Antipathies;
In falling out with that or this,
And finding somewhat still amiss:
More peevish, cross, and spleenatick.
Then Dog distract, or Monky sick.
That with more care keep Holy-day
The wrong, then others the right way:
Compound for Sins, they are inclin'd to,
By damning those they have no mind to;
Still so perverse and opposite,
As if they worshipp'd God for spight,
The self-same thing they will abhor
One way, and long another for.
Free-will they one way disavow,
Another, nothing else allow.
All Piety consists therein
In them, in other Men all Sin.
Rather then fail, they will defie
That which they love most tenderly,

Quarrel with *minc'd Pies,* and disparage
Their best and dearest friend, *Plum-porridge;*
Fat *Pig* and *Goose* it self oppose,
And blaspheme *Custard* through the *Nose.*
Th' Apostles of this fierce Religion,
Like *Mahomet's,* were Ass and Widgeon,
To whom our Knight by fast instinct
Of Wit and Temper was so linkt,
As if Hypocrisy and Non-sence
Had got th' Advouson of his Conscience.

Thus was he gifted and accouter'd,
We mean on th' inside, not the outward.

                              (Part I, canto i, lines 65–235)

[Portrait of Sidrophel]

He had been long t'wards *Mathematicks,*
Opticks, Philosophy, and *Staticks,*
Magick, Horoscopie, Astrology,
And was *old Dog* at *Physiologie;*
But, as a *Dog* that turns the spit,
Bestirs himself, and plys his feet,
To climb the *Wheel;* but all in vain,
His own weight brings him down again:
And still he's in the self-same place,
Where at his setting out he was.
So in the *Circle* of the *Arts,*
Did he advance his nat'ral Parts;
Till falling back still, for retreat,
He fell to *Juggle, Cant,* and *Cheat;*
For, as those *Fowls* that live in Water
Are never wet, he did but smatter;
What e're he labour'd to appear,
His understanding still was clear.

Yet none a deeper knowledge boasted,
Since old *Hodg Bacon,* and *Bod Grosted.*
Th' *Intelligible world* he knew,
And all, men dream on't, to be true:
That in this *World,* there's not a *Wart,*
That has not there a Counterpart;
Nor can there on the *face* of Ground,
An Individual *Beard* be found,
That has not, in that Forrain *Nation,*
A fellow of the self-same fashion;
So *cut,* so *color'd,* and so *curl'd,*
As those are, in th' *Inferior World.*
H' had read *Dee's* Prefaces before
The *Dev'l,* and *Euclide* o're and o're.
And, all th' *Intrigues,* 'twixt him and *Kelly,*
Lescus and th' *Emperor,* would tell ye.
But with the *Moon* was more familiar
Then e'r was *Almanack well-willer.*
Her Secrets understood so clear,
That some believ'd he had been there.
Knew when she was in fittest mood,
For cutting *Corns* or letting *blood,*
When for anointing *Scabs* or *Itches,*
Or to the *Bum* applying *Leeches;*
When *Sows* and *Bitches* may be spade,
And in what Sign best *Cider's* made,
Whether the *Wane* be, or *Increase,*
Best to sett *Garlick,* or sow *Pease.*
Who first found out the *Man i' th' Moon,*
That to the *Ancients* was unknown;
How many *Dukes,* and *Earls* and *Peers,*
Are in the *Planetary Spheres:*
Their *Airy Empire* and command
Their sev'ral strengths by Sea and Land;
What factions th' have, and what they drive **at**

In publick Vogue, and what in private;
With what Designs and Interests,
Each Party manages Contests.
He made an *Instrument* to know
If the *Moon* shine at full or no,
That would as soon as e're she shon, strait
Whether 'twere Day or Night demonstrate;
Tell what her *D'ameter* t' an Inch is,
And prove she is not made of *Green Cheese.*
It would demonstrate, that the *Man in
The Moon*'s a *Sea Mediterranean.*
And that it is no *Dog,* nor *Bitch,*
That stands behind him at his breech;
But a huge *Caspian Sea,* or *Lake*
With *Arms* which Men for *Legs* mistake,
How large a *Gulph* his Tail composes,
And what a goodly *Bay* his Nose is;
How many *German* Leagues by th' scale,
Cape-Snout's from *Promontory-Tayl:*
He made a *Planetary Gin*
Which *Rats* would run their cwn heads in,
And come o' purpose to be taken,
Without th' expence of Cheese or Bacon;
With *Lute-strings* he would counterfeit
Maggots, that crawl on dish of meat,
Quote Moles and Spots, on any place
O' th' body, by the *Index-face:*
Detect lost *Maidenheads,* by sneezing,
Or breaking wind, of *Dames,* or pissing.
Cure *Warts* and *Corns,* with application
Of *Med'cines,* to th' *Imagination.*
Fright *Agues* into *Dogs,* and scare
With *Rimes,* the *Tooth-ach* and *Catarrh.*
Chase evil *spirits* away by dint
Of *Cickle Horseshooe, Hollow-flint.*

Spit fire out of a *Walnut-shell*,
Which made the *Roman* Slaves rebell.
And fire a Mine in *China*, here,
With Sympathetick *Gunpowder*.
He knew whats'ever's to be known,
But much more then he knew, would own.
What Med'cine 'twas that *Paracelsus*
Could make a man with, as he tells us.
What figur'd *Slats* are best to make,
On wat'ry surface, *Duck* or *Drake*.
What *Bowling-stones*, in running race
Upon a *Board*, have swiftest pace.
Whether a *Pulse* beat in the black
List, of a Dapl'd *Louse's* back.
If *Systole* or *Diastole* move
Quickest, when he's in wrath, or love:
When two of them do run a race,
Whether they *Gallop*, *Trot*, or *Pace*.
How many scores a *Flea* will jump,
Of his own length, from Head to Rump;
Which *Socrates*, and *Chærephon*
In vain, essay'd so long agon;
Whether his *Snout* a perfect *Nose* is,
And not an Elephants *Proboscis*,
How many different *Specieses*
Of Maggots breed in rotten Cheese,
And which are next of kin to those,
Engendred in a *Chandler's* nose.
Or those not seen, but understood,
That live in *Vineger* and *Wood*.

(Part II, canto iii, lines 199–322)

Robert Herrick

(1591–1674)

The Argument of His Book

I sing of *Brooks,* of *Blossomes, Birds,* and *Bowers:*
Of *April, May,* of *June,* and *July-*Flowers.
I sing of *May-poles, Hock-carts, Wassails, Wakes,*
Of *Bride-grooms, Brides,* and of their *Bridall-cakes.*
I write of *Youth,* of *Love,* and have Accesse
By these, to sing of cleanly-*Wantonnesse.*
I sing of *Dewes,* of *Raines,* and piece by piece
Of *Balme,* of *Oyle,* of *Spice,* and *Amber-Greece.*
I sing of *Times trans-shifting;* and I write
How *Roses* first came *Red,* and *Lillies White.*
I write of *Groves,* of *Twilights,* and I sing
The Court of *Mab,* and of the *Fairie-King.*
I write of *Hell;* I sing (and ever shall)
Of *Heaven,* and hope to have it after all.

To Daffadills

Faire Daffadills, we weep to see
    You haste away so soone:
As yet the early-rising Sun
    Has not attain'd his Noone.
        Stay, stay,
    Untill the hasting day
        Has run

168

But to the Even-song;
And, having pray'd together, we
        Will goe with you along.

We have short time to stay, as you,
    We have as short a Spring;
As quick a growth to meet Decay,
    As you, or any thing.
        We die,
        As your hours doe, and drie
            Away,
    Like to the Summers raine;
Or as the pearles of Mornings dew
    Ne'r to be found againe.

To Anthea

Now is the time, when all the lights wax dim;
And thou (*Anthea*) must withdraw from him
Who was thy servant. Dearest, bury me
Under that *Holy-oke,* or *Gospel-tree:*
Where (though thou see'st not) thou may'st think upon
Me, when thou yeerly go'st Procession:
Or for mine honour, lay me in that Tombe
In which thy sacred Reliques shall have roome:
For my Embalming (Sweetest) there will be
No Spices wanting, when I'm laid by thee.

Upon Julia's Clothes

When as in silks my *Julia* goes,
Then, then (me thinks) how sweetly flowes
That liquefaction of her clothes.

Next, when I cast mine eyes and see
That brave Vibration each way free;
O how that glittering taketh me!

The Night-Piece, to Julia

Her Eyes the Glow-worme lend thee,
The Shooting Starres attend thee;
    And the Elves also,
    Whose little eyes glow,
Like the sparks of fire, befriend thee.

No *Will-o'-th'-Wispe* mis-light thee;
Nor Snake, or Slow-worme bite thee:
    But on, on thy way
    Not making a stay,
Since Ghost ther's none to affright thee.

Let not the darke thee cumber;
What though the Moon do's slumber?
    The Starres of the night
    Will lend thee their light,
Like Tapers cleare without number.

Then *Julia* let me wooe thee,
Thus, thus to come unto me:
    And when I shall meet
    Thy silv'ry feet,
My soule Ile poure into thee.

A Conjuration, to Electra

By those soft Tods of wooll
With which the aire is full:
By all those Tinctures there,
That paint the Hemisphere:
By Dewes and drisling Raine,
That swell the Golden Graine:
By all those sweets that be
I' th' flowrie Nunnerie:
By silent Nights, and the
Three Formes of Heccate:
By all Aspects that blesse
The sober Sorceresse,
While juice she straines, and pith
To make her Philters with:
By Time, that hastens on
Things to perfection:
And by your self, the best
Conjurement of the rest:
O my Electra! be
In love with none but me.

The Lilly in a Christal

You have beheld a smiling *Rose*
	When Virgins hands have drawn
	O'r it a Cobweb-Lawne:
And here, you see, this Lilly shows,

Tomb'd in a *Christal* stone,
More faire in this transparent case,
Then when it grew alone;
And had but single grace.

You see how *Creame* but naked is;
Nor daunces in the eye
Without a Strawberrie:
Or some fine tincture, like to this,
Which draws the sight thereto,
More by that wantoning with it;
Then when the paler hieu
No mixture did admit.

You see how *Amber* through the streams
More gently stroaks the sight,
With some conceal'd delight;
Then when he darts his radiant beams
Into the boundlesse aire:
Where either too much light his worth
Doth all at once impaire,
Or set it little forth.

Put Purple Grapes, or Cherries in-
To Glasse, and they will send
More beauty to commend
Them, from that cleane and subtile skin,
Then if they naked stood,
And had no other pride at all,
But their own flesh and blood,
And tinctures naturall.

Thus Lillie, Rose, Grape, Cherry, Creame,
And Straw-berry do stir
More love, when they transfer
A weak, a soft, a broken beame;
Then if they sho'd discover

At full their proper excellence;
    Without some Scean cast over,
    To juggle with the sense.

Thus let this *Christal'd Lillie* be
    A Rule, how far to teach,
    Your nakednesse must reach:
And that, no further, then we see
    Those glaring colours laid
By Arts wise hand, but to this end
    They sho'd obey a shade;
    Lest they too far extend.

So though y'are white as Swan, or Snow,
    And have the power to move
    A world of men to love:
Yet, when your Lawns and Silks shal flow;
    And that white cloud divide
Into a doubtful Twi-light; then,
    Then will your hidden Pride
    Raise greater fires in men.

To Meddowes

Ye have been fresh and green,
    Ye have been fill'd with flowers:
And ye the Walks have been
    Where Maids have spent their houres.

You have beheld, how they
    With *Wicker Arks* did come
To kisse, and beare away
    The richer Couslips home.

Y'ave heard them sweetly sing,
   And seen them in a Round:
Each Virgin, like a Spring,
   With Hony-succles crown'd.

But now, we see, none here,
   Whose silv'rie feet did tread,
And with dishevell'd Haire,
   Adorn'd this smoother Mead.

Like Unthrifts, having spent,
   Your stock, and needy grown,
Y'are left here to lament
   Your poore estates, alone.

To the Virgins, to Make Much of Time

Gather ye Rose-buds while ye may,
   Old Time is still a flying:
And this same flower that smiles to day,
   To morrow will be dying.

The glorious Lamp of Heaven, the Sun,
   The higher he's a getting;
The sooner will his Race be run,
   And neerer he's to Setting.

That Age is best, which is the first,
   When Youth and Blood are warmer;
But being spent, the worse, and worst
   Times, still succeed the former.

Then be not coy, but use your time;
   And while ye may, goe marry:
For having lost but once your prime,
   You may for ever tarry.

Corinna's Going a Maying

Get up, get up for shame, the Blooming Morne
Upon her wings presents the god unshorne.
     See how *Aurora* throwes her faire
     Fresh-quilted colours through the aire:
     Get up, sweet-Slug-a-bed, and see
     The Dew-bespangling Herbe and Tree.
Each Flower has wept, and bow'd toward the East,
Above an houre since; yet you not drest,
     Nay! not so much as out of bed?
     When all the Birds have Mattens seyd,
     And sung their thankfull Hymnes: 'tis sin,
     Nay, profanation to keep in,
When as a thousand Virgins on this day,
Spring, sooner then the Lark, to fetch in May.

Rise; and put on your Foliage, and be seene
To come forth, like the Spring-time, fresh and greene;
     And sweet as *Flora*. Take no care
     For Jewels for your Gowne, or Haire:
     Feare not; the leaves will strew
     Gemms in abundance upon you:
Besides, the childhood of the Day has kept,
Against you come, some *Orient Pearls* unwept:
     Come, and receive them while the light
     Hangs on the Dew-locks of the night:
     And *Titan* on the Eastern hill
     Retires himselfe, or else stands still
Till you come forth. Wash, dresse, be briefe in praying:
Few Beads are best, when once we goe a Maying.

Come, my *Corinna*, come; and comming, marke
How each field turns a street; each street a Parke
    Made green, and trimm'd with trees: see how
    Devotion gives each House a Bough,
    Or Branch: Each Porch, each doore, ere this,
    An Arke a Tabernacle is
Made up of white-thorn neatly enterwove;
As if here were those cooler shades of love.
    Can such delights be in the street,
    And open fields, and we not see't?
    Come, we'll abroad; and let's obay
    The Proclamation made for May:
And sin no more, as we have done, by staying;
But my *Corinna,* come, let's goe a Maying.

There's not a budding Boy, or Girle, this day,
But is got up, and gone to bring in May.
    A deale of Youth, ere this, is come
    Back, and with *White-thorn* laden home.
    Some have dispatcht their Cakes and Creame,
    Before that we have left to dreame:
And some have wept, and woo'd, and plighted Troth,
And chose their Priest, ere we can cast off sloth:
    Many a green-gown has been given;
    Many a kisse, both odde and even:
    Many a glance too has been sent
    From out the eye, Loves Firmament:
Many a jest told of the Keyes betraying
This night, and Locks pickt, yet w'are not a Maying.

Come, let us goe, while we are in our prime;
And take the harmlesse follie of the time.
    We shall grow old apace, and die
    Before we know our liberty.
    Our life is short; and our dayes run
    As fast away as do's the Sunne:

And as a vapour, or a drop of raine
Once lost, can ne'r be found againe:
    So when or you or I are made
    A fable, song, or fleeting shade;
    All love, all liking, all delight
    Lies drown'd with us in endlesse night.
Then while time serves, and we are but decaying;
Come, my *Corinna*, come, let's goe a Maying.

A *Nuptiall Song, or Epithalamie, on Sir Clipseby Crew and His Lady*

What's that we see from far? the spring of Day
Bloom'd from the East, of faire Injewel'd May
    Blowne out of April; or some New-
    Star fill'd with glory to our view,
        Reaching at heaven,
To adde a nobler Planet to the seven?
    Say, or doe we not descrie
Some Goddesse, in a cloud of Tiffanie
        To move, or rather the
    Emergent *Venus* from the Sea?

'Tis she! 'tis she! or else some more Divine
Enlightned substance; mark how from the Shrine
    Of holy Saints she paces on,
    Treading upon *Vermilion*
        And *Amber;* Spice-
ing the Chafte Aire with fumes of Paradise.
    Then come on, come on, and yeeld
A savour like unto a blessed field,
        When the bedabled Morne
    Washes the golden eares of corne.

See where she comes; and smell how all the street
Breathes Vine-yards and Pomgranats: O how sweet!
    As a fir'd Altar, is each stone,
    Perspiring pounded Cynamon.
           The Phenix nest,
Built up of odours, burneth in her breast.
    Who therein wo'd not consume
His soule to Ash-heaps in that rich perfume?
        Bestroaking Fate the while
    He burnes to Embers on the Pile.

Himen, O Himen! Tread the sacred ground;
Shew thy white feet, and head with Marjoram crown'd:
    Mount up thy flames, and let thy Torch
    Display the Bridegroom in the porch,
        In his desires
More towring, more disparkling then thy fires:
    Shew her how his eyes do turne
And roule about, and in their motions burne
        Their balls to Cindars: haste,
    Or else to ashes he will waste.

Glide by the banks of Virgins then, and passe
The Shewers of Roses, lucky-foure-leav'd grasse:
    The while the cloud of younglings sing,
    And drown yee with a flowrie Spring:
        While some repeat
Your praise, and bless you, sprinkling you with Wheat:
    While that others doe divine;
Blest is the Bride, on whom the Sun doth shine;
        And thousands gladly wish
    You multiply, as doth a Fish.

And beautious Bride we do confess y'are wise,
In dealing forth these bashfull jealousies:
    In Lov's name do so; and a price

Set on your selfe, by being nice:
            But yet take heed;
What now you seem, be not the same indeed,
      And turne *Apostate:* Love will
Part of the way be met; or sit stone-still.
           On then, and though you slow-
      ly go, yet, howsoever, go.

And now y'are enter'd; see the Codled Cook
Runs from his *Torrid Zone*, to prie, and look,
      And blesse his dainty Mistresse: see,
      The Aged point out, This is she,
            Who now must sway
The House (Love shield her) with her Yea and Nay:
      And the smirk Butler thinks it
Sin, in's Nap'rie, not to express his wit;
           Each striving to devise
      Some gin, wherewith to catch your eyes.

To bed, to bed, kind Turtles, now, and write
This the shortest day, and this the longest night;
      But yet too short for you: 'tis we,
      Who count this night as long as three,
           Lying alone,
Telling the Clock strike Ten, Eleven, Twelve, One.
      Quickly, quickly then prepare;
And let the Young-men and the Bride-maids share
           Your Garters; and their joynts
      Encircle with the Bride-grooms Points.

By the Brides eyes, and by the teeming life
Of her green hopes, we charge ye, that no strife,
      (Farther then Gentlenes tends) gets place
      Among ye, striving for her lace:
           O doe not fall
Foule in these noble pastimes, lest ye call
      Discord in, and so divide

The youthfull Bride-groom, and the fragrant Bride:
      Which Love fore-fend, but spoken
  Be't to your praise, no peace was broken.

Strip her of Spring-time, tender-whimpring-maids,
Now *Autumne's* come, when all those flowrie aids
    Of her Delayes must end; Dispose
      That *Lady-smock,* that *Pansie,* and that *Rose*
        Neatly apart;
But for *Prick-madam,* and for *Gentle-heart;*
    And soft-*Maidens-blush,* the Bride
Makes holy these, all others lay aside:
      Then strip her, or unto her
  Let him come, who dares undo her.

And to enchant yee more, see every where
About the Roofe a *Syren* in a Sphere;
    (As we think) singing to the dinne
    Of many a warbling *Cherubim:*
      O marke yee how
The soule of Nature melts in numbers: now
    See, a thousand *Cupids* flye,
To light their Tapers at the Brides bright eye.
      To Bed; or her they'l tire,
  Were she an Element of fire.

And to your more bewitching, see, the proud
Plumpe Bed beare up, and swelling like a cloud,
    Tempting the two too modest; can
    Yee see it brusle like a Swan,
      And you be cold
To meet it, when it woo's and seemes to fold
    The Armes to hugge it? throw, throw
Your selves into the mighty over-flow
      Of that white Pride, and Drowne
  The night, with you, in floods of Downe.

The bed is ready, and the maze of Love
Lookes for the treaders; every where is wove
    Wit and new misterie; read, and
    Put in practise, to understand
            And know each wile,
Each hieroglyphick of a kisse or smile;
    And do it to the full; reach
High in your own conceipt, and some way teach
        Nature and Art, one more
    Play then they ever knew before.

If needs we must for Ceremonies-sake,
Blesse a *Sack-posset;* Luck go with it; take
    The Night-Charme quickly; you have spells,
    And magicks for to end, and hells,
          To passe; but such
And of such Torture as no one would grutch
    To live therein for ever: Frie
And consume, and grow again to die,
        And live, and in that case,
    Love the confusion of the place.

But since It must be done, dispatch, and sowe
Up in a sheet your Bride, and what if so
    It be with Rock, or walles of Brasse,
    Ye Towre her up, as *Danae* was;
         Thinke you that this,
Or hell it selfe a powerfull Bulwarke is?
    I tell yee no; but like a
Bold bolt of thunder he will make his way,
        And rend the cloud, and throw
    The sheet about, like flakes of snow.

All now is husht in silence; *Midwife-moone,*
With all her *Owle-ey'd* issue begs a boon
    Which you must grant; that's entrance; with

Which extract, all we can call pith
        And quintiscence
Of Planetary bodies; so commence
    All faire *Constellations*
Looking upon yee, That two Nations
        Springing from two such Fires,
    May blaze the vertue of their Sires.

An *Epitaph* upon a *Virgin*

Here a solemne Fast we keepe,
While all beauty lyes asleep
Husht be all things; (no noyse here)
But the toning of a teare:
Or a sigh of such as bring
Cowslips for her covering.

A *Ternarie* of *Littles,*
upon a *Pipkin* of *Jellie* Sent to a *Lady*

A little Saint best fits a little Shrine,
A little prop best fits a little Vine,
As my small Cruse best fits my little Wine.

A little Seed best fits a little Soyle,
A little Trade best fits a little Toyle:
As my small Jarre best fits my little Oyle.

A little Bin best fits a little Bread,
A little Garland fits a little Head:
As my small stuffe best fits my little Shed.

A little Hearth best fits a little Fire,
A little Chappell fits a little Quire,
As my small Bell best fits my little Spire.

A little streame best fits a little Boat;
A little lead best fits a little Float;
As my small Pipe best fits my little note.

A little meat best fits a little bellie,
As sweetly Lady, give me leave to tell ye,
This little Pipkin fits this little Jellie.

Lovers How They Come and Part

A *Gyges* Ring they beare about them still,
To be, and not seen when and where they will.
They tread on clouds, and though they sometimes fall,
They fall like dew, but make no noise at all.
So silently they one to th' other come,
As colours steale into the Peare or Plum,
And Aire-like, leave no pression to be seen
Where e're they met, or parting place has been.

His Sailing from Julia

When that day comes, whose evening sayes I'm gone
Unto that watrie Desolation:
Devoutly to thy Closet-gods then pray,
That my wing'd Ship may meet no Remora.
Those Deities which circum-walk the Seas,
And look upon our dreadfull passages,

Will from all dangers re-deliver me,
For one drink offering pourèd out by thee.
Mercie and Truth live with thee! and forbeare
(In my short absence) to unsluce a teare:
But yet for Loves-sake, let thy lips doe this,
Give my dead picture one engendring kisse:
Work that to life, and let me ever dwell
In thy remembrance (Julia). So farewell.

To His Conscience

Can I not sin, but thou wilt be
My private *Protonotarie?*
Can I not wooe thee to passe by
A short and sweet iniquity?
I'le cast a mist and cloud, upon
My delicate transgression,
So utter dark, as that no eye
Shall see the hug'd impietie:
Gifts blind the wise, and bribes do please,
And winde all other witnesses:
And wilt not thou, with gold, be ti'd
To lay thy pen and ink aside?
That in the mirk and tonguelesse night,
Wanton I may, and thou not write?
It will not be: And, therefore, now,
For times to come, I'le make this Vow,
From aberrations to live free;
So I'le not feare the Judge, or thee.

Thomas Carew

(1595?–1639?)

The Spring

Now that the winter's gone, the earth hath lost
Her snow-white robes; and now no more the frost
Candies the grasse, or casts an ycie creame
Upon the silver lake or chrystall streame:
But the warme sunne thawes the benummed earth,
And makes it tender; gives a second birth
To the dead swallow; wakes in hollow tree
The drowsie cuckow and the humble-bee.
Now doe a quire of chirping minstrels sing,
In tryumph to the world, the youthfull Spring:
The vallies, hills, and woods in rich araye
Welcome the comming of the long'd-for May.
Now all things smile; onely my Love doth lowre;
Nor hath the scalding noon-day sunne the power
To melt that marble yce, which still doth hold
Her heart congeal'd, and makes her pittie cold.
The oxe, which lately did for shelter flie
Into the stall, doth now securely lie
In open field; and love no more is made
By the fire-side, but in the cooler shade.
Amyntas now doth by his Cloris sleepe
Under a sycamoure, and all things keepe
Time with the season: only shee doth carry
June in her eyes, in her heart January.

185

Epitaph on Maria Wentworth

Loe here the precious dust is laid,
Whose purely tempered Clay was made
So fine, that it the guest betraid.

Else the Soul grew so fast within,
It broke the outward shell of sin,
And so was hatch'd a Cherubin.

In height it soar'd to God above;
In depth, it did to knowledge move,
And spread in breadth to general love.

Before a pious Duty shin'd
To Parents, courtesie behind,
On either side an equal mind.

Good to the poor, to kindred dear,
To servants kind, to friendship clear,
To nothing but her self severe.

So though a Virgin, yet a Bride
To every Grace she justify'd
A chaste Polygamy, and dy'd.

Learn from hence (Reader) what small trust
We owe this world, where vertue must
Frail as our flesh crumble to dust.

A Song

Aske me no more where Jove bestowes,
When June is past, the fading rose;
For in your beautie's orient deepe
These flowers, as in their causes, sleepe.

Aske me no more whither doth stray
The golden atoms of the day;
For, in pure love, heaven did prepare
Those powders to inrich your haire.

Aske me no more whither doth hast
The nightingale when May is past;
For in your sweet dividing throat
She winters and keepes warme her note.

Aske me no more where those starres light,
That downewards fall in dead of night;
For in your eyes they sit, and there
Fixed become as in their sphere.

Aske me no more if east or west
The Phenix builds her spicy nest;
For unto you at last shee flies,
And in your fragrant bosome dyes.

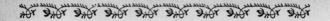

Sir John Suckling

(1609–1642)

Song

Why so pale and wan, fond Lover?
    Prethee why so pale?
Will, when looking well can't move her,
    Looking ill prevail;
    Prethee why so pale?

Why so dull and mute young Sinner?
    Prethee why so mute?
Will, when speaking well can't win her,
    Saying nothing do't:
    Prethee why so mute?

Quit, quit for shame, this will not move,
    This cannot take her;
If of her selfe she will not love,
    Nothing can make her:
    The Devil take her.

Sonnet

Oh! for some honest Lovers Ghost,
    Some kind unbodied post
    Sent from the shades below!

188

I strangely long to know
Whether the nobler Chaplets wear,
Those that their mistress scorn did bear,
    Or those that were us'd kindly.

For what so e'ere they tell us here
    To make those sufferings dear,
    'Twill there I fear be found,
    That to the being crown'd
T'have lov'd alone will not suffice,
Unless we also have been wise,
    And have our loves enjoy'd.

What posture can we think him in,
    That here unlov'd agen
    Departs, and's thither gone
    Where each sits by his own?
On how can that *Elizium* be
Where I my Mistress still must see
    Circled in others Arms.

For there the Judges all are just,
    And *Sophonisba* must
    Be his whom she held dear;
    Not his who lov'd her here:
The sweet *Philoclea* since she dy'd,
Lies by her Pirocles his side,
    Not by *Amphialus.*

Some Bayes (perchance) or Myrtle bough
    For difference crowns the brow
    Of those kind souls that were
    The noble Martyrs here;
And if that be the only odds
(As who can tell) the kinder Gods,
    Give me the woman here.

That none beguiled be

That none beguiled be by times quick flowing,
Lovers have in their hearts a clock still going;
    For though time be nimble, his motions
                Are quicker
                And thicker
    Where love hath his notions:

Hope is the main-spring on which moves desire,
And these do the less wheels, Fear, Joy, inspire;
    The ballance is thought, evermore
                Clicking
                And striking,
    And ne're giving o're.

Occasion's the hand which still's moving round,
Till by it the critical hour may be found,
    And when that falls out, it will strike
                Kisses,
                Strange blisses,
    And what you best like.

'Tis now since I sate down

'Tis now since I sate down before
    That foolish Fort, a heart;
(Time strangely spent) a year, and more,
    And still I did my part:

Made my approaches, from her hand
    Unto her lip did rise,

And did already understand
    The language of her eyes.

Proceeded on with no less Art,
    My Tongue was Engineer;
I thought to undermine the heart
    By whispering in the ear.

When this did nothing, I brought down
    Great Cannon-oaths, and shot
A thousand thousand to the Town,
    And still it yielded not.

I then resolv'd to starve the place
    By cutting off all kisses,
Praying and gazing on her face,
    And all such little blisses.

To draw her out, and from her strength,
    I drew all batteries in:
And brought my self to lye at length
    As if no siege had been.

When I had done what man could do,
    And thought the place mine own,
The Enemy lay quiet too,
    And smil'd at all was done.

I sent to know from whence and where,
    These hopes, and this relief?
A Spy inform'd, Honor was there,
    And did command in chief.

March, march (quoth I) the word straight give,
    Lets lose no time but leave her;
The Giant upon air will live,
    And hold it out for ever.

To such a place our Camp remove
　　As will no siege abide;
I hate a fool that starves her Love
　　Onely to feed her pride.

Out upon it

Out upon it, I have lov'd
　　Three whole days together;
And am like to love three more,
　　If it prove fair weather.

Time shall moult away his wings
　　Ere he shall discover
In the whole wide world agen
　　Such a constant Lover.

But the spite on't is, no praise
　　Is due at all to me:
Love with me had made no staies,
　　Had it any been but she.

Had it any been but she,
　　And that very Face,
There had been at least ere this
　　A dozen dozen in her place.

Richard Lovelace

(1618–1657)

To Lucasta, Going to the Warres

Tell me not (Sweet) I am unkinde,
    That from the Nunnerie
Of thy chaste breast, and quiet minde,
    To Warre and Armes I flie.

True; a new Mistresse now I chase,
    The first Foe in the Field;
And with a stronger Faith imbrace
    A Sword, a Horse, a Shield.

Yet this Inconstancy is such,
    As you too shall adore;
I could not love thee (Deare) so much,
    Lov'd I not Honour more.

To My Truly Valiant, Learned Friend, Who in His Book Resolv'd the Art Gladiatory into the Mathematics

Hark, Reader! wilt be learn'd i' th' wars?
    A gen'ral in a gown?
Strike a league with Arts and Scarres,
    And snatch from each a Crowne?

Wouldst be a wonder? Such a one
 As should win with a Looke?
A Bishop in a garison,
 And Conquer by the Booke?

Take then this Mathematick shield,
 And henceforth by its rules,
Be able to dispute i' th' field,
 And Combate in the Schooles.

Whilst peaceful Learning once againe,
 And the Souldier so concord,
As that he fights now with her Penne,
 And she writes with his Sword.

La Bella Bona Roba

I cannot tell who loves the Skeleton
Of a poor Marmoset, nought but boan, boan.
Give me a nakednesse with her cloath's on.

Such whose white-sattin upper coat of skin,
Cuts upon Velvet rich Incarnadin,
Ha's yet a Body (and of Flesh) within.

Sure it is meant good Husbandry in men,
Who do incorporate with Aëry leane,
T' repair their sides, and get their Ribb agen.

Hard hap unto that Huntsman that Decrees
Fat joys for all his swet, when as he sees,
After his 'Say, nought but his Keepers Fees.

Then Love I beg, when next thou tak'st thy Bow,
Thy angry shafts, and dost Heart-chasing go,
Passe *Rascall Deare*, strike me the largest Doe.

Lucasta Laughing

Heark how she laughs aloud,
    Although the world puts on its shrowd;
Wept at by the fantastick Crowd,
    Who cry, One drop let fall
From her, might save the Universal Ball.
            She laughs again
        At our ridiculous pain;
    And at our merry misery
        She laughs until she cry;
            Sages, forbear
        That ill-contrived tear,
            Although your fear,
Doth barricadoe Hope from your soft Ear.
That which still makes her mirth to flow,
    Is our sinister-handed woe,
Which downwards on its head doth go;
    And ere that it is sown, doth grow.
        This makes her spleen contract,
            And her just pleasure feast;
        For the unjustest act
            Is still the pleasant'st jest.

The Snayl

Wise Emblem of our Politick World,
Sage Snayl, within thine own self curl'd;
Instruct me softly to make hast,
Whilst these my Feet go slowly fast.

Compendious Snayl! thou seem'st to me,
Large *Euclids* strickt Epitome;
And in each Diagram, dost Fling
Thee from the point unto the Ring.
A Figure now Triangulare,
An Oval now, and now a Square;
And then a Serpentine doth crawl
Now a straight Line, now crook'd, now all.

 Preventing Rival of the Day,
Th'art up and openest thy Ray,
And ere the Morn cradles the Moon,
Th'art broke into a Beauteous Noon.
Then when the Sun sups in the Deep,
Thy Silver Horns e're *Cinthia's* peep;
And thou from thine own liquid Bed
New *Phœbus* heav'st thy pleasant Head.

 Who shall a Name for thee create,
Deep Riddle of Mysterious State?
Bold Nature that gives common Birth
To all products of Seas and Earth,
Of thee, as Earth-quakes, is affraid,
Now will thy dire Deliv'ry aid.

 Thou thine own daughter then, and Sire,
That Son and Mother art intire,
That big still with thy self dost go,
And liv'st an aged Embrio;
That like the Cubbs of *India*,
Thou from thy self a while dost play:
But frighted with a Dog or Gun,
In thine own Belly thou dost run,
And as thy House was thine own womb,
So thine own womb, concludes thy tomb.

 But now I must (analys'd King)
Thy Œconomick Virtues sing;
Thou great stay'd Husband still within,

Thou, thee, that's thine dost Discipline;
And when thou art to progress bent,
Thou mov'st thy self and tenement,
As Warlike *Scythians* travayl'd, you
Remove your Men and City too;
Then after a sad Dearth and Rain,
Thou scatterest thy Silver Train;
And when the Trees grow nak'd and old,
Thou cloathest them with Cloth of Gold,
Which from thy Bowels thou dost spin,
And draw from the rich Mines within.
    Now hast thou chang'd thee Saint; and made
Thy self a Fane that's cupula'd;
And in thy wreathed Cloister thou
Walkest thine own Gray fryer too;
Strickt, and lock'd up, th'art Hood all ore
And ne'r Eliminat'st thy Dore.
On Sallads thou dost feed severe,
And 'stead of Beads thou drop'st a tear,
And when to rest, each calls the Bell,
Thou sleep'st within thy Marble Cell;
Where in dark contemplation plac'd,
The sweets of Nature thou dost tast;
Who now with Time thy days resolve,
And in a Jelly thee dissolve.
Like a shot Star, which doth repair
Upward, and Rarifie the Air.

Another

The Centaur, Syren, I foregoe,
Those have been sung, and lowdly too;
Nor of the mixed Sphynx Ile write,

Nor the renown'd Hermaphrodite:
Behold, this Huddle doth appear
Of Horses, Coach, and Charioteer;
That moveth him by traverse Law,
And doth himself both drive and draw;
Then when the Sun the South doth winne,
He baits him hot in his own Inne;
I heard a grave and austere Clark,
Resolv'd him Pilot both and Barque;
That like the fam'd Ship of *Trevere*,
Did on the Shore himself Lavere:
Yet the Authentick do beleeve,
Who keep their Judgement in their Sleeve,
That he is his own Double man,
And sick, still carries his Sedan:
Or that like Dames i' th' Land of Luyck,
He wears his everlasting Huyck:
But banisht, I admire his fate
Since neither Ostracisme of State,
Nor a perpetual exile,
Can force this Virtue change his Soyl;
For wheresoever he doth go,
He wanders with his Country too.

A Loose Saraband

Nay, prethee Dear, draw nigher,
    Yet closer, nigher yet;
Here is a double Fire,
    A dry one and a wet:
True lasting Heavenly Fuel
Puts out the Vestal jewel,

When once we twining marry
Mad Love with wilde Canary.

Off with that crowned Venice
   'Till all the House does flame,
Wee'l quench it straight in Rhenish,
   Or what we must not name:
Milk lightning still asswageth,
So when our fury rageth,
As th'only means to cross it,
Wee'l drown it in Love's posset.

Love never was Well-willer,
   Unto my Nag or mee,
Ne'r watter'd us i'th' Cellar,
   But the cheap Buttery:
At th'head of his own Barrells,
Where broach'd are all his Quarrels,
Should a true noble Master
Still make his Guest his Taster.

See all the World how't staggers,
   More ugly drunk than we,
As if far gone in daggers,
   And blood it seem'd to be:
We drink our glass of Roses,
Which nought but sweet discloses,
Then in our Loyal Chamber,
Refresh us with Loves Amber.

Now tell me, thou fair Cripple,
   That dumb canst scarcely see
Th'almightinesse of Tipple,
   And th' ods 'twixt thee and thee:
What of Elizium's missing?
Still Drinking and still Kissing;

Adoring plump *October;*
Lord! what is man and Sober?

Now, is there such a Trifle
　　As Honour, the fools Gyant?
What is there left to rifle,
　　When Wine makes all parts plyant?
Let others Glory follow,
In their false riches wallow,
And with their grief be merry;
Leave me but Love and Sherry.

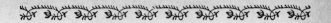

Edmund Waller

(1606–1687)

Song

Go lovely Rose,
Tell her that wastes her time and me,
  That now she knows
When I resemble her to thee,
  How sweet and fair she seems to be.

  Tell her that's young,
And shuns to have her Graces spy'd,
  That hadst thou sprung
In Desarts, where no men abide,
  Thou must have uncommended dy'd.

  Small is the worth
Of Beauty from the light retir'd;
  Bid her come forth,
Suffer her self to be desir'd,
  And not blush so to be admir'd.

  Then die, that she,
The common fate of all things rare,
  May read in thee
How small a part of time they share,
  That are so wondrous sweet and fair.

Of a Fair Lady Playing with a Snake

Strange that such Horror and such Grace
Should dwell together in one place,
A Furies Arm, an Angels Face.

'Tis innocence and youth which makes
In *Chloris's* fancy such mistakes,
To start at Love, and play with Snakes.

By this and by her coldness barr'd,
Her servants have a task too hard,
The Tyrant has a double guard.

Thrice happy Snake, that in her sleeve
May boldly creep, we dare not give
Our thoughts so unconfin'd a leave:

Contented in that nest of Snow
He lies, as he his bliss did know,
And to the wood no more would go.

Take heed, (fair *Eve*) you do not make
Another Tempter of this Snake,
A marble one so warm'd would speak.

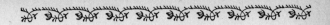

Charles Cotton

(1630–1687)

Resolution in Four Sonnets, of a Poetical Question Put to Me by a Friend, Concerning Four Rural Sisters

I

Alice is tall and upright as a Pine,
White as blaunch'd Almonds, or the falling Snow,
Sweet as are Damask Roses when they blow,
And doubtless fruitful as the swelling Vine.

Ripe to be cut, and ready to be press'd,
Her full cheek'd beauties very well appear,
And a year's fruit she loses e'ery year,
Wanting a man t'improve her to the best.

Full fain she would be husbanded, and yet,
Alas! she cannot a fit Lab'rer get
To cultivate her to her own content:

Fain would she be (God wot) about her task,
And yet (forsooth) she is too proud to ask,
And (which is worse) too modest to consent.

II

Marg'ret of humbler stature by the head
Is (as it oft falls out with yellow hair)

203

Than her fair Sister, yet so much more fair,
As her pure white is better mixt with red.

This, hotter than the other ten to one,
Longs to be put unto her Mothers trade,
And loud proclaims she lives too long a Maid,
Wishing for one t'untie her Virgin Zone.

She finds Virginity a kind of ware
That's very very troublesome to bear,
And being gone, she thinks will ne'er be mist:

And yet withall the Girl has so much grace,
To call for help I know she wants the face,
Though ask'd, I know not how she would resist.

III

Mary is black, and taller than the last,
Yet equal in perfection and desire,
To the one's melting snow, and t'other's fire,
As with whose black their fairness is defac'd:

She pants as much for love as th'other two,
But she so vertuous is, or else so wise,
That she will win or will not love a prize,
And but upon good terms will never doe:

Therefore who her will conquer ought to be
At least as full of love and wit as she,
Or he shall ne'er gain favour at her hands:

Nay, though he have a pretty store of brains,
Shall only have his labour for his pains,
Unless he offer more than she demands.

IV

Martha is not so tall, nor yet so fair
As any of the other lovely three,
Her chiefest Grace is poor simplicity,
Yet were the rest away, she were a Star.

She's fair enough, only she wants the art
To set her Beauties off as they can doe,
And that's the cause she ne'er heard any woo,
Nor ever yet made conquest of a heart:

And yet her bloud's as boiling as the best,
Which, pretty soul, does so disturb her rest,
And makes her languish so, she's fit to die.

Poor thing, I doubt she still must lie alone,
For being like to be attack'd by none,
Sh'as no more wit to ask than to deny.

Evening

The Day's grown old, the fainting Sun
Has but a little way to run,
And yet his Steeds, with all his skill,
Scarce lug the Chariot down the Hill.

With Labour spent, and Thirst opprest,
Whilst they strain hard to gain the West,
From Fetlocks hot drops melted light,
Which turn the Meteors in the Night.

The Shadows now so long do grow,
That Brambles like tall Cedars show,
Mole-hills seem Mountains, and the Ant
Appears a monstrous Elephant.

A very little little Flock
Shades thrice the ground that it would stock;
Whilst the small Stripling following them,
Appears a mighty *Polypheme*.

These being brought into the Fold,
And by the thrifty Master told,
He thinks his Wages are well paid,
Since none are either lost, or stray'd.

Now lowing Herds are each-where heard,
Chains rattle in the Villains Yard,
The Cart's on Tayl set down to rest,
Bearing on high the Cuckolds Crest.

The hedge is stript, the Clothes brought in,
Nought's left without should be within,
The Bees are hiv'd, and hum their Charm,
Whilst every House does seem a Swarm.

The Cock now to the Roost is prest:
For he must call up all the rest;
The Sow's fast pegg'd within the Sty,
To still her squeaking Progeny.

Each one has had his Supping Mess,
The Cheese is put into the Press,
The Pans and Bowls clean scalded all,
Rear'd up against the Milk-house Wall.

And now on Benches all are sat
In the cool Air to sit and chat,
Till *Phœbus*, dipping in the West,
Shall lead the World the way to Rest.

John Dryden
(1631–1700)

FROM Absalom and Achitophel

Of these the false *Achitophel* was first:
A Name to all succeeding Ages curst.
For close Designs, and crooked Counsels fit;
Sagacious, Bold, and Turbulent of wit:
Restless, unfixt in Principles and Place;
In Pow'r unpleased, impatient of Disgrace.
A fiery Soul, which working out its way,
Fretted the Pigmy-Body to decay;
And o'r informed the Tenement of Clay.
A daring Pilot in extremity;
Pleas'd with the Danger, when the Waves went high
He sought the Storms: but, for a Calm unfit,
Would steer too nigh the Sands, to boast his Wit.
Great Wits are sure to Madness near alli'd;
And thin Partitions do their Bounds divide;
Else, why should he, with Wealth and Honour blest,
Refuse his Age the needfull hours of Rest?
Punish a Body which he cou'd not please,
Bankrupt of Life, yet Prodigal of ease?
And all to leave what with his Toil he won
To that unfeather'd two-legg'd thing, a Son:
Got, while his Soul did huddl'd Notions try;
And born a shapeless Lump, like Anarchy.
In Friendship false, implacable in Hate:
Resolv'd to Ruine or to Rule the State.

To Compass this, the Triple Bond he broke;
The Pillars of the Publick Safety shook:
And fitted *Israel* for a Foreign Yoke.
Then, seiz'd with Fear, yet still affecting Fame,
Usurp'd a Patriot's All-atoning Name.

(Book I, lines 150–79)

   Doeg, though without knowing how or why,
Made still a blund'ring kind of Melody;
Spurd boldly on, and Dash'd through Thick and Thin,
Through Sense and Non-sense, never out nor in;
Free from all meaning, whether good or bad,
And in one word, Heroically mad,
He was too warm on Picking-work to dwell,
But Faggotted his Notions as they fell,
And, if they Rhim'd and Rattl'd, all was well.
Spightfull he is not, though he wrote a Satyr,
For still there goes some *thinking* to ill-Nature:
He needs no more than Birds and Beasts to think,
All his occasions are to eat and drink.
If he call Rogue and Rascal from a Garrat,
He means you no more Mischief than a Parat:
The words for Friend and Foe alike were made,
To Fetter 'em in Verse is all his Trade.
For Almonds he'll cry Whore to his own Mother:
And call young *Absalom* King *David's* Brother.
Let him be Gallows-Free by my consent,
And nothing suffer, since he nothing meant:
Hanging Supposes humane Soul and reason,
This Animal's below committing Treason.
Shall he be hang'd who never cou'd Rebell?
That's a preferment for *Achitophel*.
The Woman that Committed Buggary,
Was rightly Sentenc'd by the Law to die;
But 'twas hard Fate that to the Gallows led

The Dog that never heard the Statute read.
Railing in other Men may be a crime,
But ought to pass for mere instinct in him;
Instinct he follows and no farther knows,
For to write Verse with him is to *Transprose*.
'Twere pity treason at his Door to lay
Who *makes Heaven's gate a Lock to its own Key:*
Let him rayl on, let his invective muse
Have four and Twenty letters to abuse,
Which if he Jumbles to one line of Sense,
Indict him of a Capital Offence.
In Fire-works give him leave to vent his spight,
Those are the only Serpents he can write;
The height of his ambition is we know
But to be Master of a Puppet-show;
On that one Stage his works may yet appear,
And a months Harvest keeps him all the Year.

Now stop your noses, Readers, all and some,
For here's a tun of Midnight work to come,
Og from a Treason Tavern rowling home.
Round as a Globe, and Liquored ev'ry chink,
Goodly and Great he Sayls behind his Link;
With all this Bulk there's nothing lost in *Og*,
For ev'ry inch that is not Fool is Rogue:
A Monstrous mass of foul corrupted matter,
As all the Devils had spew'd to make the batter.
When wine has given him courage to Blaspheme,
He curses God, but God before Curst him;
And if man cou'd have reason, none has more,
That made his Paunch so rich and him so poor.
With wealth he was not trusted, for Heav'n knew
What 'twas of Old to pamper up a *Jew;*
To what would he on Quail and Pheasant swell,
That ev'n on Tripe and Carrion cou'd rebell?

But though Heaven made him poor, (with rev'rence
    speaking,)
He never was a Poet of God's making;
The Midwife laid her hand on his Thick Skull,
With this Prophetick blessing—*Be thou Dull;*
Drink, Swear, and Roar, forbear no lew'd delight
Fit for thy Bulk, doe anything but write.
Thou art of lasting Make, like thoughtless men,
A strong Nativity—but for the Pen;
Eat Opium, mingle Arsenick in thy Drink,
Still thou mayst live, avoiding Pen and Ink.
I see, I see, 'tis Counsell given in vain,
For Treason botcht in Rhime will be thy bane;
Rhime is the Rock on which thou art to wreck,
'Tis fatal to thy Fame and to thy Neck.
Why should thy Metre good King *David* blast?
A Psalm of his will Surely be thy last.
Dar'st thou presume in verse to meet thy foes,
Thou whom the Penny Pamphlet foil'd in prose?
Doeg, whom God for Mankinds mirth has made,
O'er-tops thy tallent in thy very Trade;
Doeg to thee, thy paintings are so Course,
A Poet is, though he's the Poets Horse.
A Double Noose thou on thy Neck dost pull
For Writing Treason and for Writing dull;
To die for Faction is a common Evil,
But to be hang'd for Non-sense is the Devil.
Hadst thou the Glories of thy King exprest,
Thy praises had been Satyr at the best;
But thou in Clumsy verse, unlickt, unpointed,
Hast Shamefully defi'd the Lord's Anointed:
I will not rake the Dunghill of thy Crimes,
For who would reade thy Life that reads thy rhimes?
But of King *David's* Foes be this the Doom,

May all be like the Young-man *Absalom;*
And for my Foes may this their Blessing be,
To talk like *Doeg* and to Write like Thee.

(Book II, lines 412–509)

FROM *The Hind and the Panther*

One evening, while the cooler shade she sought,
Revolving many a melancholy thought,
Alone she walk'd, and look'd around in vain,
With ruful visage for her vanish'd train:
None of her sylvan subjects made their court;
Leveés and coucheés pass'd without resort.
So hardly can Usurpers manage well
Those whom they first instructed to rebel:
More liberty begets desire of more,
The hunger still encreases with the store.
Without respect they brush'd along the wood,
Each in his clan, and fill'd with loathsome food,
Ask'd no permission to the neighbouring flood.
The *Panther,* full of inward discontent,
Since they wou'd goe, before 'em wisely went:
Supplying want of pow'r by drinking first,
As if she gave 'em leave to quench their thirst.
Among the rest, the *Hind,* with fearful face
Beheld from far the common wat'ring place,
Nor durst approach; till with an awful roar
The sovereign *Lyon* bad her fear no more.
Encourag'd thus she brought her younglings nigh,
Watching the motions of her Patron's eye,
And drank a sober draught; the rest amaz'd

Stood mutely still, and on the stranger gaz'd:
Survey'd her part by part, and sought to find
The ten-horn'd monster in the harmless *Hind*,
Such as the *Wolfe* and *Panther* had design'd:
They thought at first they dream'd, for 'twas offence
With them, to question certitude of sense,
Their guide in faith; but nearer when they drew,
And had the faultless object full in view,
Lord, how they all admir'd her heav'nly hiew!
Some, who before her fellowship disdain'd,
Scarce, and but scarce, from in-born rage restrain'd,
Now frisk'd about her and old kindred feign'd.
Whether for love or int'rest, every sect
Of all the salvage nation shew'd respect:
The Vice-roy *Panther* could not awe the herd,
The more the company the less they fear'd.
The surly *Wolfe* with secret envy burst,
Yet cou'd not howl, the *Hind* had seen him first:
But what he durst not speak, the *Panther* durst.
    For when the herd suffis'd, did late repair
To ferney heaths and to their forest lare,
She made a mannerly excuse to stay,
Proff'ring the *Hind* to wait her half the way:
That since the Skie was clear, an hour of talk
Might help her to beguile the tedious walk.
With much good-will the motion was embrac'd,
To chat a while on their adventures pass'd:
Nor had the grateful *Hind* so soon forgot
Her friend and fellow-suff'rer in the plot.
Yet wondring how of late she grew estrang'd,
Her forehead cloudy, and her count'nance chang'd,
She thought this hour th' occasion would present
To learn her secret cause of discontent,
Which, well she hop'd, might be with ease redress'd,
Considering Her a well-bred civil beast,

And more a Gentlewoman than the rest.
After some common talk what rumours ran,
The Lady of the spotted-muff began.

(Part I, lines 511–end)

Dame, said the *Panther*, times are mended well
Since late among the *Philistines* you fell.
The Toils were pitch'd, a spacious tract of ground
With expert Huntsmen was encompass'd round;
The Enclosure narrow'd; the sagacious pow'r
Of Hounds, and Death drew nearer ev'ry Hour.
'Tis true, the younger *Lyon* scap'd the snare,
But all your priestly Calves lay strugling there;
As sacrifices on their Altars laid;
While you their careful mother wisely fled
Not trusting destiny to save your head.
For, whate'er Promises you have apply'd
To your unfailing Church, the surer side
Is four fair Legs in danger to provide.
And whate'er tales of *Peter's* Chair you tell,
Yet, saving Reverence of the Miracle,
The better luck was yours to 'scape so well.
   As I remember, said the sober *Hind*,
Those Toils were for your own dear self design'd,
As well as me; and with the self same throw,
To catch the Quarry and the Vermin too,
(Forgive the sland'rous Tongues that call'd you so).
Howe'er you take it now, the common Cry
Then ran you down for your rank Loyalty;
Besides, in Popery they thought you nurst,
(As evil tongues will ever speak the worst,)
Because some forms, and ceremonies some
You kept, and stood in the main question dumb.
Dumb you were born indeed; but thinking long

The *Test,* it seems, at last has loos'd your tongue.
And, to explain what your forefathers meant,
By real presence in the Sacrament,
(After long fencing push'd against a wall,)
Your *salvo* comes, that he's not there at all:
There chang'd your faith, and what may change may
    fall.
Who can believe what varies every day,
Nor ever was, nor will be at a stay?

    Tortures may force the tongue untruths to tell,
And I ne'er own'd my self infallible,
Reply'd the *Panther;* grant such Presence were,
Yet in your sense I never own'd it there.
A real *vertue* we by faith receive.
And that we in the sacrament believe.

    Then, said the *Hind,* as you the matter state,
Not only *Jesuits* can equivocate;
For *real,* as you now the Word expound,
From Solid Substance dwindles to a Sound.
Methinks an *Esop's* fable you repeat;
You know who took the Shadow for the Meat;
Your Churchs substance thus you change at will,
And yet retain your former figure still.
I freely grant you spoke to save your Life,
For then you lay beneath the Butchers Knife.
Long time you fought, redoubl'd Batt'ry bore,
But, after all, against your self you swore;
Your former self, for ev'ry Hour your form
Is chop'd and chang'd, like Winds before a storm.
Thus Fear and Int'rest will prevail with some,
For all have not the Gift of Martyrdom.

    The *Panther* grin'd at this, and thus reply'd,
That men may err was never yet deny'd.
But, if that common principle be true,
The Cannon, Dame, is level'd full at you.

But, shunning long disputes, I fain wou'd see
That wond'rous Wight, infallibility.
Is he from Heav'n this mighty Champion come
Or lodg'd below in subterranean *Rome?*
First, seat him somewhere, and derive his Race,
Or else conclude that nothing has no place.
   Suppose, (though I disown it,) said the *Hind,*
The certain Mansion were not yet assign'd,
The doubtful residence no proof can bring
Against the plain existence of the thing.
Because *Philosophers* may disagree,
If sight b' emission or reception be,
Shall it be thence infer'd I do not see?
But you require an Answer positive,
Which yet, when I demand, you dare not give,
For Fallacies in Universals live.
I then affirm that this unfailing guide
In Pope and gen'ral Councils must reside;
Both lawful, both combin'd; what one decrees
By numerous Votes, the other Ratifies:
On this undoubted Sense the Church relies.
'Tis true, some Doctors in a scantier space,
I mean in each apart contract the Place.
Some, who to greater length extend the Line,
The Churches after acceptation join.
This last Circumference appears too wide,
The Church diffus'd is by the Council ty'd;
As members by their Representatives
Oblig'd to Laws which Prince and Senate gives:
Thus some contract, and some enlarge the space;
In Pope and Council who denies the place,
Assisted from above with God's unfailing grace?
Those Canons all the needful points contain;
Their sense so obvious, and their words so plain,
That no disputes about the doubtful Text

Have, hitherto, the lab'ring world perplex'd:
If any shou'd in after times appear,
New Councils must be call'd, to make the meaning
    clear.
Because in them the pow'r supreme resides;
And all the promises are to the Guides.
This may be taught with sound and safe Defence:
But mark how sandy is your own pretence.
Who setting Councils, Pope, and Church aside,
Are ev'ry Man his own presuming Guide.
The sacred Books, you say, are full and plain,
And ev'ry needful point of Truth contain;
All who can read, Interpreters may be:
Thus though your several Churches disagree,
Yet ev'ry Saint has to himself alone
The Secret of this Philosophick Stone.
These Principles your jarring Sects unite,
When diff'ring Doctors and Disciples fight.
Though *Luther, Zuinglius, Calvin,* holy Chiefs,
Have made a Battel Royal of Beliefs;
Or like wild Horses sev'ral ways have whirl'd
The tortur'd Text about the Christian World;
Each *Jehu* lashing on with furious force,
That *Turk* or *Jew* cou'd not have us'd it worse.
No matter what dissension leaders make
Where ev'ry private man may save a stake:
Rul'd by the Scripture and his own advice,
Each has a blind by-path to Paradise;
Where driving in a Circle slow or fast,
Opposing Sects are sure to meet at last.
A wondrous charity you have in Store
For all reform'd to pass the narrow Door:
So much, that *Mahomet* had scarcely more.
For he, kind Prophet, was for damning none,
But *Christ* and *Moyses* were to save their own:

Himself was to secure his chosen race,
Though reason good for *Turks* to take the place,
And he allow'd to be the better man
In virtue of his holier *Alcoran.*

   True, said the *Panther,* I shall ne'er deny
My Breth'ren may be sav'd as well as I:
Though *Huguenots* contemn our ordination,
Succession, ministerial vocation,
And *Luther,* more mistaking what he read,
Misjoins the sacred Body with the Bread;
Yet, *Lady,* still remember I maintain
The Word in needfull points is only plain.

   Needless or needful I not now contend,
For still you have a loophole for a friend,
(Rejoyn'd the Matron) but the rule you lay
Has led whole flocks and leads them still astray
In weighty points, and full damnation's way.
For did not *Arius* first, *Socinus* now
The Son's eternal god-head disavow,
And did not these by Gospel Texts alone
Condemn our doctrine, and maintain their own?
Have not all hereticks the same pretence,
To plead the Scriptures in their own defence?
How did the *Nicene* council then decide
That strong debate, was it by Scripture try'd?
No, sure to those the Rebel would not yield,
Squadrons of Texts he marshal'd in the field;
That was but civil war, an equal set,
Where Piles and piles, and Eagles Eagles met.
With Texts point-blank and plain he fac'd the Foe:
And did not *Sathan* tempt our Saviour so?
The good old Bishops took a simpler way,
Each ask'd but what he heard his Father say,
Or how he was instructed in his youth,
And by tradition's force upheld the truth.

The *Panther* smil'd at this, and when, said she,
Were those first Councils disallow'd by me?
Or where did I at sure tradition strike,
Provided still it were Apostolick?
    Friend, said the *Hind*, you quit your former ground,
Where all your faith you did on Scripture found,
Now, 'tis tradition joined with holy writ,
But thus your memory betrays your wit.
    No, said the *Panther*, for in that I view
When your tradition's forg'd, and when 'tis true.
I set 'em by the rule, and as they square
Or deviate from undoubted doctrine there,
This Oral fiction, that old Faith declare.
(*Hind.*) The Council steered, it seems, a diff'rent course,
They try'd the Scripture by tradition's force;
But you tradition by the Scripture try;
Pursu'd, by Sects, from this to that you fly,
Nor dare on one foundation to rely.
The Word is then depos'd, and in this view
You rule the Scripture, not the Scripture you.
Thus said the *Dame*, and, smiling, thus pursu'd,
I see tradition then is disallow'd,
When not evinc'd by Scripture to be true,
And Scripture, as interpreted by you.
But here you tread upon unfaithfull ground;
Unless you cou'd infallibly expound.
Which you reject as odious Popery,
And throw that doctrine back with scorn on me.
Suppose we on things traditive divide,
And both appeal to Scripture to decide;
By various texts we both uphold our claim
Nay, often ground our titles on the same:
After long labour lost, and times expence,
Both grant the words and quarrel for the sense.
Thus all disputes for ever must depend;

For no dumb rule can controversies end.
Thus when you said tradition must be try'd
By Sacred Writ, whose sense your selves decide,
You said no more, but that your selves must be
The judges of the Scripture sense, not we.
Against our church tradition you declare,
And yet your Clerks would sit in *Moyses* chair:
At least 'tis prov'd against your argument,
The rule is far from plain, where all dissent.

   If not by Scriptures, how can we be sure,
(Replied the *Panther*) what tradition's pure?
For you may palm upon us new for old,
All, as they say, that glitters is not gold.

   How but by following her, reply'd the dame,
To whom deriv'd from sire to son they came;
Where ev'ry age do's on another move,
And trusts no farther than the next above;
Where all the rounds like *Jacob's* ladder rise,
The lowest hid in earth, the topmost in the skyes?

   Sternly the salvage did her answer mark,
Her glowing eye-balls, glitt'ring in the dark,
And said but this, since lucre was your trade,
Succeeding times such dreadfull gaps have made
'Tis dangerous climbing: to your sons and you
I leave the ladder, and its omen too.

   (*Hind.*) The *Panther's* breath was ever fam'd for
     sweet,
But from the *Wolf* such wishes oft I meet:
You learn'd this language from the blatant beast,
Or rather did not speak, but were possess'd.
As for your answer, 'tis but barely urg'd;
You must evince tradition to be forg'd;
Produce plain proofs; unblemished authors use
As ancient as those ages they accuse;
Till when 'tis not sufficient to defame:

An old possession stands, till Elder quitts the claim.
Then for our int'rest, which is nam'd alone
To load with envy, we retort your own.
For when traditions in your faces fly,
Resolving not to yield, you must decry:
As when the cause goes hard, the guilty man
Excepts, and thins his jury all he can;
So when you stand of other aid bereft,
You to the twelve Apostles would be left.
Your friend the *Wolfe* did with more craft provide
To set those toys traditions quite aside:
And *Fathers* too, unless when reason spent
He cites 'em but sometimes for ornament.
But, Madam *Panther*, you, though more sincere,
Are not so wise as your Adulterer:
The private spirit is a better blind
Than all the dodging tricks your authours find.
For they, who left the Scripture to the crowd,
Each for his own peculiar judge allow'd;
The way to please 'em was to make 'em proud.
Thus, with full sails, they ran upon the shelf;
Who cou'd suspect a couzenage from himself?
On his own reason safer 'tis to stand,
Than be deceiv'd and damn'd at second hand.
But you who *Fathers* and traditions take
And garble some, and some you quite forsake,
Pretending church auctority to fix,
And yet some grains of private spirit mix,
Are like a *Mule* made up of diff'ring seed,
And that's the reason why you never breed;
At least not propagate your kind abroad,
For home-dissenters are by statutes aw'd.
And yet they grow upon you ev'ry day,
While you (to speak the best) are at a stay,
For sects that are extremes, abhor a middle way.

Like tricks of state, to stop a raging flood,
Or mollify a mad-brain'd Senate's mood:
Of all expedients never one was good.
Well may they argue, (nor can you deny)
If we must fix on church auctority,
Best on the best, the fountain, not the flood,
That must be better still, if this be good.
Shall she command who has herself rebell'd?
Is *Antichrist* by *Antichrist* expell'd?
Did we a lawfull tyranny displace,
To set aloft a bastard of the race?
Why all these wars to win the Book, if we
Must not interpret for our selves, but she?
Either be wholly slaves or wholly free.
For *purging* fires traditions must not fight:
But they must prove Episcopacy's right:
Thus those led horses are from service freed;
You never mount 'em but in time of need.
Like mercenary's, hir'd for home defence,
They will not serve against their native Prince.
Against domestick foes of *Hierarchy*
These are drawn forth, to make fanaticks fly;
But, when they see their country-men at hand,
Marching against 'em under church-command,
Streight they forsake their colours and disband.

Thus she, nor cou'd the *Panther* well enlarge;
With weak defence against so strong a charge;
But said, for what did Christ his Word provide,
If still his church must want a living guide?
And if all saving doctrines are not there,
Or sacred Pen-men could not make 'em clear,
From after-ages we should hope in vain
For truths, which men inspir'd, cou'd not explain.

Before the Word was written, said the *Hind*,
Our Saviour preached his Faith to humane kind;

From his Apostles the first age receiv'd
Eternal truth, and what they taught, believ'd.
Thus by tradition faith was planted first,
Succeeding flocks succeeding Pastours nurs'd.
This was the way our wise Redeemer chose,
(Who sure could all things for the best dispose,)
To fence his fold from their encroaching foes.
He cou'd have writ himself, but well foresaw
Th' event would be like that of *Moyses* law;
Some difference wou'd arise, some doubts remain,
Like those which yet the jarring *Jews* maintain.
No written laws can be so plain, so pure,
But wit may gloss and malice may obscure;
Not those indited by his first command,
A Prophet grav'd the text, an Angel held his hand.
Thus faith was e'er the written word appear'd,
And men believ'd, not what they read, but heard,
But since the Apostles cou'd not be confin'd,
To these, or those, but severally design'd
Their large commission round the world to blow;
To spread their faith they spread their labours too.
Yet still their absent flock their pains did share,
They hearken'd still, for love produces care.
And as mistakes arose, or discords fell,
Or bold seducers taught 'em to rebel,
As charity grew cold or faction hot,
Or long neglect their lessons had forgot,
For all their wants they wisely did provide,
And preaching by Epistles was supply'd:
So great Physicians cannot all attend,
But some they visit and to some they send.
Yet all those letters were not writ to all;
Nor first intended, but occasional,
Their absent sermons, nor if they contain
All needfull doctrines, are those doctrines plain.

Clearness by frequent preaching must be wrought,
They writ but seldom, but they daily taught.
And what one Saint has said of holy *Paul*,
He darkly writ, is true apply'd to all.
For this obscurity cou'd heav'n provide
More prudently than by a living guide,
As doubts arose, the difference to decide?
A guide was therefore needfull, therefore made;
And, if appointed, sure to be obey'd.
Thus, with due reverence to th' Apostles writ,
By which my sons are taught, to which, submit;
I think, those truths their sacred works contain,
The church alone can certainly explain;
That following ages, leaning on the past,
May rest upon the Primitive at last.
Nor wou'd I thence the word no rule infer,
But none without the church interpreter.
Because, as I have urg'd before, 'tis mute,
And is it self the subject of dispute.
But what th' Apostles their successors taught,
They to the next, from them to us is brought,
Th' undoubted sense which is in Scripture sought.
From hence the church is arm'd, when errours rise,
To stop their entrance, and prevent surprise;
And safe entrench'd within, her foes without defies.
By these all festring sores her counsels heal,
Which time or has discloas'd, or shall reveal,
For discord cannot end without a last appeal.
Nor can a council national decide,
But with subordination to her Guide:
(I wish the cause were on that issue try'd.)
Much less the scripture; for suppose debate
Betwixt pretenders to a fair estate,
Bequeath'd by some Legator's last intent;
(Such is our dying Saviour's Testament:)

The will is prov'd, is open'd, and is read;
The doubtfull heirs their diff'ring titles plead:
All vouch the words their int'rest to maintain,
And each pretends by those his cause is plain.
Shall then the testament award the right?
No, that's the *Hungary* for which they fight;
The field of battel, subject of debate;
The thing contended for, the fair estate.
The sense is intricate, 'tis onely clear
What vowels and what consonants are there.
Therefore 'tis plain, its meaning must be try'd
Before some judge appointed to decide.

   Suppose, (the fair Apostate said,) I grant,
The faithfull flock some living guide should want,
Your arguments an endless chase persue:
Produce this vaunted Leader to our view,
This mighty *Moyses* of the chosen crew.

   The Dame, who saw her fainting foe retir'd,
With force renew'd, to victory aspir'd;
(And looking upward to her kindred sky,
As once our Saviour own'd his Deity,
Pronounc'd his words—*she whom ye seek am I*.)
Nor less amazed this voice the *Panther* heard
Than were those *Jews* to hear a god declar'd.
Then thus the matron modestly renew'd;
Let all your prophets and their sects be view'd,
And see to which of 'em your selves think fit
The conduct of your conscience to submit:
Each Proselyte wou'd vote his Doctor best,
With absolute exclusion to the rest:
Thus wou'd your *Polish* Diet disagree,
And end, as it began, in Anarchy;
Your self the fairest for election stand,
Because you seem crown-gen'ral of the land;
But soon against your superstitious lawn

Some Presbyterian Sabre wou'd be drawn:
In your establish'd laws of sov'raignty
The rest some fundamental flaw wou'd see,
And call Rebellion gospel-liberty.
To church-decrees your articles require
Submission modify'd, if not entire;
Homage deny'd, to censures you proceed;
But when *Curtana* will not doe the deed,
You lay that pointless clergy-weapon by,
And to the laws, your sword of justice fly,
Now this your sects the more unkindly take,
(Those prying varlets hit the blots you make)
Because some ancient friends of yours declare,
Your onely rule of faith the Scriptures are,
Interpreted, by men of judgment sound,
Which ev'ry sect will for themselves expound:
Nor think less rev'rence to their doctours due
For sound interpretation, than to you.
If then, by able heads, are understood
Your brother prophets, who reform'd abroad;
Those able heads expound a wiser way,
That their own sheep their shepherd shou'd obey.
But if you mean your selves are onely sound,
That doctrine turns the reformation round,
And all the rest are false reformers found.
Because in sundry points you stand alone,
Not in communion join'd with any one;
And therefore must be all the church, or none.
Then, till you have agreed whose judge is best,
Against this forc'd submission they protest:
While *sound* and *sound* a different sense explains,
Both play at hard-head till they break their brains:
And from their Chairs each other's force defy,
While unregarded thunders vainly fly.
I pass the rest, because your Church alone

Of all usurpers best cou'd fill the throne.
But neither you, nor any sect beside
For this high office can be qualify'd
With necessary Gifts requir'd in such a Guide.
For that which must direct the whole, must be
Bound in one bond of faith and unity:
But all your sev'ral Churches disagree.
The *Consubstantiating* Church and Priest
Refuse communion to the *Calvinist;*
The *French* reform'd, from Preaching you restrain,
Because you judge their Ordination vain;
And so they judge of yours, but Donors must ordain.
In short, in Doctrine, or in Discipline,
Not one reform'd can with another join:
But all from each, as from Damnation fly;
No Union they pretend, but in *Non-Popery.*
Nor, should their Members in a Synod meet,
Cou'd any Church presume to mount the Seat
Above the rest, their discords to decide;
None wou'd obey, but each would be the Guide:
And face to face dissensions would encrease;
For only distance now preserves the Peace.
All in their Turns accusers and accus'd:
Babel was never half so much confus'd.
What one can plead, the rest can plead as well;
For amongst equals lies no last appeal,
And all confess themselves are fallible.
Now, since you grant some necessary Guide,
All who can err are justly laid aside:
Because a trust so sacred to confer
Shows want of such a sure Interpreter,
And how can he be needful who can err?
Then granting that unerring guide we want,
That such there is you stand obliged to grant:
Our Saviour else were wanting to supply

Our needs and obviate that Necessity.
It then remains that Church can only be
The guide which owns unfailing certainty;
Or else you slip your hold, and change your side,
Relapsing from a necessary Guide.
But this annex'd Condition of the Crown,
Immunity from Errours, you disown,
Here then you shrink, and lay your weak pretensions
    down.
For petty Royalties you raise debate;
But this unfailing Universal State
You shun: nor dare succeed to such a glorious weight.
And for that cause those Promises detest
With which our Saviour did his Church invest:
But strive t' evade, and fear to find 'em true,
As conscious they were never meant to you:
All which the mother church asserts her own,
And with unrivall'd claim ascends the throne.
So when of old th' Almighty Father sate
In Council, to redeem our ruin'd state,
Millions of millions, at a distance round,
Silent the sacred Consistory crown'd,
To hear what mercy mixt with Justice cou'd propound.
All prompt with eager pity, to fulfil
The full extent of their Creatour's will:
But when the stern conditions were declar'd,
A mournful whisper through the host was heard,
And the whole hierarchy, with heads hung down,
Submissively declin'd the pondrous proffer'd crown.
Then, not till then, th' eternal Son from high
Rose in the strength of all the Deity;
Stood forth t' accept the terms, and underwent
A weight which all the frame of heav'n had bent,
Nor he Himself cou'd bear, but as omnipotent.
Now, to remove the least remaining doubt,

That even the blear-ey'd sects may find her out,
Behold what heavenly rays adorn her brows,
What from his Wardrobe her belov'd allows
To deck the wedding-day of his unspotted spouse.
Behold what marks of Majesty she brings;
Richer than antient heirs of Eastern kings:
Her right hand holds the sceptre and the keys,
To show whom she commands, and who obeys:
With these to bind or set the sinner free,
With that t' assert spiritual Royalty.

   One in herself, not rent by Schism, but sound,
Entire, one solid shining Diamond,
Not Sparkles shattered into Sects like you,
One is the Church, and must be to be true:
One central principle of unity.

   As undivided, so from errours free,
As one in faith, so one in sanctity.
Thus she, and none but she, th' insulting Rage
Of Hereticks oppos'd from Age to Age:
Still when the Giant-brood invades her Throne,
She stoops from Heav'n and meets 'em half way down,
And with paternal Thunder vindicates her Crown.
But like *Egyptian* Sorcerers you stand,
And vainly lift aloft your Magick Wand,
To sweep away the Swarms of Vermin from the Land.
You cou'd like them, with like infernal Force
Produce the Plague, but not arrest the Course.
But when the Boils and Botches, with disgrace
And publick Scandal sat upon the Face,
Themselves attack'd, the *Magi* strove no more,
They saw God's Finger, and their Fate deplore;
Themselves they cou'd not Cure of the dishonest sore.

   Thus one, thus pure, behold her largely spread
Like the fair Ocean from her Mother-Bed;
From East to West triumphantly she rides,

All Shoars are water'd by her wealthy Tides.

    The Gospel-sound, diffus'd from Pole to Pole,
Where winds can carry and where waves can roll.
The self same doctrin of the Sacred Page
Convey'd to ev'ry clime, in ev'ry age.

    Here let my sorrow give my satyr place,
To raise new blushes on my *British* race;
Our Sailing Ships like common shoars we use,
And through our distant Colonies diffuse
The draughts of Dungeons and the stench of stews,
Whom, when their home-bred honesty is lost,
We disembogue on some far *Indian* coast;
Thieves, Pandars, Palliards, sins of ev'ry sort;
Those are the manufactures we export;
And these the *Missioners* our zeal has made:
For, with my Countrey's pardon be it said,
Religion is the least of all our trade.

    Yet some improve their traffick more than we,
For they on gain, their only God, rely:
And set a publick price on piety.
Industrous of the needle and the chart,
They run full sail to their *Japponian* Mart;
Prevention fear, and prodigal of fame
Sell all of Christian to the very name;
Nor leave enough of that to hide their naked shame.

    Thus of three marks, which in the Creed we view,
Not one of all can be apply'd to you:
Much less the fourth; in vain alas you seek
Th' ambitious title of Apostolick:
God-like descent! 'tis well your bloud can be
Prov'd noble in the third or fourth degree:
For all of ancient that you had before,
(I mean what is not borrow'd from our store)
Was Errour fulminated o'er and o'er,
Old Heresies condemned in ages past,

By care and time recover'd from the blast.

'Tis said with ease, but never can be prov'd,
The church her old foundations has remov'd,
And built new doctrines on unstable sands:
Judge that, ye winds and rains; you prov'd her, yet she
    stands.
Those ancient doctrines charg'd on her for new,
Shew when, and how, and from what hands they grew.
We claim no pow'r, when Heresies grow bold,
To coin new faith, but still declare the old.
How else cou'd that obscene disease be purg'd
When controverted texts are vainly urg'd?
To prove tradition new, there's somewhat more
Requir'd, than saying, 'twas not us'd before.
Those monumental arms are never stirr'd,
Till Schism or Heresie call down *Goliah's* sword.

    Thus, what you call corruptions, are in truth,
The first plantations of the gospel's youth,
Old standard faith: but cast your eyes again,
And view those errours which new sects maintain,
Or which of old disturb'd the churches peaceful reign;
And we can point each period of the time,
When they began, and who begot the crime;
Can calculate how long the eclipse endur'd,
Who interpos'd, what digits were obscur'd:
Of all which are already pass'd away,
We know the rise, the progress and decay.

    Despair at our foundations then to strike,
Till you can prove your faith Apostolick;
A limpid stream drawn from the native source;
Succession lawfull in a lineal course.
Prove any Church, oppos'd to this our head,
So one, so pure, so unconfin'dly spread,
Under one chief of the spiritual state,
The members all combin'd, and all subordinate.

Show such a seamless coat, from schism so free,
In no communion joined with heresie:
If such a one you find, let truth prevail:
Till when, your weights will in the balance fail:
A church unprincipl'd kicks up the scale.

    But if you cannot think (nor sure you can
Suppose in God what were unjust in man,)
That he, the fountain of eternal grace,
Should suffer falsehood for so long a space
To banish truth and to usurp her place;
That nine successive ages should be lost
And preach damnation at their proper cost;
That all your erring ancestours should die
Drown'd in the Abyss of deep Idolatry;
If piety forbid such thoughts to rise,
Awake, and open your unwilling eyes:
God has left nothing for each age undone,
From this to that wherein he sent his Son:
Then think but well of him, and half your work is done.

    See how his Church, adorn'd with ev'ry grace,
With open arms, a kind forgiving face,
Stands ready to prevent her long-lost sons embrace.
Not more did *Joseph* o'er his brethren weep,
Nor less himself cou'd from discovery keep,
When in the crowd of suppliants they were seen,
And in their crew his best-beloved *Benjamin.*
That pious *Joseph* in the church behold,
To feed your famine, and refuse your gold;
The *Joseph* you exil'd, the *Joseph* whom you sold.

    Thus, while with heav'nly charity she spoke,
A streaming blaze the silent shadows broke;
Shot from the skyes; a cheerful azure light;
The birds obscene to forests wing'd their flight,
And gaping graves receiv'd the wand'ring guilty
      spright.

Such were the pleasing triumphs of the sky
For *James* his late nocturnal victory;
The pledge of his Almighty patron's love,
The fire-works with his angel made above.
I saw myself the lambent easie light
Gild the brown horrour and dispell the night;
The messenger with speed the tidings bore;
News which three lab'ring nations did restore;
But heav'ns own *Nuntius* was arrived before.

By this, the *Hind* had reached her lonely cell;
And vapours rose, and dews unwholesome fell,
When she, by frequent observation wise,
As one who long on heav'n had fix'd her eyes,
Discern'd a change of weather in the skyes.
The Western borders were with crimson spread,
The moon descending look'd all flaming red;
She thought good manners bound her to invite
The stranger Dame to be her guest that night.
'Tis true, coarse dyet and a short repast,
(She said) were weak inducements to the tast
Of one so nicely bred, and so unus'd to fast;
But what plain fare her cottage cou'd afford,
A hearty welcome at a homely board
Was freely hers; and to supply the rest,
An honest meaning, and an open breast.
Last, with content of mind, the poor man's Wealth;
A grace-cup to their common Patron's health.
This she desired her to accept, and stay,
For fear she might be wilder'd in her way,
Because she wanted an unerring guide,
And then the dew-drops on her silken hide
Her tender constitution did declare,
Too Lady-like a long fatigue to bear,
And rough inclemencies of raw nocturnal air.
But most she fear'd that, travelling so late,

Some evil-minded beasts might lye in wait,
And without witness wreak their hidden hate.
    The *Panther,* though she lent a listening ear,
Had more of *Lyon* in her than to fear:
Yet wisely weighing, since she had to deal
With many foes, their numbers might prevail,
Returned her all the thanks she cou'd afford;
And took her friendly hostess at her word,
Who ent'ring first her lowly roof, (a shed
With hoary moss and winding Ivy spread,
Honest enough to hide an humble Hermit's head,)
Thus graciously bespoke her welcome guest:
So might these walls, with your fair presence blest,
Become your dwelling-place of everlasting rest,
Not for a night, or quick revolving year,
Welcome an owner, not a sojourner.
This peaceful Seat my poverty secures,
War seldom enters but where wealth allures;
Nor yet dispise it, for this poor aboad
Has oft receiv'd and yet receives a god;
A god, victorious of the stygian race,
Here laid his sacred limbs, and sanctified the place.
This mean retreat did mighty *Pan* contain;
Be emulous of him, and pomp disdain,
And dare not to debase your soul to gain.
    The silent stranger stood amaz'd to see
Contempt of wealth, and wilfull poverty:
And, though ill habits are not soon controll'd,
A while suspended her desire of gold.
But civilly drew in her sharpn'd paws,
Not violating hospitable laws,
And pacify'd her tail and lick'd her frothy jaws.
    The *Hind* did first her country Cates provide;
Then couch'd her self securely by her side.

(Part II, entire)

To My Dear Friend Mr. Congreve

ON HIS COMEDY CALLED
THE DOUBLE-DEALER

Well then, the promis'd Hour is come at last;
The present Age of Wit obscures the past:
Strong were our Syres, and as they fought they Writ,
Conqu'ring with Force of Arms and Dint of Wit:
Theirs was the Giant Race before the Flood;
And thus, when *Charles* Return'd, our Empire stood.
Like *Janus,* he the stubborn Soil manur'd,
With Rules of Husbandry the Rankness cur'd:
Tam'd us to Manners, when the Stage was rude,
And boistrous *English* Wit with Art indu'd.
Our Age was cultivated thus at length,
But what we gain'd in Skill we lost in Strength.
Our Builders were with Want of Genius curst;
The second Temple was not like the first;
Till you, the best *Vitruvius,* come at length,
Our Beauties equal, but excel our Strength.
Firm *Dorique* Pillars found Your solid Base,
The fair *Corinthian* crowns the higher Space;
Thus all below is Strength, and all above is Grace.
In easie Dialogue is *Fletcher's* Praise:
He mov'd the Mind, but had no Pow'r to raise.
Great *Johnson* did by Strength of Judgment please,
Yet, doubling *Fletcher's* Force, he wants his Ease.
In diff'ring Talents both adorn'd their Age,
One for the Study, t'other for the Stage.
But both to *Congreve* justly shall submit,
One match'd in Judgment, both o'er-match'd in Wit.

In Him all Beauties of this Age we see,
Etherege his Courtship, *Southern's* Purity,
The Satyre, Wit, and Strength of Manly *Wycherly.*
All this in blooming Youth you have Atchiev'd;
Nor are your foil'd Contemporaries griev'd;
So much the Sweetness of your Manners move,
We cannot Envy you, because we Love.
Fabius might joy in *Scipio,* when he saw
A Beardless Consul made against the Law,
And join his Suffrage to the Votes of *Rome,*
Though he with *Hannibal* was overcome.
Thus old *Romano* bow'd to *Raphael's* Fame,
And Scholar to the Youth he taught, became.

 O that your Brows my Lawrel had sustain'd,
Well had I been depos'd, if you had reign'd!
The Father had descended for the Son,
For only You are lineal to the Throne.
Thus, when the State one *Edward* did depose,
A greater *Edward* in his Room arose:
But now, not I, but Poetry is curst;
For *Tom* the Second reigns like *Tom* the First.
But let 'em not mistake my Patron's Part,
Nor call his Charity their own Desert.
Yet this I Prophesie: Thou shalt be seen,
(Tho' with some short Parenthesis between:)
High on the Throne of Wit; and, seated there,
Nor mine (that's little) but thy Lawrel wear.
Thy first Attempt an early Promise made;
That early Promise this has more than paid.
So bold, yet so judiciously you dare,
That your least Praise, is to be Regular.
Time, Place, and Action may with Pains be wrought,
But Genius must be born, and never can be taught.
This is Your Portion, this Your Native Store:
Heav'n, that but once was Prodigal before,

To *Shakespear* gave as much; she cou'd not give him
　　more.
　Maintain your Post: that's all the Fame you need;
For 'tis impossible you shou'd proceed.
Already I am worn with Cares and Age,
And just abandoning th' ungrateful Stage:
Unprofitably kept at Heav'n's Expence,
I live a Rent-charge on his Providence:
But You, whòm ev'ry Muse and Grace adorn,
Whom I foresee to better Fortune born.
Be kind to my Remains; and oh defend,
Against your Judgment, your departed Friend!
Let not th' insulting Foe my Fame pursue;
But shade those Lawrels which descend to You:
And take for Tribute what these Lines express;
You merit more; nor cou'd my Love do less.

To the Memory of Mr. Oldham

Farewell, too little and too lately known,
Whom I began to think and call my own:
For sure our Souls were near alli'd, and thine
Cast in the same poetick mold with mine.
One common Note on either Lyre did strike,
And Knaves and Fools we both abhorr'd alike.
To the same Goal did both our Studies drive:
The last set out the soonest did arrive.
Thus *Nisus* fell upon the slippery place,
Whilst his young Friend perform'd and won the Race.
O early ripe! to thy abundant Store
What could advancing Age have added more?
It might (what Nature never gives the Young)
Have taught the Numbers of thy Native Tongue.

But Satire needs not those, and Wit will shine
Through the harsh Cadence of a rugged Line.
A noble Error, and but seldom made,
When Poets are by too much force betray'd.
Thy gen'rous Fruits, though gather'd ere their prime,
Still shew'd a Quickness; and maturing Time
But mellows what we write to the dull Sweets of
   Rhyme.
Once more, hail, and farewell! farewell, thou young,
But ah! too short, *Marcellus* of our Tongue!
Thy Brows with Ivy and with Laurels bound;
But Fate and gloomy Night encompass thee around.

A Song for St. Cecilia's Day

November 22, 1687

From Harmony, from heav'nly Harmony
   This universal Frame began;
  When Nature underneath a heap
   Of jarring Atomes lay,
  And cou'd not heave her Head,
The tuneful Voice was heard from high,
   Arise, ye more than dead.
Then cold and hot and moist and dry
  In order to their Stations leap,
   And MUSICK's pow'r obey.
From Harmony, from heavenly Harmony
   This universal Frame began:
   From Harmony to Harmony
Through all the Compass of the Notes it ran,
The Diapason closing full in Man.

What Passion cannot MUSICK raise and quell?
  When *Jubal* struck the corded Shell,
 His listening Brethren stood around,
  And, wond'ring, on their Faces fell
 To worship that Celestial Sound:
Less than a God they thought there could not dwell
  Within the hollow of the Shell,
  That spoke so sweetly, and so well.
What Passion cannot MUSICK raise and quell?

  The TRUMPETS loud Clangor
   Excites us to Arms
  With shrill Notes of Anger
   And mortal Alarms.
  The double double double beat
   Of the thund'ring DRUM
   Cryes, heark the Foes come;
Charge, Charge, 'tis too late to retreat.

  The soft complaining FLUTE
  In dying Notes discovers
  The Woes of hopeless Lovers,
Whose Dirge is whisper'd by the warbling LUTE.

  Sharp VIOLINS proclaim
Their jealous Pangs and Desperation,
Fury, frantick Indignation,
Depth of Pains and Height of Passion,
  For the fair, disdainful Dame.

  But oh! what Art can teach
  What human Voice can reach
   The sacred ORGANS Praise?
  Notes inspiring holy Love,
Notes that wing their heavenly Ways
  To mend the Choires above.

Orpheus cou'd lead the savage race,
And Trees unrooted left their Place,
  Sequacious of the Lyre;
But bright CECILIA rais'd the Wonder high'r:
When to her Organ vocal Breath was given,
An Angel heard, and straight appear'd
  Mistaking Earth for Heav'n.

GRAND CHORUS

As from the Pow'r of Sacred Lays
 The Spheres began to move,
And sung the great Creator's Praise
 To all the bless'd above;
So, when the last and dreadful Hour
This crumbling Pageant shall devour,
The TRUMPET shall be heard on high,
The dead shall live, the living die,
And MUSICK shall untune the Sky.

To the Pious Memory of the Accomplisht Young Lady Mrs. Anne Killigrew Excellent in the Two Sister-Arts of Poesie and Painting

AN ODE

Thou youngest Virgin-Daughter of the Skies,
 Made in the last Promotion of the *Blest;*
Whose Palms, new pluckt from Paradise,
In spreading *Branches* more sublimely rise,
 Rich with Immortal Green above the rest:
Whether, adopted to some Neighbouring Star,
Thou rol'st above us in thy wand'ring Race,

Or, in Procession fixt and regular,
Mov'd with the Heavens Majestick pace;
   Or, call'd to more Superiour *Bliss,*
Thou tread'st, with Seraphims, the vast *Abyss:*
Whatever happy region is thy place,
Cease thy Celestial Song a little space;
(Thou wilt have time enough of Hymns Divine,
Since Heav'ns Eternal Year is thine.)
Hear then a Mortal Muse thy praise rehearse
      In no ignoble Verse;
But such as thy own voice did practise here,
When thy first Fruits of Poesie were given,
To make thyself a welcome Inmate there;
   While yet a young Probationer,
    And Candidate of Heav'n.

  If by Traduction came thy Mind,
   Our Wonder is the less to find
A Soul so charming from a Stock so good;
Thy Father was transfus'd into thy *Blood:*
So wert thou born into the tuneful strain,
(An early, rich, and inexhausted Vein.)
  But if thy Præ-existing Soul
Was form'd, at first, with Myriads more,
  It did through all the Mighty Poets roul
Who *Greek* or *Latine* Laurels wore,
And was that *Sappho* last, which once it was before.
  If so, then cease thy flight, *O Heav'n-born Mind!*
Thou hast no *Dross* to purge from thy Rich Ore:
  Nor can thy Soul a fairer Mansion find
  Than was the *Beauteous* Frame she left behind:
Return, to fill or mend the Quire of thy Celestial kind.

  May we presume to say, that at thy *Birth,*
New joy was sprung in HEAV'N as well as here on *Earth?*
For sure the Milder Planets did combine

On thy *Auspicious* Horoscope to shine,
And ev'n the most Malicious were in Trine.
Thy *Brother-Angels* at thy *Birth*
   Strung each his Lyre, and tun'd it high,
      That all the People of the Skie
Might know a Poetess was born on Earth.
      And then if ever, Mortal Ears
      Had heard the Music of the Spheres!
      And if no clust'ring Swarm of *Bees*
   On thy sweet Mouth distill'd their golden Dew,
      'Twas that, such vulgar Miracles
      Heav'n had not Leasure to renew:
   For all the *Blest* Fraternity of Love
Solemniz'd there thy *Birth*, and kept thy Holyday
      above.

      O Gracious God! How far have we
      Prophan'd thy Heav'nly Gift of Poesy!
      Made prostitute and profligate the Muse,
      Debas'd to each obscene and impious use,
      Whose Harmony was first ordain'd *Above,*
      For Tongues of *Angels* and for *Hymns* of *Love!*
Oh wretched We! why were we hurry'd down
      This lubrique and adult'rate age,
   (Nay, added fat Pollutions of our own)
      T' increase the steaming Ordures of the Stage?
What can we say t' excuse our *Second Fall?*
Let this thy *Vestal*, Heav'n, atone for all:
   Her *Arethusian* Stream remains unsoil'd,
   Unmixt with Forreign Filth and undefil'd,
Her Wit was more than Man, her Innocence a Child.

Art she had none, yet wanted none,
   For Nature did that Want supply:
So rich in Treasures of her Own,
   She might our boasted Stores defy:

Such Noble Vigour did her Verse adorn,
That it seem'd borrow'd, where 'twas only born.
Her Morals too were in her *Bosom* bred
   By great Examples daily fed,
What in the best of *Books*, her Father's Life, she read.
   And to be read her self she need not fear;
   Each Test, and ev'ry Light, her Muse will bear,
   Though *Epictetus* with his Lamp were there.
   Ev'n Love (for Love sometimes her Muse exprest),
Was but a Lambent-flame which play'd about her
         Breast:
   Light as the Vapours of a Morning Dream,
   So cold herself, whilst she such Warmth exprest,
   'Twas *Cupid* bathing in *Diana's* Stream.

Born to the Spacious Empire of the Nine,
One wou'd have thought, she should have been content
To manage well that Mighty Government;
But what can young ambitious Souls confine?
   To the next Realm she stretcht her Sway,
   For *Painture* near adjoyning lay,
A plenteous Province, and alluring Prey.
A *Chamber of Dependences* was fram'd,
(As Conquerors will never want Pretence,
   When arm'd, to justifie th' Offence),
And the whole Fief, in right of Poetry she claim'd.
   The Country open lay without Defence;
For Poets frequent In-rodes there had made,
   And perfectly cou'd represent
   The Shape, the Face, with ev'ry Lineament;
And all the large Demains which the Dumb-sister
         sway'd;
   All bow'd beneath her Government,
   Receiv'd in Triumph wheresoe're she went.
Her Pencil drew whate're her Soul design'd

And oft the *happy Draught* surpass'd the *Image* in her
        Mind.
  The *Sylvan* Scenes of Herds and Flocks
  And fruitful Plains and barren Rocks,
  Of shallow *Brooks* that flow'd so clear,
  The bottom did the top appear;
  Of deeper too and ampler Floods
  Which as in Mirrors, shew'd the Woods;
  Of lofty Trees, with Sacred Shades
  And Perspectives of pleasant Glades,
  Where Nymphs of brightest Form appear,
  And shaggy Satyrs standing near,
  Which them at once admire and fear.
  The Ruines too of some Majestick Piece,
  Boasting the Pow'r of ancient *Rome* or *Greece,*
  Whose Statues, Freezes, Columns, broken lie,
  And, tho' defac'd, the Wonder of the Eye;
  What *Nature, Art,* bold *Fiction,* e're durst frame,
  Her forming Hand gave Feature to the Name.
  So strange a Concourse ne're was seen before,
But when the peopl'd *Ark* the whole Creation bore.

  The Scene then chang'd; with bold Erected Look
Our Martial King the sight with Reverence strook:
For, not content t' express his Outward Part,
Her hand call'd out the Image of his Heart,
His Warlike Mind, his Soul devoid of Fear,
His High-designing *Thoughts* were figur'd there,
As when, by Magick, Ghosts are made appear.
  Our Phenix queen was portrai'd too so bright,
Beauty alone cou'd *Beauty* take so right:
Her Dress, her Shape, her matchless Grace,
Were all observ'd, as well as heav'nly Face.
With such a Peerless Majesty she stands,
As in that Day she took the Crown from Sacred hands:

Before a Train of Heroins was seen,
In *Beauty* foremost, as in Rank, the Queen!
   Thus nothing to her Genius was deny'd,
But like a *Ball* of Fire, the farther thrown,
Still with a greater *Blaze* she shone,
   And her bright Soul broke out on ev'ry side.
What next she had design'd, Heaven only knows:
To such Immod'rate Growth her Conquest rose
That Fate alone its Progress cou'd oppose.

Now all those Charms, that blooming Grace,
The well-proportion'd Shape and beauteous Face,
Shall never more be seen by Mortal Eyes;
In Earth the much-lamented Virgin lies!
   Not Wit nor Piety cou'd Fate prevent;
   Nor was the cruel *Destiny* content
   To finish all the Murder at a blow,
   To sweep at once her *Life* and *Beauty* too;
But, like a hardn'd Fellon, took a pride
   To work more Mischievously slow,
And plunder'd first, and then destroy'd.
O double Sacriledge on things Divine,
To rob the Relique, and deface the Shrine!
   But thus *Orinda* dy'd:
Heav'n, by the same Disease, did both translate,
As equal were their Souls, so equal was their fate.

Mean time, her *Warlike Brother* on the Seas
His waving Streamers to the Winds displays,
And vows for his Return, with vain Devotion, pays.
   Ah, Generous Youth! that Wish forbear,
   The Winds too soon will waft thee here!
   Slack all thy Sails, and fear to come,
Alas, thou know'st not, thou art wreck'd at home!
No more shalt thou behold thy Sister's Face,
Thou hast already had her last Embrace.

But look aloft, and if thou ken'st from far,
Among the *Pleiad's,* a New-kindl'd star,
If any sparkles, than the rest, more bright,
'Tis she that shines in that propitious Light.

When in mid-Air the Golden Trump shall sound,
   To raise the Nations under ground;
   When in the Valley of *Jehosaphat*
The Judging God shall close the book of Fate;
   And there the last *Assizes* keep
   For those who Wake and those who Sleep;
   When ratling *Bones* together fly
   From the four Corners of the Skie,
When Sinews o're the Skeletons are spread,
Those cloath'd with Flesh, and Life inspires the Dead;
   The Sacred Poets first shall hear the Sound,
   And formost from the Tomb shall bound:
   For they are cover'd with the lightest ground;
   And streight, with in-born Vigour, on the Wing,
   Like mounting Larks, to the New Morning sing.
   There *Thou,* sweet Saint, before the Quire shalt go,
   As Harbinger of Heav'n, the Way to show,
   The Way which thou so well hast learn'd below.

FROM *The Conquest of Granada*

[*Song of the Zambra Dance*]

Beneath a Myrtle shade
Which Love for none but happy Lovers made,
I slept, and straight my Love before me brought
Phillis the object of my waking thought;
Undress'd she came my flames to meet,

While Love strow'd flow'rs beneath her feet;
Flow'rs, which so press'd by her, became more sweet.

From the bright Visions head
A careless vail of Lawn was loosely spread:
From her white temples fell her shaded hair,
Like cloudy sunshine not too brown nor fair:
Her hands, her lips did love inspire;
Her ev'ry grace my heart did fire:
But most her eyes which languish'd with desire.

Ah, Charming fair, said I,
How long can you my bliss and yours deny?
By Nature and by love this lonely shade
Was for revenge of suffring Lovers made:
Silence and shades with love agree:
Both shelter you and favour me;
You cannot blush because I cannot see.

No, let me dye, she said,
Rather than lose the spotless name of Maid:
Faintly methought she spoke, for all the while
She bid me not believe her, with a smile.
Then dye, said I, she still deny'd:
And is it thus, thus, thus she cry'd
You use a harmless Maid, and so she dy'd!

I wak'd, and straight I knew
I lov'd so well it made my dream prove true:
Fancy, the kinder Mistress of the two,
Fancy had done what *Phillis* wou'd not do!
Ah, Cruel Nymph, cease your disdain,
While I can dream you scorn in vain:
Asleep or waking you must ease my pain.

FROM *Amphitryon*

[*Mercury's Song to Phaedra*]

Fair *Iris* I love, and hourly I dye,
But not for a Lip, nor a languishing Eye:
She's fickle and false, and there we agree;
For I am as false, and as fickle as she:
We neither believe what either can say;
And, neither believing, we neither betray.

'Tis civil to swear, and say things of course;
We mean not the taking for better for worse.
When present, we love; when absent, agree:
I think not of *Iris*, nor *Iris* of me:
The Legend of Love no Couple can find
So easie to part, or so equally join'd.

The Secular Masque

Enter Janus.
JANUS. *Chronos, Chronos,* mend thy Pace,
An hundred times the rowling Sun
Around the Radiant Belt has run
In his revolving Race.
Behold, behold, the Goal in sight,
Spread thy Fans, and wing thy flight.
Enter Chronos, with a Scythe in his hand, and a great
Globe on his Back, which he sets down at his entrance.
CHRONOS. Weary, weary of my weight,

Let me, let me drop my Freight,
   And leave the World behind.
I could not bear
Another Year
The Load of Human-kind.
Enter Momus Laughing.
MOMUS. Ha! ha! ha! Ha! ha! ha! well hast thou done,
   To lay down thy Pack,
   And lighten thy Back,
The World was a Fool, e'er since it begun,
And since neither *Janus,* nor *Chronos,* nor I,
   Can hinder the Crimes,
   Or mend the Bad Times,
'Tis better to Laugh than to Cry.
CHORUS OF ALL 3. *'Tis better to Laugh than to Cry.*
JANUS. Since *Momus* comes to laugh below,
   Old Time begin the Show,
That he may see, in every Scene,
What Changes in this Age have been,
CHRONOS. Then Goddess of the Silver Bow begin.
               Horns, or Hunting-Musique within.
Enter Diana.
DIANA. With Horns and with Hounds I waken the Day.
And hye to my Woodland walks away;
I tuck up my Robe, and am buskin'd soon,
And tye to my Forehead a wexing Moon.
I course the fleet Stagg, unkennel the Fox,
And chase the wild Goats or'e summets of Rocks,
With shouting and hooting we pierce thro' the Sky;
And Eccho turns Hunter, and doubles the Cry.
CHORUS OF ALL. *With shouting and hooting, we pierce*
   through the Skie,
And Eccho turns Hunter, and doubles the Cry.
JANUS. Then our Age was in it's Prime,
CHRONOS. Free from Rage.

DIANA. And free from Crime.

MOMUS. A very Merry, Dancing, Drinking,
Laughing, Quaffing, and unthinking Time.

CHORUS OF ALL. *Then our Age was in it's Prime,*
Free from Rage, and free from Crime,
A very Merry, Dancing, Drinking,
Laughing, Quaffing, and unthinking Time.

> *Dance of Diana's Attendants. Enter Mars.*

MARS. Inspire the Vocal Brass, Inspire;
The World is past its Infant Age:
  Arms and Honour,
  Arms and Honour,
Set the Martial Mind on Fire,
And kindle Manly Rage.
Mars has lookt the Sky to Red;
And Peace, the Lazy Good, is fled.
Plenty, Peace, and Pleasure fly;
  The Sprightly Green
In *Woodland-Walks,* no more is seen;
The Sprightly Green, has drunk the *Tyrian* Dye.

CHORUS OF ALL. *Plenty, Peace, etc.*

MARS. Sound the Trumpet, Beat the Drum,
Through all the World around;
Sound a Reveille, Sound, Sound,
  The Warrior God is come.

CHORUS OF ALL. *Sound the Trumpet, etc.*

MOMUS. Thy Sword within the Scabbard keep,
  And let Mankind agree;
Better the World were fast asleep,
  Than kept awake by Thee.
The Fools are only thinner,
  With all our Cost and Care;
But neither side a winner,
  For Things are as they were.

CHORUS OF ALL. *The Fools are only, etc.*

Enter Venus.

VENUS. Calms appear, when Storms are past;
Love will have his Hour at last:
Nature is my kindly Care;
Mars destroys, and I repair;
Take me, take me, while you may,
Venus comes not ev'ry Day.

CHORUS FOR ALL. *Take her, take her, etc.*

CHRONOS. The World was then so light,
I scarcely felt the Weight;
Joy rul'd the Day, and Love the Night.
But since the Queen of Pleasure left the Ground,
 I faint, I lag,
 And feebly drag
The pond'rous Orb around.

MOMUS. All, all, of a piece throughout;
Pointing to Diana. Thy Chase had a Beast in View;
To Mars. Thy Wars brought nothing about;
To Venus. Thy Lovers were all untrue.

JANUS. 'Tis well an Old Age is out,

CHRONOS. And time to begin a New.

CHORUS OF ALL. *All, all, of a piece throughout;*
Thy Chase had a Beast in View;
Thy Wars brought nothing about;
Thy Lovers were all untrue.
'Tis well an Old Age is out,
And time to begin a New.

 Dance of Huntsmen, Nymphs, Warriours and Lovers.

FROM *King Arthur*

[*Song of Venus*]

Fairest Isle, all Isles Excelling,
  Seat of Pleasures, and of Loves;
Venus here, will chuse her Dwelling,
  And forsake her *Cyprian* Groves.

Cupid, from his Fav'rite Nation,
  Care and Envy will Remove;
Jealousie that poysons Passion,
  And Despair that dies for Love.

Gentle Murmurs, sweet Complaining,
  Sighs that blow the Fire of Love;
Soft Repulses, kind Disdaining,
  Shall be all the Pains you prove.

Ev'ry Swain shall pay his Duty,
  Grateful every Nymph shall prove;
And as these Excel in Beauty,
  Those shall be Renown'd for Love.

John Wilmot,
Earl of Rochester
(1647–1680)

Love and Life. A Song

All my past Life is mine no more,
  The flying Hours are gone:
Like transitory Dreams giv'n o'er,
Whose Images are kept in store,
  By Memory alone.

The Time that is to come is not;
  How can it then be mine?
The present Moment's all my Lot;
And that, as fast as it is got,
  Phillis, is only thine.

Then talk not of Inconstancy,
  False Hearts, and broken Vows;
If I, by Miracle, can be
This live-long Minute true to thee,
  'Tis all that Heav'n allows.

A Satyr Against Mankind

Were I, who to my Cost already am
One of those strange, prodigious Creatures *Man*,
A Spirit free, to chuse for my own Share,

What sort of Flesh and Blood I pleas'd to wear,
I'd be a Dog, a Monkey, or a Bear,
Or any thing, but that vain Animal,
Who is so proud of being Rational.
The Senses are too gross; and he'll contrive
A Sixth, to contradict the other Five:
And before certain Instinct, will prefer
Reason, which Fifty times for One does err.
Reason, an *Ignis fatuus* of the Mind,
Which leaves the Light of Nature, Sense, behind.
Pathless, and dang'rous, wand'ring ways, it takes,
Through Error's fenny Bogs, and thorny Brakes:
Whilst the misguided Follower climbs with Pain,
Mountains of Whimsies, heapt in his own Brain:
Stumbling from Thought to Thought, falls headlong
        down
Into Doubt's boundless Sea, where like to drown
Books bear him up a-while, and make him try
To swim with Bladders of Philosophy:
In hopes still to o'ertake the skipping Light,
The Vapour dances in his dazzled Sight,
Till spent, it leaves him to eternal Night.
Then old Age, and Experience, hand in hand,
Lead him to Death, and make him understand,
After a Search so painful, and so long,
That all his Life he has been in the wrong.
Hudled in Dirt, this reas'ning Engine lies,
Who was so proud, so witty, and so wise:
Pride drew him in, as Cheats their Bubbles catch,
And made him venture to be made a Wretch:
His Wisdom did his Happiness destroy,
Aiming to know the World he should enjoy.
And *Wit* was his vain frivolous Pretence,
Of pleasing others at his own Expence.
For *Wits* are treated just like *Common Whores;*

First they're enjoy'd, and then kickt out of Doors.
The Pleasure past, a threat'ning Doubt remains,
That frights th'Enjoyer with succeeding Pains.
Women, and *Men of Wit,* are dang'rous Tools,
And ever fatal to admiring Fools.
Pleasure allures, and when the Fops escape,
'Tis not that they're belov'd, but fortunate;
And therefore what they fear, at Heart, they hate.
But now, methinks, some formal Band and Beard
Takes me to Task; Come on, Sir, I'm prepar'd:
Then by your Favour, any thing that's writ
Against this gibing, gingling knack, call'd *Wit,*
Likes me abundantly; but you'll take care
Upon this Point, not to be too severe,
Perhaps my Muse were fitter for this part:
For, I profess, I can be very smart
On *Wit,* which I abhor with all my Heart.
I long to lash it, in some sharp Essay,
But your grand Indiscretion bids me stay,
And turns my Tide of Ink another way.
What Rage ferments in your degen'rate Mind,
To make you rail at Reason and Mankind?
Blest glorious Man, to whom alone kind Heav'n
An everlasting Soul hath freely giv'n;
Whom his great Maker took such care to make,
That from himself he did the Image take,
And this fair Frame in shining Reason drest,
To dignifie his Nature above Beast.
Reason, by whose aspiring Influence,
We take a Flight beyond material Sense,
Dive into Mysteries, then soaring pierce
The flaming Limits of the Universe,
Search Heav'n and Hell, find out what's acted there,
And give the World true grounds of Hope and Fear.

Hold, mighty Man, I cry; all this we know,
From the pathetick pen of *Ingelo*,
From *Patrick's* Pilgrim, *Sibb's* Soliloquies,
And 'tis this very Reason I despise,
This supernat'ral Gift, that makes a Mite
Think he's the Image of the Infinite;
Comparing his short Life, void of all Rest,
To the Eternal and the ever Blest;
This busie puzling Stirrer up of Doubt,
That frames deep Mysteries, then finds 'em out,
Filling with frantick Crouds of thinking Fools,
The reverend Bedlams, Colleges and Schools,
Born on whose Wings, each heavy Sot can pierce
The Limits of the boundless Universe:
So charming Ointments make an old Witch fly,
And bear a cripled Carkass through the Sky.
'Tis this exalted Pow'r, whose Business lies
In Nonsense and Impossibilities:
This made a whimsical Philosopher,
Before the spacious World his Tub prefer:
And we have many modern Coxcombs, who
Retire to think, 'cause they have nought to do.
But Thoughts were giv'n for Actions Government;
Where Action ceases, Thought's impertinent.
Our Sphere of Action is Life's Happiness,
And he that thinks beyond, thinks like an Ass.
Thus whilst against false Reas'ning I inveigh,
I own right Reason, which I would obey;
That Reason, which distinguishes by Sense,
And gives us Rules of Good and Ill from thence;
That bounds Desires with a reforming Will,
To keep them more in Vigour, not to kill:
Your Reason hinders; mine helps to enjoy,
Renewing Appetites, yours would destroy.

My Reason is my Friend, yours is a Cheat:
Hunger calls out, my Reason bids me eat;
Perversely yours, your Appetite does mock;
This asks for Food, that answers What's a Clock?

   This plain distinction, Sir, your Doubt secures;
'Tis not true Reason I despise, but yours.
Thus, I think Reason righted: But for Man,
I'll ne'er recant, defend him if you can.
For all his Pride, and his Philosophy,
'Tis evident Beasts are, in their degree,
As Wise at least, and Better far than he.
Those Creatures are the wisest, who attain,
By surest Means, the Ends at which they aim.
If therefore *Jowler* finds, and kills his Hare,
Better than *Meres* suplies Committee-Chair;
Though one's a Statesman, th'other but a Hound,
Jowler in Justice will be wiser found.
You see how far Man's Wisdom here extends:
Look next if Human Nature makes amends;
Whose Principles are most generous and just;
And to whose Morals you wou'd sooner trust.
Be Judge your self, I'll bring it to the Test,
Which is the basest Creature; Man, or Beast:
Birds feed on Birds, Beasts on each other prey;
But savage Man alone, does Man betray.
Prest by Necessity, *They* kill for Food;
Man undoes Man, to do himself no good.
With Teeth and Claws by Nature arm'd, *They* hunt
Nature's Allowance, to supply their Want:
But Man, with Smiles, Embraces, Friendships, Praise,
Inhumanly, his Fellow's Life betrays:
With voluntary Pains works his Distress;
Not through Necessity, but Wantonness.
For Hunger, or for Love, *They* bite or tear,

Whilst wretched Man is still in Arms for Fear:
For Fear he arms, and is of Arms afraid;
From Fear to Fear successively betray'd.
Base Fear, the Source whence his best Passions came,
His Boasted Honour, and his dear-bought Fame:
The Lust of Pow'r, to which he's such a Slave,
And for the which alone he dares be brave:
To which his various Projects are design'd,
Which makes him gen'rous, affable, and kind:
For which he takes such Pains to be thought Wise,
And scrues his Actions, in a forc'd Disguise:
Leads a most tedious Life, in Misery,
Under laborious, mean Hypocrisie.
Look to the Bottom of his vast Design,
Wherein Man's Wisdom, Pow'r, and Glory join;
The Good he acts, the Ill he does endure,
'Tis all from Fear, to make himself secure.
Meerly for Safety, after Fame they thirst;
For all Men would be Cowards if they durst:
And Honesty's against all common Sense:
Men must be Knaves; 'tis in their own Defence,
Mankind's dishonest; if you think it fair,
Amongst known Cheats, to play upon the square,
You'll be undone—
Nor can weak Truth your Reputation save;
The Knaves will all agree to call you Knave.
Wrong'd shall he live, insulted o'er, opprest,
Who dares be less a Villain than the rest.
Thus here you see what Human Nature craves,
Most Men are Cowards, all Men shou'd be Knaves.
The Difference lies, as far as I can see,
Not in the Thing it self, but the Degree;
And all the Subject Matter of Debate,
Is only who's a Knave of the First Rate.

The Maim'd Debauchee

As some brave *Admiral,* in former War
  Depriv'd of Force, but prest with Courage still,
Two Rival Fleets appearing from afar,
  Crawls to the top of an adjacent Hill;

From whence (with Thoughts full of Concern) he
    views
  The wise and daring Conduct of the Fight:
And each bold Action to his Mind renews,
  His present Glory, and his past Delight.

From his fierce Eyes Flashes of Rage he throws,
  As from black Clouds when Lightning breaks away,
Transported thinks himself amidst his Foes,
  And absent, yet enjoys the bloody Day.

So when my Days of Impotence approach,
  And I'm by Love and Wine's unlucky chance
Driv'n from the pleasing Billows of Debauch,
  On the dull Shoar of lazy Temperance;

My Pains at last some Respite shall afford,
  While I behold the Battels you maintain:
When Fleets of Glasses sail around the Board,
  From whose Broad-sides Volleys of Wit shall rain.

Nor shall the sight of honourable Scars,
  Which my too forward Valour did procure,
Frighten new-listed Soldiers from the Wars;
  Past Joys have more than paid what I endure.

Shou'd some brave Youth (worth being drunk) prove
    nice,

And from his fair Inviter meanly shrink,
'Twould please the Ghost of my departed Vice,
   If, at my Counsel, he repent and drink.

Or shou'd some cold-complexion'd Sot forbid,
   With his dull Morals, our Night's brisk Alarms;
I'll fire his Blood, by telling what I did,
   When I was strong, and able to bear Arms.

I'll tell of Whores attack'd their Lords at home,
   Bawds Quarters beaten up, and Fortress won;
Windows demolish'd, Watches overcome,
   And handsom Ills by my Contrivance done.

With Tales like these I will such Heat inspire,
   As to important Mischief shall incline;
I'll make him long some ancient Church to fire,
   And fear no Lewdness they're call'd to by Wine.

Thus Statesman-like I'll saucily impose,
   And, safe from Danger, valiantly advise;
Shelter'd in Impotence urge you to Blows,
   And, being good for nothing else, be Wise.

Upon Nothing

Nothing! thou Elder Brother ev'n to Shade,
Thou hadst a being ere the World was made,
And (well fixt) art alone, of Ending not afraid.

Ere Time and Place were, Time and Place were not,
When Primitive *Nothing* something streight begot,
Then all proceeded from the great united—What.

Something, the gen'ral Attribute of all,
Sever'd from thee, its sole Original,
Into thy boundless self must undistinguish'd fall.

Yet Something did thy mighty Pow'r command,
And from thy fruitful Emptiness's Hand,
Snatch'd Men, Beasts, Birds, Fire, Air, and Land.

Matter, the wickedest Off-spring of thy Race,
By Form assisted, flew from thy Embrace,
And Rebel Light obscur'd thy reverend dusky Face.

With Form and Matter, Time and Place did join;
Body, thy Foe, with thee did Leagues combine,
To spoil thy peaceful Realm, and ruin all thy Line.

But Turn-Coat Time assists the Foe in vain,
And, brib'd by thee, assists thy short-liv'd Reign,
And to thy hungry Womb drives back thy Slaves again.

Tho' Mysteries are barr'd from Laick Eyes,
And the Divine alone, with Warrant, pries
Into thy Bosom, where the Truth in private lies:

Yet this of thee the Wise may freely say,
Thou from the Virtuous nothing tak'st away,
And to be part with thee the Wicked wisely pray.

Great Negative, how vainly wou'd the Wise
Enquire, define, distinguish, teach, devise?
Didst thou not stand to point their dull Philosophies.

Is, or *is not*, the Two great Ends of Fate,
And, true or false, the Subject of Debate,
That perfect, or destroy, the vast Designs of Fate;

When they have rack'd the *Politician's* Breast,
Within thy Bosom most securely rest,
And, when reduc'd to thee, are least unsafe and best.

But, *Nothing*, why does *Something* still permit,
That Sacred Monarchs should at Council sit,
With Persons highly thought at best for nothing fit.

Whilst weighty *Something* modestly abstains,
From Princes Coffers, and from Statesmen's Brains,
And Nothing there like stately *Nothing* reigns.

Nothing, who dwell's with Fools in grave Disguise,
For whom they reverend Shapes, and Forms devise,
Lawn Sleeves, and Furrs, and Gowns, when they like
   thee look wise.

French Truth, *Dutch* Prowess, *British* Policy,
Hibernian Learning, *Scotch* Civility,
Spaniards Dispatch, *Danes* Wit, are mainly seen in thee.

The Great Man's Gratitude to his best Friend,
Kings Promises, Whores Vows, towards thee they bend,
Flow swiftly into thee, and in thee ever end.

John Sheffield,
Duke of Buckingham

(1648–1721)

On Mr. Hobbs, and His Writings

Such is the Mode of these censorious Days,
The Art is lost of knowing how to praise;
Poets are envious now, and Fools alone
Admire at Wit, because themselves have none.
Yet whatsoe'er is by vain Criticks thought,
Praising is harder much than finding Fault;
In homely Pieces ev'n the *Dutch* excel,
Italians only can draw Beauty well.
   As Strings, alike wound up, so equal prove,
That one resounding makes the other move;
From such a Cause our Satires please so much,
We sympathize with each ill-natur'd Touch;
And as the sharp Infection spreads about,
The Reader's Malice helps the Writer out.
To blame, is easy; to commend, is bold;
Yet, if the Muse inspires it, who can hold?
To Merit we are bound to give Applause,
Content to suffer in so just a Cause.
   While in dark Ignorance we lay afraid
Of Fancies, Ghosts, and ev'ry empty Shade;
Great HOBBS appear'd, and by plain Reason's Light
Put such fantastick Forms to shameful Flight.

Fond is their Fear, who think Men needs must be
To Vice enslav'd, if from vain Terrors free;
The Wise and Good, Morality will guide,
And Superstition all the World beside.

In other Authors, tho' the Thought be good,
'Tis not sometimes so eas'ly understood;
That Jewel oft unpolish'd has remain'd;
Some Words should be left out, and some explain'd;
So that in Search of Sense, we either stray,
Or else grow weary in so rough a Way.
But here sweet Eloquence does always smile,
In such a choice, yet unaffected Style,
As must both Knowledge and Delight impart,
The Force of Reason, with the Flow'rs of Art;
Clear as a beautiful transparent Skin,
Which never hides the Blood, yet holds it in:
Like a delicious Stream it ever ran,
As smooth as Woman, but as strong as Man.

BACON himself, whose universal Wit
Does Admiration through the World beget,
Scarce more his Age's Ornament is thought,
Or greater Credit to his Country brought.

While Fame is young, too weak to fly away,
Malice pursues her, like some Bird of Prey;
But once on Wing, then all the Quarrels cease;
Envy herself is glad to be at Peace,
Gives over, weary'd with so high a Flight,
Above her Reach, and scarce within her Sight.
HOBBS to this happy Pitch arriv'd at last,
Might have look'd down with Pride on Dangers past:
But such the Frailty is of Human Kind,
Men toil for Fame, which no Man lives to find;
Long rip'ning under-ground this *China* lies;
Fame bears no Fruit, till the vain Planter dies.

Thus Nature, tir'd with his unusual Length
Of Life, which put her to her utmost Strength,
Such Stock of Wit unable to supply,
To spare herself, was glad to let him die.

Matthew Prior

(1664–1721)

An English Ballad, on the Taking of Namur by the King of Great Britain, 1695

Dulce est desipere in loco.

Some Folks are drunk, yet do not know it:
    So might not *Bacchus* give You Law?
Was it a Muse, O lofty Poet,
    Or Virgin of St. *Cyr*, You saw?
Why all this Fury? What's the Matter,
    That Oaks must come from *Thrace* to dance?
Must stupid Stocks be taught to flatter?
    And is there no such Wood in *France*?
Why must the Winds all hold their Tongue?
    If they a little Breath should raise;
Would that have spoil'd the Poet's Song;
    Or puff'd away the Monarch's Praise?

Pindar, that Eagle, mounts the Skies;
    While Virtue leads the noble Way:
Too like a Vultur *Boileau* flies,
    Where sordid Interest shows the Prey.
When once the Poet's Honour ceases,
    From Reason far his Transports rove:
And *Boileau*, for eight hundred Pieces,
    Makes *Louis* take the Wall of Jove.

Neptune and *Sol* came from above,
    Shap'd like *Megrigny* and *Vauban*:

265

They arm'd these Rocks; then show'd old *Jove*
　　Of *Marli* Wood, the Wond'rous Plan.
Such Walls, these three wise Gods agreed,
　　By Human Force could ne'er be shaken:
But You and I in *Homer* read
　　Of Gods, as well as Men, mistaken.
Sambre and *Maese* their Waves may join;
　　But ne'er can *William's* Force restrain:
He'll pass them Both, who pass'd the *Boyn:*
　　Remember this, and arm the *Sein.*

Full fifteen thousand lusty Fellows
　　With Fire and Sword the Fort maintain:
Each was a *Hercules,* You tell us;
　　Yet out they march'd like common Men.
Cannons above, and Mines below
　　Did Death and Tombs for Foes contrive:
Yet Matters have been order'd so,
　　That most of Us are still alive.

If *Namur* be compar'd to *Troy;*
　　Then *Britain's* Boys excell'd the *Greeks:*
Their Siege did ten long Years employ:
　　We've done our Bus'ness in ten Weeks.
What Godhead does so fast advance,
　　With dreadful Pow'r those Hills to gain?
'Tis little *Will,* the Scourge of *France;*
　　No Godhead, but the first of Men.
His mortal Arm exerts the Pow'r,
　　To keep ev'n *Mons's* Victor under:
And that same *Jupiter* no more
　　Shall fright the World with impious Thunder.

Our King thus trembles at *Namur,*
　　Whilst *Villeroy,* who ne'er afraid is,
To *Bruxelles* marches on secure,

To bomb the Monks, and scare the Ladies.
After this glorious Expedition,
  One Battle makes the Marshal Great:
He must perform the King's Commission:
  Who knows, but *Orange* may retreat?
Kings are allow'd to feign the Gout,
  Or be prevail'd with not to Fight:
And mighty *Louis* hop'd, no doubt,
  That *William* wou'd preserve that Right.

From *Seyn* and *Loyre*, to *Rhone* and *Po*,
  See every Mother's Son appear:
In such a Case ne'er blame a Foe,
  If he betrays some little Fear.
He comes, the mighty *Vill'roy* comes;
  Finds a small River in his Way:
So waves his Colours, beats his Drums;
  And thinks it prudent there to stay.
The *Gallic* Troops breath Blood and War:
  The Marshal cares not to march faster·
Poor *Vill'roy* moves so slowly here,
  We fancy'd all, it was his Master.

Will no kind Flood, no friendly Rain
  Disguise the Marshal's plain Disgrace?
No Torrents swell the low *Mehayne?*
  The World will say, he durst not pass.
Why will no *Hyades* appear,
  Dear Poet, on the Banks of *Sambre?*
Just as they did that mighty Year,
  When You turn'd *June* into *December.*
The Water-*Nymphs* are too unkind
  To *Vill'roy;* are the Land-*Nymphs* so?
And fly They All, at Once Combin'd
  To shame a General, and a Beau?

Truth, Justice, Sense, Religion, Fame
    May join to finish *William's* Story:
Nations set free may bless his Name;
    And *France* in Secret own his Glory.
But *Ipres, Mastrich,* and *Cambray,*
    Besançon, Ghent, St. Omers, Lysle,
Courtray, and *Dole*—Ye Criticks, say,
    How poor to this was *Pindar's* Style?
With Eke's and Also's tack thy Strain,
    Great Bard; and sing the deathless Prince,
Who lost *Namur* the same Campaign,
    He bought *Dixmude,* and plunder'd *Deynse.*

I'll hold Ten Pound, my Dream is out:
    I'd tell it You, but for the Rattle
Of those confounded Drums: no doubt
    Yon' bloody Rogues intend a Battel.
Dear me! a hundred thousand *French*
    With Terror fill the neighb'ring Field;
While *William* carries on the Trench,
    'Till both the Town and Castle yield.
Vill'roy to *Boufflers* should advance,
    Says *Mars,* thro' Cannons Mouths in Fire;
Id est, one Mareschal of *France*
    Tells t'other, He can come no nigher.

Regain the Lines the shortest Way,
    Vill'roy; or to *Versailles* take Post:
For, having seen it, Thou can'st say
    The Steps, by which *Namur* was lost.
The Smoke and Flame may vex thy Sight:
    Look not once back: but as thou goest,
Quicken the Squadrons in their Flight;
    And bid the D—l take the slowest.
Think not what Reason to produce,
    From *Louis* to conceal thy Fear:

He'll own the Strength of thy Excuse;
　　Tell him that *William* was but there.

Now let us look for *Louis'* Feather,
　　That us'd to shine so like a Star:
The Gen'rals could not get together,
　　Wanting that Influence, great in War.
O Poet! Thou had'st been discreeter,
　　Hanging the Monarch's Hat so high;
If Thou had'st dubb'd thy Star, a Meteor,
　　That did but blaze, and rove, and die.

To animate the doubtful Fight,
　　Namur in vain expects that Ray:
In vain *France* hopes, the sickly Light
　　Shou'd shine near *William's* fuller Day.
It knows *Versailles,* it's proper Station;
　　Nor cares for any foreign Sphere:
Where You see *Boileau's* Constellation,
　　Be sure no Danger can be near.

The *French* had gather'd all their Force;
　　And *William* met them in their Way:
Yet off they brush'd, both Foot and Horse.
　　What has Friend *Boileau* left to say?
When his high Muse is bent upon't,
　　To sing her King, that Great Commander,
Or on the Shores of *Hellespont,*
　　Or in the Valleys near *Scamander;*
Wou'd it not spoil his noble Task,
　　If any foolish *Phrygian* there is,
Impertinent enough to ask,
　　How far *Namur* may be from *Paris?*

Two Stanza's more before we end,
　　Of Death, Pikes, Rocks, Arms, Bricks, and Fire:
Leave 'em behind You, honest Friend:

And with your Country-Men retire.
Your Ode is spoilt; *Namur* is freed;
    For *Dixmuyd* something yet is due:
So good Count *Guiscard* may proceed;
    But *Boufflers*, Sir, one Word with you.—

'Tis done. In Sight of these Commanders,
    Who neither Fight, nor raise the Siege,
The Foes of *France* march safe thro' *Flanders*;
    Divide to *Bruxelles*, or to *Liege*.
Send, *Fame*, this News to *Trianon*;
    That *Boufflers* may new Honours gain:
He the same Play by Land has shown,
    As *Tourville* did upon the Main.
Yet is the Marshal made a Peer:
    O *William*, may the Arms advance;
That He may lose *Dinant* next Year,
    And so be Constable of *France*.

Written in the Beginning of Mezeray's History of France

Whate'er thy Countrymen have done
By Law and Wit, by Sword and Gun,
    In Thee is faithfully recited:
And all the living World, that view
Thy Work, give Thee the Praises due,
    At once Instructed and Delighted.

Yet for the Fame of all these Deeds,
What Beggar in the *Invalides*,
    With Lameness broke, with Blindness smitten,
Wish'd ever decently to die,

To have been either *Mezeray*,
    Or any Monarch He has written?

It's strange, dear Author, yet it true is,
That, down from *Pharamond* to *Louis*,
    All covet Life, yet call it Pain:
All feel the Ill, yet shun the Cure:
Can Sense this Paradox endure?
    Resolve Me, *Cambray*, or *Fontaine*.

The Man in graver Tragic known
(Tho' his best Part long since was done)
    Still on the Stage desires to tarry:
And He who play'd the *Harlequin*,
After the Jest still loads the Scene
    Unwilling to retire, tho' weary.

A Better Answer (to Cloe Jealous)

Dear *Cloe*, how blubber'd is that pretty Face?
    Thy Cheek all on Fire, and Thy Hair all uncurl'd:
Pr'ythee quit this Caprice, and (as *Old Falstaf* says)
    Let Us e'en talk a little like Folks of This World.

How canst Thou presume, Thou hast leave to destroy
    The Beauties, which *Venus* but lent to Thy keeping?
Those Looks were design'd to inspire Love and Joy:
    More ord'nary Eyes may serve People for weeping.

To be vext at a Trifle or two that I writ,
    Your Judgment at once, and my Passion You wrong;
You take that for Fact, which will scarce be found Wit:
    Od's Life! must One swear to the Truth of a Song?

What I speak, my fair *Cloe*, and what I write, shews
    The Diff'rence there is betwixt Nature and Art:

I court others in Verse; but I love Thee in Prose:
   And They have my Whimsies; but Thou hast my
      Heart.

The God of us Verse-men (You know, Child) the *Sun*,
   How after his Journeys He sets up his Rest:
If at Morning o'er Earth 'tis his Fancy to run;
   At Night he reclines on his *Thetis's* Breast.

So when I am weary'd with wand'ring all Day;
   To Thee my Delight in the Evening I come:
No Matter what Beauties I saw in my Way:
   They were but my Visits; but Thou art my Home.

Then finish, Dear *Cloe*, this Pastoral War;
   And let us like *Horace* and *Lydia* agree:
For Thou art a Girl as much brighter than Her,
   As He was a Poet sublimer than Me.

Jinny the Just

Releas'd from the noise of the Butcher and Baker
Who, my old Friends be thank'd, did seldom forsake her
And from the soft Duns of my Landlord the Quaker

From chiding the Footmen and watching the Lasses,
From Nell that burn'd Milk, and Tom that broke
   Glasses
(Sad mischiefs thro which a good housekeeper passes!)

From some real Care but more fancy'd vexation,
From a life Party Colour'd half reason half passion
Here lies after all the best Wench in the Nation

From the Rhine to the Po, from the Thames to the
   Rhone

Joanna or Janneton, Jinny or Joan,
'Twas all one to her by what name She was known

For the Idiom of words very little She heeded
Provided the Matter She drove at succeeded
She took and gave Languages just as She needed

So for Kitching and Market, for bargain and Sale
She paid English or Dutch or French down on the Nail
But in telling a Story she sometimes did fail

Then begging Excuse as she happen'd to Stammer
With respect to her betters but none to her Grammer
Her blush helpt her out and her Jargon became her

Her Habit and Mien she endeavour'd to frame
To the different Gout of the place where She came
Her outside stil chang'd, but her inside the same

At The Hague in her Slippers and hair as the Mode is
At Paris all Falbalow'd fine as a Goddess
And at censuring London in smock sleeves and Bodice

She order'd Affairs that few People cou'd tell
In what part about her that mixture did dwell
Of Vrough or Mistress, or Medemoiselle

For her Sirname and race let the Heraults e'en Answer
Her own proper worth was enough to advance her
And he who lik'd her, little valu'd her Grandsire.

But from what House so ever her lineage may come
I wish my own Jinny but out of her Tomb,
Tho all her Relations were there in her Room

Of such terrible beauty She never cou'd boast
As with absolute Sway o'er all hearts rules the roast,
When J—— bawls out to the Chair for a Toast

But of good Household Features her Person was made
Nor by Faction cry'd up nor of Censure afraid
And her beauty was rather for Use than Parade

Her Blood so well mix't and flesh so well Pasted
That tho her Youth faded her Comliness lasted
The blew was wore off but the Plum was well tasted

Less smooth than her Skin and less white than her
    breast
Was this pollisht stone beneath which she lyes prest
Stop, Reader, and Sigh while thou thinkst on the rest

With a just trim of Virtue her Soul was endu'd
Not affectedly Pious nor secretly lewd,
She cut even between the Cocquet and the Prude.

Her Will with her Duty so equally stood
That seldom oppos'd She was commonly good
And did pritty well, doing just what she wou'd

Declining all Pow'r she found means to perswade
Was then most regarded when most she Obey'd
The Mistress in truth when she seem'd but the Maid

Such care of her own proper Actions She took
That on other folks' lives She had no time to look
So Censure and Praise were struck out of her Book

Her thought stil confin'd to its own little Sphere
She minded not who did Excell or did Err
But just as the matter related to her

Then, too, when her Private Tribunal was rear'd
Her Mercy so mix'd with her judgment appear'd
That her Foes were condemn'd and her friends always
    clear'd

Her Religion so well with her learning did suite
That in Practice sincere, and in Controverse Mute
She shew'd She knew better to live than dispute

Some parts of the Bible by heart She recited
And much in historical Chapters delighted
But in points about Faith She was something short
  sighted

So Notions and modes She refer'd to the Schools
And in matters of Conscience adher'd to Two Rules
To advise with no Biggots, and jest with no Fools

And scrupling but little, enough she believ'd
By Charity ample smal sins She retriev'd
And when she had New Cloaths She always receiv'd

Thus stil whilst her Morning unseen fled away
In ord'ring the Linnen and making the Tea
That she scarce cou'd have time for the Psalms of the
  Day

And while after Dinner the Night came so soon
That half she propos'd very seldom was done
With twenty God bless Me's how this day is gone

While she read and Accounted and payd and abated
Eat and drank, Play'd and Work't, laught and Cry'd,
  lov'd and hated,
As answer'd the end of her being Created

In the midst of her Age came a cruel Desease
Which neither her Julips nor recepts cou'd appease
So down dropt her Clay, may her Soul be at peace

Retire from this Sepulchre all the Prophane
You that love for Debauch or that marry for gain
Retire lest Ye trouble the Manes of J——

But Thou that know'st Love above Intrest or lust
Strew the Myrtle and Rose on this once belov'd Dust
And shed one pious tear upon Jinny the Just

Tread soft on her Grave, and do right to her honor
Let neither rude hand nor ill Tongue light upon her
Do all the smal Favors that now can be done her

And when what Thou lik't shal return to her Clay
For so I'm perswaded she must do one Day
What ever fantastic J—— Asgil may say

When as I have done now, thou shalt set up a Stone
For something however distinguisht or known
May some Pious Friend the Misfortune bemoan
And make thy Concern by reflexion his own.

To a Child of Quality

FIVE YEARS OLD; THE AUTHOR FORTY

Lords, knights, and squires, the num'rous band,
    That wear the fair Miss *Mary's* fetters,
Were summon'd, by her high command,
    To show their passions by their letters.

My pen amongst the rest I took,
    Lest those bright eyes that cannot read
Shou'd dart their kindling fires, and look,
    The power they have to be obey'd.

Nor quality, nor reputation,
    Forbid me yet my flame to tell,
Dear five years old befriends my passion,
    And I may write till she can spell.

For while she makes her silk-worms beds
   With all the tender things I swear,
Whilst all the house my passion reads,
   In papers round her baby's hair,

She may receive and own my flame,
   For tho' the strictest prudes shou'd know it,
She'll pass for a most virtuous dame,
   And I for an unhappy poet.

Then too alas! when she shall tear
   The lines some younger rival sends,
She'll give me leave to write I fear,
   And we shall still continue friends;

For, as our diff'rent ages move,
   'Tis so ordain'd, wou'd fate but mend it,
That I shall be past making love
   When she begins to comprehend it.

An Epitaph

Stet quicunque volet potens
Aulæ culmine lubrico, etc.
      —SENECA

Interr'd beneath this Marble Stone,
Lie Saunt'ring *Jack,* and Idle *Joan.*
While rolling Threescore Years and One
Did round this Globe their Courses run;
If Human Things went Ill or Well;
If changing Empires rose or fell;
The Morning past, the Evening came,
And found this Couple still the same.
They Walk'd and Eat, good Folks: What then?

Why then They Walk'd and Eat again:
They soundly slept the Night away:
They did just Nothing all the Day:
And having bury'd Children Four,
Wou'd not take the Pains to try for more.
Nor Sister either had, nor Brother:
They seem'd just Tally'd for each other.

    Their Moral and Œconomy
Most perfectly They made agree:
Each Virtue kept it's proper Bound,
Nor Trespass'd on the other's Ground.
Nor Fame, nor Censure They regarded:
They neither Punish'd, nor Rewarded.
He car'd not what the Footmen did:
Her Maids She neither prais'd, nor chid:
So ev'ry Servant took his Course;
And bad at First, They all grew worse.
Slothful Disorder fill'd His Stable;
And sluttish Plenty deck'd Her Table.
Their Beer was strong; Their Wine was *Port;*
Their Meal was large; their Grace was short.
They gave the Poor the Remnant-meat,
Just when it grew not fit to eat.

    They paid the Church and Parish-rate;
And took, but read not the Receit;
For which They claim'd their *Sunday's* Due,
Of slumb'ring in an upper Pew.

    No Man's Defects sought They to know;
So never made Themselves a Foe.
No Man's good Deeds did They commend;
So never rais'd Themselves a Friend.
Nor cherish'd They Relations poor:
That might decrease Their present Store:

Nor Barn nor House did They repair:
That might oblige Their future Heir.

They neither Added, nor Confounded:
They neither Wanted, nor Abounded.
Each *Christmas* They Accompts did clear;
And wound their Bottom round the Year.
Nor Tear, nor Smile did They imploy
At News of Public Grief, or Joy.
When Bells were rung, and Bonfires made;
If ask'd, They ne'er deny'd Their Aid:
Their Jugg was to the Ringers carry'd;
Whoever either Dy'd, or Marry'd.
Their Billet at the Fire was found;
Whoever was Depos'd, or Crown'd.

Nor Good, nor Bad, nor Fools, nor Wise;
They wou'd not learn, nor cou'd advise:
Without Love, Hatred, Joy, or Fear,
They led—a kind of—as it were:
Nor Wish'd nor Car'd, nor Laugh'd, nor Cry'd:
And so They liv'd; and so They dy'd.

FROM *Solomon on the Vanity of the World*

Pass We the Ills, which each Man feels or dreads,
The Weight or fall'n, or hanging o'er our Heads;
The Bear, the Lyon, Terrors of the Plain,
The Sheepfold scatter'd, and the Shepherd slain;
The frequent Errors of the pathless Wood,
The giddy Precipice, and the dang'rous Flood:
The noisom Pest'lence, that in open War
Terrible, marches thro' the Mid-day Air,
And scatters Death; the Arrow that by Night

Cuts the dank Mist, and fatal wings it's Flight;
The billowing Snow, and Violence of the Show'r,
That from the Hills disperse their dreadful Store,
And o'er the Vales collected Ruin pour;
The Worm that gnaws the ripening Fruit, sad Guest,
Canker or Locust hurtful to infest
The Blade; while Husks elude the Tiller's Care,
And Eminence of Want distinguishes the Year.

Pass we the slow Disease, and subtil Pain,
Which our weak Frame is destin'd to sustain;
The cruel Stone, with congregated War
Tearing his bloody Way; the cold Catarrh,
With frequent Impulse, and continu'd Strife,
Weak'ning the wasted Seats of irksome Life;
The Gout's fierce Rack, the burning Feaver's Rage,
The sad Experience of Decay; and Age,
Her self the soarest Ill; while Death, and Ease,
Oft and in vain invok'd, or to appease,
Or end the Grief, with hasty Wings receed
From the vext Patient, and the sickly Bed.

Nought shall it profit, that the charming Fair,
Angelic, softest Work of Heav'n, draws near
To the cold shaking paralytic Hand,
Senseless of Beauty's Touch, or Love's Command,
Nor longer apt, or able to fulfill
The Dictates of its feeble Master's Will.

Nought shall the Psaltry, and the Harp avail,
The pleasing Song, or well repeated Tale;
When the quick Spirits their warm March forbea
And numbing Coldness has unbrac'd the Ear.

The verdant Rising of the flow'ry Hill,
The Vale enamell'd, and the Crystal Rill,
The Ocean rolling, and the shelly Shoar,

Beautiful Objects, shall delight no more;
When the lax'd Sinews of the weaken'd Eye
In wat'ry Damps, or dim Suffusion lye.
Day follows Night; the Clouds return again
After the falling of the later Rain:
But to the Aged-blind shall ne'er return
Grateful Vicissitude: He still must mourn
The Sun, and Moon, and ev'ry Starry Light
Eclips'd to Him, and lost in everlasting Night.

Behold where Age's wretched Victim lies:
See his Head trembling, and his half-clos'd Eyes:
Frequent for Breath his panting Bosom heaves:
To broken Sleeps his remnant Sense He gives;
And only by his Pains, awaking finds He Lives.

Loos'd by devouring Time the silver Cord
Dissever'd lies: unhonor'd from the Board
The Crystal Urn, when broken, is thrown by;
And apter Utensils their Place supply.
These Things and Thou must share One equal Lot;
Dye and be lost, corrupt and be forgot;
While still another, and another Race
Shall now supply, and now give up the Place.
From Earth all came, to Earth must all return;
Frail as the Cord, and brittle as the Urn.

(*Book III, lines 119–185*)

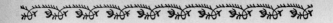

Anne Finch, Countess of Winchilsea

(1661–1720)

The Petition for an Absolute Retreat

INSCRIBED TO THE RIGHT HONOURABLE
CATHARINE COUNTESS OF THANET,
MENTION'D IN THE POEM UNDER
THE NAME OF ARMINDA

Give me, O indulgent Fate!
Give me yet, before I Dye,
A sweet, but absolute Retreat,
'Mongst Paths so lost, and Trees so high,
That the World may ne'er invade,
Through such Windings and such Shade,
My unshaken Liberty.

No Intruders thither come!
Who visit, but to be from home;
None who their vain Moments pass,
Only studious of their Glass;
News, that charm to listning Ears,
That false Alarm to Hopes and Fears;
That common Theme for every Fop,
From the Statesman to the Shop,
In those Coverts ne'er be spread,
Of who's Deceas'd, or who's to Wed;

Be no Tidings thither brought,
But silent as a Midnight Thought,
Where the World may ne'er invade,
Be those Windings, and that Shade.

Courteous Fate! afford me there
A *Table* spread without my Care,
With what the neighb'ring Fields impart,
Whose Cleanliness be all its Art,
When, of old, the Calf was drest,
(Tho' to make an Angel's Feast)
In the plain, unstudied Sauce
Nor *Treufle,* nor *Morilla* was;
Nor cou'd the mighty Patriarch's Board
One far-fetch'd *Ortolane* afford.
Courteous Fate, then give me there
Only plain, and wholesome Fare.
Fruits indeed (wou'd Heaven bestow)
All that did in *Eden* grow,
All but the *Forbidden Tree,*
Wou'd be coveted by me;
Grapes, with juice so crouded up,
As breaking thro' the native Cup;
Figs (yet growing) candy'd o'er,
By the Sun's attracting Pow'r;
Cherries, with the downy Peach,
All within my easie Reach;
Whilst creeping near the humble Ground,
Shou'd the Strawberry be found
Springing whereso'er I stray'd,
Thro' those Windings and that Shade.

For my Garments; let them be
What may with the Time agree;
Warm when *Phœbus* does retire,
And is ill-supply'd by Fire:

But when he renews the Year,
And verdant all the Fields appear;
Beauty every thing resumes,
Birds have dropt their Winter-Plumes;
When the Lilly full display'd,
Stands in purer White array'd,
Than that Vest, which heretofore
The Luxurious Monarch wore,
When from *Salem's* Gates he drove,
To the soft Retreat of Love,
Lebanon's all burnish'd House,
And the dear *Egyptian* Spouse.
Cloath me, Fate, tho' not so Gay;
Cloath me light, and fresh as *May:*
In the Fountains let me view
All my Habit cheap and new;
Such as, when sweet *Zephers* fly,
With their Motions may comply;
Gently waving, to express
Unaffected Carelessness:
No Perfumes have there a Part,
Borrow'd from the *Chymist's* Art;
But such as rise from flow'ry Beds,
Or the falling *Jasmin* Sheds!
'Twas the Odour of the Field,
Esau's rural Coat did yield,
That inspir'd his Father's Pray'r,
For Blessings of the Earth and Air:
Of Gums, or Pouders had it smelt;
The Supplanter, then unfelt,
Easily had been descry'd,
For One that did in Tents abide;
For some beauteous Handmaids Joy,
And his Mother's darling Boy.
Let me then no Fragrance wear,

But what the Winds from Gardens bear,
In such kind, surprizing Gales,
As gather'd from *Fidentia's* Vales,
All the Flowers that in them grew;
Which intermixing, as they flew,
In wreathen Garlands dropt agen,
On *Lucullus*, and his Men;
Who, chear'd by the victorious Sight,
Trebl'd Numbers put to Flight.
Let me, when I must be fine,
In such natural Colours shine;
Wove, and painted by the Sun,
Whose resplendent Rays to shun,
When they do too fiercely beat,
Let me find some close Retreat,
Where they have no Passage made,
Thro' those Windings, and that Shade.

      Give me there (since Heaven has shown
It was not Good to be alone)
A *Partner* suited to my Mind,
Solitary, pleas'd and kind;
Who, partially, may something see
Preferr'd to all the World in me;
Slighting, by my humble Side,
Fame and Splendor, Wealth and Pride.
When but Two the Earth possest,
'Twas their happiest Days, and best;
They by Bus'ness, nor by Wars,
They by no Domestick Cares,
From each other e'er were drawn,
But in some Grove, or flow'ry Lawn,
Spent the swiftly flying Time,
Spent their own, and Nature's Prime,
In Love; that only Passion giv'n

To perfect Man, whilst Friends with Heaven.
Rage, and Jealousie, and Hate,
Transports of his fallen State,
(When by *Satan's* Wiles betray'd)
Fly those Windings, and that Shade!

    Thus from Crouds, and Noise remov'd,
Let each Moment be improv'd;
Every Object still produce
Thoughts of Pleasure, and of Use:
When some River slides away,
To encrease the boundless Sea;
Think we then how Time do's haste,
To grow eternity at last.
By the Willows, on the Banks,
Gather'd into social Ranks,
Playing with the gentle Winds,
Strait the Boughs, and smooth the Rinds,
Moist each Fibre, and each Top,
Wearing a luxurious Crop,
Let the time of Youth be shown,
The time alas! too soon outgrown;
Whilst a lonely stubborn Oak,
Which no Breezes can provoke,
No less Gusts persuade to move,
Than those, which in a Whirlwind drove,
Spoil'd the old Fraternal Feast,
And left alive but one poor Guest;
Rivell'd the distorted Trunk,
Sapless Limbs all bent, and shrunk,
Sadly does the Time presage
Of our too near approaching Age.
When a helpless Vine is found,
Unsupported on the Ground,
Careless all the Branches spread,

Subject to each haughty Tread,
Bearing neither Leaves nor Fruit,
Living only in the Root;
Back reflecting let me say,
So the sad *Ardelia* lay;
Blasted by a Storm of Fate,
Felt, thro' all the *British* State;
Fall'n, neglected, lost, forgot,
Dark Oblivion all her Lot;
Faded till *Arminda's* Love
(Guided by the Pow'rs above)
Warm'd anew her drooping Heart,
And Life diffus'd thro' every Part;
Mixing Words, in wise Discourse,
Of such Weight and wondrous Force,
As could all her Sorrows charm,
And transitory Ills disarm;
Chearing the delightful Day,
When dispos'd to be more Gay,
With Wit, from an unmeasured Store,
To Woman ne'er allow'd before.
What Nature, or refining Art,
All that Fortune cou'd impart,
Heaven did to *Arminda* send;
Then gave her for *Ardelia's* Friend:
To her Cares the Cordial drop,
Which else had overflow'd the Cup.
So, when once the son of *Jess*,
Every Anguish did oppress,
Hunted by all kinds of Ills,
Like a *Partridge* on the Hills;
Trains were laid to catch his Life,
Baited with a Royal Wife,
From his House and Country torn,
Made a Heathen Prince's Scorn;

Fate, to answer all these Harms,
Threw a *Friend* into his Arms.
Friendship still has been design'd,
The support of Human-kind;
The safe Delight, the useful Bliss,
The next World's Happiness, and this.
Give then, O indulgent Fate!
Give a Friend in that Retreat
(Tho' withdrawn from all the rest)
Still a Clue, to reach my Breast.
Let a Friend be still convey'd
Thro' those Windings, and that Shade!

Where, may I remain secure,
Waste, in humble Joys and pure,
A Life, that can no Envy yield;
Want of Affluence my Shield.
Thus had *Crassus* been content,
When from *Marius* Rage he went,
With the Seat that Fortune gave,
The commodious ample Cave,
Form'd in a divided Rock,
By some mighty Earthquake's Shock,
Into Rooms of every Size,
Fair, as Art cou'd e'er devise,
Leaving, in the marble Roof
('Gainst all Storms and Tempests proof)
Only Passage for the Light,
To refresh the chearful Sight,
Whilst Three Sharers in his Fate,
On th' Escape with Joy dilate,
Beds of Moss their Bodies bore,
Canopy'd with Ivy o'er;
Rising Springs, that round them play'd,
O'er the native Pavement stray'd;

When the Hour arriv'd to Dine,
Various Meats, and sprightly Wine,
On some neighb'ring Cliff they spy'd;
Every Day a-new supply'd
By a Friend's entrusted Care;
Had He still continu'd there,
Made that lonely wond'rous Cave
Both his Palace and his Grave;
Peace and Rest he might have found
(Peace and Rest are under Ground)
Nor have been in that Retreat,
Fam'd for a Proverbial Fate;
In pursuit of Wealth been caught,
And punish'd with a golden Draught.
Nor had He, who Crowds cou'd blind,
Whisp'ring with a snowy Hind,
Made 'em think that from above
(Like the great Imposter's Dove)
Tydings to his Ears she brought,
Rules by which he march'd and fought,
After *Spain* he had o'er-run,
Cities sack'd, and Battles won,
Drove *Rome's* Consuls from the Field,
Made her darling *Pompey* yield,
At a fatal, treach'rous Feast,
Felt a Dagger in his Breast;
Had he his once-pleasing Thought
Of Solitude to Practice brought;
Had no wild Ambition sway'd,
In those Islands had he stay'd,
Justly call'd the Seats of Rest,
Truly Fortunate and Blest,
By the ancient Poets giv'n
As their best discover'd Heav'n.
Let me then, indulgent Fate!

Let me still, in my Retreat,
From all roving thoughts be freed,
Or Aims, that may Contention breed:
Nor be my Endeavours led
By Goods, that perish with the Dead!
Fitly might the Life of Man
Be indeed esteem'd a Span,
If the present Moment were
Of Delight his only Share;
If no other Joys he knew
Than what round about him grew:
But as those, who Stars wou'd trace
From a subterranean Place,
Through some Engine lift their Eyes
To the outward glorious Skies;
So th'immortal Spirit may,
When descended to our Clay,
From a rightly govern'd Frame
View the Height, from whence she came;
To her Paradise be caught,
And things unutterable taught.
Give me then, in that Retreat,
Give me, O indulgent Fate!
For all Pleasures left behind,
Contemplations of the Mind.
Let the Fair, the Gay, the Vain
Courtship and Applause obtain;
Let th'Ambitious rule the Earth;
Let the giddy Fool have Mirth;
Give the Epicure his Dish,
Every one their sev'ral Wish;
Whilst my Transports I employ
On that more extensive Joy,
When all Heav'n shall be survey'd
From those Windings and that Shade.

A *Nocturnal Reverie*

In such a *Night*, when every louder Wind
Is to its distant Cavern safe confin'd;
And only gentle *Zephyr* fans his Wings,
And lonely *Philomel* still waking, sings;
Or from some Tree, fam'd for the *Owl's* delight,
She hollowing clear, directs the Wand'rer right:
In such a *Night*, when passing clouds give place,
Or thinly vail the heav'ns mysterious Face;
When in some River, overhung with Green,
The waving Moon and trembling Leaves are seen;
When freshen'd Grass now bears itself upright,
And makes cool Banks to pleasing Rest invite,
Whence springs the *Woodbine* and the *Bramble-Rose*,
And where the sleepy *Cowslip* shelter'd grows;
Whilst now a paler Blue the *Foxglove* takes,
Yet checquers still with Red the dusky brakes
When scatter'd *Glow-worms*, but in Twilight fine,
Shew trivial Beauties watch their Hour to shine;
Whilst *Salisb'ry* stands the Test of every Light
In perfect Charms and perfect Virtue bright:
When Odours, which declin'd repelling Day,
Thro' temp'rate Air uninterrupted stray;
When darken'd Groves their softest Shadows wear,
And falling Waters we distinctly hear;
When thro' the Gloom more venerable shows
Some ancient Fabrick awful in Repose,
While Sunburnt Hills their swarthy Looks conceal,
And swelling Haycocks thicken up the Vale:
When the loos'd *Horse* now, as his Pasture leads,
Comes slowly grazing thro' th'adjoining Meads,

Whose stealing Pace, and lengthen'd Shade we fear,
Till torn up Forage in his Teeth we hear:
When nibbling *Sheep* at large pursue their Food,
And unmolested Kine rechew the Cud;
When *Curlews* cry beneath the Village-walls,
And to her straggling Brood the *Partridge* calls;
Their shortliv'd Jubilee the Creatures keep,
Which but endures, whilst Tyrant-*Man* do's sleep;
When a sedate Content the Spirit feels,
And no fierce Light disturb, whilst it reveals;
But silent Musings urge the Mind to seek
Something, too high for Syllables to speak;
Till the free Soul to a compos'dness charm'd,
Finding the Elements of Rage disarm'd
O'er all below a solemn Quiet grown,
Joys in the inferiour World, and thinks it like her Own;
In such a *Night* let Me abroad remain,
Till Morning breaks, and All's confus'd again;
Our Cares, our Toils, our Clamours are renew'd,
Or Pleasures, seldom reach'd, again pursu'd.

Joseph Addison

(1672–1719)

The spacious Firmament on high

The spacious Firmament on high,
With all the blue Ethereal Sky,
And spangled Heavens, a shining Frame,
Their great Original proclaim.
Th' unweary'd Sun, from Day to Day,
Does his Creator's Power display;
And publishes, to every Land,
The Work of an Almighty Hand.

Soon as the Evening Shades prevail,
The Moon takes up the wond'rous Tale;
And Nightly, to the list'ning Earth,
Repeats the Story of her Birth:
Whilst all the Stars, that round her burn,
And all the Planets, in their turn,
Confirm the Tidings as they roll,
And spread the Truth from Pole to Pole.

What tho', in solemn Silence, all
Meet round the dark Terrestrial Ball;
What tho', no real Voice, nor Sound,
Amidst their radiant Orbs be found:
In Reason's Ear they all rejoice,
And utter forth a glorious Voice;
For ever Singing as they Shine,
The Hand that made us is Divine.

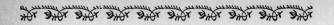

Jonathan Swift
(1667–1745)

FROM On Poetry: A Rapsody

All Human Race wou'd fain be *Wits*,
And Millions miss, for one that hits.
Young's universal Passion, *Pride*,
Was never known to spread so wide.
Say *Britain*, cou'd you ever boast,——
Three *Poets* in an Age at most?
Our chilling Climate hardly bears
A *Sprig* of Bays in Fifty Years:
While ev'ry Fool his Claim alledges,
As if it grew in common Hedges.
What Reason can there be assign'd
For this Perverseness in the Mind?
Brutes find out where their Talents lie:
A *Bear* will not attempt to fly:
A founder'd *Horse* will oft debate,
Before he tries a five-barr'd Gate:
A *Dog* by Instinct turns aside,
Who sees the Ditch too deep and wide.
But *Man* we find the only Creature,
Who, led by *Folly*, fights with *Nature*;
Who, when *she* loudly cries, *Forbear*,
With Obstinacy fixes there;
And, where his *Genius* least inclines,
Absurdly bends his whole Designs.

Not *Empire* to the Rising-Sun,
By Valour, Conduct, Fortune won;
Nor highest *Wisdom* in Debates
For framing Laws to govern States;
Nor Skill in Sciences profound,
So large to grasp the Circle round;
Such heavenly Influence require,
As how to strike the *Muses Lyre.*

Not Beggar's Brat, on Bulk begot;
Nor Bastard of a Pedlar *Scot;*
Nor Boy brought up to cleaning Shoes,
The Spawn of *Bridewell,* or the Stews;
Nor Infants dropt, the spurious Pledges
Of *Gipsies* littering under Hedges,
Are so disqualified by Fate
To rise in *Church,* or *Law,* or *State,*
As he, whom *Phebus* in his Ire
Hath *blasted* with poetick Fire.

What hope of Custom in the *Fair,*
While not a Soul demands your Ware?
Where you have nothing to produce
For private Life, or publick Use?
Court, City, Country want you not;
You cannot bribe, betray, or plot.
For Poets, Law makes no Provision:
The Wealthy have you in Derision.
Of State-Affairs you cannot smatter,
Are awkward when you try to flatter.
Your Portion, taking *Britain* round,
Was just one annual Hundred Pound.
Now not so much as in Remainder
Since *Cibber* brought in an Attainder;
For ever fixt by Right Divine,

(A Monarch's Right) on *Grubstreet* Line.
Poor starv'ling Bard, how small thy Gains!
How unproportion'd to thy Pains!

And here a *Simile* comes Pat in:
Tho' *Chickens* take a Month to fatten,
The Guests in less than half an Hour
Will more than half a Score devour.
So, after toiling twenty Days,
To earn a Stock of Pence and Praise,
Thy Labours, grown the Critick's Prey,
Are swallow'd o'er a Dish of Tea;
Gone, to be never heard of more,
Gone, where the *Chickens* went before.

How shall a new Attempter learn
Of diff'rent Spirits to discern,
And how distinguish, which is which,
The Poet's Vein, or scribling Itch?
Then hear an old experienc'd Sinner
Instructing thus a young Beginner.

Consult yourself, and if you find
A powerful Impulse urge your Mind,
Impartial judge within your Breast
What Subject you can manage best;
Whether your Genius most inclines
To Satire, Praise, or hum'rous Lines;
To Elegies in mournful Tone,
Or Prologue sent from Hand unknown.
Then rising with *Aurora's* Light,
The Muse invok'd, sit down to write;
Blot out, correct, insert, refine,
Enlarge, diminish, interline;
Be mindful, when Invention fails,
To scratch your Head, and bite your Nails.

Your Poem finish'd, next your Care
Is needful, to transcribe it fair.
In modern Wit all printed Trash, is
Set off with num'rous *Breaks*——and *Dashes*—

To Statesmen wou'd you give a Wipe,
You print it in *Italick Type*.
When Letters are in vulgar Shapes,
'Tis ten to one the Wit escapes;
But when in *Capitals* exprest,
The dullest Reader smoaks the Jest;
Or else perhaps he may invent
A better than the Poet meant,
As learned Commentators view
In *Homer* more than *Homer* knew.

Your Poem in its modish Dress,
Correctly fitted for the Press,
Convey by Penny-Post to *Lintot,*
But let no Friend alive look into't.
If *Lintot* thinks 'twill quit the Cost,
You need not fear your Labour lost:
And, how agreeably surpriz'd
Are you to see it advertiz'd!
The Hawker shews you one in Print,
As fresh as Farthings from the Mint:
The Product of your Toil and Sweating;
A Bastard of your own begetting.

Be sure at *Will's* the following Day,
Lie Snug, and hear what Criticks say.
And if you find the general Vogue
Pronounces you a stupid Rogue;
Damns all your Thoughts as low and little,
Sit still, and swallow down your Spittle.
Be silent as a Politician,
For talking may beget Suspicion:

Or praise the Judgment of the Town,
And help yourself to run it down.
Give up your fond paternal Pride,
Nor argue on the weaker Side;
For Poems read without a Name
We justly praise, or justly blame:
And Criticks have no partial Views,
Except they know whom they abuse.
And since you ne'er provok'd their Spight,
Depend upon't their Judgment's right:
But if you blab, you are undone;
Consider that a Risk you run.
You lose your Credit all at once;
The Town will mark you for a Dunce:
The vilest Doggrel *Grubstreet* sends,
Will pass for yours with Foes and Friends.
And you must bear the whole Disgrace,
'Till some fresh Blockhead takes your Place.

Your Secret kept, your Poem sunk,
And sent in Quires to line a Trunk;
If still you be dispos'd to rhime,
Go try your Hand a second Time.
Again you fail, yet Safe's the Word,
Take Courage, and attempt a Third.
But first with Care imploy your Thoughts,
Where Criticks mark'd your former Faults.
The trivial Turns, the borrow'd Wit,
The *Similes* that nothing fit;
The *Cant* which ev'ry Fool repeats,
Town-Jests, and Coffee-house Conceits;
Descriptions tedious, flat and dry,
And introduc'd the Lord knows why;
Or where we find your Fury set
Against the harmless Alphabet;

On A's and B's your Malice vent,
While Readers wonder whom you meant.
A publick, or a private *Robber;*
A *Statesman,* or a South-Sea *Jobber.*
A *Prelate,* who no God believes;
A——,or Den of Thieves.
A Pick-Purse at the Bar, or Bench;
A Duchess, or a Suburb-Wench.
Or oft when Epithets you link,
In gaping Lines to fill a Chink;
Like stepping Stones to save a Stride,
In Streets where Kennels are too wide:
Or like a Heel-piece to support
A Cripple with one Foot too short:
Or like a Bridge that joins a Marish
To Moorlands of a diff'rent Parish.
So have I seen ill-coupled Hounds,
Drag diff'rent Ways in miry Grounds.
So Geographers in *Afric*-Maps
With Savage-Pictures fill their Gaps;
And o'er unhabitable Downs
Place Elephants for want of Towns.

(*Lines* 1–180)

A Satirical Elegy on the Death of a Late Famous General

His Grace! impossible! what dead!
Of old age too, and in his bed!
And could that Mighty Warrior fall?
And so inglorious, after all!
Well, since he's gone, no matter how,
The last loud trump must wake him now:

And, trust me, as the noise grows stronger,
He'd wish to sleep a little longer.
And could he be indeed so old
As by the news-papers we're told?
Threescore, I think, is pretty high;
'Twas time in conscience he should die.
This world he cumber'd long enough;
He burnt his candle to the snuff;
And that's the reason, some folks think,
He left behind *so great a s . . . k.*
Behold his funeral appears,
Nor widow's sighs, nor orphan's tears,
Wont at such times each heart to pierce,
Attend the progress of his herse.
But what of that, his friends may say,
He had those honours in his day.
True to his profit and his pride,
He made them weep before he dy'd.

Come hither, all ye empty things,
Ye bubbles rais'd by breath of Kings;
Who float upon the tide of state,
Come hither, and behold your fate.
Let pride be taught by this rebuke,
How very mean a thing's a Duke;
From all his ill-got honours flung,
Turn'd to that dirt from whence he sprung.

Stella's Birth-day

Written A.D. 1720–21

All Travellers at first incline
Where'e'er they see the fairest Sign,
And if they find the Chambers neat,

And like the Liquor and the Meat
Will call again and recommend
The Angel-Inn to ev'ry Friend:
And though the Painting grows decayd
The House will never loose it's Trade;
Nay, though the treach'rous Rascal Thomas
Hangs a new Angel two doors from us
As fine as Dawbers Hands can make it
In hopes that Strangers may mistake it,
They think it both a Shame and Sin
To quit the true old Angel-Inn.

　　Now, this is Stella's Case in Fact;
An Angel's Face, a little crack't;
(Could Poets or could Painters fix
How Angels look at thirty six)
This drew us in at first to find
In such a Form an Angel's Mind
And ev'ry Virtue now supplyes
The fainting Rays of Stella's Eyes:
See, at her Levee crowding Swains
Whom Stella freely entertains
With Breeding, Humor, Wit, and Sense,
And puts them to so small Expence,
Their Minds so plentifully fills,
And makes such reasonable Bills
So little gets for what she gives
We really wonder how she lives;
And, had her Stock been less, no doubt
She must have long ago run out.

　　Then, who can think we'll quit the Place
When Doll hangs out a newer Face
Nail'd to her Window full in Sight
All Christian People to invite;
Or stop and light at Cloe's Head
With Scraps and Leaving to be fed.

Then Cloe, still go on to prate
Of thirty six, and thirty eight;
Pursue thy Trade of Scandall picking,
Thy Hints that Stella is no Chickin,
Your Innuendo's when you tell us
That Stella loves to talk with Fellows
But let me warn thee to believe
A Truth for which thy Soul should grieve,
That, should you live to see the Day
When Stella's Locks must all be grey
When Age must print a furrow'd Trace
On ev'ry Feature of her Face;
Though you and all your senceless Tribe
Could Art or Time or Nature bribe
To make you look like Beauty's Queen
And hold for ever at fifteen.
No Bloom of Youth can ever blind
The Cracks and Wrinckles of your Mind,
All Men of Sense will pass your Dore
And crowd to Stella's at fourscore.

Stella's Birth-day

March 13, 1726-27

This Day, whate'er the Fates decree,
Shall still be kept with Joy by me:
This Day then, let us not be told,
That you are sick, and I grown old,
Nor think on our approaching Ills,
And talk of Spectacles and Pills;
To morrow will be Time enough
To hear such mortifying Stuff.

Yet since from Reason may be brought
A better and more pleasing Thought,
Which can in spite of all Decays,
Support a few remaining Days:
From not the gravest of Divines,
Accept for once some serious Lines.

Although we now can form no more
Long schemes of Life, as heretofore;
Yet you, while Time is running fast,
Can look with Joy on what is past.

Were future Happiness and Pain,
A mere Contrivance of the Brain,
As Atheists argue, to entice,
And fit their Proselytes for Vice;
(The only Comfort they propose,
To have Companions in their Woes.)
Grant this the Case, yet sure 'tis hard,
That Virtue, stil'd its own Reward,
And by all Sages understood
To be the chief of human Good,
Should acting, die, nor leave behind
Some lasting Pleasure in the Mind,
Which by Remembrance will assuage,
Grief, Sickness, Poverty, and Age;
And strongly shoot a radiant Dart,
To shine through Life's declining Part.

Say, *Stella*, feel you no Content,
Reflecting on a Life well spent?
Your skilful Hand employ'd to save
Despairing Wretches from the Grave;
And then supporting with your Store,
Those whom you dragg'd from Death before:
(So Providence on Mortals waits,

Preserving what it first creates)
Your gen'rous Boldness to defend
An innocent and absent Friend;
That courage which can make you just,
To Merit humbled in the Dust:
The Detestation you express
For Vice in all its glitt'ring Dress:
That Patience under tort'ring Pain,
Where stubborn Stoicks would complain.

Must these like empty Shadows pass,
Or forms reflected from a Glass?
Or mere Chimæra's in the Mind,
That fly and leave no Marks behind?
Does not the Body thrive and grow
By Food of twenty Years ago?
And, had it not been still supply'd,
It must a thousand Times have dy'd.
Then, who with Reason can maintain,
That no Effects of Food remain?
And, is not Virtue in Mankind
The Nutriment that feeds the Mind?
Upheld by each good Action past,
And still continued by the last:
Then, who with Reason can pretend,
That all Effects of Virtue end?

Believe me *Stella* when you show
That true Contempt for Things below,
Nor prize your Life for other Ends
Than merely to oblige your Friends;
Your former Actions claim their Part,
And join to fortify your Heart.
For Virtue in her daily Race,
Like *Janus*, bears a double Face;
Looks back with Joy where she has gone,

And therefore goes with Courage on.
She at your sickly Couch will wait,
And guide you to a better State.

O then, whatever Heav'n intends,
Take Pity on your pitying Friends;
Nor let your Ills affect your Mind,
To fancy they can be unkind.
Me, surely me, you ought to spare,
Who gladly would your Suff'rings share;
Or give my Scrap of Life to you,
And think it far beneath your Due;
You, to whose Care so oft I owe,
That I'm alive to tell you so.

To Their Excellencies the Lords Justices of Ireland, the Humble Petition of Frances Harris, Who Must Starve, and Die a Maid if It Miscarries

Humbly Sheweth.
That I went to warm my self in Lady *Betty's* Chamber, because I was cold,
And I had in a Purse, seven Pound, four Shillings and six Pence, besides Farthings, in Money, and Gold;
So because I had been buying things for my *Lady* last Night,
I was resolved to tell my Money, to see if it was right:
Now you must know, because my Trunk has a very bad Lock,
Therefore all the Money, I have, which, *God* knows, is a very small Stock,

I keep in a Pocket ty'd about my Middle, next my
    Smock.

So when I went to put up my Purse, as *God* would have
    it, my Smock was unript,

And, instead of putting it into my Pocket, down it slipt:

Then the Bell rung, and I went down to put my *Lady*
    to Bed,

And, God knows, I thought my Money was as safe as
    my Maidenhead.

So when I came up again, I found my Pocket feel very
    light,

But when I search't, and miss'd my Purse, *Lord!* I
    thought I should have sunk outright:

Lord! Madam, says *Mary,* how d'ye do? Indeed, says I,
    never worse;

But pray, *Mary,* can you tell what I have done with
    my Purse!

Lord help me, said *Mary,* I never stirr'd out of this
    Place!

Nay, said I, I had it in Lady *Betty's* Chamber, that's a
    plain Case.

So *Mary* got me to Bed, and cover'd me up warm,

However, she stole away my Garters, that I might do
    my self no Harm:

So I tumbl'd and toss'd all Night, as you may very well
    think,

But hardly ever set my Eyes together, or slept a Wink.

So I was a-dream'd, methought, that we went and
    search'd the Folks round,

And in a Corner of Mrs. *Duke's* Box, ty'd in a Rag, the
    Money was found.

So next Morning we told *Whittle,* and he fell a Swear-
    ing;

Then my Dame *Wadgar* came, and she, you know, is
    thick of Hearing;

Dame, said I, as loud as I could bawl, do you know
    what a Loss I have had?

Nay, said she, my Lord *Collway's* Folks are all very sad,

For my Lord *Dromedary* comes a *Tuesday* without fail;

Pugh! said I, but that's not the Business that I ail.

Says *Cary,* says he, I have been a Servant this Five and
    Twenty Years, come Spring,

And in all the Places I liv'd, I never heard of such a
    Thing.

Yes, says the *Steward,* I remember when I was at my
    Lady *Shrewsbury's,*

Such a thing as this happen'd, just about the time of
    Goosberries.

So I went to the Party suspected, and I found her full
    of Grief;

(Now you must know, of all Things in the World, I hate
    a Thief.)

However, I was resolv'd to bring the Discourse slily
    about,

Mrs. *Dukes,* said I, here's an ugly Accident has hap-
    pen'd out;

'Tis not that I value the Money three Skips of a Louse;

But the Thing I stand upon, is the Credit of the House;

'Tis true, seven Pound, four Shillings, and six Pence,
    makes a great Hole in my Wages,

Besides, as they say, Service is no Inheritance in these
    Ages.

Now, Mrs. *Dukes,* you know, and every Body under-
    stands,

That tho' 'tis hard to judge, yet Money can't go without
    Hands.

The *Devil* take me, said she, (blessing her self,) if I
    ever saw't!

So she roar'd like a *Bedlam,* as tho' I had call'd her all
    to naught;

So you know, what could I say to her any more,

I e'en left her, and came away as wise as I was before.

Well: But then they would have had me gone to the
Cunning Man;

No, said I, 'tis the same Thing, the *Chaplain* will be
here anon.

So the *Chaplain* came in; now the Servants say, he is
my Sweet-heart,

Because he's always in my Chamber, and I always take
his Part;

So, as the *Devil* would have it, before I was aware, out
I blunder'd,

Parson, said I, can you cast a *Nativity,* when a Body's
plunder'd?

(Now you must know, he hates to be call'd *Parson,* like
the *Devil.*)

Truly, says he, Mrs. *Nab,* it might become you to be
more civil:

If your Money be gone, as a Learned *Divine* sayd, d'ye
see,

You are no *Text* for my Handling, so take that from me:

I was never taken for a Conjurer before, I'd have you
to know.

Lord, said I, don't be angry, I'm sure I never thought
you so;

You know, I honour the Cloth, I design to be a *Parson's*
Wife,

I never took one in *Your Coat* for a *Conjurer* in all my
Life.

With that, he twisted his Girdle at me like a Rope, as
who should say,

Now you may go hang your self for me, and so went
away.

Well; I thought I should have swoon'd; *Lord,* said I,
what shall I do?

I have lost my *Money,* and shall lose my *True-Love* too.

Then my *Lord* call'd me; *Harry,* said my *Lord,* don't cry,

I'll give something towards thy Loss; and says my *Lady,* so will I.

Oh but, said I, what if after all my Chaplain won't *come to?*

For that, he said (an't please your *Excellencies*) I must Petition You.

The Premises tenderly consider'd, I desire your *Excellencies* Protection,

And that I may have a Share in next *Sunday's* Collection:

And over and above, that I have your *Excellencies* Letter,

With an Order for the *Chaplain* aforesaid; or instead of Him, a Better:

And then your poor *Petitioner,* both Night and Day,

Or the *Chaplain,* (for 'tis his *Trade*) as in Duty bound, shall ever *Pray.*

Phillis, or, the Progress of Love

Desponding Phillis was endu'd
With ev'ry Talent of a Prude,
She trembled when a Man drew near;
Salute her, and she turn'd her Ear:
If o'er against her you were plac't
She durst not look above your Wast;
She'd rather take you to her Bed
Than let you see her dress her Head;
In Church you heard her thro the Crowd

Repeat the Absolution loud;
In Church, secure behind her Fan
She durst behold that Monster, Man:
There practic'd how to place her Head,
And bit her Lips to make them red:
Or on the Matt devoutly kneeling
Would lift her Eyes up to the Ceeling,
And heave her Bosom unaware
For neighb'ring Beaux to see it bare.
    At length a lucky Lover came,
And found Admittance from the Dame.
Suppose all Partyes now agreed,
The Writings drawn, the Lawyer fee'd,
The Vicar and the Ring bespoke:
Guess how could such a Match be broke.
See then what Mortals place their bliss in!
Next morn betimes the Bride was missing,
The Mother scream'd, the Father chid,
Where can this idle Wench be hid?
No news of Phil. The Bridegroom came,
And thought his Bride had sculk't for shame,
Because her Father us'd to say
The Girl had such a Bashfull way.
    Now, John the Butler must be sent
To learn the Way that Phillis went;
The Groom was wisht to saddle Crop,
For John must neither light nor stop;
But find her where so'er she fled,
And bring her back, alive or dead.
See here again the Dev'l to do;
For truly John was missing too:
The Horse and Pillion both were gone
Phillis, it seems, was fled with John.
Old Madam who went up to find
What Papers Phil had left behind,

A Letter on the Toylet sees
To my much honor'd Father, These:
('Tis always done, Romances tell us,
When Daughters run away with Fellows)
Fill'd with the choicest common-places,
By others us'd in the like Cases.
That, long ago a Fortune-teller
Exactly said what now befell her,
And in a Glass had made her see
A serving-Man of low Degree:
It was her Fate; must be forgiven;
For Marriages are made in Heaven:
His Pardon begg'd, but to be plain,
She'd do't if 'twere to do again.
Thank God, 'twas neither Shame nor Sin,
For John was come of honest Kin:
Love never thinks of Rich and Poor,
She'd beg with John from Door to Door:
Forgive her, if it be a Crime,
She'll never do't another Time,
She ne'r before in all her Life
Once disobey'd him, Maid nor Wife.
One Argument she summ'd up all in,
The Thing was done and past recalling:
And therefore hop'd she would recover
His Favor, when his Passion's over.
She valued not what others thought her;
And was—His most obedient Daughter.
  Fair Maidens all attend the Muse
Who now the wandring Pair pursues:
Away they rode in homely Sort
Their Journy long, their Money short;
The loving Couple well bemir'd,
The Horse and both the Riders tir'd:
Their Vittels bad, their Lodging worse,

Phil cry'd, and John began to curse;
Phil wish't, that she had strained a Limb
When first she ventur'd out with him.
John wish't, that he had broke a Leg
When first for her he quitted Peg.

But what Adventures more befell 'um
The Muse has now not time to tell 'um.
How Jonny wheadled, threatned, fawn'd,
Till Phillis all her Trinkets pawn'd:
How oft she broke her marriage Vows
In kindness to maintain her Spouse;
Till Swains unwholsome spoyld the Trade,
For now the Surgeon must be paid;
To whom those Perquisites are gone
In Christian Justice due to John.

When Food and Rayment now grew scarce
Fate put a Period to the Farce;
And with exact Poetick Justice:
For John is Landlord, Phillis Hostess;
They keep at Stains the old blue Boar,
Are Cat and Dog, and Rogue and Whore.

Verses on the Death of Dr. Swift, D.S.P.D.

*Occasioned by reading a Maxim in Rochefoucault: Dans
l'adversité de nos meilleurs amis nous trouvons quelque chose,
qui ne nous deplaist pas. (In the Adversity of our best
Friends, we find something that doth not displease us.)*

As *Rochefoucault* his Maxims drew
From Nature, I believe 'em true:
They argue no corrupted Mind
In him; the Fault is in Mankind.

This Maxim more than all the rest
Is thought too base for human Breast;

"In all Distresses of our Friends
We first consult our private Ends,
While nature kindly bent to ease us,
Points out some Circumstance to please us."

If this perhaps your Patience move
Let Reason and Experience prove.

We all behold with envious Eyes,
Our *Equal* rais'd above our *Size;*
Who wou'd not at a crowded Show,
Stand high himself, keep others low?
I love my Friend as well as you,
But would not have him stop my View;
Then let him have the higher Post;
I ask but for an Inch at most.

If in a Battle you should find,
One, whom you love of all Mankind,
Had some heroick Action done,
A Champion kill'd, or Trophy won;
Rather than thus be over-topt,
Would you not wish his Lawrels cropt?

Dear honest *Ned* is in the Gout,
Lies rackt with Pain, and you without:
How patiently you hear him groan!
How glad the Case is not your own!

What Poet would not grieve to see,
His Brethren write as well as he?
But rather than they should excel,
He'd wish his Rivals all in Hell.

Her End when Emulation misses,
She turns to Envy, Stings and Hisses:
The strongest Friendship yields to Pride,
Unless the Odds be on our Side.

Vain human Kind! Fantastick Race!
Thy various Follies, who can trace?
Self-love, Ambition, Envy, Pride,
Their Empire in our Hearts divide:
Give others Riches, Power, and Station,
'Tis all on me an Usurpation.
I have no Title to aspire;
Yet, when you sink, I seem the higher.
In *Pope*, I cannot read a Line,
But with a Sigh, I wish it mine:
When he can in one Couplet fix
More Sense than I can do in Six:
It gives me such a jealous Fit,
I cry, Pox take him, and his Wit.

Why must I be outdone by *Gay*,
In my own hum'rous biting Way?

Arbuthnot is no more my Friend,
Who dares to Irony pretend;
Which I was born to introduce,
Refin'd it first, and shew'd its Use.

St. John, as well as *Pultney* knows,
That I had some repute for Prose;
And till they drove me out of Date,
Could maul a Minister of State:
If they have mortify'd my Pride,
And made me throw my Pen aside;
If with such Talents Heav'n hath blest 'em
Have I not Reason to detest 'em?

To all my Foes, dear Fortune, send
Thy Gifts, but never to my Friend:
I tamely can endure the first,
But, this with Envy makes me burst.

Thus much may serve by way of Proem,
Proceed we therefore to our Poem.

The Time is not remote, when I
Must by the Course of Nature dye:
When I foresee my special Friends,
Will try to find their private Ends:
Tho' it is hardly understood,
Which way my Death can do them good;
Yet, thus methinks, I hear 'em speak;
See, how the Dean begins to break:
Poor Gentleman, he droops apace,
You plainly find it in his Face:
That old Vertigo in his Head,
Will never leave him, till he's dead:
Besides, his Memory decays,
He recollects not what he says;
He cannot call his Friends to Mind;
Forgets the Place where last he din'd:
Plyes you with Stories o'er and o'er,
He told them fifty Times before.
How does he fancy we can sit,
To hear his out-of-fashion'd Wit?
But he takes up with younger Fokes,
Who for his Wine will bear his Jokes:
Faith, he must make his Stories shorter,
Or change his Comrades once a Quarter:
In half the Time, he talks them round;
There must another Sett be found.

For Poetry, he's past his Prime,
He takes an Hour to find a Rhime:
His Fire is out, his Wit decay'd,
His Fancy sunk, his Muse a Jade.
I'd have him throw away his Pen;
But there's no talking to some Men.

And, then their Tenderness appears,
By adding largely to my Years:
"He's older than he would be reckon'd,
And well remembers *Charles* the Second.

He hardly drinks a Pint of Wine;
And that, I doubt, is no good Sign.
His Stomach too begins to fail:
Last Year we thought him strong and hale;
But now, he's quite another Thing;
I wish he may hold out till Spring."

Then hug themselves, and reason thus;
"It is not yet so bad with us."

In such a Case they talk in Tropes,
And, by their Fears express their Hopes:
Some great Misfortune to portend,
No Enemy can match a Friend;
With all the Kindness they profess,
The Merit of a lucky Guess,
(When daily Howd'y's come of Course,
And Servants answer; *Worse and Worse*)
Wou'd please 'em better than to tell,
That, *God* be prais'd, the Dean is well.
Then he who prophecy'd the best,
Approves his Foresight to the rest:
"You know, I always fear'd the worst,
And often told you so at first":
He'd rather chuse that I should dye,
Than his Prediction prove a Lye.
Not one foretels I shall recover;
But, all agree, to give me over.

Yet shou'd some Neighbour feel a Pain,
Just in the Parts, where I complain;
How many a Message would he send?

What hearty Prayers that I should mend?
Enquire what Regimen I kept;
What gave me Ease, and how I slept?
And more lament, when I was dead,
Than all the Sniv'llers round my Bed.

My good Companions, never fear,
For though you may mistake a Year;
Though your Prognosticks run too fast,
They must be verify'd at last.

"Behold the fatal Day arrive!
How is the Dean? He's just alive.
Now the departing Prayer is read:
He hardly breathes. The Dean is dead.
Before the Passing-Bell begun,
The News thro' half the Town has run.
O, may we all for Death prepare!
What has he left? And who's his Heir?
I know no more than what the News is,
'Tis all bequeath'd to publick Uses.
To publick Use! A perfect Whim!
What had the Publick done for him!
Meer Envy, Avarice, and Pride!
He gave it all:—But first he dy'd,
And had the Dean, in all the Nation,
No worthy Friend, no poor Relation?
So ready to do Strangers good,
Forgetting his own Flesh and Blood?"

Now Grub-Street Wits are all employ'd;
With Elegies, the Town is cloy'd:
Some Paragraph in ev'ry Paper,
To *curse* the *Dean,* or *bless* the *Drapier.*

The Doctors tender of their Fame,
Wisely on me lay all the Blame:

"We must confess his Case was nice;
But he would never take Advice:
Had he been rul'd, for ought appears,
He might have liv'd these Twenty Years:
For when we open'd him we found,
That all his vital Parts were sound."

From *Dublin* soon to *London* spread,
'Tis told at Court, the Dean is dead.

Kind Lady *Suffolk* in the Spleen,
Runs laughing up to tell the Queen.
The Queen, so Gracious, Mild, and Good,
Cries, "Is he gone? 'Tis time he shou'd.
He's dead you say; why let him rot;
I'm glad the Medals were forgot.
I promis'd them, I own; but when?
I only was the Princess then;
But now as Consort of the King,
You know 'tis quite a different Thing."

Now, *Chartres* at Sir *Robert's* Levee,
Tells, with a Sneer, the Tidings heavy:
"Why, is he dead without his Shoes?
(Cries *Bob*) I'm Sorry for the News;
Oh, were the Wretch but living still,
And in his Place my good Friend *Will;*
Or, had a Mitre on his Head
Provided *Bolingbroke* were dead."

Now *Curl* his Shop from Rubbish drains;
Three genuine Tomes of *Swift's* Remains.
And then to make them pass the glibber,
Revis'd by *Tibbalds, Moore,* and *Cibber.*
He'll treat me as he does my Betters.
Publish my Will, my Life, my Letters.

Revive the Libels born to dye;
Which *Pope* must bear, as well as I.

Here shift the Scene, to represent
How those I love, my Death lament.
Poor *Pope* will grieve a Month; and *Gay*
A Week; and *Arbuthnot* a Day.

St. John himself will scarce forbear,
To bite his Pen, and drop a Tear.
The rest will give a Shrug and cry,
I'm sorry; but we all must dye.
Indifference clad in Wisdom's Guise,
All Fortitude of Mind supplies:
For how can stony Bowels melt,
In those who never Pity felt;
When *We* are lash'd, *They* kiss the Rod;
Resigning to the Will of God.

The Fools, my Juniors by a Year,
Are tortur'd with Suspence and Fear.
Who wisely thought my Age a Screen,
When Death approach'd, to stand between:
The Screen remov'd, their Hearts are trembling,
They mourn for me without dissembling.

My female Friends, whose tender Hearts
Have better learn'd to act their Parts.
Receive the News in *doleful Dumps*,
"The Dean is dead, (*and what is Trumps?*)
Then Lord have Mercy on his Soul.
(Ladies I'll venture for the *Vole*.)
Six Deans they say must bear the Pall.
(I wish I knew what *King* to call.)
Madam, your Husband will attend
The Funeral of so good a Friend.

No Madam, 'tis a shocking Sight,
And he's engag'd To-morrow Night!
My Lady *Club* wou'd take it ill,
If he shou'd fail her at *Quadrill.*
He lov'd the Dean. (*I lead a Heart.*)
But dearest Friends, they say, must part.
His Time was come, he ran his Race;
We hope he's in a better Place."

Why do we grieve that Friends should dye?
No Loss more easy to supply.
One Year is past; a different Scene;
No further mention of the Dean;
Who now, alas, no more is mist,
Than if he never did exist.
Where's now this Fav'rite of *Apollo?*
Departed; *and his Works must follow:*
Must undergo the common Fate;
His Kind of Wit is out of Date.
Some Country Squire to *Lintot* goes,
Enquires for *Swift* in Verse and Prose:
Says *Lintot,* "I have heard the Name:
He dy'd a Year ago." The same.
He searcheth all his Shop in vain;
"Sir you may find them in *Duck-lane:*
I sent them with a Load of Books,
Last *Monday* to the Pastry-cooks.
To fancy they cou'd live a Year!
I find you're but a Stranger here.
The Dean was famous in his Time;
And had a Kind of Knack at Rhyme:
His way of Writing now is past;
The Town hath got a better Taste:
I keep no antiquated Stuff;
But, spick and span I have enough.

Pray, do but give me leave to shew 'em;
Here's *Colley Cibber's* Birth-day Poem.
This Ode you never yet have seen,
By *Stephen Duck*, upon the Queen.
Then, here's a Letter finely penn'd
Against the *Craftsman* and his Friend;
It clearly shews that all Reflection
On Ministers, is disaffection.
Next, here's Sir *Robert's* Vindication,
And Mr. *Henly's* last Oration:
The Hawkers have not got 'em yet,
Your Honour please to buy a Set?

"Here's *Wolston's* Tracts, the twelfth Edition;
'Tis read by ev'ry Politician:
The Country Members, when in Town,
To all their Boroughs send them down:
You never met a Thing so smart;
The Courtiers have them all by Heart:
Those Maids of Honour (who can read)
Are taught to use them for their Creed.
The Rev'rend Author's good Intention,
Hath been rewarded with a Pension:
He doth an Honour to his Gown,
By bravely running *Priest-craft* down:
He shews, as sure as *God's* in *Gloc'ster*,
That *Jesus* was a Grand Impostor:
That all his Miracles were Cheats,
Perform'd as Juglers do their Feats:
The Church had never such a Writer:
A Shame, he hath not got a Mitre!"

Suppose me dead; and then suppose
A Club assembled at the *Rose*;
Where from Discourse of this and that,
I grow the Subject of their Chat:

And, while they toss my Name about,
With Favour some, and some without;
One quite indiff'rent in the Cause,
My Character impartial draws:

  "The Dean, if we believe Report,
Was never ill receiv'd at Court:
As for his Works in Verse and Prose,
I own my self no Judge of those:
Nor, can I tell what Criticks thought 'em;
But, this I know, all People bought 'em;
As with a moral View design'd
To cure the Vices of Mankind:
His Vein, ironically grave,
Expos'd the Fool, and lash'd the Knave:
To steal a Hint was never known,
But what he writ was all his own.

  "He never thought an Honour done him,
Because a Duke was proud to own him:
Would rather slip aside, and chuse
To talk with Wits in dirty Shoes:
Despis'd the Fools with Stars and Garters,
So often seen caressing *Chartres:*
He never courted Men in Station,
Nor Persons had in Admiration;
Of no Man's Greatness was afraid,
Because he sought for no Man's Aid.
Though trusted long in great Affairs,
He gave himself no haughty Airs:
Without regarding private Ends,
Spent all his Credit for his Friends:
And only chose the Wise and Good;
No Flatt'rers; no Allies in Blood;
But succour'd Virtue in Distress,
And seldom fail'd of good Success;

As Numbers in their Hearts must own,
Who, but for him, had been unknown.

"With Princes kept a due Decorum,
But never stood in Awe before 'em:
He follow'd *David's* Lesson just,
In Princes never put thy Trust.
And, would you make him truly sower;
Provoke him with *a slave in Power:*
The *Irish* Senate, if you nam'd,
With what Impatience he declaim'd!
Fair LIBERTY was all his Cry;
For her he stood prepar'd to die;
For her he boldly stood alone;
For her he oft expos'd his own.
Two Kingdoms, just as Faction led,
Had set a Price upon his Head;
But, not a Traytor cou'd be found,
To sell him for Six Hundred Pound.

"Had he but spar'd his Tongue and Pen,
He might have rose like other Men:
But, Power was never in his Thought:
And, Wealth he valu'd not a Groat:
Ingratitude he often found,
And pity'd those who meant the Wound:
But, kept the Tenor of his Mind,
To merit well of human Kind:
Nor made a Sacrifice of those
Who still were true, to please his Foes.
He labour'd many a fruitless Hour
To reconcile his Friends in Power;
Saw Mischief by a Faction brewing,
While they pursu'd each others Ruin.
But, finding vain was all his Care,
He left the Court in meer Despair.

"And, oh! how short are human Schemes!
Here ended all our golden Dreams.
What *St. John's* Skill in State Affairs,
What *Ormond's Valour, Oxford's* Cares,
To save their sinking Country lent,
Was all destroy'd by one Event.
Too soon that precious Life was ended,
On which alone, our Weal depended.
When up a dangerous Faction starts,
With Wrath and Vengeance in their Hearts:
By solemn League and Covenant bound,
To ruin, slaughter, and confound;
To turn Religion to a Fable,
And make the Government a *Babel:*
Pervert the Law, disgrace the Gown,
Corrupt the Senate, rob the Crown;
To sacrifice old *England's* Glory,
And make her infamous in Story.
When such a Tempest shook the Land,
How could unguarded Virtue stand?

"With Horror, Grief, Despair the Dean
Beheld the dire destructive Scene:
His Friends in Exile, or the Tower,
Himself within the Frown of Power;
Pursu'd by base envenom'd·Pens,
Far to the Land of Slaves and Fens;
A servile Race in Folly nurs'd,
Who truckle most, when treated worst.

"By Innocence and Resolution,
He bore continual Persecution;
While Numbers to Preferment rose;
Whose Merits were, to be his Foes.
When, *ev'n his own familiar Friends*
Intent upon their private Ends;

Like Renegadoes now he feels,
Against him lifting up their Heels.

"The Dean did by his Pen defeat
An infamous destructive Cheat.
Taught Fools their Int'rest how to know;
And gave them Arms to ward the Blow.
Envy hath own'd it was his doing,
To save that helpless Land from Ruin,
While they who at the Steerage stood,
And reapt the Profit, sought his Blood.

"To save them from their evil Fate,
In him was held a Crime of State.
A wicked Monster on the Bench,
Whose Fury Blood could never quench;
As vile and profligate a Villain,
As modern *Scroggs,* or old *Tressilian;*
Who long all Justice had discarded,
Nor fear'd he GOD, *nor Man regarded;*
Vow'd on the Dean his Rage to vent,
And make him of his Zeal repent;
But Heav'n his Innocence defends,
The grateful People stand his Friends:
Not Strains of Law, nor Judges Frown,
Nor Topicks brought to please the Crown,
Nor Witness hir'd, nor Jury pick'd,
Prevail to bring him in convict.

"In Exile with a steady Heart,
He spent his Life's declining Part;
Where, Folly, Pride, and Faction sway,
Remote from *St. John, Pope,* and *Gay.*

"His Friendship there to few confin'd,
Were always of the midling Kind:
No Fools of Rank, a mungril Breed,

Who fain would pass for Lords indeed:
Where Titles give no Right or Power,
And Peerage is a wither'd Flower,
He would have held it a Disgrace,
If such a Wretch had known his Face.
On Rural Squires, that Kingdom's Bane,
He vented oft his Wrath in vain:
Biennial Squires, to Market brought;
Who sell their Souls and Votes for Naught;
The Nation stript go joyful back,
To rob the Church, their Tenants rack,
Go Snacks with Thieves and Rapparees,
And, keep the Peace, to pick up Fees:
In every Jobb to have a Share,
A Jayl or Barrack to repair;
And turn the Tax for publick Roads.
Commodious to their own Abodes.

"Perhaps I may allow, the Dean
Had too much Satyr in his Vein;
And seem'd determin'd not to starve it,
Because no Age could more deserve it.
Yet, Malice never was his Aim;
He lash'd the Vice but spar'd the Name.
No Individual could resent,
Where Thousands equally were meant.
His Satyr points at no Defect,
But what all Mortals may correct;
For he abhorr'd that senseless Tribe,
Who call it Humour when they jibe:
He spar'd a Hump or crooked Nose,
Whose Owners set not up for Beaux.
True genuine Dulness mov'd his Pity,
Unless it offer'd to be witty.
Those, who their Ignorance confess'd,

He ne'er offended with a Jest;
But laugh'd to hear an Idiot quote,
A Verse from *Horace*, learn'd by Rote.

"He knew an hundred pleasant Stories,
With all the Turns of *Whigs* and *Tories:*
Was chearful to his dying Day,
And Friends would let him have his Way.

"He gave the little Wealth he had,
To build a House for Fools and Mad:
And shew'd by one satyric Touch,
No Nation wanted it so much:
That Kingdom he hath left his Debtor,
I wish it soon may have a Better."

Alexander Pope

(1688–1744)

FROM Windsor Forest

See! from the brake the whirring pheasant springs,
And mounts exulting on triumphant wings:
Short is his joy; he feels the fiery wound,
Flutters in blood, and panting beats the ground.
Ah! what avail his glossy, varying dyes,
His purple crest, and scarlet-circled eyes,
The vivid green his shining plumes unfold,
His painted wings, and breast that flames with gold?
    Nor yet, when moist Arcturus clouds the sky,
The woods and fields their pleasing toils deny.
To plains with well-breath'd beagles we repair,
And trace the mazes of the circling hare:
(Beasts, urg'd by us, their fellow-beasts pursue,
And learn of man each other to undo.)
With slaught'ring guns th' unweary'd fowler roves,
When frosts have whiten'd all the naked groves;
Where doves in flocks the leafless trees o'ershade,
And lonely woodcocks haunt the wat'ry glade.
He lifts the tube, and levels with his eye;
Strait a short thunder breaks the frozen sky:
Oft, as in airy rings they skim the heath,
The clam'rous Lapwings feel the leaden death:
Oft, as the mounting larks their notes prepare,
They fall, and leave their little lives in air.

(Lines 111–34)

328

Eloïsa to Abelard

In these deep solitudes and awful cells,
Where heav'nly-pensive contemplation dwells,
And ever musing melancholy reigns;
What means this tumult in a Vestal's veins?
Why rove my thoughts beyond this last retreat?
Why feels my heart its long-forgotten heat?
Yet, yet I love!—From Abelard it came,
And Eloïsa yet must kiss the name.

    Dear fatal name! rest ever unreveal'd,
Nor pass these lips in holy silence seal'd:
Hide it, my heart, within that close disguise,
Where mix'd with God's, his lov'd Idea lies:
O write it not, my hand—the name appears
Already written—wash it out, my tears!
In vain lost Eloïsa weeps and prays,
Her heart still dictates, and her hand obeys.

    Relentless walls! whose darksome round contains
Repentant sighs, and voluntary pains:
Ye rugged rocks! which holy knees have worn;
Ye grots and caverns shagg'd with horrid thorn!
Shrines! where their vigils pale-ey'd virgins keep,
And pitying saints, whose statues learn to weep!
Tho' cold like you, unmov'd and silent grown,
I have not yet forgot myself to stone.
All is not Heav'n's while Abelard has part,
Still rebel nature holds out half my heart;
Nor pray'rs nor fasts its stubborn pulse restrain,
Nor tears for ages taught to flow in vain.

    Soon as thy letters trembling I unclose,
That well-known name awakens all my woes.

Oh name for ever sad! for ever dear!
Still breath'd in sighs, still usher'd with a tear.
I tremble too, where'er my own I find,
Some dire misfortune follows close behind.
Line after line my gushing eyes o'erflow,
Led thro' a sad variety of woe:
Now warm in love, now with'ring in my bloom,
Lost in a convent's solitary gloom!
There stern Religion quench'd th' unwilling flame,
There died the best of passions, Love and Fame.
     Yet write, oh write me all, that I may join
Griefs to thy griefs, and echo sighs to thine.
Nor foes nor fortune take this pow'r away;
And is my Abelard less kind than they?
Tears still are mine, and those I need not spare,
Love but demands what else were shed in pray'r;
No happier task these faded eyes pursue;
To read and weep is all they now can do.
     Then share thy pain, allow that sad relief;
Ah, more than share it, give me all thy grief.
Heav'n first taught letters for some wretch's aid,
Some banish'd lover, or some captive maid;
They live, they speak, they breathe what love inspires.
Warm from the soul, and faithful to its fires,
The Virgin's wish without her fears impart,
Excuse the blush, and pour out all the heart,
Speed the soft intercourse from soul to soul,
And waft a sigh from Indus to the Pole.
     Thou know'st how guiltless first I met thy flame,
When Love approach'd me under Friendship's name;
My fancy form'd thee of angelic kind,
Some emanation of th' all-beauteous Mind.
Those smiling eyes, attemp'ring ev'ry ray,
Shone sweetly lambent with celestial day.
Guiltless I gaz'd; heav'n listen'd while you sung;

And truths divine came mended from that tongue.
From lips like those what precept fail'd to move?
Too soon they taught me 'twas no sin to love:
Back thro' the paths of pleasing sense I ran,
Nor wish'd an Angel whom I lov'd a Man.
Dim and remote the joys of saints I see;
Nor envy them that heav'n I lose for thee.

How oft, when press'd to marriage, have I said,
Curse on all laws but those which love has made!
Love, free as air, at sight of human ties,
Spreads his light wings, and in a moment flies.
Let wealth, let honour, wait the wedded dame,
August her deed, and sacred be her fame;
Before true passion all those views remove,
Fame, wealth, and honour! what are you to Love?
The jealous God, when we profane his fires,
Those restless passions in revenge inspires,
And bids them make mistaken mortals groan,
Who seek in love for aught but love alone.
Should at my feet the world's great master fall,
Himself, his throne, his world, I'd scorn 'em all:
Not Cæsar's empress would I deign to prove;
No, make me mistress to the man I love;
If there be yet another name more free,
More fond than mistress, make me that to thee!
Oh! happy state! when souls each other draw,
When love is liberty, and nature, law:
All then is full, possessing, and possess'd,
No craving void left aking in the breast:
Ev'n thought meets thought ere from the lips it part,
And each warm wish springs mutual from the heart.
This sure is bliss (if bliss on earth there be)
And once the lot of Abelard and me.

Alas, how chang'd! what sudden horrors rise!
A naked Lover bound and bleeding lies!

Where, where was Eloïse? her voice, her hand,
Her ponyard had oppos'd the dire command.
Barbarian, stay! that bloody stroke restrain;
The crime was common, common be the pain.
I can no more; by shame, by rage suppress'd,
Let tears and burning blushes speak the rest.

    Canst thou forget that sad, that solemn day,
When victims at yon altar's foot we lay?
Canst thou forget what tears that moment fell,
When, warm in youth, I bade the world farewell?
As with cold lips I kiss'd the sacred veil,
The shrines all trembled, and the lamps grew pale:
Heav'n scarce believ'd the Conquest it survey'd,
And Saints with wonder heard the vows I made.
Yet then, to those dread altars as I drew,
Not on the Cross my eyes were fix'd, but you;
Not grace, or zeal, love only was my call,
And if I lose thy love, I lose my all.
Come! with thy looks, thy words, relieve my woe;
Those still at least are left thee to bestow.
Still on that breast enamour'd let me lie,
Still drink delicious poison from thy eye,
Pant on thy lip, and to thy heart be press'd;
Give all thou canst—and let me dream the rest.
Ah no! instruct me other joys to prize,
With other beauties charm my partial eyes,
Full in my view set all the bright abode,
And make my soul quit Abelard for God.

    Ah, think at least thy flock deserves thy care,
Plants of thy hand, and children of thy pray'r.
From the false world in early youth they fled,
By thee to mountains, wilds, and deserts led.
You rais'd these hallow'd walls; the desert smil'd,
And Paradise was open'd in the Wild.
No weeping orphan saw his father's stores

Our shrines irradiate, or emblaze the floors;
No silver saints, by dying misers giv'n,
Here brib'd the rage of ill-requited heav'n:
But such plain roofs as Piety could raise,
And only vocal with the Maker's praise.
In these lone walls (their day's eternal bound),
These moss-grown domes with spiry turrets crown'd,
Where awful arches make a noon-day night,
And the dim windows shed a solemn light;
Thy eyes diffus'd a reconciling ray,
And gleams of glory brighten'd all the day.
But now no face divine contentment wears,
'Tis all blank sadness, or continual tears.
See how the force of others' pray'rs I try,
(O pious fraud of am'rous charity!)
But why should I on others' pray'rs depend?
Come thou, my father, brother, husband, friend!
Ah let thy handmaid, sister, daughter move,
And all those tender names in one, thy love!
The darksome pines that o'er yon rocks reclin'd
Wave high, and murmur to the hollow wind,
The wand'ring streams that shine between the hills,
The grots that echo to the tinkling rills,
The dying gales that pant upon the trees,
The lakes that quiver to the curling breeze;
No more these scenes my meditation aid,
Or lull to rest the visionary maid,
But o'er the twilight groves and dusky caves,
Long-sounding isles, and intermingled graves,
Black Melancholy sits, and round her throws
A death-like silence, and a dread repose:
Her gloomy presence saddens all the scene,
Shades ev'ry flow'r, and darkens ev'ry green,
Deepens the murmur of the falling floods,
And breathes a browner horror on the woods.

Yet here for ever, ever must I stay;
Sad proof how well a lover can obey!
Death, only death, can break the lasting chain;
And here, ev'n then, shall my cold dust remain,
Here all its frailties, all its flames resign,
And wait till 'tis no sin to mix with thine.

Ah wretch! believ'd the spouse of God in vain,
Confess'd within the slave of love and man.
Assist me, heav'n! but whence arose that pray'r?
Sprung it from piety, or from despair?
Ev'n here, where frozen chastity retires,
Love finds an altar for forbidden fires.
I ought to grieve, but cannot what I ought;
I mourn the lover, not lament the fault;
I view my crime, but kindle at the view,
Repent old pleasures, and sollicit new;
Now turn'd to heav'n, I weep my past offense,
Now think of thee, and curse my innocence.
Of all affliction taught a lover yet,
'Tis sure the hardest science to forget!
How shall I lose the sin, yet keep the sense,
And love th' offender, yet detest th' offense?
How the dear object from the crime remove,
Or how distinguish penitence from love?
Unequal task! a passion to resign,
For hearts so touch'd, so pierc'd, so lost as mine.
Ere such a soul regains its peaceful state,
How often must it love, how often hate!
How often hope, despair, resent, regret,
Conceal, disdain,—do all things but forget.
But let heav'n seize it, all at once 'tis fir'd;
Not touch'd, but rapt; not waken'd, but inspir'd!
Oh come! oh teach me nature to subdue,
Renounce my love, my life, myself—and you.
Fill my fond heart with God alone, for he

Alone can rival, can succeed to thee.
    How happy is the blameless Vestal's lot!
The world forgetting, by the world forgot.
Eternal sun-shine of the spotless mind!
Each pray'r accepted, and each wish resign'd;
Labour and rest, that equal periods keep;
"Obedient slumbers that can wake and weep";
Desires compos'd, affections ever ev'n;
Tears that delight, and sighs that waft to heav'n.
Grace shines around her with serenest beams,
And whisp'ring Angels prompt her golden dreams.
For her th' unfading rose of Eden blooms,
And wings of Seraphs shed divine perfumes;
For her the Spouse prepares the bridal ring,
For her white virgins Hymenæals sing,
To sounds of heav'nly harps she dies away,
And melts in visions of eternal day.
    Far other dreams my erring soul employ,
Far other raptures, of unholy joy:
When at the close of each sad, sorrowing day,
Fancy restores what vengeance snatch'd away,
Then conscience sleeps, and leaving nature free,
All my loose soul unbounded springs to thee.
O curst, dear horrors of all-conscious night!
How glowing guilt exalts the keen delight!
Provoking Dæmons all restraint remove,
And stir within me ev'ry source of love.
I hear thee, view thee, gaze o'er all thy charms,
And round thy phantom glue my clasping arms.
I wake:—no more I hear, no more I view,
The phantom flies me, as unkind as you.
I call aloud; it hears not what I say:
I stretch my empty arms; it glides away.
To dream once more I close my willing eyes;
Ye soft illusions, dear deceits, arise!

Alas, no more! methinks we wand'ring go
Thro' dreary wastes, and weep each other's woe,
Where round some mold'ring tow'r pale ivy creeps,
And low-brow'd rocks hang nodding o'er the deeps.
Sudden you mount, you beckon from the skies;
Clouds interpose, waves roar, and winds arise.
I shriek, start up, the same sad prospect find,
And wake to all the griefs I left behind.

   For thee the fates, severely kind, ordain
A cool suspense from pleasure and from pain;
Thy life a long dead calm of fix'd repose;
No pulse that riots, and no blood that glows.
Still as the sea, ere winds were taught to blow,
Or moving spirit bade the waters flow;
Soft as the slumbers of a saint forgiv'n,
And mild as op'ning gleams of promis'd heav'n.

   Come, Abelard! for what hast thou to dread?
The torch of Venus burns not for the dead.
Nature stands check'd; Religion disapproves;
Even thou art cold—yet Eloïsa loves.
Ah hopeless, lasting flames! like those that burn
To light the dead, and warm th' unfruitful urn.

   What scenes appear where'er I turn my view!
The dear Ideas, where I fly, pursue,
Rise in the grove, before the altar rise,
Stain all my soul, and wanton in my eyes.
I waste the Matin lamp in sighs for thee,
Thy image steals between my God and me,
Thy voice I seem in ev'ry hymn to hear,
With ev'ry bead I drop too soft a tear.
When from the censer clouds of fragrance roll,
And swelling organs lift the rising soul;
One thought of thee puts all the pomp to flight,
Priests, tapers, temples, swim before my sight:
In seas of flame my plunging soul is drown'd,

While Altars blaze, and Angels tremble round.
    While prostrate here in humble grief I lie,
Kind, virtuous drops just gath'ring in my eye,
While praying, trembling, in the dust I roll,
And dawning grace is op'ning on my soul:
Come, if thou dar'st, all charming as thou art!
Oppose thyself to heav'n; dispute my heart;
Come, with one glance of those deluding eyes
Blot out each bright Idea of the skies;
Take back that grace, those sorrows, and those tears;
Take back my fruitless penitence and pray'rs;
Snatch me, just mounting, from the blest abode;
Assist the fiends, and tear me from my God!
    No, fly me, fly me, far as Pole from Pole;
Rise Alps between us! and whole oceans roll!
Ah come not, write not, think not once of me,
Nor share one pang of all I felt for thee.
Thy oaths I quit, thy memory resign;
Forget, renounce me, hate whate'er was mine.
Fair eyes, and tempting looks (which yet I view!)
Long lov'd, ador'd ideas! all adieu!
O Grace serene! oh virtue heav'nly fair!
Divine oblivion of low-thoughted care!
Fresh blooming Hope, gay daughter of the sky!
And Faith, our early immortality!
Enter each mild, each amicable guest;
Receive, and wrap me in eternal rest!
    See in her Cell sad Eloïsa spread,
Propt on some tomb, a neighbour of the dead!
In each low wind methinks a Spirit calls,
And more than Echoes talk along the walls.
Here, as I watch'd the dying lamps around,
From yonder shrine I heard a hollow sound.
"Come, sister come! (it said, or seem'd to say)
Thy place is here, sad sister come away!

Once like thy self, I trembled, wept, and pray'd,
Love's victim then, tho' now a sainted maid:
But all is calm in this eternal sleep;
Here grief forgets to groan, and love to weep,
Ev'n superstition loses ev'ry fear:
For God, not man, absolves our frailties here."

I come, I come! prepare your roseate bow'rs.
Celestial palms, and ever-blooming flow'rs.
Thither, where sinners may have rest, I go,
Where flames refin'd in breasts seraphic glow.
Thou, Abelard! the last sad office pay,
And sooth my passage to the realms of day;
See my lips tremble, and my eye-balls roll,
Suck my last breath, and catch my flying soul!
Ah no—in sacred vestments may'st thou stand,
The hallow'd taper trembling in thy hand,
Present the Cross before my lifted eye,
Teach me at once, and learn of me to die.
Ah then, thy once-lov'd Eloïsa see!
It will be then no crime to gaze on me.
See from my cheek the transient roses fly!
See the last sparkle languish in my eye!
Till ev'ry motion, pulse, and breath, be o'er;
And ev'n my Abelard be lov'd no more.
O Death all-eloquent! you only prove
What dust we doat on, when 'tis man we love.

Then too, when fate shall thy fair frame destroy,
(That cause of all my guilt, and all my joy)
In trance extatic may thy pangs be drown'd,
Bright clouds descend, and Angels watch thee round,
From op'ning skies may streaming glories shine,
And Saints embrace thee with a love like mine.

May one kind grave unite each hapless name,
And graft my love immortal on thy fame!
Then, ages hence, when all my woes are o'er,

When this rebellious heart shall beat no more;
If ever chance two wand'ring lovers brings
To Paraclete's white walls and silver springs,
O'er the pale marble shall they join their heads,
And drink the falling tears each other sheds;
Then sadly say, with mutual pity mov'd,
"Oh may we never love as these have lov'd!"
From the full choir when loud Hosannas rise,
And swell the pomp of dreadful sacrifice,
Amid that scene if some relenting eye
Glance on the stone where our cold reliks lie,
Devotion's self shall steal a thought from heav'n,
One human tear shall drop and be forgiv'n.
And sure if fate some future Bard shall join
In sad similitude of griefs to mine,
Condemn'd whole years in absence to deplore,
And image charms he must behold no more:
Such if there be, who loves so long, so well;
Let him our sad, our tender story tell;
The well-sung woes will soothe my pensive ghost;
He best can paint 'em who shall feel 'em most.

The Rape of the Lock

AN HEROI-COMICAL POEM

Nolueram, Belinda, tuos violare capillos;
Sed juvat, hoc precibus me tribuisse tuis.
                        —MARTIAL, *Epigrams* XII, 84.

CANTO I

What dire Offense from am'rous Causes springs,
What mighty Contests rise from Trivial Things,
I sing—This Verse to *Caryll*, Muse! is due;

This, ev'n *Belinda* may vouchsafe to view:
Slight is the Subject, but not so the Praise,
If she inspire, and he approve my *Lays*.

Say what strange Motive, Goddess! cou'd compel
A well-bred *Lord* t'assault a gentle *Belle*?
Oh say what stranger Cause, yet unexplor'd,
Cou'd make a gentle *Belle* reject a *Lord*?
In Tasks so bold, can Little Men engage,
And in soft Bosoms dwells such mighty Rage?

Sol thro' white Curtains shot a tim'rous ray,
And op'd those Eyes that must eclipse the Day:
Now Lapdogs give themselves the rowsing Shake,
And sleepless Lovers, just at Twelve, awake:
Thrice rung the Bell, the Slipper knock'd the Ground,
And the press'd Watch return'd a silver Sound.
Belinda still her downy Pillow prest,
Her Guardian *Sylph* prolong'd the balmy Rest.
'Twas he had summon'd to her silent Bed
The Morning-Dream that hover'd o'er her Head,
A Youth more glitt'ring than a *Birth-night Beau*,
(That ev'n in Slumber caus'd her Cheek to glow)
Seem'd to her Ear his winning Lips to lay,
And thus in Whispers said, or seem'd to say.

"Fairest of Mortals, thou distinguish'd Care
Of thousand bright Inhabitants of Air!
If e'er one Vision touch'd thy infant Thought,
Of all the Nurse and all the Priest have taught,
Of airy Elves by Moonlight Shadows seen,
The silver Token, and the circled Green,
Or Virgins visited by Angel-Pow'rs,
With Golden Crowns and Wreaths of heav'nly Flow'rs,
Hear and believe! thy own Importance know,
Nor bound thy narrow Views to things below.
Some secret Truths, from Learned Pride conceal'd,
To Maids alone and Children are reveal'd:

What tho' no credit doubting Wits may give?
The Fair and Innocent shall still believe.
Know then, unnumber'd Spirits round thee fly,
The light *Militia* of the lower Sky:
These, tho' unseen, are ever on the Wing,
Hang o'er the *Box*, and hover round the *Ring*.
Think what an Equipage thou hast in Air,
And view with scorn Two Pages and a Chair.
As now your own, our beings were of old,
And once inclos'd in Woman's beauteous Mould;
Thence, by a soft Transition, we repair
From earthly Vehicles to these of Air.
Think not, when Woman's transient Breath is fled,
That all her Vanities at once are dead:
Succeeding Vanities she still regards,
And tho' she plays no more, o'erlooks the Cards.
Her joy in gilded Chariots, when alive,
And love of *Ombre*, after Death survive.
For when the Fair in all their Pride expire,
To their first Elements their Souls retire:
The Sprights of fiery Termagants in Flame
Mount up, and take a *Salamander's* Name.
Soft yielding Minds to water glide away,
And sip, with *Nymphs*, their Elemental Tea.
The graver Prude sinks downward to a *Gnome*,
In search of Mischief still on Earth to roam.
The light Coquettes in *Sylphs* aloft repair,
And sport and flutter in the Fields of Air.
  "Know further yet; Whoever fair and chaste
Rejects Mankind, is by some *Sylph* embrac'd:
For Spirits, freed from Mortal Laws, with ease
Assume what Sexes and what Shapes they please.
What guards the Purity of melting Maids,
In Courtly Balls, and Midnight Masquerades,
Safe from the treach'rous Friend, the daring Spark,

The Glance by Day, the Whisper in the Dark;
When kind Occasion prompts their warm Desires,
When Musick softens, and when Dancing fires?
'Tis but their *Sylph*, the wise Celestials know,
Tho' *Honour* is the Word with Men below.

  "Some Nymphs there are, too conscious of their Face,
For Life predestin'd to the *Gnomes'* Embrace.
These swell their Prospects and exalt their Pride,
When Offers are disdain'd, and Love deny'd:
Then gay Ideas crowd the vacant Brain;
While Peers, and Dukes, and all their sweeping Train,
And Garters, Stars, and Coronets appear,
And in soft Sounds, "*Your* Grace" salutes their Ear.
'Tis these that early taint the Female Soul,
Instruct the Eyes of young *Coquettes* to roll,
Teach Infant-Cheeks a bidden Blush to know,
And little Hearts to flutter at a *Beau*.

  "Oft, when the World imagine Women stray,
The *Sylphs* thro' mystick Mazes guide their Way,
Thro' all the giddy Circle they pursue,
And old Impertinence expel by new.
What tender Maid but must a Victim fall
To one Man's Treat, but for another's Ball?
When *Florio* speaks, what Virgin could withstand,
If gentle *Damon* did not squeeze her Hand?
With varying Vanities, from ev'ry Part,
They shift the moving Toyshop of their Heart;
Where Wigs with Wigs, with Sword-knots Sword-knots
      strive,
Beaus banish Beaus, and Coaches Coaches drive.
This erring Mortals Levity may call,
Oh blind to Truth! the *Sylphs* contrive it all.

  "Of these am I, who thy Protection claim,
A watchful Sprite, and *Ariel* is my Name.
Late, as I rang'd the Crystal Wilds of Air,

In the clear Mirror of thy ruling Star
I saw, alas! some dread Event impend,
Ere to the Main this morning Sun descend.
But Heav'n reveals not what, or how, or where:
Warn'd by the *Sylph,* oh Pious Maid beware!
This to disclose is all thy Guardian can.
Beware of all, but most beware of Man!"

  He said; when *Shock,* who thought she slept too long,
Leapt up, and wak'd his Mistress with his Tongue.
'Twas then, *Belinda!* if Report say true,
Thy Eyes first open'd on a *Billet-doux;*
Wounds, Charms, and *Ardors* were no sooner read,
But all the Vision vanish'd from thy Head.

  And now, unveil'd, the *Toilet* stands display'd,
Each Silver Vase in mystic Order laid.
First, rob'd in White, the Nymph intent adores,
With Head uncover'd, the *Cosmetic* Pow'rs.
A heav'nly image in the Glass appears,
To that she bends, to that her Eyes she rears;
Th' inferior Priestess, at her Altar's side,
Trembling begins the sacred Rites of Pride.
Unnumber'd Treasures ope at once, and here
The various Off'rings of the World appear;
From each she nicely culls with curious Toil,
And decks the Goddess with the glitt'ring Spoil.
This Casket *India's* glowing Gems unlocks,
And all *Arabia* breathes from yonder Box.
The Tortoise here and Elephant unite,
Transform'd to *Combs,* the speckled, and the white.
Here Files of Pins extend their shining Rows,
Puffs, Powders, Patches, Bibles, Billet-doux.
Now awful Beauty puts on all its Arms;
The Fair each moment rises in her Charms,
Repairs her Smiles, awakens ev'ry Grace,
And calls forth all the Wonders of her Face;

Sees by Degrees a purer Blush arise,
And keener Lightnings quicken in her eyes.
The busy *Sylphs* surround their darling Care;
These set the Head, and those divide the Hair,
Some fold the Sleeve, whilst others plait the Gown;
And *Betty's* prais'd for Labours not her own.

CANTO II

Not with more Glories, in th' Ethereal Plain,
The Sun first rises o'er the purpled Main,
Than, issuing forth, the Rival of his Beams
Launch'd on the Bosom of the silver *Thames.*
Fair Nymphs, and well-dress't Youths around her shone,
But ev'ry Eye was fix'd on her alone.
On her white Breast a sparkling Cross she wore,
Which *Jews* might kiss, and Infidels adore.
Her lively Looks a sprightly Mind disclose,
Quick as her Eyes, and as unfix'd as those:
Favours to none, to all she Smiles extends,
Oft she rejects, but never once offends.
Bright as the Sun, her Eyes the Gazers strike,
And, like the Sun, they shine on all alike.
Yet graceful Ease, and Sweetness void of Pride,
Might hide her Faults, if *Belles* had Faults to hide:
If to her share some Female Errors fall,
Look on her Face, and you'll forget 'em all.
    This Nymph, to the destruction of Mankind,
Nourish'd two Locks, which graceful hung behind
In equal Curls, and well conspir'd to deck
With shining Ringlets the smooth Iv'ry Neck.
Love in these Labyrinths his Slaves detains,
And mighty Hearts are held in slender Chains.
With hairy springes we the Birds betray,
Slight Lines of Hair surprize the Finny Prey,

Fair Tresses Man's Imperial Race ensnare,
And beauty draws us with a single hair.

Th' Advent'rous *Baron* the bright Locks admir'd,
He saw, he wish'd, and to the Prize aspir'd:
Resolv'd to win, he meditates the way,
By Force to ravish, or by Fraud betray;
For when Success a Lover's Toil attends,
Few ask, if Fraud or Force attain'd his Ends.

For this, ere *Phœbus* rose, he had implor'd
Propitious Heav'n, and ev'ry Pow'r ador'd,
But chiefly *Love*—to *Love* an Altar built,
Of twelve vast French Romances, neatly gilt.
There lay three Garters, half a Pair of Gloves;
And all the Trophies of his former Loves;
With tender *Billet-doux* he lights the Pyre,
And breathes three am'rous Sighs to raise the Fire.
Then prostrate falls, and begs with ardent Eyes
Soon to obtain, and long possess the Prize:
The Pow'rs gave Ear, and granted half his Pray'r,
The rest, the Winds dispers'd in empty Air.

But now secure the painted Vessel glides,
The Sun-beams trembling on the floating Tydes:
While melting Musick steals upon the Sky,
And soften'd Sounds along the Waters die;
Smooth flow the Waves, the Zephyrs gently play,
Belinda smil'd, and all the World was gay.
All but the *Sylph*—With careful Thoughts opprest,
Th' impending Woe sat heavy on his Breast.
He summons strait his Denizens of Air;
The lucid Squadrons round the Sails repair;
Soft o'er the Shrouds Aërial Whispers breathe,
That seem'd but *Zephyrs* to the Train beneath.
Some to the Sun their Insect-Wings unfold,
Waft on the Breeze, or sink in Clouds of Gold;
Transparent Forms, too fine for mortal sight,

Their fluid Bodies half dissolv'd in Light.
Loose to the Wind their airy Garments flew,
Thin glitt'ring Textures of the filmy Dew;
Dipt in the richest Tincture of the Skies,
Where Light disports in ever-mingling Dyes,
While ev'ry Beam new transient Colours flings,
Colours that change whene'er they wave their Wings.
Amid the Circle, on the gilded Mast,
Superior by the head, was *Ariel* plac'd;
His Purple Pinions op'ning to the Sun,
He rais'd his Azure Wand, and thus begun:
  "Ye *Sylphs* and *Sylphids,* to your Chief give Ear,
Fays, Fairies, Genii, Elves, and *Demons,* hear!
Ye know the *Spheres,* and various Tasks assign'd
By Laws Eternal to th' Aërial kind.
Some in the Fields of purest *Æther* play,
And bask and whiten in the Blaze of Day.
Some guide the Course of wand'ring Orbs on high,
Or roll the Planets thro' the boundless Sky.
Some less refin'd, beneath the Moon's pale Light
Pursue the Stars that shoot athwart the Night,
Or suck the Mists in grosser Air below,
Or dip their Pinions in the painted Bow,
Or brew fierce Tempests on the wintry Main,
Or o'er the Glebe distill the kindly Rain.
Others on Earth o'er human Race preside,
Watch all their Ways, and all their Actions guide:
Of these the Chief the Care of Nations own,
And guard with Arms Divine the *British Throne.*
  "Our humbler Province is to tend the Fair,
Not a less pleasing, tho' less glorious Care.
To save the Powder from too rude a Gale,
Nor let th' imprison'd Essences exhale;
To draw fresh Colours from the vernal Flow'rs;
To steal from Rainbows ere they drop in Show'rs

A brighter Wash; to curl their waving Hairs,
Assist their Blushes, and inspire their Airs;
Nay oft, in Dreams, Invention we bestow,
To change a *Flounce,* or add a *Furbelow.*

"This Day, black Omens threat the brightest Fair
That e'er deserv'd a watchful Spirit's Care;
Some dire Disaster, or by Force, or Slight,
But what, or where, the Fates have wrapp'd in Night.
Whether the Nymph shall break *Diana's* Law,
Or some frail *China* Jar receive a Flaw;
Or stain her Honour, or her new Brocade,
Forget her Pray'rs, or miss a Masquerade,
Or lose her Heart, or Necklace, at a Ball;
Or whether Heav'n has doom'd that *Shock* must fall.
Haste then, ye Spirits! to your Charge repair:
The flutt'ring Fan be *Zephyretta's* Care;
The Drops to thee, *Brillante,* we consign;
And, *Momentilla,* let the Watch be thine;
Do thou, *Crispissa,* tend her fav'rite Lock;
Ariel himself shall be the Guard of *Shock.*

"To Fifty chosen *Sylphs,* of special Note,
We trust th' important Charge, the *Petticoat:*
Oft have we known that seven-fold Fence to fail,
Tho' stiff with Hoops, and arm'd with Ribs of Whale;
Form a strong Line about the Silver Bound,
And guard the wide Circumference around.

"Whatever Spirit, careless of his Charge,
His Post neglects, or leaves the fair at large,
Shall feel sharp Vengeance soon o'ertake his Sins,
Be stopp'd in *Vials,* or transfixt with Pins;
Or plung'd in Lakes of bitter *Washes* lie,
Or wedg'd whole ages in a *Bodkin's Eye:*
Gums and *Pomatums* shall his Flight restrain,
While clog'd he beats his silken Wings in vain;
Or Alom-*styptics* with contracting Pow'r

Shrink his thin Essence like a rivel'd Flow'r.
Or, as *Ixion* fix'd, the Wretch shall feel
The giddy Motion of the whirling Mill,
In Fumes of burning Chocolate shall glow,
And tremble at the Sea that froths below!"
    He spoke; the Spirits from the Sails descend;
Some, Orb in Orb, around the Nymph extend,
Some thrid the mazy Ringlets of her Hair,
Some hang upon the Pendants of her Ear;
With beating Hearts the dire Event they wait,
Anxious, and trembling for the Birth of Fate.

CANTO III

Close by those Meads forever crown'd with Flow'rs,
Where *Thames* with Pride surveys his rising Tow'rs,
There stands a Structure of Majestic Frame,
Which from the neighb'ring *Hampton* takes its Name.
Here *Britain's* Statesmen oft the Fall foredoom
Of Foreign Tyrants and of Nymphs at home;
Here thou, great *Anna!* whom three realms *obey,*
Dost sometimes Counsel take—and sometimes Tea.
    Hither the Heroes and the Nymphs resort,
To taste a while the Pleasures of a Court;
In various talk th' instructive hours they past,
Who gave the *Ball,* or paid the Visit last:
One speaks the *Glory* of the *British Queen,*
And one describes a charming *Indian Screen;*
A third interprets Motions, Looks, and Eyes;
At ev'ry Word a Reputation dies.
Snuff, or the *Fan,* supply each pause of Chat,
With singing, laughing, ogling, *and all that.*
    Mean while declining from the Noon of Day,
The Sun obliquely shoots his burning Ray;
The hungry Judges soon the Sentence sign,

And Wretches hang that Jury-men may Dine;
The Merchant from th' *Exchange* returns in Peace,
And the long Labours of the *Toilet* cease.
Belinda now, whom Thirst of Fame invites,
Burns to encounter two adventrous Knights,
At *Ombre* singly to decide their Doom;
And swells her Breast with Conquests yet to come.
Strait the three Bands prepare in Arms to join,
Each Band the number of the Sacred Nine.
Soon as she spreads her hand, th' Aërial Guard
Descend, and sit on each important Card:
First *Ariel* perch'd upon a *Matadore*,
Then each, according to the Rank they bore;
For *Sylphs*, yet mindful of their ancient Race,
Are, as when Women, wondrous fond of Place.

Behold, four *Kings* in Majesty rever'd,
With hoary Whiskers and a forky Beard;
And four fair Queens, whose hands sustain a Flow'r,
Th' expressive Emblem of their softer Pow'r;
Four *Knaves* in Garbs succinct, a trusty Band,
Caps on their heads, and Halberds in their hand;
And Particolour'd Troops, a shining Train,
Draw forth to Combat on the Velvet plain.

The skilful Nymph reviews her Force with Care:
"Let Spades be Trumps!" she said, and Trumps they
                              were.

Now move to War her sable *Matadores*,
In Show like Leaders of the swarthy *Moors*.
Spadillio first, unconquerable Lord!
Led off two captive Trumps, and swept the Board.
As many more *Manillio* forc'd to yield,
And march'd a Victor from the verdant Field.
Him *Basto* follow'd, but his fate more hard
Gain'd but one trump and one *Plebeian* Card.
With his broad Sabre next, a Chief in Years,

The hoary Majesty of *Spades* appears;
Puts forth one manly Leg, to sight reveal'd,
The rest, his many-colour'd Robe conceal'd.
The Rebel *Knave,* who dares his Prince engage,
Proves the just Victim of his Royal Rage.
Even mighty *Pam,* that Kings and Queens o'erthrew,
And mow'd down Armies in the Fights of *Lu,*
Sad Chance of War! now destitute of Aid,
Falls undistinguish'd by the Victor *Spade!*

    Thus far both Armies to *Belinda* yield;
Now to the *Baron* Fate inclines the Field.
His warlike *Amazon* her Host invades,
Th' Imperial Consort of the Crown of *Spades.*
The *Club's* black Tyrant first her Victim dy'd,
Spite of his haughty Mien, and barb'rous Pride:
What boots the Regal Circle on his Head,
His Giant Limbs, in State unwieldy spread;
That long behind he trails his pompous Robe,
And, of all Monarchs, only grasps the Globe?

    The *Baron* now his Diamonds pours apace;
Th' embroider'd *King* who shows but half his Face,
And his refulgent *Queen,* with Pow'rs combin'd,
Of broken Troops an easy Conquest find.
Clubs, Diamonds, Hearts, in wild Disorder seen,
With Throngs promiscuous strow the level Green.
Thus when dispers'd a routed army runs,
Of *Asia's* Troops, and *Africk's* Sable Sons,
With like Confusion different Nations fly,
Of various Habit, and of various Dye,
The pierc'd Battalions dis-united fall,
In heaps on heaps; one fate o'erwhelms them all.

    The *Knave* of *Diamonds* tries his wily Arts,
And wins (oh shameful Chance!) the Queen of *Hearts.*
At this, the Blood the Virgin's Cheek forsook,
A livid Paleness spreads o'er all her Look;

She sees, and trembles at th' approaching Ill,
Just in the Jaws of Ruin, and *Codille*.
And now (as oft in some distemper'd State)
On one nice *Trick* depends the gen'ral Fate.
An *Ace* of Hearts steps forth: the *King* unseen
Lurk'd in her Hand, and mourn'd his captive *Queen*.
He springs to Vengeance with an eager pace,
And falls like Thunder on the prostrate *Ace*.
The Nymph exulting fills with Shouts the Sky,
The Walls, the Woods, and long Canals reply.

   Oh thoughtless Mortals! ever blind to Fate,
Too soon dejected, and too soon elate.
Sudden, these honours shall be snatch'd away,
And curs'd forever this Victorious Day.

   For lo! the Board with Cups and Spoons is crown'd,
The Berries crackle, and the Mill turns round.
On shining Altars of *Japan* they raise
The silver Lamp; the fiery Spirits blaze.
From silver Spouts the grateful Liquors glide,
While *China's* Earth receives the smoking Tyde:
At once they gratify their Scent and Taste,
And frequent Cups prolong the rich Repaste.
Straight hover round the Fair her Airy Band;
Some, as she sipp'd, the fuming Liquor fann'd,
Some o'er her Lap their careful Plumes display'd,
Trembling, and conscious of the rich Brocade.
Coffee (which makes the Politician wise,
And see thro' all things with his half-shut Eyes)
Sent up in Vapours to the *Baron's* Brain
New Stratagems, the radiant Lock to gain.
Ah cease, rash Youth! desist ere 'tis too late,
Fear the just Gods, and think of *Scylla's* Fate!
Chang'd to a bird, and sent to flit in Air,
She dearly pays for *Nisus'* injur'd Hair!

   But when to Mischief Mortals bend their Will,

How soon they find fit Instruments of Ill!
Just then, *Clarissa* drew with tempting Grace
A two-edg'd Weapon from her shining Case;
So Ladies in Romance assist their Knight,
Present the Spear, and arm him for the Fight.
He takes the Gift with rev'rence, and extends
The little Engine on his fingers' Ends;
This just behind *Belinda's* neck he spread,
As o'er the fragrant Steams she bends her Head.
Swift to the Lock a thousand Sprites repair,
A thousand Wings, by turns, blow back the Hair,
And thrice they twitch'd the Diamond in her Ear;
Thrice she look'd back, and thrice the Foe drew near.
Just in that instant, anxious *Ariel* sought
The close Recesses of the Virgin's Thought;
As on the Nosegay in her Breast reclin'd,
He watch'd th' Ideas rising in her Mind,
Sudden he view'd, in spite of all her Art,
An Earthly Lover lurking at her Heart.
Amaz'd, confus'd, he found his Pow'r expir'd,
Resign'd to Fate, and with a Sigh retir'd.
   The Peer now spreads the glitt'ring *Forfex* wide,
T'enclose the Lock; now joins it, to divide.
Ev'n then, before the fatal Engine clos'd,
A wretched *Sylph* too fondly interpos'd;
Fate urg'd the Shears, and cut the *Sylph* in twain,
(But Airy Substance soon unites again)
The meeting Points the sacred Hair dissever
From the fair Head, for ever, and for ever!
   Then flash'd the living Lightning from her Eyes,
And screams of Horror rend th' affrighted Skies.
Not louder Shrieks to pitying Heav'n are cast,
When Husbands or when Lapdogs breathe their last,
Or when rich *China* Vessels, fal'n from high,
In glitt'ring Dust and painted Fragments lie!

"Let Wreaths of triumph now my Temples twine,
(The Victor cry'd,) the glorious Prize is mine!
While Fish in Streams, or Birds delight in Air,
Or in a Coach and Six the *British* Fair,
As long as *Atalantis* shall be read,
Or the small Pillow grace a Lady's Bed,
While Visits shall be paid on solemn Days,
When num'rous Wax-lights in bright Order blaze,
While Nymphs take Treats, or Assignations give,
So long my Honour, Name, and Praise shall live!
    "What Time wou'd spare, from Steel receives its date,
And Monuments, like Men, submit to Fate!
Steel cou'd the Labour of the Gods destroy,
And strike to Dust th' Imperial Tow'rs of *Troy;*
Steel cou'd the Works of mortal Pride confound,
And hew Triumphal Arches to the Ground.
What Wonder then, fair Nymph! thy Hairs shou'd feel
The conqu'ring Force of unresisted Steel?"

CANTO IV

But anxious Cares the pensive Nymph oppres'd,
And secret Passions labour'd in her Breast.
Not youthful Kings in Battel seiz'd alive,
Not scornful Virgins who their Charms survive,
Not ardent Lovers robb'd of all their Bliss,
Not ancient Ladies when refus'd a Kiss,
Not Tyrants fierce that unrepenting die,
Not *Cynthia* when her *Manteau's* pinn'd awry,
E'er felt such Rage, Resentment, and despair,
As Thou, sad Virgin! for thy ravish'd Hair.
    For, that sad moment, when the *Sylphs* withdrew,
And *Ariel* weeping from *Belinda* flew,
Umbriel, a dusky, melancholy Spright,
As ever sully'd the fair face of Light,

Down to the Central Earth, his proper Scene,
Repair'd to search the gloomy Cave of *Spleen*.

Swift on his sooty Pinions flitts the Gnome,
And in a Vapour reach'd the dismal dome.
No cheerful Breeze this sullen Region knows,
The dreaded *East* is all the Wind that blows.
Here, in a Grotto, sheltred close from Air,
And screen'd in Shades from Day's detested Glare,
She sighs for ever on her pensive Bed,
Pain at her Side, and *Megrim* at her Head.

Two handmaids wait the Throne: Alike in Place,
But diff'ring far in Figure and in Face.
Here stood *Ill-nature* like an ancient *Maid*,
Her wrinkled Form in *Black* and *White* array'd;
With store of Pray'rs, for Mornings, Nights, and Noons,
Her Hand is fill'd; her Bosom with Lampoons.

There *Affectation*, with a sickly Mien
Shows in her Cheek the Roses of Eighteen,
Practis'd to lisp, and hang the Head aside,
Faints into Airs, and languishes with Pride;
On the rich Quilt sinks with becoming Woe,
Wrapt in a Gown, for Sickness, and for Show.
The Fair-ones feel such maladies as these,
When each new Night-Dress gives a new Disease.

A constant *Vapour* o'er the Palace flies;
Strange Phantoms rising as the Mists arise;
Dreadful, as Hermits' Dreams in haunted Shades,
Or bright, as Visions of expiring Maids.
Now glaring Fiends, and Snakes on rolling Spires,
Pale Spectres, gaping Tombs, and purple Fires:
Now Lakes of liquid Gold, *Elysian* Scenes,
And Crystal Domes, and Angels in Machines.

Unnumber'd Throngs on ev'ry side are seen,
Of Bodies chang'd to various Forms by *Spleen*.
Here living *Teapots* stand, one Arm held out,

One bent; the Handle this, and that the Spout:
A Pipkin there, like *Homer's Tripod* walks;
Here sighs a Jar, and there a Goose-pye talks;
Men prove with Child, as pow'rful Fancy works,
And Maids turn'd Bottles, call aloud for Corks.

Safe pass'd the *Gnome* thro' this fantastick Band,
A Branch of healing *Spleenwort* in his hand.
Then thus addrest the Pow'r—"Hail wayward Queen!
Who rule the Sex to Fifty from Fifteen,
Parent of Vapours and of Female Wit,
Who give th' *Hysteric,* or *Poetic* Fit,
On various Tempers act by various ways,
Make some take Physick, others scribble Plays;
Who cause the Proud their Visits to delay,
And send the Godly in a Pett to pray.
A Nymph there is, that all thy Pow'r disdains,
And thousands more in equal Mirth maintains.
But oh! if e'er thy *Gnome* could spoil a Grace,
Or raise a Pimple on a beauteous Face,
Like Citron-Waters Matrons' Cheeks inflame,
Or change Complexions at a losing Game;
If e'er with airy Horns I planted Heads,
Or rumpled Petticoats, or tumbled Beds,
Or caus'd Suspicion when no Soul was rude,
Or discompos'd the Head-dress of a Prude,
Or e'er to costive Lapdog gave Disease,
Which not the Tears of brightest Eyes could ease:
Hear me, and touch *Belinda* with Chagrin,
That single Act gives half the World the Spleen."

The Goddess with a discontented Air
Seems to reject him, tho' she grants his Pray'r.
A wondrous Bag with both her Hands she binds,
Like that where once *Ulysses* held the Winds;
There she collects the Force of Female Lungs,
Sighs, Sobs, and Passions, and the War of Tongues.

A Vial next she fills with fainting Fears,
Soft Sorrows, melting Griefs, and flowing Tears.
The *Gnome* rejoicing bears her Gifts away,
Spreads his black Wings, and slowly mounts to Day.

　　Sunk in *Thalestris'* Arms the Nymph he found,
Her Eyes dejected, and her Hair unbound.
Full o'er their Heads the swelling Bag he rent,
And all the Furies issu'd at the Vent.
Belinda burns with more than mortal Ire,
And fierce *Thalestris* fans the rising Fire.
"Oh wretched maid!" she spread her hands, and cry'd,
(While *Hampton's* echoes, Wretched Maid! reply'd)
"Was it for this you took such constant Care
The *Bodkin, Comb,* and *Essence* to prepare;
For this your Locks in Paper Durance bound,
For this with tort'ring Irons wreath'd around?
For this with Fillets strain'd your tender Head,
And bravely bore the double Loads of Lead?
Gods! shall the Ravisher display your Hair,
While the Fops envy, and the Ladies stare!
Honour forbid! at whose unrival'd Shrine
Ease, Pleasure, Virtue, All our Sex resign.
Methinks already I your Tears survey,
Already hear the horrid things they say,
Already see you a degraded Toast,
And all your Honour in a Whisper lost!
How shall I, then, your helpless Fame defend?
'Twill then be Infamy to seem your Friend!
And shall this Prize, th' inestimable Prize,
Expos'd thro' Crystal to the gazing Eyes,
And heighten'd by the Diamond's circling Rays,
On that Rapacious Hand for ever blaze?
Sooner shall Grass in *Hide-Park Circus* grow,
And Wits take Lodgings in the Sound of *Bow;*
Sooner let Earth, Air, Sea, to *Chaos* fall,

Men, Monkeys, Lapdogs, Parrots, perish all!"
    She said; then raging to *Sir Plume* repairs,
And bids her *Beau* demand the precious Hairs:
(*Sir Plume* of *Amber Snuff-Box* justly vain,
And the nice Conduct of a *clouded* Cane)
With earnest Eyes, and round unthinking Face,
He first the Snuff-box open'd, then the Case,
And thus broke out—"My Lord, why, what the Devil?
Z—ds! damn the Lock! 'fore Gad, you must be civil!
Plague on't! 'tis past a Jest—nay prithee, Pox!
Give her the Hair"—he spoke, and rapp'd his Box.
    "It grieves me much," reply'd the peer again,
"Who speaks so well shou'd ever speak in vain.
But by this Lock, this sacred Lock, I swear,
(Which never more shall join its parted Hair;
Which never more its honours shall renew,
Clipt from the lovely Head where late it grew)
That while my Nostrils draw the vital Air,
This Hand, which won it, shall forever wear."
He spoke, and speaking, in proud Triumph spread
The long-contended Honours of her Head.
    But *Umbriel*, hateful *Gnome!* forbears not so;
He breaks the Vial whence the Sorrows flow.
Then see! the *Nymph* in beauteous Grief appears,
Her Eyes half-languishing, half-drown'd in Tears;
On her heav'd Bosom hung her drooping Head,
Which, with a Sigh, she rais'd; and thus she said:
    "Forever curs'd be this detested Day,
Which snatch'd my best, my fav'rite Curl away!
Happy! ah ten times happy, had I been,
If *Hampton-Court* these Eyes had never seen!
Yet am not I the first mistaken Maid,
By Love of Courts to num'rous Ills betray'd.
Oh had I rather un-admir'd remain'd
In some lone Isle, or distant *Northern* Land;

Where the gilt *Chariot* never marks the Way,
Where none learn *Ombre,* none e'er taste *Bohea!*
There kept my Charms conceal'd from mortal Eye,
Like Roses, that in Desarts bloom and die.
What mov'd my Mind with youthful Lords to roam?
O had I stay'd, and said my Pray'rs at home!
'Twas this, the Morning *Omens* seem'd to tell;
Thrice from my trembling hand the *Patch-box* fell;
The tott'ring *China* shook without a Wind,
Nay, *Poll* sat mute, and *Shock* was most Unkind!
A *Sylph* too warn'd me of the Threats of Fate,
In mystic Visions, now believ'd too late!
See the poor Remnants of these slighted Hairs!
My Hands shall rend what ev'n thy Rapine spares:
These, in two sable Ringlets taught to break,
Once gave new Beauties to the snowie Neck.
The Sister-Lock now sits uncouth, alone,
And in its Fellow's Fate foresees its own;
Uncurl'd it hangs, the fatal Sheers demands;
And tempts, once more, thy sacrilegious Hands.
Oh hadst thou, Cruel! been content to seize
Hairs less in sight, or any Hairs but these!"

CANTO V

She said: the pitying Audience melt in Tears,
But *Fate* and *Jove* had stopp'd the *Baron's* Ears.
In vain *Thalestris* with Reproach assails,
For who can move when fair *Belinda* fails?
Not half so fixt the *Trojan* cou'd remain,
While *Anna* begg'd and *Dido* rag'd in vain.
Then grave *Clarissa* graceful wav'd her Fan;
Silence ensu'd, and thus the Nymph began.

"Say why are Beauties prais'd and honour'd most,
The wise Man's Passion, and the vain Man's Toast?

Why deck'd with all that Land and Sea afford,
Why Angels call'd, and Angel-like ador'd?
Why round our Coaches crowd the white-glov'd Beaus,
Why bows the Side-box from its inmost Rows?
How vain are all these Glories, all our Pains,
Unless good Sense preserve what Beauty gains:
That Men may say, when we the Front-box grace,
'Behold the first in Virtue, as in Face!'
Oh! if to dance all Night, and dress all Day,
Charm'd the Smallpox, or chas'd old Age away;
Who would not scorn what Huswife's Cares produce,
Or who would learn one earthly Thing of Use?
To patch, nay ogle, might become a Saint,
Nor could it sure be such a Sin to paint.
But since, alas! frail Beauty must decay,
Curl'd or uncurl'd, since Locks will turn to grey;
Since painted, or not painted, all shall fade,
And she who scorns a Man, must die a Maid;
What then remains, but well our Pow'r to use,
And keep good Humour still whate'er we lose?
And trust me, Dear! good Humour can prevail,
When Airs, and Flights, and Screams, and Scolding fail.
Beauties in vain their pretty Eyes may roll;
Charms strike the Sight, but Merit wins the Soul."

So spoke the Dame, but no Applause ensu'd;
Belinda frown'd, *Thalestris* call'd her Prude.
"To Arms, to Arms!" the fierce Virago cries,
And swift as Lightning to the Combate flies.
All side in Parties, and begin th' Attack;
Fans clap, Silks russle, and tough Whalebones crack;
Heroes' and Heroines' shouts confus'dly rise,
And bass and treble Voices strike the Skies.
No common Weapons in their Hands are found,
Like Gods they fight, nor dread a mortal Wound.

So when bold *Homer* makes the Gods engage,

And heav'nly Breasts with human Passions rage;
'Gainst *Pallas, Mars; Latona, Hermes* Arms;
And all *Olympus* rings with loud Alarms:
Blue *Neptune* storms, the bellowing Deeps resound;
Earth shakes her nodding Tow'rs, the Ground gives
      way;
And the pale Ghosts start at the Flash of Day!
    Triumphant *Umbriel* on a Sconce's Height
Clapt his glad Wings, and sate to view the Fight:
Propt on their Bodkin Spears, the Sprights survey
The growing Combat, or assist the Fray.
    While thro' the Press enrag'd *Thalestris* flies,
And scatters Death around from both her Eyes,
A *Beau* and *Witling* perish'd in the Throng,
One dy'd in *Metaphor,* and one in *Song.*
"O cruel Nymph! a living Death I bear,"
Cry'd *Dapperwit,* and sunk beside his Chair.
A mournful Glance Sir *Fopling* upwards cast,
"Those eyes are made so killing"—was his last:
Thus on *Meander's* flow'ry Margin lies
Th' expiring Swan, and as he sings he dies.
    When bold Sir *Plume* had drawn *Clarissa* down,
Chloe stept in, and kill'd him with a frown;
She smil'd to see the doughty Hero slain,
But, at her Smile, the Beau reviv'd again.
    Now *Jove* suspends his golden Scales in Air,
Weighs the Men's Wits against the Lady's Hair;
The doubtful Beam long nods from side to side;
At length the Wits mount up, the Hairs subside.
    See fierce *Belinda* on the *Baron* flies,
With more than usual Lightning in her Eyes;
Nor fear'd the Chief th' unequal Fight to try,
Who sought no more than on his Foe to die.
But this bold Lord with manly Strength indu'd,

She with one Finger and a Thumb subdu'd:
Just where the Breath of Life his Nostrils drew,
A charge of *Snuff* the wily Virgin threw;
The *Gnomes* direct, to ev'ry Atome just,
The pungent Grains of titillating Dust.
Sudden, with starting Tears each Eye o'erflows,
And the high Dome re-echoes to his Nose.
   "Now meet thy Fate," incens'd *Belinda* cry'd,
And drew a deadly *Bodkin* from her Side.
(The same, his ancient Personage to deck,
Her grand great Grandsire wore about his Neck,
In three Seal-Rings; which after, melted down,
Form'd a vast *Buckle* for his Widow's Gown:
Her infant Grandame's *Whistle* next it grew,
The *Bells* she gingled, and the *Whistle* blew;
Then in a *Bodkin* grac'd her Mother's Hairs,
Which long she wore, and now *Belinda* wears.)
   "Boast not my Fall (he cry'd) insulting Foe!
Thou by some other shalt be laid as low.
Nor think, to die dejects my lofty Mind:
All that I dread, is leaving you behind!
Rather than so, ah let me still survive,
And burn in *Cupid's* Flames—but burn alive."
   "*Restore* the *Lock!*" she cries; and all around
"*Restore the Lock!*" the vaulted Roofs rebound.
Not fierce *Othello* in so loud a Strain
Roar'd for the Handkerchief that caus'd his Pain.
But see how oft Ambitious Aims are cross'd,
And Chiefs contend 'till all the Prize is lost!
The Lock, obtain'd with Guilt, and kept with Pain,
In ev'ry place is sought, but sought in vain:
With such a Prize no Mortal must be blest,
So Heav'n decrees! with Heav'n who can contest?
   Some thought it mounted to the Lunar Sphere,

Since all things lost on Earth are treasur'd there.
There Heroes' Wits are kept in pond'rous Vases,
And Beaus' in *Snuff-boxes* and *Tweezer-cases*.
There broken Vows, and Death-bed Alms are found,
And Lovers' Hearts with Ends of Riband bound,
The Courtier's Promises, and Sick Man's Pray'rs,
The Smiles of Harlots, and the Tears of Heirs,
Cages for Gnats, and Chains to Yoke a Flea,
Dry'd Butterflies, and Tomes of Casuistry.

 But trust the Muse—she saw it upward rise,
Tho' mark'd by none but quick, Poetic Eyes:
(So *Rome's* great Founder to the Heav'ns withdrew,
To *Proculus* alone confess'd in view.)
A sudden Star, it shot thro' liquid Air,
And drew behind a radiant *Trail of Hair*.
Not *Berenice's* Locks first rose so bright,
The Heav'ns bespangling with dishevel'd Light.
The *Sylphs* behold it kindling as it flies,
And pleas'd pursue its Progress thro' the skies.

 This the *Beau monde* shall from the *Mall* survey,
And hail with Musick its propitious Ray.
This the blest Lover shall from *Venus* take,
And send up Vows from *Rosamonda's* Lake.
This *Partridge* soon shall view in cloudless Skies,
When next he looks thro' *Galileo's* Eyes;
And hence th' Egregious Wizard shall foredoom
The fate of *Louis,* and the fall of *Rome.*

 Then cease, bright Nymph! to mourn thy ravish'd
  Hair
Which adds new Glory to the shining Sphere!
Not all the Tresses that fair Head can boast
Shall draw such Envy as the Lock you lost.
For, after all the Murders of your Eye,
When, after Millions slain, yourself shall die;
When those fair Suns shall sett, as sett they must,

And all those Tresses shall be laid in Dust;
This Lock, the Muse shall consecrate to Fame,
And 'midst the Stars inscribe *Belinda's* Name.

An Essay on Criticism

PART I

'Tis hard to say, if greater want of skill
Appear in writing or in judging ill;
But, of the two, less dang'rous is th' offence
To tire our patience, than mislead our sense.
Some few in that, but numbers err in this,
Ten censure wrong for one who writes amiss;
A fool might once himself alone expose,
Now one in verse makes many more in prose.

'Tis with our judgments as our watches, none
Go just alike, yet each believes his own.
In Poets as true genius is but rare,
True Taste as seldom is the Critic's share;
Both must alike from Heav'n derive their light,
These born to judge, as well as those to write.
Let such teach others who themselves excel,
And censure freely who have written well.
Authors are partial to their wit, 'tis true,
But are not Critics to their judgment too?

Yet if we look more closely, we shall find
Most have the seeds of judgment in their mind:
Nature affords at least a glimm'ring light;
The lines, tho' touch'd but faintly, are drawn right.
But as the slightest sketch, if justly trac'd,
Is by ill-colouring but the more disgrac'd,
So by false learning is good sense defac'd:

Some are bewilder'd in the maze of schools,
And some made coxcombs Nature meant but fools.
In search of wit these lose their common sense,
And then turn Critics in their own defence:
Each burns alike, who can, or cannot write,
Or with a Rival's, or an Eunuch's spite.
All fools have still an itching to deride,
And fain would be upon the laughing side.
If *Mævius* scribble in *Apollo's* spight,
There are, who judge still worse than he can write.

    Some have at first for Wits, then Poets past,
Turn'd Critics next, and prov'd plain fools at last.
Some neither can for Wits nor Critics pass,
As heavy mules are neither horse nor ass.
Those half-learn'd witlings, num'rous in our isle,
As half-form'd insects on the banks of Nile;
Unfinish'd things, one knows not what to call,
Their generation's so equivocal:
To tell 'em, would a hundred tongues require,
Or one vain wit's, that might a hundred tire.

    But you who seek to give and merit fame,
And justly bear a Critic's noble name,
Be sure yourself and your own reach to know,
How far your genius, taste, and learning go;
Launch not beyond your depth, but be discreet,
And mark that point where sense and dullness meet.

    Nature to all things fix'd the limits fit,
And wisely curb'd proud man's pretending wit.
As on the land while here the ocean gains,
In other parts it leaves wide sandy plains;
Thus in the soul while memory prevails,
The solid pow'r of understanding fails;
Where beams of warm imagination play,
The memory's soft figures melt away.
One science only will one genius fit;

So vast is art, so narrow human wit:
Not only bounded to peculiar arts,
But oft in those confin'd to single parts.
Like Kings, we lose the conquests gain'd before,
By vain ambition still to make them more;
Each might his sev'ral province well command,
Would all but stoop to what they understand.

First follow *Nature*, and your judgment frame
By her just standard, which is still the same:
Unerring *Nature*, still divinely bright,
One clear, unchang'd, and universal light,
Life, force, and beauty, must to all impart,
At once the source, and end, and test of Art.
Art from that fund each just supply provides,
Works without show, and without pomp presides:
In some fair body thus th' informing soul
With spirits feeds, with vigour fills the whole,
Each motion guides, and ev'ry nerve sustains;
Itself unseen, but in th' effects, remains.
Some, to whom Heav'n in wit has been profuse,
Want as much more, to turn it to its use;
For wit and judgment often are at strife,
Tho' meant each other's aid, like man and wife.
'Tis more to guide, than spur the Muse's steed;
Restrain his fury, than provoke his speed;
The winged courser, like a gen'rous horse,
Shows most true mettle when you check his course.

Those *Rules* of old discover'd, not devis'd,
Are Nature still, but Nature methodiz'd;
Nature, like Liberty, is but restrain'd
By the same Laws which first herself ordain'd.

Hear how learn'd Greece her useful rules indites,
When to repress, and when indulge our flights:
High on Parnassus' top her sons she show'd,
And pointed out those arduous paths they trod;

Held from afar, aloft, th' immortal prize,
And urg'd the rest by equal steps to rise.
Just precepts thus from great examples giv'n,
She drew from them what they deriv'd from Heav'n.
The gen'rous Critic fann'd the Poet's fire,
And taught the world with reason to admire.
Then Criticism the Muse's handmaid prov'd,
To dress her charms, and make her more belov'd:
But following wits from that intention stray'd,
Who could not win the mistress, woo'd the maid;
Against the Poets their own arms they turn'd,
Sure to hate most the men from whom they learn'd.
So modern 'Pothecaries, taught the art
By Doctor's bills to play the Doctor's part,
Bold in the practice of mistaken rules,
Prescribe, apply, and call their masters fools.
Some on the leaves of antient authors prey,
Nor time nor moths e'er spoil'd so much as they.
Some drily plain, without invention's aid,
Write dull receits how poems may be made.
These leave the sense, their learning to display,
And those explain the meaning quite away.
  You then whose judgment the right course would
    steer,
Know well each *Ancient's* proper character;
His Fable, Subject, scope in ev'ry page;
Religion, Country, genius of his Age:
Without all these at once before your eyes,
Cavil you may, but never criticize.
Be Homer's works your study and delight,
Read them by day, and meditate by night;
Thence form your judgment, thence your maxims bring,
And trace the Muses upward to their spring.
Still with itself compar'd, his text peruse;
And let your comment be the Mantuan Muse.

When first young Maro in his boundless mind
A work t' outlast immortal Rome design'd,
Perhaps he seem'd above the Critic's law,
And but from Nature's fountains scorn'd to draw:
But when t' examine ev'ry part he came,
Nature and Homer were, he found, the same.
Convinc'd, amaz'd, he checks the bold design;
And rules as strict his labour'd work confine,
As if the Stagirite o'erlook'd each line.
Learn hence for ancient rules a just esteem;
To copy nature is to copy them.
    Some beauties yet no Precepts can declare,
For there's a happiness as well as care.
Music resembles Poetry, in each
Are nameless graces which no methods teach,
And which a master-hand alone can reach.
If, where the rules not far enough extend,
(Since rules were made but to promote their end)
Some lucky License answer to the full
Th' intent propos'd, that License is a rule.
Thus Pegasus, a nearer way to take,
May boldly deviate from the common track.
From vulgar bounds with brave disorder part,
And snatch a grace beyond the reach of art,
Which, without passing thro' the judgment, gains
The heart, and all its end at once attains.
In prospects thus, some objects please our eyes,
Which out of nature's common order rise,
The shapeless rock, or hanging precipice.
Great Wits sometimes may gloriously offend,
And rise to faults true Critics dare not mend.
But tho' the Ancients thus their rules invade,
(As Kings dispense with laws themselves have made)
Moderns, beware! or if you must offend
Against the Precept, ne'er transgress its End;

Let it be seldom, and compell'd by need;
And have, at least, their precedent to plead.
The Critic else proceeds without remorse,
Seizes your fame, and puts his laws in force.
    I know there are, to whose presumptuous thoughts
Those freer beauties, ev'n in them, seem faults.
Some figures monstrous and mishap'd appear,
Consider'd singly, or beheld too near,
Which, but proportion'd to their light, or place,
Due distance reconciles to form and grace.
A prudent chief not always must display
His pow'rs in equal ranks, and fair array,
But with th' occasion and the place comply,
Conceal his force, nay seem sometimes to fly.
Those oft are stratagems which errors seem,
Nor is it Homer nods, but we that dream.
    Still green with bays each ancient Altar stands,
Above the reach of sacrilegious hands;
Secure from Flames, from Envy's fiercer rage,
Destructive War, and all-involving Age.
See, from each clime the learn'd their incense bring!
Hear, in all tongues consenting Pæans ring!
In praise so just let ev'ry voice be join'd,
And fill the gen'ral chorus of mankind.
Hail, Bards triumphant! born in happier days;
Immortal heirs of universal praise!
Whose honours with increase of ages grow,
As streams roll down, enlarging as they flow;
Nations unborn your mighty names shall sound,
And worlds applaud that must not yet be found!
Oh may some spark of your celestial fire,
The last, the meanest of your sons inspire
(That on weak wings, from far, pursues your flights;
Glows while he reads, but trembles as he writes)

To teach vain Wits a science little known,
T' admire superior sense, and doubt their own!

PART II

Of all the Causes which conspire to blind
Man's erring judgment, and misguide the mind,
What the weak head with strongest bias rules,
Is *Pride*, the never-failing vice of fools.
Whatever Nature has in worth deny'd,
She gives in large recruits of needful Pride;
For as in bodies, thus in souls, we find
What wants in blood and spirits, swell'd with wind:
Pride, where Wit fails, steps in to our defence,
And fills up all the mighty Void of sense.
If once right reason drives that cloud away,
Truth breaks upon us with resistless day.
Trust not yourself; but your defects to know,
Make use of ev'ry friend—and ev'ry foe.
A *little learning* is a dang'rous thing;
Drink deep, or taste not the Pierian spring:
There shallow draughts intoxicate the brain,
And drinking largely sobers us again.
Fir'd at first sight with what the Muse imparts,
In fearless youth we tempt the heights of Arts,
While from the bounded level of our mind,
Short views we take, nor see the lengths behind;
But more advanc'd, behold with strange surprize
New distant scenes of endless science rise!
So pleas'd at first the tow'ring Alps we try,
Mount o'er the vales, and seem to tread the sky,
Th' eternal snows appear already past,
And the first clouds and mountains seem the last:
But, those attain'd, we tremble to survey

The growing labours of the lengthen'd way,
Th' increasing prospect tires our wand'ring eyes,
Hills peep o'er hills, and Alps on Alps arise!
  A perfect Judge will read each work of Wit
With the same spirit that its author writ:
Survey the *Whole*, nor seek slight faults to find
Where nature moves, and rapture warms the mind;
Nor lose, for that malignant dull delight,
The gen'rous pleasure to be charm'd with wit.
But in such lays as neither ebb, nor flow,
Correctly cold, and regularly low,
That shunning faults, one quiet tenour keep;
We cannot blame indeed—but we may sleep.
In Wit, as Nature, what affects our hearts
Is not th' exactness of peculiar parts;
'Tis not a lip, or eye, we beauty call,
But the joint force and full result of all.
Thus when we view some well-proportion'd dome,
(The world's just wonder, and ev'n thine, O Rome!)
No single parts unequally surprize,
All comes united to th' admiring eyes;
No monstrous height, or breadth, or length appear;
The Whole at once is bold, and regular.
  Whoever thinks a faultless piece to see,
Thinks what ne'er was, nor is, nor e'er shall be.
In ev'ry work regard the writer's End,
Since none can compass more than they intend;
And if the means be just, the conduct true,
Applause, in spight of trivial faults, is due.
As men of breeding, sometimes men of wit,
T' avoid great errors, must the less commit:
Neglect the rules each verbal Critic lays,
For not to know some trifles, is a praise.
Most Critics, fond of some subservient art,
Still make the Whole depend upon a Part:

They talk of principles, but notions prize,
And all to one lov'd Folly sacrifice.

   Once on a time, La Mancha's Knight, they say,
A certain Bard encount'ring on the way,
Discours'd in terms as just, with looks as sage,
As e'er could Dennis, of the Grecian stage,
Concluding all were desp'rate sots and fools,
Who durst depart from Aristotle's rules.
Our Author, happy in a judge so nice,
Produc'd his Play, and begg'd the Knight's advice;
Made him observe the subject, and the plot,
The manners, passions, unities; what not?
All which, exact to rule, were brought about,
Were but a Combat in the lists left out.
"What! leave the Combat out?" exclaims the Knight;
"Yes, or we must renounce the Stagirite."
"Not so by Heav'n," he answers in a rage,
"Knights, squires, and steeds, must enter on the stage."
"So vast a throng the stage can ne'er contain."
"Then build a new, or act it in a plain."

   Thus Critics, of less judgment than caprice,
Curious, not knowing, not exact but nice,
Form short Ideas; and offend in arts
(As most in manners) by a love to parts.

   Some to *Conceit* alone their taste confine,
And glitt'ring thoughts struck out at ev'ry line;
Pleas'd with a work where nothing's just or fit;
One glaring Chaos and wild heap of wit.
Poets, like painters, thus, unskill'd to trace
The naked nature and the living grace,
With gold and jewels cover ev'ry part,
And hide with ornaments their want of art.
True Wit is Nature to advantage dress'd,
What oft was thought, but ne'er so well express'd;
Something, whose truth convinc'd at sight we find,

That gives us back the image of our mind.
As shades more sweetly recommend the light,
So modest plainness sets off sprightly wit.
For works may have more wit than does 'em good,
As bodies perish thro' excess of blood.

  Others for *Language* all their care express,
And value books, as women men, for Dress:
Their praise is still,—the Style is excellent;
The Sense, they humbly take upon content.
Words are like leaves; and where they most abound,
Much fruit of sense beneath is rarely found:
False Eloquence, like the Prismatic glass,
Its gaudy colours spreads on ev'ry place;
The face of nature we no more survey,
All glares alike, without distinction gay:
But true Expression, like th' unchanging Sun,
Clears and improves whate'er it shines upon,
It gilds all objects, but it alters none.
Expression is the dress of thought, and still
Appears more decent, as more suitable;
A vile conceit in pompous words express'd,
Is like a clown in regal purple dress'd:
For diff'rent styles with diff'rent subjects sort,
As several garbs with country, town, and court.
Some by old words to fame have made pretence,
Ancients in phrase, meer moderns in their sense;
Such labour'd nothings, in so strange a style,
Amaze th' unlearn'd, and make the learned smile.
Unlucky, as Fungoso in the Play,
These sparks with aukward vanity display
What the fine gentleman wore yesterday;
And but so mimic ancient wits at best,
As apes our grandsires, in their doublets drest.
In words, as fashions, the same rule will hold;
Alike fantastic, if too new, or old:

Be not the first by whom the new are try'd,
Nor yet the last to lay the old aside.
  But most by *Numbers* judge a Poet's song;
And smooth or rough, with them, is right or wrong:
In the bright Muse tho' thousand charms conspire,
Her Voice is all these tuneful fools admire;
Who haunt Parnassus but to please their ear,
Not mend their minds; as some to Church repair,
Not for the doctrine, but the music there.
These equal syllables alone require,
Tho' oft the ear the open vowels tire;
While expletives their feeble aid do join;
And ten low words oft creep in one dull line:
While they ring round the same unvary'd chimes,
With sure returns of still expected rhymes.
Where-e'er you find "the cooling western breeze,"
In the next line, it "whispers thro' the trees;"
If crystal streams "with pleasing murmurs creep,"
The reader's threaten'd (not in vain) with "sleep."
Then, at the last and only couplet fraught
With some unmeaning thing they call a thought,
A needless Alexandrine ends the song,
That, like a wounded snake, drags its slow length along.
Leave such to tune their own dull rhymes, and know
What's roundly smooth, or languishingly slow;
And praise the easy vigour of a line,
Where Denham's strength, and Waller's sweetness join.
True ease in writing comes from art, not chance,
As those move easiest who have learn'd to dance.
'Tis not enough no harshness gives offence,
The sound must seem an Echo to the sense:
Soft is the strain when Zephyr gently blows,
And the smooth stream in smoother numbers flows;
But when loud surges lash the sounding shore,
The hoarse, rough verse should like the torrent roar:

When Ajax strives some rock's vast weight to throw,
The line too labours, and the words move slow;
Not so, when swift Camilla scours the plain,
Flies o'er th' unbending corn, and skims along the main.
Hear how Timotheus' vary'd lays surprize,
And bid alternate passions fall and rise!
While, at each change, the son of Libyan Jove
Now burns with glory, and then melts with love;
Now his fierce eyes with sparkling fury glow,
Now sighs steal out, and tears begin to flow:
Persians and Greeks like turns of nature found,
And the World's victor stood subdu'd by Sound!
The pow'r of Music all our hearts allow,
And what Timotheus was, is *Dryden* now.

  Avoid *Extremes;* and shun the fault of such,
Who still are pleas'd too little or too much.
At ev'ry trifle scorn to take offence,
That always shows great pride, or little sense;
Those heads, as stomachs, are not sure the best,
Which nauseate all, and nothing can digest.
Yet let not each gay Turn thy rapture move;
For fools admire, but men of sense approve:
As things seem large which we thro' mists descry,
Dullness is ever apt to magnify.

  Some foreign writers, some our own despise;
The Ancients only, or the Moderns prize.
Thus Wit, like Faith, by each man is apply'd
To one small sect, and all are damn'd beside.
Meanly they seek the blessing to confine,
And force that sun but on a part to shine,
Which not alone the southern wit sublimes,
But ripens spirits in cold northern climes;
Which from the first has shone on ages past,
Enlights the present, and shall warm the last;
Tho' each may feel encreases and decays,

And see now clearer and now darker days.
Regard not then if Wit be old or new,
But blame the false, and value still the true.
    Some ne'er advance a Judgment of their own,
But catch the spreading notion of the Town;
They reason and conclude by precedent,
And own stale nonsense which they ne'er invent.
Some judge of authors' names, not works, and then
Nor praise nor blame the writings, but the men.
Of all this servile herd, the worst is he
That in proud dullness joins with Quality.
A constant Critic at the great man's board,
To fetch and carry nonsense for my Lord.
What woeful stuff this madrigal would be,
In some starv'd hackney sonneteer, or me?
But let a Lord once own the happy lines,
How the wit brightens! how the style refines!
Before his sacred name flies ev'ry fault,
And each exalted stanza teems with thought!
    The Vulgar thus through Imitation err;
As oft the Learn'd by being singular;
So much they scorn the croud, that if the throng
By chance go right, they purposely go wrong:
So Schismatics the plain believers quit,
And are but damn'd for having too much wit.
Some praise at morning what they blame at night;
But always think the last opinion right.
A Muse by these is like a mistress us'd,
This hour she's idoliz'd, the next abus'd;
While their weak heads, like towns unfortify'd,
'Twixt sense and nonsense daily change their side.
Ask them the cause; they're wiser still, they say;
And still to-morrow's wiser than to-day.
We think our fathers fools, so wise we grow;
Our wiser sons, no doubt, will think us so.

Once School-divines this zealous isle o'erspread;
Who knew most Sentences, was deepest read;
Faith, Gospel, all, seem'd made to be disputed,
And none had sense enough to be confuted:
Scotists and Thomists, now, in peace remain,
Amidst their kindred cobwebs in Duck-lane.
If Faith itself has diff'rent dresses worn,
What wonder modes in Wit should take their turn?
Oft, leaving what is natural and fit,
The current folly proves the ready wit;
And authors think their reputation safe,
Which lives as long as fools are pleas'd to laugh.

    Some, valuing those of their own side or mind,
Still make themselves the measure of mankind:
Fondly we think we honour merit then,
When we but praise ourselves in other men.
Parties in Wit attend on those of State,
And public faction doubles private hate.
Pride, Malice, Folly, against Dryden rose,
In various shapes of Parsons, Critics, Beaus;
But sense surviv'd, when merry jests were past;
For rising merit will buoy up at last.
Might he return, and bless once more our eyes,
New Blackmores and new Milbourns must arise:
Nay, should great Homer lift his awful head,
Zoilus again would start up from the dead.
Envy will merit, as its shade, pursue;
But like a shadow, proves the substance true;
For envy'd Wit, like Sol eclips'd, makes known
Th' opposing body's grossness, not its own.
When first that sun too pow'rful beams displays,
It draws up vapours which obscure its rays;
But ev'n those clouds at last adorn its way,
Reflect new glories, and augment the day.

    Be thou the first true merit to befriend;

His praise is lost, who stays 'till all commend.
Short is the date, alas, of modern rhymes,
And 'tis but just to let them live betimes.
No longer now that golden age appears,
When Patriarch-wits surviv'd a thousand years:
Now length of Fame (our second life) is lost,
And bare threescore is all ev'n that can boast;
Our sons their fathers' failing language see,
And such as Chaucer is, shall Dryden be.
So when the faithful pencil has design'd
Some bright Idea of the master's mind,
Where a new world leaps out at his command,
And ready Nature waits upon his hand;
When the ripe colours soften and unite,
And sweetly melt into just shade and light,
When mellowing years their full perfection give,
And each bold figure just begins to live,
The treach'rous colours the fair art betray,
And all the bright creation fades away!
  Unhappy Wit, like most mistaken things,
Attones not for that envy which it brings.
In youth alone its empty praise we boast,
But soon the short-liv'd vanity is lost:
Like some fair flow'r the early spring supplies,
That gayly blooms, but ev'n in blooming dies.
What is this Wit, which must our cares employ?
The owner's wife, that other men enjoy;
Then most our trouble still when most admir'd,
And still the more we give, the more requir'd;
Whose fame with pains we guard, but lose with ease,
Sure some to vex, but never all to please;
'Tis what the vicious fear, the virtuous shun,
By fools 'tis hated, and by knaves undone!
  If Wit so much from Ign'rance undergo,
Ah let not Learning too commence its foe!

Of old, those met rewards who could excell,
And such were prais'd who but endeavoured well:
Tho' triumphs were to gen'rals only due,
Crowns were reserv'd to grace the soldiers too.
Now, they who reach Parnassus' lofty crown
Employ their pains to spurn some others down;
And while self-love each jealous writer rules,
Contending wits become the sport of fools:
But still the worst with most regret commend,
For each ill Author is as bad a Friend.
To what base ends, and by what abject ways,
Are mortals urg'd thro' sacred lust of praise!
Ah, ne'er so dire a thirst of glory boast,
Nor in the Critic let the Man be lost.
Good-nature and good-sense must ever join;
To err is human, to forgive, divine.
   But if in noble minds some dregs remain
Not yet purg'd off, of spleen and sour disdain;
Discharge that rage on more provoking crimes,
Nor fear a dearth in these flagitious times.
No pardon vile Obscenity should find,
Tho' wit and art conspire to move your mind;
But Dullness with Obscenity must prove
As shameful sure as Impotence in love.
In the fat age of pleasure, wealth, and ease,
Sprung the rank weed, and thriv'd with large increase:
When love was all an easy Monarch's care;
Seldom at council, never in a war:
Jilts rul'd the state, and statesmen farces writ;
Nay, wits had pensions, and young Lords had wit:
The Fair sat panting at a Courtier's play,
And not a Mask went unimprov'd away:
The modest fan was lifted up no more,
And Virgins smil'd at what they blush'd before.
The following licence of a Foreign reign

Did all the dregs of bold Socinus drain;
Then unbelieving Priests reform'd the nation,
And taught more pleasant methods of salvation;
Where Heav'n's free subjects might their rights dispute,
Lest God himself should seem too absolute:
Pulpits their sacred satire learn'd to spare,
And Vice admir'd to find a flatt'rer there!
Encourag'd thus, Wit's Titans brav'd the skies,
And the press groan'd with licens'd blasphemies.
These monsters, Critics! with your darts engage,
Here point your thunder, and exhaust your rage!
Yet shun their fault, who, scandalously nice,
Will needs mistake an author into vice;
All seems infected that th' infected spy,
As all looks yellow to the jaundic'd eye.

PART III

Learn then what Morals Critics ought to show,
For 'tis but half a Judge's task, to know.
'Tis not enough, taste, judgment, learning, join;
In all you speak, let truth and candour shine:
That not alone what to your sense is due
All may allow; but seek your friendship too.

Be silent always, when you doubt your sense;
And speak, tho' sure, with seeming diffidence:
Some positive, persisting fops we know,
Who, if once wrong, will needs be always so;
But you, with pleasure own your errors past,
And make each day a Critic on the last.

'Tis not enough your counsel still be true;
Blunt truths more mischief than nice falshoods do;
Men must be taught as if you taught them not,
And things unknown propos'd as things forgot.

Without Good Breeding, truth is disapprov'd;
That only makes superior sense belov'd.
   Be niggards of advice on no pretence;
For the worst avarice is that of sense.
With mean complacence ne'er betray your trust,
Nor be so civil as to prove unjust.
Fear not the anger of the wise to raise;
Those best can bear reproof, who merit praise.
   'Twere well might Critics still this freedom take;
But Appius reddens at each word you speak,
And stares, tremendous, with a threat'ning eye,
Like some fierce Tyrant in old tapestry.
Fear most to tax an Honourable fool,
Whose right it is, uncensur'd, to be dull;
Such, without wit, are Poets when they please,
As without learning they can take Degrees.
Leave dang'rous truths to unsuccessful Satires,
And flattery to fulsome Dedicators,
Whom, when they praise, the world believes no more,
Than when they promise to give scribbling o'er.
'Tis best sometimes your censure to restrain,
And charitably let the dull be vain:
Your silence there is better than your spite,
For who can rail so long as they can write?
Still humming on, their drowzy course they keep,
And lash'd so long, like tops, are lash'd asleep.
False steps but help them to renew the race,
As, after stumbling, Jades will mend their pace.
What crouds of these, impenitently bold,
In sounds and jingling syllables grown old,
Still run on Poets, in a raging vein,
Ev'n to the dregs and squeezings of the brain,
Strain out the last dull droppings of their sense,
And rhyme with all the rage of Impotence.
   Such shameless Bards we have; and yet 'tis true,

There are as mad, abandon'd Critics too.
The bookful blockhead, ignorantly read,
With loads of learned lumber in his head,
With his own tongue still edifies his ears,
And always list'ning to himself appears.
All books he reads, and all he reads assails,
From Dryden's Fables down to Durfey's Tales.
With him, most authors steal their works, or buy;
Garth did not write his own Dispensary.
Name a new Play, and he's the Poet's friend;
Nay, show'd his faults—but when wou'd Poets mend?
No place so sacred from such fops is barr'd,
Nor is Paul's church more safe than Paul's church yard:
Nay, fly to Altars; there they'll talk you dead:
For Fools rush in where Angels fear to tread.
Distrustful sense with modest caution speaks,
It still looks home, and short excursions makes;
But rattling nonsense in full vollies breaks,
And never shock'd, and never turn'd aside,
Bursts out, resistless, with a thund'ring tide.

But where's the man, who counsel can bestow,
Still pleas'd to teach, and yet not proud to know?
Unbias'd, or by favour, or by spite;
Not dully prepossess'd, nor blindly right;
Tho' learn'd, well-bred; and tho' well-bred, sincere;
Modestly bold, and humanly severe:
Who to a friend his faults can freely show,
And gladly praise the merit of a foe?
Blest with a taste exact, yet unconfin'd;
A knowledge both of books and human kind;
Gen'rous converse; a soul exempt from pride;
And love to praise, with reason on his side?

Such once were Critics; such the happy few,
Athens and Rome in better ages knew.
The mighty Stagirite first left the shore,

Spread all his sails, and durst the deeps explore;
He steer'd securely, and discover'd far,
Led by the light of the Mæonian Star.
Poets, a race long unconfin'd, and free,
Still fond and proud of savage liberty,
Receiv'd his laws; and stood convinc'd 'twas fit,
Who conquer'd Nature, should preside o'er Wit.

    Horace still charms with graceful negligence,
And without method talks us into sense,
Will, like a friend, familiarly convey
The truest notions in the easiest way.
He who supreme in judgment, as in wit,
Might boldly censure, as he boldly writ,
Yet judg'd with coolness, tho' he sung with fire;
His Precepts teach but what his works inspire.
Our Critics take a contrary extreme,
The judge with fury, but they write with fle'me:
Nor suffers Horace more in wrong Translations
By Wits, than Critics in as wrong Quotations.

    See Dionysius Homer's thoughts refine,
And call new beauties forth from ev'ry line!

    Fancy and art in gay Petronius please,
The scholar's learning, with the courtier's ease.

    In grave Quintilian's copious work, we find
The justest rules, and clearest method join'd:
Thus useful arms in magazines we place,
All rang'd in order, and dispos'd with grace,
But less to please the eye, than arm the hand,
Still fit for use, and ready at command.

    Thee, bold Longinus! all the Nine inspire,
And bless their Critic with a Poet's fire.
An ardent Judge, who, zealous in his trust,
With warmth gives sentence, yet is always just;
Whose own example strengthens all his laws;
And is himself that great Sublime he draws.

Thus long succeeding Critics justly reign'd,
Licence repress'd, and useful laws ordain'd.
Learning and Rome alike in empire grew;
And Arts still follow'd where her Eagles flew:
From the same foes, at last, both felt their doom,
And the same age saw Learning fall, and Rome.
With Tyranny, then Superstition join'd,
As that the body, this enslav'd the mind;
Much was believ'd, but little understood,
And to be dull was constru'd to be good;
A second deluge Learning thus o'er-run,
And the Monks finish'd what the Goths begun.

At length Erasmus, that great injur'd name,
(The glory of the Priesthood, and the shame!)
Stemm'd the wild torrent of a barb'rous age,
And drove those holy Vandals off the stage.

But see! each Muse, in Leo's golden days,
Starts from her trance, and trims her wither'd bays!
Rome's ancient Genius, o'er its ruins spread,
Shakes off the dust, and rears his rev'rend head.
Then Sculpture and her sister-arts revive;
Stones leap'd to form, and rocks began to live;
With sweeter notes each rising Temple rung;
A Raphael painted, and a Vida sung.
Immortal Vida! on whose honour'd brow
The Poet's bays and Critic's ivy grow:
Cremona now shall ever boast thy name,
As next in place to Mantua, next in fame!

But soon by impious arms from Latium chas'd,
Their ancient bounds the banish'd Muses pass'd;
Thence Arts o'er all the northern world advance,
But Critic learning flourish'd most in France:
The rules a nation, born to serve, obeys;
And Boileau still in right of Horace sways.
But we, brave Britons, foreign laws despis'd,

And kept unconquer'd, and unciviliz'd;
Fierce for the liberties of wit, and bold,
We still defy'd the Romans, as of old.
Yet some there were, among the sounder few
Of those who less presum'd, and better knew,
Who durst assert the juster ancient cause,
And here restor'd Wit's fundamental laws.
Such was the Muse, whose rules and practice tell,
"Nature's chief Master-piece is writing well."
Such was Roscommon, not more learn'd than good,
With manners gen'rous as his noble blood;
To him the wit of Greece and Rome was known,
And ev'ry author's merit, but his own.
Such late was Walsh—the Muse's judge and friend,
Who justly knew to blame or to commend;
To failings mild, but zealous for desert;
The clearest head, and the sincerest heart.
This humble praise, lamented Shade! receive,
This praise at least a grateful Muse may give:
The Muse whose early voice you taught to sing,
Prescrib'd her heights, and prun'd her tender wing,
(Her guide now lost) no more attempts to rise,
But in low numbers short excursions tries:
Content, if hence th' unlearn'd their wants may view,
The learn'd reflect on what before they knew:
Careless of censure, nor too fond of fame;
Still pleas'd to praise, yet not afraid to blame;
Averse alike to flatter, or offend;
Not free from faults, nor yet too vain to mend.

FROM An Essay on Man

To Henry St. John, Lord Bolingbroke

EPISTLE I

Argument of the Nature and State of Man,
with Respect to the Universe

Of man in the abstract—I. That we can judge only with re-
gard to our own system, being ignorant of the relations of
systems and things, ver. 17, etc.—II. That Man is not to be
deemed imperfect, but a Being suited to his place and rank
in the creation, agreeable to the general Order of things, and
conformable to Ends and Relations to him unknown, ver. 35,
etc.—III. That it is partly upon his ignorance of future
events, and partly upon the hope of a future state, that all
his happiness in the present depends, ver. 77, etc.—IV. The
pride of aiming at more knowledge, and pretending to more
Perfection, the cause of Man's error and misery. The impiety
of putting himself in the place of God, and judging of the
fitness or unfitness, perfection or imperfection, justice or in-
justice of his dispensations, ver. 109, etc.—V. The absurdity
of conceiting himself the final cause of the creation, or ex-
pecting that perfection in the moral world which is not in
the natural, ver. 131, etc.—VI. The unreasonableness of his
complaints against Providence, while on the one hand he de-
mands the Perfections of the Angels, and on the other the
bodily qualifications of the Brutes; though, to possess any of
the sensitive faculties in a higher degree, would render him
miserable, ver. 173, etc.—VII. That throughout the whole
visible world, an universal order and gradation in the sensual
and mental faculties is observed, which causes a subordina-
tion of creature to creature, and of all creatures to Man. The
gradations of sense, instinct, thought, reflection, reason: that
Reason alone countervails all the other faculties, ver. 207.—
VIII. How much further this order and subordination of liv-
ing creatures may extend, above and below us; were any part

*of which broken, not that part only, but the whole connected
creation must be destroyed, ver. 233.—IX. The extravagance,
madness, and pride of such a desire, ver. 250.—X. The consequence of all, the absolute submission due to Providence,
both as to our present and future state, ver. 281, etc., to the
end.*

Awake, my St. John! leave all meaner things
To low ambition, and the pride of Kings.
Let us (since Life can little more supply
Than just to look about us and to die)
Expatiate free o'er all this scene of Man;
A mighty maze! but not without a plan;
A Wild, where weeds and flow'rs promiscuous shoot,
Or Garden, tempting with forbidden fruit.
Together let us beat this ample field,
Try what the open, what the covert yield;
The latent tracts, the giddy heights, explore
Of all who blindly creep, or sightless soar;
Eye Nature's walks, shoot Folly as it flies,
And catch the Manners living as they rise;
Laugh where we must, be candid where we can;
But vindicate the ways of God to Man.
  I. Say first, of God above, or Man below,
What can we reason, but from what we know?
Of Man, what see we, but his station here,
From which to reason, or to which refer?
Thro' worlds unnumber'd tho' the God be known,
'Tis ours to trace him only in our own.
He, who thro' vast immensity can pierce,
See worlds on worlds compose one universe,
Observe how system into system runs,
What other planets circle other suns,
What vary'd Being peoples ev'ry star,
May tell why Heav'n has made us as we are.
But of this frame the bearings, and the ties,

The strong connections, nice dependencies,
Gradations just, has thy pervading soul
Look'd thro'? or can a part contain the whole?
   Is the great chain, that draws all to agree,
And drawn supports, upheld by God, or thee?
   II. Presumptuous Man! the reason wouldst thou find,
Why form'd so weak, so little, and so blind?
First, if thou canst, the harder reason guess,
Why form'd no weaker, blinder, and no less?
Ask of thy mother earth, why oaks are made
Taller or stronger than the weeds they shade?
Or ask of yonder argent fields above,
Why JOVE's Satellites are less than JOVE?
   Of systems possible, if 'tis confest
That Wisdom infinite must form the best,
Where all must full or not coherent be,
And all that rises, rise in due degree;
Then, in the scale of reas'ning life, 'tis plain,
There must be, somewhere, such a rank as Man:
And all the question (wrangle e'er so long)
Is only this, if God has plac'd him wrong?
   Respecting Man, whatever wrong we call,
May, must be right, as relative to all.
In human works, tho' labour'd on with pain,
A thousand movements scarce one purpose gain;
In God's, one single can its end produce;
Yet serves to second too some other use.
So Man, who here seems principal alone,
Perhaps acts second to some sphere unknown,
Touches some wheel, or verges to some goal;
'Tis but a part we see, and not a whole.
   When the proud steed shall know why Man restrains
His fiery course, or drives him o'er the plains;
When the dull Ox, why now he breaks the clod,
Is now a victim, and now Ægypt's god:

Then shall Man's pride and dullness comprehend
His actions', passions', being's, use and end;
Why doing, suff'ring, check'd, impell'd; and why
This hour a slave, the next a deity.

    Then say not Man's imperfect, Heav'n in fault;
Say rather, Man's as perfect as he ought:
His knowledge measur'd to his state and place;
His time a moment, and a point his space.
If to be perfect in a certain sphere,
What matter, soon or late, or here or there?
The blest to-day is as completely so,
As who began a thousand years ago.

    III. Heav'n from all creatures hides the book of Fate,
All but the page prescrib'd, their present state:
From brutes what men, from men what spirits know:
Or who could suffer Being here below?
The lamb thy riot dooms to bleed to-day,
Had he thy Reason, would he skip and play?
Pleas'd to the last, he crops the flow'ry food,
And licks the hand just rais'd to shed his blood.
Oh blindness to the future! kindly giv'n,
That each may fill the circle mark'd by Heav'n:
Who sees with equal eye, as God of all,
A hero perish, or a sparrow fall,
Atoms or systems into ruin hurl'd,
And now a bubble burst, and now a world.

    Hope humbly then; with trembling pinions soar;
Wait the great teacher Death, and God adore.
What future bliss, he gives not thee to know,
But gives that Hope to be thy blessing now.
Hope springs eternal in the human breast:
Man never Is, but always To be blest:
The soul, uneasy and confin'd from home,
Rests and expatiates in a life to come.

    Lo! the poor Indian! whose untutor'd mind

Sees God in clouds, or hears him in the wind;
His soul, proud Science never taught to stray
Far as the solar walk, or milky way;
Yet simple Nature to his hope has giv'n,
Behind the cloud-topt hill, and humbler heav'n;
Some safer world in depth of woods embrac'd,
Some happier island in the wat'ry waste,
Where slaves once more their native land behold,
No fiends torment, no Christians thirst for gold!
To Be, contents his natural desire,
He asks no Angel's wing, no Seraph's fire;
But thinks, admitted to that equal sky,
His faithful dog shall bear him company.

   IV. Go, wiser thou! and, in thy scale of sense,
Weigh thy Opinion against Providence;
Call Imperfection what thou fancy'st such,
Say, here he gives too little, there too much:
Destroy all creatures for thy sport or gust,
Yet cry, If Man's unhappy, God's unjust;
If Man alone engross not Heav'n's high care,
Alone made perfect here, immortal there:
Snatch from his hand the balance and the rod,
Re-judge his justice, be the God of God!
   In Pride, in reas'ning Pride, our error lies;
All quit their sphere, and rush into the skies.
Pride still is aiming at the blest abodes,
Men would be Angels, Angels would be Gods.
Aspiring to be Gods, if Angels fell,
Aspiring to be Angels, Men rebel:
And who but wishes to invert the laws
Of ORDER, sins against th' Eternal Cause.

   V. Ask for what end the heav'nly bodies shine,
Earth for whose use? Pride answers, " 'Tis for mine:
For me kind Nature wakes her genial pow'r,
Suckles each herb, and spreads out ev'ry flow'r;

Annual for me, the grape, the rose renew,
The juice nectareous, and the balmy dew;
For me, the mine a thousand treasures brings;
For me, health gushes from a thousand springs;
Seas roll to waft me, suns to light me rise;
My foot-stool earth, my canopy the skies."

But errs not Nature from this gracious end,
From burning suns when livid deaths descend,
When earthquakes swallow, or when tempests sweep
Towns to one grave, whole nations to the deep?
"No," 'tis reply'd, "the first Almighty Cause
Acts not by partial, but by gen'ral laws;
Th' exceptions few; some change since all began,
And what created perfect?"—Why then Man?
If the great end be human Happiness,
Then Nature deviates; and can Man do less?
As much that end a constant course requires
Of show'rs and sun-shine, as of Man's desires;
As much eternal springs and cloudless skies,
As Men forever temp'rate, calm, and wise.
If plagues or earthquakes break not Heav'n's design,
Why then a Borgia, or a Catiline?
Who knows but he, whose hand the lightning forms,
Who heaves old Ocean, and who wings the storms;
Pours fierce Ambition in a Cæsar's mind,
Or turns young Ammon loose to scourge mankind?
From pride, from pride, our very reas'ning springs;
Account for moral, as for nat'ral things:
Why charge we Heav'n in those, in these acquit?
In both, to reason right is to submit.

Better for Us, perhaps, it might appear,
Were there all harmony, all virtue here;
That never air or ocean felt the wind;
That never passion discompos'd the mind.
But ALL subsists by elemental strife;

And Passions are the elements of Life.
The gen'ral ORDER, since the whole began,
Is kept in Nature, and is kept in Man.
  VI. What would this Man? Now upward will he soar,
And little less than Angel, would be more;
Now looking downwards, just as griev'd appears
To want the strength of bulls, the fur of bears.
Made for his use all creatures if he call,
Say what their use, had he the pow'rs of all?
Nature to these, without profusion, kind,
The proper organs, proper pow'rs assign'd;
Each seeming want compensated of course,
Here with degrees of swiftness, there of force;
All in exact proportion to the state;
Nothing to add, and nothing to abate.
Each beast, each insect, happy in its own:
Is Heav'n unkind to Man, and Man alone?
Shall he alone, whom rational we call,
Be pleas'd with nothing, if not bless'd with all?
  The bliss of Man (could Pride that blessing find)
Is not to act or think beyond mankind;
No pow'rs of body or of soul to share,
But what his nature and his state can bear.
Why has not Man a microscopic eye?
For this plain reason, Man is not a Fly.
Say what the use, were finer optics giv'n,
T' inspect a mite, not comprehend the heav'n?
Or touch, if tremblingly alive all o'er,
To smart and agonize at ev'ry pore?
Or quick effluvia darting thro' the brain,
Die of a rose in aromatic pain?
If Nature thunder'd in his op'ning ears,
And stunn'd him with the music of the spheres,
How would he wish that Heav'n had left him still
The whisp'ring Zephyr, and the purling rill?

Who finds not Providence all good and wise,
Alike in what it gives, and what denies?
   VII. Far as Creation's ample range extends,
The scale of sensual, mental pow'rs ascends:
Mark how it mounts, to Man's imperial race,
From the green myriads in the peopled grass:
What modes of sight betwixt each wide extreme,
The mole's dim curtain, and the lynx's beam:
Of smell, the headlong lioness between,
And hound sagacious on the tainted green:
Of hearing, from the life that fills the flood,
To that which warbles thro' the vernal wood:
The spider's touch, how exquisitely fine!
Feels at each thread, and lives along the line:
In the nice bee, what sense so subtly true
From pois'nous herbs extracts the healing dew:
How Instinct varies in the grov'ling swine,
Compar'd, half-reas'ning elephant, with thine!
'Twixt that, and Reason, what a nice barrier;
Forever sep'rate, yet forever near!
Remembrance and Reflection how ally'd;
What thin partitions Sense from Thought divide:
And Middle natures, how they long to join,
Yet never pass th' insuperable line!
Without this just gradation, could they be
Subjected, these to those, or all to thee?
The pow'rs of all subdu'd by thee alone,
Is not thy Reason all these pow'rs in one?
   VIII. See, thro' this air, this ocean, and this earth,
All matter quick, and bursting into birth.
Above, how high, progressive life may go!
Around, how wide! how deep extend below!
Vast chain of Being, which from God began,
Natures æthereal, human, angel, man,
Beast, bird, fish, insect! what no eye can see,

No glass can reach; from Infinite to thee,
From thee to Nothing!—On superior pow'rs
Were we to press, inferior might on ours:
Or in the full creation leave a void,
Where, one step broken, the great scale's destroy'd:
From Nature's chain whatever link you strike,
Tenth or ten thousandth, breaks the chain alike.

    And, if each system in gradation roll
Alike essential to th' amazing Whole,
The least confusion but in one, not all
That system only, but the Whole must fall.
Let Earth unbalanc'd from her orbit fly,
Planets and Suns run lawless thro' the sky,
Let ruling Angels from their spheres be hurl'd,
Being on Being wreck'd, and world on world,
Heav'n's whole foundations to their center nod,
And Nature trembles to the throne of God;
All this dread ORDER break—for whom? for thee?
Vile worm!—oh Madness! Pride! Impiety!

    IX. What if the foot, ordain'd the dust to tread,
Or hand, to toil, aspir'd to be the head?
What if the head, the eye, or ear repin'd
To serve mere engines to the ruling Mind?
Just as absurd for any part to claim
To be another, in this gen'ral frame:
Just as absurd, to mourn the tasks or pains,
The great directing MIND of ALL ordains.

    All are but parts of one stupendous whole,
Whose body Nature is, and God the soul;
That, chang'd thro' all, and yet in all the same;
Great in the earth, as in th' æthereal frame;
Warms in the sun, refreshes in the breeze,
Glows in the stars, and blossoms in the trees,
Lives thro' all life, extends thro' all extent,
Spreads undivided, operates unspent;

Breathes in our soul, informs our mortal part,
As full, as perfect, in a hair as heart;
As full, as perfect, in vile Man that mourns,
As the rapt Seraph that adores and burns:
To him no high, no low, no great, no small;
He fills, he bounds, connects, and equals all.

　　x. Cease then, nor ORDER Imperfection name:
Our proper bliss depends on what we blame.
Know thy own point: This kind, this due degree
Of blindness, weakness, Heav'n bestows on thee.
Submit.—In this, or any other sphere,
Secure to be as blest as thou canst bear:
Safe in the hand of one disposing Pow'r,
Or in the natal, or the mortal hour.
All Nature is but Art, unknown to thee;
All Chance, Direction, which thou canst not see;
All Discord, Harmony not understood;
All partial Evil, universal Good:
And, spite of Pride, in erring Reason's spite,
One truth is clear, WHATEVER IS, IS RIGHT.

EPISTLE II

Argument of the Nature and State of Man with Respect to
Himself, as an Individual

I. *The business of Man not to pry into God, but to study*
himself. His Middle Nature; his Powers and Frailties, ver.
1–19. The Limits of his Capacity, ver. 19, etc.—II. The two
Principles of Man, Self-love and Reason, both necessary, ver.
53, etc. Self-love the stronger, and why, ver. 67, etc. Their
end the same, ver. 81, etc.—III. The Passions, and their use,
ver. 93–130. The predominant Passion, and its force, ver.
132–160. Its Necessity, in directing Men to different pur-
poses, ver. 165, etc. Its providential Use, in fixing our Prin-
ciple, and ascertaining our Virtue, ver. 177.—IV. Virtue and
Vice joined in our mixed Nature; the limits near, yet the
things separate and evident: What is the office of Reason,

   i. Know then thyself, presume not God to scan;
The proper study of Mankind is Man.
Plac'd on this isthmus of a middle state,
A Being darkly wise, and rudely great:
With too much knowledge for the Sceptic side,
With too much weakness for the Stoic's pride,
He hangs between; in doubt to act, or rest,
In doubt to deem himself a God, or Beast;
In doubt his Mind or Body to prefer;
Born but to die, and reas'ning but to err;
Alike in ignorance, his reason such,
Whether he thinks too little, or too much:
Chaos of Thought and Passion, all confus'd;
Still by himself abus'd, or disabus'd;
Created half to rise, and half to fall;
Great lord of all things, yet a prey to all;
Sole judge of Truth, in endless Error hurl'd:
The glory, jest, and riddle of the world!
   Go, wondrous creature! mount where Science guides,
Go, measure earth, weigh air, and state the tides;
Instruct the planets in what orbs to run,
Correct old Time, and regulate the Sun;
Go, soar with Plato to th' empyreal sphere,
To the first good, first perfect, and first fair;
Or tread the mazy round his follow'rs trod,
And quitting sense call imitating God;
As Eastern priests in giddy circles run,
And turn their heads to imitate the Sun.

Go, teach Eternal Wisdom how to rule—
Then drop into thyself, and be a fool!
   Superior beings, when of late they saw
A mortal Man unfold all Nature's law,
Admir'd such wisdom in an earthly shape,
And show'd a NEWTON as we shew an Ape.
   Could he, whose rules the rapid Comet bind,
Describe or fix one movement of his Mind?
Who saw its fires here rise, and there descend,
Explain his own beginning, or his end?
Alas what wonder! Man's superior part
Uncheck'd may rise, and climb from art to art;
But when his own great work is but begun,
What Reason weaves, by Passion is undone.
   Trace Science then, with Modesty thy guide;
First strip off all her equipage of Pride,
Deduct what is but Vanity, or Dress,
Or Learning's Luxury, or Idleness;
Or tricks to shew the stretch of human brain,
Mere curious pleasure, or ingenious pain;
Expunge the whole, or lop th' excrescent parts
Of all, our Vices have created Arts;
Then see how little the remaining sum,
Which serv'd the past, and must the times to come!
   II. Two Principles in human nature reign;
Self-love, to urge, and Reason, to restrain;
Nor this a good, nor that a bad we call,
Each works its end, to move or govern all:
And to their proper operation still,
Ascribe all Good; to their improper, Ill.
   Self-love, the spring of motion, acts the soul;
Reason's comparing balance rules the whole.
Man, but for that, no action could attend,
And, but for this, were active to no end:
Fix'd like a plant on his peculiar spot,

To draw nutrition, propagate, and rot;
Or, meteor-like, flame lawless thro' the void,
Destroying others, by himself destroy'd.
　　Most strength the moving principle requires;
Active its task, it prompts, impels, inspires.
Sedate and quiet the comparing lies,
Form'd but to check, delib'rate, and advise.
Self-love still stronger, as its objects nigh;
Reason's at distance, and in prospect lie:
That sees immediate good by present sense;
Reason, the future and the consequence.
Thicker than arguments, temptations throng,
At best more watchful this, but that more strong.
The action of the stronger to suspend
Reason still use, to Reason still attend.
Attention, habit and experience gains,
Each strengthens Reason, and Self-love restrains.
　　Let subtle schoolmen teach these friends to fight,
More studious to divide than to unite,
And Grace and Virtue, Sense and Reason split,
With all the rash dexterity of wit:
Wits, just like Fools, at war about a name,
Have full as oft no meaning, or the same.
Self-love and Reason to one end aspire,
Pain their aversion, Pleasure their desire;
But greedy that, its object would devour,
This taste the honey, and not wound the flow'r:
Pleasure, or wrong or rightly understood,
Our greatest evil, or our greatest good.
　　iii. Modes of Self-love the Passions we may call;
'Tis real good, or seeming, moves them all:
But since not ev'ry good we can divide,
And Reason bids us for our own provide;
Passions, tho' selfish, if their means be fair,
List under Reason, and deserve her care;

Those, that imparted, court a nobler aim,
Exalt their kind, and take some Virtue's name.

   In lazy Apathy let Stoics boast
Their Virtue fix'd; 'tis fix'd as in a frost;
Contracted all, retiring to the breast;
But strength of mind is Exercise, not Rest:
The rising tempest puts in act the soul,
Parts it may ravage, but preserves the whole.
On life's vast ocean diversely we sail,
Reason the card, but Passion is the gale;
Nor God alone in the still calm we find,
He mounts the storm, and walks upon the wind.

   Passions, like Elements, tho' born to fight,
Yet, mix'd and soften'd, in his work unite:
These 'tis enough to temper and employ;
But what composes Man, can Man destroy?
Suffice that Reason keep to Nature's road,
Subject, compound them, follow her and God.
Love, Hope, and Joy, fair pleasure's smiling train,
Hate, Fear, and Grief, the family of pain,
These mix'd with art, and to due bounds confin'd,
Make and maintain the balance of the mind:
The lights and shades, whose well accorded strife
Gives all the strength and colour of our life.

   Pleasures are ever in our hands or eyes;
And when, in act, they cease, in prospect, rise:
Present to grasp, and future still to find,
The whole employ of body and of mind.
All spread their charms, but charm not all alike;
On diff'rent senses diff'rent objects strike;
Hence diff'rent Passions more or less inflame,
As strong or weak, the organs of the frame;
And hence one MASTER PASSION in the breast,
Like Aaron's serpent, swallows up the rest.

   As Man, perhaps, the moment of his breath,

Receives the lurking principle of death;
The young disease, that must subdue at length,
Grows with his growth, and strengthens with his
     strength:
So, cast and mingled with his very frame,
The Mind's disease, its RULING PASSION came;
Each vital humour which should feed the whole,
Soon flows to this, in body and in soul:
Whatever warms the heart, or fills the head,
As the mind opens, and its functions spread,
Imagination plies her dang'rous art,
And pours it all upon the peccant part.
    Nature its mother, Habit is its nurse;
Wit, Spirit, Faculties, but make it worse;
Reason itself but gives it edge and pow'r;
As Heav'n's blest beam turns vinegar more sowr.
    We, wretched subjects tho' to lawful sway,
In this weak queen, some fav'rite still obey.
Ah! if she lend not arms, as well as rules,
What can she more than tell us we are fools?
Teach us to mourn our Nature, not to mend,
A sharp accuser, but a helpless friend!
Or from a judge turn pleader, to persuade
The choice we make, or justify it made;
Proud of an easy conquest all along,
She but removes weak passions for the strong:
So, when small humours gather to a gout,
The doctor fancies he has driv'n them out.
    Yes, Nature's road must ever be prefer'd;
Reason is here no guide, but still a guard:
'Tis hers to rectify, not overthrow,
And treat this passion more as friend than foe:
A mightier Pow'r the strong direction sends,
And sev'ral Men impels to sev'ral ends.
Like varying winds, by other passions tost,

This drives them constant to a certain coast.
Let pow'r or knowledge, gold or glory, please,
Or (oft more strong than all) the love of ease;
Thro' life 'tis follow'd ev'n at life's expence;
The merchant's toil, the sage's indolence,
The monk's humility, the hero's pride,
All, all alike, find Reason on their side.

    Th' Eternal Art, educing good from ill,
Grafts on this Passion our best principle:
'Tis thus the Mercury of Man is fix'd,
Strong grows the Virtue with his nature mix'd;
The dross cements what else were too refin'd,
And in one int'rest body acts with mind.

    As fruits, ungrateful to the planter's care,
On savage stocks inserted, learn to bear;
The surest Virtues thus from Passions shoot,
Wild Nature's vigor working at the root.
What crops of wit and honesty appear
From spleen, from obstinacy, hate, or fear!
See anger, zeal and fortitude supply;
Ev'n av'rice, prudence; sloth, philosophy;
Lust, thro' some certain strainers well refin'd
Is gentle love, and charms all womankind;
Envy, to which th' ignoble mind's a slave,
Is emulation in the learn'd or brave;
Nor Virtue, male or female, can we name,
But what will grow on Pride, or grow on Shame.

    Thus Nature gives us (let it check our pride)
The virtue nearest to our vice ally'd;
Reason the byas turns to good from ill,
And Nero reigns a Titus, if he will.
The fiery soul abhorr'd in Catiline,
In Decius charms, in Curtius is divine:
The same ambition can destroy or save,
And makes a patriot as it makes a knave.

IV. This light and darkness in our chaos join'd,
What shall divide? The God within the mind.
  Extremes in nature equal ends produce,
In Man they join to some mysterious use;
Tho' each by turns the other's bound invade,
As, in some well-wrought picture, light and shade,
And oft so mix, the diff'rence is too nice
Where ends the Virtue, or begins the Vice.
  Fools! who from hence into the notion fall,
That Vice or Virtue there is none at all.
If white and black blend, soften, and unite
A thousand ways, is there no black or white?
Ask your own heart, and nothing is so plain;
'Tis to mistake them, costs the time and pain.
  V. Vice is a monster of so frightful mien,
As, to be hated, needs but to be seen;
Yet seen too oft, familiar with her face,
We first endure, then pity, then embrace.
But where th' Extreme of Vice, was ne'er agreed:
Ask where's the North? at York, 'tis on the Tweed;
In Scotland, at the Orcades; and there,
At Greenland, Zembla, or the Lord knows where.
No creature owns it in the first degree,
But thinks his neighbour farther gone than he;
Ev'n those who dwell beneath its very zone,
Or never feel the rage, or never own;
What happier natures shrink at with affright,
The hard inhabitant contends is right.
  VI. Virtuous and vicious ev'ry Man must be,
Few in th' extreme, but all in the degree;
The rogue and fool, by fits, is fair and wise;
And ev'n the best, by fits, what they despise.
'Tis but by parts we follow good or ill;
For, Vice or Virtue, Self directs it still;
Each individual seeks a sev'ral goal;

But HEAV'N's great view is One, and that the Whole:
That counter-works each folly and caprice;
That disappoints th' effect of ev'ry vice:
That, happy frailties to all ranks apply'd;
Shame to the virgin, to the matron pride,
Fear to the statesman, rashness to the chief,
To kings presumption, and to crowds belief:
That, Virtue's ends from Vanity can raise,
Which seeks no int'rest, no reward but praise;
And build on wants, and on defects of mind,
The joy, the peace, the glory of Mankind.

   Heav'n forming each on other to depend,
A master, or a servant, or a friend,
Bids each on other for assistance call,
'Till one Man's weakness grows the strength of all.
Wants, frailties, passions, closer still ally
The common int'rest, or endear the tie.
To these we owe true friendship, love sincere,
Each home-felt joy that life inherits here;
Yet from the same we learn, in its decline,
Those joys, those loves, those int'rests to resign;
Taught half by Reason, half by mere decay,
To welcome death, and calmly pass away.

   Whate'er the Passion, knowledge, fame, or pelf,
Not one will change his neighbour with himself.
The learn'd is happy nature to explore,
The fool is happy that he knows no more;
The rich is happy in the plenty giv'n,
The poor contents him with the care of Heav'n.
See the blind beggar dance, the cripple sing,
The sot a hero, lunatic a king;
The starving chemist in his golden views
Supremely blest, the poet in his muse.

   See some strange comfort ev'ry state attend,
And Pride bestow'd on all, a common friend;

See some fit Passion ev'ry age supply,
Hope travels thro', nor quits us when we die.
    Behold the child, by Nature's kindly law,
Pleas'd with a rattle, tickled with a straw:
Some livelier play-thing gives his youth delight,
A little louder, but as empty quite:
Scarfs, garters, gold, amuse his riper stage;
And beads and pray'r-books are the toys of age:
Pleas'd with this bauble still, as that before;
Till tir'd he sleeps, and Life's poor play is o'er.
    Meanwhile Opinion gilds with varying rays
Those painted clouds that beautify our days;
Each want of happiness by Hope supply'd,
And each vacuity of sense by Pride:
These build as fast as knowledge can destroy;
In Folly's cup still laughs the bubble, joy;
One prospect lost, another still we gain;
And not a vanity is giv'n in vain;
Ev'n mean Self-love becomes, by force divine,
The scale to measure others' wants by thine.
See! and confess, one comfort still must rise,
'Tis this, Tho' Man's a fool, yet GOD IS WISE.

Epistle to Dr. Arbuthnot

BEING THE PROLOGUE TO THE SATIRES

P. Shut, shut the door, good *John!* fatigu'd, I said,
Tye up the knocker! say I'm sick, I'm dead.
The Dog-star rages! nay, 'tis past a doubt,
All Bedlam, or Parnassus, is let out:
Fire in each eye, and papers in each hand,
They rave, recite, and madden round the land.

What walls can guard me, or what shades can hide?
They pierce my thickets, thro' my Grot they glide,
By land, by water, they renew the charge,
They stop the chariot, and they board the Barge.
No place is sacred, not the Church is free,
Ev'n Sunday shines no Sabbath-day to me:
Then from the Mint walks forth the man of rhyme,
Happy! to catch me just at Dinner-time.

Is there a Parson much be-mus'd in beer,
A maudlin Poetess, a rhyming Peer,
A Clerk, foredoom'd his father's soul to cross,
Who pens a Stanza, when he should *engross*?
Is there, who, lock'd from ink and paper, scrawls
With desp'rate charcoal round his darken'd walls?
All fly to *Twit'nam*, and in humble strain
Apply to me, to keep them mad or vain.
Arthur, whose giddy Son neglects the Laws,
Imputes to me and my damn'd works the cause:
Poor Cornus sees his frantic wife elope,
And curses Wit, and Poetry, and Pope.

Friend to my Life! (which did not you prolong,
The world had wanted many an idle song)
What *Drop* or *Nostrum* can this plague remove?
Or which must end me, a Fool's wrath or love?
A dire dilemma! either way I'm sped,
If Foes, they write, if Friends, they read me dead.
Seiz'd and ty'd down to judge, how wretched I!
Who can't be silent, and who will not lye:
To laugh, were want of goodness and of grace,
And to be grave exceeds all Pow'r of face.
I sit with sad Civility, I read
With honest anguish and an aching head;
And drop at last, but in unwilling ears,
This saving counsel, "Keep your piece nine years."

"Nine years!" cries he who, high in Drury lane,

Lull'd by soft Zephyrs thro' the broken pane,
Rhymes ere he wakes, and prints before *Term* ends,
Oblig'd by hunger, and request of friends:
  "The piece, you think, is incorrect? why take it,
I'm all submission, what you'd have it, make it."

  Three things another's modest wishes bound,
My Friendship, and a Prologue, and ten Pound.
  Pitholeon sends to me: "You know his Grace,
I want a Patron; ask him for a Place."
Pitholeon libell'd me—"but here's a letter
Informs you, Sir, 'twas when he knew no better.
Dare you refuse him? Curl invites to dine,
He'll write a *Journal*, or he'll turn Divine."
  Bless me! a packet.—" 'Tis a stranger sues,
A Virgin Tragedy, an Orphan Muse."
If I dislike it, "Furies, death, and rage!"
If I approve, "Commend it to the Stage."
There (thank my stars) my whole commission ends,
The Play'rs and I are, luckily, no friends.
Fir'd that the house reject him, " 'Sdeath I'll print it,
And shame the fools—your int'rest, Sir, with Lintot."
Lintot, dull rogue! will think your price too much:
"Not, Sir, if you revise it, and retouch."
All my demurs, but double his attacks;
At last he whispers, "Do; and we go snacks."
Glad of a quarrel, strait I clap the door,
Sir, let me see your works and you no more.
  'Tis sung, when *Midas*' Ears began to spring
(Midas, a sacred person and a King),
His very Minister who spy'd them first
(Some say his Queen) was forc'd to speak, or burst.
And is not mine, my friend, a sorer case,
When ev'ry coxcomb perks them in my face?
A. Good friend forbear! you deal in dang'rous things.
I'd never name Queens, Ministers, or Kings;

Keep close to ears, and those let Asses prick.
'Tis nothing—*P.* Nothing? if they bite and kick?
Out with it, *Dunciad!* let the secret pass,
That secret to each fool, that he's an Ass:
The truth once told (and wherefore shou'd we lie?)
The Queen of Midas slept, and so may I.

   You think this cruel? take it for a rule,
No creature smarts so little as a Fool.
Let peals of laughter, Codrus! round thee break,
Thou unconcern'd canst hear the mighty crack:
Pit, box, and Gall'ry in convulsions hurl'd,
Thou stand'st unshook amidst a bursting world.
Who shames a Scribler? break one cobweb thro',
He spins the slight, self-pleasing thread anew:
Destroy his fib or sophistry, in vain,
The creature's at his dirty work again,
Thron'd in the centre of his thin designs,
Proud of a vast extent of flimzy lines!
Whom have I hurt? has Poet yet, or Peer
Lost the arch'd eyebrow, or Parnassian sneer?
And has not Colly still his lord, and whore?
His butchers Henley, his free-masons Moor?
Does not one table Bavius still admit?
Still to one Bishop Philips seem a wit?
Still Sappho—*A.* Hold! for God-sake—you'll offend,
No names—be calm—learn prudence of a friend:
I too could write, and I am twice as tall
But foes like these—*P.* One Flatt'rer's worse than all.
Of all mad creatures, if the learn'd are right,
It is the slaver kills, and not the bite.
A Fool quite angry is quite innocent:
Alas! 'tis ten times worse when they *repent.*

   One dedicates in high heroic prose,
And ridicules beyond a hundred foes:
One from all *Grubstreet* will my fame defend,

And, more abusive, calls himself my friend.
This prints my *Letters,* that expects a bribe,
And others roar aloud, "Subscribe, subscribe."
     There are, who to my person pay their court:
I cough like *Horace,* and, tho' lean, am short,
Ammon's great son one shoulder had too high,
Such *Ovid's* nose, and "Sir! you have an Eye"—
Go on, obliging creatures, make me see
All that disgrac'd my Betters, met in me.
Say for my comfort, languishing in bed,
"Just so immortal *Maro* held his head":
And when I die, be sure you let me know
Great *Homer* dy'd three thousand years ago.
     Why did I write? what sin to me unknown
Dipt me in ink, my parents', or my own?
As yet a child, nor yet a fool to fame,
I lisp'd in numbers, for the numbers came.
I left no calling for this idle trade,
No duty broke, no Father disobey'd.
The Muse but serv'd to ease some friend, not Wife,
To help me thro' this long disease, my Life,
To second, *Arbuthnot!* thy Art and Care,
And teach the Being you preserv'd, to bear.
     But why then publish? *Granville* the polite,
And knowing *Walsh,* would tell me I could write;
Well-natur'd *Garth* inflam'd with early praise,
And *Congreve* lov'd, and *Swift* endur'd my lays;
The courtly *Talbot, Somers, Sheffield* read,
Ev'n mitred *Rochester* would nod the head,
And *St. John's* self (great *Dryden's* friends before)
With open arms receiv'd one Poet more.
Happy my Studies, when by these approv'd!
Happier their Author, when by these belov'd!
From these the world will judge of Men and books,
Not from the *Burnets, Oldmixons,* and *Cooks.*

Soft were my numbers; who could take offence
While pure Description held the place of Sense?
Like gentle *Fanny's* was my flow'ry theme,
A painted mistress, or a purling stream.
Yet then did *Gildon* draw his venal quill;
I wish'd the man a dinner, and sate still:
Yet then did *Dennis* rave in furious fret;
I never answer'd, I was not in debt.
If want provok'd, or madness made them print,
I wag'd no war with *Bedlam* or the *Mint*.

Did some more sober Critic come abroad;
If wrong, I smil'd; if right, I kiss'd the rod.
Pains, reading, study are their just pretense,
And all they want is spirit, taste, and sense.
Commas and points they set exactly right,
And 'twere a sin to rob them of their mite.
Yet ne'er one sprig of laurel grac'd these ribalds,
From slashing *Bentley* down to piddling *Tibalds*:
Each wight who reads not, and but scans and spells,
Each Word-catcher, that lives on syllables,
Ev'n such small Critics some regard may claim,
Preserv'd in *Milton's* or in *Shakespear's* name.
Pretty! in Amber to observe the forms
Of hairs, or straws, or dirt, or grubs, or worms!
The things, we know, are neither rich nor rare,
But wonder how the devil they got there.

Were others angry: I excus'd them too:
Well might they rage; I gave them but their due.
A man's true merit 'tis not hard to find;
But each man's secret standard in his mind,
That Casting-weight pride adds to emptiness,
This, who can gratify? for who can *guess?*
The Bard whom pilfer'd Pastorals renown,
Who turns a *Persian* tale for half a Crown,
Just writes to make his barrenness appear,

And strains from hard-bound brains eight lines a year;
He, who still wanting, tho' he lives on theft,
Steals much, spends little, yet has nothing left:
And He, who now to sense, now nonsense leaning,
Means not, but blunders round about a meaning:
And He, whose fustian's so sublimely bad,
It is not Poetry, but prose run mad:
All these, my modest satire bade *translate*,
And own'd that nine such Poets made a *Tate*.
How did they fume, and stamp, and roar, and chafe!
And swear, not *Addison* himself was safe.

Peace to all such! But were there One whose fires
True Genius kindles and fair Fame inspires;
Blest with each talent and each art to please,
And born to write, converse, and live with ease:
Should such a man, too fond to rule alone,
Bear, like the *Turk*, no brother near the throne,
View him with scornful, yet with jealous eyes,
And hate for arts that caus'd himself to rise;
Damn with faint praise, assent with civil leer,
And without sneering, teach the rest to sneer;
Willing to wound, and yet afraid to strike,
Just hint a fault, and hesitate dislike;
Alike reserv'd to blame, or to commend,
A tim'rous foe, and a suspicious friend;
Dreading ev'n fools, by Flatterers besieg'd,
And so obliging, that he ne'er oblig'd;
Like *Cato*, give his little Senate laws,
And sit attentive to his own applause;
While Wits and Templars ev'ry sentence raise,
And wonder with a foolish face of praise—
Who but must laugh, if such a man there be?
Who would not weep, if *Atticus* were he!

What tho' my Name stood rubric on the walls,
Or plaister'd posts, with claps, in capitals?

Or smoaking forth, a hundred hawkers load,
On wings of winds came flying all abroad?
I sought no homage from the Race that write;
I kept, like *Asian* Monarchs, from their sight:
Poems I heeded (now be-rym'd so long)
No more than thou, great *George!* a birth-day song.
I ne'er with wits or witlings past my days,
To spread about the itch of verse and praise;
Nor like a puppy, daggled thro' the town,
To fetch and carry sing-song up and down;
Nor at Rehearsals sweat, and mouth'd, and cry'd
With handkerchief and orange at my side;
But sick of fops, and poetry, and prate,
To *Bufo* left the whole *Castalian* state.

    Proud as *Apollo* on his forked hill,
Sate full-blown *Bufo*, puff'd by ev'ry quill;
Fed with soft Dedication all day long,
Horace and he went hand in hand in song.
His Library (where busts of Poets dead
And a true Pindar stood without a head)
Receiv'd of wits an undistinguish'd race,
Who first his judgment ask'd, and then a place:
Much they extoll'd his pictures, much his seat,
And flatter'd ev'ry day, and some days eat:
Till grown more frugal in his riper days,
He paid some bards with port, and some with praise,
To some a dry rehearsal was assign'd,
And others (harder still) he paid in kind.
Dryden alone (what wonder?) came not nigh,
Dryden alone escap'd this judging eye:
But still the *Great* have kindness in reserve,
He help'd to bury whom he help'd to starve.

    May some choice Patron bless each gray-goose quill!
May ev'ry *Bavius* have his *Bufo* still!
So when a statesman wants a Day's defence,

Or envy holds a whole week's war with Sense,
Or simple pride for Flatt'ry makes demands;
May Dunce by dunce be whistled off my hands!
Blest be the *Great!* for those they take away,
And those they left me; for they left me *Gay;*
Left me to see neglected Genius bloom,
Neglected die, and tell it on his tomb:
Of all thy blameless life the sole return
My Verse and *Queensb'ry* weeping o'er thy urn!

 Oh, let me live my own! and die so too!
(To live and die is all I have to do:)
Maintain a Poet's dignity and ease,
And see what friends, and read what books I please:
Above a Patron, tho' I condescend
Sometimes to call a Minister my friend.
I was not born for Courts or great affairs;
I pay my debts, believe, and say my pray'rs;
Can sleep without a Poem in my head,
Nor know, if *Dennis* be alive or dead.

 Why am I ask'd what next shall see the light?
Heav'ns! was I born for nothing but to write?
Has Life no joys for me? or (to be grave)
Have I no friend to serve, no soul to save?
"I found him close with *Swift*"—"Indeed? no doubt,"
Cries prating *Balbus*, "something will come out."
'Tis all in vain, deny it as I will.
"No, such a Genius never can lie still";
And then for mine obligingly mistakes
The first Lampoon Sir *Will* or *Bubo* makes.
Poor guiltless I! and can I chuse but smile,
When ev'ry Coxcomb knows me by my *Style?*

 Curst be the Verse, how well soe'er it flow,
That tends to make one worthy man my foe,
Give Virtue scandal, Innocence a fear,
Or from the soft-ey'd Virgin steal a tear!

But he who hurts a harmless neighbour's peace,
Insults fall'n worth, or Beauty in distress,
Who loves a Lye, lame slander helps about,
Who writes a Libel, or who copies out:
That Fop, whose pride affects a Patron's name,
Yet absent, wounds an Author's honest fame:
Who can your merit *selfishly* approve,
And show the *sense* of it without the *love;*
Who has the vanity to call you friend,
Yet wants the honour, injur'd, to defend;
Who tells whate'er you think, whate'er you say,
And, if he lye not, must at least betray:
Who to the *Dean* and *silver bell* can swear,
And sees at *Cannons* what was never there;
Who reads, but with a lust to misapply,
Make Satire a Lampoon, and fiction Lye.
A lash like mine no honest man shall dread,
But all such babbling blockheads in his stead.

  Let *Sporus* tremble—*A.* What? that thing of silk,
Sporus, that mere white curd of ass's milk?
Satire or sense, alas! can *Sporus* feel?
Who breaks a butterfly upon a wheel?
P. Yet let me flap this bug with gilded wings,
This painted child of Dirt, that stinks and stings;
Whose buzz the witty and the fair annoys,
Yet wit ne'er tastes, and beauty ne'er enjoys;
So well-bred spaniels civilly delight
In mumbling of the game they dare not bite.
Eternal smiles his emptiness betray,
As shallow streams run dimpling all the way.
Whether in florid impotence he speaks,
And, as the prompter breathes, the puppet squeaks;
Or at the ear of *Eve,* familiar Toad,
Half froth, half venom, spits himself abroad,
In puns, or politics, or tales, or lies,

Or spite, or smut, or rhymes, or blasphemies.
His wit all see-saw, between *that* and *this*,
Now high, now low, now master up, now miss,
And he himself one vile Antithesis.
Amphibious thing! that acting either part,
The trifling head, or the corrupted heart,
Fop at the toilet, flatt'rer at the board,
Now trips a Lady, and now struts a Lord.
Eve's tempter thus the Rabbins have exprest,
A Cherub's face, a reptile all the rest,
Beauty that shocks you, parts that none will trust,
Wit that can creep, and pride that licks the dust.

   Not Fortune's worshiper, nor Fashion's fool,
Not Lucre's madman, nor Ambition's tool,
Not proud, nor servile; Be one Poet's praise,
That, if he pleas'd, he pleas'd by manly ways;
That Flatt'ry, ev'n to Kings, he held a shame,
And thought a Lye in verse or prose the same:
That not in Fancy's maze he wander'd long,
But stoop'd to Truth and moraliz'd his song:
That not for Fame, but Virtue's better end,
He stood the furious foe, the timid friend,
The damning critic, half approving wit,
The coxcomb hit, or fearing to be hit;
Laugh'd at the loss of friends he never had,
The dull, the proud, the wicked, and the mad;
The distant threats of Vengeance on his head,
The blow unfelt, the tear he never shed;
The tale reviv'd, the lye so oft o'erthrown,
Th' imputed trash, and dulness not his own;
The Morals blacken'd when the writings 'scape,
The libel'd person, and the pictur'd shape;
Abuse, on all he lov'd, or lov'd him, spread,
A friend in exile, or a father, dead;
The whisper, that to greatness still too near,

Perhaps, yet vibrates on his *Sov'reign's* ear—
Welcome for thee, fair *Virtue!* all the past:
For thee, fair *Virtue!* welcome ev'n the *last!*
    A. But why insult the poor, affront the great?
P. A knave's a knave, to me, in ev'ry state:
Alike my scorn, if he succeed or fail,
Sporus at court, or *Japhet* in a jail,
A hireling scribler, or a hireling peer,
Knight of the post corrupt, or of the shire;
If on a Pillory, or near a Throne,
He gain his Prince's ear, or lose his own.
    Yet soft by Nature, more a dupe than wit,
Sapho can tell you how this man was bit;
This dreaded Sat'rist *Dennis* will confess
Foe to his pride, but friend to his distress;
So humble he has knock'd at *Tibbald's* door,
Has drunk with Cibber, nay has rhym'd for Moore.
Full ten years slander'd, did he once reply?
Three thousand suns went down on Welsted's lye.
To please a Mistress one aspers'd his life;
He lash'd him not, but let her be his wife:
Let *Budgell* charge low *Grubstreet* on his quill,
And write whate'er he pleas'd, except his Will;
Let the two *Curls* of Town and Court, abuse
His father, mother, body, soul, and muse.
Yet why? that Father held it for a rule,
It was a sin to call our neighbour fool:
That harmless Mother thought no wife a whore:
Hear this, and spare his family, *James Moore!*
Unspotted names, and memorable long!
If there be force in Virtue, or in Song.
    Of gentle blood (part shed in Honour's cause,
While yet in *Britain* Honour had applause)
Each parent sprung.—*A.* What fortune, pray?
    —*P.* Their own,

And better got, than *Bestia's* from the throne.
Born to no Pride, inheriting no Strife,
Nor marrying Discord in a noble wife,
Stranger to civil and religious rage,
The good man walk'd innoxious thro' his age.
No Courts he saw, no suits would ever try,
Nor dar'd an Oath, nor hazarded a Lye.
Un-learn'd, he knew no schoolman's subtle art,
No language, but the language of the heart.
By Nature honest, by Experience wise,
Healthy by temp'rance, and by exercise;
His life, tho' long, to sickness past unknown,
His death was instant, and without a groan.
O grant me, thus to live, and thus to die!
Who sprung from Kings shall know less joy than I.
    O Friend! may each domestic bliss be thine!
Be no unpleasing Melancholy mine:
Me, let the tender office long engage,
To rock the cradle of reposing Age,
With lenient arts extend a Mother's breath,
Make Languor smile, and smooth the bed of Death,
Explore the thought, explain the asking eye,
And keep a while one parent from the sky!
On cares like these if length of days attend,
May Heav'n, to bless those days, preserve my friend,
Preserve him social, chearful, and serene,
And just as rich as when he serv'd a *Queen*.
A. Whether that blessing be deny'd or giv'n,
Thus far was right, the rest belongs to Heav'n.

FROM *Moral Essays*

EPISTLE IV: OF THE USE OF RICHES

'Tis strange, the Miser should his Cares employ
To gain those Riches he can ne'er enjoy:
Is it less strange, the Prodigal should wast
His wealth, to purchase what he ne'er can taste?
Not for himself he sees, or hears, or eats;
Artists must chuse his Pictures, Music, Meats:
He buys for Topham, Drawings and Designs,
For Pembroke Statues, dirty Gods, and Coins;
Rare monkish Manuscripts for Hearne alone,
And Books for Mead, and Butterflies for Sloane.
Think we all these are for himself? no more
Than his fine Wife, alas! or finer Whore.

For what has Virro painted, built, and planted?
Only to show, how many Tastes he wanted.
What brought Sir Visto's ill got wealth to waste?
Some Dæmon whisper'd, "Visto! have a Taste."
Heav'n visits with a Taste the wealthy fool,
And needs no Rod but Ripley with a Rule.
See! sportive fate, to punish aukward pride,
Bids Bubo build, and sends him such a Guide:
A standing sermon, at each year's expence,
That never Coxcomb reach'd Magnificence!

You show us, Rome was glorious, not profuse,
And pompous buildings once were things of Use.
Yet shall (my Lord) your just, your noble rules
Fill half the land with Imitating-Fools;
Who random drawings from your sheets shall take,

And of one beauty many blunders make;
Load some vain Church with old Theatric state,
Turn Arcs of triumph to a Garden-gate;
Reverse your Ornaments, and hang them all
On some patch'd dog-hole ek'd with ends of wall;
Then clap four slices of Pilaster on't,
That, lac'd with bits of rustic, makes a Front.
Shall call the winds thro' long arcades to roar,
Proud to catch cold at a Venetian door;
Conscious they act a true Palladian part,
And if they starve, they starve by rules of art.

   Oft have you hinted to your brother Peer,
A certain truth, which many buy too dear:
Something there is more needful than Expence,
And something previous ev'n to Taste—'tis Sense:
Good Sense, which only is the gift of Heav'n,
And tho' no Science, fairly worth the seven:
A Light, which in yourself you must perceive;
Jones and Le Nôtre have it not to give.

   To build, to plant, whatever you intend,
To rear the Column, or the Arch to bend,
To swell the Terras, or to sink the Grot;
In all, let Nature never be forgot.
But treat the Goddess like a modest fair,
Nor over-dress, nor leave her wholly bare;
Let not each beauty ev'ry where be spy'd,
Where half the skill is decently to hide.
He gains all points, who pleasingly confounds,
Surprizes, varies, and conceals the Bounds.

   Consult the Genius of the Place in all;
That tells the Waters or to rise, or fall;
Or helps th' ambitious Hill the heav'ns to scale,
Or scoops in circling theatres the Vale;
Calls in the Country, catches op'ning glades,
Joins willing woods, and varies shades from shades;

Now breaks or now directs, th' intending Lines;
Paints as you plant, and, as you work, designs.
  Still follow Sense, of ev'ry Art the Soul,
Parts answ'ring parts shall slide into a whole,
Spontaneous beauties all around advance,
Start ev'n from Difficulty, strike from Chance;
Nature shall join you; Time shall make it grow
A Work to wonder at—perhaps a STOW.
  Without it, proud Versailles! thy glory falls;
And Nero's Terraces desert their walls:
The vast Parterres a thousand hands shall make,
Lo! COBHAM comes, and floats them with a Lake:
Or cut wide views thro' Mountains to the Plain,
You'll wish your hill or shelter'd seat again.
Ev'n in an ornament its place remark,
Nor in an Hermitage set Dr. Clarke.
  Behold Villario's ten-years toil compleat;
His Quincunx darkens, his Espaliers meet;
The Wood supports the Plain, the parts unite,
And strength of Shade contends with strength of Light;
A waving Glow the bloomy beds display,
Blushing in bright diversities of day,
With silver-quiv'ring rills mæander'd o'er—
Enjoy them, you! Villario can no more;
Tir'd of the scene Parterres and Fountains yield,
He finds at last he better likes a Field.
  Thro' his young Woods how pleas'd Sabinus stray'd
Or sat delighted in the thick'ning shade,
With annual joy the red'ning shoots to greet,
Or see the stretching branches long to meet!
His Son's fine Taste an op'ner Vista loves,
Foe to the Dryads of his Father's groves;
One boundless Green, or flourish'd Carpet views,
With all the mournful family of Yews;
The thriving plants ignoble broomsticks made,

Now sweep those Alleys they were born to shade.
   At Timon's Villa let us pass a day,
Where all cry out, "What sums are thrown away!"
So proud, so grand; of that stupendous air,
Soft and Agreeable come never there.
Greatness, with Timon, dwells in such a draught
As brings all Brobdingnag before your thought.
To compass this, his building is a Town,
His pond an Ocean, his parterre a Down:
Who but must laugh, the Master when he sees,
A puny insect, shiv'ring at a breeze!
Lo, what huge heaps of littleness around!
The whole, a labour'd Quarry above ground.
Two Cupids squirt before: a Lake behind
Improves the keenness of the Northern wind.
His Gardens next your admiration call,
On ev'ry side you look, behold the Wall!
No pleasing Intricacies intervene,
No artful wildness to perplex the scene;
Grove nods at grove, each Alley has a brother,
And half the platform just reflects the other.
The suff'ring eye inverted Nature sees,
Trees cut to Statues, Statues thick as trees;
With here a Fountain, never to be play'd;
And there a Summer-house, that knows no shade;
Here Amphitrite fails thro' myrtle bow'rs;
There Gladiators fight, or die in flow'rs;
Un-water'd see the drooping sea-horse mourn,
And swallows roost in Nilus' dusty Urn.
   My Lord advances with majestic mien,
Smit with the mighty pleasure, to be seen:
But soft—by regular approach—not yet—
First thro' the length of yon hot Terrace sweat;
And when up ten steep slopes you've drag'd your
     thighs,

Just at his Study-door he'll bless your eyes.
  His Study! with what Authors is it stor'd?
In Books, not Authors, curious is my Lord;
To all their dated Backs he turns you round:
These Aldus printed, those Du Suëil has bound.
Lo some are Vellom, and the rest as good
For all his Lordship knows, but they are Wood.
For Locke or Milton 'tis in vain to look,
These shelves admit not any modern book.
  And now the Chapel's silver bell you hear,
That summons you to all the Pride of Pray'r:
Light quirks of Music, broken and uneven,
Make the soul dance upon a Jig to Heav'n.
On painted Cielings you devoutly stare,
Where sprawl the Saints of Verrio or Laguerre,
On gilded clouds in fair expansion lie,
And bring all Paradise before your eye.
To rest, the Cushion and soft Dean invite,
Who never mentions Hell to ears polite.
  But hark! the chiming Clocks to dinner call;
A hundred footsteps scrape the marble Hall:
The rich Buffet well-colour'd Serpents grace,
And gaping Tritons spew to wash your face.
Is this a dinner? this a Genial room?
No, 'tis a Temple, and a Hecatomb.
A solemn Sacrifice, perform'd in state,
You drink by measure, and to minutes eat.
So quick retires each flying course, you'd swear
Sancho's dread Doctor and his Wand were there.
Between each Act the trembling salvers ring,
From soup to sweet-wine, and God bless the King.
In plenty starving, tantaliz'd in state,
And complaisantly help'd to all I hate,
Treated, caress'd, and tir'd, I take my leave,
Sick of his civil Pride from Morn to Eve;

I curse such lavish cost, and little skill,
And swear no Day was ever past so ill.

Yet hence the Poor are cloath'd, the Hungry fed;
Health to himself, and to his Infants bread
The Lab'rer bears: What his hard Heart denies,
His charitable Vanity supplies.

Another age shall see the golden Ear
Imbrown the Slope, and nod on the Parterre,
Deep Harvests bury all his pride has plann'd,
And laughing Ceres re-assume the land.

Who then shall grace, or who improve the Soil?
Who plants like Bathurst, or who builds like Boyle.
'Tis Use alone that sanctifies Expence,
And Splendor borrows all her rays from Sense.

His Father's Acres who enjoys in peace,
Or makes his Neighbours glad, if he encrease:
Whose chearful Tenants bless their yearly toil,
Yet to their Lord owe more than to the soil
Whose ample Lawns are not asham'd to feed
The milky heifer and deserving steed;
Whose rising Forests, not for pride or show,
But future Buildings, future Navies, grow:
Let his plantations stretch from down to down,
First shade a Country, and then raise a Town.

You too proceed! make falling Arts your care,
Erect new wonders, and the old repair;
Jones and Palladio to themselves restore,
And be whate'er Vitruvius was before:
Till Kings call forth th' Ideas of your mind,
(Proud to accomplish what such hands design'd,)
Bid Harbors open, public Ways extend,
Bid Temples, worthier of the God, ascend;
Bid the broad Arch the dang'rous Flood contain,
The Mole projected break the roaring Main;
Back to his bounds their subject Sea command,

And roll obedient Rivers thro' the Land:
These Honours, Peace to happy Britain brings,
These are Imperial Works, and worthy Kings.

Epistle to Miss Blount

ON HER LEAVING THE TOWN
AFTER THE CORONATION

As some fond Virgin, whom her mother's care
Drags from the Town to wholesome Country air,
Just when she learns to roll a melting eye,
And hear a spark, yet think no danger nigh;
From the dear man unwilling she must sever,
Yet takes one kiss before she parts for ever:
Thus from the world fair Zephalinda flew,
Saw others happy, and with sighs withdrew;
Not that their pleasures caus'd her discontent,
She sigh'd not that they stay'd, but that she went.

She went, to plain-work, and to purling brooks,
Old-fashion'd halls, dull Aunts, and croaking rooks:
She went from Op'ra, Park, Assembly, Play,
To morning walks, and pray'rs three hours a day;
To part her time 'twixt reading and bohea,
To muse, and spill her solitary tea,
Or o'er cold coffee trifle with the spoon,
Count the slow clock, and dine exact at noon;
Divert her eyes with pictures in the fire,
Hum half a tune, tell stories to the squire;
Up to her godly garret after sev'n,
There starve and pray, for that's the way to heav'n.

Some Squire, perhaps, you take delight to rack;
Whose game is Whisk, whose treat a toast in sack;

Who visits with a Gun, presents you birds,
Then gives a smacking buss, and cries,—No words!
Or with his hound comes hallowing from the stable,
Makes love with nods, and knees beneath a table;
Whose laughs are hearty, tho' his jests are coarse,
And loves you best of all things—but his horse.

　　In some fair ev'ning, on your elbow laid,
You dream of Triumphs in the rural shade;
In pensive thought recall the fancy'd scene,
See Coronations rise on ev'ry green;
Before you pass th' imaginary sights
Of Lords, and Earls, and Dukes, and garter'd Knights,
While the spread fan o'ershades your closing eyes;
Then give one flirt, and all the vision flies.
Thus vanish sceptres, coronets, and balls,
And leave you in lone woods, or empty walls!

　　So when your Slave, at some dear idle time,
(Not plagu'd with head-achs, or the want of rhyme)
Stands in the streets, abstracted from the crew,
And while he seems to study, thinks of you;
Just when his fancy points your sprightly eyes,
Or sees the blush of soft Parthenia rise,
Gay pats my shoulder, and you vanish quite,
Streets, Chairs, and Coxcombs rush upon my sight;
Vex'd to be still in town, I knit my brow,
Look sour, and hum a Tune, as you may now.

The Challenge

A COURT BALLAD

To the tune of "To all you Ladies now at Land"

To *one* fair Lady out of Court,
    And *two* fair Ladies in,
We think the *Turk* and *Pope* a Sport,
    And Wit and Love no Sin;
·Come, these soft Lines, with nothing stiff in,
To *Bellenden, Lepell,* and *Griffin.*
        With a fa, la, la.

What passes in the dark third Row,
    And what behind the Scene,
Couches and cripled Chairs I know,
    And Garrets hung with Green;
I know the Swing of sinful Hack,
Where many Damsels cry Alack.
        With a fa, la, la.

Then why to Court should I repair,
    Where's such ado with *Townshend,*
To hear each Mortal stamp and swear,
    And every speech with *Zoons* end;
To hear 'em rail at honest *Sunderland,*
And rashly blame the Realm of *Blunderland.*
        With a fa, la, la.

Alas! like *Schutz,* I cannot pun,
    Like *Grafton* court the *Germans;*
Tell *Pickenbourg* how Slim she's grown,
    Like *Meadowes* run to Sermons;

To Court ambitious Men may roam,
But *I* and *Marlbro'* stay at Home.
    With a fa, la, la.

In Truth, by what I can discern,
    Of Courtiers 'twixt you *Three,*
Some Wit you have, and more may learn
    From Court, than *Gay* or *Me:*
Perhaps, in Time, you'll leave high Diet,
To sup with us on Milk and Quiet.
    With a fa, la, la.

At *Leicester-Fields,* a House full high,
    With door all painted green,
Where Ribbons wave upon the Tye,
    (A *Milliner* I mean);
There may you meet us *Three* to *Three,*
For *Gay* can well make *Two* of Me.
    With a fa, la, la.

But shou'd you catch the Prudish Itch,
    And each become a Coward,
Bring sometimes with you Lady *Rich,*
    And sometimes Mistress *Howard;*
For Virgins to keep Chaste, must go
Abroad with such as are not so.
    With a fa, la, la.

And thus, fair Maids, my Ballad ends;
    God send the King safe Landing;
And make all honest Ladies friends
    To Armies that are Standing;
Preserve the Limits of these Nations,
And take off Ladies Limitations.
    With a fa, la, la.

Epigram

When other Ladies to the Shades go down,
Still *Flavia, Chloris, Celia* stay in Town;
Those Ghosts of Beauty ling'ring there abide,
And haunt the places where their Honour dy'd.

FROM *The Dunciad*

To Dr. Jonathan Swift

BOOK THE FOURTH

Yet, yet a moment, one dim Ray of Light
Indulge, dread Chaos, and eternal Night!
Of darkness visible so much be lent,
As half to shew, half veil the deep Intent.
Ye Pow'rs! whose Mysteries restor'd I sing,
To whom Time bears me on his rapid wing,
Suspend a while your Force inertly strong,
Then take at once the Poet and the Song.
    Now flam'd the Dog-star's unpropitious ray,
Smote ev'ry Brain, and wither'd ev'ry Bay;
Sick was the Sun, the Owl forsook his bow'r,
The moon-struck Prophet felt the madding hour:
Then rose the Seed of Chaos, and of Night,
To blot out Order, and extinguish Light,
Of dull and venal a new World to mold,
And bring Saturnian days of Lead and Gold.
    She mounts the Throne: her head a Cloud conceal'd,

In broad Effulgence all below reveal'd,
('Tis thus aspiring Dulness ever shines)
Soft on her lap her Laureat son reclines.

  Beneath her foot-stool, *Science* groans in Chains,
And *Wit* dreads Exile, Penalties and Pains.
There foam'd rebellious *Logic*, gagg'd and bound;
There, stript, fair *Rhet'ric* languish'd on the ground;
His blunted Arms by *Sophistry* are born,
And shameless *Billingsgate* her Robes adorn.
Morality, by her false Guardians drawn,
Chicane in Furs, and *Casuistry* in Lawn,
Gasps, as they straiten at each end the cord,
And dies, when *Dulness* gives her Page the word.
Mad *Mathesis* alone was unconfin'd,
Too mad for mere material chains to bind,
Now to pure Space lifts her extatic stare,
Now running round the Circle, finds it square.
But held in ten-fold bonds the *Muses* lie,
Watch'd both by Envy's and by Flatt'ry's eye:
There to her heart sad Tragedy addrest
The dagger wont to pierce the Tyrant's breast;
But sober History restrain'd her rage,
And promis'd Vengeance on a barb'rous age.
There sunk Thalia, nerveless, cold, and dead,
Had not her Sister Satyr held her head:
Nor could'st thou, CHESTERFIELD! a tear refuse,
Thou wept'st, and with thee wept each gentle Muse.

  When lo! a Harlot form soft sliding by,
With mincing step, small voice, and languid eye:
Foreign her air, her robe's discordant pride
In patch-work flutt'ring, and her head aside:
By singing Peers up-held on either hand,
She tripp'd and laugh'd, too pretty much to stand:
Cast on the prostrate Nine a scornful look,
Then thus in quaint Recitativo spoke.

"O *Cara! Cara!* silence all that train:
Joy to great Chaos! let Division reign:
Chromatic tortures soon shall drive them hence,
Break all their nerves, and fritter all their sense:
One Trill shall harmonize joy, grief, and rage,
Wake the dull Church, and lull the ranting Stage;
To the same notes thy sons shall hum, or snore,
And all thy yawning daughters cry, *encore.*
Another Phoebus, thy own Phoebus, reigns,
Joys in my jigs, and dances in my chains.
But soon, ah soon, Rebellion will commence,
If Music meanly borrows aid from Sense:
Strong in new Arms, lo! Giant HANDEL stands,
Like bold Briareus, with a hundred hands;
To stir, to rouze, to shake the Soul he comes,
And Jove's own Thunders follow Mar's Drums.
Arrest him, Empress; or you sleep no more"—
She heard, and drove him to th' Hibernian shore.

And now had Fame's posterior Trumpet blown,
And all the nations summon'd to the Throne.
The young, the old, who feel her inward sway,
One instinct seizes, and transports away.
None need a guide, by sure Attraction led,
And strong impulsive gravity of Head:
None want a place, for all their Centre found,
Hung to the Goddess, and coher'd around.
Not closer, orb in orb, conglob'd are seen
The buzzing Bees about their dusky Queen.

The gath'ring number, as it moves along,
Involves a vast involuntary throng,
Who gently drawn, and straggling less and less,
Roll in her Vortex, and her pow'r confess.
Not those alone who passive own her laws,
But who, weak rebels, more advance her cause.
Whate'er of dunce in College or in Town

Sneers at another, in toupee or gown;
Whate'er of mungril no one class admits,
A wit with dunces, and a dunce with wits.
　　Nor absent they, no members of her state,
Who pay her homage in her sons, the Great;
Who false to Phoebus, bow the knees to Baal;
Or impious, preach his Word without a call.
Patrons, who sneak from living worth to dead,
With-hold the pension, and set up the head;
Or vest dull Flatt'ry in the sacred Gown;
Or give from fool to fool the Laurel crown.
And (last and worse) with all the cant of wit,
Without the soul, the Muse's Hypocrit.
　　There march'd the bard and blockhead, side by side,
Who rhym'd for hire, and patroniz'd for pride.
Narcissus, prais'd with all a Parson's pow'r,
Look'd a white lilly sunk beneath a show'r.
There mov'd Montalto with superior air;
His stretch'd-out arm display'd a Volume fair;
Courtiers and Patriots in two ranks divide,
Thro' both he pass'd, and bow'd from side to side:
But as in graceful act, with awful eye
Compos'd he stood, bold Benson thrust him by:
On two unequal crutches propt he came,
Milton's on this, on that one Johnston's name.
The decent Knight retir'd with sober rage,
"What! no respect," he cry'd, " for Shakespear's page?"
But (happy for him as the times went then)
Appear'd Apollo's May'r and Aldermen,
On whom three hundred gold-capt youths await,
To lug the pond'rous volume off in state.
　　When Dulness, smiling—"Thus revive the Wits!
But murder first, and mince them all to bits;
As erst Medea (cruel, so to save!)
A new Edition of old Æson gave;

Let standard-Authors, thus, like trophies born,
Appear more glorious as more hack'd and torn.
And you, my Critics! in the checquer'd shade,
Admire new light thro' holes yourselves have made.
   "Leave not a foot of verse, a foot of stone,
A Page, a Grave, that they can call their own;
But spread, my sons, your glory thin or thick,
On passive paper, or on solid brick.
So by each Bard an Alderman shall sit,
A heavy Lord shall hang at ev'ry Wit,
And while on Fame's triumphal Car they ride,
Some Slave of mine be pinion'd to their side."
   Now crowds on crowds around the Goddess press,
Each eager to present the first Address.
Dunce scorning Dunce beholds the next advance,
But Fop shews Fop superior complaisance.
When lo! a Spectre rose, whose index-hand
Held forth the Virtue of the dreadful wand;
His beaver'd brow a birchin garland wears,
Dropping with Infant's blood, and Mother's tears.
O'er ev'ry vein a shudd'ring horror runs;
Eton and Winton shake thro' all their Sons.
All Flesh is humbled, Westminster's bold race
Shrink, and confess the Genius of the place:
The pale Boy-Senator yet tingling stands,
And holds his breeches close with both his hands.
   Then thus. "Since Man from beast by Words is known,
Words are Man's province, Words we teach alone.
When Reason doubtful, like the Samian letter,
Points him two ways, the narrower is the better.
Plac'd at the door of Learning, youth to guide,
We never suffer it to stand too wide.
To ask, to guess, to know, as they commence,
As Fancy opens the quick springs of Sense,
We ply the Memory, we load the brain,

Bind rebel Wit, and double chain on chain,
Confine the thought, to exercise the breath;
And keep them in the pale of Words till death,
Whate'er the talents, or howe'er designed,
We hang one jingling padlock on the mind:
A Poet the first day, he dips his quill;
And what the last? a very Poet still.
Pity! the charm works only in our wall,
Lost, lost too soon in yonder House or Hall.
There truant WYNDHAM ev'ry Muse gave o'er,
There TALBOT sunk, and was a Wit no more!
How sweet an Ovid, MURRAY was our boast!
How many Martials were in PULT'NEY lost!
Else sure some Bard, to our eternal praise,
In twice ten thousand rhyming nights and days,
Had reach'd the Work, the All that mortal can;
And South beheld that Master-piece of Man.

  "Oh (cry'd the Goddess) for some pedant Reign!
Some gentle JAMES, to bless the land again;
To stick the Doctor's Chair into the Throne,
Give law to Words, or war with Words alone,
Senates and Courts with Greek and Latin rule,
And turn the Council to a Grammar School!
For sure, if Dulness sees a grateful Day,
'Tis in the shade of Arbitrary Sway.
O! if my sons may learn one earthly thing,
Teach but that one, sufficient for a King;
That which my Priests, and mine alone, maintain,
Which as it dies, or lives, we fall, or reign:
May you, may Cam, and Isis preach it long!
'The RIGHT DIVINE of Kings to govern wrong.'"

  Prompt at the call, around the Goddess roll
Broad hats, and hoods, and caps a sable shoal:
Thick and more thick the black blockade extends,
A hundred head of Aristotle's friends.

Nor wert thou, Isis! wanting to the day,
(Tho' Christ-church long kept prudishly away.)
Each staunch Polemic, stubborn as a rock,
Each fierce Logician, still expelling Locke,
Came whip and spur, and dash'd thro' thin and thick
On German Crouzaz, and Dutch Burgersdyck.
As many quit the streams that murm'ring fall
To lull the sons of Marg'ret and Clare-hall,
Where Bentley late tempestuous wont to sport
In troubled waters, but now sleeps in Port.
Before them march'd that awful Aristarch;
Plow'd was his front with many a deep Remark:
His Hat, which never vail'd to human pride,
Walker with rev'rence took, and lay'd aside.
Low bow'd the rest: He, kingly, did but nod;
So upright Quakers please both Man and God.
"Mistress! dismiss that rabble from your throne:
Avaunt—is Aristarchus yet unknown?
Thy mighty Scholiast, whose unweary'd pains
Made Horace dull, and humbled Milton's strains.
Turn what they will to Verse, their toil is vain
Critics like me shall make it Prose again.
Roman and Greek Grammarians! know your Better.
Author or something yet more great than Letter;
While tow'ring o'er your Alphabet, like Saul,
Stands our Digamma, and o'er-tops them all.
'Tis true, on Words is still our whole debate.
Disputes of *Me* or *Te*, of *aut* or *at*,
To sound or sink in *cano*, O or A,
Or give up Cicero to C or K.
Let Freind affect to speak as Terence spoke,
And Alsop never but like Horace joke:
For me, what Virgil, Pliny may deny,
Manilius or Solinus shall supply:
For Attic Phrase in Plato let them seek,

I poach in Suidas for unlicens'd Greek.
In ancient Sense if any needs will deal,
Be sure I give them Fragments, not a Meal;
What Gellius or Stobæus hash'd before,
Or chew'd by blind old Scholiasts o'er and o'er,
The critic Eye, that microscope of Wit,
Sees hairs and pores, examines bit by bit:
How parts relate to parts, or they to whole,
The body's harmony, the beaming soul,
Are things which Kuster, Burman, Wasse shall see,
When Man's whole frame is obvious to a *Flea.*

    "Ah, think not, Mistress! more true Dulness lies
In Folly's Cap, than Wisdom's grave disguise.
Like buoys, that never sink into the flood,
On Learning's surface we but lie and nod,
Thine is the genuine head of many a house,
And much Divinity without a *Nous*
Nor could a BARROW work on ev'ry block,
Nor has one ATTERBURY spoil'd the flock.
See! still thy own, the heavy Canon roll,
And Metaphysic smokes involve the Pole.
For thee we dim the eyes, and stuff the head
With all such reading as was never read:
For thee explain a thing till all men doubt it:
And write about it, Goddess, and about it:
So spins the silk-worm small its slender store,
And labours till it clouds itself all o'er.

    "What tho' we let some better sort of fool
Thrid ev'ry science, run thro' ev'ry school?
Never by tumbler thro' the hoops was shown
Such skill in passing all, and touching none.
He may indeed (if sober all this time)
Plague with Dispute, or persecute with Rhyme.
We only furnish what he cannot use,
Or wed to what he must divorce, a Muse:

Full in the midst of Euclid dip at once,
And petrify a Genius to a Dunce:
Or set on Metaphysic ground to prance,
Show all his paces, not a step advance.
With the same CEMENT, ever sure to bind,
We bring to one dead level ev'ry mind.
Then take him to devellop, if you can,
And hew the Block off, and get out the Man.
But wherefore waste I words? I see advance
Whore, Pupil, and lac'd Governor from France.
Walker! our hat"—nor more he deign'd to say,
But, stern as Ajax' spectre, strode away.

In flow'd at once a gay embroider'd race,
And titt'ring push'd the Pedants off the place:
Some would have spoken, but the voice was drown'd
By the French horn, or by the op'ning hound.
The first came forwards, with as easy mien,
As if he saw St. James's and the Queen.
When thus th' attendant Orator begun,
"Receive, great Empress! thy accomplish'd Son:
Thine from the birth, and sacred from the rod,
A dauntless infant! never scar'd with God.
The Sire saw, one by one, his Virtues wake:
The Mother begg'd the blessing of a Rake.
Thou gav'st that Ripeness, which so soon began,
And ceas'd so soon, he ne'er was Boy, nor Man,
Thro' School and College, thy kind cloud o'ercast,
Safe and unseen the young Æneas past:
Thence bursting glorious, all at once let down,
Stunn'd with his giddy Larum half the town.
Intrepid then, o'er seas and lands he flew:
Europe he saw, and Europe saw him too.
There all thy gifts and graces we display,
Thou, only thou, directing all our way!
To where the Seine, obsequious as she runs,

Pours at great Bourbon's feet her silken sons;
Or Tyber, now no longer Roman, rolls
Vain of Italian Arts, Italian Souls:
To happy Convents, bosom'd deep in vines,
Where slumber Abbots, purple as their wines:
To Isles of fragrance, lilly-silver'd vales,
Diffusing languor in the panting gales:
To lands of singing, or of dancing slaves,
Love-whisp'ring woods, and lute-resounding waves.
But chief her shrine where naked Venus keeps,
And Cupids ride the Lyon of the Deeps;
Where, eas'd of Fleets, the Adriatic main
Wafts the smooth Eunuch and enamour'd swain.
Led by my hand, he saunter'd Europe round,
And gather'd ev'ry Vice on Christian ground;
Saw ev'ry Court, heard ev'ry King declare
His royal Sense, of Op'ra's or the Fair;
The Stews and Palace equally explor'd,
Intrigu'd with glory, and with spirit whor'd;
Try'd all *hors-d'œuvres,* all *liqueurs* defin'd,
Judicious drank, and greatly-daring din'd;
Dropt the dull lumber of the Latin store,
Spoil'd his own language, and acquir'd no more;
All Classic learning lost on Classic ground;
And last turn'd *Air,* the Echo of a Sound!
See now, half cur'd, and perfectly well-bred,
With nothing but a Solo in his head;
As much Estate, and Principle, and Wit,
As Jansen, Fleetwood, Cibber shall think fit;
Stol'n from a Duel, follow'd by a Nun,
And, if a Borough chuse him, not undone!
See, to my country happy I restore
This glorious Youth, and add one Venus more.
Her too receive (for her my soul adores)
So may the sons of sons of sons of whores,

Prop thine, O Empress! like each neighbour Throne,
And make a long Posterity thy own."

   Pleas'd, she accepts the Hero, and the Dame,
Wraps in her Veil, and frees from sense of Shame.

   Then look'd, and saw a lazy, lolling sort,
Unseen at Church, at Senate, or at Court,
Of ever-listless Loit'rers, that attend
No Cause, no Trust, no Duty, and no Friend.
Thee too, my Paridel! she mark'd thee there,
Stretch'd on the rack of a too easy chair.
And heard thy everlasting yawn confess
The Pains and Penalties of Idleness.
She pity'd! but her Pity only shed
Benigner influence on thy nodding head.

   But Annius, crafty Seer, with ebon wand,
And well-dissembled em'rald on his hand,
False as his Gems, and canker'd as his Coins,
Came, cramm'd with capon, from where Pollio dines.
Soft, as the wily Fox is seen to creep,
Where bask on sunny banks the simple sheep,
Walk round and round, now prying here, now there,
So he; but pious, whisper'd first his pray'r.

   "Grant, gracious Goddess! grant me still to cheat,
O may thy cloud still cover the deceit!
Thy choicer mists on this assembly shed,
But pour them thickest on the noble head.
So shall each youth, assisted by our eyes,
See other Cæsars, other Homers rise;
Thro' twilight ages hunt th' Athenian fowl,
Which Chalcis Gods, and Mortals call an Owl,
Now see an Attys, now a Cecrops clear,
Nay, Mahomet! the Pigeon at thine ear;
Be rich in ancient brass, tho' not in gold,
And keep his Lares, tho' his house be sold;
To headless Phœbe his fair bride postpone,

Honour a Syrian Prince above his own;
Lord of an Otho, if I vouch it true;
Blest in one Niger, till he knows of two."
    Mummius o'erheard him; Mummius, Fool-renown'd,
Who like his Cheops stinks above the ground,
Fierce as a startled Adder, swell'd, and said,
Rattling an ancient Sistrum at his head:
    "Speak'st thou of Syrian Princes? Traitor base!
Mine, Goddess! mine is all the horned race;
True, he had wit, to make their value rise;
From foolish Greeks to steal them, was as wise;
More glorious yet, from barb'rous hands to keep,
When Sallee Rovers chas'd him on the deep.
Then taught by Hermes, and divinely bold,
Down his own throat he risqu'd the Grecian Gold,
Receiv'd each Demi-God, with pious care,
Deep in his Entrails—I rever'd them there,
I bought them, shrouded in that living shrine,
And, at their second birth, they issue mine."
    "Witness great Ammon! by whose horns I swore,
(Reply'd soft Annius) this our paunch before
Still bears them, faithful; and that thus I eat,
Is to refund the Medals with the meat.
To prove me, Goddess! clear of all design,
Bid me with Pollio sup, as well as dine:
There all the Learn'd shall at the labour stand,
And Douglas lend his soft, obstetric hand."
    The Goddess smiling seem'd to give consent;
So back to Pollio, hand in hand they went.
    Then thick as Locusts black'ning all the ground,
A tribe, with weeds and shells fantastic crown'd,
Each with some wond'rous gift approach'd the Pow'r,
A Nest, a Toad, a Fungus, or a Flow'r.
But far the foremost, two, with earnest zeal,
And aspect ardent to the Throne appeal.

The first thus open'd: "Hear thy suppliant's call,
Great Queen, and common Mother of us all!
Fair from its humble bed I rear'd this Flow'r,
Suckled, and chear'd, with air, and sun, and show'r,
Soft on the paper ruff its leaves I spread,
Bright with the gilded button tipt its head.
Then thron'd in glass, and nam'd it CAROLINE:
Each maid cry'd, Charming! and each youth, Divine!
Did Nature's pencil ever blend such rays,
Such vary'd light in one promiscuous blaze?
Now prostrate! dead! behold that Caroline:
No Maid cries, charming! and no Youth, divine!
And lo the wretch! whose vile, whose insect lust
Lay'd this gay daughter of the Spring in dust.
Oh punish him, or to th' Elysian shades
Dismiss my soul, where no Carnation fades."
    He ceas'd and wept. With innocence of mien,
Th' Accus'd stood forth, and thus addressed the Queen.
    "Of all th' enamel'd race, whose silv'ry wing
Waves to the tepid Zephyrs of the spring,
Or swims along the fluid atmosphere,
Once brightest shin'd this child of Heat and Air.
I saw, and started from its vernal bow'r
The rising game, and chac'd from flow'r to flow'r.
It fled, I follow'd; now in hope, now pain;
It stopt, I stopt; it mov'd, I mov'd again.
At last it fix'd, 'twas on what plant it pleas'd,
And where it fix'd, the beauteous bird I seiz'd:
Rose or Carnation was below my care;
I meddle, Goddess! only in my sphere.
I tell the naked fact without disguise,
And, to excuse it, need but shew the prize;
Whose spoils this Paper offers to your eye,
Fair ev'n in death! this peerless *Butterfly*."
    "My sons! (she answer'd) both have done your parts:

Live happy both, and long promote our arts.
But hear a Mother, when she recommends
To your fraternal care, our sleeping friends.
The common Soul, of Heaven's more frugal make,
Serves but to keep fools pert, and knaves awake:
A drowzy Watchman, that just gives a knock,
And breaks our rest, to tell us what's a clock.
Yet by some object ev'ry brain is stirr'd;
The dull may waken to a Humming-bird;
The most recluse, discreetly open'd, find
Congenial matter in the Cockle-kind;
The mind, in Metaphysics at a loss,
May wander in a wilderness of Moss;
The head that turns at super-lunar things,
Poiz'd with a tail, may steer on Wilkins' wings.
    "O! would the Sons of Men once think their *Eyes*
And Reason giv'n them but to study *Flies!*
See Nature in some partial narrow shape,
And let the Author of the Whole escape:
Learn but to trifle; or, who most observe,
To wonder at their Maker, not to serve."
    "Be that my task (replies a gloomy Clerk,
Sworn foe to Myst'ry, yet divinely dark;
Whose pious hope aspires to see the day
When Moral Evidence shall quite decay,
And damns implicit faith, and holy lies,
Prompt to impose, and fond to dogmatize:)
Let others creep by timid steps, and slow,
On plain Experience lay foundations low,
By common sense to common knowledge bred,
And last, to Nature's Cause thro' Nature led.
All-seeing in thy mists, we want no guide,
Mother of Arrogance, and Source of Pride!
We nobly take the high Priori Road,
And reason downward, till we doubt of God:

Make Nature still incroach upon his plan;
And shove him off as far as e'er we can:
Thrust some Mechanic Cause into his place;
Or bind in Matter, or diffuse in Space.
Or, at one bound o'er-leaping all his laws,
Make God Man's Image, Man the final Cause,
Find Virtue local, all Relation scorn,
See all in *Self,* and but for self be born:
Of nought so certain as our *Reason* still,
Of nought so doubtful as of *Soul* and *Will.*
Oh hide the God still more! and make us see
Such as Lucretius drew, a God like Thee:
Wrapt up in Self, a God without a Thought,
Regardless of our merit or default.
Or that bright Image to our fancy draw,
Which Theocles in raptur'd vision saw,
While thro' Poetic scenes the Genius roves,
Or wanders wild in Academic Groves;
That NATURE our Society adores,
Where Tindal dictates and Silenus snores."
  Rous'd at his name, up rose the bowzy Sire,
And shook from out his Pipe the seeds of fire;
Then snapt his box, and strok'd his belly down:
Rosy and rev'rend, tho' without a Gown.
Bland and familiar to the throne he came,
Led up the Youth, and call'd the Goddess *Dame.*
Then thus. "From Priest-craft happily set free,
Lo! ev'ry finish'd Son returns to thee:
First slave to Words, then vassal to a Name,
Then dupe to Party; child and man the same;
Bounded by Nature, narrow'd still by Art,
A trifling head, and a contracted heart.
Thus bred, thus taught, how many have I seen,
Smiling on all, and smil'd on by a Queen?
Mark'd out for Honours, honour'd for their Birth,

To thee the most rebellious things on earth:
Now to thy gentle shadow all are shrunk,
All melted down, in Pension, or in Punk!
So K——, so B——, sneak'd into the grave,
A Monarch's half, and half a Harlot's slave.
Poor W—— nipt in Folly's broadest bloom,
Who praises now? his Chaplain on his Tomb.
Then take them all, oh take them to thy breast!
Thy *Magus*, Goddess! shall perform the rest."

   With that, a WIZARD OLD his *Cup* extends;
Which whoso tastes, forgets his former friends,
Sire, Ancestors, Himself. One cast his eyes
Up to a *Star*, and like Endymion dies,
A *Feather*, shooting from another's head,
Extracts his brain; and Principle is fled;
Lost is his God, his Country, ev'rything;
And nothing left but Homage to a King!
The vulgar herd turn off to roll with Hogs,
To run with Horses, or to hunt with Dogs;
But, sad example! never to escape
Their Infamy, still keep the human shape.

   But she, good Goddess, sent to ev'ry child
Firm Impudence, or Stupefaction mild;
And strait succeeded, leaving shame no room,
Cibberian forehead, or Cimmerian gloom.

   Kind Self-conceit to some her glass applies,
Which no one looks in with another's eyes:
But as the Flatt'rer or Dependant paint,
Beholds himself a Patriot, Chief, or Saint.

   On others Int'rest her gay liv'ry flings,
Int'rest, that waves on Party-colour'd wings:
Turn'd to the Sun, she casts a thousand dyes,
And, as she turns, the colours fall or rise.

   Others the Syren Sisters warble round,
And empty heads console with empty sound.

No more, alas! the voice of Fame they hear,
The balm of Dulness trickling in their ear.
Great C——, H——, P——, R——, K——,
Why all your Toils? your Sons have learn'd to sing.
How quick Ambition hastes to ridicule!
The Sire is made a Peer, the Son a Fool.

On some, a Priest succinct in amice white
Attends; all flesh is nothing in his sight!
Beeves, at his touch, at once to jelly turn,
And the huge Boar is shrunk into an Urn:
The board with specious miracles he loads,
Turns Hares to Larks, and Pigeons into Toads.
Another (for in all what one can shine?)
Explains the *Seve* and *Verdeur* of the Vine.
What cannot copious Sacrifice atone?
Thy Treufles, Perigord! thy Hams, Bayonne!
With French Libation, and Italian Strain,
Wash Bladen white, and expiate Hays's stain.
Knight lifts the head, for what are crouds undone,
To three essential Partridges in one?
Gone ev'ry blush, and silent all reproach,
Contending Princes mount them in their Coach.

Next bidding all draw near on bended knees,
The Queen confers her *Titles* and *Degrees*.
Her children first of more distinguish'd sort,
Who study Shakespeare at the Inns of Court,
Impale a Glow-worm, or Vertù profess,
Shine in the dignity of F. R. S.
Some, deep Free-masons, join the silent race
Worthy to fill Pythagoras's place:
Some Botanists, or Florists at the least,
Or issue Members of an Annual feast.
Nor past the meanest unregarded, one
Rose a Gregorian, one a Gormogon.
The last, not least in honour or applause,

Isis and Cam made Doctors of her Laws.
 Then, blessing all, " Go, Children of my care!
To Practice now from Theory repair.
All my commands are easy, short, and full:
My Sons! be proud, be selfish, and be dull.
Guard my Prerogative, assert my Throne:
This Nod confirms each Privilege your own.
The Cap and Switch be sacred to his Grace;
With Staff and Pumps the Marquis leads the Race;
From Stage to Stage the licens'd Earl may run,
Pair'd with his Fellow-Charioteer the Sun;
The learned Baron Butterflies design,
Or draw to silk Arachne's subtile line;
The Judge to dance his brother Sergeant call;
The Senator at Cricket urge the Ball;
The Bishop stow (Pontific Luxury!)
An hundred Souls of Turkeys in a pyre;
The sturdy Squire to Gallic masters stoop,
And drown his Lands and Manors in a Soupe.
Others import yet nobler arts from France,
Teach Kings to fiddle, and make Senates dance.
Perhaps more high some daring son may soar,
Proud to my list to add one Monarch more:
And nobly conscious, Princes are but things
Born for First Ministers, as Slaves for Kings,
Tyrant supreme! shall three Estates command,
And MAKE ONE MIGHTY DUNCIAD OF THE LAND!"
 More she had spoke, but yawn'd—All Nature nods:
What Mortal can resist the Yawn of Gods?
Churches and Chapels instantly it reach'd;
(St. James's first, for leaden Gilbert preach'd)
Then catch'd the Schools; the Hall scarce kept awake;
The Convocation gap'd, but could not speak:
Lost was the Nation's Sense, nor could be found,
While the long solemn Unison went round:

Wide, and more wide, it spread o'er all the realm;
Ev'n Palinurus nodded at the Helm:
The Vapour mild o'er each Committee crept;
Unfinish'd Treaties in each Office slept;
And Chiefless Armies doz'd out the Campaign;
And Navies yawn'd for Orders on the Main.

O Muse! relate (for you can tell alone,
Wits have short Memories, and Dunces none)
Relate, who first, who last resign'd to rest;
Whose Heads she partly, whose completely blest;
What Charms could Faction, what Ambition lull,
The Venal quiet, and intrance the Dull;
Till drown'd was Sense, and Shame, and Right, and
    Wrong—
O sing, and hush the Nations with thy Song!

·   ·   ·   ·   ·   ·

In vain, in vain,—the all-composing Hour
Resistless falls: the Muse obeys the Pow'r.
She comes! she comes! the sable Throne behold
Of *Night* Primæval, and of *Chaos* old!
Before her, *Fancy's* gilded clouds decay,
And all its varying Rain-bows die away.
Wit shoots in vain its momentary fires,
The meteor drops, and in a flash expires.
As one by one, at dread Medea's strain,
The sick'ning stars fade off th' ethereal plain;
As Argus' eyes, by Hermes' wand opprest,
Clos'd one by one to everlasting rest;
Thus at her felt approach, and secret might,
Art after *Art* goes out, and all is Night:
See skulking *Truth* to her old cavern fled,
Mountains of Casuistry heap'd o'er her head!
Philosophy, that lean'd on Heav'n before,
Shrinks to her second cause, and is no more.

Physic of *Metaphysic* begs defence,
And *Metaphysic* calls for aid on *Sense!*
See *Mystery* to *Mathematics* fly!
In vain! they gaze, turn giddy, rave, and die.
Religion blushing veils her sacred fires,
And unawares *Morality* expires.
Nor *public* Flame, nor *private,* dares to shine;
Nor *human* Spark is left, nor Glimpse *divine!*
Lo! thy dread Empire, chaos! is restor'd;
Light dies before thy uncreating word:
Thy hand, great Anarch! lets the curtain fall;
And Universal Darkness buries All.

John Gay
(1685–1732)

Mr. Pope's Welcome from Greece

Long hast thou, friend, been absent from thy soil,
  Like patient Ithacus at siege of Troy;
I have been witness of thy six years' toil,
  Thy daily labours and thy night's annoy,
Lost to thy native land with great turmoil,
  On the wide sea, oft threat'ning to destroy:
Methinks with thee I've trod Sigæan ground,
And heard the shores of Hellespont resound.

Did I not see thee when thou first sett'st sail
  To seek adventures fair in Homer's land?
Did I not see thy sinking spirits fail
  And wish thy bark had never left the strand?
Ev'n in mid ocean didst thou quail
  And oft lift up thy holy eye and hand,
Praying the Virgin dear and saintly choir,
Back to the port to bring thy bark entire.

Cheer up, my friend, thy dangers now are o'er;
  Methinks—nay, sure the rising coasts appear;
Hark how the guns salute from either shore
  As thy trim vessel cuts the Thames so fair:

446

Shouts answ'ring shouts from Kent and Essex roar,
    And bells break loud from ev'ry gust of air:
Bonfires do blaze, and bones and cleavers ring,
As at the coming of some mighty king.

Now pass we Gravesend with a friendy wind,
    And Tilbury's white fort, and long Blackwall;
Greenwich where dwells the friend of humankind,
    More visited than either park or hall.
Withers the good, and (with him ever join'd)
    Facetious Disney greet thee first of all:
I see his chimney smoke, and hear him say:
"Duke! that's the room for Pope, and that for Gay.

"Come in, my friends, here shall ye dine and lie,
    And here shall breakfast and here dine again,
And sup and breakfast on (if ye comply),
    For I have still some dozens of champagne."
His voice still lessens as the ship sails by;
    He waves his hand to bring us back in vain;
For now I see, I see proud London's spires;
Greenwich is lost, and Deptford Dock retires.

Oh, what a concourse swarms on yonder quay!
    The sky re-echoes with new shouts of joy:
By all this show, I ween, 'tis Lord Mayor's Day;
    I hear the voice of trumpet and hautboy.
No, now I see them near—oh, these are they
    Who come in crowds to welcome thee from Troy.
Hail to the bard whom long as lost we mourn'd,
From siege, from battle, and from storm return'd.

Of goodly dames and courteous knights I view
    The silken petticoat and broider'd vest;
Yea, peers and mighty dukes, with ribbons blue
    (True blue, fair emblem of unstained breast).
Others I see as noble and more true,

By no court badge distinguish'd from the rest:
First see I Methuen of sincerest mind,
As Arthur grave, as soft as womankind.

What lady's that to whom he gently bends?
  Who knows not her? Ah, those are Wortley's eyes.
How art thou honour'd, number'd with her friends;
  For she distinguishes the good and wise.
The sweet-tongu'd Murray near her side attends:
  Now to my heart the glance of Howard flies;
Now Hervey, fair of face, I mark full well
With thee, youth's youngest daughter, sweet Lepell.

I see two lovely sisters hand in hand,
  The fair-hair'd Martha and Teresa brown;
Madge Bellenden, the tallest of the land;
  And smiling Mary soft and fair as down.
Yonder I see the cheerful Duchess stand,
  For friendship, zeal, and blithesome humours known:
Whence that loud shout in such a hearty strain?
Why, all the Hamiltons are in her train.

See next the decent Scudamore advance
  With Winchilsea, still meditating song,
With her perhaps Miss Howe came there by chance,
  Nor knows with whom, nor why she comes along.
Far off from these see Santlow fam'd for dance,
  And frolic Bicknell, and her sister young,
With other names by me not to be nam'd,
Much lov'd in private, not in public fam'd.

But now behold the female band retire,
  And the shrill music of their voice is still'd!
Methinks I see fam'd Buckingham admire,
  That in Troy's ruins thou hast not been kill'd.
Sheffield who knows to strike the living lyre
  With hand judicious like thy Homer skill'd:

Bathurst impetuous, hastens to the coast,
Whom you and I strive who shall love the most.

See gen'rous Burlington with goodly Bruce
    (But Bruce comes wafted in a soft sedan),
Dan Prior next, belov'd by every Muse,
    And friendly Congreve, unreproachful man!
(Oxford by Cunningham hath sent excuse),
    See hearty Watkins come with cup and can;
And Lewis who has never friend forsaken;
And Laughton whispering asks—"Is Troy Town taken?"

Earl Warwick comes, of free and honest mind,
    Bold, gen'rous Craggs whose heart was ne'er
        disguis'd,
Ah, why, sweet St. John cannot I thee find?
    St. John for ev'ry social virtue priz'd—
Alas! to foreign climates he's confin'd,
    Or else to see thee here I well surmis'd;
Thou too, my Swift, dost breathe Bœotian air,
When wilt thou bring back wit and humour here?

Harcourt I see for eloquence renown'd,
    The mouth of justice, oracle of law!
Another Simon is beside him found,
    Another Simon like as straw to straw.
How Lansdown smiles with lasting laurel crown'd!
    What mitred prelate there commands our awe?
See Rochester approving nods the head,
And ranks one modern with the mighty dead.

Carlton and Chandos thy arrival grace;
    Hanmer, whose eloquence the unbiass'd sways;
Harley, whose goodness opens in his face
    And shows his heart the seat where virtue stays.
Ned Blount advances next with hasty pace,
    In haste, yet saunt'ring, hearty in his ways.

I see the friendly Carylls come by dozens,
Their wives, their uncles, daughters, sons, and cousins.

Arbuthnot there I see, in physic's art,
    As Galen learned or fam'd Hippocrate;
Whose company drives sorrow from the heart
    As all disease his med'cines dissipate:
Kneller amid the triumph bears his part
    Who could (were mankind lost) anew create;
What can th' extent of his vast soul confine?
A painter, critic, engineer, divine!

Thee Jervas hails, robust and debonair,
    "Now have we conquer'd Homer, friends!" he cries;
Dartneuf, gay joker, joyous Ford is there,
    And wond'ring Maine so fat, with laughing eyes,
(Gay, Maine, and Cheney, boon companions dear,
    Gay fat, Maine fatter, Cheney huge of size),
Yea, Dennis, Gildon (hearing thou hast riches),
And honest hatless Cromwell with red breeches.

O Wanley, whence com'st thou with shorten'd hair,
    And visage from thy shelves with dust besprent?
"Forsooth," quoth he, "from placing Homer there,
    As ancients to compyle is mine intent;
Of ancients only hath Lord Harley care,
    But hither me hath my meeke lady sent:—
In manuscript of Greek rede we thilke same,
But book reprint best plesyth my gude dame."

Yonder I see among th' expecting crowd
    Evans with laugh jocose and tragic Young;
High buskin'd Booth, grave Mawbert, wand'ring Frowde
    And Titcombe's belly waddles slow along.
See Digby faints at Southerne talking loud,
    Yea, Steele and Tickell mingle in the throng,

Tickell, whose skiff (in partnership they say)
Set forth for Greece, but founder'd on the way.

Lo, the two Doncastles in Berkshire known!
　Lo, Bickford, Fortescue of Devon land!
Lo, Tooker, Eckershall, Sykes, Rawlinson!
　See hearty Morley take thee by the hand!
Ayrs, Graham, Buckridge, joy thy voyage done;
　But who can count the leaves, the stars, the sand?
Lo, Stonor, Fenton, Caldwell, Ward, and Broome;
Lo, thousands more, but I want rhyme and room!

How lov'd, how honour'd thou! yet be not vain!
　And sure thou art not, for I hear thee say—
"All this, my friends, I owe to Homer's strain,
　On whose strong pinions I exalt my lay.
What from contending cities did he gain?
　And what rewards his grateful country pay?
None, none were paid—why then all this for me?
These honours, Homer, had been just to thee."

FROM *The Shepherd's Week*

THURSDAY, OR, THE SPELL

HOBNELIA

　Hobnelia seated in a dreary Vale,
In pensive Mood rehears'd her piteous Tale,
Her piteous Tale the Winds in Sighs bemoan,
And pining Eccho answers Groan for Groan.

　I rue the Day, a rueful Day I trow,
The woful Day, a Day indeed of Woe!
When *Lubberkin* to Town his Cattle drove,

A Maiden fine bedight he hapt to love;
The Maiden fine bedight his Love retains,
And for the Village he forsakes the Plains.
Return, my *Lubberkin,* these Ditties hear;
Spells will I try, and Spells shall ease my Care.
   With my sharp Heel I three times mark the Ground,
And turn me thrice around, around, around.

When first the Year, I heard the Cuckow sing,
And call with welcome Note the budding Spring,
I straitway set a running with such Haste,
Deb'rah that won the Smock scarce ran so fast.
'Till spent for lack of Breath, quite weary grown,
Upon a rising Bank I sat adown,
Then doff'd my Shoe, and by my Troth, I swear,
Therein I spy'd this yellow frizled Hair,
As like to *Lubberkin's* in Curl and Hue,
As if upon his comely Pate it grew.
   With my sharp Heel I three times mark the Ground,
And turn me thrice around, around, around.

At Eve last *Midsummer* no Sleep I sought,
But to the Field a Bag of Hemp-seed brought,
I scatter'd round the Seed on ev'ry side,
And three times in a trembling Accent cry'd.
This Hempseed with my Virgin Hands I sow,
Who shall my True-love be, the Crop shall mow.
I strait look'd back, and if my Eyes speak Truth,
With his keen Scythe behind me came the Youth.
   With my sharp Heel I three times mark the Ground,
And turn me thrice around, around, around.

Last *Valentine,* the Day when Birds of Kind
Their Paramours with mutual Chirpings find;
I rearly rose, just at the break of Day,
Before the Sun had chas'd the Stars away;

A-field I went, amid the Morning Dew
To milk my Kine (for so should Huswives do)
Thee first I spy'd, and the first Swain we see,
In spite of Fortune shall our True-love be;
See, *Lubberkin*, each Bird his Partner take,
And can'st thou then thy Sweetheart dear forsake?
   With my sharp Heel I three times mark the Ground,
And turn me thrice around, around, around.

   Last *May-day* fair I search'd to find a Snail
That might my secret Lover's Name reveal;
Upon a Gooseberry Bush a Snail I found,
For always Snails near sweetest Fruit abound.
I seiz'd the Vermine, home I quickly sped,
And on the Hearth the milk-white Embers spread.
Slow crawl'd the Snail, and if I right can spell,
In the soft Ashes mark'd a curious *L*:
Oh, may this wondrous Omen lucky prove!
For *L* is found in *Lubberkin* and *Love*.
   With my sharp Heel I three times mark the Ground,
And turn me thrice around, around, around.

   Two Hazel-Nuts I threw into the Flame,
And to each Nut I gave a Sweet-heart's Name.
This with the loudest Bounce me sore amaz'd,
That in a Flame of brightest Colour blaz'd.
As blaz'd the Nut so may thy Passion grow,
For 'twas *thy Nut* that did so brightly glow.
   With my sharp Heel I three times mark the Ground,
And turn me thrice around, around, around.

   As Peascods once I pluck'd, I chanc'd to see
One that was closely fill'd with three times three,
Which when I crop'd I safely home convey'd,
And o'er my Door the Spell in secret laid.
My Wheel I turn'd, and sung a Ballad new,

While from the Spindle I the Fleeces drew;
The Latch mov'd up, when who should first come in,
But in his proper Person, —— *Lubberkin.*
I broke my Yarn surpriz'd the Sight to see.
Sure Sign that he would break his Word with me.
Eftsoons I join'd it with my wonted Slight,
So may again his Love with mine unite!
   With my sharp Heel I three times mark the Ground,
And turn me thrice around, around, around.

   This *Lady-fly* I take from off the Grass,
Whose spotted Back might scarlet Red surpass:
Fly, Lady-bird, *North, South, or East or West,*
Fly where the Man is found that I love best.
He leaves my Hand, see to the *West* he's flown,
To call my True-love from the faithless Town.
   With my sharp Heel I three times mark the Ground,
And turn me thrice around, around, around.

   This mellow Pippin, which I pare around,
My Shepherd's Name shall flourish on the Ground.
I fling th' unbroken Paring o'er my Head,
Upon the Grass a perfect *L* is read;
Yet on my Heart a fairer *L* is seen
Than what the Paring marks upon the Green.
   With my sharp Heel I three times mark the Ground,
And turn me thrice around, around, around.

   This Pippin shall another Tryal make,
See from the Core two Kernels brown I take;
This on my Cheek for *Lubberkin* is worn,
And *Boobyclod* on t' other side is born.
But *Boobyclod* soon drops upon the Ground,
A certain Token that his Love's unfound,
While *Lubberkin* sticks firmly to the last;
Oh were his Lips to mine but join'd so fast!

With my sharp Heel I three times mark the Ground,
And turn me thrice around, around, around.

As *Lubberkin* once slept beneath a Tree,
I twitch'd his dangling Garter from his Knee;
He wist not when the hempen String I drew,
Now mine I quickly doff of Inkle Blue;
Together fast I tye the Garters twain,
And while I knit the Knot repeat this Strain.
Three times a True-love's Knot I tye secure,
Firm be the Knot, firm may his Love endure.
With my sharp Heel I three times mark the Ground,
And turn me thrice around, around, around.

As I was wont, I trudg'd last Market-Day
To Town, with New-laid Eggs preserv'd in Hay.
I made my Market long before 'twas Night,
My Purse grew heavy and my Basket light.
Strait to the Pothecary's Shop I went,
And in Love-Powder all my Mony spent;
Behap what will, next Sunday after Prayers,
When to the Ale-house *Lubberkin* repairs,
These *Golden Flies* into his Mug I'll throw,
And soon the Swain with fervent Love shall glow.
With my sharp Heel I three times mark the Ground,
And turn me thrice around, around, around.

But hold—our *Light-Foot* barks, and cocks his Ears,
O'er yonder Stile see *Lubberkin* appears.
He comes, he comes, *Hobnelia's* not bewray'd,
Nor shall she crown'd with Willow die a Maid.
He vows, he swears, he'll give me a green Gown,
Oh dear! I fall *adown, adown, adown!*

The Birth of the Squire

AN ECLOGUE IN IMITATION
OF THE POLLIO OF VIRGIL

Ye sylvan Muses, loftier strains recite,
Not all in shades, and humble cotts delight.
Hark! the bells ring; along the distant grounds
The driving gales convey the swelling sounds;
Th' attentive swain, forgetful of his work,
With gaping wonder, leans upon his fork.
What sudden news alarms the waking morn?
To the glad Squire a hopeful heir is born.
Mourn, mourn, ye stags; and all ye beasts of the chace,
This hour destruction brings on all your race:
See the pleas'd tenants duteous off'rings bear,
Turkeys and geese and grocer's sweetest ware;
With the new health the pond'rous tankard flows,
And old *October* reddens ev'ry nose.
Beagles and spaniels round his cradle stand,
Kiss his moist lip and gently lick his hand;
He joys to hear the shrill horn's ecchoing sounds,
And learns to lisp the names of all the hounds.
With frothy ale to make his cup o'er-flow,
Barley shall in paternal acres grow:
The bee shall sip the fragrant dew from the flow'rs,
To give metheglin for his morning hours;
For him the clustring hop shall climb the poles,
And his own orchard sparkle in his bowles.
　　His Sire's exploits he now with wonder hears,
The monstrous tales indulge his greedy ears;
How when youth strung his nerves and warm'd his
　　　　veins,

He rode the mighty *Nimrod* of the plains:
He leads the staring infant through the hall,
Points out the horny spoils that grace the wall;
Tells, how this stag thro' three whole Countys fled,
What rivers swam, where bay'd and where he bled.
Now he the wonders of the fox repeats,
Describes the desp'rate chase, and all his cheats;
How in one day beneath his furious speed,
He tir'd sev'n coursers of the fleetest breed;
How high the pale he leapt, how wide the ditch,
When the hound tore the haunches of the witch!
These storys which descend from son to son,
The forward boy shall one day make his own.

　　Ah, too fond mother, think the time draws nigh,
That calls the darling from thy tender eye;
How shall his spirit brook the rigid rules,
And the long tyranny of grammar schools?
Let younger brothers o'er dull authors plod,
Lash'd into *Latin* by the tingling rod;
No, let him never feel that smart disgrace:
Why should he wiser prove than all his race?

　　When rip'ning youth with down o'ershades his chin,
And ev'ry female eye incites to sin;
The milk-maid (thoughtless of her future shame)
With smacking lip shall raise his guilty flame;
The dairy, barn, the hay-loft and the grove
Shall oft' be conscious of their stolen love.
But think, *Priscilla,* on that dreadful time,
When pangs and watry qualms shall own thy crime;
How wilt thou tremble when thy nipple's prest,
To see the white drops bathe thy swelling breast!
Nine moons shall publickly divulge her shame,
And the young Squire forestal a father's name.

　　When twice twelve times the reaper's sweeping hand
With level'd harvests has bestrown the land,

On fam'd St. *Hubert's* feast, his winding horn
Shall cheer the joyful hound and wake the morn:
This memorable day his eager speed
Shall urge with bloody heel the rising steed.
O check the foamy bit, nor tempt thy fate,
Think on the murders of a five-bar gate!
Yet prodigal of life, the leap he tries,
Low in the dust his groveling honour lies,
Headlong he falls, and on the rugged stone
Distorts his neck, and cracks the collar bone;
O vent'rous youth, thy thirst of game allay,
Mayst thou survive the perils of this day!
He shall survive; and in late years be sent
To snore away Debates in *Parliament*.

  The time shall come, when his more solid sense
With nod important shall the laws dispense;
A Justice with grave Justices shall sit,
He praise their wisdom, they admire his wit.
No greyhound shall attend the tenant's pace,
No rusty gun the farmer's chimney grace;
Salmons shall leave their covers void of fear,
Nor dread the thievish net or triple spear;
Poachers shall tremble at his awful name,
Whom vengeance now o'ertakes for murder'd game.

  Assist me, *Bacchus*, and ye drunken Pow'rs,
To sing his friendships and his midnight hours!
  Why dost thou glory in thy strength of beer,
Why dost thou glory in thy strength of beer,
Firm-cork'd, and mellow'd till the twentieth year;
Brew'd or when *Phœbus* warms the fleecy sign,
Or when his languid rays in *Scorpio* shine.
Think on the mischiefs which from hence have sprung!
It arms with curses dire the wrathful tongue;
Foul scandal to the lying lip affords,
And prompts the mem'ry with injurious words.

O where is wisdom, when by this o'erpower'd?
The State is censur'd, and the maid deflower'd!
And wilt thou still, O Squire, brew ale so strong?
Hear then the dictates of prophetic song.
  Methinks I see him in his hall appear,
Where the long table floats in clammy beer,
'Midst mugs and glasses shatter'd o'er the floor,
Dead-drunk his servile crew supinely snore;
Triumphant, o'er the prostrate brutes he stands,
The mighty bumper trembles in his hands;
Boldly he drinks, and like his glorious Sires,
In copious gulps of potent ale expires.

FROM *The Beggar's Opera*

SONGS

If any Wench *Venus's* Girdle wear,
  Though she be never so ugly,
Lillies and Roses will quickly appear,
  And her face look wond'rous smuggly.
Beneath the left Ear, so fit but a Cord,
  (A Rope so charming a Zone is!)
The Youth in his Cart hath the Air of a Lord,
  And we cry, There dies an *Adonis!*

Were I laid on *Greenland's* Coast,
  And in my Arms embrac'd my Lass;
Warm amidst eternal Frost,
  Too soon the Half Year's Night would pass.
Were I sold on *Indian* Soil,
  Soon as the burning Day was clos'd,
I could mock the sultry Toil,

When on my Charmer's Breast repos'd.
And I would love you all the Day,
Every Night would kiss and play,
If with me you'd fondly stray
Over the Hills and far away.

Before the Barn-Door crowing,
    The Cock by Hens attended,
His Eyes around him throwing,
    Stands for a while suspended:
Then One he singles from the Crew,
    And cheers the happy Hen;
With how do you do, and how do you do,
    And how do you do again.

Thus when the Swallow, seeking Prey,
    Within the Sash is closely pent,
His Consort with bemoaning Lay,
    Without sits pining for th' Event.
Her chatt'ring Lovers all around her skim;
She heeds them not (poor Bird) her Soul's with him.

Isaac Watts

(1674–1748)

The Sluggard

'Tis the voice of the Sluggard; I heard him complain,
"You have wak'd me too soon; I must slumber again."
As the door on its hinges, so he on his bed,
Turns his sides, and his shoulders, and his heavy head.

"A little more sleep, and a little more slumber,"
Thus he wastes half his days, and his hours without
     number,
And when he gets up, he sits folding his hands,
Or walks about sant'ring, or trifling he stands.

I pass'd by his garden, and saw the wild brier,
The thorn and the thistle grow broader and higher;
The clothes than hang on him are turning to rags;
And his money still wastes, till he starves, or he begs.

I made him a visit, still hoping to find
He had took better care for improving his mind:
He told me his dreams, talk'd of eating and drinking;
But he scarce reads his Bible, and never loves thinking.

Said I then to my heart, "Here's a lesson for me,
That man's but a picture of what I might be.
But thanks to my friends for their care in my breeding,
Who taught me betimes to love working and reading."

461

ISAAC WATTS

A Cradle Hymn

Hush! my dear, lie still and slumber;
Holy angels guard thy bed!
Heav'nly blessings without number
Gently falling on thy head.

Sleep, my babe; thy food and raiment,
House and home thy friends provide,
All without thy care or payment;
All thy wants are well supply'd.

How much better thou'rt attended
Than the Son of God could be,
When from heaven he descended,
And became a child like thee.

Soft and easy is thy cradle:
Coarse and hard thy Saviour lay;
When his birth-place was a stable,
And his softest bed was hay.

Blessed Babe! what glorious features,
Spotless fair, divinely bright!
Must he dwell with brutal creatures?
How could angels bear the sight?

Was there nothing but a manger
Cursed sinners could afford,
To receive the heav'nly stranger?
Did they thus affront their Lord?

Soft, my child; I did not chide thee,
Tho' my song might sound too hard;

'Tis thy $\genfrac{}{}{0pt}{}{\text{mother}^1}{\text{nurse}}$ that sits beside thee,
And her arm shall by thy guard.

Yet to read the shameful story,
How the Jews abus'd their King,
How they serv'd the Lord of glory,
Makes me angry while I sing.

See the kinder shepherds round him,
Telling wonders from the sky;
There they sought him, there they found him,
With his virgin Mother by.

See the lovely Babe a-dressing;
Lovely Infant, how he smil'd!
When he wept, the Mother's blessing
Sooth'd and hush'd the holy child.

Lo, he slumbers in his manger,
Where the horned oxen feed;
Peace, my Darling! here's no danger,
Here's no ox anear thy bed.

'Twas to save thee, child, from dying,
Save my dear from burning flame,
Bitter grones, and endless crying,
That my blest Redeemer came.

Mayst thou live to know and fear him,
Trust and love him all thy days!
Then go dwell forever near him,
See his face and sing his praise!

---

[1] Here you may use the words, brother, sister, neighbour, friend, etc.—WATTS.

I could give thee thousand kisses,
Hoping what I most desire:
Not a mother's fondest wishes,
Can to greater joys aspire.

Man Frail and God Eternal

Our God, our Help in Ages past,
Our Hope for Years to come,
Our Shelter from the Stormy Blast,
And our eternal Home.

Under the Shadow of thy Throne
Thy Saints have dwelt secure;
Sufficient is thine Arm alone,
And our Defence is sure.

Before the Hills in order stood,
Or Earth receiv'd her Frame,
From everlasting Thou art God,
To endless years the same.

Thy Word commands our Flesh to Dust,
Return ye sons of Men:
All Nations rose from Earth at first,
And turn to Earth again.

A thousand ages in thy Sight
Are like an Evening gone;
Short as the Watch that ends the Night
Before the rising Sun.

The busy Tribes of Flesh and Blood
With all their Lives and Cares
Are carried downwards by thy Flood,
And lost in following Years.

Time like an ever-rolling Stream
    Bears all its Sons away;
They fly forgotten as a Dream
    Dies at the opening Day.

Like flow'ry Fields the Nations stand
    Pleas'd with the Morning-light;
The Flowers beneath the Mower's Hand
    Ly withering e'er 'tis Night.

Our God, our Help in Ages past,
    Our Hope for Years to come,
Be thou our Guard while Troubles last,
    And our eternal Home.

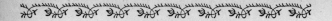

John Byrom

(1692–1763)

A Hymn for Christmas Day

Christians awake! Salute the happy Morn
Whereon the *Saviour* of the World was born!
Rise, to adore the Mystery of Love,
Which Hosts of Angels chanted from above;
With them the joyful Tidings first begun
Of *God* Incarnate, and the Virgin's Son.
Then to the watchful Shepherds it was told,
Who heard th'Angelic Herald's Voice: "Behold!
I bring good tidings of a *Saviour's* Birth
To you and all the Nations upon Earth;
This Day hath *God* fulfill'd his promis'd Word;
This Day is born a *Saviour, Christ* the *Lord.*
In David's City, Shepherds, ye shall find
The long-foretold Redeemer of Mankind;
Wrapt up in swaddling-clothes, the Babe Divine
Lies in a Manger; this shall be your Sign."
He spake, and straightway the Celestial Choir
In Hymns of Joy, unknown before, conspire;
The Praises of Redeeming Love they sung,
And Heav'ns whole Orb with Hallelujahs rung.
"*God's* highest Glory" was their Anthem still,
"Peace upon Earth, and mutual *Goodwill!*"
To *Bethlehem* straight th'enlighten'd Shepherds ran
To see the wonder *God* had wrought for Man;
And found with *Joseph* and the blessed Maid,

Her *Son*, the *Saviour*, in a Manger laid.
Amaz'd, the wond'rous Story they proclaim,
The first Apostles of his Infant Fame;
While *Mary* keeps and ponders in her Heart
The heav'nly Vision which the Swains impart.
They to their Flocks, still praising *God*, return,
And their glad Hearts within their Bosoms burn.
    Let us, like these good Shepherds, then, employ
Our grateful Voices to proclaim the Joy;
Like *Mary*, let us ponder in our Mind
God's wond'rous love in saving lost Mankind.
Artless and watchful as these favour'd Swains,
While Virgin Meekness in the Heart remains,
Trace we the Babe, who has retriev'd our Loss,
From his poor Manger to His bitter Cross;
Treading His Steps, assisted by His Grace,
Till Man's first heav'nly State again takes Place!
Then, may we hope, th'Angelic Thrones among,
To sing, redeem'd, a glad Triumphal Song.
He That was born upon this joyful Day
Around us all His Glory shall display;
Sav'd by His Love, incessant we shall sing
Of Angels and of Angel-men the King.

Charles Wesley
(1707–1788)

Wrestling Jacob

Come O Thou Traveller unknown,
　Whom still I hold but cannot see,
My company before is gone,
　And I am left alone with Thee;
With Thee all night I mean to stay,
And wrestle till the break of day.

I need not tell Thee who I am,
　My misery or sin declare,
Thyself hast call'd me by my name,
　Look on Thy hands, and read it there;
But who, I ask Thee, who art Thou?
Tell me Thy name, and tell me now.

In vain Thou strugglest to get free,
　I never will unloose my hold;
Art Thou the Man that died for me?
　The secret of Thy love unfold;
Wrestling I will not let Thee go
Till I Thy name, Thy nature know.

Wilt Thou not yet to me reveal
　Thy new, unutterable name?
Tell me, I still beseech Thee, tell;
　To know it not resolved I am;
Wrestling I will not let Thee go
Till I Thy name, Thy nature know.

'Tis all in vain to hold Thy tongue,
　Or touch the hollow of my thigh;
Though every sinew be unstrung,
　Out of my arms Thou shalt not fly;
Wrestling I will not let Thee go
Till I Thy name, Thy nature know.

What though my shrinking flesh complain,
　And murmur to contend so long,
I rise superior to my pain,
　When I am weak then I am strong;
And when my all of strength shall fail,
I shall with the God-man prevail.

My strength is gone, my nature dies,
　I sink beneath Thy weighty hand,
Faint to revive, and fall to rise;
　I fall, and yet by faith I stand,
I stand, and will not let Thee go,
Till I Thy name, Thy nature know.

Yield to me now; for I am weak,
　But confident is my despair:
Speak to my heart, in blessings speak,
　Be conquer'd by my instant prayer;
Speak, or Thou never hence shalt move,
And tell me if Thy name is Love.

'Tis Love! 'tis Love! Thou diedst for me;
　I hear Thy whisper in my heart:
The morning breaks, the shadows flee:
　Pure *Universal Love* Thou art;
To me, to all Thy bowels move;
Thy nature, and Thy name is Love.

My prayer hath power with God; the grace
　Unspeakable I now receive,

Through faith I see Thee face to face;
   I see Thee face to face, and live:
In vain I have not wept and strove;
Thy nature, and Thy name is Love.

I know Thee, Saviour, who Thou art,
   Jesus, the feeble sinner's Friend;
Nor wilt Thou with the night depart,
   But stay, and love me to the end;
Thy mercies never shall remove;
Thy nature, and Thy name is Love.

The Sun of Righteousness on me
   Hath rose with healing in His wings;
Wither'd my nature's strength, from Thee
   My soul its life and succour brings;
My help is laid up all above;
Thy nature, and Thy name is Love.

Contented now upon my thigh
   I halt, till life's short journey end;
All helplessness, all weakness, I
   On Thee alone for strength depend,
Nor have I power from Thee to move;
Thy nature, and Thy name is Love.

Lame as I am, I take the prey,
   Hell, earth, and sin with ease o'ercome;
I leap for joy, pursue my way,
   And as a bounding hart fly home,
Through all eternity to prove,
Thy nature, and Thy name is Love.

A Morning Hymn

Christ, whose glory fills the skies,
    Christ, the true, the only Light,
Sun of Righteousness, arise,
    Triumph o'er the shades of night:
Dayspring from on high, be near;
Daystar, in my heart appear.

Dark and cheerless is the morn,
    Unaccompanied by Thee;
Joyless is the day's return,
    Till Thy mercy's beams I see;
Till they inward light impart,
Glad my eyes, and warm my heart.

Visit then this soul of mine;
    Pierce the gloom of sin and grief;
Fill me, Radiancy divine;
    Scatter all my unbelief:
More and more Thyself display,
Shining to the perfect Day.

In Temptation

Jesu, Lover of my soul,
    Let me to Thy bosom fly,
While the nearer waters roll,
    While the tempest still is high.
Hide me, O my Saviour, hide,
    Till the storm of life is past:
Safe into the haven guide;
    O receive my soul at last.

Other refuge have I none:
   Hangs my helpless soul on Thee.
Leave, ah leave me not alone,
   Still support and comfort me.
All my trust on Thee is stayed,
   All my help from Thee I bring;
Cover my defenceless head
   With the shadow of Thy wing.

Wilt Thou not regard my call?
   Wilt Thou not accept my prayer?
Lo, I sink, I faint, I fall!
   Lo, on Thee I cast my care.
Reach me out Thy gracious hand!
   While I of Thy strength receive,
Hoping against hope I stand,
   Dying, and behold I live!

Thou, O Christ, art all I want;
   More than all in Thee I find.
Raise the fallen, cheer the faint,
   Heal the sick, and lead the blind.
Just and holy is Thy Name;
   I am all unrighteousness:
False and full of sin I am;
   Thou art full of truth and grace.

Plenteous grace with Thee is found,
   Grace to cover all my sin:
Let the healing streams abound,
   Make and keep me pure within.
Thou of Life the Fountain art:
   Freely let me take of Thee:
Spring Thou up within my heart
   Rise to all eternity.

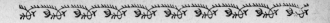

Matthew Green

(1696–1737)

FROM *The Spleen*

But now more serious let me grow,
And what I think, my Memmius, know.

Th' enthusiast's hopes, and raptures wild,
Have never yet my reason foil'd.
His springy soul dilates like air,
When free from weight of ambient care;
And, hush'd in meditations deep,
Slides into dreams, as when asleep;
Then, fond of new discov'ries grown,
Proves a Columbus of her own,
Disdains the narrow bounds of place,
And thro' the wilds of endless space,
Borne up on metaphysic wings,
Chases light forms, and shadowy things;
And in the vague excursion caught,
Brings home some rare exotic thought:
The melancholy man such dreams,
As brightest evidence esteems;
Fain would he see some distant scene
Suggested by his restless spleen,
And fancy's telescope applies
With tinctur'd glass to cheat his eyes.
Such thoughts, as love the gloom of night,
I close examine by the light.
For who, tho' brib'd by gain to lye,

Dare sun-beam written truths deny,
And execute plain common sense
On faith's mere hearsay evidence?

That superstition mayn't create,
And club its ills with those of fate,
I many a notion take to task,
Made dreadful by its visor-mask:
Thus scruple, spasm of the mind,
Is cur'd, and certainty I find;
Since optic reason shews me plain
I dreaded spectres of the brain;
And legendary fears are gone,
Tho' in tenacious childhood sown.
Thus in opinions I commence
Freeholder in the proper sense,
And neither suit nor service do,
Nor homage to pretenders shew,
Who boast themselves by spurious roll
Lords of the manor of the soul;
Preferring sense, from chin that's bare,
To nonsense thron'd in whisker'd hair.

To thee, Creator uncreate!
O Entium Ens divinely great!—
Hold, Muse, nor melting pinions try,
Nor near the blazing glory fly,
Nor straining break thy feeble bow,
Unfeather'd arrows far to throw;
Thro' fields unknown nor madly stray,
Where no ideas mark the way;
With tender eyes, and colours faint,
And trembling hands forbear to paint.
Who features veil'd by light can hit?
Where can, what has no outline, sit?
My soul, the vain attempt forego,

Thyself, the fitter subject, know.
He wisely shuns the bold extreme,
Who soon lays by th' unequal theme,
Nor runs, with wisdom's Sirens caught,
On quick-sand swallowing shipwreckt thought;
But, conscious of his distance, gives
Mute praise, and humble negatives.
In one, no object of our sight,
Immutable and infinite,
Who can't be cruel, or unjust,
Calm and resign'd, I fix my trust;
To him my past and present state
I owe, and must my future fate.
A stranger into life I'm come,
Dying may be our going home,
Transported here by angry fate,
The convicts of a prior state:
Hence I no anxious thoughts bestow
On matters, I can never know.
Thro life's foul ways, like vagrant, pass'd,
He'll grant a settlement at last;
And with sweet ease the wearied crown,
By leave to lay his being down.
If doom'd to dance th' eternal round
Of life, no sooner lost than found;
And dissolution soon to come,
Like spunge, wipes out life's present sum,
But can't our state of pow'r bereave
An endless series to receive:
Then if hard dealt with here by fate,
We ballance in another state,
And consciousness must go along,
And sign th' acquittance for the wrong;
He for his creatures must decree
More happiness than misery,

Or be supposed to create,
Curious to try, what 'tis to hate,
And do an act, which rage infers,
'Cause lameness halts, or blindness errs.

Thus, thus I steer my bark, and sail
On even keel with gentle gale.
At helm I make my reason sit,
My crew of passions all submit.
If dark and blust'ring prove some nights
Philosophy puts forth her lights;
Experience holds the cautious glass,
To shun the breakers, as I pass;
And frequent throws the wary lead,
To see what dangers may be hid.
And once in seven years I'm seen
At Bath, or Tunbridge to careen.
Tho' pleas'd to see the dolphins play,
I mind my compass and my way;
With store sufficient for relief
And wisely still prepar'd to reef;
Nor wanting the dispersive bowl
Of cloudy weather in the soul,
I make (may heaven propitious send
Such wind and weather to the end)
Neither becalm'd, nor over-blown,
Life's voyage to the world unknown.

(Lines 716–end)

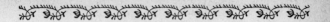

John Dyer

(1700?–1758)

FROM *The Fleece*

Ah gentle shepherd, thine the lot to tend,
Of all, that feel distress, the most assail'd,
Feeble, defenceless: lenient be thy care:
But spread around thy tend'rest diligence
In flow'ry spring-time, when the new-dropt lamb,
Tott'ring with weakness by his mother's side,
Feels the fresh world about him; and each thorn,
Hillock, or furrow, trips his feeble feet:
O guard his meek sweet innocence from all
Th'innum'rous ills, that rush around his life,
Mark the quick kite, with beak and talons prone,
Circling the skies to snatch him from the plain;
Observe the lurking crows; beware the brake;
There the sly fox the careless minute waits;
Nor trust thy neighbour's dog, nor earth, nor sky;
Thy bosom to a thousand cares divide.

(Lines 410–25)

Grongar Hill

Silent Nymph, with curious eye!
Who, the purple ev'ning, lie
On the mountain's lonely van,

Beyond the noise of busy man,
Painting fair the form of things,
While the yellow linnet sings,
Or the tuneful nightingale
Charms the forest with her tale;
Come with all thy various hues,
Come, and aid thy sister Muse;
Now while Phœbus riding high,
Gives lustre to the land and sky,
Grongar Hill invites my song.
Draw the landskip bright and strong;
Grongar, in whose mossy cells,
Sweetly-musing Quiet dwells;
Grongar, in whose silent shade,
For the modest Muses made,
So oft I have the evening still,
At the fountain of a rill,
Sate upon a flow'ry bed,
With my hand beneath my head,
While stray'd my eyes o'er Towy's flood,
Over mead, and over wood,
From house to house, from hill to hill,
Till Contemplation had her fill.

About his chequer'd sides I wind,
And leave his brooks and meads behind,
And groves, and grottoes where I lay,
And vistoes shooting beams of day:
Wide and wider spreads the vale,
As circles on a smooth canal:
The mountains round, unhappy fate!
Sooner or later, of all height,
Withdraw their summits from the skies,
And lessen as the others rise:
Still the prospect wider spreads,
Adds a thousand woods and meads,

Still it widens, widens still,
And sinks the newly-risen hill.

    Now I gain the mountain's brow,
What a landskip lies below!
No clouds, no vapours intervene,
But the gay, the open scene
Does the face of nature show
In all the hues of heaven's bow!
And swelling to embrace the light,
Spreads around beneath the sight.

    Old castles on the cliff arise,
Proudly tow'ring in the skies!
Rushing from the woods, the spires
Seem from hence ascending fires!
Half his beams Apollo sheds
On the yellow mountain-heads!
Gilds the fleeces of the flocks;
And glitters on the broken rocks!

    Below me trees unnumber'd rise,
Beautiful in various dyes:
The gloomy pine, the poplar blue,
The yellow beech, the sable yew,
The slender fir, that taper grows,
The sturdy oak, with wide-spread boughs,
And beyond the purple grove,
Haunt of Phillis, queen of love!
Gaudy as the op'ning dawn,
Lies a long and level lawn
On which a dark hill, steep and high,
Holds and charms the wand'ring eye!
Deep are his feet in Towy's flood,
His sides are cloath'd with waving wood,
And ancient towers crown his brow,
That cast an awful look below;
Whose ragged walls the ivy creeps,

And with her arms from falling keeps;
So both a safety from the wind
On mutual dependence find.

    'Tis now the raven's bleak abode;
'Tis now th'apartment of the toad;
And there the fox securely feeds;
And there the pois'nous adder breeds,
Conceal'd in ruins, moss, and weeds;
While, ever and anon, there falls
Huge heaps of hoary moulder'd walls.
Yet time has seen, that lifts the low,
And level lays the lofty brow,
Has seen this broken pile compleat,
Big with the vanity of state:
But transient is the smile of fate!
A little rule, a little sway,
A sunbeam in a winter's day,
Is all the proud and mighty have
Between the cradle and the grave.

    And see the rivers how they run
Thro' woods and meads, in shade and sun,
Sometimes swift, and sometimes slow,
Wave succeeding wave, they go
A various journey to the deep,
Like human life to endless sleep!
Thus is nature's vesture wrought,
To instruct our wand'ring thought;
Thus she dresses green and gay,
To disperse our cares away.

    Ever charming, ever new,
When will the landskip tire the view!
The fountain's fall, the river's flow,
The woody vallies, warm and low;
The windy summit, wild and high,
Roughly rushing on the sky!

The pleasant seat, the ruin'd tow'r,
The naked rock, the shady bow'r;
The town and village, dome and farm,
Each gives each a double charm,
As pearls upon a Æthiop's arm.

  See on the mountain's southern side,
Where the prospect opens wide,
Where the ev'ning gilds the tide;
How close and small the hedges lie!
What streaks of meadows cross the eye!
A step, methinks, may pass the stream,
So little distant dangers seem;
So we mistake the future's face,
Ey'd thro' hope's deluding glass;
As yon summits soft and fair,
Clad in colours of the air,
Which, to those who journey near,
Barren, brown, and rough appear;
Still we tread the same coarse way;
The present's still a cloudy day.

  O may I with myself agree,
And never covet what I see.
Content me with an humble shade,
My passions tam'd, my wishes laid;
For while our wishes wildly roll,
We banish quiet from the soul:
'Tis thus the busy beat the air;
And misers gather wealth and care.

  Now, ev'n now, my joys run high,
As on the mountain turf I lie;
While the wanton Zephyr sings,
And in the vale perfumes his wings;
While the waters murmur deep;
While the shepherd charms his sheep;
While the birds unbounded fly,

And with musick fill the sky,
Now, ev'n now, my joys run high.
　　Be full, ye courts, be great who will;
Search for Peace with all your skill:
Open wide the lofty door,
Seek her on the marble floor.
In vain you search, she is not there;
In vain you search the domes of care!
Grass and flowers Quiet treads,
On the meads and mountain-heads,
Along with Pleasure, close ally'd,
Ever by each other's side:
And often, by the murm'ring rill,
Hears the thrush, while all is still,
Within the groves of Grongar Hill.

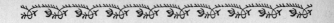

James Thomson

(1700–1748)

FROM *The Seasons*

From SPRING

As rising from the vegetable World
My Theme ascends, with equal Wing ascend,
My panting Muse; and hark, how loud the Woods
Invite you forth in all your gayest Trim.
Lend me your Song, ye Nightingales! oh pour
The mazy-running Soul of Melody
Into my varied Verse! while I deduce,
From the first Note the hollow Cuckoo sings,
The Symphony of Spring, and touch a Theme
Unknown to Fame, *the Passion of the Groves.*

When first the Soul of Love is sent abroad,
Warm thro the vital Air, and on the Heart
Harmonious seizes, the gay Troops begin,
In gallant Thought, to plume the painted Wing;
And try again the long-forgotten Strain,
At first faint-warbled. But no sooner grows
The soft Infusion prevalent, and wide,
Than, all alive, at once their Joy o'erflows
In Musick unconfin'd. Up-springs the Lark,
Shrill-voic'd, and loud, the Messenger of Morn;
Ere yet the Shadows fly, he mounted sings
Amid the dawning Clouds, and from their Haunts
Calls up the tuneful Nations. Every Copse

Deep-tangled, Tree irregular, and Bush
Bending with dewy Moisture, o'er the Heads
Of the coy Quiristers that lodge within,
Are prodigal of Harmony. The Thrush
And Wood-lark, o'er the kind contending Throng
Superior heard, run thro' the sweetest Length
Of Notes; when listening *Philomela* deigns
To let them joy, and purposes, in Thought
Elate, to make her Night excel their Day.
The Black-bird whistles from the thorny Brake;
The mellow Bullfinch answers from the Grove:
Nor are the Linnets, o'er the flow'ring Furze
Pour'd out profusely, silent. Join'd to these
Innumerous Songsters, in the freshening Shade
Of new-sprung Leaves, their Modulations mix
Mellifluous. The Jay, the Rook, the Daw,
And each harsh Pipe discordant heard alone,
Aid the full Concert: while the Stock-dove breathes
A melancholy Murmur thro' the whole.

   'Tis Love creates their Melody, and all
This Waste of Music is the Voice of Love;
That even to Birds, and Beasts, the tender Arts
Of pleasing teaches. Hence the glossy kind
Try every winning way inventive Love
Can dictate, and in Courtship to their Mates
Pour forth their little Souls. First, wide around,
With distant Awe, in airy Rings they rove,
Endeavouring by a thousand Tricks to catch
The cunning, conscious, half-averted Glance
Of their regardless Charmer. Should she seem
Softening the least Approvance to bestow,
Their Colours burnish, and by Hope inspir'd,
They brisk advance; then, on a sudden struck,
Retire disorder'd; then again approach;

In fond rotation spread the spotted Wing,
And shiver every Feather with Desire.

Connubial Leagues agreed, to the deep Woods
They haste away, all as their Fancy leads,
Pleasure, or Food, or secret Safety prompts;
That *Nature's great Command* may be obey'd,
Nor all the sweet Sensations they perceive
Indulg'd in vain. Some to the Holly-Hedge
Nestling repair, and to the Thicket some;
Some to the rude Protection of the Thorn
Commit their feeble Offspring. The cleft Tree
Offers its kind Concealment to a Few,
Their Food its Insects, and its Moss their Nests.
Others apart far in the grassy Dale,
Or roughening Waste, their humble Texture weave.
But most in woodland Solitudes delight,
In unfrequented Glooms, or shaggy Banks,
Steep, and divided by a babbling Brook,
Whose Murmurs soothe them all the live-long Day,
When by kind Duty fix'd. Among the Roots
Of Hazel, pendant o'er the plaintive Stream,
They frame the first Foundation of their Domes;
Dry Sprigs of Trees, in artful Fabrick laid,
And bound with Clay together. Now 'tis nought
But restless Hurry thro the busy Air,
Beat by unnumber'd Wings. The Swallow sweeps
The slimy Pool, to build his hanging House
Intent. And often, from the careless Back
Of Herds and Flocks, a thousand tugging Bills
Pluck Hair and Wool; and oft, when unobserv'd,
Steal from the Barn a Straw: till soft and warm,
Clean, and compleat, their Habitation grows.

As thus the patient Dam assiduous sits,
Not to be tempted from her tender Task,

Or by sharp Hunger, or by smooth Delight,
Tho the whole loosen'd Spring around Her blows,
Her sympathizing Lover takes his Stand
High on th' opponent Bank, and ceaseless sings
The tedious Time away; or else supplies
Her place a moment, while she sudden flits
To pick the scanty Meal. Th' appointed Time
With pious Toil fulfill'd, the callow Young,
Warm'd and expanded into perfect Life,
Their brittle Bondage break, and come to Light,
A helpless Family, demanding Food
With constant Clamour. O what Passions then,
What melting Sentiments of kindly Care,
On the new Parents seize! Away they fly
Affectionate, and undesiring bear
The most delicious Morsel to their Young,
Which equally distributed, again
The Search begins. Even so a gentle Pair,
By Fortune sunk, but form'd of generous Mold,
And charm'd with Cares beyond the vulgar Breast,
In some lone Cott amid the distant Woods,
Sustain'd alone by providential *Heaven*,
Oft, as they weeping eye their infant Train,
Check their own Appetites and give them all.

   Nor Toil alone they scorn: exalting Love,
By the great *Father of the Spring* inspir'd,
Gives instant Courage to the *fearful* Race,
And to the *simple* Art. With stealthy Wing,
Should some rude Foot their woody Haunts molest,
Amid a neighbouring Bush they silent drop,
And whirring thence, as if alarm'd, deceive
Th' unfeeling School-Boy. Hence, around the Head
Of wandering Swain, the white-wing'd Plover wheels

Her sounding Flight, and then directly on
In long Excursion skims the level Lawn,
To tempt him from her Nest. The Wild-Duck, hence,
O'er the rough Moss, and o'er the trackless Waste
The Heath-Hen flutters, (pious Fraud!) to lead
The hot pursuing Spaniel far astray.

Be not the Muse asham'd, here to bemoan
Her Brothers of the Grove, by tyrant Man
Inhuman caught, and in the narrow Cage
From Liberty confin'd, and boundless Air.
Dull are the pretty Slaves, their Plumage dull,
Ragged, and all its brightening Lustre lost;
Nor is that sprightly Wildness in their Notes,
Which, clear and vigorous, warbles from the Beech.
Oh then, ye Friends of Love and Love-taught Song,
Spare the soft Tribes, this barbarous Art forbear!
If on your Bosom Innocence can win,
Music engage, or Piety persuade.

But let not chief the Nightingale lament
Her ruin'd Care, too delicately fram'd
To brook the harsh Confinement of the Cage.
Oft when, returning with her loaded Bill,
Th' astonish'd Mother finds a vacant Nest,
By the hard Hand of unrelenting Clowns
Robb'd, to the Ground the vain Provision falls;
Her Pinions ruffle, and low-drooping scarce
Can bear the Mourner to the poplar Shade;
Where, all abandon'd to Despair, she sings
Her Sorrows thro the Night; and, on the Bough,
Sole-sitting, still at every dying Fall
Takes up again her lamentable Strain
Of winding Woe; till wide around the Woods
Sigh to her Song, and with her Wail resound.

But now the feather'd Youth their former Bounds,
Ardent, disdain; and, weighing oft their Wings,
Demand the free Possession of the Sky.
This one glad Office more, and then dissolves
Parental Love at once, now needless grown.
Unlavish *Wisdom* never works in vain.
'Tis on some Evening, sunny, grateful, mild,
When nought but Balm is breathing thro the Woods,
With yellow Lustre bright, that the new Tribes
Visit the spacious Heavens, and look abroad
On Nature's Common, far as they can see,
Or wing, their Range, and Pasture. O'er the Boughs
Dancing about, still at the giddy Verge
Their Resolution fails; their Pinions still,
In loose Libration stretch'd, to trust the Void
Trembling refuse: till down before them fly
The Parent-Guides, and chide, exhort, command,
Or push them off. The surging Air receives
The Plumy Burden; and their self-taught Wings
Winnow the waving Element. On Ground
Alighted, bolder up again they lead,
Farther and farther on, the lengthening Flight;
Till vanish'd every Fear, and every Power
Rouz'd into Life and Action, light in Air
Th' acquitted Parents see their soaring Race,
And once rejoicing never know them more.

(Lines 569–751)

FROM *The Castle of Indolence*

Sometimes the Pencil, in cool airy Halls,
Bade the gay Bloom of Vernal Landskips rise,
Or Autumn's vary'd Shades imbrown the Walls:

Now the black Tempest strikes the astonish'd Eyes;
Now down the Steep the flashing Torrent flies;
The trembling Sun now plays o'er Ocean blue,
And now rude Mountains frown amid the Skies;
Whate'er *Lorrain* light-touch'd with softening Hue,
Or savage *Rosa* dash'd, or learned *Poussin* drew.

Each Sound too here to Languishment inclin'd,
Lull'd the weak Bosom, and induced Ease.
Aereal Music in the warbling Wind,
At Distance rising oft, by small Degrees,
Nearer and nearer came, till o'er the Trees
It hung, and breath'd such Soul-dissolving Airs,
As did, alas! with soft Perdition please:
Entangled deep in its inchanting Snares,
The listening Heart forgot all Duties and all Cares.

A certain Music, never known before,
Here sooth'd the pensive melancholy Mind;
Full easily obtain'd. Behoves no more,
But sidelong, to the gently-waving Wind,
To lay the well-tun'd Instrument reclin'd;
From which, with airy flying Fingers light,
Beyond each mortal Touch the most refin'd,
The God of Winds drew Sounds of deep Delight:
Whence, with just Cause, *The Harp of Ælous* it hight.

Ah me! what Hand can touch the Strings so fine?
Who up the lofty Diapason roll
Such sweet, such sad, such solemn Airs divine,
Then let them down again into the Soul?
Now rising Love they fan'd; now pleasing Dole
They breath'd in tender Musings, through the Heart;
And now a graver sacred Strain they stole,
As when Seraphic Hands an Hymn impart:
Wild warbling Nature all, above the Reach of Art!

Such the gay Splendor, the luxurious State,
Of *Caliphs* old, who on the *Tygris*' Shore,
In mighty *Bagdat*, populous and great,
Held their bright Court, where was of Ladies store;
And Verse, Love, Music still the Garland wore:
When Sleep was coy, the Bard, in Waiting there,
Chear'd the lone Midnight with the Muse's Lore;
Composing Music bade his Dreams be fair,
And Music lent new Gladness to the Morning Air.

(Canto I, stanzas 38–42)

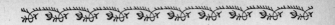

Samuel Johnson
(1709–1784)

A Short Song of Congratulation

Long-expected one and twenty
Ling'ring year at last is flown,
Pomp and Pleasure, Pride and Plenty
Great Sir John, are all your own.

Loosen'd from the Minor's tether,
Free to mortgage or to sell,
Wild as wind, and light as feather
Bid the slaves of thrift farewell.

Call the Bettys, Kates, and Jennys
Ev'ry name that laughs at Care,
Lavish of your Grandsire's guineas,
Show the spirit of an heir.

All that prey on vice and folly
Joy to see their quarry fly,
Here the Gamester light and jolly
There the Lender grave and sly.

Wealth, Sir John, was made to wander,
Let it wander as it will;
See the Jocky, see the Pander,
Bid them come, and take their fill.

When the bonny Blade carouses,
Pockets full, and Spirits high,

What are acres? What are houses?
  Only dirt, or wet or dry.

If the Guardian or the Mother
  Tell the woes of wilful waste,
Scorn the counsel and their pother,
  You can hang or drown at last.

On the Death of Dr. Robert Levet

Condemn'd to hope's delusive mine,
  As on we toil from day to day,
By sudden blasts, or slow decline,
  Our social comforts drop away.

Well tried through many a varying year,
  See LEVET to the grave descend;
Officious, innocent, sincere,
  Of ev'ry friendless name the friend.

Yet still he fills affection's eye,
  Obscurely wise, and coarsely kind;
Nor, letter'd arrogance, deny
  Thy praise to merit unrefin'd.

When fainting nature call'd for aid,
  And hov'ring death prepar'd the blow,
His vig'rous remedy display'd
  The power of art without the show.

In misery's darkest caverns known,
  His useful care was ever nigh,
Where hopeless anguish pour'd his groan,
  And lonely want retir'd to die.

No summons mock'd by chill delay,
　No petty gain disdain'd by pride,
The modest wants of ev'ry day
　The toil of ev'ry day supplied.

His virtues walk'd their narrow round,
　Nor made a pause, nor left a void;
And sure th' Eternal Master found
　The single talent well employ'd.

The busy day, the peaceful night,
　Unfelt, uncounted, glided by;
His frame was firm, his powers were bright,
　Tho' now his eightieth year was nigh.

Then with no throbbing fiery pain,
　No cold gradations of decay,
Death broke at once the vital chain,
　And free'd his soul the nearest way.

London

A POEM IN IMITATION
OF THE THIRD SATIRE OF JUVENAL

Quis ineptae
Tam patiens urbis, tam ferreus ut teneat se?
　　　　　　—JUVENAL

Tho' grief and fondness in my breast rebel,
When injur'd THALES bids the town farewell,
Yet still my calmer thoughts his choice commend,
I praise the hermit, but regret the friend,
Resolved at length, from vice and LONDON far,
To breathe in distant fields a purer air,

And, fix'd on Cambria's solitary shore,
Give to St. David one true Briton more.

    For who would leave, unbrib'd, Hibernia's land,
Or change the rocks of Scotland for the Strand?
There none are swept by sudden fate away,
But all whom hunger spares, with age decay:
Here malice, rapine, accident, conspire,
And now a rabble rages, now a fire;
Their ambush here relentless ruffians lay,
And here the fell attorney prowls for prey;
Here falling houses thunder on your head,
And here a female atheist talks you dead.

    While THALES waits the wherry that contains
Of dissipated wealth the small remains,
On Thames's banks, in silent thought we stood,
Where Greenwich smiles upon the silver flood:
Struck with the seat that gave Eliza birth,
We kneel, and kiss the consecrated earth;
In pleasing dreams the blissful age renew,
And call Britannia's glories back to view;
Behold her cross triumphant on the main,
The guard of commerce, and the dread of Spain,
Ere masquerades debauch'd, excise oppress'd,
Or English honour grew a standing jest.

    A transient calm the happy scenes bestow,
And for a moment lull the sense of woe.
At length awaking, with contemptuous frown,
Indignant THALES eyes the neighb'ring town.

    Since worth, he cries, in these degen'rate days,
Wants ev'n the cheap reward of empty praise;
In those curs'd walls, devote to vice and gain,
Since unrewarded science toils in vain;
Since hope but sooths to double my distress,
And ev'ry moment leaves my little less;
While yet my steady steps no staff sustains,

And life still vig'rous revels in my veins;
Grant me, kind heaven, to find some happier place,
Where honesty and sense are no disgrace;
Some pleasing bank where verdant osiers play,
Some peaceful vale with nature's paintings gay;
Where once the harrass'd Briton found repose,
And safe in poverty defy'd his foes;
Some secret cell, ye pow'rs, indulgent give.
Let —— live here, for —— has learn'd to live.
Here let those reign, whom pensions can incite
To vote a patriot black, a courtier white;
Explain their country's dear-bought rights away,
And plead for pirates in the face of day;
With slavish tenets taint our poison'd youth,
And lend a lye the confidence of truth.

Let such raise palaces, and manors buy,
Collect a tax, or farm a lottery,
With warbling eunuchs fill a licens'd stage,
And lull to servitude a thoughtless age.

Heroes, proceed! what bounds your pride shall hold?
What check restrain your thirst of pow'r and gold?
Behold rebellious virtue quite o'erthrown,
Behold our fame, our wealth, our lives your own.

To such, a groaning nation's spoils are giv'n,
When publick crimes inflame the wrath of heav'n:
But what, my friend, what hope remains for me,
Who start at theft, and blush at perjury?
Who scarce forbear, tho' BRITAIN's Court he sing,
To pluck a titled Poet's borrow'd wing;
A Statesman's logick unconvinc'd can hear,
And dare to slumber o'er the Gazetteer;
Despise a fool in half his pension dress'd,
And strive in vain to laugh at H——y's jest.

Others with softer smiles, and subtler art,
Can sap the principles, or taint the heart;

With more address a lover's note convey,
Or bribe a virgin's innocence away.
Well may they rise, while I, whose rustick tongue
Ne'er knew to puzzle right, or varnish wrong,
Spurn'd as a beggar, dreaded as a spy,
Love unregarded, unlamented die.

    For what but social guilt the friend endears?
Who shares Orgilio's crimes, his fortune shares.
But thou, should tempting villainy present
All Marlb'rough hoarded, or all Villiers spent,
Turn from the glitt'ring bribe thy scornful eye,
Nor sell for gold, what gold could never buy,
The peaceful slumber, self-approving day,
Unsullied fame, and conscience ever gay.

    The cheated nation's happy fav'rites, see!
Mark whom the great caress, who frown on me!
LONDON! the needy villain's gen'ral home,
The common shore of Paris and of Rome;
With eager thirst, by folly or by fate,
Sucks in the dregs of each corrupted state.
Forgive my transports on a theme like this,
I cannot bear a French metropolis.

    Illustrious EDWARD! from the realms of day,
The land of heroes and of saints survey;
Nor hope the British lineaments to trace,
The rustick grandeur, or the surly grace,
But lost in thoughtless ease, and empty show,
Behold the warrior dwindled to a beau;
Sense, freedom, piety, refin'd away,
Of France the mimick, and of Spain the prey.

    All that at home no more can beg or steal,
Or like a gibbet better than a wheel;
Hiss'd from the stage, or hooted from the court,
Their air, their dress, their politicks import;
Obsequious, artful, voluble and gay,

On Britain's fond credulity they prey.
No gainful trade their industry can 'scape,
They sing, they dance, clean shoes, or cure a clap;
All sciences a fasting Monsieur knows,
And bid him go to hell, to hell he goes.

Ah! what avails it, that, from slav'ry far,
I drew the breath of life in English air;
Was early taught a Briton's right to prize,
And lisp the tale of HENRY's victories;
If the gull'd conqueror receives the chain,
And flattery subdues when arms are vain?

Studious to please, and ready to submit,
The supple Gaul was born a parasite:
Still to his int'rest true, where'er he goes,
Wit, brav'ry, worth, his lavish tongue bestows;
In ev'ry face a thousand graces shine,
From ev'ry tongue flows harmony divine.
These arts in vain our rugged natives try,
Strain out with fault'ring diffidence a lye,
And get a kick for awkward flattery.

Besides, with justice, this discerning age
Admires their wond'rous talents for the stage:
Well may they venture on the mimick's art,
Who play from morn to night a borrow'd part;
Practis'd their master's notions to embrace,
Repeat his maxims, and reflect his face;
With ev'ry wild absurdity comply,
And view each object with another's eye;
To shake with laughter ere the jest they hear,
To pour at will the counterfeited tear,
And as their patron hints the cold or heat,
To shake in dog-days, in December sweat.

How, when competitors like these contend,
Can surly virtue hope to fix a friend?
Slaves that with serious impudence beguile,

And lye without a blush, without a smile;
Exalt each trifle, ev'ry vice adore,
Your taste in snuff, your judgment in a whore;
Can Balbo's eloquence applaud, and swear
He gropes his breeches with a monarch's air.

  For arts like these preferr'd, admir'd, caress'd,
They first invade your table, then your breast;
Explore your secrets with insidious art,
Watch the weak hour, and ransack all the heart;
Then soon your ill-plac'd confidence repay,
Commence your lords, and govern or betray.

  By numbers here from shame or censure free,
All crimes are safe, but hated poverty.
This, only this, the rigid law pursues,
This, only this, provokes the snarling muse.
The sober trader at a tatter'd cloak,
Wakes from his dream, and labours for a joke;
With brisker air the silken courtiers gaze,
And turn the varied taunt a thousand ways.
Of all the griefs that harrass the distress'd,
Sure the most bitter is a scornful jest;
Fate never wounds more deep the gen'rous heart,
Than when a blockhead's insult points the dart.

  Has heaven reserv'd, in pity to the poor,
No pathless waste, or undiscover'd shore;
No secret island in the boundless main?
No peaceful desart yet unclaim'd by SPAIN?
Quick let us rise, the happy seats explore,
And bear oppression's insolence no more.
This mournful truth is ev'ry where confess'd,
SLOW RISES WORTH, BY POVERTY DEPRESS'D:
But here more slow, where all are slaves to gold,
Where looks are merchandise, and smiles are sold;
Where won by bribes, by flatteries implor'd,
The groom retails the favours of his lord.

But hark! th' affrighted crowd's tumultuous cries
Roll thro' the streets, and thunder to the skies;
Rais'd from some pleasing dream of wealth and pow'r,
Some pompous palace, or some blissful bow'r,
Aghast you start, and scarce with aking sight
Sustain th' approaching fire's tremendous light;
Swift from pursuing horrors take your way,
And leave your little ALL to flames a prey;
Then thro' the world a wretched vagrant roam,
For where can starving merit find a home?
In vain your mournful narrative disclose,
While all neglect, and most insult your woes.

   Should heaven's just bolts Orgilio's wealth confound,
And spread his flaming palace on the ground,
Swift o'er the land the dismal rumour flies,
And publick mournings pacify the skies;
The laureat tribe in servile verse relate,
How virtue wars with persecuting fate;
With well-feign'd gratitude the pension'd band
Refund the plunder of the beggar'd land.
See! while he builds, the gaudy vassals come,
And crowd with sudden wealth the rising dome;
The price of boroughs and of souls restore,
And raise his treasures higher than before.
Now bless'd with all the baubles of the great,
The polish'd marble, and the shining plate,
Orgilio sees the golden pile aspire
And hopes from angry heav'n another fire.

   Could'st thou resign the park and play content,
For the fair banks of Severn or of Trent;
There might'st thou find some elegant retreat,
Some hireling senator's deserted seat;
And stretch thy prospects o'er the smiling land,
For less than rent the dungeons of the Strand;
There prune thy walks, support thy drooping flow'rs,

Direct thy rivulets, and twine thy bow'rs;
And, while thy grounds a cheap repast afford,
Despise the dainties of a venal lord:
There ev'ry bush with nature's musick rings,
There ev'ry breeze bears health upon its wings;
On all thy hours security shall smile,
And bless thine evening walk and morning toil.

Prepare for death, if here at night you roam,
And sign your will before you sup from home.
Some fiery fop, with new commission vain,
Who sleeps on brambles till he kills his man;
Some frolick drunkard, reeling from a feast,
Provokes a broil, and stabs you for a jest.
Yet ev'n these heroes, mischievously gay,
Lords of the street, and terrors of the way;
Flush'd as they are with folly, youth and wine,
Their prudent insults to the poor confine;
Afar they mark the flambeau's bright approach,
And shun the shining train, and golden coach.

In vain, these dangers past, your doors you close,
And hope the balmy blessings of repose:
Cruel with guilt, and daring with despair,
The midnight murd'rer bursts the faithless bar;
Invades the sacred hour of silent rest,
And leaves, unseen, a dagger in your breast.

Scarce can our fields, such crowds at Tyburn die,
With hemp the gallows and the fleet supply.
Propose your schemes, ye Senatorian band,
Whose Ways and Means support the sinking land;
Lest ropes be wanting in the tempting spring,
To rig another convoy for the k——g.

A single jail, in ALFRED's golden reign,
Could half the nation's criminals contain;
Fair Justice then, without constraint ador'd,
Held high the steady scale, but deep'd the sword;

No spies were paid, no special juries known,
Blest age! but ah! how diff'rent from our own!
   Much could I add,—but see the boat at hand,
The tide retiring, calls me from the land:
Farewell!—When youth, and health, and fortune spent,
Thou fly'st for refuge to the wilds of Kent;
And tir'd like me with follies and with crimes,
In angry numbers warn'st succeeding times;
Then shall thy friend, nor thou refuse his aid,
Still foe to vice, forsake his Cambrian shade;
In virtue's cause once more exert his rage,
Thy satire point, and animate thy page.

The Vanity of Human Wishes

THE TENTH SATIRE OF JUVENAL IMITATED

   Let observation with extensive view,
Survey mankind, from China to Peru;
Remark each anxious toil, each eager strife,
And watch the busy scenes of crouded life;
Then say how hope and fear, desire and hate,
O'erspread with snares the clouded maze of fate,
Where wav'ring man, betray'd by vent'rous pride,
To tread the dreary paths without a guide,
As treach'rous phantoms in the mist delude,
Shuns fancied ills, or chases airy good;
How rarely reason guides the stubborn choice,
Rules the bold hand, or prompts the suppliant voice;
How nations sink, by darling schemes oppress'd,
When vengeance listens to the fool's request.
Fate wings with ev'ry wish th' afflictive dart,
Each gift of nature, and each grace of art,

With fatal heat impetuous courage glows,
With fatal sweetness elocution flows,
Impeachment stops the speaker's pow'rful breath,
And restless fire precipitates on death.

But scarce observ'd, the knowing and the bold
Fall in the gen'ral massacre of gold;
Wide-wasting pest! that rages unconfin'd,
And crouds with crimes the records of mankind;
For gold his sword the hireling ruffian draws,
For gold the hireling judge distorts the laws;
Wealth heap'd on wealth, nor truth nor safety buys,
The dangers gather as the treasures rise.

Let hist'ry tell where rival kings command,
And dubious title shakes the madded land,
When statutes glean the refuse of the sword,
How much more safe the vassal than the lord;
Low skulks the hind beneath the rage of pow'r,
And leaves the wealthy traytor in the Tow'r,
Untouch'd his cottage, and his slumbers sound,
Tho' confiscation's vultures hover round.

The needy traveller, serene and gay,
Walks the wild heath, and sings his toil away.
Does envy seize thee? crush th' upbraiding joy,
Increase his riches and his peace destroy;
Now fears in dire vicissitude invade,
The rustling brake alarms, and quiv'ring shade,
Nor light nor darkness bring his pain relief,
One shews the plunder, and one hides the thief.

Yet still one gen'ral cry the skies assails,
And gain and grandeur load the tainted gales;
Few know the toiling statesman's fear or care,
Th' insidious rival and the gaping heir.

Once more, Democritus, arise on earth,
With chearful wisdom and instructive mirth,
See motley life in modern trappings dress'd,

And feed with varied fools th' eternal jest:
Thou who couldst laugh where want enchain'd caprice,
Toil crush'd conceit, and man was of a piece;
Where wealth unlov'd without a mourner dy'd,
And scarce a sycophant was fed by pride;
Where ne'er was known the form of mock debate,
Or seen a new-made mayor's unwieldy state;
Where change of fav'rites made no change of laws,
And senates heard before they judg'd a cause;
How wouldst thou shake at Britain's modish tribe,
Dart the quick taunt, and edge the piercing gibe?
Attentive truth and nature to descry,
And pierce each scene with philosophic eye.
To thee were solemn toys or empty shew,
The robes of pleasure and the veils of woe:
All aid the farce, and all thy mirth maintain,
Whose joys are causeless, or whose griefs are vain.

Such was the scorn that fill'd the sage's mind,
Renew'd at ev'ry glance on humankind;
How just that scorn ere yet thy voice declare,
Search every state, and canvas ev'ry pray'r.

Unnumber'd suppliants croud Preferment's gate,
Athirst for wealth, and burning to be great;
Delusive Fortune hears th' incessant call,
They mount, they shine, evaporate, and fall.
On ev'ry stage the foes of peace attend,
Hate dogs their flight, and insult mocks their end.
Love ends with hope, the sinking statesman's door
Pours in the morning worshiper no more;
For growing names the weekly scribbler lies,
To growing wealth the dedicator flies,
From every room descends the painted face,
That hung the bright Palladium of the place,
And smoak'd in kitchens, or in auctions sold,
To better features yields the frame of gold;

For now no more we trace in ev'ry line
Heroic worth, benevolence divine:
The form distorted justifies the fall,
And detestation rids th' indignant wall.

But will not Britain hear the last appeal,
Sign her foes doom, or guard her fav'rites zeal?
Through Freedom's sons no more remonstrance rings,
Degrading nobles and controuling kings;
Our supple tribes repress their patriot throats,
And ask no questions but the price of votes;
With weekly libels and septennial ale,
Their wish is full to riot and to rail.

In full-blown dignity, see Wolsey stand,
Law in his voice, and fortune in his hand:
To him the church, the realm, their pow'rs consign,
Thro' him the rays of regal bounty shine,
Turn'd by his nod the stream of honour flows,
His smile alone security bestows:
Still to new heights his restless wishes tow'r,
Claim leads to claim, and pow'r advances pow'r;
Till conquest unresisted, left him none to seize.
At length his sov'reign frowns—the train of state
Mark the keen glance, and watch the sign to hate.
Where-e'er he turns he meets a stranger's eye,
His suppliants scorn him, and his followers fly;
At once is lost the pride of aweful state,
The golden canopy, the glitt'ring plate,
The regal palace, the luxurious board,
The liv'ried army, and the menial lord.
With age, with cares, with maladies oppress'd,
He seeks the refuge of monastic rest.
Grief aids disease, remember'd folly stings.
And his last sighs reproach the faith of kings.

Speak thou, whose thoughts at humble peace repine,
Shall Wolsey's wealth, with Wolsey's end be thine?

Or liv'st thou now, with safer pride content,
The wisest justice on the banks of Trent?
For why did Wolsey near the steeps of fate,
On weak foundations raise th' enormous weight?
Why but to sink beneath misfortune's blow,
With louder ruin to the gulphs below?

What gave great Villiers to th' assassin's knife,
And fixed disease on Harley's closing life?
What murder'd Wentworth, and what exil'd Hyde,
By kings protected, and to kings ally'd?
What but their wish indulg'd in courts to shine,
And pow'r too great to keep, or to resign?

When first the college rolls receive his name,
The young enthusiast quits his ease for fame;
Through all his veins the fever of renown
Burns from the strong contagion of the gown;
O'er Bodley's dome his future labours spread,
And Bacon's mansion trembles o'er his head.
Are these thy views? proceed, illustrious youth,
And virtue guard thee to the throne of Truth!
Yet should thy soul indulge the gen'rous heat,
Till captive Science yields her last retreat;
Should Reason guide thee with her brightest ray,
And pour on misty Doubt resistless day;
Should no false Kindness lure to loose delight,
Nor Praise relax, nor Difficulty fright;
Should tempting Novelty thy cell refrain,
And Sloth effuse her opiate fumes in vain;
Should Beauty blunt on fops her fatal dart,
Nor claim the triumph of a letter'd heart;
Should no Disease thy torpid veins invade,
Nor Melancholy's phantoms haunt thy shade;
Yet hope not life from grief or danger free,
Nor think the doom of man revers'd for thee:
Deign on the passing world to turn thine eyes,

And pause awhile from letters, to be wise;
There mark what ills the scholar's life assail,
Toil, envy, want, the patron, and the jail.
See nations slowly wise, and meanly just,
To buried merit raise the tardy bust.
If dreams yet flatter, once again attend,
Hear Lydiat's life, and Galileo's end.

    Nor deem, when learning her last prize bestows,
The glitt'ring eminence exempt from foes;
See when the vulgar 'scape, despis'd or aw'd,
Rebellion's vengeful talons seize on Laud.
From meaner minds, tho' smaller fines content,
The plunder'd palace or sequester'd rent;
Mark'd out by dangerous parts he meets the shock,
And fatal Learning leads him to the block:
Around his tomb let Art and Genius weep,
But hear his death, ye blockheads, hear and sleep.

    The festal blazes, the triumphal show,
The ravish'd standard, and the captive foe,
The senate's thanks, the gazette's pompous tale,
With force resistless o'er the brave prevail.
Such bribes the rapid Greek o'er Asia whirl'd,
For such the steady Romans shook the world;
For such in distant lands the Britons shine,
And stain with blood the Danube or the Rhine;
This pow'r has praise, that virtue scarce can warm
Till fame supplies the universal charm.
Yet Reason frowns on War's unequal game,
Where wasted nations raise a single name,
And mortgag'd states their grandsires wreaths regret,
From age to age in everlasting debt;
Wreaths which at last the dear-bought right convey
To rust on medals, or on stones decay.

    On what foundation stands the warrior's pride,
How just his hopes let Swedish Charles decide;

A frame of adamant, a soul of fire,
No dangers fright him, and no labours tire;
O'er love, o'er fear, extends his wide domain,
Unconquer'd lord of pleasure and of pain;
No joys to him pacific scepters yield,
War sounds the trump, he rushes to the field;
Behold surrounding kings their pow'r combine,
And one capitulate, and one resign;
Peace courts his hand, but spreads her charms in vain;
"Think nothing gain'd," he cries, "till nought remain,
On Moscow's walls till Gothic standards fly,
And all be mine beneath the polar sky."
The march begins in military state,
And nations on his eye suspended wait;
Stern Famine guards the solitary coast,
And Winter barricades the realms of Frost;
He comes, not want and cold his course delay;—
Hide, blushing Glory, hide Pultowa's day:
The vanquish'd hero leaves his broken bands,
And shews his miseries in distant lands;
Condemn'd a needy supplicant to wait,
While ladies interpose, and slaves debate.
But did not Chance at length her error mend?
Did no subverted empire mark his end?
Did rival monarchs give the fatal wound?
Or hostile millions press him to the ground?
His fall was destin'd to a barren strand,
A petty fortress, and a dubious hand;
He left the name, at which the world grew pale,
To point a moral, or adorn a tale.

   All times their scenes of pompous woes afford,
From Persia's tyrant to Bavaria's lord.
In gay hostility, and barb'rous pride,
With half mankind embattled at his side,
Great Xerxes comes to seize the certain prey,

And starves exhausted regions in his way;
Attendant Flatt'ry counts his myriads o'er,
Till counted myriads sooth his pride no more;
Fresh praise is try'd till madness fires his mind,
The waves he lashes, and enchains the wind;
New pow'rs are claim'd, new pow'rs are still bestow'd,
Till rude resistance lops the spreading god;
The daring Greeks deride the martial show,
And heap their vallies with the gaudy foe;
Th' insulted sea with humbler thoughts he gains,
A single skiff to speed his flight remains;
Th' incumber'd oar scarce leaves the dreaded coast
Through purple billows and a floating host.

The bold Bavarian, in a luckless hour,
Tries the dread summits of Cesarean pow'r,
With unexpected legions bursts away,
And sees defenceless realms receive his sway;
Short sway! fair Austria spreads her mournful charms,
The queen, the beauty, sets the world in arms;
From hill to hill the beacons rousing blaze
Spreads wide the hope of plunder and of praise;
The fierce Croatian, and the wild Hussar,
And all the sons of ravage croud the war;
The baffled prince in honour's flatt'ring bloom
Of hasty greatness finds the fatal doom,
His foes derision, and his subjects blame,
And steals to death from anguish and from shame.

Enlarge my life with multitude of days,
In health, in sickness, thus the suppliant prays;
Hides from himself his state, and shuns to know,
That life protracted is protracted woe.
Time hovers o'er, impatient to destroy,
And shuts up all the passages of joy:
In vain their gifts the bounteous seasons pour,
The fruit autumnal, and the vernal flow'r,

With listless eyes the dotard views the store,
He views, and wonders that they please no more;
Now pall the tasteless meats, and joyless wines,
And Luxury with sighs her slave resigns.
Approach, ye minstrels, try the soothing strain,
Diffuse the tuneful lenitives of pain:
No sounds alas would touch th' impervious ear,
Though dancing mountains witness'd Orpheus near;
Nor lute nor lyre his feeble pow'rs attend,
Nor sweeter musick of a virtuous friend,
But everlasting dictates croud his tongue,
Perversely grave, or positively wrong.
The still returning tale, and ling'ring jest,
Perplex the fawning niece and pamper'd guest,
While growing hopes scarce awe the gath'ring sneer,
And scarce a legacy still hint the last offence,
The daughter's petulance, the son's expence,
Improve his heady rage with treach'rous skill,
And mould his passions till they make his will.

    Unnumber'd maladies his joints invade,
Lay siege to life and press the dire blockade;
But unextinguish'd Avarice still remains,
And dreaded losses aggravate his pains;
He turns, with anxious heart and cripled hands,
His bonds of debt, and mortgages of lands;
Or views his coffers with suspicious eyes,
Unlocks his gold, and counts it till he dies.

    But grant, the virtues of a temp'rate prime
Bless with an age exempt from scorn or crime;
An age that melts with unperceiv'd decay,
And glides in modest Innocence away;
Whose peaceful day Benevolence endears,
Whose night congratulating Conscience cheers;
The gen'ral fav'rite as the gen'ral friend:
Such age there is, and who shall wish its end?

Yet ev'n on this her load Misfortune flings,
To press the weary minutes flagging wings:
New sorrow rises as the day returns,
A sister sickens, or a daughter mourns.
Now kindred Merit fills the sable bier,
Now lacerated Friendship claims a tear.
Year chases year, decay pursues decay,
Still drops some joy from with'ring life away;
New forms arise, and diff'rent views engage,
Superfluous lags the vet'ran on the stage,
Till pitying Nature signs the last release,
And bids afflicted worth retire to peace.

But few there are whom hours like these await,
Who set unclouded in the gulphs of fate.
From Lydia's monarch should the search descend,
By Solon caution'd to regard his end,
In life's last scene what prodigies surprise,
Fears of the brave, and follies of the wise?
From Marlb'rough's eyes the streams of dotage flow,
And Swift expires a driv'ler and a show.

The teeming mother, anxious for her race,
Begs for each birth the fortune of a face:
Yet Vane could tell what ills from beauty spring;
And Sedley curs'd the form that pleas'd a king.
Ye nymphs of rosy lips and radiant eyes,
Whom Pleasure keeps too busy to be wise,
Whom Joys with soft varieties invite,
By day the frolick, and the dance by night,
Who frown with vanity, who smile with art,
And ask the latest fashion of the heart,
What care, what rules your heedless charms shall save,
Each nymph your rival, and each youth your slave?
Against your fame with fondness hate combines,
The rival batters, and the lover mines.
With distant voice neglected Virtue calls,

Less heard and less, the faint remonstrance falls;
Tir'd with contempt, she quits the slipp'ry reign
And Pride and Prudence take her seat in vain.
In croud at once, where none the pass defend,
The harmless Freedom, and the private Friend.
The guardians yield, by force superior ply'd;
By Int'rest, Prudence; and by Flatt'ry, Pride.
Now beauty falls betray'd, despis'd, distress'd,
And hissing Infamy proclaims the rest.

   Where then shall Hope and Fear their objects find?
Must dull Suspence corrupt the stagnant mind?
Must helpless man, in ignorance sedate,
Roll darkling down the torrent of his fate?
Must no dislike alarm, no wishes rise,
No cries attempt the mercies of the skies?
Enquirer, cease, petitions yet remain,
Which heav'n may hear, nor deem religion vain.
Still raise for good the supplicating voice,
But leave to heav'n the measure and the choice,
Safe in his pow'r, whose eyes discern afar
The secret ambush of a specious pray'r.
Implore his aid, in his decisions rest,
Secure whate'er he gives, he gives the best.
Yet when the sense of sacred presence fires,
And strong devotion to the skies aspires,
Pour forth thy fervours for a healthful mind,
Obedient passions, and a will resign'd;
For love, which scarce collective man can fill;
For patience sov'reign o'er transmuted ill;
For faith, that panting for a happier seat,
Counts death kind Nature's signal of retreat:
These goods for man the laws of heav'n ordain,
These goods he grants, who grants the pow'r to gain;
With these celestial wisdom calms the mind,
And makes the happiness she does not find.

Mark Akenside

(1721–1770)

Hymn to Science

Science! thou fair effusive ray
From the great source of mental day,
   Free, gen'rous, and refin'd,
Descend with all thy treasures fraught,
Illumine each bewilder'd thought,
   And bless my lab'ring mind.

But first with thy resistless light,
Disperse those phantoms from my sight,
   Those mimic shades of thee,
The scholiast's learning, sophist's cant,
The visionary bigot's rant,
   The monk's philosophy.

Oh! let thy pow'rful charms impart
The patient head, the candid heart,
   Devoted to thy sway,
Which no weak passions e'er mislead,
Which still with dauntless steps proceed
   Where Reason points the way.

Give me to learn each secret cause;
Let Number's, Figure's, Motion's laws
   Reveal'd before me stand;
These to great Nature's scenes apply,
And round the globe, and thro' the sky,
   Disclose her working hand.

Next, to thy nobler search resign'd,
The busy, restless, human mind
　　Thro' ev'ry maze pursue;
Detect perception where it lies,
Catch the ideas as they rise,
　　And all their changes view.

Say from what simple springs began
The vast ambitious thoughts of man,
　　Which range beyond controul,
Which seek eternity to trace,
Dive thro' th' infinity of space,
　　And strain to grasp the whole?

Her secret stores let Mem'ry tell,
Bid Fancy quit her fairy cell,
　　In all her colours drest,
While, prompt her sallies to controul,
Reason, the judge, recalls the soul
　　To Truth's severest test.

Then launch thro' Being's wide extent;
Let the fair scale, with just ascent,
　　And cautious steps be trod,
And from the dead, corporeal mass,
Thro' each progressive order pass
　　To Instinct, Reason, God.

There, Science! veil thy daring eye,
Nor dive too deep, nor soar too high,
　　In that divine abyss,
To Faith content thy beams to lend,
Her hopes t'assure, her steps befriend,
　　And light her way to bliss.

Then downwards take thy flight again;
Mix with the policies of men,

  And social Nature's ties:
The plan, the genius of each state,
Its int'rest and its pow'rs, relate,
   Its fortunes and its rise.

Thro' private life pursue thy course,
Trace ev'ry action to its source,
   And means and motives weigh;
Put tempers, passions, in the scale,
Mark what degrees in each prevail,
   And fix the doubtful sway.

That last, best effort of thy skill,
To form the life and rule the will,
   Propitious Pow'r! impart;
Teach me to cool my passion's fires,
Make me the judge of my desires,
   The master of my heart.

Raise me above the vulgar's breath,
Pursuit of fortune, fear of death,
   And all in life that's mean:
Still true to Reason be my plan,
Still let my action speak the man,
   Thro' ev'ry various scene.

Hail! queen of Manners, light of Truth;
Hail! charm of age, and guide of youth;
   Sweet refuge of distress:
In bus'ness, thou exact, polite;
Thou giv'st retirement its delight,
   Prosperity its grace.

Of wealth, pow'r, freedom, thou the cause;
Foundress of order, cities, laws;
   Of arts inventress, thou!
Without thee what were humankind?

How vast their wants, their thoughts how blind,
   Their joys how mean, how few!

Sun of the soul! thy beams unveil;
Let others spread the daring sail
   On Fortune's faithless sea,
While undeluded, happier I
From the vain tumult timely fly,
   And sit in peace with thee.

Inscription for a Grotto

To me, whom in their lays the shepherds call
Actæa, daughter of the neighbouring stream,
This cave belongs. The fig-tree and the vine,
Which o'er the rocky entrance downward shoot,
Were plac'd by Glycon. He with cowslips pale,
Primrose, and purple lychnis, deck'd the green
Before my threshold, and my shelving walls
With honeysuckle cover'd. Here at noon,
Lull'd by the murmur of my rising fount,
I slumber: here my clustering fruits I tend;
Or from the humid flowers, at break of day,
Fresh garlands weave, and chase from all my bounds
Each thing impure or noxious. Enter in,
O stranger, undismay'd. Nor bat nor toad
Here lurks: and if thy breast of blameless thoughts
Approve thee, not unwelcome shalt thou tread
My quiet mansion: chiefly, if thy name
Wise Pallas and the immortal muses own.

To the Evening Star

To-night retir'd the queen of heaven
   With young Endymion stays:
And now to Hesper is it giv'n
Awhile to rule the vacant sky,
Till she shall to her lamp supply
   A stream of brighter rays.

O Hesper, while the starry throng
   With awe thy path surrounds,
Oh listen to my suppliant song,
If haply now the vocal sphere
Can suffer thy delighted ear
   To stoop to mortal sounds.

So may the bridegroom's genial strain
   Thee still invoke to shine:
So may the bride's unmarried train
To Hymen chaunt their flattering vow,
Still that his lucky torch may glow
   With lustre pure as thine.

Far other vows must I prefer
   To thy indulgent power.
Alas, but now I paid my tear
On fair Olympia's virgin tomb:
And lo, from thence, in quest I roam
   Of Philomela's bower.

Propitious send thy golden ray,
   Thou purest light above:
Let no false flame seduce to stray

Where gulph or steep lie hid for harm:
But lead where music's healing charm
   May soothe afflicted love.

To them, by many a grateful song
   In happier season's vow'd,
These lawns, Olympia's haunts, belong:
Oft by yon silver stream we walk'd,
Or fix'd, while Philomela talk'd,
   Beneath yon copses stood.

Nor seldom, where the beechen boughs
   That roofless tow'r invade,
We came, while her enchanting Muse
The radiant moon above us held:
Till by a clam'rous owl compell'd,
   She fled the solemn shade.

But hark; I hear her liquid tone.
   Now, Hesper, guide my feet
Down the red marle with moss o'ergrown,
Through yon wild thicket next the plain,
Whose hawthorns choke the winding lane
   Which leads to her retreat.

See the green space: on either hand
   Inlarg'd it spreads around:
See, in the midst she takes her stand,
Where one old oak his awful shade
Extends o'er half the level mead
   Inclos'd in woods profound.

Hark, how through many a melting note
   She now prolongs her lays:
How sweetly down the void they float!
The breeze their magic path attends:

The stars shine out: the forest bends:
　　The wakeful heifers gaze.

Who'er thou art whom chance may bring
　　To this sequester'd spot,
If then the plaintive Syren sing,
Oh softly tread beneath her bower,
And think of heaven's disposing power,
　　Of man's uncertain lot.

Oh think, o'er all this mortal stage,
　　What mournful scenes arise:
What ruin waits on kingly rage:
How often virtue dwells with woe:
How many griefs from knowledge flow:
　　How swiftly pleasure flies.

O sacred bird, let me at eve,
　　Thus wand'ring all alone,
Thy tender counsel oft receive,
Bear witness to thy pensive airs,
And pity Nature's common cares
　　Till I forget my own.

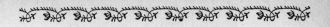

Joseph Warton

(1722–1800)

The Enthusiast, or, The Lover of Nature

Ye green-rob'd Dryads, oft at dusky eve
By wondering shepherds seen, to forests brown,
To unfrequented meads, and pathless wilds,
Lead me from gardens deck'd with art's vain pomps.
Can gilt alcoves, can marble-mimick gods,
Parterres embroider'd, obelisks, and urns,
Of high relief; can the long, spreading lake
Or vista lessening to the sight; can Stow,
With all her Attick fanes, such raptures raise,
As the thrush-haunted copse, where lightly leaps
The fearful fawn the rustling leaves along,
And the brisk squirrel sports from bough to bough,
While from an hollow oak, whose naked roots
O'erhang a pensive rill, the busy bees
Hum drowsy lullabies? The bards of old,
Fair Nature's friends, sought such retreats, to charm
Sweet Echo with their songs; oft too they met
In summer evenings, near sequester'd bow'rs.
Or mountain-nymph, or muse, and eager learn'd
The moral strains she taught to mend mankind.
As to a secret grot Ægeria stole
With patriot Numa, and in silent night
Whisper'd him sacred laws, he list'ning sat,
Rapt with her virtuous voice, old Tiber lean'd
Attentive on his urn, and hush'd his waves.

Rich in her weeping country's spoils, Versailles
May boast a thousand fountains, that can cast
The tortur'd waters to the distant heav'ns;
Yet let me choose some pine-top'd precipice
Abrupt and shaggy, whence a foamy stream,
Like Anio, tumbling roars; or some bleak heath,
Where straggling stands the mournful juniper,
Or yew-tree scath'd; while in clear prospect round,
From the grove's bosom spires emerge, and smoak
In bluish wreaths ascends, ripe harvests wave,
Low, lonely cottages, and ruin'd tops
Of Gothick battlements appear, and streams
Beneath the sunbeams twinkle—the shrill lark,
That wakes the wood-man to his early task,
Or love-sick Philomel, whose luscious lays
Soothe lone night-wanderers, the moaning dove
Pitied by listening milk-maid, far excell
The deep-mouth'd viol, the soul-lulling lute,
And battle-breathing trumpet. Artful sounds!
That please not like the choristers of air,
When first they hail th' approach of laughing May.
　　Can Kent design like Nature? Mark where Thames
Plenty and pleasure pours thro' Lincoln's meads;
Can the great artist, tho' with taste supreme
Endu'd, one beauty to this Eden add?
Tho' he, by rules unfetter'd, boldly scorns
Formality and method, round and square
Disdaining, plans irregularly great.
　　Creative Titian, can thy vivid strokes,
Or thine, O graceful Raphael, dare to vie
With the rich tints that paint the breathing mead?
The thousand-colour'd tulip, violet's bell
Snow-clad and meek, the vermeil-tinctur'd rose,
And golden crocus?—Yet with these the maid,
Phillis or Phœbe, at a feast or wake,

Her jetty locks enamels; fairer she,
In innocence and homespun vestments dress'd,
Than if cœrulean saphires at her ears
Shone pendent, or a precious diamond-cross
Heav'd gently on her panting bosom white.

    Yon shepherd idly stretch'd on the rude rock,
Listening to dashing waves, and sea-mews clang
High-hovering o'er his head, who views beneath
The dolphin dancing o'er the level brine,
Feels more true bliss than the proud admiral,
Amid his vessels bright with burnish'd gold
And silken streamers, tho' his lordly nod
Ten thousand war-worn mariners revere.
And great Æneas gaz'd with more delight
On the rough mountain shagg'd with horrid shades
(Where cloud-compelling Jove, as fancy dream'd,
Descending, shook his direful Ægis black)
Than if he enter'd the high Capitol
On golden columns rear'd, a conquer'd world
Exhausted, to enrich its stately head.
More pleas'd he slept in poor Evander's cott
On shaggy skins, lull'd by sweet nightingales,
Than if a Nero, in an age refin'd,
Beneath a gorgeous canopy had plac'd
His royal guest, and bade his minstrels sound
Soft slumb'rous Lydian airs, to soothe his rest.

    Happy the first of men, ere yet confin'd
To smoaky cities; who in sheltering groves,
Warm caves, and deep-sunk vallies liv'd and lov'd,
By cares unwounded; what the sun and showers,
And genial earth untillag'd, could produce,
They gather'd grateful, or the acorn brown,
Or blushing berry; by the liquid lapse
Of murm'ring waters call'd to slake their thirst,
Or with fair nymphs their sun-brown limbs to bathe;

With nymphs who fondly clasp'd their fav'rite youths,
Unaw'd by shame, beneath the beechen shade,
Nor wiles, nor artificial coyness knew.
Then doors and walls were not; the melting maid
Nor frown of parents fear'd, nor husband's threats;
Nor had curs'd gold their tender hearts allur'd:
Then beauty was not venal. Injur'd love,
O! whither, God of raptures, art thou fled?
While Avarice waves his golden wand around,
Abhorr'd magician, and his costly cup
Prepares with baneful drugs, t' enchant the souls
Of each low-thoughted fair to wed for gain.
  In earth's first infancy (as sung the bard
Who strongly painted what he boldly thought),
Tho' the fierce north oft smote with iron whip
Their shiv'ring limbs, tho' oft the bristly boar
Or hungry lion 'woke them with their howls,
And scar'd them from their moss-grown caves, to rove
Houseless and cold in dark tempestuous nights;
Yet were not myriads in embattl'd fields
Swept off at once, nor had the raging seas
O'erwhelm'd the found'ring bark and shrieking crew;
In vain the glassy ocean smil'd to tempt
The jolly sailor, unsuspecting harm,
For commerce ne'er had spread her swelling sails,
Nor had the wond'ring Nereids ever heard
The dashing oar: then famine, want, and pine,
Sunk to the grave their fainting limbs; but us,
Diseaseful dainties, riot, and excess,
And feverish luxury destroy. In brakes,
Or marshes wild unknowingly they crop'd
Herbs of malignant juice; to realms remote
While we for powerful poisons madly roam,
From every noxious herb collecting death.
What tho' unknown to those primeval sires

The well-arch'd dome, peopled with breathing forms
By fair Italia's skillful hand, unknown
The shapely column, and the crumbling busts
Of awful ancestors in long descent?
Yet why should man, mistaken, deem it nobler
To dwell in palaces, and high-roof'd halls,
Than in God's forests, architect supreme!
Say, is the Persian carpet, than the field's
Or meadow's mantle gay, more richly wov'n;
Or softer to the votaries of ease
Than bladed grass, perfum'd with dew-drop'd flow'rs?
O taste corrupt! that luxury and pomp
In specious names of polish'd manners veil'd,
Should proudly banish Nature's simple charms!
All-beauteous Nature! by thy boundless charms
Oppress'd, O where shall I begin thy praise,
Where turn th' ecstatick eye, how ease my breast
That pants with wild astonishment and love!
Dark forests, and the opening lawn, refresh'd
With ever-gushing brooks, hill, meadow, dale,
The balmy bean-field, the gay-clover'd close,
So sweetly interchang'd, the lowing ox,
The playful lamb, the distant water-fall
Now faintly heard, now swelling with the breeze,
The sound of pastoral reed from hazel-bower,
The choral birds, the neighing steed, that snuffs
His dappled mate, stung with intense desire,
The ripen'd orchard when the ruddy orbs
Betwixt the green leaves blush, the azure skies,
The cheerful sun that thro' earth's vitals pours
Delight and health and heat; all, all conspire
To raise, to soothe, to harmonize the mind,
To lift on wings of praise, to the great sire
Of being and of beauty, at whose nod
Creation started from the gloomy vault

Of dreary Chaos, while the grisly king
Murmur'd to feel his boisterous power confin'd.
    What are the lays of artful Addison,
Coldly correct, to Shakespear's warblings wild?
Whom on the winding Avon's willow'd banks
Fair fancy found, and bore the smiling babe
To a close cavern: (still the shepherds shew
The sacred place, whence with religious awe
They hear, returning from the field at eve,
Strange whisp'rings of sweet musick thro' the air)
Here, as with honey gather'd from the rock,
She fed the little prattler, and with songs
Oft sooth'd his wondering ears, with deep delight
On her soft lap he sat, and caught the sounds.
    Oft near some crouded city would I walk,
Listening the far-off noises, rattling cars,
Loud shouts of joy, sad shrieks of sorrow, knells
Full slowly tolling, instruments of trade,
Striking mine ears with one deep-swelling hum.
Or wand'ring near the sea, attend the sounds
Of hollow winds, and ever-beating waves.
Ev'n when wild tempests swallow up the plains,
And Boreas' blasts, big hail, and rains combine
To shake the groves and mountains, would I sit,
Pensively musing on th' outrageous crimes
That wake heav'n's vengeance: at such solemn hours,
Dæmons and goblins thro' the dark air shriek,
While Hecat, with her black-brow'd sisters nine,
Rides o'er the earth, and scatters woes and death.
Then too, they say, in drear Ægyptian wilds
The lion and the tiger prowl for prey
With roarings loud! the list'ning traveller
Starts fear-struck, while the hollow-echoing vaults
Of pyramids encrease the deathful sounds.
    But let me never fail in cloudless nights,

When silent Cynthia in her silver car
Thro' the blue concave slides, when shine the hills,
Twinkle the streams, and woods look tip'd with gold,
To seek some level mead, and there invoke
Old Midnight's sister Contemplation sage
(Queen of the rugged brow, and stern-fix'd eye)
To lift my soul above this little earth,
This folly-fetter'd world: to purge my ears,
That I may hear the rolling planets' song,
And tuneful turning spheres: if this be barr'd,
The little Fayes that dance in neighbouring dales,
Sipping the night-dew, while they laugh and love,
Shall charm me with aërial notes.—As thus
I wander musing, lo, what awful forms
Yonder appear! sharp-ey'd Philosophy
Clad in dun robes, an eagle on his wrist,
First meets my eye; next, virgin Solitude
Serene, who blushes at each gazer's sight;
Then Wisdom's hoary head, with crutch in hand,
Trembling, and bent with age; last, Virtue's self,
Smiling, in white array'd, who with her leads
Sweet Innocence, that prattles by her side,
A naked boy!—Harass'd with fear, I stop,
I gaze, when Virtue thus—"Whoe'er thou art,
Mortal, by whom I deign to be beheld
In these my midnight-walks; depart, and say
That henceforth I and my immortal train
Forsake Britannia's isle; who fondly stoops
To Vice, her favourite paramour."—She spoke,
And as she turn'd, her round and rosy neck,
Her flowing train, and long ambrosial hair,
Breathing rich odours, I enamour'd view.

     O who will bear me then to western climes
(Since Virtue leaves our wretched land), to fields
Yet unpolluted with Iberian swords:

To isles of innocence, from mortal view
Deeply retir'd, beneath a plantane's shade,
Where Happiness and Quiet sit enthron'd,
With simple Indian swains, that I may hunt
The boar and tiger thro' Savannah's wild,
Thro' fragrant desarts and thro' citron-groves.
There, fed on dates and herbs, would I despise
The far-fetch'd cates of Luxury, and hoards
Of narrow-hearted Avarice; nor heed
The distant din of the tumultuous world.
So when rude whirlwinds rouze the roaring main,
Beneath fair Thetis sits, in coral caves,
Serenely gay, nor sinking sailors' cries
Disturb her sportive nymphs, who round her form
The light fantastick dance, or for her hair
Weave rosy crowns, or with according lutes
Grace the soft warbles of her honied voice.

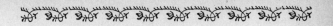

Thomas Warton

(1728–1790)

Verses on Sir Joshua Reynolds's
Painted Window at New-College, Oxford

Ah stay thy treacherous hand, forbear to trace
Those faultless forms of elegance and grace!
Ah, cease to spread the bright transparent mass,
With Titian's pencil, o'er the speaking glass!
Nor steal, by strokes of art with truth combin'd,
The fond illusions of my wayward mind!
For long, enamour'd of a barbarous age,
A faithless truant to the classic page;
Long have I lov'd to catch the simple chime
Of minstrel-harps, and spell the fabling rhyme;
To view the festive rites, the knightly play,
That deck'd heroic Albion's elder day;
To mark the mouldering halls of Barons bold,
And the rough castle, cast in giant mould;
With Gothic manners Gothic arts explore,
And muse on the magnificence of yore.

But chief, enraptur'd have I lov'd to roam,
A lingering votary, the vaulted dome,
Where the tall shafts, that mount in massy pride,
Their mingling branches shoot from side to side;
Where elfin sculptors, with fantastic clew,
O'er the long roof their wild embroidery drew;
Where *Superstition* with capricious hand

527

In many a maze the wreathed window plann'd,
With hues romantic ting'd the gorgeous pane,
To fill with holy light the wondrous fane;
To aid the builder's model, richly rude,
By no Vitruvian symmetry subdued;
To suit the genius of the mystic pile:
Whilst as around the far-retiring ile,
And fretted shrines, with hoary trophies hung,
Her dark illumination wide she flung,
With new solemnity, the nooks profound,
The caves of death, and the dim arches frown'd.
From bliss long felt unwillingly we part:
Ah, spare the weakness of a lover's heart!
Chase not the phantoms of my fairy dream,
Phantoms that shrink at Reason's painful gleam!
That softer touch, insidious artist, stay,
Nor to new joys my struggling breast betray!

Such was a pensive bard's mistaken strain.—
But, oh, of ravish'd pleasures why complain?
No more the matchless skill I call unkind
That strives to disenchant my cheated mind.
For when again I view thy chaste Design,
The just proportion, and the genuin line;
Those native portraitures of Attic art,
That from the lucid surface seem to start;
Those tints, that steal no glories from the day,
Nor ask the sun to lend his streaming ray;
The doubtful radiance of contending dyes,
That faintly mingle, yet distinctly rise;
'Twixt light and shade the transitory strife;
The feature blooming with immortal life:
The stole in casual foldings taught to flow,
Not with ambitious ornaments to glow;
The tread majestic, and the beaming eye

That lifted speaks its commerce with the sky:
Heaven's golden emanation, gleaming mild
O'er the mean cradle of the virgin's child:
Sudden, the sombrous imagery is fled,
Which late my visionary rapture fed:
Thy powerful hand has broke the Gothic chain,
And brought my bosom back to truth again:
To truth, by no peculiar taste confin'd,
Whose universal pattern strikes mankind;
To truth, whose bold and unresisted aim
Checks frail caprice, and fashion's fickle claim;
To truth, whose Charms deception's magic quell,
And bind coy Fancy in a stronger spell.

Ye brawny Prophets, that in robes so rich,
At distance due, possess the crisped nich;
Ye Rows of Patriarch's that sublimely rear'd
Diffuse a proud primeval length of beard:
Ye Saints, who clad in crimson's bright array,
More pride than humble poverty display;
Ye Virgins meek, that wear the palmy crown
Of patient faith, and yet so fiercely frown:
Ye Angels, that from clouds of gold recline,
But boast no semblance to a race divine.
Ye tragic Tales of legendary lore,
That draw devotion's ready tear no more:
Ye Martyrdoms of unenlighten'd days,
Ye Miracles that now no wonder raise:
Shapes, that with one broad glare the gazer strike,
Kings, Bishops, Nuns, Apostles, all alike!
Ye Colours, that th'unwary sight amaze,
And only dazzle in the noontide blaze!
No more the Sacred Window's round disgrace,
But yield to Grecian groupes the shining space.
Lo, from the canvas Beauty shifts her throne,

Lo, Picture's powers a new formation own!
Behold, she prints upon the crystal plain,
With her own energy, th'expressive stain!
The mighty Master spreads his mimic toil
More wide, nor only blends the breathing oil;
But calls the lineaments of life compleat
From genial alchymy's creative heat;
Obedient forms to the bright fusion gives,
While in the warm enamel Nature lives.

Reynolds, 'tis thine, from the broad window's height,
To add new lustre to religious light:
Not of its pomp to strip this ancient shrine,
But bid that pomp with purer radiance shine:
With arts unknown before, to reconcile
The willing Graces to the Gothic pile.

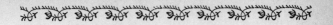

William Collins

(1721–1759)

Ode Written in the Beginning of the Year 1746

How sleep the Brave, who sink to Rest,
By all their Country's Wishes blest!
When *Spring*, with dewy Fingers cold,
Returns to deck their hallow'd Mold,
She there shall dress a sweeter Sod,
Than *Fancy's* Feet have ever trod.

By Fairy Hands their Knell is rung,
By Forms unseen their Dirge is sung;
There *Honour* comes, a Pilgrim grey,
To bless the Turf that wraps their Clay,
And *Freedom* shall a-while repair,
To dwell a weeping Hermit there!

Ode to Evening

If ought of Oaten Stop, or Pastoral Song,
May hope, O pensive *Eve*, to sooth thine Ear,
    Like thy own brawling Springs,
    Thy Springs, and dying Gales,
O *Nymph* reserv'd, while now the bright-hair'd Sun
Sits in yon western Tent, whose cloudy Skirts,

With Brede ethereal wove,
  O'erhang his wavy Bed:
Now Air is hush'd, save where the weak-ey'd Bat,
With short shrill Shriek flits by on leathern Wing,
  Or where the Beetle winds
  His small but sullen Horn,
As oft he rises 'midst the twilight Path,
Against the Pilgrim born in heedless Hum:
  Now teach me, *Maid* compos'd,
  To breathe some soften'd Strain,
Whose Numbers stealing thro' thy darkning Vale,
May not unseemly with its Stillness suit,
  As musing slow, I hail
  Thy genial lov'd Return!

For when thy folding Star arising shews
His paly Circlet, at his warning Lamp
  The fragrant *Hours*, and *Elves*
  Who slept in Buds the Day,
And many a *Nymph* who wreaths her Brows with
  Sedge,
And sheds the fresh'ning Dew, and lovelier still,
  The *Pensive Pleasures* sweet
  Prepare thy shadowy Car.

Then let me rove some wild and heathy Scene,
Or find some Ruin 'midst its dreary Dells,
  Whose Walls more awful nod
  By thy religious Gleams.
Or if chill blustring Winds, or driving Rain,
Prevent my willing Feet, be mine the Hut,
  That from the Mountain's Side,
  Views Wilds, and swelling Floods,
And Hamlets brown, and dim-discover'd Spires,
And hears their simple Bell, and marks o'er all
  Thy Dewy Fingers draw
  The gradual dusky Veil.

While *Spring* shall pour his Show'rs, as oft he wont,
And bathe thy breathing Tresses, meekest *Eve!*
 While *Summer* loves to sport,
 Beneath thy ling'ring Light:
While sallow *Autumn* fills thy Lap with Leaves,
Or *Winter* yelling thro' the troublous Air,
 Affrights thy shrinking Train,
 And rudely rends thy Robes.
So long regardful of thy quiet Rule,
Shall *Fancy, Friendship, Science*, smiling *Peace*,
 Thy gentlest Influence own,
 And love thy fav'rite Name!

Ode on the Poetical Character

[STROPHE]

As once, if not with light Regard
I read aright that gifted Bard,
(Him whose School above the rest
His Loveliest *Elfin* Queen has blest.)
One, only One, unrival'd Fair,
Might hope the magic Girdle wear,
At solemn Turney hung on high,
The Wish of each love-darting Eye;

Lo! to each other Nymph in turn applied,
 As if, in Air unseen, some hov'ring Hand,
Some chaste and Angel-Friend to Virgin-Fame,
 With whisper'd Spell had burst the starting Band,
It left unblest her loath'd dishonour'd Side;
  Happier hopeless Fair, if never
  Her baffled Hand with vain Endeavour
Had touch'd that fatal Zone to her denied!

Young *Fancy* thus, to me Divinest Name,
 To whom, prepar'd and bath'd in Heav'n,
 The Cest of amplet Pow'r is giv'n:
 To few the God-like Gift assigns,
 To gird their blest prophetic Loins,
And gaze her visions wild, and feel unmix'd her Flame!

[EPODE]

The Band, as Fairy Legends say,
Was wove on that creating Day,
When He, who call'd with Thought to Birth
Yon tented Sky, this laughing Earth,
And drest with Springs, and Forests tall,
And pour'd the Main engirting all,
Long by the lov'd *Enthusiast* woo'd,
Himself in some Diviner Mood,
Retiring, sate with her alone,
And plac'd her on his Saphire Throne,
The whiles, the vaulted Shrine around,
Seraphic Wires were heard to sound,
Now sublimest Triumph swelling,
Now on Love and Mercy dwelling;
And she, from out the veiling Cloud,
Breath'd her magic Notes aloud:
And Thou, Thou rich-hair'd Youth of Morn,
And all thy subject Life was born!
The dang'rous Passions kept aloof,
Far from the sainted growing Woof:
But near it sate Ecstatic *Wonder*,
List'ning the deep applauding Thunder:
And *Truth*, in sunny Vest array'd,
By whose the Tarsel's Eyes were made;
All the shad'wy Tribes of *Mind*,
In braided Dance their Murmurs join'd,
And all the bright uncounted *Pow'rs*,

Who feed on Heav'n's ambrosial Flow'rs.
Where is the Bard, whose Soul can now
Its high presuming Hopes avow?
Where He who thinks, with Rapture blind,
This hallow'd Work for Him design'd?

[ANTISTROPHE]

High on some Cliff, to Heav'n up-pil'd,
Of rude Access, of Prospect wild,
Where, tangled round the jealous Steep,
Strange Shades o'erbrow the Valleys deep,
And holy *Genii* guard the Rock,
Its Gloomes embrown, its Springs unlock,
While on its rich ambitious Head,
An *Eden,* like his own, lies spread:

I view that Oak, the fancied Glades among,
  By which as *Milton* lay, His Ev'ning Ear,
From many a Cloud that drop'd Ethereal Dew,
  Nigh spher'd in Heav'n its native Strains could hear:
On which that ancient Trump he reach'd was hung;
    Thither oft his Glory greeting,
    From Waller's Myrtle Shades retreating,
With many a Vow from Hope's aspiring Tongue,

My trembling Feet his guiding Steps pursue;
    In vain—Such Bliss to One alone,
    Of all the Sons of Soul was known,
    And Heav'n, and *Fancy,* kindred Pow'rs,
    Have now o'erturn'd th' inspiring Bow'rs,
Or curtain'd close such Scene from ev'ry future View.

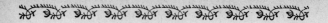

Thomas Gray

(1716–1771)

Ode on the Death of a Favourite Cat, Drowned in a Tub of Gold Fishes

'Twas on a lofty vase's side,
Where China's gayest art had dy'd
   The azure flowers, that blow;
Demurest of the tabby kind,
The pensive Selima reclin'd,
   Gazed on the lake below.

Her conscious tail her joy declar'd;
The fair round face, the snowy beard,
   The velvet of her paws,
Her coat, that with the tortoise vies,
Her ears of jet, and emerald eyes,
   She saw; and purr'd applause.

Still had she gaz'd; but 'midst the tide
Two angel forms were seen to glide,
   The Genii of the stream:
Their scaly armour's Tyrian hue
Thro' richest purple to the view
   Betray'd a golden gleam.

The hapless Nymph with wonder saw:
A whisker first and then a claw,
   With many an ardent wish,
She stretch'd in vain to reach the prize.

What female heart can gold despise?
 What Cat's averse to fish?

Presumptuous Maid! with looks intent
Again she stretch'd, again she bent,
 Nor knew the gulf between.
(Malignant Fate sat by, and smil'd)
The slipp'ry verge her feet beguil'd,
 She tumbled headlong in.

Eight times emerging from the flood
She mew'd to ev'ry watry God,
 Some speedy aid to send.
No Dolphin came, no Nereid stirr'd:
Nor cruel *Tom*, nor *Susan* heard.
 A Fav'rite has no friend!

From hence, ye Beauties, undeceiv'd,
Know, one false step is ne'er retriev'd,
 And be with caution bold.
Not all that tempts your wand'ring eyes
And heedless hearts, is lawful prize;
 Nor all, that glisters, gold.

The Triumphs of Owen

A FRAGMENT

Owen's praise demands my song,
Owen swift, and Owen strong;
Fairest flower of Roderic's stem,
Gwyneth's shield, and Britain's gem.
He nor heaps his brooded stores,
Nor on all profusely pours;

Lord of every regal art,
Liberal hand, and open heart.

Big with hosts of mighty name,
Squadrons three against him came;
This the force of Eirin hiding,
Side by side as proudly riding,
On her shadow long and gay
Lochlin plows the watry way;
There the Norman sails afar
Catch the winds, and join the war:
Black and huge along they sweep,
Burthens of the angry deep.

Dauntless on his native sands
The Dragon-Son of Mona stands;
In glitt'ring arms and glory drest,
High he rears his ruby crest.
There the thund'ring strokes begin,
There the press, and there the din;
Talymalfra's rocky shore
Echoing to the battle's roar.
Where his glowing eye-balls turn,
Thousand Banners round him burn.
Where he points his purple spear,
Hasty, hasty Rout is there,
Marking with indignant eye
Fear to stop, and shame to fly.
There Confusion, Terror's child,
Conflict fierce, and Ruin wild,
Agony, that pants for breath,
Despair and honourable Death.

Elegy Written in a Country Church-Yard

The Curfew tolls the knell of parting day,
The lowing herd wind slowly o'er the lea,
The plowman homeward plods his weary way,
And leaves the world to darkness and to me.

Now fades the glimmering landscape on the sight,
And all the air a solemn stillness holds,
Save where the beetle wheels his droning flight,
And drowsy tinklings lull the distant folds;

Save that from yonder ivy-mantled tow'r
The mopeing owl does to the moon complain
Of such, as wand'ring near her secret bow'r,
Molest her ancient solitary reign.

Beneath those rugged elms, that yew-tree's shade,
Where heaves the turf in many a mould'ring heap,
Each in his narrow cell for ever laid,
The rude Forefathers of the hamlet sleep.

The breezy call of incense-breathing Morn,
The swallow twitt'ring from the straw-built shed,
The cock's shrill clarion, or the echoing horn,
No more shall rouse them from their lowly bed.

For them no more the blazing hearth shall burn,
Or busy housewife ply her evening care:
No children run to lisp their sire's return,
Or climb his knees the envied kiss to share.

Oft did the harvest to their sickle yield,
Their furrow oft the stubborn glebe has broke;

How jocund did they drive their team afield!
How bow'd the woods beneath their sturdy stroke!

Let not Ambition mock their useful toil,
Their homely joys, and destiny obscure;
Nor Grandeur hear with a disdainful smile,
The short and simple annals of the poor.

The boast of heraldry, the pomp of pow'r,
And all that beauty, all that wealth e'er gave,
Awaits alike th' inevitable hour.
The paths of glory lead but to the grave.

Nor you, ye Proud, impute to These the fault,
If Mem'ry o'er their Tomb no Trophies raise,
Where thro' the long-drawn isle and fretted vault
The pealing anthem swells the note of praise.

Can storied urn or animated bust
Back to its mansion call the fleeting breath?
Can Honour's voice provoke the silent dust,
Or Flatt'ry sooth the dull cold ear of Death?

Perhaps in this neglected spot is laid
Some heart once pregnant with celestial fire;
Hands, that the rod of empire might have sway'd,
Or wak'd to extasy the living lyre.

But Knowledge to their eyes her ample page
Rich with the spoils of time did ne'er unroll;
Chill Penury repress'd their noble rage,
And froze the genial current of the soul.

Full many a gem of purest ray serene,
The dark unfathom'd caves of ocean bear:
Full many a flower is born to blush unseen,
And waste its sweetness on the desert air.

Some village-Hampden, that with dauntless breast
The little Tyrant of his fields withstood;
Some mute inglorious Milton here may rest,
Some Cromwell guiltless of his country's blood.

Th' applause of list'ning senates to command,
The threats of pain and ruin to despise,
To scatter plenty o'er a smiling land,
And read their hist'ry in a nation's eyes,

Their lot forbad: nor circumscrib'd alone
Their growing virtues, but their crimes confin'd;
Forbad to wade through slaughter to a throne,
And shut the gates of mercy on mankind,

The struggling pangs of conscious truth to hide,
To quench the blushes of ingenuous shame,
Or heap the shrine of Luxury and Pride
With incense kindled at the Muse's flame.

Far from the madding crowd's ignoble strife,
Their sober wishes never learn'd to stray;
Along the cool sequester'd vale of life
They kept the noiseless tenor of their way.

Yet ev'n these bones from insult to protect
Some frail memorial still erected nigh,
With uncouth rhimes and shapeless sculpture deck'd,
Implores the passing tribute of a sigh.

Their name, their years, spelt by th' unletter'd muse,
The place of fame and elegy supply:
And many a holy text around she strews,
That teach the rustic moralist to die.

For who to dumb Forgetfulness a prey,
This pleasing anxious being e'er resign'd,

Left the warm precincts of the chearful day,
Nor cast one longing ling'ring look behind?

On some fond breast the parting soul relies,
Some pious drops the closing eye requires;
Ev'n from the tomb the voice of Nature cries,
Ev'n in our Ashes live their wonted Fires.

For thee, who mindful of th' unhonour'd Dead
Dost in these lines their artless tale relate;
If chance, by lonely contemplation led,
Some kindred Spirit shall inquire thy fate,

Haply some hoary-headed Swain may say,
"Oft have we seen him at the peep of dawn
Brushing with hasty steps the dews away
To meet the sun upon the upland lawn.

"There at the foot of yonder nodding beech
That wreathes its old fantastic roots so high,
His listless length at noontide would he stretch,
And pore upon the brook that babbles by.

"Hard by yon wood, now smiling as in scorn,
Mutt'ring his wayward fancies he would rove,
Now drooping, woeful wan, like one forlorn,
Or craz'd with care, or cross'd in hopeless love.

"One morn I miss'd him on the custom'd hill,
Along the heath and near his fav'rite tree;
Another came; nor yet beside the rill,
Nor up the lawn, nor at the wood was he;

"The next with dirges due in sad array
Slow thro' the church-way path we saw him born.
Approach and read (for thou can'st read) the lay,
Grav'd on the stone beneath yon aged thorn."

THE EPITAPH

Here rests his head upon the lap of Earth
A Youth to Fortune and to Fame unknown.
Fair Science frown'd not on his humble birth,
And Melancholy mark'd him for her own.

Large was his bounty, and his soul sincere,
Heav'n did a recompence as largely send:
He gave to Mis'ry all he had, a tear,
He gain'd from Heav'n ('twas all he wish'd) a friend.

No farther seek his merits to disclose,
Or draw his frailties from their dread abode,
(There they alike in trembling hope repose,)
The bosom of his Father and his God.

Ode on a Distant Prospect of Eton College

Ye distant spires, ye antique towers,
That crown the watry glade,
Where grateful Science still adores
Her HENRY's holy Shade;
And ye, that from the stately brow
Of WINDSOR's heights th' expanse below
Of grove, of lawn, of mead survey,
Whose turf, whose shade, whose flowers among
Wanders the hoary Thames along
His silver-winding way.

Ah happy hills, ah pleasing shade,
Ah fields belov'd in vain,
Where once my careless childhood stray'd,

A stranger yet to pain!
I feel the gales, that from ye blow,
A momentary bliss bestow,
As waving fresh their gladsome wing,
My weary soul they seem to sooth,
And, redolent of joy and youth,
To breathe a second spring.

Say, Father THAMES, for thou hast seen
Full many a sprightly race
Disporting on thy margent green
The paths of pleasure trace,
Who foremost now delight to cleave
With pliant arm thy glassy wave?
The captive linnet which enthrall?
What idle progeny succeed
To chase the rolling circle's speed,
Or urge the flying ball?

While some on earnest business bent
Their murm'ring labours ply
'Gainst graver hours, that bring constraint
To sweeten liberty:
Some bold adventurers disdain
The limits of their little reign,
And unknown regions dare descry:
Still as they run they look behind,
They hear a voice in every wind,
And snatch a fearful joy.

Gay hope is theirs by fancy fed,
Less pleasing when possest;
The tear forgot as soon as shed,
The sunshine of the breast:
Theirs buxom health of rosy hue,
Wild wit, invention ever-new,

And lively chear of vigour born;
The thoughtless day, the easy night,
The spirits pure, the slumbers light,
That fly th' approach of morn.

Alas, regardless of their doom,
The little victims play!
No sense have they of ills to come,
Nor care beyond to-day:
Yet see how all around 'em wait
The Ministers of human fate,
And black Misfortune's baleful train!
Ah, shew them where in ambush stand
To seize their prey the murth'rous band!
Ah, tell them, they are men!

These shall the fury Passions tear,
The vulturs of the mind,
Disdainful Anger, pallid Fear,
And Shame that sculks behind;
Or pineing Love shall waste their youth,
Or Jealousy with rankling tooth,
That inly gnaws the secret heart,
And Envy wan, and faded Care,
Grim-visag'd comfortless Despair,
And Sorrow's piercing dart.

Ambition this shall tempt to rise,
Then whirl the wretch from high,
To bitter Scorn a sacrifice,
And grinning Infamy.
The stings of Falshood those shall try,
And hard Unkindness' alter'd eye,
That mocks the tear it forc'd to flow;
And keen Remorse with blood defil'd,
And moody Madness laughing wild
Amid severest woe.

Lo, in the vale of years beneath
A griesly troop are seen,
The painful family of Death,
More hideous than their Queen:
This racks the joints, this fires the veins,
That every labouring sinew strains,
Those in the deeper vitals rage:
Lo, Poverty, to fill the band,
That numbs the soul with icy hand,
And slow-consuming Age.

To each his suff'rings: all are men,
Condemn'd alike to groan,
The tender for another's pain;
Th' unfeeling for his own.
Yet ah! why should they know their fate?
Since sorrow never comes too late,
And happiness too swiftly flies.
Thought would destroy their paradise.
No more; where ignorance is bliss,
'Tis folly to be wise.

Sonnet on the Death of Richard West

In vain to me the smileing Mornings shine,
    And redning Phœbus lifts his golden Fire:
The Birds in vain their amorous Descant joyn;
    Or chearful Fields resume their green Attire:
These Ears, alas! for other Notes repine,
    A different Object do these Eyes require.
My lonely Anguish melts no Heart, but mine;
    And in my Breast the imperfect Joys expire.
Yet Morning smiles the busy Race to chear,

And new-born Pleasure brings to happier Men:
The Fields to all their wonted Tribute bear:
  To warm their little Loves the Birds complain:
I fruitless mourn to him, that cannot hear,
  And weep the more because I weep in vain.

John Wolcot (Peter Pindar)

(1738–1819)

A TOWN ECLOGUE

[*Introduction and Anecdotes*]

When *Johnson* sought (as Shakespear says) *that bourn,*
From whence, alas! no travellers return:
In *humbler* English, when the *Doctor* died,
Apollo whimper'd and the *Muses* cried;
Parnassus mop'd for days, in business slack,
And like a *herse*, the hill was hung with *black.*
Minerva sighing for her *fav'rite* son,
Pronounc'd, with lengthen'd face, the world *undone:*
Her *owl*, too, hooted in so loud a stile,
That people might have heard the *bird, a mile:*
Jove wip'd his eyes so red, and told his *wife,*
He ne'er made *Johnson's equal,* in his life;
And that 'twould be a *long time* first, if *ever,*
His art could form a fellow *half so clever:*
Venus, of all the little Loves, the *dam,*
With all the *Graces,* sobb'd for *brother* Sam:
Such were the heav'nly howlings for his death,
As if *Dame Nature* had *resign'd* her *breath.*
Nor less sonorous was the grief, I ween,
Amidst the natives of our *earthly* scene:
From beggars, to the GREAT who hold the helm,

548

One *Johnso-mania* rag'd through all the realm!
"*Who,* (cried the world) can match his prose or rhime?
O'er wits of modern days, he tow'rs *sublime!*
An *oak,* wide spreading o'er the *shrubs* below,
That round his roots, with puny foliage, blow:
A *Pyramid,* amidst some barren waste,
That frowns o'er *huts* the sport of ev'ry blast:
A mighty *Atlas,* whose aspiring head,
O'er distant regions, casts an awful shade.
By *kings* and beggars lo! his tales are told,
And ev'ry sentence glows a *grain of gold!*
Blest! who his philosophic phiz can *take,*
Catch ev'n his weaknesses—his *noddle's shake,*
The lengthen'd lip of scorn, the forehead's scowl,
The low'ring eye's contempt, and bear-like growl.
In vain, the *critics* aim their toothless rage!
Mere *sprats,* that venture war with *whales* to wage:
Unmov'd he stands, and feels their force, *no more*
Than some huge rock amidst the *wat'ry roar,*
That calmly bears the tumults of the *deep,*
And howling *tempests,* that as well may *sleep.*"

　　Strong, midst the *Rambler's cronies,* was the rage
To fill with his *bons mots,* and tales, the page:
Mere flies, that buzz'd around his setting ray,
And bore a *splendor,* on their wings, away:
Thus round his *orb,* the pigmy *planets* run,
And catch their little lustre from the SUN.

　　At length, rush'd forth two *candidates* for fame,
A *Scotchman,* one; and one a *London Dame:*
That, by th' emphatic *Johnson,* christ'ned *Bozzy;*
This, by the *Bishop's* License, *Dame Piozzi;*
Whose *widow'd* name, by topers lov'd, was *Thrale,*
Bright in the annals of *election ale:*
A name, by *marriage,* that gave up the *ghost!*

In *poor Pedocchio*,[1]—no! *Piozzi*, lost!
Each seiz'd with ardor wild, the grey goose quill:
Each sat to work the *intellectual mill:*
That *pecks* of *bran* so coarse, began to pour,
To *one poor* solitary grain of *flour.*

    Forth rush'd to light, their books—but *who* should
      say,
Which bore the palm of anecdote away?
This, to decide, the *rival wits* agreed,
Before *Sir John* their tales and jokes to read,
And let the *Knight's* opinion in the strife,
Declare the prop'rest pen to write *Sam's life:* . . .

BOZZY

    At supper, rose a dialogue on witches,
When *Crosbie* said, there could not be such b–tch–s;
And that 'twas *blasphemy* to think *such hags*
Could stir up storms, and on their *broomstick nags*
Gallop along the air with wondrous pace,
And boldly fly in *God Almighty's* face:
But *Johnson* answer'd him, "There *might be* witches,
Nought prov'd the non existence of the b–tch–s."

MADAME PIOZZI

    In Lincolnshire, a lady show'd our friend
A grotto, that she wish'd him to *commend:*
Quoth she, "How *cool* in summer this abode!"
"Yes, Madam, (answer'd *Johnson*) for a *toad*."

BOZZY

    As at *Argyle's* grand house, my hat I took,
To seek my alehouse; thus began the Duke,

---

[1] The author was nearly committing a blunder—fortunate indeed was his recollection; as *Pedocchio* signifies in the Italian language, that most contemptible of animals, a *louse*. [Author's note.]

"Pray, Mr. Boswell, won't you have some tea?"
To this, I made my bow, and did agree—
Then to the drawing room, we both retreated,
Where *Lady Betty Hamilton* was seated
Close by the *Duchess,* who, in deep discourse,
Took no more notice of me than a *horse.*
Next day *myself,* and Doctor *Johnson* took
Our hats, to go and wait upon the Duke:
Next to himself, the *Duke* did *Johnson* place,
But I, thank God, sat *second* to his *Grace.*
The place was due, most surely to my merits—
And faith, I was in very pretty spirits:
I plainly saw (my penetration such is)
I was not yet in favour with the *Duchess.*
Thought I, I am not disconcerted yet—
Before we part, I'll give her *Grace* a *sweat*—
Then looks of intrepidity I put on,
And ask'd her, if she'd have a plate of mutton.
This was a glorious deed must be confess'd!
I knew I was the *Duke's,* and not *her* guest!
Knowing—as I'm. a man of tip-top breeding,
That *great folks* drink no healths whilst they are feed-
        ing;
I took my glass, and looking at her *Grace,*
I star'd her like a *devil* in the face:
And in *respectful* terms, as was my duty,
Said I, my *Lady Duchess,* I salute ye:
Most audible, indeed, was my salute,
For which some folks will say I was a brute:
But faith, it dash'd her, as I knew it wou'd,
But then I knew, that I was flesh and blood.

MADAME PIOZZI

One day, with spirits low, and sorrow fill'd,
I told him that I had a *cousin kill'd:*

"My dear," quoth he, "for heav'n's sake hold your *can-
      ing;*
Were all your cousins kill'd, they'd not be *wanting:*
Though *Death* on each of them should set his *mark,*
Though ev'ry one were spitted like a lark—
Roasted, and given that dog there, for a meal;
The loss of them, the world would never feel—
Trust me, dear Madam, all your *dear relations,*
Are nits—are *nothings* in the eye of *nations.*"
Again, says I one day—"I do believe,
A good acquaintance that I have, will *grieve,*
To hear her *friend* hath lost a *large estate:*"
"Yes, (answer'd he) lament *as much* her *fate,*
As did your *horse* (I freely will allow)
To hear of the *miscarriage* of your *cow.*"

BOZZY

Of *Doctor Johnson,* having giv'n a sketch,
Permit me, Reader, of *myself,* to preach—
The world will certainly receive with glee,
The slightest bit of history of *Me.*
Think of a *gentleman* of ancient blood!
Prouder of *title,* than of being *good.*
A *gentleman* just thirty-three years old:
Married four years, and as a Tyger, bold;
Whose bowels yearn'd *Great Britain's* foes to tame,
And from the cannon's mouth to swallow flame;
To get his limbs by broad swords carv'd in wars
Like some old bedstead, and to *boast* his scars;
And proud immortal actions to atchieve,
See his hide bor'd by bullets, like a sieve.
But lo! his father, a *well-judging* Judge,
Forbade his son from Edinburgh to budge—
Resolv'd the French should not his b–ckside claw;
So bound his *son* apprentice to the law.

This *gentleman* had been in foreign parts,
And, like *Ulysses,* learnt a world of arts:
Much wisdom, his vast travels having brought him,
He was not *half* the fool, the people *thought* him—
Of prudence, this *same gentleman* was *such,*
He rather had *too little,* than *too much.*
Bright was this *gentleman's* imagination,
Well calculated for the *highest* station:
Indeed so *lively,* give the dev'l his due,
He ten times more would utter, than was *true.*
Which forc'd him frequently against his will,
Poor man! to swallow many a bitter pill—
One bitter pill among the rest, he took,
Which was to cut some *scandal* from his book.—
By *Doctor Johnson* he is well pourtray'd:
Quoth he, "Of *Bozzy* it may well be said,
That through the most *inhospitable* scene,
One never can be troubled with the spleen,
Nor ev'n the greatest difficulties *chafe at,*
Whilst *such an animal* is near, to *laugh at.*"

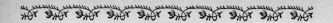

Christopher Smart
(1722–1771)

The Nativity of Our Lord

Where is this stupendous stranger,
    Swains of Solyma, advise,
Lead me to my Master's manger,
    Shew me where my Saviour lies?

O Most Mighty! O MOST HOLY!
    Far beyond the seraph's thought,
Art thou then so mean and lowly
    As unheeded prophets taught?

O the magnitude of meekness!
    Worth from worth immortal sprung;
O the strength of infant weakness,
    If eternal is so young!

If so young and thus eternal,
    Michael tune the shepherd's reed,
Where the scenes are ever vernal,
    And the loves be love indeed!

See the God blasphemed and doubted
    In the schools of Greece and Rome;
See the pow'rs of darkness routed,
    Taken at their utmost gloom.

Nature's decorations glisten
    Far above their usual trim;

Birds on box and laurel listen,
  As so near the cherubs hymn.

Boreas now no longer winters
  On the desolated coast;
Oaks no more are riv'n in splinters
  By the whirlwind and his host.

Spinks and ouzels sing sublimely,
  "We too have a Saviour born;"
Whiter blossoms burst untimely
  On the blest Mosaic thorn.

God all-bounteous, all-creative,
  Whom no ills from good dissuade.
Is incarnate, and a native
  Of the very world he made.

FROM *Jubilate Agno*

LET ELIZUR REJOICE WITH THE PARTRIDGE

Let Elizur rejoice with the Partridge, who is a prisoner
  of state and is proud of his keepers.
For I am not without authority in my jeopardy, which I
  derive inevitably from the glory of the name of the
  Lord.
Let Shedeur rejoice with Pyrausta, who dwelleth in a
  medium of fire, which God hath adapted for him.
For I bless God whose name is Jealous—and there is a
  zeal to deliver us from everlasting burnings.
Let Shelumiel rejoice with Olor, who is of a goodly
  savour, and the very look of him harmonizes the mind.
For my existimation is good even amongst the slanderers

and my memory shall arise for a sweet savour unto the Lord.

Let Jael rejoice with the Plover, who whistles for his live, and foils the marksmen and their guns.

For I bless the PRINCE of PEACE and pray that all the guns may be nail'd up, save such [as] are for the rejoicing days.

Let Raguel rejoice with the Cock of Portugal—God send good Angels to the allies of England!

For I have abstained from the blood of the grape and that even at the Lord's table.

Let Hobab rejoice with Necydalus, who is the Greek of a Grub.

For I have glorified God in GREEK and LATIN, the consecrated languages spoken by the Lord on earth.

Let Zurishaddai with the Polish Cock rejoice—The Lord restore peace to Europe.

For I meditate the peace of Europe amongst family bickerings and domestic jars.

Let Zuar rejoice with the Guinea Hen—The Lord add to his mercies in the WEST!

For the HOST is in the WEST—the Lord make us thankful unto salvation.

Let Chesed rejoice with Strepsiceros, whose weapons are the ornaments of his peace.

For I preach the very GOSPEL of CHRIST without comment and with this weapon shall I slay envy.

Let Hagar rejoice with Gnesion, who is the right sort of eagle, and towers the highest.

For I bless God in the rising generation, which is on my side.

Let Libni rejoice with the Redshank, who migrates not but is translated to the upper regions.

For I have translated in the charity, which makes things better and I shall be translated myself at the last.

Let Nahshon rejoice with the Seabreese, the Lord give
the sailors of his Spirit.

For he that walked upon the sea, hath prepared the
floods with the Gospel of peace.

Let Helon rejoice with the Woodpecker—the Lord
encourage the propagation of trees!

For the merciful man is merciful to his beast, and to the
trees that give them shelter.

Let Amos rejoice with the Coote—prepare to meet thy
God, O Israel.

For he hath turned the shadow of death into the morning, the Lord is his name.

Let Ephah rejoice with Buprestis, the Lord endue us
with temperance and humanity, till every cow can
have her mate!

For I am come home again, but there is nobody to kill
the calf or to pay the musick.

Let Sarah rejoice with the Redwing, whose harvest is
in the frost and snow.

For the hour of my felicity, like the womb of Sarah,
shall come at the latter end.

Let Rebekah rejoice with Iynx, who holds his head on
one side to deceive the adversary.

For I shou'd have avail'd myself of waggery, had not
malice been multitudinous.

Let Shuah rejoice with Boa, which is the vocal serpent.

For there are still serpents that can speak—God bless
my head, my heart and my heel.

Let Ehud rejoice with Onocrotalus, whose braying is
for the glory of God, because he makes the best
musick in his power.

For I bless God that I am of the same seed as Ehud,
Mutius Scævola, and Colonel Draper.

Let Shamgar rejoice with Otis, who looks about him for

the glory of God, and sees the horizon compleat at once.

For the word of God is a sword on my side—no matter what other weapon a stick or a straw.

Let Bohan rejoice with the Scythian Stag—he is beef and breeches against want and nakedness.

For I have adventured myself in the name of the Lord, and he hath mark'd me for his own.

Let Achsah rejoice with the Pigeon who is an antidote to malignity and will carry a letter.

For I bless God for the Postmaster general and all conveyancers of letters under his care especially Allen and Shelvock.

Let Tohu rejoice with the Grouse—the Lord further the cultivating of heaths and the peopling of deserts.

For my grounds in New Canaan shall infinitely compensate for the flats and maynes of Staindrop Moor.

Let Hillel rejoice with Ammodytes, whose colour is deceitful and he plots against the pilgrim's feet.

For the praise of God can give to a mute fish the notes of a nightingale.

Let Eli rejoice with Leucon—he is an honest fellow, which is a rarity.

For I have seen the White Raven and Thomas Hall of Willingham and am myself a greater curiosity than both.

Let Jemuel rejoice with Charadrius, who is from the HEIGHT and the sight of him is good for the jaundice.

For I look up to heaven which is my prospect to escape envy by surmounting it.

Let Pharaoh rejoice with Anataria, whom God permits to prey upon the ducks to check their increase.

For if Pharaoh had known Joseph, he woud have blessed God and me for the illumination of the people.

Let Lotan rejoice with Sauterelle. Blessed be the name
of the Lord from the Lote-tree to the Palm.

For I pray God to bless improvements in gardening until
London be a city of palm-trees.

Let Dishon rejoice with the Landrail, God give his grace
to the society for preserving the game.

For I pray to give his grace to the poor of England, that
Charity be not offended and that benevolence may
increase.

Let Hushim rejoice with the King's Fisher, who is of
royal beauty, tho' plebeian size.

For in my nature I quested for beauty, but God, God
hath sent me to sea for pearls.

Let Machir rejoice with Convolvulus, from him to the
ring of Saturn, which is the girth of Job; to the signet
of God from Job and his daughters BLESSED BE JESUS.

For there is a blessing from the STONE of JESUS which is
founded upon hell to the precious jewell on the right
hand of God.

Let Atad bless with Eleos, the nightly Memorialist
ελεησον κυριε.

For the nightly Visitor is at the window of the impeni-
tent, while I sing a psalm of my own composing.

Let Jamim rejoice with the Bittern blessed be the name
of Jesus for Denver Sluice, Ruston, and the draining
of the fens.

For there is a note added to the scale, which the Lord
hath made fuller, stronger and more glorious.

Let Ohad rejoice with Byturos who eateth the vine and
is a minister of temperance.

For I offer my goat as he browses the vine, bless the
Lord from chambering and drunkeness.

Let Zohar rejoice with Cychramus who cometh with the
quails on a particular affair.

For there is a traveling for the glory of God without going to Italy or France.

Let Serah, the daughter of Asher, rejoice with Ceyx, who maketh his cabin in the Halcyon's hold.

For I bless the children of Asher for the evil I did them and the good I might have received at their hands.

Let Magdiel rejoice with Ascarides, which is the life of the bowels—the worm hath a part in our frame.

For I rejoice like a worm in the rain in him that cherishes and from him that tramples.

Let Becher rejoice with Oscen who terrifies the wicked, as trumpet and alarm the coward.

For I am ready for the trumpet and alarm to fight, to die and to rise again.

Let Shaul rejoice with Circos, who hath clumsy legs, but he can wheel it the better with his wings.

For the banish'd of the Lord shall come about again, for so he hath prepared for them.

Let Hamul rejoice with the Crystal, who is pure and translucent.

For sincerity is a jewel which is pure and transparent, eternal and inestimable.

Let Ziphion rejoice with the Tit-Lark who is a groundling, but he raises the spirits.

For my hands and my feet are perfect as the sublimity of Naphtali and the felicity of Asher.

Let Mibzar rejoice with the Cadess, as is their number, so are their names, blessed be the Lord Jesus for them all.

For the names and number of animals are as the names and number of the stars.

Let Jubal rejoice with Cæcilia, the woman and the slow-worm praise the name of the Lord.

For I pray the Lord Jesus to translate my MAGNIFICAT into verse and represent it.

Let Arodi rejoice with the Royston Crow, there is a society of them at Trumpington and Cambridge.

For I bless the Lord Jesus from the bottom of Royston Cave to the top of King's Chapel.

Let Areli rejoice with the Criel, who is a dwarf that towereth above others.

For I am a little fellow, which is intitled to the great mess by the benevolence of God my father.

Let Phuvah rejoice with Platycerotes, whose weapons of defence keep them innocent.

For I this day made over my inheritance to my mother in consideration of her infirmities.

Let Shimron rejoice with the Kite, who is of more value than many sparrows.

For I this day made over my inheritance to my mother in consideration of her age.

Let Sered rejoice with the Wittal—a silly bird is wise unto his own preservation.

For I this day made over my inheritance to my mother in consideration of her poverty.

Let Elon rejoice with Attelabus, who is the Locust without wings.

For I bless the thirteenth of August, in which I had the grace to obey the voice of Christ in my conscience.

Let Jahleel rejoice with the Woodcock, who liveth upon suction and is pure from his diet.

For I bless the thirteenth of August, in which I was willing to run all hazards for the sake of the name of the Lord.

Let Shuni rejoice with the Gull, who is happy in not being good for food.

For I bless the thirteenth of August, in which I was willing to be called a fool for the sake of Christ.

Let Ezbon rejoice with Musimon, who is from the ram and she-goat.

For I lent my flocks and my herds and my lands at once
unto the Lord.

Let Barkos rejoice with the Black Eagle, which is the
least of his species and the best-natured.

For nature is more various than observation tho' ob-
servers be innumerable.

Let Bedan rejoice with Ossifrage—the bird of prey and
the man of prayer.

For Agricola is Γηωργος.

Let Naomi rejoice with Pseudosphece who is between
a wasp and a hornet.

For I pray God to bless POLLY in the blessing of Naomi
and assign her to the house of DAVID.

Let Ruth rejoice with the Tumbler—it is a pleasant thing
to feed him and be thankful.

For I am in charity with the French who are my
foes and Moabites because of the Moabitish
woman.

Let Ram rejoice with the Fieldfare, who is a good gift
from God in the season of scarcity.

For my Angel is always ready at a pinch to help me out
and to keep me up.

Let Manoah rejoice with Cerastes, who is a Dragon with
horns.

For CHRISTOPHER must slay the Dragon with a PHEON'S
head.

Let Talmai rejoice with Alcedo, who makes a cradle for
its young, which is rock'd by the winds.

For they have seperated me and my bosom, whereas the
right comes by setting us together.

Let Bukki rejoice with the Buzzard, who is clever, with
the reputation of a silly fellow.

For Silly fellow! Silly fellow! is against me and belongeth
neither to me nor my family.

Let Michal rejoice with Leucocruta who is a mixture of beauty and magnanimity.

For he that scorneth the scorner hath condescended to my low estate.

Let Abiah rejoice with Morphnus who is a bird of passage to the Heavens.

For Abiah is the father of Joab and Joab of all Romans and English Men.

Let Hur rejoice with the Water-wag-tail, who is a neighbour, and loves to be looked at.

For they pass me by in their tour, and the good Samaritan is not yet come.

Let Dodo rejoice with the purple Worm, who is cloathed sumptuously, tho he fares meanly.

For I bless God in behalf of TRINITY COLLEGE in CAMBRIDGE and the society of PURPLES in LONDON.

Let Ahio rejoice with the Merlin who is a cousin german of the hawk.

For I have a nephew CHRISTOPHER to whom I implore the grace of God.

Let Joram rejoice with the Water Rail, who takes his delight in the river.

For I pray God bless the CAM—Mr HIGGS and Mr and Mrs WASHBOURNE as the drops of the dew.

Let Chileab rejoice with Ophion who is clean made, less than an hart, and a Sardinian.

For I pray God bless the king of Sardinia and make him an instrument of his peace.

Let Shephatiah rejoice with the little Owl, which is the wingged Cat.

For I am possessed of a cat, surpassing in beauty, from whom I take occasion to bless Almighty God.

Let Ithream rejoice with the great Owl, who understandeth that which he professes.

For I pray God for the professors of the University of Cambridge to attend and to amend.

Let Abigail rejoice with Lethophagus—God be gracious to the widows indeed.

For the Fatherless Children and widows are never deserted of the Lord.

(Antiphonal lines 1–70, Fragment A)

FOR I WILL CONSIDER MY CAT JEOFFRY

For I will consider my Cat Jeoffry.

For he is the servant of the Living God, duly and daily serving him.

For at the first glance of the glory of God in the East he worships in his way.

For is this done by wreathing his body seven times round with elegant quickness.

For then he leaps up to catch the musk, which is the blessing of God upon his prayer.

For he rolls upon prank to work it in.

For having done duty and received blessing he begins to consider himself.

For this he performs in ten degrees.

For first he looks upon his fore-paws to see if they are clean.

For secondly he kicks up behind to clear away there.

For thirdly he works it upon stretch with the fore paws extended.

For fourthly he sharpens his paws by wood.

For fifthly he washes himself.

For sixthly he rolls upon wash.

For seventhly he fleas himself, that he may not be interrupted upon the beat.

For eighthly he rubs himself against a post.

For ninthly he looks up for his instructions.

For tenthly he goes in quest of food.

For having consider'd God and himself he will consider his neighbour.

For if he meets another cat he will kiss her in kindness.

For when he takes his prey he plays with it to give it chance.

For one mouse in seven escapes by his dallying.

For when his day's work is done his business more properly begins.

For [he] keeps the Lord's watch in the night against the adversary.

For he counteracts the powers of darkness by his electrical skin and glaring eyes.

For he counteracts the Devil, who is death, by brisking about the life.

For in his morning orisons he loves the sun and the sun loves him.

For he is of the tribe of Tiger.

For the Cherub Cat is a term of the Angel Tiger.

For he has the subtlety and hissing of a serpent, which in goodness he suppresses.

For he will not do destruction, if he is well-fed, neither will he spit without provocation.

For he purrs in thankfulness, when God tells him he's a good Cat.

For he is an instrument for the children to learn benevolence upon.

For every house is incompleat without him and a blessing is lacking in the spirit.

For the Lord commanded Moses concerning the cats at the departure of the Children of Israel from Egypt.

For every family had one cat at least in the bag.

For the English Cats are the best in Europe.

For he is the cleanest in the use of his fore-paws of any quadrupede.

For the dexterity of his defence is an instance of the love of God to him exceedingly.

For he is the quickest to his mark of any creature.

For he is tenacious of his point.

For he is a mixture of gravity and waggery.

For he knows that God is his Saviour.

For there is nothing sweeter than his peace when at rest.

For there is nothing brisker than his life when in motion.

For he is of the Lord's poor and so indeed is he called by benevolence perpetually—Poor Jeoffry! poor Jeoffry! the rat has bit thy throat.

For I bless the name of the Lord Jesus that Jeoffry is better.

For the divine spirit comes about his body to sustain it in compleat cat.

For his tongue is exceeding pure so that it has in purity what it wants in musick.

For he is docile and can learn certain things.

For he can set up with gravity which is patience upon approbation.

For he can fetch and carry, which is patience in employment.

For he can jump over a stick which is patience upon proof positive.

For he can spraggle upon waggle at the word of command.

For he can jump from an eminence into his master's bosom.

For he can catch the cork and toss it again.

For he is hated by the hypocrite and miser.

For the former is affraid of detection.

For the latter refuses the charge.

For he camels his back to bear the first notion of business.

For he is good to think on, if a man would express
himself neatly.

For he made a great figure in Egypt for his signal serv-
ices.

For he killed the Icneumon-rat very pernicious by land.

For his ears are so acute that they sting again.

For from this proceeds the passing quickness of his attention.

For by stroaking of him I have found out electricity.

For I perceived God's light about him both wax and
fire.

For the Electrical fire is the spiritual substance, which
God sends from heaven to sustain the bodies both of
man and beast.

For God has blessed him in the variety of his movements.

For, tho he cannot fly, he is an excellent clamberer.

For his motions upon the face of the earth are more
than any other quadrupede.

For he can tread to all the measures upon the musick.

For he can swim for life.

For he can creep.

(Lines 697–770, Fragment B')

A Song to David

O Thou, that sit'st upon a throne,
With harp of high majestic tone,
    To praise the King of kings:
And voice of heav'n-ascending swell,
Which, while its deeper notes excell,
    Clear, as a clarion, rings:

To bless each valley, grove, and coast,
And charm the cherubs to the post
   Of gratitude in throngs;
To *keep* the days on Zion's Mount,
And send the year to his account,
   With dances and with songs:

O Servant of God's holiest charge,
The minister of praise at large,
   Which thou mayst now receive;
From thy blest mansion hail and hear,
From topmost eminence appear
   To this the wreath I weave.

Great, valiant, pious, good, and clean,
Sublime, contemplative, serene,
   Strong, constant, pleasant, wise!
Bright effluence of exceeding grace;
Best man!—the swiftness and the race,
   The peril, and the prize!

Great—from the lustre of his crown,
From Samuel's horn, and God's renown,
   Which is the people's voice;
For all the host, from rear to van,
Applauded and embrac'd the man—
   The man of God's own choice.

Valiant—the word, and up he rose—
The fight—he triumph'd o'er the foes,
   Whom God's just laws abhor;
And arm'd in gallant faith, he took
Against the boaster, from the brook,
   The weapons of the war.

Pious—magnificent and grand;
'Twas he the famous temple plann'd:

(The seraph in his soul)
Foremost to give his Lord his dues,
Foremost to bless the welcome news,
    And foremost to condole.

Good—from Jehudah's genuine vein,
From God's best nature good in grain,
    His aspect and his heart;
To pity, to forgive, to save,
Witness En-gedi's conscious cave,
    And Shimei's blunted dart.

Clean—if perpetual prayer be pure,
And love, which could itself inure
    To fasting and to fear—
Clean in his gestures, hands, and feet,
To smite the lyre, the dance complete,
    To play the sword and spear.

Sublime—invention ever young,
Of vast conception, tow'ring tongue,
    To God th' eternal theme;
Notes from yon exaltations caught,
Unrival'd royalty of thought,
    O'er meaner strains supreme.

Contemplative—on God to fix
His musings, and above the six
    The sabbath-day he blest;
'Twas then his thoughts self-conquest prun'd,
And heav'nly melancholy tun'd,
    To bless and bear the rest.

Serene—to sow the seeds of peace,
Rememb'ring, when he watch'd the fleece,
    How sweetly Kidron purl'd—
To further knowledge, silence vice,

And plant perpetual paradise
   When God had calm'd the world.

Strong—in the Lord, who could defy
Satan, and all his powers that lie
   In sempiternal night;
And hell, and horror, and despair
Were as the lion and the bear
   To his undaunted might.

Constant—in love to God THE TRUTH,
Age, manhood, infancy, and youth—
   To Jonathan his friend
Constant, beyond the verge of death;
And Ziba and Mephibosheth,
   His endless fame attend.

Pleasant—and various as the year;
Man, soul, and angel, without peer,
   Priest, champion, sage and boy;
In armour, or in ephod clad,
His pomp, his piety was glad;
   Majestic was his joy.

Wise—in recovery from his fall,
Whence rose his eminence o'er all,
   Of all the most revil'd;
The light of Israel in his ways,
Wise are his precepts, pray'r and praise,
   And counsel to his child.

His muse, bright angel of his verse,
Gives balm for all the thorns that pierce,
   For all the pangs that rage;
Blest light, still gaining on the gloom,
The more than Michal of his bloom,
   Th' Abishag of his age.

He sung of God—the mighty source
Of all things—the stupendous force
    On which all strength depends;
From whose right arm, beneath whose eyes,
All period, pow'r, and enterprize
    Commences, reigns, and ends.

Angels—their ministry and meed,
Which to and fro with blessings speed,
    Or with their citterns wait;
Where Michael with his millions bows,
Where dwells the seraph and his spouse,
    The cherub and her mate.

Of man—the semblance and effect
Of God and Love—the Saint elect
    For infinite applause—
To rule the land, and briny broad,
To be laborious in his laud,
    And heroes in his cause.

The world—the clust'ring spheres he made,
The glorious light, the soothing shade,
    Dale, champaign, grove, and hill;
The multitudinous abyss,
Where secrecy remains in bliss,
    And wisdom hides her skill.

Trees, plants, and flow'rs—of virtuous root;
Gem yielding blossom, yielding fruit,
    Choice gums and precious balm;
Bless ye the nosegay in the vale,
And with the sweetness of the gale
    Enrich the thankful psalm.

Of fowl—e'en ev'ry beak and wing
Which cheer the winter, hail the spring,

That live in peace or prey;
They that make music, or that mock,
The quail, the brave domestic cock,
   The raven, swan, and jay.

Of fishes—ev'ry size and shape,
Which Nature frames of light escape,
   Devouring man to shun:
The shells are in the wealthy deep,
The shoals upon the surface leap,
   And love the glancing sun.

Of beasts—the beaver plods his task;
While the sleek tigers roll and bask,
   Nor yet the shades arouse;
Her cave the mining coney scoops;
Where o'er the mead the mountain stoops.
   The kids exult and brouse.

Of gems—their virtue and their price,
Which hid in earth from man's device,
   Their darts of lustre sheathe;
The jasper of the master's stamp,
The topaz blazing like a lamp
   Among the mines beneath.

Blest was the tenderness he felt
When to his graceful harp he knelt,
   And did for audience call;
When satan with his hand he quell'd,
And in serene suspense he held
   The frantic throes of Saul.

His furious foes no more malign'd
As he such melody divin'd,
   And sense and soul detain'd;
Now striking strong, now soothing soft,

He sent the godly sounds aloft,
　Or in delight refrain'd.

When up to heav'n his thoughts he pil'd,
From fervent lips fair Michal smil'd,
　As blush to blush she stood;
And chose herself the queen, and gave
Her utmost from her heart, "so brave,
　And plays his hymns so good."

The pillars of the Lord are seven,
Which stand from earth to topmost heav'n;
　His wisdom drew the plan;
His WORD accomplish'd the design,
From brightest gem to deepest mine,
　From CHRIST enthron'd to man.

Alpha, the cause of causes, first
In station, fountain, whence the burst
　Of light, and blaze of day;
Whence bold attempt, and brave advance,
Have motion, life, and ordinance,
　And heav'n itself its stay.

Gamma supports the glorious arch
On which angelic legions march,
　And is with sapphires pav'd;
Thence the fleet clouds are sent adrift,
And thence the painted folds, that lift
　The crimson veil, are wav'd.

Eta with living sculpture breathes,
With verdant carvings, flow'ry wreathes
　Of never-wasting bloom;
In strong relief his goodly base
All instruments of labour grace,
　The trowel, spade, and loom.

Next Theta stands to the Supreme—
Who form'd, in number, sign, and scheme,
   Th' illustrious lights that are;
And one address'd his saffron robe,
And one, clad in a silver globe,
   Held rule with ev'ry star.

Iota's tun'd to choral hymns
Of those that fly, while he that swims
   In thankful safety lurks;
And foot, and chapitre, and niche,
The various histories enrich
   Of God's recorded works.

Sigma presents the social droves,
With him that solitary roves,
   And man of all the chief;
Fair on whose face, and stately frame,
Did God impress his hallow'd name,
   For ocular belief.

OMEGA! GREATEST and the BEST,
Stands sacred to the day of rest,
   For gratitude and thought;
Which bless'd the world upon his pole,
And gave the universe his goal,
   And clos'd th' infernal draught.

O DAVID, scholar of the Lord!
Such is thy science, whence reward
   And infinite degree;
O strength, O sweetness, lasting ripe!
God's harp thy symbol, and thy type
   The lion and the bee!

There is but One who ne'er rebell'd,
But One by passion unimpell'd,

By pleasures unentic't;
He from himself his semblance sent,
Grand object of his own content,
    And saw the God in CHRIST.

Tell them I Am, JEHOVAH said
To MOSES; while earth heard in dread,
    And smitten to the heart,
At once above, beneath, around,
All Nature, without voice or sound,
    Replied, O Lord, THOU ART.

Thou art—to give and to confirm,
For each his talent and his term;
    All flesh thy bounties share:
Thou shalt not call thy brother fool;
The porches of the Christian school
    Are meekness, peace, and pray'r.

Open, and naked of offense,
Man's made of mercy, soul, and sense;
    God arm'd the snail and wilk;
Be good to him that pulls thy plough;
Due food and care, due rest, allow
    For her that yields thee milk.

Rise up before the hoary head,
And God's benign commandment dread,
    Which says thou shalt not die:
"Not as I will, but as thou wilt,"
Pray'd He whose conscience knew no guilt;
    With whose bless'd pattern vie.

Use all thy passions!—love is thine,
And joy, and jealousy divine;
    Thine hope's eternal fort,
And care thy leisure to disturb,

With fear concupiscence to curb,
  And rapture to transport.

Act simply, as occasion asks;
Put mellow wine in season'd casks;
  Till not with ass and bull:
Remember thy baptismal bond;
Keep from commixtures foul and fond,
  Nor work thy flax with wool.

Distribute: pay the Lord his tithe,
And make the widow's heart-strings blithe;
  Resort with those that weep:
As you from all and each expect,
For all and each thy love direct,
  And render as you reap.

The slander and its bearer spurn,
And propagating praise sojourn
  To make thy welcome last;
Turn from old Adam to the New;
By hope futurity pursue;
  Look upwards to the past.

Control thine eye, salute success,
Honour the wiser, happier bless,
  And for thy neighbour feel;
Grutch not of mammon and his leaven,
Work emulation up to heaven
  By knowledge and by zeal.

O David, highest in the list
Of worthies, on God's ways insist,
  The genuine word repeat.
Vain are the documents of men,
And vain the flourish of the pen
  That keeps the fool's conceit.

Praise above all—for praise prevails;
Heap up the measure, load the scales,
    And good to goodness add:
The gen'rous soul her Saviour aids,
But peevish obloquy degrades;
    The Lord is great and glad.

For ADORATION all the ranks
Of angels yield eternal thanks,
    And DAVID in the midst;
With God's good poor, which, last and least
In man's esteem, thou to thy feast,
    O blessed bridegroom, bid'st.

For ADORATION seasons change,
And order, truth, and beauty range,
    Adjust, attract, and fill:
The grass the polyanthus cheques;
And polish'd porphyry reflects,
    By the descending rill.

Rich almonds colour to the prime
For ADORATION; tendrils climb,
    And fruit-trees pledge their gems;
And Ivis with her gorgeous vest
Builds for her eggs her cunning nest,
    And bell-flow'rs bow their stems.

With vinous syrup cedars spout;
From rocks pure honey gushing out,
    For ADORATION springs:
All scenes of painting crowd the map
Of nature; to the mermaid's pap
    The scaléd infant clings.

The spotted ounce and playsome cubs
Run rustling 'mongst the flow'ring shrubs,

And lizards feed the moss;
For ADORATION beasts embark,
While waves upholding halcyon's ark
 No longer roar and toss.

While Israel sits beneath his fig,
With coral root and amber sprig,
 The wean'd advent'rer sports;
Where to the palm the jasmin cleaves,
For ADORATION 'mongst the leaves
 The gale his peace reports.

Increasing days their reign exalt,
Nor in the pink and mottled vault
 Th' opposing spirits tilt;
And, by the coasting reader spy'd,
The silverlings and crusions glide
 For ADORATION gilt.

For ADORATION, rip'ning canes
And cocoa's purest milk detains
 The western pilgrim's staff;
Where rain in clasping boughs inclos'd,
And vines with oranges dispos'd,
 Embow'r the social laugh.

Now labour his reward receives,
For ADORATION counts his sheaves
 To peace, her bounteous prince;
The nectarine his strong tint imbibes,
And apples of ten thousand tribes,
 And quick peculiar quince.

The wealthy crops of whit'ning rice,
'Mongst thyine woods and groves of spice
 For ADORATION grow;
And, marshall'd in the fencéd land,

The peaches and pomegranates stand,
   Where wild carnations blow.

The laurels with the winter strive,
The crocus burnishes alive
   Upon the snow-clad earth.
For ADORATION myrtles stay
To keep the garden from dismay,
   And bless the sight from dearth.

The pheasant shows his pompous neck;
And ermine, jealous of a speck,
   With fear eludes offense:
The sable, with his glossy pride,
For ADORATION is descried,
   Where frosts the wave condense.

The cheerful holly, pensive yew,
And holy thorn, their trim renew;
   The squirrel hoards his nuts:
All creatures batten o'er their stores,
And careful Nature all her doors
   For ADORATION shuts.

For ADORATION, David's psalms
Lift up the heart to deeds of alms;
   And he, who kneels and chants,
Prevails his passions to control,
Finds meat and med'cine to the soul,
   Which for translation pants.

For ADORATION, beyond match,
The scholar bullfinch aims to catch
   The soft flute's iv'ry touch;
And, careless on the hazel spray,
The daring redbreast keeps at bay
   The damsel's greedy clutch.

For ADORATION, in the skies,
The Lord's philosopher espies
　　The Dog, the Ram, and Rose;
The planet's ring, Orion's sword;
Nor is his greatness less ador'd
　　In the vile worm that glows.

For ADORATION, on the strings
The western breezes work their wings,
　　The captive ear to soothe.—
Hark! 'tis a voice—how still, and small—
That makes the cataracts to fall,
　　Or bids the sea be smooth!

For ADORATION, incense comes
From bezoar, and Arabian gums;
　　And on the civet's furr.
But as for pray'r, or ere it faints,
Far better is the breath of saints
　　Than galbanum and myrrh.

For ADORATION, from the down
Of dam'sins to th' anana's crown,
　　God sends to tempt the taste;
And while the luscious zest invites,
The sense, that in the scene delights,
　　Commands desire be chaste.

For ADORATION, all the paths
Of grace are open, all the baths
　　Of purity refresh;
And all the rays of glory beam
To deck the man of God's esteem,
　　Who triumphs o'er the flesh.

For ADORATION, in the dome
Of Christ the sparrows find an home;

And on his olives perch:
The swallow also dwells with thee,
O man of God's humility,
   Within his Saviour CHURCH.

Sweet is the dew that falls betimes,
And drops upon the leafy limes;
   Sweet Hermon's fragrant air:
Sweet is the lily's silver bell,
And sweet the wakeful tapers smell
   That watch for early pray'r.

Sweet the young nurse with love intense,
Which smiles o'er sleeping innocence;
   Sweet when the lost arrive:
Sweet the musician's ardour beats,
While his vague mind's in quest of sweets,
   The choicest flow'rs to hive.

Sweeter in all the strains of love
The language of thy turtle dove
   Pair'd to thy swelling chord;
Sweeter with ev'ry grace endu'd
The glory of thy gratitude,
   Respir'd unto the Lord.

Strong is the horse upon his speed;
Strong in pursuit the rapid glede,
   Which makes at once his game;
Strong the tall ostrich on the ground;
Strong through the turbulent profound
   Shoots xiphias to his aim.

Strong is the lion—like a coal
His eyeball—like a bastion's mole
   His chest against the foes:
Strong, the gier-eagle on his sail,

Strong against tide, th' enormous whale
  Emerges as he goes.

But stronger still, in earth and air,
And in the sea, the man of pray'r,
  And far beneath the tide;
And in the seat to faith assign'd,
Where ask is have, where seek is find
  Where knock is open wide.

Beauteous the fleet before the gale;
Beauteous the multitudes in mail,
  Rank'd arms and crested heads:
Beauteous the garden's umbrage mild,
Walk, water, meditated wild,
  And all the bloomy beds.

Beauteous the moon full on the lawn;
And beauteous, when the veil's withdrawn,
  The virgin to her spouse:
Beauteous the temple deck'd and fill'd,
When to the heav'n of heav'ns they build
  Their heart-directed vows.

Beauteous, yea beauteous more than these,
The shepherd king upon his knees,
  For his momentous trust;
With wish of infinite conceit,
For man, beast, mute, the small and great,
  And prostrate dust to dust.

Precious the bounteous widow's mite;
And precious, for extreme delight,
  The largess from the churl:
Precious the ruby's blushing blaze,
And alba's blest imperial rays,
  And pure cerulean pearl.

Precious the penitential tear;
And precious is the sigh sincere,
   Acceptable to God:
And precious are the winning flow'rs,
In gladsome Israel's feast of bow'rs,
   Bound on the hallow'd sod.

More precious that diviner part
Of David, ev'n the Lord's own heart,
   Great, beautiful, and new:
In all things where it was intent,
In all extremes, in each event,
   Proof—answ'ring true to true.

Glorious the sun in mid career;
Glorious th' assembled fires appear;
   Glorious the comet's train:
Glorious the trumpet and alarm;
Glorious th' almighty stretch'd-out arm;
   Glorious th' enraptur'd main:

Glorious the northern lights a-stream;
Glorious the song, when God's the theme;
   Glorious the thunder's roar;
Glorious hosannah from the den;
Glorious the catholic amen;
   Glorious the martyr's gore:

Glorious—more glorious, is the crown
Of Him that brought salvation down
   By meekness, call'd thy Son;
Thou that stupendous truth believ'd,
And now the matchless deed's achiev'd,
   DETERMIN'D, DAR'D, *and* DONE.

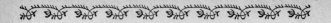

William Cowper

(1731–1800)

FROM *Hope*

Though clasp'd and cradled in his nurse's arms,
He shine with all a cherub's artless charms,
Man is the genuine offspring of revolt,
Stubborn and sturdy, a wild ass's colt;
His passions, like the watery stores that sleep
Beneath the smiling surface of the deep,
Wait but the lashes of a wintry storm,
To frown and roar, and shake his feeble form.
From infancy through childhood's giddy maze,
Froward at school, and fretful in his plays,
The puny tyrant burns to subjugate
The free republic of the whip-gig state.
If one, his equal in athletic frame,
Or, more provoking still, of nobler name,
Dare step across his arbitrary views,
An Iliad, only not in verse, ensues:
The little Greeks look trembling at the scales,
Till the best tongue, or heaviest hand prevails.

(*Lines 179–96*)

The Poplar Field

The poplars are fell'd; farewell to the shade,
And the whispering sound of the cool colonnade!
The winds play no longer and sing in the leaves,
Nor Ouse on his bosom their image receives.

Twelve years have elapsed since I first took a view
Of my favourite field, and the bank where they grew;
And now in the grass behold they are laid,
And the tree is my seat that once lent me a shade!

The blackbird has fled to another retreat,
Where the hazels afford him a screen from the heat,
And the scene where his melody charm'd me before
Resounds with his sweet flowing ditty no more.

My fugitive years are all hasting away,
And I must ere long lie as lowly as they,
With a turf on my breast, and a stone at my head,
Ere another such grove shall arise in its stead.

'Tis a sight to engage me, if any thing can,
To muse on the perishing pleasures of man;
Though his life be a dream, his enjoyments, I see,
Have a being less durable even than he.

Verses Supposed to Be Written
by Alexander Selkirk, During His Solitary
Abode in the Island of Juan Fernandez

I am monarch of all I survey,
    My right there is none to dispute;
From the center all round to the sea,
    I am lord of the fowl and the brute.
O Solitude! where are the charms
    That sages have seen in thy face?
Better dwell in the midst of alarms,
    Than reign in this horrible place.

I am out of humanity's reach,
    I must finish my journey alone,
Never hear the sweet music of speech;
    I start at the sound of my own.
The beasts, that roam over the plain,
    My form with indifference see;
They are so unacquainted with man,
    Their tameness is shocking to me.

Society, friendship, and love,
    Divinely bestow'd upon man,
Oh, had I the wings of a dove,
    How soon would I taste you again!
My sorrows I then might assuage
    In the ways of religion and truth,
Might learn from the wisdom of age,
    And be cheer'd by the sallies of youth.

Religion! what treasure untold
    Resides in that heavenly word!

More precious than silver and gold,
   Or all that this earth can afford.
But the sound of the church-going bell
   These valleys and rocks never heard,
Never sigh'd at the sound of a knell,
   Or smil'd when a sabbath appear'd.

Ye winds, that have made me your sport,
   Convey to this desolate shore
Some cordial endearing report
   Of a land I shall visit no more.
My friends, do they now and then send
   A wish or a thought after me?
Oh, tell me I yet have a friend,
   Though a friend I am never to see.

How fleet is a glance of the mind!
   Compar'd with the speed of its flight,
The tempest itself lags behind,
   And the swift-wing'd arrows of light.
When I think of my own native land,
   In a moment I seem to be there;
But alas! recollection at hand
   Soon hurries me back to despair.

But the sea-fowl is gone to her nest,
   The beast is laid down in his lair,
Even here is a season of rest,
   And I to my cabin repair.
There's mercy in every place;
   And mercy, encouraging thought!
Gives even affliction a grace,
   And reconciles man to his lot.

Epitaph on a Hare

Here lies, whom hound did ne'er pursue,
  Nor swifter greyhound follow,
Whose foot ne'er tainted morning dew,
  Nor ear heard huntsman's halloo;

Old Tiney, surliest of his kind,
  Who, nursed with tender care,
And to domestic bounds confined,
  Was still a wild Jack hare.

Though duly from my hand he took
  His pittance every night,
He did it with a jealous look,
  And, when he could, would bite.

His diet was of wheaten bread,
  And milk, and oats, and straw;
Thistles, or lettuces instead,
  With sand to scour his maw.

On twigs of hawthorn he regaled,
  On pippins' russet peel,
And, when his juicy salads fail'd,
  Sliced carrot pleased him well.

A Turkey carpet was his lawn,
  Whereon he loved to bound,
To skip and gambol like a fawn,
  And swing his rump around.

His frisking was at evening hours,
  For then he lost his fear,

But most before approaching showers,
 Or when a storm drew near.

Eight years and five round-rolling moons
 He thus saw steal away,
Dozing out all his idle noons,
 And every night at play.

I kept him for his humour's sake,
 For he would oft beguile
My heart of thoughts that made it ache,
 And force me to a smile.

But now beneath his walnut shade
 He finds his long last home,
And waits, in snug concealment laid,
 Till gentler Puss shall come.

He, still more aged, feels the shocks
 From which no care can save,
And, partner once of Tiney's box,
 Must soon partake his grave.

Lines Written
Under the Influence of Delirium

Hatred and vengeance, my eternal portion,
Scarce can endure delay of execution,
Wait with impatient readiness to seize my
    Soul in a moment.

Damned below Judas; more abhorred than he was,
Who for a few pence sold his holy Master!
Twice-betrayed Jesus me, the last delinquent,
    Deems the profanest.

Man disavows, and Deity disowns me,
Hell might afford my miseries a shelter;
Therefore Hell keeps her ever-hungry mouths all
        Bolted against me.

Hard lot! encompass'd with a thousand dangers;
Weary, faint, trembling with a thousand terrors,
I'm called, if vanquish'd, to receive a sentence
        Worse than Abiram's.

Him the vindictive rod of angry justice
Sent quick and howling to the centre headlong;
I, fed with judgment, in a fleshy tomb, am
        Buried above ground.

The Contrite Heart

Isaiah, 57:15

The Lord will happiness divine
   On contrite hearts bestow;
Then tell me, gracious God, is mine
   A contrite heart, or no?

I hear, but seem to hear in vain,
   Insensible as steel;
If ought is felt, 'tis only pain,
   To find I cannot feel.

I sometimes think myself inclined
   To love thee, if I could;
But often feel another mind,
   Averse to all that's good.

My best desires are faint and few,
   I fain would strive for more;

But when I cry, "My strength renew!"
    Seem weaker than before.

Thy saints are comforted, I know,
    And love thy house of prayer;
I therefore go where others go,
    But find no comfort there.

O make this heart rejoice or ache;
    Decide this doubt for me;
And if it be not broken, break,—
    And heal it if it be!

Light Shining out of Darkness

God moves in a mysterious way
    His wonders to perform;
He plants his footsteps in the sea,
    And rides upon the storm.

Deep in unfathomable mines
    Of never-failing skill,
He treasures up his bright designs,
    And works his sovereign will.

Ye fearful saints, fresh courage take,
    The clouds ye so much dread
Are big with mercy, and shall break
    In blessings on your head.

Judge not the Lord by feeble sense,
    But trust him for his grace;
Behind a frowning providence
    He hides a smiling face.

His purposes will ripen fast,
    Unfolding every hour;
The bud may have a bitter taste,
    But sweet will be the flower.

Blind unbelief is sure to err,
    And scan his work in vain:
God is his own interpreter,
    And He will make it plain.

Walking with God

Genesis 5:24

Oh! for a closer walk with God,
    A calm and heav'nly frame;
A light to shine upon the road
    That leads me to the Lamb!

Where is the blessedness I knew
    When first I saw the Lord?
Where is the soul-refreshing view
    Of Jesus, and his word?

What peaceful hours I once enjoy'd!
    How sweet their mem'ry still!
But they have left an aching void,
    The world can never fill.

Return, O holy Dove, return,
    Sweet messenger of rest;
I hate the sins that made thee mourn,
    And drove thee from my breast.

The dearest idol I have known,
    Whate'er that idol be;

Help me to tear it from thy throne,
    And worship only thee.

So shall my walk be close with God,
    Calm and serene my frame;
So purer light shall mark the road
    That leads me to the Lamb.

FROM *The Task*

GOD MADE THE COUNTRY

God made the country, and man made the town.
What wonder then that health and virtue, gifts
That can alone make sweet the bitter draught
That life holds out to all, should most abound
And least be threaten'd in the fields and groves?
Possess ye, therefore, ye, who, borne about
In chariots and sedans, know no fatigue
But that of idleness, and taste no scenes
But such as art contrives, possess ye still
Your element; there only can ye shine;
There only minds like yours can do no harm.
Our groves were planted to console at noon
The pensive wanderer in their shades. At eve
The moonbeam, sliding softly in between
The sleeping leaves, is all the light they wish,
Birds warbling all the music. We can spare
The splendour of your lamps; they but eclipse
Our softer satellite. Your songs confound
Our more harmonious notes: the thrush departs
Scar'd, and th' offended nightingale is mute.
There is a public mischief in your mirth;
It plagues your country. Folly such as yours,

Grac'd with a sword, and worthier of a fan,
Has made, which enemies could ne'er have done,
Our arch of empire, steadfast but for you,
A mutilated structure, soon to fall.

(Book I, lines 749–74)

THE WINTER MORNING WALK

'Tis morning; and the sun with ruddy orb
Ascending fires the horizon: while the clouds
That crowd away before the driving wind,
More ardent as the disk emerges more,
Resemble most some city in a blaze,
Seen through the leafless wood. His slanting ray
Slides ineffectual down the snowy vale,
And tinging all with his own rosy hue,
From every herb and every spiry blade
Stretches a length of shadow o'er the field.
Mine, spindling into longitude immense,
In spite of gravity and sage remark
That I myself am but a fleeting shade,
Provokes me to a smile. With eye askance
I view the muscular proportioned limb
Transformed to a lean shank. The shapeless pair
As they designed to mock me, at my side
Take step for step; and as I near approach
The cottage, walk along the plastr'd wall,
Preposterous sight! the legs without the man.
The verdure of the plain lies buried deep
Beneath the dazzling deluge; and the bents
And coarser grass upspearing o'er the rest,
Of late unsightly and unseen, now shine
Conspicuous, and in bright apparel clad
And fledged with icy feathers, nod superb.
The cattle mourn in corners where the fence

Screens them, and seem half-petrified to sleep
In unrecumbent sadness. There they wait
Their wonted fodder, not like hungering man,
Fretful if unsupplied, but silent, meek,
And patient of the slow-paced swain's delay.
He from the stack carves out the accustomed load,
Deep-plunging and again deep-plunging oft
His broad keen knife into the solid mass.
Smooth as a wall the upright remnant stands,
With such undeviating and even force
He severs it away: no needless care,
Lest storms should overset the leaning pile
Deciduous, or its own unbalanced weight.
Forth goes the woodman, leaving unconcerned
The cheerful haunts of man, to wield the axe
And drive the wedge in yonder forest drear,
From morn to eve his solitary task.
Shaggy and lean and shrewd, with pointed ears
And tail cropp'd short, half lurcher and half cur,
His dog attends him. Close behind his heel
Now creeps he slow; and now with many a frisk
Wide-scampering snatches up the drifted snow
With ivory teeth, or ploughs it with his snout;
Then shakes his powder'd coat and barks for joy.
Heedless of all his pranks the sturdy churl
Moves right toward the mark; nor stops for aught,
But now and then with pressure of his thumb
To adjust the fragrant charge of a short tube
That fumes beneath his nose; the trailing cloud
Streams far behind him, scenting all the air.
Now from the roost, or from the neighbouring pale,
Where, diligent to catch the first faint gleam
Of smiling day, they gossipp'd side by side,
Come trooping at the housewife's well-known call
The feather'd tribes domestic. Half on wing

And half on foot, they brush the fleecy flood
Conscious, and fearful of too deep a plunge.
The sparrows peep, and quit the sheltering eaves
To seize the fair occasion. Well they eye
The scatter'd grain, and, thievishly resolved
To escape the impending famine, often scared
As oft return, a pert voracious kind.
Clean riddance quickly made, one only care
Remains to each, the search of sunny nook,
Or shed impervious to the blast. Resign'd
To sad necessity, the cock forgoes
His wonted strut, and, wading at their head
With well-considered steps, seems to resent
His alter'd gait and stateliness retrenched.
How find the myriads that in summer cheer
The hills and valleys with their ceaseless songs
Due sustenance, or where subsist they now?
Earth yields them nought: the imprison'd worm is safe
Beneath the frozen clod; all seeds of herbs
Lie covered close, and berry-bearing thorns
That feed the thrush, (whatever some suppose,)
Afford the smaller minstrels no supply.
The long protracted rigour of the year
Thins all their numerous flocks. In chinks and holes
Ten thousand seek an unmolested end
As instinct prompts, self buried ere they die.
The very rooks and daws forsake the fields,
Where neither grub nor root nor earth-nut now
Repays their labour more; and perch'd aloft
By the way-side, or stalking in the path,
Lean pensioners upon the traveller's track,
Pick up their nauseous dole, though sweet to them,
Of voided pulse or half-digested grain.
The streams are lost amid the splendid blank
O'erwhelming all distinction. On the flood

Indurated and fixt, the snowy weight
Lies undissolved, while silently beneath
And unperceived, the current steals away.
Not so, where scornful of a check it leaps
The mill-dam, dashes on the restless wheel,
And wantons in the pebbly gulf below.
No frost can bind it there; its utmost force
Can but arrest the light and smoky mist ·
That in its fall the liquid sheet throws wide.
And see where it has hung the embroidered banks
With forms so various, that no powers of art,
The pencil or the pen, may trace the scene!
Here glittering turrets rise, upbearing high
(Fantastic misarrangement!) on the roof
Large growth of what may seem the sparkling trees
And shrubs of fairy land. The crystal drops
That trickle down the branches, fast congeal'd
Shoot into pillars of pellucid length,
And prop the pile they but adorned before.
Here grotto within grotto safe defies
The sun-beam; there emboss'd and fretted wild
The growing wonder takes a thousand shapes
Capricious, in which fancy seeks in vain
The likeness of some object seen before.
Thus nature works as if to mock at art,
And in defiance of her rival powers;
By these fortuitous and random strokes
Performing such inimitable feats
As she with all her rules can never reach.
Less worthy of applause, though more admired
Because a novelty, the work of man,
Imperial mistress of the fur-clad Russ!
Thy most magnificent and mighty freak,
The wonder of the north. No forest fell
When thou would'st build; no quarry sent its stores

To enrich thy walls: but thou didst hew the floods,
And make thy marble of the glassy wave.
In such a palace Aristaeus found
Cyrene, when he bore the plaintive tale
Of his lost bees to her maternal ear.
In such a palace poetry might place
The armoury of Winter, where his troops
The gloomy clouds find weapons, arrowy sleet
Skin-piercing volley, blossom-bruising hail,
And snow that often blinds the traveller's course,
And wraps him in an unexpected tomb.
Silently as a dream the fabric rose;
No sound of hammer or of saw was there.
Ice upon ice, the well-adjusted parts
Were soon conjoined, nor other cement ask'd
Than water interfused to make them one.
Lamps gracefully disposed and of all hues
Illumined every side. A watery light
Gleamed through the clear transparency, that seemed
Another moon new-risen, or meteor fallen
From heaven to earth, of lambent flame serene.
So stood the brittle prodigy; though smooth
And slippery the materials, yet frost-bound
Firm as a rock. Nor wanted aught within
That royal residence might well befit,
For grandeur or for use. Long wavy wreaths
Of flowers that feared no enemy but warmth,
Blushed on the panels. Mirror needed none
Where all was vitreous; but in order due
Convivial table and commodious seat
(What seemed at least commodious seat,) were there,
Sofa and couch and high-built throne august.
The same lubricity was found in all,
And all was moist to the warm touch; a scene
Of evanescent glory, once a stream,

And soon to slide into a stream again.
Alas! 'twas but a mortifying stroke
Of undesigned severity, that glanced
(Made by a monarch,) on her own estate,
On human grandeur and the courts of kings.
'Twas transient in its nature, as in show
'Twas durable; as worthless as it seemed
Intrinsically precious; to the foot
Treacherous and false; it smiled and it was cold.
   Great princes have great playthings. Some have
      played
At hewing mountains into men, and some
At building human wonders mountain-high.
Some have amused the dull sad years of life,
Life spent in indolence, and therefore sad,
With schemes of monumental fame, and sought
By pyramids and mausolean pomp,
Short-lived themselves, to immortalize their bones.
Some seek diversion in the tented field,
And make the sorrows of mankind their sport.
But war's a game, which, were their subjects wise,
Kings should not play at. Nations would do well
To extort their truncheons from the puny hands
Of heroes, whose infirm and baby minds
Are gratified with mischief, and who spoil
Because men suffer it, their toy the world.

                    (Book V, *lines* 1–192)

The Castaway

Obscurest night involv'd the sky,
   Th' Atlantic billows roar'd,
When such a destin'd wretch as I,

Wash'd headlong from on board,
Of friends, of hope, of all bereft,
His floating home forever left.

No braver chief could Albion boast
   Than he with whom he went,
Nor ever ship left Albion's coast,
   With warmer wishes sent.
He lov'd them both, but both in vain,
Nor him beheld, nor her again.

Not long beneath the whelming brine,
   Expert to swim, he lay;
Nor soon he felt his strength decline,
   Or courage die away;
But wag'd with death a lasting strife,
Supported by despair of life.

He shouted; nor his friends had fail'd
   To check the vessel's course,
But so the furious blast prevail'd
   That, pitiless perforce,
They left their outcast mate behind,
And scudded still before the wind.

Some succour yet they could afford;
   And, such as storms allow,
The cask, the coop, the floated cord,
   Delay'd not to bestow.
But he (they knew) nor ship nor shore,
Whate'er they gave, should visit more.

Nor, cruel as it seem'd, could he
   Their haste himself condemn,
Aware that flight, in such a sea,
   Alone could rescue them;

Yet bitter felt it still to die
Deserted, and his friends so nigh.

He long survives, who lives an hour
   In ocean, self-upheld;
And so long he, with unspent pow'r,
   His destiny repell'd;
And ever, as the minutes flew,
Entreated help, or cried—"Adieu!"

At length, his transient respite past,
   His comrades, who before
Had heard his voice in ev'ry blast,
   Could catch the sound no more;
For then, by toil subdu'd, he drank
The stifling wave, and then he sank.

No poet wept him; but the page
   Of narrative sincere,
That tells his name, his worth, his age,
   Is wet with Anson's tear:
And tears by bards or heroes shed
Alike immortalize the dead.

I therefore purpose not, or dream,
   Descanting on his fate,
To give the melancholy theme
   A more enduring date;
But misery still delights to trace
Its semblance in another's case.

No voice divine the storm allay'd,
   No light propitious shone;
When, snatch'd from all effectual aid,
   We perish'd, each alone;
But I beneath a rougher sea,
And whelm'd in deeper gulfs than he.

Oliver Goldsmith

(1730?–1774)

The Deserted Village

Sweet Auburn, loveliest village of the plain,
Where health and plenty cheared the labouring swain,
Where smiling spring its earliest visit paid,
And parting summer's lingering blooms delayed,
Dear lovely bowers of innocence and ease,
Seats of my youth, when every sport could please,
How often have I loitered o'er thy green,
Where humble happiness endeared each scene!
How often have I paused on every charm,
The sheltered cot, the cultivated farm,
The never-failing brook, the busy mill,
The decent church that topt the neighbouring hill,
The hawthorn bush, with seats beneath the shade,
For talking age and whispering lovers made!
How often have I blest the coming day,
When toil remitting lent its turn to play,
And all the village train, from labour free
Led up their sports beneath the spreading tree,
While many a pastime circled in the shade,
The young contending as the old surveyed;
And many a gambol frolicked o'er the ground,
And slights of art and feats of strength went round;
And still as each repeated pleasure tired,
Succeeding sports the mirthful band inspired;
The dancing pair that simply sought renown

By holding out to tire each other down;
The swain mistrustless of his smutted face,
While secret laughter tittered round the place;
The bashful virgin's side-long looks of love,
The matron's glance that would those looks reprove!
These were thy charms, sweet village; sports like these,
With sweet succession, taught even toil to please;
These round thy bowers their chearful influence shed,
These were thy charms—But all these charms are fled.

Sweet smiling village, loveliest of the lawn,
Thy sports are fled, and all thy charms withdrawn;
Amidst thy bowers the tyrant's hand is seen,
And desolation saddens all thy green:
One only master grasps the whole domain,
And half a tillage stints thy smiling plain;
No more thy glassy brook reflects the day,
But choaked with sedges, works its weedy way;
Along thy glades, a solitary guest,
The hollow-sounding bittern guards its nest;
Amidst thy desert walks the lapwing flies,
And tires their ecchoes with unvaried cries.
Sunk are thy bowers, in shapeless ruin all,
And the long grass o'ertops the mouldering wall;
And, trembling, shrinking from the spoiler's hand,
Far, far away, thy children leave the land.

Ill fares the land, to hastening ills a prey,
Where wealth accumulates, and men decay:
Princes and lords may flourish, or may fade;
A breath can make them, as a breath has made;
But a bold peasantry, their country's pride,
When once destroyed, can never be supplied.

A time there was, ere England's griefs began,
When every rood of ground maintained its man;
For him light labour spread her wholesome store,
Just gave what life required, but gave no more:

His best companions, innocence and health;
And his best riches, ignorance of wealth.

But times are altered; trade's unfeeling train
Usurp the land and dispossess the swain;
Along the lawn, where scattered hamlets rose,
Unwieldy wealth, and cumbrous pomp repose;
And every want to oppulence allied,
And every pang that folly pays to pride.
Those gentle hours that plenty bade to bloom,
Those calm desires that asked but little room,
Those healthful sports that graced the peaceful scene,
Lived in each look, and brightened all the green;
These, far departing seek a kinder shore,
And rural mirth and manners are no more.

Sweet Auburn! parent of the blissful hour,
Thy glades forlorn confess the tyrant's power.
Here as I take my solitary rounds,
Amidst thy tangling walks, and ruined grounds,
And, many a year elapsed, return to view
Where once the cottage stood, the hawthorn grew,
Remembrance wakes with all her busy train,
Swells at my breast, and turns the past to pain.

In all my wanderings round this world of care,
In all my griefs—and God has given my share—
I still had hopes, my latest hours to crown,
Amidst these humble bowers to lay me down;
To husband out life's taper at the close,
And keep the flame from wasting by repose.
I still had hopes, for pride attends us still,
Amidst the swains to shew my book-learned skill,
Around my fire an evening groupe to draw,
And tell of all I felt, and all I saw;
And, as an hare whom hounds and horns pursue,
Pants to the place from whence at first she flew,
I still had hopes, my long vexations past,

Here to return—and die at home at last.
  O blest retirement, friend to life's decline,
Retreats from care that never must be mine,
How happy he who crowns, in shades like these,
A youth of labour with an age of ease;
Who quits a world where strong temptations try,
And, since 'tis hard to combat, learns to fly!
For him no wretches, born to work and weep,
Explore the mine, or tempt the dangerous deep;
No surly porter stands in guilty state
To spurn imploring famine from the gate,
But on he moves to meet his latter end,
Angels around befriending virtue's friend;
Bends to the grave with unperceived decay,
While resignation gently slopes the way;
And, all his prospects brightening to the last,
His Heaven commences ere the world be past!
  Sweet was the sound, when oft at evening's close,
Up yonder hill the village murmur rose;
There, as I past with careless steps and slow,
The mingling notes came soften'd from below;
The swain responsive as the milk-maid sung,
The sober herd that lowed to meet their young,
The noisy geese that gabbled o'er the pool,
The playful children just let loose from school,
The watch-dog's voice that bayed the whispering wind,
And the loud laugh that spoke the vacant mind,
These all in sweet confusion sought the shade,
And filled each pause the nightingale had made.
But now the sounds of population fail,
No chearful murmurs fluctuate in the gale,
No busy steps the grass-grown foot-way tread,
For all the bloomy flush of life is fled.
All but yon widowed, solitary thing
That feebly bends beside the plashy spring;

She, wretched matron, forced in age, for bread,
To strip the brook with mantling cresses spread,
To pick her wintry faggot from the thorn,
To seek her nightly shed, and weep till morn;
She only left of all the harmless train,
The sad historian of the pensive plain.

   Near yonder copse, where once the garden smiled,
And still where many a garden-flower grows wild;
There, where a few torn shrubs the place disclose,
The village preacher's modest mansion rose.
A man he was, to all the country dear,
And passing rich with forty pounds a year;
Remote from towns he ran his godly race,
Nor e'er had changed, nor wished to change his place;
Unpractised he to fawn, or seek for power,
By doctrines fashioned to the varying hour;
Far other aims his heart had learned to prize,
More skilled to raise the wretched than to rise.
His house was known to all the vagrant train,
He chid their wanderings, but relieved their pain;
The long-remembered beggar was his guest,
Whose beard descending swept his aged breast;
The ruined spendthrift, now no longer proud,
Claim'd kindred there, and had his claims allowed;
The broken soldier, kindly bade to stay,
Sate by his fire, and talked the night away;
Wept o'er his wounds, or, tales of sorrow done,
Shouldered his crutch, and shewed how fields were
     won.
Pleased with his guests, the good man learned to glow,
And quite forgot their vices in their woe;
Careless their merits, or their faults to scan,
His pity gave ere charity began.

   Thus to relieve the wretched was his pride,
And even his failings leaned to Virtue's side;

But in his duty prompt at every call,
He watched and wept, he prayed and felt, for all.
And, as a bird each fond endearment tries,
To tempt its new-fledged offspring to the skies;
He tried each art, reproved each dull delay,
Allured to brighter worlds, and led the way.

Beside the bed where parting life was layed,
And sorrow, guilt, and pain, by turns, dismayed
The reverend champion stood. At his control,
Despair and anguish fled the struggling soul;
Comfort came down the trembling wretch to raise,
And his last faultering accents whispered praise.

At church, with meek and unaffected grace,
His looks adorned the venerable place;
Truth from his lips prevailed with double sway,
And fools, who came to scoff, remained to pray.
The service past, around the pious man,
With steady zeal, each honest rustic ran;
Even children followed, with endearing wile,
And plucked his gown, to share the good man's smile.
His ready smile a parent's warmth exprest,
Their welfare pleased him, and their cares distrest;
To them his heart, his love, his griefs were given,
But all his serious thoughts had rest in Heaven.
As some tall cliff that lifts its awful form,
Swells from the vale, and midway leaves the storm,
Tho' round its breast the rolling clouds are spread,
Eternal sunshine settles on its head.

Beside yon straggling fence that skirts the way,
With blossomed furze unprofitably gay,
There, in his noisy mansion, skill'd to rule,
The village master taught his little school;
A man severe he was, and stern to view,
I knew him well, and every truant knew;
Well had the boding tremblers learned to trace

The day's disasters in his morning face;
Full well they laughed, with counterfeited glee,
At all his jokes, for many a joke had he:
Full well the busy whisper circling round,
Conveyed the dismal tidings when he frowned;
Yet he was kind, or if severe in aught,
The love he bore to learning was in fault;
The village all declared how much he knew;
'Twas certain he could write, and cypher too;
Lands he could measure, terms and tides presage,
And even the story ran that he could gauge.
In arguing too, the parson owned his skill,
For even tho' vanquished, he could argue still;
While words of learned length and thundering sound,
Amazed the gazing rustics ranged around;
And still they gazed, and still the wonder grew,
That one small head could carry all he knew.
    But past is all his fame. The very spot
Where many a time he triumphed, is forgot.
Near yonder thorn, that lifts its head on high,
Where once the sign-post caught the passing eye,
Low lies that house where nut-brown draughts inspired,
Where grey-beard mirth and smiling toil retired,
Where village statesmen talked with looks profound,
And news much older than their ale went round.
Imagination fondly stoops to trace
The parlour splendours of that festive place;
The white-washed wall, the nicely sanded floor,
The varnished clock that clicked behind the door;
The chest contrived a double debt to pay,
A bed by night, a chest of drawers by day;
The pictures placed for ornament and use,
The twelve good rules, the royal game of goose;
The hearth, except when winter chill'd the day,
With aspen boughs, and flowers, and fennel gay,

While broken tea-cups, wisely kept for shew,
Ranged o'er the chimney, glistened in a row.
 Vain transitory splendours! Could not all
Reprieve the tottering mansion from its fall!
Obscure it sinks, nor shall it more impart
An hour's importance to the poor man's heart;
Thither no more the peasant shall repair
To sweet oblivion of his daily care;
No more the farmer's news, the barber's tale,
No more the woodman's ballad shall prevail;
No more the smith his dusky brow shall clear,
Relax his ponderous strength, and lean to hear;
The host himself no longer shall be found
Careful to see the mantling bliss go round;
Nor the coy maid, half willing to be prest,
Shall kiss the cup to pass it to the rest.
 Yes! let the rich deride, the proud disdain,
These simple blessings of the lowly train;
To me more dear, congenial to my heart,
One native charm, than all the gloss of art;
Spontaneous joys, where Nature has its play,
The soul adopts, and owns their first-born sway;
Lightly they frolic o'er the vacant mind,
Unenvied, unmolested, unconfined.
But the long pomp, the midnight masquerade,
With all the freaks of wanton wealth arrayed,
In these, ere triflers half their wish obtain,
The toiling pleasure sickens into pain;
And even while fashion's brightest arts decoy,
The heart distrusting asks, if this be joy.
 Ye friends to truth, ye statesmen, who survey
The rich man's joys encrease, the poor's decay,
'Tis yours to judge, how wide the limits stand
Between a splendid and a happy land.
Proud swells the tide with loads of freighted ore,

And shouting Folly hails them from her shore;
Hoards even beyond the miser's wish abound,
And rich men flock from all the world around.
Yet count our gains. This wealth is but a name
That leaves our useful products still the same.
Not so the loss. The man of wealth and pride
Takes up a space that many poor supplied;
Space for his lake, his park's extended bounds,
Space for his horses, equipage, and hounds;
The robe that wraps his limbs in silken sloth,
Has robbed the neighbouring fields of half their growth;
His seat, where solitary sports are seen,
Indignant spurns the cottage from the green;
Around the world each needful product flies,
For all the luxuries the world supplies.
While thus the land, adorned for pleasure, all
In barren splendour feebly waits the fall.
  As some fair female unadorned and plain,
Secure to please while youth confirms her reign,
Slights every borrowed charm that dress supplies,
Nor shares with art the triumph of her eyes.
But when those charms are past, for charms are frail,
When time advances, and when lovers fail,
She then shines forth, sollicitous to bless,
In all the glaring impotence of dress.
Thus fares the land, by luxury betrayed;
In nature's simplest charms at first arrayed;
But verging to decline, its splendours rise,
Its vistas strike, its palaces surprize;
While, scourged by famine from the smiling land,
The mournful peasant leads his humble band;
And while he sinks, without one arm to save,
The country blooms—a garden, and a grave.
  Where then, ah where, shall poverty reside,
To scape the pressure of contiguous pride?

If to some common's fenceless limits strayed,
He drives his flock to pick the scanty blade,
Those fenceless fields the sons of wealth divide,
And ev'n the bare-worn common is denied.
    If to the city sped—What waits him there?
To see profusion that he must not share;
To see ten thousand baneful arts combined
To pamper luxury, and thin mankind;
To see those joys the sons of pleasure know,
Extorted from his fellow-creature's woe.
Here, while the courtier glitters in brocade,
There the pale artist plies the sickly trade;
Here, while the proud their long-drawn pomps display,
There the black gibbet glooms beside the way.
The dome where Pleasure holds her midnight reign,
Here, richly deckt, admits the gorgeous train;
Tumultuous grandeur crowds the blazing square,
The rattling chariots clash, the torches glare.
Sure scenes like these no troubles e'er annoy!
Sure these denote one universal joy!
Are these thy serious thoughts?—Ah, turn thine eyes
Where the poor houseless shivering female lies.
She once, perhaps, in village plenty blest,
Has wept at tales of innocence distrest;
Her modest looks the cottage might adorn,
Sweet as the primrose peeps beneath the thorn;
Now lost to all; her friends, her virtue fled,
Near her betrayer's door she lays her head,
And, pinch'd with cold, and shrinking from the shower,
With heavy heart deplores that luckless hour
When idly first, ambitious of the town,
She left her wheel and robes of country brown.
    Do thine, sweet Auburn, thine, the loveliest train,
Do thy fair tribes participate her pain?
Even now, perhaps, by cold and hunger led,

At proud men's doors they ask a little bread!
  Ah, no. To distant climes, a dreary scene,
Where half the convex world intrudes between,
Through torrid tracts with fainting steps they go,
Where wild Altama murmurs to their woe.
Far different there from all that charm'd before,
The various terrors of that horrid shore;
Those blazing suns that dart a downward ray,
And fiercely shed intolerable day;
Those matted woods where birds forget to sing,
But silent bats in drowsy clusters cling;
Those poisonous fields with rank luxuriance crowned,
Where the dark scorpion gathers death around;
Where at each step the stranger fears to wake
The rattling terrors of the vengeful snake;
Where crouching tigers wait their hapless prey,
And savage men, more murderous still than they;
While oft in whirls the mad tornado flies,
Mingling the ravaged landscape with the skies.
Far different these from every former scene,
The cooling brook, the grassy vested green,
The breezy covert of the warbling grove,
That only shelter'd thefts of harmless love.
  Good Heaven! what sorrows gloom'd that parting
    day,
That called them from their native walks away;
When the poor exiles, every pleasure past,
Hung round their bowers, and fondly looked their last,
And took a long farewell, and wished in vain
For seats like these beyond the western main;
And shuddering still to face the distant deep,
Returned and wept, and still returned to weep.
The good old sire the first prepared to go
To new found worlds, and wept for others woe.
But for himself, in conscious virtue brave,

He only wished for worlds beyond the grave.
His lovely daughter, lovelier in her tears,
The fond companion of his helpless years,
Silent went next, neglectful of her charms,
And left a lover's for a father's arms.
With louder plaints the mother spoke her woes,
And blest the cot where every pleasure rose;
And kist her thoughtless babes with many a tear,
And claspt them close, in sorrow doubly dear;
Whilst her fond husband strove to lend relief
In all the silent manliness of grief.

   O luxury! thou curst by Heaven's decree,
How ill exchanged are things like these for thee!
How do thy potions, with insidious joy,
Diffuse their pleasures only to destroy!
Kingdoms, by thee, to sickly greatness grown,
Boast of a florid vigour not their own;
At every draught more large and large they grow,
A bloated mass of rank unwieldy woe;
Till sapped their strength, and every part unsound,
Down, down they sink, and spread a ruin round.

   Even now the devastation is begun,
And half the business of destruction done;
Even now, methinks, as pondering here I stand,
I see the rural virtues leave the land:
Down where yon anchoring vessel spreads the sail,
That idly waiting flaps with every gale,
Downward they move, a melancholy band,
Pass from the shore, and darken all the strand.
Contented toil, and hospitable care,
And kind connubial tenderness, are there;
And piety with wishes placed above,
And steady loyalty, and faithful love.
And thou, sweet Poetry, thou loveliest maid,
Still first to fly where sensual joys invade;

Unfit in these degenerate times of shame,
To catch the heart, or strike for honest fame;
Dear charming nymph, neglected and decried,
My shame in crowds, my solitary pride;
Thou source of all my bliss, and all my woe,
That found'st me poor at first, and keep'st me so;
Thou guide by which the nobler arts excell,
Thou nurse of every virtue, fare thee well!
Farewell, and O where'er thy voice be tried,
On Torno's cliffs, or Pambamarca's side,
Whether were equinoctial fervours glow,
Or winter wraps the polar world in snow,
Still let thy voice, prevailing over time,
Redress the rigours of the inclement clime;
Aid slighted truth with thy persuasive strain,
Teach erring man to spurn the rage of gain;
Teach him, that states of native strength possest,
Tho' very poor, may still be very blest;
That trade's proud empire hastes to swift decay,
As ocean sweeps the labour'd mole away;
While self-dependent power can time defy,
As rocks resist the billows and the sky.

Index of Titles and First Lines

615

Some other books published by Penguin
are described on the following pages.

Some volumes in
THE VIKING PORTABLE LIBRARY

POETS OF THE ENGLISH LANGUAGE
Edited by W.H. Auden and Norman Holmes Pearson.

MEDIEVAL AND RENAISSANCE POETS.   015.049 8

ELIZABETHAN AND JACOBEAN POETS.   015.050 1

RESTORATION AND AUGUSTAN POETS.   015.051 X

ROMANTIC POETS.   015.052 8

VICTORIAN AND EDWARDIAN POETS.   015.053 6

HENRY JAMES
Edited by Morton Dauwen Zabel. Revised by Lyall H. Powers.   015.055 2

ROMAN READER
Edited by Basil Davenport.   015.056 0

CERVANTES
Translated and edited by Samuel Putnam.   015.057 9

MELVILLE
Edited by Jay Leyda.   015.058 7

GIBBON
Edited by Dero A. Saunders.   015.060 9

RENAISSANCE READER
Edited by James Bruce Ross and Mary Martin McLaughlin.   015.061 7

THE GREEK HISTORIANS
Edited by M. I. Finley.   015.065 X

STEPHEN CRANE
Edited by Joseph Katz.   015.068 4

VICTORIAN READER
Edited by Gordon S. Haight.   015.069 2

NORTH AMERICAN INDIAN READER
Edited by Frederick W. Turner III.   015.077 3

WALT WHITMAN
Edited by Mark Van Doren. Revised edition.   015.078 1

THOMAS JEFFERSON
Edited by Merrill D. Peterson.   015.080 3

CHAUCER
Edited and translated by Theodore Morrison. Revised edition.   015.081 1

THE PENGUIN BOOK OF BALLADS

Edited and introduced by Geoffrey Grigson

This original selection includes not only English and Scottish ballads from the sixteenth and seventeenth centuries but also many modern and American ones. Most of these ballads are of unknown authorship and have been handed down orally through the years. (The exact definition of the word *ballad* is a poem that tells a story in short stanzas and simple words, with repetition and with strong rhythms.)

THE PENGUIN BOOK OF ELIZABETHAN VERSE

Edited and introduced by Edward Lucie-Smith

An extremely rich anthology bringing together not only poems by great poets such as Campion, Dekker, Golding, and Shakespeare but also works by many less famous men. Extraordinary variety appears in the editor's selections because the word *Elizabethan,* instead of referring to a style, is interpreted here as encompassing "poets whose reputations were made or largely sustained during the reign of Elizabeth."

THE PENGUIN BOOK OF ENGLISH ROMANTIC VERSE

Edited and introduced by David Wright

This comprehensive anthology redefines Romanticism and the Romantic period. The period is traditionally seen as beginning with the publication of *Lyrical Ballads* in 1798 and ending with the death of Byron in 1824; but David Wright opens his selections with Pope's "Elegy to the Memory of an Unfortunate Lady" and goes on to include work by thirty-five other poets, the last of whom is Emily Brontë.

SCOTTISH LOVE POEMS
A Personal Anthology

Edited and introduced by Antonia Fraser

The celebrated author of *Cromwell* and *Mary, Queen of Scots* has assembled this unique anthology. Its purpose, she says, "is first and foremost to give pleasure. It has a secondary intention: to demonstrate the romantic richness of Scottish love poetry down the ages to the present day." (She calls it "personal" because the choice of poets is entirely her own and no poem has been retained out of dutiful respect for tradition.) The poems are grouped neither chronologically nor alphabetically but by "categories of love": Celebrations of Love; Wooings; First Love; Longing and Waiting; Encounters; Romantics; Unromantics; Marriages; The Nature of Love; Obsessions; Warnings; Laments; Unrequited Love; Fainthearts; Doomed Love; Farewells; Love Lost; Love in Abeyance; Change and Paradox; Old Loves; and Enduring Love. Included are not only beautiful poems by Burns, Byron, Scott, and Stevenson but also many less familiar ones, some by young poets writing today.

Poet to Poet

In each volume of Penguin's Poet to Poet series, an eminent living poet presents his own edition of the work of a British or American poet of the past. The series' guiding idea is that the response of one poet to the work of another can be doubly illuminating. Thus, by their choice of poet, their selection of verses, and the critical and personal reactions expressed in their introductions, today's poets provide unique insights both into their own work and into that of great poets whom they admire. Among the currently available titles . . .

CRABBE. *Selected by C. Day Lewis*

HENRYSON. *Selected by Hugh MacDiarmid*

WORDSWORTH. *Selected by Lawrence Durrell*

THE PENGUIN BOOK OF LOVE POETRY

Edited and introduced by Jon Stallworthy

This intriguing anthology defines a love poem as "any poem about any aspect of one human being's desire for another." Chosen from various epochs, the selections are international and are grouped according to these categories: Intimations, Declarations, Persuasions, Celebrations, Aberrations, Separations, Desolations, and Reverberations. The poets themselves range from Chaucer to Octavio Paz, from Ronsard to Lawrence Ferlinghetti, from Sappho to W. H. Auden. Read together, their poems prove that, as Jon Stallworthy puts it, "love is a country where anything can happen."

THREE RESTORATION COMEDIES

Edited and introduced by Gāmini Salgādo

Because of their glittering language, their delightful bawdiness, and their bold social criticisms, the plays in this volume rank with the very best English comedies. Included are Wycherley's *The Country Wife*, Congreve's *Love for Love*, and Etherege's *The Man of Mode*, which introduces the prototypical Restoration dandy, Sir Fopling Flutter.